MAYA NICOLE

CW01499202

ASCEND

CELESTIAL ACADEMY BOOK 1

CELESTIAL ACADEMY

THE COMPLETE SERIES

MAYA NICOLE

❀ Created with Vellum

AUTHOR'S NOTE

Celestial Academy is a why choose romance with MM content. That means the main character will have a happily ever after with three or more men and two of the men will also be together.

Some scenes may trigger some readers due to PTSD WWII flashbacks, abduction, bullying, violence, and a relationship with a teacher in a college academy setting.

Recommended for readers 18+ for adult content and language.

CHAPTER 1

DANICA

ick. Tick. Tick.
    I stared down at the beige and gray flecked linoleum tiles as the sound of the seconds ticking by echoed in my ears. I ran a hand over my jean-clad thigh, smoothing a miniscule wrinkle.

Glancing at the clock, the red hand taunted me as it made its slow circle around for fifty-eight beats before hesitating and then clicking twice in quick succession as the minute hand moved forward. It was torture listening to it. It's like one day a clockmaker said, 'Hey! Let's make the loudest clock possible to put in schools!'

It seemed louder in here with the office staff quietly chatting, answering phone calls, and clicking away on their computers. They glanced up occasionally to check on me, to make sure I was still in the rather comfortable armchair situated outside Mr. Miller's closed office door. I itched to take my phone out of my backpack to check to see what people were saying on Twitter, but didn't dare pull it out in the office.

It was an office I was all too familiar with. It was a chair that might as well be engraved with my name. It was a well-known fact that the chairs in high school offices were specifically designed to create a false sense of comfort before the guillotine came crashing down. That was how I felt, as if my head was about to be lopped off *A Tale of Two Cities* style.

Mr. Miller and I saw each other more often than I'd care to admit. He told me he didn't like seeing me in his office so much. That he saw me more than he saw his own son, which I find to be a gross exaggeration. Last time I was here for disrupting class, he said that I was an adult now. That I needed to get my act together before I ended up in a different type of concrete building. A concrete building where they didn't care that my dad worked all the time and left me practically to my own devices.

My own devices put me near the bottom of the entire senior class and at the bottom of a discipline flowchart he referred to every time I was sent to him. I was a smart woman, even though my grades might not have reflected that. I knew what was coming. I was actually surprised it hadn't happened already. The flowchart dictated what action Mr. Miller had to take, no matter his sympathies towards me. He warned me every time I was suspended that my time was running out to turn myself around.

Maybe I would just get my GED. Would I even *pass* the GED test? I could get a job. Could I get a job without a GED?

My body jerked as a secretary slammed a file cabinet shut, the metal on metal echoing in the sterile environment of the hall. I let out a long breath of air and picked a piece of lint off my shirt with my bruised hand. It still stung, but the ice the nurse gave me helped. Too bad ice wouldn't help what was about to happen.

My last suspension was my last chance and now the glint of metal sat ready and waiting above my outstretched neck. They called my dad, even though I was eighteen now. I begged them to call my former caregiver like they did before my eighteenth birthday, but they refused. I was screwed.

My dad was a busy man with an important job, and the last time he came for something I'd done, his wrath was merciless and I was grounded for months. That was back when I was kicked out of the private school where they didn't dick around or put up with the same "juvenile delinquent" behavior as public schools did.

My friends always bitched about their parents and their rules. Their consequences. Well, I had them beat. My dad tortured souls for a living. Dealt their punishments. Condemned them to suffer in the fiery pits of hell.

Literally.

My eyes snapped up as I heard the front door of the office open. I couldn't see him from where I was sitting, but I felt him. The smallest whispers of discomfort spiraled up my spine and caused my shoulder blades to tingle with an itch I couldn't quite scratch. I slouched down slightly in the chair as his voice carried across the room and into the hall.

"I'm here for my daughter, Danica Deville." I shut my eyes as his smooth, yet slightly gravelly voice drew the attention of several of the office staff.

Whatever initial reactions they had to his demanding tone quickly vanished as they took in his tall, lithe frame, and his mesmerizing dark eyes. They sat up a little taller in their chairs and patted their hair to make sure it was in place.

The principal's secretary stood and fumbled with the latch on the swinging door that blocked the lobby from the back offices. "She's right through here, sir. If you could have a seat, Mr. Miller will be right with you," she said with a slight tremble in her voice.

My heart stuttered as my father came into view. He flashed a white smile at the secretary that crinkled the corners of his eyes and caused a small dimple in his left cheek. The secretary placed one of her trembling hands on her chest as if it would stop the fluttering of her heart. I covered my mouth with my hand, a smile threatening to escape at her display. It was hard not to laugh when he came into a room and put people under his spell.

My dad made his way towards me, his shiny brown shoes making a clicking noise on the floor, much like the ticking of the clock. Today he was wearing a brown three-piece suit, the color reminding me of a blonde coffee bean, with a navy tie tucked neatly into the suit vest. He sat down in the chair next to me, the scent of firewood and cinnamon hitting my nose.

"Danica."

I bit my lip and shifted in my seat. He probably would have much rather been attending to the souls down in hell than in a stuffy school office dealing with my transgressions.

"I'm sorry." The words came out as a breath. I only half meant the words. I was sorry he was here, not for what I had done. I was also sorry for turning out to be a failure of epic proportions.

I clasped my hands in my lap and kept my eyes focused on them. I could feel my father's eyes burning into the side of my head. I knew when he looked away because the slight warmth his gaze caused dissipated.

The principal's door opened and I lifted my eyes to meet those of my best friend, Ava. Her blue eyes were red from crying. She looked past me at my father and her eyes went wide before snapping back to mine. She gave me a very slow shake of her head before exiting the office. If she had a tail, it would have been tucked between her legs.

Ava was caught in the crossfires, dragged into the middle of something I was keeping her out of. She had a scholarship to a top university to protect. Her headshake was all that was needed to let me know that the guillotine was locked and loaded.

"Mr. Deville. If you and Danica could step into my office." Mr. Miller stood by his open office door and gestured inside.

I entered in front of my dad, as he stopped and shook Mr. Miller's hand in a firm handshake that I'm sure left my principal feeling uneasy, but he didn't show it as he took his place behind his desk.

The room was silent, the only sound the faint office noises on the other side of the closed door. During my three and a half years at Montecito High, the principal's office had remained the same, except for the man behind the desk. He looked tired now.

I reached out and straightened Mr. Miller's name plate. He steepled his fingers just under his nose and then let out a long sigh.

"Mr. Deville, I'm sorry to call you in like this. I know you're a very busy man."

"Please, call me Michael," he replied, flashing another award-winning grin that didn't reach his eyes. He was not happy to be here.

"Michael," Mr. Miller said, testing the name out. By the way his eyes narrowed the tiniest bit, it was clear he didn't think my father's name was actually Michael. It was like he could sense the wrongness of it on his tongue.

It's not like my dad could go around calling himself Lucifer Deville. It would raise too many eyebrows and garner too much attention. He decided his name would be Michael when he was here. It was akin to giving the angel the middle finger.

I was sure the angels were well aware that Lucifer visited this place, but left him alone unless he gave them reason not to. I would have thought him using the name Michael would piss some of the angels off, especially Michael, but perhaps it wasn't worth their time or effort.

"As you know, we have tried many interventions to help Danica succeed, and she has already been granted an additional chance by the expulsion review board. Given she continues to disregard rules, her failing grades in almost all of her courses, and her assault of a young man this morning, the district is going through with expelling her."

"I see." My dad was no longer smiling. Instead, his eyes were on me again, sending a sharp slap of heat to my head. It didn't hurt, but was uncomfortable.

At that moment I didn't know if failing out of senior year and being expelled simultaneously was rock bottom, or the fire that was smoldering next to me was. I braved another glance in his direction, keeping my chin down, and saw the pupils of his eyes dilate inside the smoky gray of his irises. He was assessing me, no doubt thinking of how he was going to punish his half human, half devil daughter.

At least torture was out of the question, not that he'd ever do that. We weren't entirely sure I was immortal anyway. I was uncharted territory. Something that shouldn't even be possible. Yet here I was. Lucifer's daughter.

He released me from his stare and looked back at Mr. Miller. "She assaulted someone? That is out of character, even for her."

"Well, as you know, she has been showing increasingly troublesome behavior over the past several years."

Out of the corner of my eye, I caught my dad clenching his jaw ever so slightly. No, he didn't know because I didn't tell him and my caregiver was too nervous around him to tell him. He knew about the expulsion hearing; it was mandatory since a joint was found in my locker, but he hadn't even attended that.

"This morning, one of the boys she has been in verbal altercations with before approached Danica and handed her a flier to his church. She punched him and broke his nose." He paused. "The boy's family has decided not to press charges, since she will no longer be attending school here."

"You punched a boy because he gave you a flier for a church?" Lucifer may have sounded calm, but his voice was a slightly lower timbre that caused goosebumps on my arms.

I gritted my teeth and swallowed the bile that had slowly worked its way into my throat. My father may very well be the devil, but never once had I heard him speak ill of the big man upstairs. At least, not in front of me. I couldn't tell him the real reason John had offered me that flier, he'd kill him.

I shrugged. Nothing I could say at this point would help. Ava telling Mr. Miller that John had done more than just hand me a church flier certainly didn't get me out of being expelled. John was the golden boy of the school. No adult would believe a juvenile delinquent like me. Especially if I told them the church was not a church but a front for drug dealing.

Lucifer cleared his throat and turned his gaze back to Mr. Miller, who was watching our exchange with piqued curiosity. My dad had this detached manner about him, where he didn't show his emotions, even when the situation called for it. He'd probably act the same if we were sitting discussing my college prospects. Which by the way, were non-existent, especially now.

"I'll just need you to sign this document. One of our school resource officers is cleaning out her locker and will bring her personal belongings." Mr. Miller slid a paper across the desk and my dad took a pen out of the inner breast pocket of his blazer.

He never signed anything with other people's pens. He said it was too risky, that there was always a potential for blood shed. As if a high school principal would put some kind of spell or something on a pen. He took a moment to skim the page and then signed his name in flowing cursive that was much too pretty to be that of Satan himself. He slid the paper over to me and offered me his pen.

I let out a long sigh and signed my name under his. I slouched in my chair as the paper was slid back across the desk and Mr. Miller signed his name. It was all too simple, sealing my fate with a flourish of a pen. No senior prom. No senior week. No graduation. No future.

Mr. Miller left the office to make copies of the document, leaving me alone with my dad.

"Sit up. You did this of your own accord, now deal with it." To an outsider, his words would have sounded passive, almost bored. But his eyes were glossy and his face too stoic.

I sat up and glanced over as he looked at his watch. Today he was sporting his Louis Moinet Meteoris; it had a piece of a meteorite from Mars in it. Seemed a little extravagant to me, but it was one of his favorites. He had a thing for fancy watches and there was no better place to keep them safe than his lair in hell. Sometimes I felt he took better care of his watches than he did his own flesh and blood.

Once Mr. Miller returned with copies and a bag of random junk I had in my locker, we left the office and walked towards the student parking lot.

"Keys." Lucifer held out his hand as I dug in the front pocket of my backpack for them. Tears pricked at the corners of my eyes as I handed them over.

We got into my black Nissan GT-R and I threw my bag in the backseat. Lucifer was peeling out of the parking lot before I could even get my seatbelt buckled.

"Jesus! Don't hurt my baby!" I gripped onto the door handle as he drifted around a corner.

He laughed and took his foot off the gas. "Yours? Last time I checked, the pink slip was in my name. And you can't tell me you don't drive it like this. You are my daughter, after all."

I might be his daughter, but I was at least a semi-sane driver. He drove like a bat out of hell.

The rest of the ten-minute drive to our house was quiet, the only sounds in the car the faint sound of the radio that was practically turned all the way down. He wasn't a fan of popular music or small talk. When we got to the gates leading up the long drive to the house, my stomach clenched.

He pulled into the garage, still silent, his jaw set, and I followed him into the kitchen where he turned on his espresso machine. I sat at the island and watched as he made himself a cup of espresso. He then grabbed me a Diet Dr. Pepper out of the refrigerator and slid it across the smooth surface of the island.

I knew he was going to ream me after he finished his drink, but despite that, I had missed him. He visited once a week for dinner with me, but the rest of the time he spent reigning over hell and his army of demons. FaceTime and texting just weren't the same as having him around.

When I was little, I used to wonder where he was all the time. The first time I realized he was different was when I was about six. Surprisingly, I had convinced him to go to my elementary school harvest festival. It was warm, but he still chose to wear a suit. He always wore a suit and I had never seen him wear anything else.

It was there, in the middle of the carnival when he was buying me ice cream, that I realized he was different than the other parents. The other parents didn't seem to think it was weird he was wearing an expensive suit while they were in jeans and T-shirts. In fact, they had looked at him as if he was the most beautiful man they had laid eyes on. Even the men.

It's not that he *looked* different than a human, but there was just something about him and his presence that sent emotions soaring. Especially if a person had done something that was of questionable morals. Most of the time he blocked me from having to feel this aspect of himself, but I could tell he was letting just a little bit of his fear inducing spell, or whatever it was, leak out.

I took a long gulp of my drink and put the can on the counter, popping the tab off and fiddling with it. I watched as he rinsed his cup and put it in the dishwasher.

"What's your plan?" He leaned against the counter opposite the island, crossing his legs at the ankles.

I continued to fiddle with the tab, spinning it on the counter. "I guess get a job. Any job openings in hell?" A laugh left my lips and died a silent death as he stared at me. There was no way he was going to let me live or work in hell. No. That would be impossible.

I had only been to hell once. For five minutes. Five minutes of pain.

"What about college? Get your GED and then enroll in some classes."

Here I was having a conversation with the devil about taking college courses as if everything was normal. Everything was definitely not normal.

"I don't like school. You know that. Maybe I can help your demons with some of the jobs they do here." I looked at him hopefully.

"Absolutely not. You aren't meant to..." His voice trailed off and he stared past me and into the living room before running a hand over his face. "You're not meant for that life."

I cleared my throat. "You're the devil."

"That doesn't mean I want you to be. Your mother would skin me alive."

My chest felt tight and I grabbed my soda and took another drink. "My mother is dead."

He ran his hands over his tie, pulling it from his vest and loosening it around his neck before dropping his hands to his sides and clenching them open and closed a few times.

"A fact I'm very well aware of." He pulled his phone out of his pocket and swiped across the screen. "I've been thinking that maybe it's time I reach out to the others."

He rarely talked about them, but from what I could tell from the brief mentions of them, they weren't enemies, but they weren't friends either.

"What do you mean reach out to them?" I narrowed my eyes at him before following him into the living room as he pressed buttons.

He glanced up briefly from the screen before he held it up to his ear, the faint sound of the ring-back filling the quiet room. I plopped down in my seat on the couch and pulled a pillow into my lap, hugging it to my chest. He went to the window and opened the curtains to look out at the backyard.

When he started talking to whoever he had called, his grip tightened on his phone and his voice sounded like it was shaking slightly. I squeezed the pillow tighter.

After a few strings of bullshit small talk he got to the point. "I have a daughter... I don't know how it happened... Yes, I'm sure she's mine... She doesn't have wings..." He finished his conversation and inhaled a sharp breath before slowly turning to face me with a tight smile on his face.

"Chamuel will be here in five minutes." He set his phone on the coffee table and sat on the edge of a chair. He straightened his tie and shoved it back in his vest.

I watched his movement before scooting over to the cushion at the end of the couch nearest him. "You invited an *angel* here to the house?" I shrugged out of my sweater, suddenly feeling hot, and ran my hand over my mouth. "Why would you do that?"

He shut his eyes before shaking his head as he spoke. "My blood hasn't changed Danica. That makes you half-angel. Maybe I've been wrong in keeping this from them. Especially since I can't be here all the time and your attraction to trouble."

I stood up, sending the pillow I was holding to the floor and crossed my arms over my chest. "So *now* you suddenly show interest in how much trouble I'm causing?"

He opened his mouth and then shut it. After clearing his throat, he said, "You're walking around punching people in the face. Who knows what else you've been doing. So, yes, I'm concerned."

I let out a laugh at the absurdity of the whole conversation. The devil was concerned that I had punched someone in the face. At what

I was doing when he left me alone eighty percent of the time to be raised by nannies and caregivers.

"And where were you?"

He flinched at my words but didn't say anything before he stood and went back to stare out the window.

"Let me know once you and the angel decide my fate." I kicked the pillow out of my way and ran up to my bedroom, slamming the door shut behind me.

I really should have stayed downstairs.

CHAPTER 2

DANICA

*M*y inability to not act impulsively really got me into a pickle, and not just a slice of pickle on a hamburger, but a world record-sized gherkin of a pickle. Had I stayed downstairs, then maybe I could have at least argued with what Lucifer and Chamuel decided was best for me. Instead, I had given them all the power to make my life miserable.

Yes, I was of legal age. Yes, I could say no. But could I really? I had no family to speak of besides Lucifer, and independent living without a high school diploma in the Santa Barbara area was an impossibility. So pretty much, I was screwed.

I pulled the tape dispenser across the box and sealed it shut, the sound making my ears want to bleed. Maybe I could invent a quiet packing tape dispenser and not be shipped off to hell.

I had never had to pack my belongings before. We had always lived in this house; well, I had, at least. I had kissed my first boy and lost my virginity here. I had gotten drunk and high here. All things that a father who was present shouldn't have allowed to happen.

I put together another box and dumped my underwear and bras into it before throwing a stack of tank tops and t-shirts on top. I really needed to pare down my collection; it was borderline excessive. Some people liked their shoes, I liked feeling sexy at all moments of the day by way of a lot of lace in every color under the sun. At least I'd have cute underwear underneath the hideous uniforms at the training school I was being shipped off to.

I hadn't even known there were schools for angels until Lucifer sat me down on the couch later that night and dropped the bomb on me. Los Angeles Celestial Academy, one of four academies for college-aged guardian angels. Located in the Angeles National Forest under special protective wards, it was where the top angels were sent to hone their angel knowledge and skills.

I was definitely not a top angel. I wasn't even sure I qualified as one given I had no wings and hadn't died. There were two ways to become an angel: being created or ascending upon death. Once a soul had ascended they were faced with a choice to remain in heaven or serve a greater cause and become a guardian angel on Earth.

I don't see how Chamuel thought sending me to an academy to become some kind of savior was in mine or the world's best interest. What could I offer someone in their time of need? A toke from a joint I used to attempt to stay focused on my school work? Maybe a swig of vodka from a water bottle? It was doubtful my soul would even make it to heaven if I died. I wasn't bad per se, but I certainly wasn't good or angel material.

Besides having an extra class to study for my GED (which Lucifer was adamant about), I'd be subject to tortures such as Defensive Flight Techniques, The Portrayal of Angels in Modern Literature, Introduction to Demonology, and General World Studies. Shoot. Me. Now. I had barely even made it to trigonometry.

Ava entering my bedroom snapped me out of my pity party and I snatched my hot chocolate with extra whipped cream from her hands. There were most likely not any Starbucks where I was going unless I wanted to drive thirty minutes into the city.

"Are you sure you really have to go? You're eighteen, you could just get a job," Ava said flopping down in my desk chair and taking the straw out of her drink to lick the whip cream from it.

I sighed and dumped my jean drawer into another box, not caring that by doing so I was wasting space. I looked at Ava and wondered what she would think or say if she knew the truth about me, about Lucifer. She was so strait-laced it would probably rock her world. We were unlikely friends to say the least.

"You've met my dad, right? He doesn't care that I'm eighteen. What he says goes." I taped the box shut and grabbed a red Sharpie to write on it. "Plus, it's not like I can get a job that pays well without a GED."

Ava leaned forward to see what I had written and snorted a laugh. I couldn't wait to see the reaction of the angels as boxes labeled with dildos, bondage, and porn were carried down the hall.

"What is he, a mobster or something? Just tell him you aren't going and move out. I bet my parents would let you stay with us for a while." She stood and grabbed the Sharpie from me before adding the word 'hardcore' to the box labeled 'porn.'

"It's a little more complicated than that." I looked around my room, making sure I wasn't forgetting anything. "I think I'm all packed."

Ava put her arms around me. "Promise you won't forget about me."

"Don't *you* forget about me." The musical quality of my voice caused us to both belt out *Don't You (Forget About Me)* by Simple Minds a la *Breakfast Club*. It was a fitting song for us to sing considering I was about to endure the longest detention in the history of detentions.

THE SUV that came to pick up my boxes was a pearlescent white monstrosity that screamed angel, and not just because two angels were driving it. The two men that were sent to pick up my boxes kept staring at me when they thought I wasn't looking, and not because they found me attractive. Although I'd like to think that maybe a small part of them did.

It also didn't help that I had every box labeled inappropriately. So inappropriately, that one of the men had stepped out into the hallway and made a call. Surely angels had sex and had senses of humor.

I followed behind the SUV for the almost two-hour drive from Montecito to Angeles National Forest. Had they seriously set up a school there because of the name? Hell, the school might have even been there before Los Angeles was even a city.

My stomach tightened as we drove on the two-lane highway and turned down a gravel road. Dirt and rocks hit the sides of my car and I flinched thinking of how tortured my car must be feeling. Black was the worst color for dust.

As we traveled down the dirt road, I felt rather than saw the shift in the air as we passed through the wards that hid the campus amongst the trees. As we came down a hill, it came into view and I couldn't help but let my mouth fall open.

There were ten massive brick buildings that spread out across a wide area with large swaths of grass and trees. I'd been entertaining the thought that it might look like Hogwarts, but it looked like something straight out of the English countryside. The grass was so green it felt out of place in the drought-stricken area. Maybe that was why Southern California was perpetually dry; the angels were stealing all the water.

I followed the SUV to a smaller brick building set off from the rest of the buildings and parked in an empty spot. There were only a few other cars, most being SUVs. I guess they didn't need cars here since they had wings and all that jazz. Even if I did have wings, I'd still want a car.

I slid out of my car just as a man walked out the door and walked over to us. I licked my lips as he approached. He was singlehandedly the most attractive male specimen I had ever laid eyes on. His dark brown hair was cut short and looked like he had run his fingers through it. His beard was close cut and well groomed. He looked muscular with wide shoulders and a narrowed waist under his blue Dodgers sweatshirt. I bet he had abs. Men with shoulders like that *always* had abs.

His brown eyes quickly took me in from head to toe before he met my eyes. I wondered what he was expecting when he was given the task of greeting me. I felt naked instead of having on a pair of skinny jeans and crop top that bared about an inch of my stomach. I should have put on a longer shirt.

No. No, I wouldn't change who I was just because I was in the presence of angels. They were humans once; surely they had seen some skin.

"I would have taken you for an Angels fan, not the Dodgers." I smiled lightly and stood a little straighter.

His mouth turned up slightly before falling flat again, and he shoved his hands in the pockets of his jeans. "I'm Tobias Armstrong. I'll be your advisor and instructor for one of your courses."

His voice was... well you know how there's that phrase, voice of an angel? There's some truth to it. It made my breath catch and I cleared my throat, hoping he hadn't noticed. I took a step forward and reached out my hand.

"Danica Deville." Instead of taking my hand in a handshake, he shifted from one foot to the other before pulling a key and fob out of his pocket and holding it out over my outstretched hand.

A dull ache started building in my chest because, what the hell? Who doesn't shake someone's hand when offered? I turned my hand palm up and he dropped the keys into it. I stared at them in my open hand before I curled my fingers around them, my hand shaking ever so slightly.

I had known going to this school was going to be difficult given who I was, but after my interactions with the movers and now this guy, I wondered what the students were going to be like.

"This is the faculty and staff building. The dean felt it was better to have you here than in the student dorms." He offered no other explanation, and he didn't need to.

The ache spread like someone was sitting on my chest and my feet felt heavy. He turned and walked towards the door he had exited from. They were scared of me. Scared of what I might do to the other students here.

"Are you coming?" He glanced back at me with slightly raised eyebrows.

I nodded and plastered on a smile before following him. He scanned his own fob and we entered a large common room. I was immediately drawn to the large fireplace with chairs and couches angled towards it. I'd probably never get to enjoy it since I would be living with my teachers.

I groaned internally at the thought of being under their scrutiny at all times. I probably couldn't get away with smoking or sneaking out. Pasadena wasn't that far away, but any hopes of at least somewhat enjoying this torture-fest were slowly dwindling away.

"Where is everyone?" I asked as we approached a large split staircase. There wasn't another person in sight; surprising since it was Sunday.

"Working." It didn't seem he was going to give me much more than that.

"Isn't Sunday supposed to be a day of rest? Hell, Chick-fil-a is closed but an angel school has people working?" I bit the inside of my cheek after the words left my mouth. He grunted but didn't respond. I was setting a really good first impression and probably digging my grave deeper.

I increased my pace to catch up to him so I wouldn't be tempted to watch his ass as we walked up the stairs. There was no denying that he was attractive. We went to the right and into a hallway that had several doors. The only sounds were our shoes on the hardwood floors. It was a ghost town.

We stopped at the last door and he moved out of the way so I could open the door. I was pleasantly surprised at the size of the room and the attached bathroom. They may have stuck me with the teachers and staff, but at least the room was decent enough. The furniture was white wood and included a full-sized bed, dresser, desk, futon, and a small kitchenette.

Tobias didn't move an inch from his spot near the opened door as I looked around and pulled the curtains open to let light in. I could see clear across campus to what looked like a football field.

"Does this work for you? Chamuel didn't really tell us what to expect."

I glanced over at him as he shifted from one foot to the other. He looked down the hall and then back at me. Clearly, I made him nervous.

"I'm a little disappointed with the size of the bed. I guess my days of orgies are over." I walked towards him and he quickly backed up into the hall, a slight pink tint creeping onto his cheeks just above his beard line.

"Uhh... well. You don't necessarily need a bed for that." Eyes wide and looking at the floor, his hand went to the back of his neck. He rubbed it before he brought it to his beard and then ran his hand through his hair.

I brushed past him and he leaned back slightly as my arm touched his shirt. It was subtle, the tiniest of movements, but it was enough to be noticeable. And painful. Was I really so revolting?

I took off down the hall without a word as the two angels tasked to moving me in walked by with narrowed glances. If Lucifer's goal was to punish me, well, this was doing the job.

Once I returned to my room after sitting in my car while the SUV was unloaded, I looked through the binder left on the desk. There were so many rules and protocols. No smoking. No drinking. Lights out at eleven on weeknights. Blah. Blah. Blah. Who did these angels think they were, a military school for misfits?

I was eighteen years old and from what little I did know about this school, it was for college-aged angels. What could they possibly do if an angel broke a rule? Ground them?

I opened the window and let in the fresh air, suddenly feeling like the walls of the room were closing in on me. I still couldn't shake the hurt I had felt when Mr. Armstrong had visibly been repulsed by me. It's not like I had horns or even looked evil. Lucifer wasn't even evil.

Sure, he had a dark side. Anyone cast out of heaven would. If anything, the other angels should be grateful that he controlled the dark depths of hell so well. There hadn't been a major incident with demons in centuries.

Still at the window, my eyes were drawn to the football field in the distance where a group of angels were playing what looked like football but while flying through the air. I had never seen an angel all angelic like, with wings out. From my room they looked like giant winged birds.

I had asked Lucifer once if I could see his wings, but he refused. I wasn't even sure he still had wings. My knowledge of angels was limited to what I could get out of my father, which wasn't much.

My knowledge of demons was top notch. All of the time I spent grounded was spent reading books Lucifer provided.

I turned back to the binder, ignoring the rest of the sections that probably would have answered all my questions and pulled the campus map out. The campus itself was sprawling, but most of my classes were in a center building aptly named Uriel Hall.

My stomach growled as I located the dining hall on the map. I tucked the map and my phone in the back pocket of my jeans before throwing on my black leather jacket and heading out the door. There were no signs of any staff members as I made my way out of the building.

The pathways weaving their way between buildings and around large grassy areas reminded me of old college campuses I had searched up on the internet. Despite my low GPA and nonexistent college plans, I still perused the websites since college was all Ava talked about.

This campus seemed out of place here in the mountains, hidden by magic I didn't yet understand. The brick building the dining hall and administrative offices were housed in loomed ahead of me. Five stories of aged brick and large windows rose into the sky with an angel statute perched at the top. I assumed it was Ariel, since the building was Ariel Hall. I bet they didn't have a Lucifer Hall here.

As I approached, the delicious aromas of food filled my nose. I could really go for a cheeseburger and Diet Dr. Pepper. I hoped angel food was no different than what humans ate. If they ate twigs and berries I was probably going to exist on cereal and frozen food. My room did have a kitchenette, but I could basically only cook ramen, and even then I managed to mess it up somehow.

I was almost to the small set of stone steps leading into the building when a group of seven angels landed in front of me by the door. I stopped in my tracks and stared slack-jawed at their expansive white wings. They spanned five or six feet on each side of their torsos. Somehow they managed not to bump into each other. One of the boys had wings that almost appeared silver in the fading light of the evening. They folded them back behind themselves and they seemed to disappear as I blinked.

I was considering how to get around their group as some of the boys pushed and shoved each other, when one of the girls in the group gasped as she made eye contact with me. She nudged the girl next to her and they started whispering in a completely obvious way. The five boys they were with continued to rough house and throw a football around as the two girls walked towards me.

Maybe they wouldn't know who I was. Who was I kidding? They knew *exactly* who I was. Every student on this campus probably knew Lucifer's flesh and blood was going to be attending. Maybe they had even gotten a warning notice to be on high alert.

"You must be the new girl we've heard so much about. I'm Delilah and this is Abby." A tall blond introduced herself and the other girl but neither made any move to get closer than a few feet away from me.

Both girls were gorgeous and had glowing skin and hair that looked like it belonged in a shampoo commercial. They held themselves like their shit didn't stink and appraised me by giving me the once over.

I smiled, my face feeling tight under the forced movement. "Danica. Are you all first years?"

Abby looked me up and down with raised eyebrows and pursed lips. "She looks normal. I was expecting her to be scary."

The girls laughed and I went to move around them to find the path blocked by the five male angels that had finally realized what was going on. Great, more attention.

"Well, what's this? The antichrist in the flesh!" One of the angels sneered and crossed his arms over his chest.

My fake smile quickly faded as I stared at the five male angels in front of me. They were all striking, and stood stoically with matching frowns on their faces.

"Can you move, please?" I really wanted to lash out at their commentary, but had to be better than that. They were expecting me to do something. Typically I would, but that was how I got into this whole situation in the first place.

"Or what? You'll unleash your demons to make us?" They all laughed like it was the funniest thing in the world.

I shrugged, deciding my words weren't worth wasting on them, and walked onto the grass to get around them. Their laughter faded as I entered into the dining commons. Heads immediately turned to check out where the laughter had come from in the brief moment the door had been opened.

I made my way to the food line that was similar to the dining commons I had seen on a field trip to UC Santa Barbara. A field trip that was wasted on me since I was not college material. I piled my plate with food and filled a cup with Diet Dr. Pepper before scanning the room for a place to sit.

I decided to sit in the corner at the end of a long table that was already occupied at one end. Right as I was about to sit down, a girl grabbed my arm, causing some of my drink to slosh out of the side of my cup.

"Don't sit there. The Divine 7 sit there. Come sit with us." She gestured to a round table somewhat in the middle of the room.

I stifled a groan. Middle of the room meant center of attention, which I already seemed to be. Eyes followed me as I walked and several students rose a little, trying to look at what was on my tray. What did they think I ate? I guess I couldn't blame them since I had the same question about them.

Once I sat down, I let out a sigh of relief and took a drink. Three sets of curious eyes watched me as I slowly put my cup back down.

"I'm Danica. Thanks for saving me?" I didn't mean for it to come out as a question but based on my warm reception at this school so far, I wasn't sure what this group's motives were.

"Oh, we saved you all right. I'm Brooklyn, by the way. Class III," the girl who had invited me to the table said.

"Ethan, Class II."

"Cora, Class II."

"What do you mean by class? Your year?" I took a bite of the pasta with chicken I had picked. It was surprisingly good, for you know, angel food.

"Class just specifies how we came to be angels. Class I are created by The Man himself, Class II died before they were age twelve, Class III died after twelve and are deemed pure enough to serve," Ethan explained. "Did your advisor not tell you what Class you were?"

"No." I spun my fork around my noodles, creating a very impressive bite that was almost picture worthy. "I think he was scared of me so I didn't get too many details about things here."

My three eating companions all looked at each other before going back to their own dinners. My shoulders were just starting to relax when the group from outside started to file past with their food.

"It eats real food! Holy shit, man." One of the guys nudged the guy next to him and they both stared openly as I took a bite.

I narrowed my eyes slightly and then started chewing my food with my mouth open. If they wanted to stare, I'd at least give them something to look at. Cora laughed as the two boys took off towards the back corner with disgust on their faces. I watched as all seven of the group from outside sat where I had first tried to sit. That was a close call.

"Why are they called the Divine 7? They don't seem very divine." I put my fork down and took a bite out of the chocolate chip cookie I had grabbed for dessert. It seemed like a good time to have my cookie after enduring their bullshit.

"*They* call themselves the Divine 7 because they have the highest divinity rankings. Of course, that doesn't really take into consideration how shitty they might act on the sly. The two girls are the worst. Oliver and Levi aren't that horrible, but they also don't put a stop to anything. Oliver is the only Class I angel at any of the academies. We're still trying to figure out why he's here. They renumbered the class system this year since he is the first since the original archangels." Brooklyn looked over her shoulder at the table. "Oliver is the one examining his bread, and Levi is next to him."

I glanced briefly in that direction and Levi was staring at me, which he quickly tried to hide by looking away. Oliver really was examining his bread, which he sniffed before taking a bite. It wasn't a normal look and sniff, like a regular person might do. It was as if he had never seen it before in his life. I tilted my head slightly, trying to figure that one out.

"Can I ask you a question?" Ethan looked directly at me and was immediately nudged in the side by Brooklyn who then gave him a very annoyed look. I appreciated that at least Brooklyn seemed to somewhat understand what I was going through.

"Sure. I don't mind questions from people who are nice to me." I finished the last bite of my cookie and braced myself for the questions I knew were going to come. I didn't mind as long as they were in good faith.

Ethan leaned forward on his forearms so our conversation couldn't be heard at the other tables. I had no clue if angels had super-sonic hearing. I guess I also had a lot of questions to ask them.

"Did you actually like, *live* in hell?" I barely caught his question over the noise in the dining room. At least he was being discreet.

I couldn't help it, I laughed. "No I didn't. I went for maybe five minutes once before getting violently ill. I'm half human. I assume I'd get just as sick going to heaven."

Cora let out a relieved breath and Brooklyn just stared at me. If eyes could actually bug out of heads, Ethan's would have.

"So you lived with your mom, who's... human?"

"My mom died during childbirth so my dad hired caregivers. I lived right outside of Santa Barbara in Montecito my entire life."

"So you don't actually see... *him*?" Ethan was elbowed again by Brooklyn.

"He's not like Voldemort. You can say Lucifer and he won't suddenly appear and torture you." I laughed. The table next to us looked over at the mention of Lucifer's name. I hadn't spoken quietly enough. I lowered my voice enough so that only the three across from me could hear. "He comes for dinner once a week and we text and FaceTime all the time."

"Cell phones work in hell?" Cora had been quiet up until now. She seemed to be processing everything I had said.

I nodded. I used to wonder about how technology worked in another plane of existence. My dad told me it was magic. I wasn't entirely sure that explanation was accurate, but honestly, I don't think I wanted to know how the internet and cell service worked there.

Brooklyn changed the topic of conversation after that and we discussed our class schedules. I had two classes with her, one with Cora, and one with Ethan. I also learned that I'd only have to deal with Oliver and Levi in classes because the other five were second or third-year students with different classes. I left the dining room feeling hopeful that maybe this new school wouldn't be so bad after all.

CHAPTER 3

DANICA

I woke up to the sounds of birds chirping somewhere outside my cracked-open window. It was the beginning of February, so it was a little chilly, but not having a window open made me feel claustrophobic. Plus, I liked piling the blankets on. It made me feel cozy and relaxed.

I went to the generously sized closet and looked longingly at the clothes I used to wear to school. Jeans, T-shirts, hoodies. Instead of having freedom of choice here at the lovely Academy of Asshole Angels, I had to wear a uniform. It was so cliché I wanted to vomit.

I pulled a uniform out and threw it on the bed before going to my box of underwear and bras I had yet to put in a drawer. I wanted to Marie Kondo the shit out of my drawers, but hadn't gotten around to it yet. What I was sure of was that every piece of lingerie I owned sparked joy within me and would not be going anywhere.

I dumped the box and found a matching set of red lace boy shorts and a bra. I considered putting the pile back in the box, but it really was my best intention to organize and fold them later. After putting them on, I eyed the uniform laying haphazardly across the bed. Thick white wool skirt with silver and navy-blue trim, white button up, blue blazer with silver crest on breast pocket.

First off, a man must have decided on a white skirt. I'd have to strongly consider getting a pair of those period panties as an extra precaution. Secondly, it looked like something a captain of a yacht might wear. I was experiencing serious FML in that moment, but at least the uniform was thick enough that I didn't have to wear boring undergarments.

I let out a curse as I picked up the shirt and jacket, realizing the back had two slits with about an inch of overlapping fabric, no doubt for angel wings to pop through. After putting on the sailor attire, I grabbed a Diet Dr. Pepper and a granola bar. One of the perks of being in the teacher building was a small kitchenette which had a half-sized fridge, sink, and two electric burners. Not that I'd use it much, but who knows, maybe I'd give cooking a shot.

I popped the top on my soda and took a long gulp as I went into the bathroom. Yes, I had an addiction to Diet Dr. Pepper. Some people liked their coffee, I liked my red and white can of crisp goodness.

I brushed out my brown hair and pulled it back into a loose pony-tail at the base of my neck before putting on my makeup. I toned it back much more than usual, skipping the black eyeliner and fake eyelashes.

I grabbed my bag and was out the door with plenty of time to spare. I had to walk to class, unlike my winged peers, although I noticed a lot were walking as I approached Uriel Hall.

This was going to be tough. I was not only starting midyear, having missed the entire first semester, but three weeks of the current semester had already passed. Not going to lie, school was tough for me. It would have taken a miracle for me to graduate with Ds and Cs had I not been expelled. Most likely I would have been retaking a few classes in summer school.

It's not that I didn't *want* to do well in school, but I found it hard to concentrate. In high school, the teachers didn't seem to care. There were meetings. There was testing. They never blamed me, but medicine wasn't an option because it didn't work. Different seating didn't work. Videos and audio recordings of the class didn't work. The only thing that helped, even if just a little, was marijuana. Too bad it was

ASCEND

still illegal for my age in California. Not that it had stopped me from getting my hands on any before, but then again that had led to me being scouted by a drug conglomerate.

I entered the building and made my way up two flights of stairs to room 306. Introduction to Demonology. I was actually excited, it being in my wheelhouse and all. Having some prior knowledge on the subject made me feel a little more confident as I pulled open the door.

Once inside the classroom I was immediately disappointed there were tables with two chairs at each. I hated partners. Well, really they hated me. It was a fairly large classroom with multiple tiers of tables curving in a crescent shape, much like a typical university. I looked to the front of the room and in the corner behind the teacher's desk sat Tobias Armstrong. *Great.* I was sure this class wouldn't be biased at all.

I walked over to the desk and stood by it while he typed something on his laptop. I cleared my throat and he looked up. His expression was hard to read. The day before he had recoiled and been annoyed with my presence, it seemed. Now, he had his teacher face on.

"Is there assigned seating?" Because God forbid I sit in someone's seat and taint it with my evil.

"Good morning, Danica." He went back to typing on his computer.

Yeah, maybe I should have greeted him. My elementary teachers always used to make us greet each other daily, but this wasn't elementary school anymore. Why did I need to say good morning to someone that looked at me like I was a piece of dog shit on the bottom of his shoe?

"Why don't you take a seat in the front row." He stopped typing and handed me a small stack with a book and folder.

I grabbed it from him rather roughly and sat off to the side, near the wall. I flipped through the book first. It was a run of the mill text book. Was there ever a class that didn't use a textbook? The teacher's job was to teach not force me to read chapters from an overly wordy book.

I flipped open the folder and found several pages of notes dated over the last three weeks. There was also a syllabus and list of assignments. Two had a line drawn through them with 'excused' written next to them. Thank goodness for small miracles. If I had to make up three weeks' worth of reading and assignments I'd lose it. Or I just wouldn't do it.

I took my spiral notebook and my pouch of Flair pens out of my bag and flipped the notebook open. I started at the corner of the page and started drawing a vine around the perimeter. Class must have started while I was doodling because the next thing I knew, Mr. Armstrong was tapping on the table in front of me. I looked up and met his gaze with raised eyebrows.

"You might want to take notes, Ms. Deville." I hated when teachers used students' last names.

I heard a few sniggers from behind me at the mention of my last name and watched as Mr. Armstrong narrowed his eyes in their direction before walking back to the center of the room. He smoothed down the front of his blue dress shirt and cleared his throat.

"In your reading last week, you should have read about Corpus Unguis demons. Who can tell me what physical features this demon has?" Mr. Armstrong went back to his desk and labeled a diagram that was being projected on the front board with the words 'physical features'.

I quickly flipped to the index of the book he had given me and found the page the Corpus Unguis demon was on. Skimming the page, I sighed. There were so many details that were incorrect or just flat out missing. That particular demon was complex and having half a page devoted to it was like having only a chapter about the Civil War in a history textbook. The angels' version of demon history was watered down just like a typical high school textbook.

A student near the middle of the room was called on and I turned slightly in my seat. Several sets of eyes stared back at me as I glanced around the room. None of my new friends were in this class. I did spot Oliver but quickly turned around before he could notice I had looked his way.

No one sat next to me.

Figures.

At least I'd have a seat for my bag.

Wasn't that the worst feeling in the world? Walking into a class-room and having no one sit next to you? I tried not to let it bother me, but it was becoming blatantly obvious I was the pariah of the school. I had been here less than twenty-four hours.

"A Corpus Unguis has five small heads with long tongues that have razor like protrusions on the ends. It has thick, almost clear skin that is impenetrable."

"Very nice. Now, why does this species have that type of exoskele-ton?" He wrote down what the student said and turned back to the class.

Another student was called on. "It eats the fingernails from its victims."

I watched as he wrote on his notes. I raised my hand.

"Yes, Danica?" Oh, thank fuck he was using my first name. "Something to add?"

"It actually only has one head with five mouths. Its head is shaped like a hammerhead shark. I can see how it could be confused as having five heads though. Plus it doesn't eat the fingernails. It pries them off, chews them up, then spreads the substance over its armor to strengthen it. It actually has a serpent like body which is exposed in a few places."

The room was so silent I could hear my own heartbeat thudding in my chest. Fuck. Now I was *that* student.

"Why the fingernails?" I turned to see Oliver looking at me. "How do we kill it?"

"Usually it steps in when the soul has done something that warrants nonuse of their hands. An eye for an eye type of situation. To kill it..." I bit my lip. I wasn't sure how happy Lucifer would be if I divulged how. "I'm not sure how."

"Oh, I'm pretty sure you know how. Sounds like you are well acquainted with them. Your last boyfriend was probably a Corpus Unguis." At Oliver's words the class exploded into laughter.

"Enough!" Mr. Armstrong stood from his desk and stood in the front center of the room, rubbing his hands along his short beard. "Mr. Morgan, that will be five points off your divinity score."

"But, Mr. Armstrong, she's-" He protested before being cut off.

"I don't care what your reason is. I won't tolerate bullying in this classroom. If anything we should be grateful we have someone who is knowledgeable about something we hopefully will never encounter."

The rest of the class I continued my flowering vines and wrote down, instead of volunteering, the errors in the book. I could see how so many demons were misrepresented. They were all confined to hell and it's not like Lucifer had written the textbook. I'd have to let Mr. Armstrong borrow the book I had on demons. It would blow his mind.

Once class ended, I ripped my notes out of my notebook and set them on his desk as I left the classroom.

BESIDES THE HUSHED whispers and the occasional use of the word devil, I made it out of Uriel Hall and across the quad area to the gymnasium. I didn't love or hate gym class, but this class was Defensive and Offensive Flight Techniques. It was gym on crack.

There was one big problem.

I didn't have wings.

I made my way to the locker rooms and found Brooklyn already in her workout clothes. She greeted me and I quickly changed. Luckily there was no dress code for PE, so I threw on leggings and a tank top.

"How was your first class?" Brooklyn and her friends were the only ones so far to not throw hate my way, which was a relief. At least I had a few people on my side, or at the very least, in neutral territory.

She seemed to be on the quiet, shy side and reminded me a tad of Ava. She was shorter than me and had a head full of luscious curls that she wore in a sloppy bun on the top of her head.

"Oliver had five points taken away because he made some comment about the fingernail demon being my boyfriend. It's like we're in junior high." I shrugged like it was no big deal and I steered us towards the teacher, who looked awfully young to be teaching. "There's a student teaching?"

"Coach Ferguson? He's a Class II. He's about twenty-five in angel years."

I stopped in my tracks and grabbed her arm. "Run that by me again."

"He died when he was ten, drowned in a river. He's been an angel for twenty-five years, so he is thirty-five in human years, if that helps. Angels stop maturing in their early twenties. If they are older when they die they just stay that way, like Mr. Armstrong. All the really old Class IIIs go to a different academy."

"How'd he die?" I didn't know if that was a rude question, but if I was going to be asked if I had a pet hellhound or if I had horns, then any of my questions were fair game.

She shrugged. "Coach Ferguson told us his story the first day of school. Mr. Armstrong doesn't share much about his time before he became an angel. But I think I heard him say he was twenty-seven when he died."

We waited behind a student already talking to the coach. His eyes widened slightly when he saw me, but he finished his conversation before turning to me.

"Danica Deville, is it?"

I nodded in reply.

When he started to turn away, I cleared my throat. "Sir, I don't have, uh... I don't have wings."

A hush fell around the gymnasium. I hadn't even realized everyone was watching me so intently. This room sure did echo too.

"What do you mean you don't have wings? They let you in here without wings? How can you fly with no wings? This is an academy to be a guardian angel!" I was so tempted to roll my eyes at his stupid questions. Had I been back at my old school, I would have, and then I would have promptly been kicked out of class.

"Flap my arms really hard?" I raised my eyebrows and smiled. He didn't seem amused.

"You are an angel, right? What class are you?"

Crap, crap, crap. I had forgotten to find that little important piece of information out. I had meant to ask Mr. Armstrong.

Brooklyn, sensing my anxiety, stepped forward a little. "Sir, she is half angel. I don't think they have a classification for her yet. Maybe today I can practice hand-to-hand combat with her since she missed first semester?"

"Good thinking, Russo." He gave me one last look before turning his back to me.

We made our way over to an area off the main gym. I had tried karate when I was younger and hated it. It was too controlled. What I really wanted was to learn how to throw down on the fly. I already knew how to throw a good punch at the nose though.

"Thanks. You deserve ten points for that," I said as we approached the door.

I heard footsteps behind us and turned to see Levi and two other boys. I turned back towards Brooklyn and nearly collided with her stopped body at the entrance to the area we were headed.

I heard laughter and my stomach clenched. Brooklyn spun around and glared at the three boys holding their stomachs in laughter. I stepped into the room where training dummies were spread at regular intervals and mats lined the floors. Taped to the dummy's heads were pictures of Lucifer.

Except it wasn't Lucifer. It was a red monster with a contorted face, horns, and red eyes. I went to each one and ripped the paper off. I didn't hear what Brooklyn said to them because my ears had done the strange, fuzzy ringing that happens when I get really pissed off, but the boys seemed to be laughing even harder. I walked over to them and stepped too close for comfort, because their laughing immediately stopped and they backed up a step.

"Maybe I should summon my father here to show you what he *really* looks like. And trust me, you don't want to see him when he's pissed off." The boys paled at my words and backed up another foot.

They didn't need to know that Lucifer didn't have a demon form, or a different face. That's actually what made him so terrifying. He looked almost normal. The almost being that he had a penchant for fancy-ass suits and exuberant watches all while permeating hearts and souls with fear.

I wadded up the photos and threw them at Levi who jumped back to avoid their touch. I only wished I had the ability to throw fire balls. I turned on my heel and went back into the room with Brooklyn.

"That was... epic."

I gave her a tight smile but it was forced. I didn't want to use Lucifer as a threat, but these angels weren't leaving me with any other choice.

The rest of my classes and lunch passed without incident. Word had spread that I had threatened Levi and his two friends.

Good. Let them be scared.

At least if they were scared of me they would stop being assholes.

CHAPTER 4

TOBIAS

*T*his semester was really shaping up to be a shit-show of a semester. Just last week, the dean had called me into her office to meet with her and Chamuel. They told me I would be the advisor of Lucifer's daughter.

Lucifer's daughter.

I still couldn't quite wrap my head around that one. Angels weren't fertile. How the hell did Lucifer get a human pregnant? Had he used dark magic? Demon blood?

Chamuel didn't seem to know, nor did he care. He was all about peace and love. I'm not exactly sure what his thought process was behind allowing her to come to the most prestigious of all the celestial academies. We had standards here and after looking at her rather thick cumulative folder from her *human* education, she was far below what we would ever allow.

Besides lackluster grades that resulted in her frequenting summer school, she had a discipline record a mile long. A few suspensions with a day here, three days there. It painted a picture of a troubled young woman.

Pot in locker.

Defiance.

Disruption.

Assault.

Did Chamuel truly think we could fix this girl? She might have angel blood in her, but she certainly wasn't angelic. Maybe he was losing his touch because this place was definitely not the place for a half-blood angel that didn't even have wings.

On Sunday, when she had arrived, I had actually been surprised that she looked normal. A little better than normal. I guess I expected her to be goth or something. I wouldn't say angels ran around in skin tight pants that showed the sharp curve between their ass and hamstrings or crop tops that bared a flat stomach begging to be touched.

As she walked towards me that first day, I had known I was in trouble with this... woman. She stirred something deep within me that I hadn't even felt when I was human. It repulsed me. She repulsed me. Not because of who she was, but because I was the adult in this situation and she was, well, she was my student.

At least that's what I kept trying to tell myself.

Walking back to my room, I found myself thinking about her. She was already being bullied for who she was. Oliver might be top of the class, but his behavior was completely out of line and I don't think he was even aware how out of line he was. We had the other Divine 7 to thank for that.

They were supposed to be guiding him. Instead they were corrupting him. I wanted to intervene, but there were explicit orders from upstairs that he was to find his own path. Things probably weren't going to end well for him.

Even the other instructors were out of line. At lunch, Trey Ferguson had done nothing but complain about the half-breed in his class. She had no wings. She had an attitude. I couldn't argue with him there, she certainly had that.

Then there was Patricia Fisher, the Portrayal of Angels and Demons in Modern Literature instructor. She had docked Danica ten points she didn't even have because the girl had made a comment about her dad not being red. I hadn't docked her points for speaking out in *my* class.

I entered the common room of my building and nodded politely at the other staff members lounging on the soft leather sofas. Normally, I'd join them, but I wanted to work on updating our files on demons after the new information I learned today. Danica Deville might not be our ideal student, but she knew things we didn't.

Turning right at the top of the stairs, I stopped in my tracks as Danica stood outside her door and was wiggling to pull pants on under her skirt. A flash of red caught my eye but her gaze snapped to mine and I looked away.

What the hell was she doing changing in the hall?

And were those feathers on the ground?

Trailing out her door to where she was standing was a small trail of white feathers. Had she gotten her wings? If she had, then I needed to get her to the infirmary because that much shedding wasn't typical.

"Oh, hi, Mr. Armstrong." She zipped up her pants and stared at me as I started walking down the hall to my door.

She was at the end of the hall, I was in the middle. I stopped at my door but then turned to look at her before speaking.

"May I ask what you're doing?"

Now that I was closer I could see a few feathers in her brown hair and red blotches under her eyes, as if she'd been crying. My chest constricted at the sight and I felt the unwavering desire to step closer to her. To wrap her in my arms.

"Come and see for yourself. I'm just going to change my shirt in the stairwell." Her normal confident vibrato was absent from her voice as she spoke. I watched as she opened the door to the stairwell and slipped inside.

I peeked into her room but then moved to stand in the doorway, taking in the sight.

White down feathers lay all over the room. Everything, and I mean everything, had feathers on it. Her bed. Her dresser drawers that were pulled out. Her desk. Her bathroom.

My eyes went to the open window and I cursed under my breath. I hadn't thought to tell her to keep her window shut and locked, but how was I to know someone would do something so cruel?

I moved out of the way as she came out of the stairwell with a black tank top on that had a picture of the devil and the words "I'm horny" on it. I felt her eyes land on my quirked lips as I stared at her chest.

"So, yeah." She crossed her arms over her chest, which only made my focus on her breasts worse because it pushed them up. They'd probably fit perfectly in my hands.

No. No they wouldn't.

I looked down the hall, away from her. "I can call the custodian to come and clean this up."

"No! I... just let me take care of it." Her voice cracked and that made me ache to reach out and touch her.

To touch her, just like I had wanted to on Sunday.

God, how I had wanted to touch her.

"I'll get us some supplies to clean this up."

I went to the supply closet, which was right across from her room, and grabbed black trash bags, brooms, and dust pans. I was a shitty advisor. I should have shown her around yesterday. Instead, I had run for the hills because she made my dick twitch.

We worked in silence for a few minutes before I let out a frustrated grunt and threw the broom down. "Who the fuck did this?"

I hadn't been that angry out in the hall, but now that we were trying to clean up the feathers, I was furious. Down feathers were the most annoying of all feathers. They stuck to everything and were so fluffy it was hard to pick them up, even with a broom and dustpan.

"I think it's pretty obvious angels did it, don't you?" She threw her broom down too, but with much less force than I had, and went to her refrigerator. "The assholes better not have put feathers in here."

She let out a puff of air as she opened the door and there were no feathers. Once the door was open, several drifted to the inside of the door at the bottom.

"Want a soda or water?" She took out a Diet Dr. Pepper and a bottle of water and held them out to me.

I grabbed the water and she looked relieved I hadn't taken the soda. I tilted my head a bit to the side and took her in as she popped the top and drank half the can in one go. She could have been a spokesmodel in a commercial with how sexy she looked drinking it.

"Why are you helping me?" she asked before putting her can on the counter and grabbing a bowl out of the cupboard.

She reached down and scooped up a bowl of feathers. Her face cracked into a grin at her ingenuity.

"Why would I not help you?" I started scooping feathers again.

"You're a dick."

I wasn't expecting that, that was for sure.

I paused mid scoop and looked up at her looking down at me. "What do you mean?"

"You think I'm repulsive. You all do." She spoke in an even tone that didn't give away any emotion. Either she was strong as fuck or had already come to terms with how the others felt about her.

"I don't think that. What gave you that impression?" My chest felt a little tight. Had I given her that idea? If she only knew how completely untrue her words were.

"The way you talk to me, look at me, flinch away when I get close." She lowered to her knees and continued scooping. "I would have at least expected the teachers to be more accepting."

I remained quiet. What was I going to tell her anyway? That the looks I gave her were more of an outward expression of the disgust I felt towards myself for getting a hard on for her? That when she got close to me I wanted to move away so I didn't do something stupid?

I couldn't tell her any of that.

Sure she was eighteen and of age, but I was her teacher.

Plus, I was old. Like died when I was twenty-seven during World War II old.

She let out a frustrated sigh and sat down in the feathers.

"How do angels get their wings?" Her hands lowered to the feathers beside her and she gathered them in her hands and watched the feathers drift down as she released them.

I continued to work and stopped near the dresser. "Well, there's a few ways..."

I struggled to find my words at the sight of her panties and bras laying in a heap on the floor. They were covered with feathers, but it was pretty obvious she liked lace. So much lace.

I turned quickly and moved away, hoping she wouldn't notice. She did.

"I'm lucky they didn't do anything to those, otherwise I'd have to go commando."

The thought of her without panties under that white skirt of hers made my dick twitch and start to harden. *Shit.*

"So, wings. Well, some are born with them. Class I, like Oliver Morgan. Class II usually get them immediately upon entering heaven. The rest of us have to go through a vetting process to make sure we are worthy."

"Lucifer didn't exactly explain all this stuff to me." She glanced up at me before she turned her attention back to playing with the feathers at her sides.

I hoped the way I was holding the trash bag was covering up my growing erection because I still couldn't get the image of her in that skirt with no panties out of my mind. Or how I'd love to bend her over my desk and-

What the heck was happening to me?

"I guess the easiest way to explain it is a person must have more light in their past than darkness. If there's more darkness they are sent to hell. If we are deemed worthy, then we're given tasks or jobs to increase the light. It might be as simple as singing in the choir for a year or maybe a series of selfless acts."

"You mean like a blow job? If that isn't a selfless act, I don't know what is." She laughed as she looked at me, a tinge of pink touching her cheeks. I felt all the blood drain from my face and straight down, making my erection throb.

She stood then and walked towards me and my breath caught in my throat. She reached her hand towards my face, and as much as I wanted to pull away, I stood still. Her pinky finger lightly touched my

bottom lip as she plucked a feather off my chin with her thumb and forefinger.

I was headed down a dark path.

Not that angels couldn't have sex.

Sex wasn't the issue here.

She was a forbidden fruit, one that if I took a bite of I would surely be damned.

"You have a feather too." The words sounded stupid coming from my mouth, but they were out there and I reached towards her hair and brushed it off.

She pulled her bottom lip between her teeth and her eyes dropped to where I had just been holding the trash bag. The trash bag that I had dropped to brush the feather out of her hair. Her eyes met mine and I was certain that I wasn't alone in my sudden desire. It hit me like a lightning bolt.

I dropped the dust pan and brought my other hand up to cup her cheek. A warm sensation ran up my arm and to the center of my chest. My wings tingled in response.

"Shit." She backed away and turned away from me. "Sometimes I don't have a filter or boundaries. I'm sorry."

"Let me touch you again." I heard my words but they didn't sound like my own. My voice had lowered slightly. I felt a need swirling inside of me. I wanted to touch her. I needed to touch her.

"As much as I want you to, Mr.-"

"Tobias," I interrupted. I already felt skeevy enough as it was. Calling me Mr. Armstrong would only make it worse.

"Okay then, Tobias. I... okay."

I stepped behind her and picked a few feathers off her tank top, my hands shaking in the process. I ran a finger across her shoulder and felt her shiver with my touch. This was such a bad idea. Did she even really want me to touch her or was she just letting me because she felt she didn't have a choice?

"Tell me if you want me to stop."

I trailed my index finger down her arm before dragging it slowly back up. My body was thrumming with an energy I had never felt before. Even as a human I had never felt like this, and certainly not as an angel. Sexual pleasure was always slightly dulled, but not now. Not with her.

"I don't want you to stop," she breathed as my hand fell away from her.

Fuck it. For once in my life I was going to let myself lose control, consequences be damned. I lowered my mouth to her shoulder and kissed it lightly, drawing a sigh from her. I gently moved her hair out of the way and kissed my way to the base of her neck. It was taking so much self-control not to spin her around and capture her lips.

My hand went back to caressing her arm as I dragged my tongue from her neck to the strap of her tank top, which I grabbed in my teeth and pulled down over her shoulder. She let out a moan as I sucked her skin and planted kisses over the goose-bumped flesh. She tasted like heaven. If heaven had a taste.

My other hand threaded through her hair and pulled her head to the side to bare her neck to me. She whimpered as I lightly scraped my teeth over the spot just below her ear before sucking her earlobe between my lips. I don't know how I had gone from completely level-headed and professional to horned up and out of my mind.

My hands went to her waist and I struggled not to devour her whole. I had never wanted a woman so bad in my life and as she shivered and moaned with my touch and my kisses, I knew she had to be feeling the same.

My hand moved to her breasts, fitting perfectly in my hands as I kneaded them through her clothing. She turned her head and our lips met, a groan escaping before I let my tongue explore hers. I pressed against her back, letting her feel my erection against her ass. She pressed back against me before turning and grabbing my hair, bringing me closer, as if we could get any closer.

We were moving towards the bed. We were moving so damn slow towards it. She pulled me down with her, our lips never breaking contact, even when feathers floated around us. I settled between her legs so perfectly that I was anxious to get her out of her jeans to see just how well we fit together.

My hands pushed her tank up over her breasts and I pulled away to look. Her chest moved up and down as her lungs caught up with what we had just done. I traced my finger in a circle on her smooth stomach before trailing it up to her red-lace clad breasts.

I met her eyes and smiled. "No white?" I joked before lowering my mouth to the waist line of her jeans. She moaned as I licked the skin right above where her jeans touched. Her skin tasted like roses and what reminded me of licorice.

"What if I wanted you to wear white panties for me, or maybe no panties at all?" I glanced up at her again; desire was written all over her face.

I dragged my lips up her belly and kissed under her bra as I reached behind her and unclasped it. A sigh left her as she sat up and took off her tank. She grabbed the straps of her bra and slowly moved it down her arms to reveal her peaked nipples. I ran the back of my hand along the outside of her breast and she shivered. My thumb gently brushed over her nipple, causing her back to arch, bringing her closer to me.

"No more teasing. I want you to fuck me before I explode," she growled before grabbing a hand full of my hair and pushing my mouth to her breast.

If there was any doubt about her innocence or unwillingness, it quickly vanished.

I sucked and nipped at her puckered nipples as I unbuttoned her pants and pushed my hand between her legs. The lace between her legs was soaked through with her arousal. And I wanted to taste it. I wanted to taste all of her.

"You're so fucking wet," I murmured against her breast.

She moaned as I ran my finger up and down her hot, wet slit before pulling my hand out enough to slide back down into her panties. My fingers slid over a small patch of hair before my index finger dipped between her folds, her hips rising to encourage me further. Our lips met again in a forceful kiss.

Her hands slid down my back and cupped my ass cheeks. I took her bottom lip in my teeth as I plunged two of my fingers into her pussy. There was no turning back now; I was all in with where this was headed.

"Tobias, please." I wasn't sure if she wanted more from my hand, my mouth, or my dick inside of her.

"Tell me what you want, baby. There's no rush." My thumb found her clit and worked it in circles.

Her hands slipped around to my belt buckle and she fumbled with it as she dealt with the pleasure I was bringing her. I used my free hand to help her and undid my slacks. Her hands slipped inside and found my bare cock, ready and waiting for her.

"I need this inside of me." She grabbed the base of my cock and began to work her hand at the same pace as I was moving my fingers.

I let out a groan before pulling my hand out of her pants and pulling her to her feet. I ripped back the quilt on her bed, sending feathers flying, but at least now we wouldn't get them in our ass cracks.

"Do we need protection? I have an implant, but..." She tilted her head back slightly to look at me, her cheeks flushed with heat.

How on God's green Earth did I let it get this far? Far enough that we were discussing using a condom, which she had no clue we didn't even need because angels were infertile.

Only now I was questioning that because how else had *she* happened? She must have read the hesitation on my face because she backed up a step.

"Unless you don't want to. I know it all happened a little fast." She bit her lip and started to pull her pants back up.

I was completely fucking this up. I felt like this was my first time, that awkward moment when you have to stop to fumble with the condom because putting a condom on a dick was way different than putting it on a banana.

"We don't need condoms."

Before I could mess up further, I pulled her back towards me and kissed her. I pushed down her jeans and panties and took off my pants. We sank to the bed and I put the tip of my cock against her opening.

Her phone rang and her face suddenly changed from sweet antici-pation to annoyance. I pushed inside of her and we both sighed in satisfaction. What felt like lightning bolts shot through my dick and up between my shoulder blades. My wings ached to come out, but that might have ruined it for her.

Her phone rang again and she threw an arm over her eyes and let out a moan. Not a moan of pleasure, but a moan of frustration. I listened closer and heard the song, *Runnin' With the Devil* by Van Halen.

Crap. Her dad was calling.

Did he know?

Oh, sweet baby Jesus, did the devil know that I was currently buried balls deep inside his little girl?

I pulled out and rolled over next to her, both of us panting. My dick was still hard, but now I was slightly scared that he was going to show up and kick my ass. Or probably sic a Corpus Unguis demon on me since I had my hands all over her.

The phone rang a third time and she finally jumped up and went to her backpack to dig it out of the front pocket.

"For fuck's sake, *Lucifer*. What the hell is it?" she snapped into the phone.

I sat up abruptly, surprised she'd talk to him like that. Wasn't she scared of him? I mean, he controlled demons that chewed on finger-nails like a cow chews on cud. I shuddered and felt my erection start to deflate. I didn't want it to, it's just now I was thinking about having my fingernails ripped off for touching her.

She rolled her eyes as she listened to her dad, Lucifer. The devil.

"Everything's fine. Great actually. Well, except for the name calling, oh, and the feathers covering my room. But I've made some friends." She looked at me and winked.

It gave me a little relief, that wink, but not enough to salvage the moment. Maybe that was a good thing; this was rather spur of the moment. I don't do spur of the moment. I should have asked her out for coffee or to dinner.

She listened to him talk again. "I appreciate your concern, but I

have it handled... No, I won't punch anyone in the nose. I promise...
You're way too overprotective... Love you too, bye."

She hung up and walked back over to the bed, sitting on the side,
her back to me.

"Kind of a mood killer, isn't it?" She looked over her shoulder at
me and down at my limp dick. "It's like he sensed a sin was about to be
committed."

"What do you mean he sensed a sin?" I stood, panic flaring in
my gut.

The last thing I needed was to piss off Lucifer, or any of the
archangels, and end up without my wings. I saw what that did to a
man and it wasn't pretty.

"It was a joke. We should finish cleaning this up. Maybe try to find
one of those shop vacuums to use." She didn't sound like she wanted
to finish cleaning it up but stood and went into the bathroom, shutting the door partway.

I heard the sink water, so I grabbed my pants, shook them out and
slid them back on. I grabbed her clothing off the floor and shook
them off the best I could. My heart was beating wildly as I grabbed
her red lace panties. I looked back at the cracked bathroom door to
make sure she wasn't looking and shoved them in my pocket. I left my
shirt untucked to hide the fact there was something there.

When she came back out she looked for a few moments for them
but then just grabbed another pair from her pile. How had we so
quickly gone from zero to sixty? I was feeling whiplash and I was
pretty sure I wanted it again.

CHAPTER 5

DANICA

I hated when time seemed to slow infinitely when you were impatiently awaiting the weekend. It slowed even more when you had to deal with assholes and the fiery gaze of a particular teacher.

My encounter at the beginning of the week with Tobias was only that. An encounter. Sure, I had felt something beyond anything I had felt with a simple touch before, but I barely knew him. He barely knew me. It was not beyond my often-impulsive self to recognize that starting something with a teacher, my advisor nonetheless, was playing with fire.

And I'd probably be the one who got burned.

All week I had done my best to avoid him in the hall. It's not that I didn't want him, because I did. Every time I saw him my skin ached for him to touch it, but my mind was on other things. Like why the Divine 7 thought it was their duty to torture me.

On Tuesday before Demonology had started, Oliver very loudly announced that he was in desperate need of new pillows and asked for recommendations. Tobias looked murderous most of class, but did nothing, at least from what I could tell.

Then on Wednesday at lunch, Abby, Julian, and Levi walked by the table and dumped a plate of deviled eggs on me. Where they had even gotten them was beyond me since there had been none available when I went through the lunch line. I had wanted to retaliate but then Lucifer's warning echoed in my head.

The one he gave when he interrupted the pleasure train to an orgasm. The way Tobias had been touching me, kissing me. *Le-sigh*. Damn him to hell for calling.

Every time they said or did something, his voice echoed in my head. "Danica, don't get yourself kicked out of this school. This is your last chance." I wasn't sure what he meant by 'last chance' but I *really* didn't want to find out. There was only so far you could push the devil, and I think I had met my life quota ten-fold.

Thursday was freaking fantastic, and I should have known that it was the calm before the storm. The storm being my last class, which just happened to be independent study in the library. It was my least favorite class because I was studying for my GED, which meant I had to focus. My focus was even worse because all I could think about was Tobias.

When he had touched me it was like fireworks had gone off in my body. No one had ever made me feel like that before. He worshipped my body, and despite barely knowing him, I felt some weird comfort being near him.

I was just finishing up a lesson on the computer when I heard something behind me. I hadn't even heard the library door open, so they had to have already been inside. Before I could even register the sensation to flee, a black bag was yanked over my head and I was jerked out of my chair by my arm.

Either the librarian was away or they had distracted her, because when I screamed, no one came. All there was, was laughter. Gleeful laughter. By now I knew that laughter well.

My hands were tied behind my back and then the bag was pulled up and a ball gag put in my mouth. I'd never be able to enjoy a ball gag now, thanks to those assholes.

Once they were gone, I managed to get the bag off my head by bending in half and shaking my head vigorously. The damn librarian was nowhere to be seen, so my only option was to wander into the hall.

I wish I hadn't.

I wish I had just stayed until the librarian came back.

At least some students in the hall looked at me in pity. Most laughed and took pictures with their phones. It would be spread around the school in a matter of minutes.

Someone finally untied my hands, and when I yanked the ball gag out of my mouth, well, no wonder it was so hilarious to everyone. It was in the shape of an apple.

I would have maybe even thought it was brilliant if they hadn't done it to me.

FRIDAY. Possibly the best day of the week. Well, besides Saturday and Sunday. Even school on Fridays didn't bother me too much since most teachers were always burnt out, which usually meant easy assignments or a video.

Teachers except Tobias Armstrong. A pop quiz on a Friday was not the way I had envisioned my day starting. I had half-expected a movie with demons. Tests and I didn't exactly see eye to eye. At least it was short-answer.

I found that short-answer was the best for me. I could embellish the hell out of my answers and usually at least get a few points. It's how I maintained my stellar 2.3 grade point average in high school.

When class ended, I pretended like I was finishing up my quiz until the last student had exited and then handed it to Tobias.

"I won't be marked down for my descriptions being a little different than the book's, will I?" This was my main worry during the quiz, but I hadn't wanted to ask in front of everyone.

I was trying to lay low after the apple gag incident the afternoon before. I was going to be called Eve for weeks because of it. I didn't need everyone calling me an idiot too.

Tobias grabbed my paper and glanced over it. "No, but I will mark down for all these feather doodles you put everywhere." He smiled up at me, a glint in his eye.

Smiling was something he needed to do more often. It brought a light to his eyes that made me want to reach out and caress his cheek. He stared back down at my paper. "You've been avoiding me, Danica."

I ran my finger over the corner of the desk and then examined my nails to avoid his gaze. I felt it though. Felt it right between my legs.

"Come here." His voice was quietly commanding, which made my heart start to beat wildly. What if I refused and stayed where I was? It was tempting to defy him, but instead I moved around the side of the desk to stand near the drawers.

He grabbed my hand and pulled me closer. The same overwhelming need to be touched flared in my body, running up my arm, into my chest, to my core.

"Why have you been avoiding me?" He still had ahold of my hand so I couldn't escape.

"I haven't." I looked him square in the eyes, hoping he couldn't see what he was doing to me. I cleared my throat. "Is there anything I can do to make up for the lost points?"

"You can earn some extra credit." He let go of my hand and gripped my hip.

I was losing my resolve fast. This was why I had avoided him. Just his presence got me all worked up. It hadn't even been that long since I got laid, but I felt like it had been years. Monday's festivities didn't count.

"Get on the desk."

A jolt of excitement shot up through my toes and straight to my clit. We were in an unlocked classroom, but I wanted to get on the desk just to see what he was going to do. The thought of doing anything lascivious in a classroom at an angel school made me feel breathless. So, I slid my ass up onto the desk, my feet dangling off the side.

He rolled his chair away from his desk and slid it over in front of me, putting his hands on my knees. I took a sharp inhale of breath as he slid his hands up my bare legs, pushing them apart as he went. He let out a groan when his hands reached my panties and he slowly pulled them off, sticking them in his pocket.

My eyes narrowed on him and he smirked before he ran his tongue up my leg. I was already trembling and he hadn't even touched my pussy yet, but when he did I had to put the end of my jacket sleeve in my mouth to keep from crying out.

I thought his hands were brilliant, but his tongue was sinful. He pulled his mouth away and stood from the chair, kicking it back with his foot. I resisted the urge to touch my clit to finish the task he had abandoned.

"Is this part of my extra credit?"

He grabbed me around my waist, pulled me off the desk and bent me over so my chest was pressed into the stacks of papers on it. My body shook with anticipation as he lifted my skirt around my waist and ran his hand over my bare ass.

"Is your phone on silent?" he whispered in my ear, amusement in his voice, and pressed his erection against my ass.

I nodded, words alluding me in that moment, and he gripped my hip before thrusting into me, causing me to let a moan escape. I pushed his papers out of the way and brought my blazer-covered arm to my mouth to muffle my sounds as he thrust into me over and over again.

The last thing we needed was to be caught. I knew he didn't have a class, but the risk was there. A risk that sent a thrill through me. When I came, I came hard, sending Tobias to his own climax.

He rested against me while he caught his breath then handed me a few tissues. I cleaned up and pulled my skirt down. I had just thrown the tissues away when the classroom door opened and Oliver Morgan, of all people, walked in.

He stopped in his tracks and his eyes went from me to Tobias, who was still buckling his belt, to the desk with papers shoved to one side, then back to me.

His face turned red as he went to where he had sat and picked up a notebook that was left on the desk. "Forgot my notebook."

Without giving us another look he walked out of the classroom, slamming the door behind him hard enough that I jumped in surprise.

"Shit. Fuck. Shit." I grabbed my bag and smoothed my skirt. "I'm late for PE."

That's not why I was freaked out. Now the whole school was going to know I was sleeping with a teacher. As if they didn't already have enough ammunition against me.

"Hey, don't freak out. Oliver isn't going to say anything." Tobias started straightening the papers on his desk. "And before you ask, yes, I'm sure. I know some things that he probably doesn't want everyone to know about."

My anxiety suddenly ebbed and my curiosity reared its ugly head. "Oh, really. Like what?"

He laughed and leaned towards me to give me a much too tame kiss. It was probably for the best since I was already fifteen minutes late to PE.

"Can't tell you." He finished straightening his papers and sat down in his chair. "Let me take you out to dinner tomorrow. Tonight I'm on call."

"Like a date?" My heart started beating a little faster and I crossed my arms over my chest, thinking he could see the change. He nodded. "Yeah, I'd like that."

"Good. I'll text you later. And Dani?" He grabbed my hand as I started to walk away. I turned and met his chocolate brown eyes. "Don't avoid me again."

I left the room on wobbly knees but managed to make it to PE with enough time left to be scowled at by Coach Ferguson.

At lunch, I was nervous. Tobias's assurances did nothing to stop the pit of anxiety in my stomach. Plus, I had something planned to get a little sweet revenge. I hadn't been entirely sure I was even going to do it. That was until the apple gag was shoved in my mouth.

The deviled eggs I could deal with. Hell, even the feathers in my room was more of just an annoyance to get under my skin. But physically restraining me and putting their hands on me? That was where I drew the line between childish pranks and something more sinister.

"What are your plans for this weekend? There's a party Saturday night we were going to go to." Cora interrupted my train of thought and I jerked my attention back to the lunch conversation. Angels had parties? Color me surprised.

"I have a dinner date Saturday night but if I get back in enough time I can meet up with you guys."

Cora and Brooklyn leaned forward in their seats.

"Do we know him or her?" Brooklyn looked like she was about to burst. She was all about the boys. She had never had a boyfriend, so I couldn't blame her for her curiosity.

Earlier in the week she had asked me about my love life, and when I told her I had slept with three men, she about died. Well, if she could have died again.

"No. It's our first date so I don't really have much to tell you besides he's hot." I imagined their faces if I told them the truth.

Honestly, I never had imagined myself with an older man, at least not one nine years older or however old he was in angel years. I couldn't help that I was attracted to him and wanted to know everything about him. He seemed to have no qualms about my age, at least from what I could tell. I decided to put my plan in motion instead of dwelling further on something that, at the end of the day, didn't bother me.

I reached down and grabbed the large manila envelope in my bag. When I was deciding on the vessel for the feathers, I had run through a million different scenarios. They were already going to be suspicious when I approached their table.

"What are you up to?" Ethan narrowed his eyes in my direction. Was I that obvious? "You have a shit-eating grin on your face."

"You'll see." I held the envelope between my knees and finished scarfing down my sandwich.

As if fate had determined this was an excellent idea, all seven angels waltzed through the dining room to their table with their trays.

I had gone over my plan several times during my last class before lunch.

"I'll be right back."

I made my way to the Divine 7's table, and by the time I stood behind an empty chair next to Abby, the table had gone silent and six sets of eyes stared at me. All except Oliver.

"Eve, what do you want?" Delilah spat. Her eyes dropped to the envelope in my hand.

In the most irritatingly-sweet voice I possessed, I spoke. "I'm so happy you asked. Yesterday was a massive awakening for me." I shook my head as if I was disappointed in myself. "Until I saw myself with that apple in my mouth, I never thought about how our sins can affect those around us."

I looked at each of them before continuing. They at least weren't stopping me. "And all this time, for eighteen years, all I've done is sin, sin, sin. I thought who better to help me atone for my sins than the highest-ranking angels in this academy."

I held up the envelope, which was bulging. Their eyes followed it. "So I wrote down all of my sins on strips of paper and I figure if you can help me with one at a time then maybe, just maybe, I'll get my wings. The thought of going even one more day without them. It pains me." I put my other hand over my heart. Maybe a career in acting was in my future.

"You aren't serious, are you? You have that many sins?" Levi gestured to the envelope and had a look of amusement on his face.

"I don't even think I remembered all of them, honestly. Oh!" I made a noise of excitement. "I have one more I need to add that happened just today. I think maybe I should just tell you guys what I did and we can take care of it now."

At my words, Oliver's head snapped up and his eyes widened.

"Or even better!" I dropped the smile from my face. "How about I show you."

With my final words I started shaking the envelope down the length of the table as if it were a salt shaker. A few of the guys scooted back from the table, but most of the group sat stoically. Shocked. Flabbergasted. Probably already plotting my demise.

I sprinkled the last of the feathers on Oliver's and Levi's trays before dropping the envelope in front of Oliver. "And Oliver? I do hope your new pillows *satisfy* you."

I probably shouldn't have said that, but clearly he was uncomfortable with what he had seen this morning. If he had only walked in a few minutes before he would have seen a whole hell of a lot more.

I turned and walked back to my table, the entire dining area staring at me in silence. Some with scowls, some with admiration. They had heard it all. Hell, most of them probably knew about the feathers.

"Ms. Deville." Dean Whittaker seemed to appear out of nowhere and walked towards me with a deep frown on her face. "Please come with me."

Damn.

But it was totally worth it.

CHAPTER 6

DANICA

*E*vidence. That was what Dean Whittaker said was lacking in my defense. I, on the other hand, had evidence against me. It's hard not to when you dump a giant envelope of feathers out on your enemies' food and the dean sees it happen with her very own eyes.

That was what they were now. My enemies.

Dean Whittaker said she wanted to give me a chance. A chance at what? A chance at sitting back and letting bully angels torment me? I kept my mouth shut, because unlike my former principal, the dean did not shoot the breeze or even care.

If she would have cared she wouldn't have brushed off my accusations of bullying like they were insignificant pieces of lint that landed on her shoulder. That was what she had called them. Accusations. The problems that plagued human schools seemed to plague celestial schools too. Only it made it so much worse that they were angels.

Instead of even an ounce of sympathy for me—I had even showed her the pictures of the feathers and the apple gag—she took twenty-five divinity points from me and said she was assigning me a peer mentor because my points were at a critical level.

Critical my ass.

When points dropped too much, angels were sent to the high court for judgement on what action should be taken. Los Angeles Celestial Academy was the top academy for training angels to become guardians, but if a student wasn't showing promise they could be sent back to heaven or not be given any guardian tasks. Divinity points were the way they kept track. I didn't even have wings, so did points even apply to me? I didn't dare ask.

I left the administrative offices feeling deflated. It was rare my heart was so irrevocably twisted to the point it hurt to breathe. Not even when I was expelled, or that time the school resource officer threatened to throw me in a juvenile detention facility if I was ever found with pot again.

This was different. The very essence of who I was, was being attacked. Villainized. And for what? For being different? I honestly didn't even feel I was that different. Yes, I made mistakes, maybe even more than average, but did that make me evil? I didn't *feel* evil.

When I got back to my room, I pulled up FaceTime. It rang twice before Lucifer answered. I stared at the wall behind his desk which was covered in art depicting him. He got a kick out of it. To me it was just a reminder of how everyone saw my father and now how they saw me.

"Dani, just a second." His voice sounded far away, like he was on the other side of his office.

When he did appear, he was buttoning the top two buttons on a dress shirt. I briefly wondered if he had just gotten up or if he had been working. Lord knows why he would need to change his shirt after working.

"I'm leaving," I stated bluntly. Really no use in beating around the bush.

He sat in his chair and put laced fingers under his chin, searching my face. I was glad he couldn't interfere with my emotions through the computer screen.

"And where will you go? Back to Montecito? What will you do?"

I had been thinking about that question since he told me he was sending me to the Celestial Academy. "I have money. I'll just get a job at Starbucks or something, so I'm not bored."

"You hate the smell of coffee." His voice was neutral, which always made me leery of what he was thinking. "And what do you mean, you have money? Your money is *my* money."

"But you have so much of it, you can share with your only daughter, can't you? I *am* your only child, aren't I?" It was childish, but at one point in time, I had thought he had another family because he was never around.

Now I knew why he was never around.

He sighed and ran his hands over his face. "You'll stay there or I will have to cut you off."

I gaped at him. Lucifer was loaded. He had multiple aliases throughout the world and the sum of his wealth was astronomical. It would put Bezos to shame.

"I'm not like them. They hate me because you're my dad and I don't even have wings to at least somewhat fit in." My voice caught in my throat and I fought to hold back tears. Lucifer didn't do well with tears. At least not from me.

"Danica... you don't need wings to fly."

"Don't go getting all mushy and philosophical on me." I laughed and wiped a stray tear that had fallen.

"I don't want this life for you." He gestured around him, referring to a life in hell. "At least try until the end of the semester. Maybe they just need time to adjust."

As much as I hated the idea of staying more time in this hell, I agreed. Maybe I just needed a way to relieve the stress this place was bringing me.

∾

AFTER I HAD cereal for dinner, because I most definitely wasn't going to eat in the dining hall, I drove about thirty minutes from the academy to a mall in Pasadena. I pulled my car into the parking structure and felt relief flood me. Shopping always cheered me up and I'd get to be around people who had no idea who I was.

As I made my way inside the mall, my phone buzzed with a text from Tobias. *Are you ok? I heard what happened.*

I shot a quick text back. *Fine. Shopping. I'll text you later.*

I'll admit it. I had a shopping problem. In particular when it came to a certain lingerie store. Their new line, with angel in the name of course, just released and I was beyond excited to add all the colors to my already vast collection.

The pink polka-dot walls and scents of fruit and floral instantly brought a smile to my face. I grabbed a mesh bag to put my bounty in and started with the panties.

"Can I help you find anything in particular?" I looked up and smiled at the saleswoman standing at the end of the display.

"No, thanks. I got it."

"Let me know if you need any help." She walked away but didn't go far before her eyes were watching me while she straightened panties and bras in the next display over. I guess I'd watch me too if I saw a teenager practically shoveling underwear into a bag.

Next time I'd just order online. There were eight colors. I had to have them all. As soon as I opened the drawers holding the bras the saleswoman approached me again.

I was starting to feel irritated. "You know what, you can help me." I handed her the bag. "Hold this for me."

I finished loading the bag up and made my way towards the cash register, but something caught my eye on a mannequin. Besides bras and panties, I'd never purchased anything else lingerie related. Teenage boys didn't really stop to appreciate what was under the clothes, but a certain man did.

It was a teddy that would have made a really inappropriate swimsuit with cutouts all over the front, lace to barely cover the important parts, and only strings in the back.

"Oh, that would look great on you," the saleswoman, who's name tag read Natasha, suggested. Now that she realized I wasn't going to make a run for it with the bag, she was my best friend.

"It's not something I normally wear." There was only red, white, and black so I grabbed the white. "I'd like to wear this one out of here."

Once I paid, the girl let me into one of the dressing rooms and I changed into it. Surprisingly, it was comfortable. I bit my lip thinking of what Tobias might think. Before I could talk myself out of it, I snapped a picture of myself, front and back, and sent Tobias the pictures.

After I put my clothes on over the teddy, I got a text back from him. *What time are you going to be back tonight?*

I sent back a devil and an angel emoji and put my phone away before I took things too far. The last thing I needed was to start sexting with him. Sending sexy pictures to my Demonology instructor was far enough already.

Leaving the store, I felt great. Nothing like a bag full of sexy things to give you a pick-me-up. I hopped on the descending escalator and looked out over the hustle and bustle of the evening mall. A baby cried in his mother's arms. A girl with a group of other teenagers shoved a corn dog in her mouth causing the other teens to laugh. A group of men leaned against the wall near a sports clothing store staring at their phones. I should have invited Brooklyn and Cora to shop with me.

There was something so normal about being here among the throngs of shoppers. Not having to worry what the Divine 7 might do next or what the other angels might say or do. If I left the academy, it could all be over. If I left then I wouldn't have money to shop. What a catch-22.

I hit a few more stores before encountering an arcade and getting sucked into the world of video games. If they could just find a way to teach school only using video games, I'd be set and have straight As.

"We're closing in like two minutes," a teenage boy about my age said, tapping on the side of Street Fighter II. I had been playing old-school games for hours.

I picked my bags up and made my way out into the mall, the stores already closed with rolling security grilles. The lights were dimmed and a few people milled about chatting, and some power walked like it was an indoor track. I looked at the time and it was just shy of eleven, the arcade had extended hours. I hadn't even realized I'd been playing that long. Amazing how video games seem to be on a different time continuum than real life.

I exited into the parking garage and took the elevator to the fifth floor. The doors slid open and I spotted my car, alone in the center of gray concrete walls and white lines. The echo of my shoes was the only sound besides distant screeching of tires on the floors below.

I was halfway to my car when the hairs on the back of my neck stood on end. I clutched my keys in my hand, my thumb poised over the alarm. I turned my head and looked over my shoulder. Nothing.

I wondered if men always felt like they had to look over their shoulders like women did. For once I would like to walk into a dark place and not wonder what lurked. The garage was eerily silent now, the only sounds the distant honking and whoosh of cars on the street below. I unlocked my car as I approached. And then I heard it.

It was the faintest sound, like leaves blowing across the pavement. My heart leapt into my throat as I threw open my car door and started lowering myself into the bucket seat with my bags drawn to my chest.

My head jerked back violently as a hand gripped my ponytail and pulled me back and up, my forehead hitting the edge of the car. My bags fell from my grip and onto the driver's seat and pavement next to the open door. A fine mist sprayed on my face, like water from a squirt bottle and I let out a scream as my head hit the pavement, sending a sharp pain through my skull.

There was no time to fight back. One second I was about to sit in my car, and the next I was thrown to the rough cement of the parking garage. My head went fuzzy and my eye sockets began throbbing. Another scream was lodged in my throat, but the only sound escaping me was short, rasping breaths.

Three men stood over me, their faces sneering and angry. They weren't that much older than me, but they looked rough, like they had lived twice or three times over. Two grabbed at my arms and legs. Adrenaline surged through me and I kicked and punched in a lame attempt at stopping them, but having just smashed my skull and there being three of them, I was up shit's creek without a paddle.

My crossbody purse lay under me, but nothing in there would help me. I didn't have pepper spray in my purse. It was in my car because the idea of it accidently exploding wigged me out. An irrational and stupid fear.

"Where the hell are her wings? Usually they pop out by now." The man not restraining me shoved a wadded-up cloth in my mouth before he zip tied my ankles and my hands.

"I don't fucking know, man. She hit her head pretty hard. Let's go."

The pressure of the zip ties dug into my skin and liquid dripped off of them, warming my skin where it touched. They picked me up like I was a trussed pig and carried me down the set of stairs near the elevator. A gray van waited with an open back door at the bottom of the stairs.

I'd never quite experienced true, all-encompassing fear before. Not the kind you have when you walk through one of the haunted houses at theme parks, or the kind you feel when the school resource officer's drug sniffing dog finds weed in your locker. No, this fear reached deep inside and made my teeth ache.

They threw me in the back of the van and slammed the door shut. I curled into a ball and coughed around the gag, my sobs making it hard to breathe. I tried spitting the rag out of my mouth but it just made me gag more.

I heard the front door of the van open and then a scream. Loud sounds and shouts erupted from outside and the van shook several times before everything was silent besides the small sounds escaping around my gag.

I had really reached my limit with the gags.

The door of the van opened and a fourth man looked down at me, shadows from the hood he was wearing hiding his face.

"I'm not going to hurt you." He had a blade and as he leaned in the bed of the van I kicked both legs out at him like I was a dolphin, connecting with his chest. He grunted but grabbed my legs anyway and cut off the zip tie. "Are you going to let me cut the one off your hands?"

I scrambled back away from him, trying to catch my breath through the gag and my running nose. I was going to die if I didn't get air. I might already be dead. My head felt like it was going to explode like a pumpkin smashed in the middle of the street.

The man waited while I looked at him with wide eyes. He had a bloody cut over his eye that was slowly trickling down his cheek and onto his black hooded sweatshirt. I could see the men who had attacked me laying in a heap just behind him. Literally, they were piled in a heap. Dead, I think.

Who was this guy? Batman?

I finally scooted forward because, between sobs and the gag, I was starting to feel dizzy, but that could have also been from hitting my head. I turned around and he sliced through the thick black plastic. I quickly yanked the cloth out of my mouth, taking in gulps of air.

He slid his knife behind him and raised his empty hands in front of him, backing up several feet from the van. I followed and sat on the edge, my hands on my knees, still trying to steady my heart and catch my breath.

"Who are you?" I managed to get out and stood up.

Standing up lasted all of three seconds before my knees gave out and my world went dark.

"Listen, *asshole*, I'm giving you the courtesy of a phone call so don't try to pull that bull shit with me... I told you, it was three Fallen... Yes, they were working together... Yes, I'm fucking sure... fuck you Toby, I'm not part of whatever it is they were up to, you should know that... Fine. I'll see you in five. Land on the roof, the door leads straight in."

My eyes opened and I let out a moan as the dim light in the room hit my eyes. My eyes quickly scanned what was in my line of sight. Brick walls, shiny duct work, giant industrial ceiling fan. My eyes were slightly blurred but beyond the black wire railing surrounding a bedroom of sorts, the room was massive. Then it became clear I was on a very large, very comfortable bed.

The vigilante snapped his eyes to the bed from where he was leaning against the railing and made his way to the side I was on. His bed. I was in Batman's bed.

"Your boyfriend will be here in a few minutes. I hope you don't mind. I got into your phone and since he was your last text, I called him." A smirk spread across his face as he spoke.

I should have known using a fingerprint to lock my phone was a stupid idea. It seemed safe at the time. He had called Tobias because of Tobias's text messages.

My eyes widened and the smallest of thrills shot through me knowing what the smirk was about. He had seen the last texts in my phone. I felt heat rising to my cheeks.

"I'm surprised you've been out so long. Usually angels heal up pretty quick." He placed my cell phone on the nightstand and ran his hands through his disheveled dark blond hair that came to his shoulders. "You want to try to sit up?"

I nodded, my brain not quite caught up yet with everything. I must have hit my head harder than I thought. He had saved me. Brought me to his home. Called... Toby?

I pushed myself up with a groan and scooted back against the pillows and metal headboard that matched the railing around the perimeter of the room.

"You know Tobias?"

I took a better look around. It was one giant open room with a kitchen, dining room, living room, and the bedroom. It appeared to be some kind of old building; the windows were similar to what an old warehouse or factory might have.

"Do I know Toby? You could say that. I'm Asher." He held out his hand and I put my hand in his.

His handshake was firm and sent tingles up my arm. Probably from the complete exhaustion my body felt. *Probably.*

"Danica." I let my hand fall to my lap and squinted my eyes up at him. He had a really sharp jaw and his eyes were a slate blue, almost gray. "You shouldn't have let me sleep so long. I think I have a pretty bad concussion. How long was I out?"

"About an hour. I honestly thought you'd be awake after a few minutes." He shrugged his shoulders and scratched the side of his scruffy face.

He stood awkwardly at the side of the bed like he wanted to sit but wasn't sure if he should. He finally sat at the end of it.

I stared at him for several long seconds before speaking. "They were fallen angels? The guys that attacked me? What did you do with them?"

"They were. I killed them so now they are dead. Probably in hell."

"I should call my dad so he can personally torture them." I flinched after the words left my lips. I wished sometimes I didn't just blurt out the first thing that popped into my head.

His eyes widened slightly, drawing my attention to where he had a small cut above his eye. He shifted a little and I could tell he was thinking about who my father was. Since I had such a damn big mouth, I told him.

"Lucifer is my father. I'm half human, half angel, or something. Do you think that's why the fallen attacked me?"

If my admission made him nervous he didn't let it show. "There was an attack a few days ago. Angels can sense each other. Fallen can't sense other angels very well but if they are close enough they can feel others."

"Is that why I feel all tingly and wired up when I'm around you or Tobias? No other angels have really gotten close enough to me."

Another one of his smirks spread across his face and he chuckled. "Tingly, huh? When I say *sense,* I mean our brains register another angel in the area and when we see them they have a glow about them."

If I could have died of embarrassment, I would have. I wasn't typically a blusher, but I felt my face burn red. Twice now he had made me blush.

Asher's chuckles abruptly stopped as the metal door across the room slammed open, causing him to jump. Tobias walked in and down the metal stairs. As soon as he got close enough, I could see the worry etched on his face.

He glared at Asher and then practically laid on top of me, pulling me into a hug.

"Are you okay?"

"Jesus, man. She isn't going to be if you manhandle her like that." Asher got off the bed and made his way down two steps and to the kitchen. He grabbed a glass that was half full of brown liquid and drank it in one gulp. Then he refilled it and did it again.

"My head hurts, but I'm fine. Thanks to Asher." I felt I needed to add that last bit because the tension was so thick you could have cut it with a knife.

"You're welcome," Asher said from across the room.

Tobias rolled his eyes at Asher's words and let me go before standing.

"Is her car here or back at the mall?"

"It's here. I drove her back in it. I also picked up all the lingerie that had spilled out of one of the bags and put them in the trunk," Asher said, making his way back to the bed and standing near the two steps leading down.

I wanted to crawl under a rock.

Tobias ignored Asher's comment and held out his hand. "Let's get you home."

I grabbed his hand and he pulled me to my feet. He let go and my body plopped right back on the bed like my muscles and bones were made of jelly.

He tried to pick me up and I waved him away with my hand. My entire being ached and the thought of having to sit in a car and feel the movement and lights made me nauseous.

"She has a pretty bad concussion, and apparently she can't heal. Maybe she should stay here the rest of the night. I'll sleep on the couch. Or maybe *you* can sleep on the couch."

"Over my dead body." Tobias crossed his arms and turned his body towards Asher to glare at him.

Asher was purposely trying to piss off Tobias, but why? I hadn't known Tobias all that long but he was pretty calm, not letting his emotions explode. There was something about Asher though that was making him narrow his eyes and stiffen his spine.

"Have you forgotten already? Been there done that." Asher leaned against the brick wall behind him, propping one of his feet up with his knee bent like he had been waiting for this for a long time.

Tobias walked to the end of the bed and stopped at the end closest to Asher, clenching his fists at his sides. The last thing I needed was for them to come to blows and not even be able to break them apart. Not that I'd be stupid enough to throw myself in the middle of two men who probably knew how to throw punches.

"Guys, can you just put your dicks away for now. You're making my headache worse. How do you two even know each other anyway?"

"You didn't tell her how you *died* yet? Shit, man. Seems like something you should tell the woman who's sending you sexy lingerie pics, doesn't it?"

Tobias moved so quickly it made my head hurt even more, and punched Asher in the jaw, sending his head to the side and back into the brick wall. He slid down the wall and sat on the floor rubbing his jaw, a smile on his face.

I shook my head and laid back down on the bed, kicking my shoes off. If they wanted to beat the shit out of each other, I really didn't care. All I wanted was to sleep.

CHAPTER 7

ASHER

*D*eath. It's something most angels have to go through to get to the angel part. Well, except for those created as angels. I didn't know what hell was like but being a fallen angel was not my cup of tea. In fact, most nights it was half a bottle of whiskey or a twelve pack.

It's hard for angels at first. Realizing our lives were ripped away from us, floating around in heaven, waiting for enough time to pass so we could make a choice. A choice to serve as a guardian on Earth or a choice to serve in heaven. I chose the former, by the way.

Any painful memories surrounding or leading up to our deaths are erased and all we're left with is the knowledge of how it happened and the memories of our life before. That's hard enough, the lost life.

Unless you're Fallen.

Then the missing memories come back.

Which is why I drink like a fish and fuck like a rabbit.

I looked over at Toby, who after sucker punching me in the fucking jaw, poured himself a whiskey without asking, and joined me on the large sectional sofa. I hadn't seen him in ten or so years and the first thing he does is punch me and steal my alcohol.

I really couldn't blame him for punching me though. I would have done worse, but I'm a dick. Tobias Armstrong is not. He is a saint, well, except for the student he seems to be sleeping with.

We fought together in World War II. He was like an older brother to me, taking me under his hypothetical, but now literal, wing. We survived D-Day, liberated towns, and died during the Battle of the Bulge.

It was cold that day, snow blanketing the ground when the Germans closed in on us. I don't even remember the exact date, not sure I even knew then what day of the week it was. Hell, it might have even been Christmas. We were well into the Battle of the Bulge though, and losing. At least we won the war. Well, the other soldiers did.

I stared down into my whiskey glass, Toby's presence bringing me back to that particular day.

"WE'RE GOING TO DIE, Toby. I don't want to fucking die." I was sniveling like a pansy-ass as debris, gunfire, and explosions rained down on our platoon.

"Shut up. We'll be fine. We've lasted this long." Tobias climbed back up the side of the bank and fired his gun. The sound was deafening. "Fuck."

I took his place as he reloaded his gun. This had been going on for what felt like hours, but was probably more like ten minutes. He'd shoot. I'd reload. I'd shoot. He'd reload. On and on it went. They kept advancing. My hands were numb, my shoulder throbbed, but on we went.

We had to. You don't watch most of your platoon die and just give up. We'd fight for them, for what they had lost.

I was out of ammo again and Toby went right back to his spot. I was just about done reloading when my body was thrown across the shallow agricultural trench we were using as a foxhole of sorts. It wasn't doing that good of a job, clearly.

My ears rang, my eyes burned, a blinding flash of pain careened down my back.

I'd told him we were going to die today. He didn't believe me.

A heavy weight landed on me and jerked several times before falling still.

I pried my eyes open and Toby stared back at me with wide, glassy eyes. Vacant eyes. Eyes I was too familiar with seeing. Another one of my brothers taken. I pushed at him, his body heavy.

"Toby?" I felt his hot blood seeping through my jacket and shirt. So much blood. Too much blood.

I needed to move. If the Germans decided to search the carnage, they'd take me. I didn't have it in me to be a prisoner. I struggled under Toby's weight, but I couldn't move my legs.

I stopped struggling and stared up at the gray sky. It would snow soon.

A HAND WAS PLACED on my shoulder and I jerked back to reality, sloshing the amber liquid in my glass onto my hand. Fucking idiot would know not to touch me if he had the memories of that shit storm. Lucky bastard.

PTSD was a mother fucking bitch and I couldn't even get help because who the fuck is going to believe that a mid-twenties looking man fought in WWII? Yeah. Exactly. No to the fucking one.

"Sorry, I shouldn't have-" He realized his errors a little too late.

"You're right, you shouldn't have." I leaned forward and set my glass on the coffee table before wiping my shaking, wet hand on my jeans. "So, you and Lucifer's daughter... interesting."

He made a grunting noise in reply and took a drink from his glass. He was still sitting next to me, he must have moved when I zoned out, a mere inch from my leg. I could have strangled his ass. I shifted farther from him.

I looked over my shoulder at her sleeping on my bed, her body curled around one of my pillows. What would it be like to lay next to her and have her curl around me like that? Probably a really fucking bad idea is what it would be.

I looked over at my former best friend, my brother in arms. He was still rocking his beard, close shaven and neat. I hadn't known him before the war, but from the pictures he had shown me from before our time deployed together, he hadn't changed at all.

I, on the other hand, probably looked like a drunken vagrant. I used to be a handsome, strapping young fellow with hair like Cary Grant. The ladies loved me. Come to think of it, the ladies still loved me, and I still loved them. They just couldn't handle that I was completely fucking broken.

"You aren't worried they're going to take your wings? Banging a student has to be against some kind of rule."

"She's eighteen. We're both consenting adults. It doesn't matter if I'm a teacher or not." His words didn't hold any conviction and fell flat. He must have lay up at night convincing himself of those things.

I snorted back a laugh. "Keep telling yourself that. Trust me, you do *not* want to fall."

The worst part of falling wasn't losing use of the wings or any special abilities, it was the sudden bombardment of the memories and complete and utter isolation. Most didn't survive beyond the first few weeks, but those of us that did, were broken.

That's probably why the Fallen were trying to kidnap angels. I didn't even want to think about *why* they were kidnapping angels or what they were doing to them. I had stopped two abductions now and they had probably gotten away with several.

"I think it'd take a lot more than a relationship with a student to lose my wings. Don't you?"

"Just don't murder anyone you aren't supposed to and you'll be fine."

Killing as an angel was strictly forbidden. When we were given an assignment to help a human, it didn't mean taking the law into our own hands. Which is exactly what I did. I was supposed to help a woman flee, not kill her husband, even if he had beaten her black and blue.

"You've tried appealing?" Toby finally looked at me. He had been avoiding looking at me, probably because he felt pity. He sure as hell didn't feel guilty.

When I first fell, he came to see me to check on me. That didn't go so well. Hence why we hadn't seen each other in ten years.

"I gave up after the second appeal." I shrugged. "It is what it is. I'm getting things on track."

A comfortable silence fell over the room. The only sounds were the sips he was taking of his drink. I considered turning on the TV because I certainly wasn't going to be able to sleep now, but then he had to go and open his big-ass mouth again.

I had known the moment would come eventually. Ten years ago when I fell, he hadn't dared ask, especially as I tore up a motel room in a blinding rage.

"What happened?"

He didn't even have to elaborate. I knew exactly what he was asking. I stood and walked over to the kitchen, grabbing the bottle of whiskey that sat half empty on the counter. I sat back down in the crook of the sectional sofa, facing him, leg bent in front of me to give me a barrier. I'd kick his ass if he tried to touch me again. He reached over with his glass and I filled it back up.

"Do you want to know how you died or how I died?" I lifted the bottle to my lips and took a long swig. It burned more than usual tonight.

"Me."

I described the day to him, not leaving out any detail. The day was always vivid in my mind, even after all this time. Down to what we had eaten. What wasn't vivid was what I had eaten for breakfast that current morning. It's funny what the brain holds onto.

"Your body landed on mine. You died pretty instantly, lots of blood. I'm not sure if you landed on me because something threw your body at me or if you dived on top of me. Only you'd know that answer."

He ran his hand through his hair and we both took a drink at the same time.

"And you?"

I let out a pained laugh. "I wasn't as lucky as you were. I couldn't move from the waist down, so I was stuck there under you. It didn't exactly hurt. I was in shock that it was even happening. The pain only started when the snow started falling."

"Fuck."

"Yeah." I took another swig of whiskey and then put the cap back on. "I blamed you for a while."

"For what?" He seemed confused.

"For landing on me. I don't know what I would have done if I had gotten out from under you though. Probably would have been tortured by Krauts."

"It makes no sense." He wiped at his eyes as if he was about to shed some tears. He always was a sensitive bastard.

"What doesn't? It was war."

"I meant that it makes no sense to me that when an angel falls, something so traumatic and painful is given back to them."

"Maybe they figure it's better than sending us straight to hell. I can tell you it's probably not." As I spoke, I looked back over at Danica. I was still trying to wrap my head around that one.

"She's not... evil," he said softly.

"I didn't think she was. Lucifer is Fallen, right? He didn't have his death to torment him. That's probably why they stuck him for an eternity in hell. She didn't grow up in hell, did she?"

"Not literal hell. Her mom died when she was born and her dad could only be around so much. She got kicked out of high school."

I looked back over at her, feeling drawn to her. To make sure she was safe. I felt the tight muscles in my jaw relax and I let out a sigh.

"You feel it too, don't you?" Toby looked at me with a slight narrowing of his eyes, more of a thoughtful narrowing, as if he was running through things in his head. Not a narrowing like he was going to punch me again.

I knew exactly what he was talking about. It was what she had described when she told me what she thought sensing other angels was like. Tingly and almost giddy, and I never felt giddy.

"Yes. What is it?"

I didn't know whether to be concerned with it or accept it as normal. I should probably have been concerned. Even when I was an angel I had felt detached from everyone, missing my old life. My wife. My family. But around her I felt connected. They needed to seriously invest in training angel therapists.

"I'm not sure. There's someone else too, but she doesn't seem to be aware of it yet." He sounded jealous, but also angry. Before I could ask him why, he continued. "He bullies her. Him and his cronies."

"Why haven't you kicked his ass? If I could come to campus, I'd do it. Not like I have anything left to lose."

He rolled his eyes at me and I felt a warmness spread in my chest. This was familiar. Normal. How we used to be.

"He's an archangel. They sent him to us hoping we could acclimate him to how the world works. Plus, he was causing problems. I guess creating an archangel at the height of human times backfired a bit. I see the way he looks at her, yet he does stupid shit to her with his friends. Honestly, I don't even know if he realizes what he's doing, he just follows the other Divine like a lost puppy. And she just takes it and gives it back to them. She's strong, Asher. Stronger than I think she even knows." A dreamy look crossed his eyes but then he seemed to snap out of it and yawned.

"Why don't you go to bed." I grabbed my headphones off the table and turned them on, the Bluetooth connecting to my phone. Music helped me sleep. It was the only way I could sleep, actually.

"You going to be all right?"

"I'm not sure my jaw will ever be the same again, but I'll be fine, brother. Go lay next to your woman."

IT TOOK me a long time to fall asleep and at best I got three hours. Worse than usual, but at least not as bad as not being able to sleep for three days straight. That had fucking sucked.

The large metal barn door leading to the bathroom slid open and Danica walked out, looking much better than she had the night before. I had given her a shirt and a pair of sweats with an elastic and drawstring waist to wear after she showered. Her damp hair was gathered around one of her shoulders, making the dark fabric of the shirt even darker.

She looked stunning. Partly because she had my clothes on and there was something sexy about seeing a woman wearing my clothes. I turned away to not appear like I was gawking and filled my coffee maker up. I was probably going to drink a whole pot of it just to counteract all the whiskey I drank the night before.

"Where's Tobias?" Her voice was stronger today, less scratchy.

"He went to grab food. How do you like your coffee?" I grabbed a second mug from the open metal shelf and went to grab the carafe but stopped when I saw the scrunched-up face she was sporting.

"Poured down the drain. You don't by a slim chance have any Diet Dr. Pepper?"

Now I scrunched up my face. Gross. "You fucking drink that shit? And here I thought we were soul mates. I have orange juice, water, and liquor. Unfortunately, I'm out of beer."

"You sure do have a dirty mouth."

I raised my eyebrows. This was really the first real conversation I was having with her. Last night she was solely focused on her almost-abduction by three now-dead Fallen. I wasn't sure if her words meant she was appalled by my sailor's tongue or if she was poking fun at me.

I decided to test the boundaries a little. "Maybe I should show you just how dirty it can be." I licked my bottom lip for effect.

Her face turned pink and then she sat down on a stool around my stainless-steel bar-height table. "This is a cool place. Where are we, in an old warehouse?"

I took a drink of my black coffee and leaned against the counter. "It's an abandoned factory. There are two units downstairs I restored too that have tenants. I have an industrial chic remodeling business."

I looked around at the large open room. It had taken me several years to finish all the work myself, but it was a good distraction and got out some of my rage. Using my hands to tear down and then restore something helped keep my broken pieces from falling all over the place.

"Construction by day, vigilante by night?"

"Something like that."

The recent influx of Fallen encounters were concerning to say the least. We were a reclusive bunch, not often building long-term relationships, and most certainly not seeking companionship with each other. So the fact that I had encountered two groups of Fallen had me on edge.

Why were they after angels? Why were they using demon blood? Where were they getting the demon blood?

She cleared her throat and I blinked and looked at her. I spaced out a lot if I wasn't doing something with my hands. Luckily that time I was thinking about last night.

"You got into my phone last night." It was a statement. Did she want a response back? Luckily, she continued. "And you went through my photos."

I wish women would just spit out what their words meant. She was clearly unhappy with my intrusion, but just how unhappy? Slap me in the face unhappy? Kick me in the balls unhappy? Did she want an apology?

"I didn't go through your photos. I opened your texts to call whoever was sending you so many. He sent a lot. Did you read them yet? What a stalker. Better watch out for that one." I grinned around the rim of my coffee cup as her face looked a bit murderous. I guess she had wanted an apology. "Look, I'm sorry. I saw it was Tobias Armstrong and I scrolled up only meaning to see the ones he had sent. I was a little bit disappointed they weren't nudes, but they were hot nonetheless."

I was glad the table was between us. "You're an ass. You know that?"

"I am aware of that fact. So you and Toby?"

"Yeah. Me and Toby." She watched me as I refilled my cup. "So, how do you two know each other? I didn't get an answer before you got punched in the face, and since he left you here alone with me, I'm guessing you know each other well."

I laughed and sat at the table on the metal stool across from her. "World War II, same platoon. That's where we both died."

Her eyes went wide and then her expression softened. "I can't even imagine what it's like being in a war zone... and during a World War? Wow."

I expected her to ask more questions, but she didn't. I respected that. Maybe one day I'd tell her about my past life. I stood abruptly and my stool fell over, hitting the concrete floor with a loud metallic sound that made us both jump, and in my haste to flee, I fell flat on my ass over the stool.

Danica rushed around the table and I held up both hands in front of me. "Just give me a minute, okay?"

Where the hell had that come from? Telling someone about my life made my skin crawl. The last time I'd shared my life with someone, they had died, right the fuck on top of me. I shut my eyes and tried to remind myself that I was fine. I was safe here in my home. The home I'd built with my bare hands.

With slightly shaky legs, I stood and righted the stool before meeting her eyes. "I'm sorry about that. Sometimes it just comes out of nowhere."

Usually I could keep myself in check. So much so that I was able to start my own business a few years ago. My workers all knew I suffered from severe PTSD, although they thought it was from Iraq, and on the days I couldn't handle things, they had my back.

Toby chose that moment to walk into my place, a pink box in one hand and a Diet Dr. Pepper in the other. His eyes went to Danica's worried face and then they shot quickly to me, concern etched in them.

"Everything okay?" He put the box and soda on the table slowly. "I got donuts."

It was like one minute there was tension in the air and the next her face lit up like a Christmas tree. She threw her arms around Toby like he had just come back from a long deployment and then they were kissing.

Oh, shit, were they kissing. If I opened the dictionary and looked up the term face-sucking, there would be a picture of them. I'd buy her every damn Diet Dr. Pepper and donut on the face of this planet if she'd kiss me like that.

Before I started thinking of her body pressed against me, her lips opening and waiting for my tongue, I lifted the lid of the donut box and the sweet sugary scent of maple and chocolate hit me right in the face. I grabbed the glazed twist with a hint of cinnamon woven into it and took a bite. A moan escaped my lips. I hadn't had a donut in a while.

Toby ripped his lips away from Danica's and looked at me with a glare as if I was inconveniencing his make-out session right in front of my fucking face.

I swallowed my bite and grinned at Toby's narrowed eyes. Serves him right for making out in front of me. "Want a bite?"

Toby rolled his eyes and then grabbed his own donut before sitting down. "What are we going to do about those Fallen?"

"Well, they are dead now and were disposed of. I didn't see who came and got them. I've searched the vans. There is nothing in them."

"Do you think there are more?"

I shrugged in response. "I guess we'll find out, won't we?"

"They sensed I was an angel. Said something about my wings not coming out when they sprayed me in the face." Danica nursed her Diet Dr. Pepper in her hands. I briefly wondered how addicted she was to it, having asked for it so early in the morning. I wasn't one to talk though. I had a bad habit of my own.

"Wait, why didn't your wings come out?" I looked back and forth between Toby and her.

"I don't have wings." I could tell immediately that it bothered her by the way her mouth turned slightly down and her eyes glossed up.

"Well, mine are bound so they can't come out. I guess we have something in common."

"That's horrible! All fallen angels have bound wings?" She looked back and forth between me and Toby. How did she know nothing about being an angel?

"Yes. It doesn't hurt. Well, until they really want to come out, then it feels like a dull ache in the shoulder blades."

"We should get going after we eat. I need to talk to Sue Whittaker about these attacks so she can get a message to Michael."

I grunted in response, my mouth full of donut. As much as I didn't want to admit it, the company was nice. Especially the brunette across from me, wearing my clothes. Lucky for me, I already programmed her number in my phone.

CHAPTER 8

DANICA

I stood frozen in front of the brightly colored paper taped to the hallway walls. There were so many, like rainbows leading down every hallway. The pot of gold at the end of the rainbow? My utter humiliation.

They had photocopied them all, all 'Notice of Disciplinary Action' forms and suspension forms, and plastered them around Uriel Hall. They were all there.

Caused physical injury to another person.

Unlawful use of an illegal substance.

Disruption of school activities.

There were so many in my file over the years that I didn't even remember most of them. I clutched my bag to my chest and made my way out of the building, keeping my eyes on the ground.

How dare they.

How dare they take something that was in my past and put it out there for the world to see? Wasn't it enough that I was here, at this school, *trying?*

I threw my bag on the floor and faceplanted onto my bed. I shut my eyes, breathed in deep, and exhaled. I could do this. I'd go back in there and take them all down once classes were in session.

My phone buzzed in my bag and I groaned. *Tobias.*

He had taken care of me all weekend. We never went on our date. Instead, he cooked for me in his room. Chicken fettuccini alfredo. Salad. Garlic bread. I felt my chest tightening and I swallowed back my tears. At some point he was going to realize that I came with a lot of baggage.

I rolled off my bed and grabbed my phone. *Don't come to class.* As if that warning would stop me in the first place.

Me: Too late for that. Still want to date a juvenile delinquent?

Tobias: Don't say that.

I turned off my phone and changed out of my uniform. It was a little chilly outside so I threw on sweats and a hoodie. I wasn't technically going to class, so no uniform was required.

It took me most of the morning to take down all of the papers spread around campus. Mainly because I hid between class times. I'd save my brave face for tomorrow. Adults are always saying to just ignore the bullies, but did that actually work? This was something deeper. This was a deep-seated hatred for Lucifer and for me. What had the devil ever done to them?

I wanted to punch each and every one of them in their glowing faces. Or leave. Leaving would be better, but part of me didn't want to leave. One thing was clear, something needed to change or I wasn't going to make it to the end of the semester.

I HID in my room the rest of the day until my last class; independent study in the library. Except now Mondays would be dedicated to peer mentoring. What that entailed hadn't exactly been made clear to me. Or maybe it was, and I had zoned out as Dean Whittaker had droned on and on.

At least my day was going better, especially after the picture Tobias sent me. Normally a dick pic would turn me off, but if anything, it just made me want him more. I'd always laughed at the movies or books where the girl falls head over heels after a few days. I understood now. When it was there, it was just *there*.

Although, a certain dirty-mouthed vigilante kept popping into my head as well, but that was probably something for a therapist to explore.

I plopped down in a leather armchair in the corner of the library and tipped my head back to let the light from the colonial-style window hit my face. What I would give to be napping right now. With a long exhale, I sat up and dug in the front section of my bag for the tiny pouch with my Flair pens. They were my version of a fidget spinner; constantly switching pens helped my focus. Plus, they made my notes look like a rainbow threw up on them. A win in my book.

They were nowhere to be found though. Hopefully they were back in my room. Or had I left them in a class? Shrugging to myself, I dropped my bag on the floor and scanned the library. It was empty as usual. Ms. Hall was just out of my line of sight, her long manicured nails creating a very faint tapping sound on her keyboard. Hopefully this week wouldn't be a repeat of last week.

The heavy wooden library door opened and I turned my head towards it.

No. Just no.

I pressed my lips together and gripped the arms of the chair, digging my fingernails into the leather. If I hadn't known him already, I would have sat up straighter, pushed my chest out, smoothed down my clothes. Then worried about my choice in wearing sweats.

Oliver Morgan was breathtaking.

He walked towards me, his lips quirked into a small smile, his blue eyes appraising my sweats. He sat down in the chair next to me and turned to face me, touching the top of his brown hair as if to check that the hair product that held it in place was still working.

I pursed my lips and crossed my legs. "Well, isn't this fucking fantastic."

He shrugged his shoulders and tilted his chin in the direction of my bag while he shrugged out of his blue blazer and laid it over the arm of the chair. The faint smell of chocolate chip cookies hit my nose.

"Did you bring the binder?"

"What binder?" My eyebrows drew together and I tilted my head slightly to the side. "Was I supposed to bring stuff?"

"The school handbook binder. Dean Whittaker said she told you to bring it with you. That's what we're going to be going over." He crossed his arms behind his head and leaned back against the back of the chair.

"Oh... I forgot."

He shut his eyes and opened them in an extra-long blink and then leaned forward again to pull his binder out of his bag. "Let's just get this over with."

He moved his chair so our knees were practically touching and opened the binder, placing it on my lap. He pointed to the first line in the table of contents. Dress code.

"Is this really necessary? I can just read it on my own." I leaned my elbow on the side of the chair and put my cheek on my fist.

He grunted and flipped the pages open to the dress code section. He then reached into his bag and pulled out a notebook and a pen and handed them to me. I ran my hand over the smooth cover of the notebook that had a pink watercolor design and a gold embossed D on it. The pen was thicker than usual, given it had ten retractable colors.

"What's this for?" I shifted in my seat. I was kicking myself for the flutters in my stomach. Why had he given me something so... personalized?

He let out a breath and pinched the bridge of his nose. "Notes. Remember you'll have a test at the end of our mentoring sessions."

"Right... So, dress code." I flipped open the small notebook and labeled the first page. "Rule 1. Wear ridiculous sailor uniforms because we're children that can't dress ourselves. Is that correct?"

"Are you going to take this seriously? We wear uniforms so we aren't distracted from our studies. God only knows what you would wear if you were given free rein." He looked at my sweats with a raised eyebrow.

I pushed down hard with my pen as I wrote. He leaned forward again and looked at the page, nodding his head slightly. I didn't know how he could read upside down; I sure couldn't. I clicked the pen a few times and drew several swirly circles on the corner of my paper.

"Are you listening?"

My head snapped up and I pulled the notebook towards my chest. "I umm... no. I wasn't listening. I mean, I was but..."

He tapped a finger on his lips before sitting back in his chair, his legs moving out from where they were against the bottom of the chair and touching mine.

"Is your endgame to go to hell and work with your father? Really, you punched a guy because he gave you a church paper or something?" His eyebrows furrowed and he reached forward and grabbed the pen I continued to click.

I looked down at the binder on my lap and brushed away an imaginary piece of eraser shaving. He didn't say anything during my silence, the only noise in the room the faint sound of steps in the hall and the printer at Ms. Hall's desk spitting out papers.

He broke the silence by nudging my foot with his, causing my head to snap up. He looked back at me, his light smattering of freckles even more prominent in the slant of light from the window.

"That is what happened, right?" He put the pen back in the middle of the binder.

"He did give me a church flier, so that's what the principal chose to believe."

He cleared his throat and sat up straighter. I could tell he really wanted to ask more questions. Only Ava and I knew the truth, and we wanted to keep it that way. We had heard rumors that those who knew and didn't join were beaten to a pulp.

I closed the binder and handed it back to him while grabbing my bag off the floor. I quickly stood while unzipping it and dropping the pen and notebook inside.

"Where are you going? We have fifteen more minutes. If Dean Whittaker-"

"I don't give a shit about Dean Whittaker or any of this. You sitting here acting like you care is a joke." My eyes darted to the door and then back to him.

He looked up at me with downturned lips and stood. "At least stay in the library so if she comes by you don't get in more trouble."

"Fine," I said through gritted teeth before turning and making my way down the rows of books labeled *Angel History*.

I grabbed a random book off a shelf and started flipping through it, stopping to look at the pictures. What was I even looking at? I slammed the book shut and read the title on the cover: *Angel Disgrace During the 1970s*. I snorted back a laugh.

"It is funny, isn't it? That they'd put that crap in a book for everyone to see."

I turned and rolled my eyes as Oliver leaned on the sturdy wooden shelf next to me. He plucked the book from my hands, frowning.

"I wonder what they'll write about me." He flipped through the book in the same way I had, furrowing his brows.

"Probably that you're an asshole that picks on the weak."

"You aren't weak. You're actually pretty strong." He shut the book with a snap and reached past me and put it on the shelf, his shirt sleeve brushing against my shoulder.

"Oh, so that's what all the bullying is for? To test my strength? You know what? I'm actually glad because now I get to see what phonies you all are. My dad is more angel than any of you."

I straightened my back and stared up at Oliver. I hadn't realized he was so tall, the top of my head coming to his chin. Someone knew what they were doing when they created him.

He stared back down at me and leaned closer.

"Maybe you're right," he said gently.

And then he kissed me.

I LAID on the soft comforter of my bed, the slight breeze outside wafting in and brushing across my skin. My lips still tingled from Oliver's very short, yet satisfying, kiss. One second his lips were on me and the next he was out the door. My mind was swirling as I brought my fingers to my lips.

The kiss had lasted only for a few seconds, but a few seconds I couldn't take back. It sent a thrill through me, kissing him there against the shelf in the library, each breath smelling of books and the faint scent of chocolate chip cookies.

Honestly, I felt a little like a harlot. Three men had occupied my mind today and I couldn't stop thinking about my body pressed up against them, their hands roaming my curves, their lips on my-

My phone buzzed on my chest and I lifted it above my face to read a text from Ava. My head hurt. Maybe my heart hurt a little too. Oliver Morgan had kissed me. And I kissed him back.

I had been texting Ava all evening about my confusion.

Aren't you sick of idiot boys? I vote for the teacher. He's a man.

She had a point, but would that even work? He was absolutely the most attentive guy I had ever been interested in. He had even left a can of soup, box of crackers, and bottle of 7 Up outside my door. I felt only slightly guilty that my stomachache had been a lie to be left alone.

I think he stole my panties.

So? That's hot. What do you think he did with those panties? He's probably not wearing them if that's what you're thinking. She followed her text with an eggplant emoji. Ava wasn't so innocent after all.

A laugh bubbled out of me. *Wow. No words.*

I need to tell you something... about John.

My stomach dropped and I sat up. I could see she was typing out a text so I waited. My hand shook slightly.

That day you punched him, Officer Flores took that flier off the ground. I'm not sure what happened exactly, but him and his dad were arrested over the weekend.

I let out a long, shaky breath of air. I knew exactly what happened. His father's drug mule business, hidden behind the veil of being a church, had imploded. Him giving me the flier like that was a threat to me to work for them or be sacrificed. When John gave you a flier, there was no choice.

I knew I should have never bought my weed from him in the first place, but I had needed it and it was high quality. If I had known they were more than just weed dealers, I would have found someone else.

My phone buzzed and another text popped up with an unknown number. I opened it and a smile spread across my face.

Asher: Hey, this is your knight in shining armor, Ash. How is your head?

Me: It's feeling better. If angels weren't such dicks it would be even better.

Asher: I won't disagree with that. What happened? Whose ass do I need to kick?

I laughed, a smile plastered on my face. *Everyone's.*

Asher: Even Toby's?

Me: What are you up to tomorrow? I'm thinking of ditching classes...

Asher: Work. I usually go to the pool hall or a bar after.

I bit my lip and went to stand by the window, looking out over the darkened campus. There were several angels milling about and one on the far side, across the far field, going into the trees.

Me: Let's hang out. Ditch work.

Asher: Can't do that but maybe when I get home. Meet at my place at 5ish?

Me: Yeah, see you then.

Now I was going to get no sleep because I was sleeping with a teacher, kissing my bully who bought me a personalized notebook and pen, and hanging out with a Fallen.

CHAPTER 9

DANICA

I must have been overzealous about hanging out with Asher because I got to his place before he did. I sat at the top of the metal stairs that led to his door and tried to calm the fluttering in my stomach.

This was just two friends hanging out. Right? Not that he was a friend yet, he was Tobias's long-lost Fallen friend. Tobias was surprisingly understanding, or at least he appeared that way when he stopped by after classes to check on me. I couldn't keep this from him, especially given their history. Which was still a big fat mystery to me. There had to be more to their stories than just that they had fought and died together in WWII.

Nothing was ever so cut and dry.

"A woman that's on time, I like that."

My eyes snapped to the bottom of the stairs and I stood, tugging my shirt so it fell back into place. I hadn't even heard him drive up in his truck.

"Or I just got lucky. There was no traffic." I adjusted the strap of my purse on my shoulder. God, why was I so nervous?

He smiled and slid his sunglasses on the top of his head. His hair was pulled back into a small man bun, which worked for him, and his

late chip cookies. Two were probably more man than I could handle, and then there was Oliver. I didn't even know how old he was. He was around my age, but he was a Class I angel, which meant he just *was*.

Tobias and I hadn't talked about *us*. The idea of being a couple was too new. We barely knew each other. But he hadn't said anything about me wanting to hang out with Asher. Because that's all this was, two people getting to know each other as friends.

I sipped the wine, the faint hint of fruit staying on the back of my tongue. I didn't usually like wine, but this almost tasted like juice. I turned on the TV to some court show and only half paid attention until the bathroom door slid open.

The soft scent of coconut and pineapple wafted into the room. Asher did not strike me as the tropical scent type, but I wasn't complaining. I turned my head and watched as he walked out with a towel around his waist, his lean, toned body on full display. I raised my wine glass to my mouth and took a prolonged sip as he walked up the two steps to the bedroom platform to a chest of drawers, his back turned towards me. He had a large tattoo of black wings covering the entirety of his back and part of his arms.

Holy mother of all things holy.

I turned so my leg was bent on the couch and watched as he dropped his towel and pulled a pair of blue jeans from a drawer. I didn't know if he thought I wouldn't look or if he was purposely baring his toned ass.

My wine was gone, but my lips were still on the rim of the glass as he slid the jeans on with no underwear. Tobias wasn't too keen on wearing them either. The jeans hit just below the two dimples in his lower back.

Quickly turning back towards the TV so I wouldn't be caught, I put my hand on my chest to try to calm myself down. The judge on TV was lecturing a couple for wasting her time with nonsense.

I didn't look away from the TV until he walked into the kitchen, buttoning the last button on his green plaid shirt, but leaving the top two undone. He grabbed the whiskey he had left on the kitchen table and drank it all at once.

"Ready to go? I was thinking we could check out this new Korean barbecue place a few blocks from here."

He offered me his hand and I took it as I got up off the couch. His callused hand was massive compared to mine and made me feel... safe. I followed him as we made our way down the stairs, still letting him hold my hand.

~

DINNER WAS INTERESTING. Not interesting in a bad way, but in a 'holy shit is he flirting with me?' and 'please, keep your leg pressed against mine' kind of way. We talked about almost everything. Food, his business, my school issues past and present, interests.

He threaded his fingers through mine, looking over at me as we made our way back down the street towards his place. The whole area was being revitalized by people like him, turning previously abandoned buildings into lively hot spots and living spaces.

"Are you going to come up or head back to school?" He had finally let my hand go and had his arm slung around my shoulder, his fingers playing with my hair. I was glad I had chosen at the last minute to wear it down.

I wasn't cold but had goosebumps on my skin from his touch. Did I want to go up to his place with the bed and the couch all in the same room, beckoning me? *Yes.* Should I? The jury was still out on that one.

I looked up at him, the white strand lights in the trees lining the street creating a soft glow on the sidewalk. His eyes sparkled and looked back at me, darkened with dilated pupils. What would it be like to have his strong, callused hands on my skin?

His hand tightened on my shoulder and he stopped, his neck stiffening and his eyes darting to the other side of the street.

"Stay right here." He moved me in front of a large window of a restaurant, the couple sitting on the other side glancing briefly at us before going back to their conversation. "I need to go check something out."

Before I could protest or ask any questions, he jogged across the street, stopping in the middle on the dashed yellow lines to wait for passing vehicles. I watched the space between two buildings he had disappeared between with a frown and then made my way across the street. It led to an alley that ran behind the buildings. I strained to hear but the only sounds were the passing of cars and the noises coming from the restaurants and bars lining the street.

On impulse, I quickly walked down the path between the buildings and peeked around the corner. My eyes widened as Asher threw a man in dark clothing into another and they fell onto the ground. He walked with clenched fists and hunched shoulders to the nearest one, grabbed his head and snapped his neck. The sound caused me to gasp and cover my mouth with my hand.

He grabbed the next man who was scrambling back like a crab and did the same thing. He piled the two limp bodies on top of a third near the wheel of the gray, windowless van blocking the alley.

I felt as if my heart was going to jump out of my chest cavity and explode. I stepped out of the darkened walkway as Asher pulled open the back doors of the van.

"I told you to stay across the street." He didn't look in my direction as he reached into the van and dragged two angels out; one had their wings extended and arms and legs zip tied, but the other didn't.

I took another step forward and gasped as they stepped into the light from a lamp post. I rushed forward and knelt by Oliver's side. He looked at me with wide eyes and tried to talk through his gag. I pulled it out.

"They came out of nowhere!" His voice was frantic and he smacked the ground with his wings, trying to sit up with his bound legs and arms.

I looked over at Asher who was staring down at Levi with a glowing silver weapon gripped in his hand. He looked confused and then turned towards Oliver and me.

"I take it you know these idiots?" Asher swiped the knife through Oliver's ties. "I'd never expect an archangel along with another angel to get taken by three Fallen. You should have felt them coming."

"We... we thought it was you two. They knocked us out before we even knew what hit us," Levi said, standing and reaching over to help Oliver up. I watched with rapt attention as Oliver shook out his shining wings and they folded back and disappeared.

Asher tucked his knife into the waist band of his pants near his hip, the faint sound of it sliding inside a sheath bringing my attention completely back to him.

"You're fucking idiots. What do they teach you at that school of yours? Fallen angels feel different." He shook his head and then turned towards me, putting his hand on his hips. "And I told you to stay back. Isn't one kidnapping attempt enough? What if they-"

"Who are you? You feel like those three... hey, where did they go?" Oliver moved his head around, looking for the heap of bodies that had suddenly vanished. He swatted Levi's chest with the back of his hand. "See. I told you following her was a bad idea."

Faster than my eyes could track, Asher had Oliver pinned against the side of the van, his feet dangling a foot off the ground. His jaw was set tight. "You were following her?" His words came out clipped and menacing.

Heat bloomed between my legs. Clearing my throat, I stepped forward and placed my hand on Asher's tense biceps.

"Let him go, Ash. It's okay." I didn't want Asher to kill them. I was curious as to why they had been following me though.

I turned to Levi and raised my eyebrows. Behind me I heard Oliver grunt as he dropped to the ground.

Levi sighed and ran a hand over his forehead. "He- we were worried. You missed class two days in a row."

My stomach clenched and I folded my arms over my chest. "You were *worried*. After all the bullshit over the past week, are you really surprised?"

"These are two of the fuckers that have been assholes? Say the word and I'll kick their asses." Asher took a step towards Levi who promptly backed up with his hands in front of him, palms out.

"We're sorry, we..." Oliver looked over to Levi and then at me. "We were stupid."

"That's an understatement." Asher grabbed my hand, lacing his fingers through mine.

Oliver's eyes looked down at our interlocking fingers and then up at me. His eyebrows arched and his frown deepened.

"You said that she was almost kidnapped?" Levi moved next to Oliver, keeping a wide distance between himself and Asher.

"Yes. There were three of them, same type of van. Why couldn't you guys get away?" I asked.

"Besides the demon blood on the zip ties, they spray something in your face. I think it makes you weaker. That's why I need my seraph blade to cut the ties," Asher explained while pulling his phone out of his back pocket. "I'm calling Tobias to come get you two. The demon blood that got on your skin will take a few hours to wear off. You won't be able to fly."

"Armstrong? Please don't!" Oliver took a step forward before Levi put an arm out across his chest, stopping him.

"Don't, Ash. I'll take them back." It was out of my mouth before I even knew what I was doing.

Asher turned to look at me and I crossed my arms under my breasts. He clenched his jaw. He put his phone back in his back pocket and muttered something unintelligible under his breath before turning and walking down the gap between the buildings we had come down.

We walked in uncomfortable silence back to his house, the two angels following us. When we reached my car, he looked past me across the street, his jaw set tight, moving slightly.

"I'll see you later." He leaned forward and brushed his lips against my cheek, the skin burning under the softness of his lips. He turned and headed towards the stairs leading up to his place.

I watched as he went and blinked several times, quelling the tears that had formed. He was disappointed our night hadn't ended well. I can't say I blamed him. I had wanted to go up those stairs with him.

We piled into my car, Levi in the back and Oliver in the front, and rode back to the school in silence.

~

WE SOMEHOW ALL ENDED UP IN Levi's room, which looked exactly like mine. So much for telling myself living in the staff building was a *good* thing. The only good thing about it was Tobias was right down the hall.

We sat in a circle on Levi's bed with a bottle of vodka. How Levi had gotten a bottle of vodka was something I would file away to explore later.

"Let's play Never Have I Ever," I said after Levi had suggested playing Try Not to Laugh.

I'd have a hard time with that one and end up drunk before I even knew what happened.

"How do you play that?" Oliver was examining the text on the label of the vodka before he handed it back to Levi.

"You say something you've never done that you think the other players have done. If they've done it, they take a drink."

"Is it safe to drink a lot of that?" Oliver had a crease between his eyebrows and was frowning at the blue bottle.

I shrugged and looked to Levi who regarded Oliver with a smile and a twinkle in his eye.

"Olly here has never drank before. We always try to get him to but he won't." He handed the bottle back to Oliver. "You start."

"Okay, let's see. Never have I ever had alcohol?" He looked back and forth between us, seeking confirmation he was playing right.

"Good job, angel. You catch on quick." I snatched the bottle out of his hands and twisted the top. After taking a quick swig, I passed it to Levi, who I was certain had had alcohol before. Why else would he have three different bottles hidden under his bed?

"I'll go next," he said, wincing after taking a drink, "Never have I ever smoked weed."

I snorted and reached for the bottle but he tipped it back and took a drink before handing it to me. I narrowed my eyes slightly at him before grabbing the bottle and doing the same, my eyes staying locked on his hazel green ones.

"Never have I ever... been to heaven." Levi snatched the bottle back from me and drank before handing it to Oliver.

Oliver looked down the opening of the bottle and then took the smallest sip I had ever seen. I laughed at his puckered expression before he coughed and then took another small sip.

"God, it burns! How can you stand it?"

"You'll see once you get enough of it in you." Levi wiggled his eyebrows and touched my knee. "Right, Dee?"

"Right." I wasn't sure I liked him calling me Dee, it felt wrong. I tilted my head slightly to the side and looked at Levi. Really looked at him. He was kind of cute with his messy curly hair on top of his head and high cheekbones, but maybe the alcohol was already speaking to me.

"Never have I ever..." Oliver bit his lip and looked between us, seeming unsure of himself. "Had sex."

I threw my head back and laughed, not at him, but at myself, because boy, had I had sex. Would have probably done it with Asher had they not ruined our evening. I snatched the bottle and took a mouthful and looked at Levi. He took the bottle and drank.

"Really?" Oliver looked equally as surprised as I was.

"I was sixteen when I died. I had a girlfriend. Plus, Delilah and I hooked up once. Never have I ever lusted after more than one person at a time." He took another drink and then preemptively handed the bottle to me.

"You're playing wrong, Levi. You're supposed to say something you haven't done or felt." I took a drink and then Oliver reached over and grabbed it.

As he took a surprisingly long drink, his eyes danced between me and Levi. *Oh, fuck.* When I had taken a drink, I had thought of him, Asher, and Tobias. He was thinking of me and Levi.

He cleared his throat. "Never have I ever wanted to kiss someone in this room." He took another long drink and held it out to Levi with a shaking hand.

I would have never expected this game to take this turn with the angels who had been assholes to me, but here we were, already onto sex. Levi drank.

"Never-" he started, but I grabbed the bottle and took one shot while I looked at Oliver.

Yeah, I did want to kiss Oliver again, but I also wanted to smack him. He was a Grade A asshole, but damn if I didn't want him. What the hell was wrong with me?

"Never have I ever regretted being such an asshole more than right now." I smirked and handed the bottle to Oliver.

They both drank and Levi leaned over and put the bottle on his nightstand. "I think if we play anymore right now, Olly might puke."

I looked at Oliver with his glossy eyes and smiled. He was literally beaming. His faint glow was brighter than usual. He looked at my lips and I ran my tongue along them, causing him to suck in a breath of air.

I leaned forward and our lips connected, both of us letting out moans as the connection we had felt in the library took over our bodies. Maybe it was because he was an angel, but if all angels got this response from my body, I was in big trouble.

My hands moved to his shoulders and I pushed him back, lying on top of the hard contours of his body. His arms went to my hips, gripping lightly at first before the deepening of our kiss moved them to my ass.

He rolled us so he was on top and moved his lips to my neck where he delivered kisses so light across my throat that it felt like he was running feathers across my skin. I moaned and opened my eyes to see what had happened to Levi. He had laid next to us, his head propped up on his hand. His eyes locked on Oliver. My attention went back to Oliver as he recaptured my lips and parted them with his tongue. His tongue collided with mine and I moved my hips up, connecting with his erection. He moaned against my lips.

"Take her shirt off." Levi's voice broke our kiss and we both looked at him.

I had just enough alcohol in me to throw caution to the wind. I was game if they were. Oliver was still staring at Levi as I reached

face was cleanly shaven. I tried to hide the fact that my eyes ran down his body, taking in his opened blue plaid flannel, gray shirt, blue jeans, and work boots marked with dirt. The flirty smirk on his face told me I didn't do a good job.

"I hope you don't mind if I shower first." He brushed past me and opened his door, holding it open. "I'm assuming you don't want me to smell."

I smiled at him as I squeezed past him and took in the clean space. The other day it had clothes thrown over a chair and floor, and empty bottles and food containers covering the counters. It had looked like he hadn't cleaned in weeks.

"You didn't have to clean for me."

"Who said I cleaned for you?" He bumped my shoulder playfully as he passed and went to the kitchen. "Drink?"

I watched as he poured himself a glass of whiskey and then went to the refrigerator. "I've got wine, beer, Diet Dr. Pepper."

My heart fluttered. He had said Diet Dr. Pepper was crap, but he had stocked his fridge with some. "I'll take some wine."

He turned and raised his eyebrows but then pulled a bottle of white wine out and grabbed a wine glass out of a top cupboard. He probably didn't use the wine glasses often.

He walked over to where I had perched on the arm of the couch and held the half-filled glass out to me. I reached out to take it, our fingers touching, but he didn't let go. His slate blue eyes, a little bluer than the other day, stared down at me, then at my lips. My legs spread slightly and he took a small step forward.

"I should go take a shower." His voice had taken on a slightly husky quality but then he stepped back and pulled his sunglasses off the top of his head. "Make yourself at home."

I let out a shaky breath after he slid the bathroom door shut and sat down on the couch. All I could think about was him in the shower. Did the muscles in his forearms extend under his shirt? Did he have any tattoos?

Never before had I longed for three guys. I hated admitting to myself that there were three but I couldn't stop thinking about choco-

down and tugged my shirt up as far as I could before he moved so I could remove it. Oliver looked down at my lace-covered breasts and let out a breath of air.

"Kiss them." Levi ran his free hand through his hair before lowering it to his pants and rubbing his evident erection through the fabric of his jeans. "Don't just stare at them."

Oliver took his finger and traced it over the top of my breasts before lowering his lips to kiss where he had just touched. I tilted my head back and then turned my head towards Levi and bit my lip. I wasn't attracted to Levi in the same way I was to Oliver, but part of me was curious what would happen.

He scooted forward and ran a finger along my bottom lip and then kissed me with such heat that I clenched my legs together, trying to lessen the overwhelming need that consumed me.

How would I even handle two guys at a time? One was hard enough as it was.

Levi moved his hands behind me, Oliver preoccupied with the swell of my breasts over the fabric of my bra. The restrictiveness of the bra went away as Olly kissed down my arm as he moved the strap down. I threw the bra to the side and watched as both guys looked at me with hunger in their eyes.

Oliver moved first, taking my left nipple in his mouth and sucking lightly. I arched my back and tangled one of my hands in his hair. Levi kissed my neck and trailed his tongue down to the same breast. He hesitated for a brief moment before he moved his lips near Oliver's.

Their lips met on my nipple and they both sighed against my skin. My hands threaded in Levi's soft curls as his lips and Oliver's began kissing around my nipple. It was hard not to watch and even harder to ignore how turned on I was by it. One of Levi's hands snaked around Oliver's neck and pulled him up towards him, their lips colliding in a needy kiss above me that had me feeling a little jealous.

Oliver broke the kiss and stared panting at Levi before his eyes cut to mine.

"It's okay." I looked between the boys and saw the lust in Levi's eyes, but not for me, for Oliver.

"I should go." Oliver slid off the bed and had his feet shoved in his shoes before we could react. "I'll see you guys in class tomorrow."

The door shut with a click and Levi rolled over and threw his hands over his face. Now that Oliver had left the room, my need to be touched evaporated.

CHAPTER 10

DANICA

I put my pillow over my face and pressed it against my ears. After Oliver's exodus the night before, Levi and I drank until we were sloppy drunk. Not my finest moment. The realization that Levi didn't turn me on was like a slap to the face. It was like all desire had evaporated once Oliver left. For a moment I had thought all angels that had dicks were going to turn me on.

I somehow managed to make it back to my room, but now someone was knocking on my door. I threw my pillow and pushed myself up. I was never going to drink again. How many times had I said that before?

My feet dragged across the floor, my eyes not quite all the way open, and I peeked out the peephole. I let out a groan because I really didn't want to see *him* right now. I turned the lock anyway and shuffled back to my bed, lying face down to block out the light that was making my eyeballs throb like someone was pumping them full of air.

The door opened with a small creak and clicked shut. The bed dipped as Tobias laid down next to me and pulled me towards him, the faint scent of mint hitting my nose.

"Time to wake up," he said, kissing my hair. I grumbled into his chest and shook my head. "Where were you last night? I called, texted, knocked. Asher called and told me what happened."

His hand went to my lower back and ran back and forth across it, sending tingles up my spine. Where the heck was my shirt? I didn't even remember taking it off. Besides making out and the hot kiss between Levi and Oliver, I didn't remember much else.

"I think I'm still drunk." I hiccupped and let out another groan as the jolt of the hiccup sent a pain through my skull. "Didn't mean to worry you."

"You got drunk with Oliver and Levi?" I nodded my response into his button up shirt and ran my hands over the smooth material on his back.

He pulled back so he could see my face. I bit my lip and saw the question in his eyes.

"We kissed. A lot." I flinched with my words. It was one thing to hold hands with Asher and flirt all night, but to make out with not one, but two different guys? Guilt was a fickle beast and it had currently set up shop in my chest. What Tobias and I had was so new, yet I felt as if I had just cheated on a long-term love.

His hand moved a stray piece of hair out of my eyes and then rested on my cheek. "They've bullied you."

"I know." I looked at the top buttons on his shirt. "But I feel something for Oliver. I don't know what it is. Safety? I feel the same thing with you. With Asher. I know it sounds crazy."

He put his finger under my chin and tilted it up to meet my eyes. "It doesn't sound crazy. I feel the same way, and I bet if you asked them they'd say the same. What about Levi?"

I shrugged. "I probably wouldn't make out with him sober." I played with a loose thread on one of his buttons, tempted to yank on it, but not wanting to pop the button off. "I can't be with all three of you, that's..." He put his finger over my lips, stopping my words.

His eyes closed and he spoke softly. "I've been around a long time, both as a human and angel, and I have never felt like this. I'm not willing to let you go because you feel the same thing with them."

102

I kissed his finger and turned my head so it was on my cheek. "What about divinity points?"

He chuckled and opened his eyes, amusement written on their glistening surface. "Your dad really didn't explain anything to you did he? You being with us hurts no one. The only person you'd be hurting is yourself. Besides, divinity points really just help you get better guardian gigs." He kissed my cheek and then sat up. "Now, let's get you showered and to class because you *will* be going to class today even if I have to drag you there myself or throw you over my shoulder."

"Is that an offer to help me shower?" I rolled onto my back and looked up at him standing over me. His eyes moved down to my chest and narrowed slightly. My eyes fell to my left breast and I let out a groan. "Yeah, about this." I ran my finger over the hickey. I wasn't even sure who had left it.

He cleared his throat and put his hand out to help me off the bed. "You don't need to explain." He pulled me up and led me into the bathroom.

He turned on the water and then started unbuttoning his shirt. I hadn't seen him without his shirt on yet, and watched in anticipation. As the sleeves slid down his arms, I watched as his right arm came into view. Stunning portraits wrapped around his muscles; four smiling faces looked back at me. A woman. Twin boys about five. A baby girl.

I stepped forward as he started unbuttoning his pants and I slid a finger down his arm, feeling a lump form in my throat. His hands stilled on his belt buckle and he looked at his arm and then at me.

"My past life. I didn't want to forget what they looked like." He wiped a stray tear that had worked its way down my cheek before continuing to undress.

I had no words. His life was stolen from him and now all he had were the memories of what could have been. It had to be hard knowing they were probably still out there somewhere, at least his children, and he couldn't see them.

"Don't look so sad about it. Until Asher fell, he checked in on them from time to time. They grieved, moved on, lived their lives. That's all I wanted for them. To be happy." His eyes brightened and he slid my panties down my legs. "You know they say the best cure for a hangover is an orgasm."

I smiled back at him and climbed in the shower after him, the warm water falling over us and instantly making my tense muscles relax. "Who says that?"

"Me." He pulled me against him and kissed me, making my knees go weak.

The shower might have been small but my orgasm was not. Tobias was right. Orgasms really did help with hangovers.

Oliver Morgan. The celestial I still knew so little about. The boy who had fled after he and his friend had kissed. The boy who had decided that today he was sitting next to me in Demonology. You know, because I wasn't already confused enough as it was.

When he slid into the seat next to me, he said nothing. He still said nothing when the whispers started. The whispers about why he was sitting next to me. The only angels that ever dared sit next to me were Brooklyn, Cora, and Ethan. I was beginning to think they were a special breed of angel.

Tobias cleared his throat at the front of the room and the class went silent. Despite his quiet nature, Tobias's presence commanded attention.

"Dean Whittaker has asked me to speak to you about recent attempted abductions of angels in Pasadena." The room erupted in chatter and he held up his hands to quiet the class back down. "As far as we know, there have been three attempted abductions. No angels have been reported missing yet, but as you know, some have assignments that require them to go off the radar. Dean Whittaker is asking you to stay on campus, and if you must go into the city, go in a large group. The Fallen seem to be attacking in groups of three."

"The Fallen aren't strong enough to abduct an angel," a girl in the back of the room commented. "Plus, we can just fly away."

Tobias's eyes briefly looked in my direction before he paced once in front of the room with his hand rubbing his bearded chin. "They are using demon blood, which weakens our defenses. Your wings won't work. You'll be too weak to fly or fight back."

"Then we attack the Fallen first," another boy said, and the class bubbled up with noises of affirmation and agreement.

I don't know why but I clutched Oliver's leg under the table and he put his hand on mine. My mind had gone to Asher. Not all Fallen were abducting angels, and if angels went on a manhunt, innocent Fallen would be hurt in the process.

"I bet Danica is in on it." I flinched as the words hit my ears and Oliver's hand tightened on top of mine. "She gets here and now we have Fallen trying to kidnap angels using demon blood? The Princess of Hell is probably their ring leader."

"That's enough!" Tobias's voice was sharp and angry. The room fell silent once more. "Danica is not behind this. They attacked her."

"She rescued me and Levi last night." Oliver didn't turn, but spoke loud enough for everyone to hear. The room was silent. I didn't turn to gauge their reactions.

"If you have any other questions or concerns you can speak to me after class." Tobias spoke with finality and then started his lesson.

I tried to concentrate on what he was lecturing about, but couldn't keep my mind off of the Fallen and the three men slowly worming their way into my heart.

I wondered if I was still in high school or at a guardian angel training academy. They were making up for the experience now, considering most of the angels here had missed high school. The stares and whispers were relentless.

When lunch rolled around, I was in a foul mood. My mood only got worse when Oliver sat down next to me. The air at the table disappeared as Brooklyn, Cora, and Ethan sucked in breaths and held them. I'm sure they had heard about the rescue and his presence at my side in Demonology, but seeing it was shocking after the events of the previous week. The other members of the Divine 7 were shooting daggers my way, even Levi. He wasn't shooting daggers when he had his tongue down my throat last night.

"Why are you sitting here?" I crammed chips in my mouth to keep myself from saying anything else.

Oliver glanced in my direction before sniffing at his sandwich and then taking a bite. He certainly was an odd duck. A cute, odd duck.

"I'm done being Divine," he said with a shrug. "Can I not sit here?"

A sound came from across the table but I kept my attention on Oliver. I narrowed my eyes. "You can't just undo what you've done to me."

"I'm aware of that, but I can at least try to make it up to you." He grabbed a cookie from a stack of five on his plate and offered it to me. "For you. I know you like them."

Brooklyn let out a snort. "So generous of you to give her one. What are you, the cookie monster?" She looked at the cookies he had stacked on his plate. They weren't small cookies either, they were the kind you buy at a cookie shop. No wonder he smelled like chocolate chip cookies.

"Who's that?" he asked as I took the cookie from him and put it on my plate.

"The blue monster on *Sesame Street*... you know... C is for cookie, that's good enough for me, oh cookie, cookie, cookie starts with C." Brooklyn impersonated the Cookie Monster causing me to almost choke on the food in my mouth.

"Huh. That sounds like an interesting show. I'll have to check it out sometime." He grabbed one of the giant cookies and shoved half of it in his mouth, causing us all to laugh. He looked so serious about it that I couldn't quite tell if he was joking.

Ethan narrowed his eyes at Oliver and then leaned back in his chair with his arms crossed. "How do we know we can trust you?"

Oliver put down the other half of the cookie and folded his hands on the table. "I'm pretty good at keeping secrets, right, Danica?" He looked over at me with raised eyebrows.

My smile faded and I stared back at Oliver for a moment before clearing my throat and looking at Ethan. I knew he was referring to Tobias.

"He can be trusted. I wouldn't go telling him your deepest darkest secrets or anything like that."

After a few minutes of tense silence at the table, Oliver spoke. "Before dinner tonight some of us are playing a pick-up game of football with the staff. You guys should come and watch us kick their butts."

Cora made a squealing noise and perked up. "We should go. You haven't had one in forever!" She turned to me. "It's eye candy central! They usually take their shirts off, and let me tell you... Coach Ferguson and Mr. Armstrong are scrumptious."

"Sitting right here, Cora." Ethan laughed as he took a bite of his food.

I looked back and forth between them. Why hadn't I noticed the way they always sat so close to each other?

IT SEEMED like the whole school turned out for the game. There were no bleachers because the angel version of football was played in the sky. The field was twice the size of a standard football field. When the players took the field they were already shirtless with their wings out.

The first thing I noticed was that most of the male staff members were incredibly attractive without shirts on. Was that a prerequisite for becoming a guardian angel? Or maybe it was just that washboard abs were necessary to play football. Tobias with his wings out gave me the female equivalent of a boner.

"Most of the women here are here for the show. It's like *Magic Mike* meets angels," Cora explained as we spread out a blanket and sat down. "They get pretty aggressive too since angels heal and all."

"I'm interested to see what happens with Oliver since he is now on team Danica and not team Divine. I bet they let him get pummeled by the staff, and you know how the staff like to go after Oliver since he's an archangel and all." Ethan sat next to Cora and pulled her close to him, putting his arm around her.

A pang of jealousy shot through me at seeing them cuddled up with each other. I wasn't typically a jealous person, but I wanted what they had. Someone to cuddle with openly and not just in clandestine moments.

A whistle blew and the angels shot into the sky. The student team included the five male Divine 7 and six others, in possession of the football. It appeared to be played very similar to actual football, but the tackles were in the air and much more violent. I cringed as the first student took a hit from Coach Ferguson, sending both of them onto the grass.

The rest of the quarter, which was shortened from a regulation game, was much of the same. The staff ended up leading three goals to two when the angels descended to take a break. Oliver made his way over to us, looking just as refreshed as when he had started. He had taken some pretty serious hits too, but since angels didn't sweat and they healed, he didn't seem fazed.

"How are you liking it so far?" He plopped down next to me on the blanket on his side and looked up at me. "Think I have a career in football?"

My eyes slid down his chest and abs to where his shorts rode low on his hips. It was almost a sin with how attractive he had been made. He was like a juicy cherry just waiting to be popped.

"It's fun to watch. You might have a career in male exotic dancing though." I bit my lip to keep myself from laughing when his face went from confused to flirtatious.

"You know, I'm a pretty good dancer. I should show you my moves sometime."

"Please make sure to do that in the privacy of your own room," Ethan groaned, throwing an empty water bottle at Oliver.

"Incoming," Brooklyn warned under her breath.

The rest of the Divine were headed in our direction as if on a mission. They walked with purpose, and at the front of their little group was Abby. They stopped a few feet from us. It was like a scene out of *Mean Girls.*

"May we help you?" I asked as casually as possible, trying to hide the fact that I wanted to jump up and beat the shit out of her smirking little face.

Abby ignored me and looked down at Oliver. "Oliver, this has to stop. You're embarrassing yourself being associated with this devil worshiper. We are concerned you're going to fall."

I snorted back a laugh and went to stand but Oliver put out his hand to stop me before he stood. He towered over the group with the next tallest being at least half a head shorter than him. He stepped forward and cleared his throat.

"You are a bitch." He spoke loud enough for every angel in the vicinity to hear and the whole area went quiet, which then in turn caused the entire field to turn their attention to the confrontation.

Abby made a noise in her throat and looked like she had been smacked but then a grin spread on her face.

"She fucked you, didn't she? Did her evil pussy put you under a spell? And here we thought you liked dick." The silence around us was deafening. It was one of those moments where I half expected a baby to start crying and snap everyone out of it. Everyone was holding their breaths.

Oliver took another step forward to get in her face but the four men of the group pulled her back and faced off with him. I stood up and grabbed Oliver's arm but he pulled it away from me.

Several staff members and Tobias landed next to us.

"What's going on here?" Tobias looked at Oliver and then at me.

"We were just getting Oliver so we could start playing again," Levi said.

"Well, let's go then!" Coach Ferguson jumped and flew into the air, the other players following him.

Oliver turned and gave me an apologetic look before following them. I stood facing Abby and Delilah.

"It's only a matter of time before he sees your evil ways, Eve. You better watch your back," Delilah spat as she and Abby backed away. They turned on their heels and took off into the crowd.

That certainly sounded like a threat.

CHAPTER 11

DANICA

J had a gut feeling when I woke up Friday morning, Friday the thirteenth nonetheless, that the day was going to go badly. I'm not usually superstitious, but with life rearing its ugly head at me for no apparent reason, I couldn't help but wonder if it was karma biting me in the ass.

I woke up to no texts back from Asher. I had texted him every day since Tuesday, but my texts went unanswered, the silence speaking louder than words. I had thought something was there between us, but I was wrong. Tobias told me Asher was "complicated." Well, I could do without complicated in my life at the moment. Things were already complicated enough without a grown man not even bothering to text me back. Even a "stop texting me" or "leave me alone, stalker" would have sufficed.

Demonology had another pop quiz. Had I read the syllabus like everyone else in the class, I would have known that every Friday there was a quiz so there really was no pop to it.

It was time for me to get my act together, buy a planner, maybe put things in my phone and set reminders. It was suggested to me before back in high school but I had never taken the time to actually do it. Maybe now was a good time to start. Tobias would help me if I asked.

Ava would have helped me too, but I always felt I was already depending on her too much when she helped me with homework assignments.

Then there was glorified PE for pompous wing-toting beings, where I was reminded daily about my lack of wings. The rest of the class did warmups together, practiced drills, played games. Sometimes they didn't even use their wings, but I was banished to the room with the mats and the dummies.

"Do you think Coach Ferguson is going to let you keep me company the rest of the semester? Shouldn't you be learning whatever flying maneuvers the other angels are?" I asked Brooklyn, who was my constant companion the past two weeks.

We had just finished the drills we were running through and were stretching on the mats. I was getting better at throwing a punch and a kick, but still felt useless defending myself. Brooklyn told me it just took time and she had been even worse at the beginning of the year. She was good, easily connecting with her targets with an intensity I hadn't seen from another female before. If she got into a fight with a human male, she would kick his ass. That at least gave me a small sliver of hope.

"Actually, I think I found a solution to that. Levi is going to start training with me so I can keep training with you." A blush creeped up her cheeks as she turned away.

I thought she hated the Divine 7 just as much as the rest of us. Hell, I had thought I hated them too and now Oliver sat with us at lunch. Levi was a mystery to me after his abrupt mood swings. One second he seemed to hate me, the next to like me, then right back to hating me again.

"When did this happen?" I hadn't told anyone besides Tobias about my drunken night with Levi and Oliver. Since then, Levi had been avoiding me besides sending scowls my way, which I was actually grateful for. It would have been awkward being near him. What would we have discussed? Him using my nipple to make out with Oliver?

"Yesterday. Don't tell anyone, but we're going on a date on

Saturday night! I know we aren't supposed to go off campus, but Levi says I will be safe with him." She spoke so surely, like she trusted him fully with her safety. I wasn't convinced.

"Levi almost got abducted on Tuesday. He didn't even put up much of a fight."

"I know. I told him we should just watch a movie here or something, but he says he isn't going to live in fear. He does have a point. We can't just sequester ourselves here on campus."

I studied the excitement on her face for several long seconds before getting up from the mats. I was surprised Levi would even want to go off campus so soon after almost being abducted.

"Just be careful. No dark, empty places."

"Yes, mom. What are you up to this weekend?" We headed towards the locker room where the rest of the class was already headed. "Are you going to see your mystery man again?"

Which mystery man was she referring to? I had three. Well, two now. "Maybe." I smiled to myself. Tobias and I had been seeing a *lot* of each other the past few days. I was still being overly cautious with Oliver and only sitting with him at lunch and in class.

We grabbed our clothes out of our lockers and I headed to one of the few showers that were in the locker room. Unlike my angel counterparts, I had to rinse off. They never sweated. Lucky bastards.

After getting dressed in my uniform, I went back to my locker to grab my bag.

"Oh my God! There's a snake!" A girl screeched, causing everyone to scream and start pushing and shoving to get out of the room.

At first I thought they were just being their normal bitchy selves and calling me a snake, but there was a literal snake in the middle of the locker room. I rolled my eyes at the chaos that erupted around me, grabbing my bag out of my gym locker.

I could have just left like the rest of them and let someone else deal with it, but the poor snake was a semi-harmless gopher snake. It was not happy with all the thundering feet, slamming lockers, and screaming girls. I could hear its hiss echoing as the locker room emptied. Gopher snakes sounded very similar to rattlesnakes when they were threatened.

"Well, buddy, looks like it's just me and you now. How'd you get in here? Please don't tell me you came from under the sinks." I got closer to the snake; his body was coiled and his head was up, assessing the threat in front of him, forked tongue tasting the air.

I could see how everyone had freaked out. He was massive and even looked very similar to a rattlesnake. Somehow, he had found himself right smack dab in the middle of the women's locker room.

I stood still until the hissing stopped and the snake started to slither out of its coiled position. Placing my hand on it about halfway, it stiffened and stilled under my hand, lifting its head again and tasting the air with its forked tongue. I waited for it to soften its muscles and start to move again. I very slowly picked it up, bringing my other hand up to support its body. It wasn't my first encounter with a snake.

"Poor guy... or gal." Since I didn't have anything to put the snake in and I was not going to sacrifice my bag, I walked back into the gym, hoping to put it outside the gym door.

Dean Whittaker and Coach Ferguson were walking quickly across the gym towards me. The dean's high heels echoed their click-clacking sounds across the large room. The dean stopped several feet from me but Coach Ferguson had no qualms about the snake in my hands.

"What the hell is wrong with you?" His voice was raised and his hands were on his hips. "Bringing a snake into school!"

I continued walking towards the gym door because the last thing I needed was for him to be yelling in my face with an agitated snake in my hands. I stepped outside into the bright sunlight and set the snake down in the grass, letting it slither out of my hands.

"Danica, you need to come with us immediately," Dean Whittaker's voice projected from the gym door, where she and Coach Ferguson stood waiting for me.

"You can't be serious." I turned around and held my hands out in disbelief. "I didn't bring that snake in the locker room!"

"We have several trustworthy witnesses that say you did. Unfortunately, you are out of chances."

Two weeks. That had to be a new record for getting kicked out of a school.

~

I<small>T WAS</small> different sitting in Dean Whittaker's office this time, knowing I had done nothing wrong. They had called Tobias and we were waiting for him to arrive after his class. How could I, the daughter of the devil, really expect to come out ahead in this situation? The dean was never going to take my word over the word of a group of angels.

When Tobias entered the dean's office, I turned and watched him approach the empty chair. He didn't meet my eyes, but his neck muscles were tense. At least one of the staff members at this godforsaken academy was in my corner.

"What's this about, Sue?" he said as he sat down next to me.

"I knew we should have never agreed to let such a loose cannon into this school and today she proved us right. She brought a rattlesnake into the women's locker room and let it loose. Someone could have been bitten!" She tapped a pen on her desk before setting it down. "I've already put a call in to the high court to decide if she should stay."

Tobias gripped the wooden arm of the chair and worked his jaw. He turned his head in my direction. "Did you take a rattlesnake into the locker room?"

I met his eyes. "First off, it was a gopher snake, completely harmless unless agitated. And no. I took it out of the locker room. It was there when I got done showering."

He turned back to look at the dean and cleared his throat. "With all due respect, I find it highly unlikely Danica would do something like this. How would she have even had the time to go and find the snake? She certainly didn't have it during her first class with me."

Dean Whittaker looked surprised and picked up a folder before dropping it on the desk edge in front of Tobias. "She has only been in attendance for two weeks and there have been countless reports and incidents involving her. Not to mention her history at her past schools. Now, I understand that Chamuel has a soft spot for Lucifer, but I've contacted Michael and he agrees that the high court needs to decide what to do with her. She doesn't show any signs of being anything other than a troubled human teenager."

In that moment, I wanted to scream. I wanted to stand up and take that folder and smack Dean Whittaker over the head. I would have if Tobias hadn't scooted his shoe over to touch mine.

"I see where you're coming from, Sue, but are you really that blind that you can't see what's going on right in front of your eyes?" My head jerked over to look at Tobias. "You allow the top angels, which are only top because of some ridiculous point system, rule this school and cloud your better judgement."

Dean Whittaker was very quiet as she stared at Tobias with a look of pure venom. Hell, I was even surprised Tobias had told her that, not that she didn't deserve his words because she most certainly did.

She finally spoke with no emotion in her voice. "Mr. Armstrong, need I remind you what happens to angels that go against the higher authority?" He shook his head, his body tense. "Very good. Her hearing is tomorrow at ten in the morning. You will go as her representative since she is unable to. Now, if you'll excuse me, I have somewhere to be."

She stood and walked out of the office, leaving us. I stood, grabbing my bag and throwing it over my shoulder. I was struggling to keep my emotions from bubbling over into a flood, but a stray tear managed to sneak out.

"Dan-" I put my hand up to stop him. He stood and took a step towards me, pain in his eyes.

I understood, I did. He cared about me, but it didn't change the fact that I wasn't an angel. I couldn't even go stand up for myself at my own hearing because I wasn't dead and couldn't go to heaven. Even if I could go plead my case, they would kick me out, I was sure of it.

"I'm just going to go start packing. I can take a hint when I'm not wanted, and I'm pretty sure this goes far beyond a hint." I left before he could stop me.

I kept my head down, going back to my room. Never had I walked with my eyes on the ground, but sometimes hiding was better than having to look at stares and looks of disgust.

I couldn't help myself, I texted Asher once I was back in my room. *They are sending Tobias tomorrow to the high court to decide my fate. Maybe I can work on your construction crew? I can't use a hammer, but you could teach me.*

He didn't respond, which I didn't expect him to since he worked. I needed to talk to someone to keep the weight that was sitting on my chest from crashing down on me, so I called Lucifer. When he answered I couldn't even talk through the sudden tears that burst from me. I rarely cried in front of him, but I guess everyone has their breaking point. After several minutes of me crying and him staying silent on the other end, I finally was able to speak and told him about the snake and about the hearing.

"Mr. Armstrong will be going in my place since-"

"I'm coming," he stated firmly, but also with a hint of sadness in his voice.

"What? You can't come. Fallen can't get past the wards or go to heaven." I was sure he was aware of that small detail.

"I'll call in a few favors. I will see you tomorrow for breakfast."

He ended the call before I could even respond. The devil was coming to breakfast.

I PACED in front of the futon where Tobias was sitting. He was adamant that he would still be going, even if my dad had it in his head that he was going to somehow be allowed to go to the heavenly realm.

I had been mad at my dad for over two weeks, but for him to come and stand up for me in a place where he wasn't going to be received with warm hugs, it said a lot. He might have been an absent father but he always showed up when I needed him.

"Aren't you nervous?" I stopped in front of him and frowned. "I feel like you should be a little more nervous, like sweating through your shirt nervous. Need to take a cold shower nervous. You're going to meet my father. I told you he was the devil, didn't I?"

He laughed and crossed his ankle onto his knee. I didn't know if I was more nervous over my dad coming to campus, my possible expulsion, or Tobias meeting him. My dad had never met any of my boyfriends because I had never told him I had any. Not that any ever lasted longer than a few months. I had a feeling that what I had with Tobias was going to last a lot longer than that though so getting it out of the way might be a good idea.

"I don't sweat. I guess I'm a little nervous about meeting my girlfriend's dad, but it'll be fine."

"Girlfriend?" I smiled down at him, my stomach fluttering. "Is that what I am now?"

I walked towards him and lowered myself to straddle his lap, wrapping my arms around his neck. He groaned and buried his face in my hair, inhaling deeply, his hands moving to my ass and squeezing.

"Get your hands off my daughter."

If I was capable of jumping ten feet in the air, I would have. I hadn't even heard the door open or felt his presence. Yet there he was, Lucifer, standing just inside the door of my room. I nearly fell getting off of Tobias's lap, who looked just as embarrassed as I was.

"Dad, how did you get in here?" I turned towards him and plastered on a smile as if he hadn't just caught a man with his hands on my ass.

Tobias stood, stiff as a board. My father ignored me and gave Tobias the once over before giving me a hug. His firewood and cinnamon scent hit my nose and I buried my nose in his charcoal gray blazer, relief flooding me. He released me and his eyes were back on Tobias again.

"Sir, I'm Tobias Armstrong." I was impressed with his ability to introduce himself with a steady tone and stick out a calm hand for a handshake.

My dad took his hand and I swear I saw Tobias wince. My dad was probably doing something to him with his special voodoo tricks.

"Mr. Armstrong, is it? Care to tell me why a teacher is manhandling a student?" He let Tobias's hand go.

He walked around the room, looking in the cabinets, the refrigerator, out the window. We both watched him, unsure of how to answer that question. We had known it would come from someone eventually and that Tobias might face repercussions because of it. He finished his perusal of the room and turned back to Tobias, ignoring the look of horror on my face.

"Dad-"

"Let the boy speak, Danica." He looked at his watch and then back at Tobias.

"Well, sir, we, well, we..." he was stuttering, his forehead creasing with the struggle of how to answer the question. I had never seen him flustered or at a loss for words. He always spoke with confidence and strength.

Meeting parents was a big deal even under normal circumstances. These were not normal circumstances by any means. I had avoided this type of situation for years, my father never even having an inkling of my love life. If he only knew that there were two others besides Tobias. Well, one now that Asher seemed to have fallen off the face of the Earth.

My dad smirked, enjoying seeing him squirm. He slung his arm around his shoulder and moved towards the door. "Let's get breakfast and your *boyfriend* and I can get to know each other a little bit better."

"In the dining hall? Is that really a good idea?" I followed them as he opened the door and walked into the hallway where two men stood waiting. They practically radiated power and had a faint glow to them, like someone had put lights under their skin. Oliver had a similar glow to him, just not as strong.

"Chamuel and Haniel will accompany us."

My eyes went wide as I took in the two archangels. They looked like normal men, just like my father, but you could tell there was an otherness about them. I just wanted to stare, but instead followed my dad, who still had his arm wrapped around Tobias like they were long-lost buddies. Poor Tobias; this had to be hell for him.

Walking to the dining hall, many students stopped to stare as we passed. They recognized Chamuel and Haniel, who my dad called Ham and Han, but they regarded my dad with curious glances and whispers. It was only a matter of time before they connected the dots that he was my father.

Once we got food, I made for my regular table, but my dad passed right by me and went to the corner seats at the Divine 7's table. I groaned internally and followed, sitting next to him on the far side of the table. I could try to explain to him that these seats belonged to a group, but instead tried to focus on saving Tobias from whatever my father had cooked up for him.

We ate in silence, but it didn't escape my notice that the entire dining room was staring at us. Maybe it was the fact that there were two recognizable archangels eating pancakes at the other end of the table. Or maybe it was the sharp-dressed man sitting next to me. As far as I knew, no one knew Lucifer's actual appearance. At one point it was probably well known, but over the millennia it was twisted. He did somewhat look like Tom Ellis though, or was it that Tom Ellis looked like him?

"And who is this?" My inner dialogue was interrupted by my dad pointing a piece of bacon in the direction of Oliver, who was walking straight towards us with a large grin on his face.

He had no clue what he was about to walk into. I groaned and put my palm against my forehead. This was not going well. He already hated Tobias. Now he was going to meet the angel that had made it his mission to make up for his wrongs.

Oliver stopped and greeted the other two archangels before putting his tray down next to Tobias, leaning over the table, and kissing me on the cheek. Tobias chuckled as he sat down next to him.

"Good morning, beautiful. Why the long face?" He was much too excited for it being so early on a Saturday morning.

My eyes were drawn to his plate which was piled with cantaloupe and only cantaloupe. Since he had been eating with me, I had noticed he ate almost the exact same things.

When I didn't answer, he finally looked at my dad and then he smiled at him with the most welcoming and gracious smile I'd ever seen. It was endearing really, his complete obliviousness.

"I'm Olly." He looked down at the archangels who were watching him curiously. I couldn't tell if they were amused by him or not, but they both had a glimmer in their eyes. "You must have been created after I left?"

"I wasn't aware another archangel was created. When were you created?" He looked down at the piles of orange fruit on Oliver's plate. "Recently is my guess."

"July. What about you?"

I nearly choked on the soda in my mouth and my dad put his hand on my back to give it a few pats as I coughed. Oliver narrowed his eyes a bit at the hand on my back but didn't say anything. Oh God, he thought my dad was putting the moves on me. Gross.

"Long before that. So, tell me, how do you know Danica? Tobias here is her boyfriend, so who are you?"

Oliver looked at me and then at Tobias. He focused back on my dad's hand on my back. I didn't even want to imagine what was going through his head. Now that I knew he had only been *created* in July, he made so much more sense. He couldn't even recognize that two familiar archangels and Tobias being in the dining room was *odd*.

"I'm a close friend. And you are?"

"Just how close of a friend are we talking? Hands on her ass type of friend?"

I was going to die. Literally, I was going to die.

"Lucifer, leave the boy alone." Haniel warned from the end of the table.

Oliver's eyeballs nearly popped out of their sockets and he dropped his fork onto his tray. I gave him a reassuring smile, which didn't seem to help.

"We should get out of here before the Divine 6 come." I finished my last piece of bacon and piled my napkin and silverware onto my plate.

"What happened to the seventh one?" My dad turned slightly towards me with raised eyebrows, which was the most emotion I'd seen from him since he arrived. He probably somehow knew they sat at the table we were at and was biding his time to scare the shit out of them. Normally I'd be all for it, but it would only make matters worse. He *was* the reason they were such assholes.

"There is a seventh. They already replaced me with a second year named Betty." Oliver had a wistful look in his eyes but then cleared his throat. "Glad to be done with them."

The air suddenly changed at the table, taking on a prickling feeling of heat. My dad was no idiot. He knew the Divine 7 were my torturers and one was sitting right across from him at that very moment. The two angels at the end of the table put their forks down and looked ready to intervene if needed, but I shook my head at them. They may have known my father well at one point, but they didn't now.

Oliver's face turned a few shades shy of a tomato. "I... sir. I'm sorry. I just... It was funny at first, you know? You have to admit a room full of feathers is pretty hilarious. I didn't want to do the apple ball gag but... I will spend every remaining moment of my time here on Earth apologizing to your daughter."

"What. Ball. Gag."

I flinched and looked to Tobias for help. He was avoiding my gaze and was looking at the table. *Coward.*

"A prank. It was a stupid prank where they shoved a gag that looked like an apple in my mouth. I'm fine, Dad. Honestly. It's probably karma for all the shit I've done."

"Sir, I can assure you-" Oliver started, but Tobias reached over and squeezed the back of his neck.

"Just stop talking," Tobias said with a sigh.

Lucifer pointed his fork at Tobias. "I like this one." He then pointed his fork at Oliver. "This one. Well, no wonder they sent him to Earth."

Oliver's face fell at his words and before I could stop him he was rushing away from the table, leaving his uneaten pile of cantaloupe.

CHAPTER 12

DANICA

I couldn't worry about what was going on with Oliver when my future lay on the chopping block. My dad struck a sore spot with the angel. It also didn't slip my mind that Tobias had mentioned knowing things about Oliver that he wouldn't want known. What had the angel done?

My thoughts of Oliver quickly vanished as we climbed the last set of stairs in Ariel Hall and exited onto the roof where we would be out of sight of curious eyes. I hadn't seen many roofs in my life, but this one had to be the cleanest roof in existence. It gleamed in the sunlight like a launch pad for the pure.

From what I had gleaned from the post-breakfast conversation, Chamuel and Haniel were taking responsibility for Lucifer through a sworn blood oath which gave them permission to kill him if anything went awry in heaven. When Haniel unsheathed a dagger that looked like it was encrusted purely in diamonds, I wasn't that surprised that all three of them sliced their hands and clasped them together.

"I'm not sure what state my wings are in. I stopped feeling them millennia ago." My dad took off his jacket, tie, and shirt, and handed them to me. He didn't wear clothing with slits for wings, since he couldn't use his. My heart ached knowing that my father was an angel, but couldn't access an essential part of who he was.

"Maybe when we're done, before we bind them again, we can have a quick race for old-time's sake." Haniel ran a hand between my father's shoulder blades as if he was searching for something. "This might hurt."

I clutched onto Tobias's hand as Haniel seemed to grab an invisible string and pull it away from my dad's shoulders before swiping the dagger through it. My dad fell to his knees, his back muscles scrunched. I was glad he wasn't facing me because I don't think I would have been able to handle whatever emotion was on his face. I took a step forward but Tobias pulled me back to him, shaking his head.

His hands fell to the smooth surface of the roof and his body seemed to vibrate with a power I couldn't understand. It was like a machine with a giant turbine was turned on, the waves radiating from him in a circular pattern.

"We should have done this in the field. It's going to knock the entire building down!" Chamuel backed up a step.

The roof beneath our feet started to shake and Tobias pulled me closer to him. It felt like an earthquake, and I might have thought it was one if I didn't see my father's body vibrating in the middle of the roof.

Just when I thought my teeth were going to break from the vibrations, everything went eerily still and silent for the briefest moment and then wings burst from his back with a flash of bright light as he stood. They flapped twice, stirring the hair around my face.

I choked on a sob, the image of the man so hated, so vilified, standing before me with pure white wings that nearly blinded me. He turned around slowly, his wings moving as if on autopilot to avoid hitting Chamuel and Haniel. He walked towards me without hesitation.

"You've always wondered what my wings look like." He stopped in front of me, bringing a hand to my cheek and wiping away the tears that were cascading down.

His face looked different somehow. He was the same, but a lightness caressed his cheeks and he had a twinkle in his eyes. A sob escaped my lips and he pulled me into his arms, wrapping his arms and wings around me.

"Shhh." He kissed the top of my head and then pulled away. "Everything is going to be fine. Shall we get this over with?"

He stepped back and Tobias followed him, giving my hand a squeeze as he passed. The four angels launched into the air and disappeared from sight.

~

WAITING for the angels to return was akin to going to the dentist. I hated it with every fiber of my being. They said it could be hours before returning, so instead of sitting around on the roof, I decided to track down Oliver.

I pulled my phone out of my back pocket and shot him a text. *Where are you? Want to wait with me?*

I was halfway back to my room when I got a response. I was thankful he hadn't pulled an Asher and ghosted me. *You can come to my room if you want. Building 2, room 403.*

Not exactly what I had in mind in terms of waiting, but after what happened in the dining hall, I couldn't really blame him for wanting to hide in his room. There were so many questions I had for him that, if I did have the balls to ask him, I wouldn't even know where to start.

He looked around twenty, yet was only about eight months old. He was at the top of the year one students, so it made no sense that he only had eight months of knowledge. Did he just pop into existence one day and already know a lot, or did he learn by sleeping with his head on books? I might hate him if he learned by osmosis.

Maybe I'd ask him why he wasn't in heaven anymore. That seemed rude though, and insensitive. So was asking him if he'd ever watched porn or masturbated. Did they have porn in heaven?

My mind was still going a mile a minute as I stepped out of the fourth-floor elevator of his building. I walked down the hall to his door, and before I could even raise my arm to knock, the door was opened.

"I felt you coming." He moved out of the way to let me in the room.

I stepped inside as he shut the door behind me and I looked around the room that was similar to mine, but decorated with blue accents. A large television was mounted to the wall in front of the futon, the Netflix logo displayed across it.

"You felt me coming? That's not creepy at all." I walked to the futon and flopped down, suddenly feeling exhausted.

He let out a small laugh and sat next to me instead of at the other end. "You can't feel us?"

I shook my head and nodded my chin towards the TV. "What are you watching?"

I reached for the controller on the coffee table and Oliver plucked it from my fingers before I could get into his account. His face turned slightly pink.

"Just some show. I was thinking of watching a DVD and then you texted."

"Liar. You were watching something sexy, weren't you?" I wiggled my eyebrows and giggled as his face turned even more pink.

Giggling was so out of character for me. I put my hand over my mouth to stop myself. I felt like I was a prepubescent teen with her first crush again.

"Don't be ashamed of it. Sex is natural. It's part of who we are." I grabbed the controller out of his hand. "And if you're watching something on Netflix with sex in it, then you need supervision, because who knows what misinformation you're getting."

"Sex isn't part of who I am. I was made out of thin air." He tried to grab the controller back but I moved it out of his reach. He let out a strangled sigh and crossed his arms.

I was so used to him being so jovial and smiling all the time that the downturned face and indifferent demeanor made something clench in my belly. I put my hand on his knee.

"The other night in Levi's room... sex *is* a part of who you are. A beautiful part of who you are."

"I didn't even like it though." He ran his hand over his face. "I mean I liked you, but then..."

"Then you kissed Levi." I searched his face, trying to figure out how he felt about kissing another guy. "How did that make you feel?"

"I didn't really feel anything." He put his hand over mine and squeezed it lightly. "Tobias told me only I would know what I liked. The shows I've been watching, it didn't seem to matter if it was a man or woman. I thought I felt something, but then Levi..."

"Sex is a funny thing like that. Sometimes we think something will turn us on and it doesn't, and then something will completely turn us on that we never expected. And what are you doing talking to Tobias about sex anyways?"

"He's my advisor. He's kind of like a big brother I guess you could say. I kind of feel bad always asking him stupid questions but he seems to know what he's doing."

"What do you mean by that?"

"Just that he's your boyfriend, and that one day that I walked in after you had, you know." He looked away at the red lettering bouncing around the screen.

"We were both stupid that day, and that's not why he and I are together. It's more than sex."

"What about that Fallen you were with on Tuesday?" He looked back at me, curiosity in his eyes.

"It's complicated, but he isn't even talking to me anymore. Like I said, sometimes you can't help what you like and don't like. If you like men, well, then you like men. If you like watching men having sex but only like having sex with women, then that's what you like. Don't think you have to fit any mold that you see on television or hear about from your friends. With that being said, how about we watch whatever it is you decided to enlighten yourself with and we can talk about it."

I pressed the button on the remote and the screensaver switched to the resume watching screen. I bit my lip, stifling back a laugh at the thought of him picking out *Sex Education*, thinking it was educational.

"I've been Googling things I'm confused about or texting Tobias to ask."

I was a little surprised about that but didn't say anything. "I'll be your Google. I've heard this show is pretty funny. Anything called *Sex Education* is probably not that educational if I'm being honest. Even if it was a show to teach you about sex, American sex education leaves a lot out, or makes you feel guilty for what turns you on."

He cleared his throat. "Do you have a lot of experience?"

I shrugged. "Probably average for my age. I mean, if you want to experiment on me, I wouldn't be opposed." I felt my face heat up with my words. Sometimes I just couldn't stop the words from tumbling out.

"I don't think I'm really ready yet. Plus, you have a boyfriend."

"Tobias says he doesn't care. I guess we'll find out soon enough."

"Soon enough?"

"Yeah." I patted his knee, leaving my hand there, and pressed the play button.

AFTER A FEW HOURS of watching Netflix and me answering way too many personal and nonpersonal questions about sex, Olly and I made our way back to the roof of Ariel Hall and sat against the wall surrounding the edge.

Hanging out with Olly was a good distraction from the nervousness that hit me like a Mack truck as we sat waiting on the roof. There had been a shift with me. Suddenly, I cared about staying in school and seeing it through.

Olly was naturally a curious person and had questions about everything, not just sex related. When he was created he was only given knowledge of heaven and a very basic knowledge of Earth and its history. He had absolutely no knowledge of the modern human world when he had started at Celestial Academy in the fall.

Whoever decided to send him to Earth didn't really consider how hard it was going to be on him. It was even worse than a prisoner rejoining society, especially since the Divine 7 had taken him under their dirty wings.

"Are you worried?" he asked, tracing a circle in my palm. I shut my eyes and put my head back against the wall.

"A little. I don't know why I care so much about this school. I've never been the school type." I had never enjoyed school, not because I didn't want to learn things or do something with my life, but because traditional teaching styles and the style I needed just didn't go hand in hand. Out of all the years spent in school, only two teachers understood my needs and really helped me.

"School is hard for you, isn't it?" I felt warmth radiating from the finger making a circle on my hand, causing my shoulders to relax.

I shrugged. "I have a hard time focusing, if you haven't noticed. I've tried everything. Pills don't work. Weed helped a little, but then again, it's illegal under twenty-one. Plus I don't really want to have to smoke something to focus long enough to read a page of a book."

"I have noticed the focus thing. I notice a lot." He moved his finger to my wrist and I bit back a whimper. Why did his touch have to feel so good?

"I've noticed. Thanks for the notebook and pen, by the way. It was thoughtful." I popped open an eye and looked at him; he was watching his finger move on my wrist.

"I'm sorry for being such a dick."

We sat in silence for a while before I put my head on his shoulder and nodded off.

I awoke to him shaking me gently. I rubbed my eyes and squinted towards the middle of the roof where the four angels stood in a circle, talking. I stood and walked towards them, silence falling over the group.

"Dad? How bad is it?"

"They're letting you stay," he said, turning towards me and letting out a sigh. He didn't seem happy.

"Just like that? They're letting me stay?" I was shocked. I was so sure they were going to kick my ass to the curb.

"We aren't at liberty to talk about what was discussed. Just know that you won't be going anywhere, but you need to at least try to stay out of trouble. The Divine 7 will be handled," Chamuel said as he and Haniel walked towards Olly. "Oliver, come with us."

"Sir," Tobias said, sticking out his hand to my dad. "Hopefully next time we meet it won't be under such circumstances."

My dad shook his hand and then turned towards me. "I need to get back. Try to stay out of trouble?"

I hugged him and handed him his clothing. He backed away, extended his wings, and launched off the building.

I turned to Tobias with my mouth gaping. "They let him keep his wings?"

"Something major happened in that room. Michael was there too. I wasn't allowed in, but when they came out they were quiet. You should have seen them on our way there though. It was like nothing I could have ever imagined. Laughing, joking with each other. It was like Lucifer had never left. The way back was pretty tense, but they wouldn't tell me what happened."

I frowned. I didn't like secrets being kept from me and that was certainly what was going on in this case. The question was, was it about me or the fact that Lucifer now had his angel wings back?

CHAPTER 13

DANICA

*S*tudying. I hated it. There was nothing worse than staring at the pages of a book and trying to make sense of what it was trying to tell you. I had been neglecting my reading all week, and here it was a beautiful Saturday afternoon and I was spending it with my nose buried in a book.

Tobias was called into a meeting shortly after my dad left and I hadn't heard anything from him in hours. I was pretty sure it had to do with Olly, but there was also the slim possibility it was about me. I can't say I felt bad for him; he chose the wrong group to attach himself to. For all I knew, he could be putting on an act and I should tread carefully.

I stretched my arms over my head and swiveled back and forth in my desk chair. The sun had set at least an hour ago. How I had managed to study for as long as I had was a miracle. I stood and went to the kitchenette for my beverage of choice and a half-eaten bag of pretzels. I dumped a pile on my math notebook and plopped back in the chair. Getting my GED was probably the hardest thing of all. I sucked at math since I often got distracted in the middle of long equations and had to restart.

I grabbed my phone and propped my feet up on the desk. I pulled open the texts I had sent Asher and sighed. It was beyond frustrating. My thumb hovered over the call button. I hated talking on the phone but I longed to hear his voice.

Before I could chicken out, I pressed the button and brought my phone to my ear. One. Two. Three. Four. I moved the phone away from my ear on the fifth ring, ready to end the call, but Asher's voice brought it right back up.

"Hey." That was it. I should have been excited he actually picked up the phone, but my stomach clenched at his less than stellar 'hey.' He had been ignoring me for days and I had thought our hangout session had gone well. Or had it been a date?

I was at a loss for words. Me, Danica Marie Deville, at a loss for words.

"Danica? Are you going to say something or did you just call to be creepy as fuck?" In the background, I heard what sounded like pool balls hitting each other, and music.

Say something, you idiot. Instead, I hung up and threw my phone on my bed. I covered my face in embarrassment, despite no one being present to make fun of me. I *was* such a creeper. Who calls someone and just breathes into the phone? Serial killers, that's who.

I shoved a few pretzels in my mouth and let them sit for a second, the salt melting off and onto my tongue. I didn't like to play games, yet I felt like I was playing games with all three angels. Would they even be on board with me seeing all of them at the same time, or would they eventually make me choose? I *should* choose, yet I constantly thought about them, dreamed about them. How was that even possible? Did I even want it to be possible?

I pulled my feet off my desk and went to the bed. I stared at the phone and then picked it up again and hit the green button. This time he answered on the first ring. It was quiet in the background, like he had left wherever he had been.

"You're an asshole." The words left my lips before I could stop them. *Typical.*

He sighed into the phone. "I thought we had already determined that. Look, I've been busy and-"

"You could have texted me that. A simple 'I'm busy' or even 'fuck off.' Something is better than nothing. I thought we had a good time the other night." I laid back on my pillows and stared at the ceiling fan. I needed to dust the blades; they must have forgotten to clean them before I moved in. Or they didn't care they were dirty.

"We did up until you didn't listen to me. Do you have any idea..." His voice trailed off and the phone went silent for a brief moment. I checked to make sure the call was still connected. "If you had been hurt or taken, that would have been on me."

"I'm not a child and I'm not going to apologize for following you."

"I didn't ask you to apologize. Besides that, it's too dangerous to be around me." He sounded dejected. I bet if I could have seen him, he would have been shoving his hand through his wavy locks.

I snorted. "Let me be the judge of that. Are you going to let me come over so we can finish our date?"

"Usually a date all happens on one day, not with four days in between. Is it really a good idea for you to come over?"

So, it was a date to him after all. It didn't slip my attention that he knew exactly how many days ago we had our date. It probably wasn't a good idea for me to go over to his place, but bad ideas never stopped me before.

"I can be there in about thirty minutes." My voice sounded hopeful.

He sighed. "If I don't answer, I'll be on the roof. Just let yourself in."

I couldn't stop the squeal that escaped my lips after hanging up with him. What the hell was happening to me?

I ENDED up stuck in Saturday night traffic and it took me almost an hour before I turned into the area Asher lived. He lived in an ideal spot, surrounded by buildings being revitalized and on a street that had come alive with restaurants and bars.

I pulled my car next to his truck and took several calming breaths before getting out. I really liked this guy, despite his smart mouth and avoidance of me.

I walked up the metal stairs to his door and knocked before trying the handle. He'd left it unlocked; I guess when you can snap necks so easily, keeping the door unlocked isn't an issue. I stepped inside, closing the door behind me and flipping the lock out of habit. The massive room was dark besides a small lamp near the bed and undercabinet lighting that reflected off the metal surface of the counters.

I set my purse on the table and walked through the empty room to the stairs leading to the roof. The only sound was the clink of my shoes on the steps and my thudding heart.

I walked onto the roof and smiled at the sight of him leaning on the rail, his forearms on the black metal. There was a small garden in one corner of the roof and a sitting area with a fire pit and a few chairs in another. There was also a hot tub with a gazebo covering it.

I approached him and cleared my throat. He didn't move from his spot, but turned his head to the side to acknowledge me before turning back towards the skyline. It was a beautiful view from the roof; part of the skyline lit up between the buildings and the fairly unpopulated area allowed just enough darkness to see the stars.

I stood next to him and leaned on the rail, my elbow brushing his. He looked over at me again, pushing his hair behind his ear when it fell in his face. I didn't speak, because I was at a loss for words again. He was a beautiful man. What do you say to someone you have such a deep yearning for?

Instead, he broke the silence. "When I was younger, before the war, I used to spend hours lying in the grass, staring up at the night sky." He ran a hand through his hair and then leaned his arms back on the railing. "I'd lie there for hours and wonder what was up there. I didn't think I'd actually find out one day. I didn't even believe in heaven." I put my hand on the crook of his elbow and squeezed gently. "I still remember the day FDR declared war. I was eating lunch at work and we were listening to the radio. We all left work and signed up to serve that same day. That was the moment when staring at the stars never felt the same."

I had watched my fair share of war movies, but had never really been around anyone who had gone to war. I couldn't even begin to wrap my head around what it was like or what it did to the mind.

"It's no excuse for me being an asshole. I can stand here and try to tell you that I won't be an asshole again, but I can't promise you that. I'm messed up, Danica, and it'll be fine if you turn around and walk away." His jaw clenched and he gripped the railing.

I kept my hand on his elbow and let the sounds of the evening wash over us. A car alarm beeped in the distance and the faint sounds of music and laughter drifted from down the street. The soft whoosh of wings flew overhead as birds, or maybe they were bats or owls, flew towards the trees in the distance.

Once I felt I could trust my voice not to shake, I pushed off the railing and stood next to his hunched over body, turning towards him. I gently pulled on his elbow until he stood and faced me.

"I can handle you being an asshole, Asher. What I can't handle is you ignoring me. You have to use your words, or at least give me some indication that it's not me." I searched his eyes for an acknowledgement of my words. They sparkled in the faint light from a single strand of string lights wrapped around the edge of the gazebo and the faint sliver of moon. "Running from things doesn't make them any better."

He reached a hand up and brushed my hair behind my ear, his hand settling on my cheek. "I don't want to run when I'm around you."

My voice left me in a whisper. "Then stop running."

His lips captured mine as the final syllable left my lips. I leaned into him, and threaded my fingers through his hair. I could run my fingers through it all day and never tire of the silky texture. My tongue probed his lips, his mouth opening and our tongues colliding. He tasted like whiskey.

His tongue retreated and his lips moved to my neck, leaving a wet trail. The chill in the night air made me shiver as he tilted my head to the side, exposing the skin and trailing his lips over it. Scooping me into his arms, never breaking contact with my neck, my ear, my lips, he walked us back inside.

At the bottom of the stairs, he set me down and we backed

towards the couch, or at least I think that was where he was leading me. I *hoped* that was where he was leading me. My nipples hardened in anticipation as he slid my jacket off my shoulders and it hit the concrete floor.

I started pulling up his shirt, which he grabbed from the back of his neck and yanked over his head. He pulled off my shirt next, letting out an appreciative grunt at the sight of my breasts covered in lace. We stopped moving when his legs hit the couch and I pushed him back, our breaths the only sounds in the room. It was like the room was in suspended animation, waiting for the clash of lips and our bodies to touch.

I lowered down on top of him, straddling his hips, my lips reconnecting with his in a bruising kiss. He groaned as he gripped my hips and his fingers dug into them. I leaned forward, my lace bra and his naked chest connecting. His lips stilled and I was suddenly ejected from my seat on his lap onto the couch cushion next to us.

He sprang off the couch like a scorpion had pinched his ass and crossed to the other side of the coffee table, his back heaving with harsh inhales of breath. He didn't face me but his back muscles gave enough of a clue to know something was wrong.

"What did I do wrong?"

"Nothing. You did nothing wrong." His voice trembled with unspoken emotion. Unspoken pain.

I stood from the couch and reached for his fisted hand. He let me take it, and standing close behind him, but far enough to not crowd him, I peeled his fingers back and threaded my fingers with his. He let out a shaky breath, his shoulders relaxing little by little.

I put my forehead against his back and my head moved with his deep breaths. He was barely holding it together.

"What's wrong?"

"I don't deserve this. You." His voice cracked with his words and a sudden sob shook his body. "I can't keep feeling this way."

My chest clenched at his words, but I didn't speak. What could I say to that? That it would be okay? I didn't know him well enough to even fathom what was plaguing him. We all had our demons, and demons weren't defeated by standing idle and watching them do their damage. I placed my other hand gently on his back, hoping the light touch would at least give him some comfort.

We stood there like that for a while, with his sobs shaking us both. When they finally faded away, he turned to me, not bothering to hide the evidence of his tears. There was something so raw, so heart-breaking about seeing him like that.

It only made the desire to be close to him flare inside of me. I reached my hand up and wiped the tears from his cheeks, his eyes shutting at the gesture, a sigh escaping his lips.

"I'm sorry." He paused as if considering whether he should explain. "I get flashbacks."

"From the war?"

"That and the hours before my death." He kept his eyes shut. "You can't be on top of me."

"Is it okay if I hug you?" He nodded and I wrapped my arms around him, burying my face in his chest.

He let out a shaky breath. "I guess I ruined the moment, didn't I?" He chuckled and buried his face in my neck, his breath tickling my skin. "Thank you."

I ran my fingers up and down his spine before tracing his shoulder blade and the muscles underneath. He moaned into my neck, his lips moving ever so slightly against the skin. I pulled away and grabbed his hand, leading him back to the couch.

I bit my lip and reached behind me, letting my bra fall from my shoulders. His eyes widened slightly as he appraised my breasts, taking in the smooth skin and pebbled nipples.

"You didn't ruin the moment." I grabbed his hand again and brought it to my breast, closing my eyes.

His rough thumb swiped over my nipple, the sensation making my core clench. He stepped forward, moving his hands to my hips, and kissed me, working his tongue between my lips. Whatever had happened a few minutes ago seemed to float away and now I was his sole focus.

His hands trailed to the button on my jeans, and in one flick he had them open and slid them down my hips, trailing kisses down my body as the fabric made its slow descent.

He stopped and pulled off my shoes before kissing my inner thighs while sliding the jeans off the rest of the way. It was a slow, torturous journey he was taking to get to the final destination between my legs. He slid his hands behind me and palmed my ass, kissing right above my slit. He was driving me mad, on his knees in front of me, kissing everywhere except where I needed him to be.

"You're a tease." I threaded my fingers in his hair and gave his head a little push.

He chuckled against my skin, the action vibrating and pulling a moan from my throat. He finally slid off my panties before standing and capturing my mouth again, nipping and sucking at my lips. One of his hands kneaded my breast while the other sat just to the side of my pussy, rubbing in a circle.

"Wait until I get you tied up to my bed. I'll remember you called me a tease."

His index finger trailed along my slit. I could feel my wetness taking over, begging to be used. His lips went to my ear, biting and nibbling as he slowly worked his finger back and forth. I moved my hips and he adjusted, just barely teasing the folds.

"Would you like that?" His tongue flicked my ear and I went weak in the knees. "I think you would." He slid two fingers into me, burying them as far as he could before curling them and slowly moving them left to right.

I didn't know what the hell was happening, but when he hit what he was searching for I gasped. He smiled against my ear.

"Too much?" I nodded and his fingers began moving in and out of me.

My breaths came out louder as his fingers slid in and out, the anticipation of his next move almost too much. I unbuttoned his pants and pushed them down, freeing his cock. I grabbed the base of it before trailing a finger underneath it and rubbing the head with my thumb.

"Now who's the tease?" I breathed as his two fingers moved to my clit, sliding it between them before stepping away from me and grab-bing two pillows off the couch.

Excitement stirred in my belly as he put them on the floor and pushed the coffee table out of the way. He grabbed my hips and moved me towards the couch, pushing me down to lay with my lower half hanging off the edge, my shoulders and upper back still on the couch. My legs quivered as he lowered to his knees in front of me, adjusting my legs. The head of his dick teased my opening, and in one swift movement, he was buried inside of me.

His hands massaged my breasts as he thrust in quick, deep move-ments. My orgasm was already building as he moved his thumb over my clit, his touch sending me over the edge. My muscles tightened and my legs tried closing but he pushed them back open as he moved faster and harder, small grunts escaping his lips.

As my orgasm ebbed, his thumb returned to my clit, working it into an oblivion as my entire body felt like it ignited. His dick filled me, moving in with quick thrusts of his hips. I cried out as another orgasm hit me, and with two more thrusts, took him with me for the ride.

"Well, fuck me," I managed to get out between breaths, scooting back on the couch.

"I just did. You already want more?" He laughed and stood before walking to the kitchen and grabbing a hand towel.

I watched with half-closed eyes as he cleaned himself and handed it to me.

"I'll never look at your couch the same way again." I stood on shaky legs and made my way to the bathroom.

After cleaning up, I returned to find him in a pair of boxer briefs, a beer in one hand and the remote control for the television in the other. I could see myself with him night after night, curled up next to him on the couch.

I pulled on my panties and bra as he watched. Then I sat next to him, stealing his beer and taking a drink.

"You spending the night?" he asked, taking the beer back from me.

"If you want me to. It's getting kind of late so I should go if not."

"Stay. I have a hard time sleeping next to someone, but we can try." He examined the controller for a few seconds before pointing it at the television and turning it on. "If it doesn't work out, I can just sleep on the couch."

I put my hand on his leg and gave it a reassuring squeeze. "Who said anything about sleeping?"

CHAPTER 14

DANICA

*F*alling asleep together didn't work out. We tried, even tried pillows in between us, but he just couldn't get comfortable. I understood, but at the same time was slightly disappointed I didn't get to cuddle with him, especially after he had worked my body like he owned it.

Getting back to campus put a damper on my mood. I had so much studying to do and still wasn't sure what was going on with Oliver or what the meeting Tobias attended was about.

Was it even worth my time to stay at a school that trained me to be something I wasn't? I was essentially just a human, with no angelic abilities as far as I could tell. I didn't plan on dying any time in the near future, so what was the purpose of me staying somewhere I was hated?

I walked into the dining hall and was surprised to see Olly already sitting with Ethan and Cora at our table. I half expected him to be missing or even sitting back at the Divine 7's table without me there. After grabbing French toast, bacon, and a bowl of fruit, I joined them.

"Where's Brooklyn?" I asked, sliding in next to Oliver and glancing at his plate of cantaloupe. I needed to ask him about that. It couldn't be healthy to eat that much fruit every day, although it wasn't like he could die.

"She should be here. Remember we're supposed to go study after we eat?" Cora turned and looked over at the Divine's table and then turned back to me. "She had her date last night, but never answered my texts about how it went."

"She probably just overslept." I glanced over at Levi to see him with his arm slung around Betty's shoulders. What a douchebag player. "If she walks in and sees that, I hope she goes over there and punches him in the dick."

"He's a player," Olly said, putting his fork down. "That's the right word, isn't it? In the last week he's been with four different people in some way."

"I almost forgot that you have the inside scoop on their deepest darkest secrets," Ethan said and then motioned towards Olly's plate. "You've eaten that every morning for days. Isn't your stomach all messed up?"

"It tastes good. Why get something else and risk it tasting bad? I don't want to waste food," Olly said, taking a defensive tone.

"I'd probably eat a plate of bacon every day if I could, but then I'd probably..." I shut my mouth for once in my life. "Anyway, maybe when we're done we should go wake Brooklyn up."

"You were going to say die," Cora pointed out. "It's okay if you say it. We're long past when we died. We wouldn't have been sent here if we were still grieving our old lives."

It still didn't help me from feeling like an ass mentioning dying in front of angels that were essentially dead people.

"Does bacon kill people?" Olly looked at the two strips on my plate.

Ethan chuckled. "God, you're strange. Bacon in and of itself doesn't kill people."

After we finished, we headed to Brooklyn's room. We knocked several times but she didn't answer.

"Did you try calling her? Some people just don't like texting." I knew this wasn't true since Brooklyn texted about anything and everything. I pulled out my phone and called her, the phone going straight to voicemail.

"Olly, maybe you can ask Levi if he knows where she is? I'm a little worried about her. She doesn't do things like this." Cora's brows pulled together in concentration. "Ethan and I will go check in the library, you two can talk to Levi and check in the gym."

We headed our separate ways. Olly called Levi and he said he hadn't seen her since the night before when he dropped her off at her room. We walked across campus to the gym. She could have decided to practice her flying techniques since she was behind after helping me with hand to hand. The gym was empty.

Brooklyn was nowhere to be found and I couldn't help the fear that filled my gut.

~

BROOKLYN WAS MISSING and the rest of us were asked not to leave campus. Olly, Tobias, and I were sitting around Tobias's table.

"Do you think Levi is lying?" Tobias had a concerned look on his face. He knew both Brooklyn and Levi, but not enough to make any determination as to their character.

Olly shrugged. "He might be. You think he has something to do with her being missing?"

"I don't know but we can't just keep sitting here acting like she's not out there somewhere. She's not here on campus, so why aren't we out there looking for her?" I stood and walked to the window, pulling the curtain aside to look out. "Maybe Levi was a dick and left her in the city and she can't get back. What the hell?" I squinted through the window that had a reflection from the light in the room and then opened it so I could get a better view.

"What is it?" Tobias came up behind me and looked in the direction I was staring.

The same hooded figure I had seen before was sneaking towards the tree line before disappearing from view.

"I think that's the same person I saw the other night sneaking off." I let the curtain fall and turned back to the room, putting my hand on Tobias's chest. "We need to go to the city and look for her. We can call Asher to help."

"That guy scares me," Olly piped up, seriousness in his voice. He had only met Asher once and it had not been under the best circumstances.

I rolled my eyes. "Seriously?" I crossed my arms over my chest. "If you plan on hanging out anymore you are going to have to get used to him."

Tobias raised his eyebrows. "I thought he wasn't answering your texts."

With all the worry over Brooklyn, I hadn't had the time to talk to Tobias about Asher. "I went over there last night."

There. The Band-Aid was ripped off. Now I was officially dating two men at once. At least they already knew each other, although their relationship was strained.

"You went to the city? You know that we're supposed to-" Olly started.

"It's not like I was walking around. Besides, Asher clearly can kick ass. I'd be more worried about going to the city with just you two," I stated, smiling at them both.

"What's that supposed to mean?" Olly looked offended. He was the one who almost got himself abducted and there were two of them.

"She thinks we're weak because all she's seen us do so far is academics. I'll have you know that before Asher fell, I used to be right out there with him. I can throw a punch. I can kick some ass. Maybe if you're lucky, I'll kick Asher's ass so you can see just how skilled I am." He looked smug, but I was doubtful. I had seen Asher fight before. "So, you and Asher are what now exactly?"

I perched on the side of his bed and looked up at him. "I guess he's my boyfriend. And you're my other boyfriend. Is that going to be a problem?"

"You're wrong. I'm your boyfriend and he's your other boyfriend. And no it's not a problem, we talked about that already. I can't say I have any experience sharing a woman, but we probably need to all have a conversation at some point."

"Two boyfriends. Is that normal?" Olly stood and stretched, a small sliver of skin showing between his pants and shirt. I licked my lips because, good lord, was he attractive. It's like heaven decided to create the most beautiful male specimen to illicit impure thoughts.

"Normal depends on who you ask. It's not conventional, but I'm not a conventional gal now, am I?"

"Oliver, you were included in that conversation too." Tobias smirked as he watched me pick at a loose string on his quilt. It was old; I probably shouldn't have been picking at it.

"I was?" He sounded very excited over the prospect. I could feel his eyes on me. "You want to go on a date with me?"

I shrugged. "I'm drawn to you for whatever reason. There has to be some weird supernatural phenomenon going on, right? Or I'm just one horny woman. Makes sense considering my dad's the devil."

Tobias laughed at my joke, but the reference to the devil having horns went straight over Oliver's head, at least I think it did because he didn't laugh.

"I would have asked about it when we were in heaven, but your dad was right there and I really didn't want to get on his bad side. Remember, he likes *me*." Tobias almost sounded childish as he made reference to the breakfast from hell.

"At least I'm not her teacher." Olly mumbled it so quietly that I barely heard it, but it was out there nonetheless.

Tobias practically flew across the room, grabbed him by the throat, and shoved him against the door. "Listen, you little fucker, you don't get to judge people after the shit you've pulled. Or have you forgotten the reason you're here in the first place?" Tobias shoved into him one last time and then let him go. He dropped like a sack of flour to the floor.

"Care to elaborate on that?" I was standing now, ready to separate the two from ripping each other apart if necessary.

"Oliver, do you want to tell her or shall I?"

Olly sat against the wall and put his head in his hands looking dejected. It couldn't have been worse than the shit I'd pulled over the years, but then again, it probably did take a lot to get kicked out of heaven.

"It can't be that bad, can it? Just tell me. Remember who you're talking to here. No judgement from me."

"Oh, but this is so much more epic than any of the crap you got in trouble for," Tobias said.

"Shut up, Tobias. Olly, what is it?" I squatted next to him and tried to pull his hands away from his face.

He sighed and dropped his hands. "I broke into the artifact room and took the Holy Grail."

I bit my lip to keep from laughing. I didn't know much about religious artifacts, but I was pretty sure the Holy Grail was a big deal. "And *why* would you do that Olly?"

He looked at the floor and mumbled something.

"What was that?" I felt like I was a mother talking to her four-year old who just broke a vase and wanted to blame it on the cat.

"I was bored and there was this rumor that it turned water to wine and I just wanted to test it out. I was tired of just flitting around up there doing nothing. So I took it, snuck to Earth to get some water and it slipped out of my grasp. I couldn't find it." He let out a shaky sigh. "They told me I was such an idiot and needed to wise up, so they sent me here to teach me a lesson."

"Wait, wait, wait." I stood from my squat and looked down at him. "You're telling me you lost the Holy Grail? How does that even happen?" Tobias was laughing now but was trying to cover it by covering his mouth. "Where were you trying to get water from?"

He looked to Tobias with a pleading look in his eyes, which only made him laugh harder. He rubbed his hands over his eyes and then looked at me again. "The Pacific Ocean."

"Don't stop there, Olly boy. Tell her the whole thing," Tobias choked out between laughs. I had never seen him laugh so hard. He had clearly heard this story before, but probably never heard it from Oliver's lips.

"Near Hawaii, I swooped down to scoop and a wave knocked me

in. I dove after it but it sank so quickly and none of us could find it. It's lost forever. I don't know why they got so mad about it. I told them they can just go to the store and buy wine now. They don't need a cup that makes it."

I joined in the laughing now. "There are probably a lot of people that would love to get ahold of a cup that turns water into wine. I wonder if the ocean will eventually turn to wine."

"There is a bright side to my punishment though. At least here I get to talk to people and have fun. Plus, I get to talk about sex with you." He looked at me and then at Tobias and smirked. Maybe Olly wasn't completely oblivious after all.

Tobias stopped laughing. "You probably don't even know what hole to stick it in."

"Tobias! Seriously, how old are you, twelve?" I stood and pulled out my phone. "I'm calling Asher. He, at least, doesn't act like a child."

Tobias snorted. "Hate to break it to you, but Asher is ten times worse. You think his foul mouth is bad, wait until all three of us are vying for your attention at once."

I raised my eyebrows and then shrugged. If they wanted to act like petulant children around each other that was their own business.

WE PULLED up outside of Asher's place and I really just wanted to get out of the car. Maybe it was the stress of everything over the past several weeks, but my irritation was at an all-time high. Their bickering started the second we got to my car and Olly called shotgun. The entire drive I wanted to throttle them both. But then I also kept imagining myself ripping their clothes off and letting them both have their way with me.

I should have taken them up on their offer to *fly* me to Asher's, but considering I was scared of heights, I declined. Instead, I was stuck in a not-so-large car with two testosterone filled males who were displaying their feathers like damn peacocks. Although, I suppose I was more of the peacock since I essentially had a harem and they were territorial like peahens.

"Is it safe to be here? It looks like one of those creepy buildings in a movie just before the heroine gets murdered with a giant knife," Olly commented as he slid out of the car. "Don't worry, Dani. I will protect you."

"What the hell have you been watching? You know all that crap is only partially based on reality, don't you?" Tobias retorted, slamming the door of my car shut which made me scowl at him. "You can't protect her. You'd probably slip and drop her."

"Can you two just knock it off?" I stomped up the stairs and banged on the door with my fist. I would normally find their banter funny and join in, but Brooklyn was missing and who knew how many other angels we hadn't been told about.

Asher opened the door with a confused look, probably at why I was banging instead of knocking. He looked behind me and then seemed to comprehend the reason and pulled me to him, kissing me on the lips. I let out a surprised squeal and leaned into his chest. Tobias cleared his throat.

"Oh, hey guys. Didn't see you there. Come on in," Asher said, moving out of the way. Great. This was a really *great* idea.

Olly walked in behind me and looked around wide-eyed like a kid in a candy store. I wondered if he had ever been in a candy store. We needed to start a list. "This place is awesome!"

There was an awkward moment between Asher and Tobias as Tobias entered. They hesitated before Asher stuck out his hand and they shook. They were totally thinking about hugging.

"You brought the idiot from the other night?" Asher asked, watching Olly move into the place like he owned it. He picked up a wood carving off an accent table and examined it before Asher snatched it from his hands and put it back.

"Asher, be nice," Tobias warned. Funny words coming from someone who hadn't been so nice himself.

Olly took a step away from Asher and held up his hands in mock surrender before angling his body towards me. "Great, now both of your boyfriends are going to gang up on me. Maybe you and I should just ditch them and ride off into the sunset together. What do you say?"

"You can all either get along with each other or-" I bit my cheek to stop myself.

"Or what, Danica?" Tobias raised his eyebrows.

What I really wanted to say was that I would spank them, but held it in. For once I didn't want to add fuel to the fire. We had shit to do, and saying something about spanking probably would not help. Instead, I said, "Let's just get this over with. Where are we going to start?"

"The Fallen have been operating in places where there aren't a lot of people around. Park after nightfall, empty parking garage, empty alley. I doubt they'll go to the same place twice, at least not so soon afterward," Asher said, moving across the room and grabbing a laptop off his desk. He moved to the kitchen table with it. While it powered on he stood and went to the refrigerator to offer us drinks.

After pouring himself a glass of whiskey, he sat back down at his laptop and paused his fingers over his keyboard. He looked over his shoulder at Tobias, then turned to face him. "So, I need to tell you about something I did a few years ago before you see my background."

Tobias looked confused, but it was Olly who spoke. "It's okay if you have naked girls on your background, or hey, even naked men. You do you. You should see my computer background."

Asher's eyes snapped to Olly and narrowed slightly before moving back to Tobias. "As you know, as a Fallen no one really keeps an eye on what I do if I stay out of trouble, so I took a little trip to Philly when I heard that Margie died."

Tobias's hand gripped his beer bottle tighter, his knuckles turning white, and I hoped it wasn't going to break. Or that he wasn't about to hit Asher over the head with it. I looked between the two men, wondering if they were going to come to blows again. Olly noticed the tension radiating off of Tobias too and backed up a few steps. Tobias always had an air of calmness about him, so to see his hackles bristling was off-putting. It had become more and more frequent lately.

"She was ninety-nine, died in her sleep. Anyway, I approached Jeffrey and told him my great grandfather served with you."

Tobias took a really long gulp of beer, at least half the bottle. "Why are you just now telling me all of this?"

"Didn't quite know how to tell you. We got to talking and he said that Margie had given them a box of pictures shortly before she passed. He let me borrow them and I got them scanned. I have been waiting for a good time to contact you about them."

"You had no right to do that," Tobias ground out between gritted teeth. He walked to the kitchen window and looked out. "So what, you have my family plastered as your background?"

Asher typed in his password and logged in. "There were quite a few pictures of our platoon in the box. I did scan all of the photos though. I'll share the folder if you want."

Tobias walked back over to the table and I pulled Olly away to sit on the couch to give them privacy. There would be time later for us to look at pictures, but the two men needed a moment. Tobias was visibly tense, but then his shoulders dropped as Asher said something and they both laughed. After a few minutes of hushed talking, Tobias turned with shining eyes and waved us over.

We gathered around Asher and watched as he pulled up a map. He zoomed in so that a mile radius was showing and pointed to the three known points of abduction.

"Why are the Fallen even taking angels?" Olly asked, then turned to me. "We should ask your dad. Maybe he might know something."

"You think my dad has something to do with this?"

"Well.. he is the OG fallen angel."

If he hadn't been talking about my father, I would have laughed.

"I think what Olly is trying to say is that at one point in time the Fallen thought they were meant to be his army, and since they are using demon blood, maybe there's something he might shed light on," Tobias said. "It's worth a try."

I stepped away from them and pulled up FaceTime on my phone.

If I was going to ask him if he was kidnapping angels or supplying demon blood to the Fallen, I would at least do it to his face.

He answered without video and the first thing we heard was screaming. "Just a second." He put us on hold, the phone going silent.

"Was that seriously just a scream?" Olly looked at me with wide eyes. "Is he in hell right now torturing someone?"

"Don't freak out so much. He usually still answers even if he's in the middle of something." I shrugged because it wasn't that big of a deal. Well, maybe it was a little bit of a big deal.

"And you're okay with him torturing souls?" Olly seemed really concerned so I put a hand on his forearm. He looked down at it and then back at me.

"It's his job."

"His job was to let the souls exist in the afterworld in isolation, not torture them."

"Not entirely my fault, boy," my father said. He must have come back on the line mid-conversation. "Danica, please tell me you aren't in trouble again. I'm getting too old for this."

I snorted back a laugh. "I'm not. My friend Brooklyn is missing and we are trying to figure out what the Fallen would want with angels and how they are getting demon blood."

"Who is there with you?" he asked and I told him. "So there are three men now? Is there a fourth? Figures Michael was only seventy-five percent accurate. The archangels are investigating this. You need to stay out of it, especially if Oliver is involved."

What. Did. He. Mean.

"Wait, a fourth? What do you mean Michael was right? You hate Michael. And what about Oliver?"

"Hate is a strong word. It's more of a strong aversion to him. Oliver isn't just a regular angel. He didn't ascend, he just *is*. Like me, Han, Ham, Michael. Any of us would probably be a major win for whatever they are up to. If they get their hands on him, that probably wouldn't go very well for him."

We all looked at each other. They almost *had* gotten their hands on him.

"What are they doing with angels, Dad?"

"We can't be sure, but we think they're using their blood. It only makes sense that's what they're doing. An angel's blood is a powerful catalyst for creation."

"What do you think they're creating?" Tobias asked.

"Whatever it is, it isn't good. I'm still interrogating all of my surface demons to see if they know where the demon blood is coming from. Demon blood has the opposite effect as angel blood."

"Wait, you have demons here on Earth? Isn't that against some kind of law?" Olly said, not realizing that he was continuing to dig himself into a hole with my father. If he wasn't careful he was going to end up at the same level of disdain as Michael.

My father laughed. "Son, if I didn't have demons dealing punishments on Earth, I'd end up with a whole hell of a lot more souls down here. When the guardians can't help the soul, I step in. I'm assuming they don't teach you that now, do they?"

"You don't have anything to do with this, do you?" I asked slowly, cautiously.

"Danica, I have angel blood myself. If I needed angel blood, I'd just use my own. Please, just... be careful. You have always had a faint angel aura about you and we don't know the composition of your blood, but it has to have some angel quality to it. If they took you and then found out you were mine..."

We ended the call after that, saying our goodbyes, and I stared at the phone for a moment before looking at three sets of inquiring eyes. "We've never had my blood tested and I've never been to a regular doctor. He's paranoid they'd somehow find a way to take me and experiment. My dad pays for a private doctor or he just heals me himself."

We turned back to our map.

"There are way too many places to look," Asher said.

"What if we should be looking for where they're taking them," I piped in. "Where do the Fallen like to live?"

"Well, if they are off the rails, then abandoned buildings. That's how I found this place. Not far from here there are some empty warehouses." He looked back at the map, not seeming to notice that he just told us he was 'off the rails' at some point. Whatever that meant.

"We have to start somewhere. How are we getting there?" I asked, not sure if I wanted to be stuck in my car with three men.

"Flying would be faster but someone is scared of heights. Funny considering she's half angel," Tobias joked, nudging me in the side with his elbow.

"Even if I did agree to fly, won't someone see us?"

"No. It's a short distance. It will be a good way to break you in. You can fly with me," Olly said.

Asher went to his closet and disappeared. He popped his head back out a few seconds later. "Toby, come get a gun." Asher disappeared again and Tobias went into the closet with him. They came back out, but both had bulges in their front pockets, and it wasn't from them being happy to see me.

"Do we not get guns?" Olly asked. I highly doubted Olly had even seen a gun up close before. He'd probably shoot his eye out.

"Do you know how to shoot a gun?" Asher asked.

"Well, no, but how hard can it be?" Olly replied, shrugging as if handling a firearm was no big deal. If he couldn't keep his grasp on a magical goblet, I would hate to see what happened if he fired a gun.

FLYING, even if just for a minute, was much different than I expected. I thought I'd feel dread at the thought of plummeting to my death, but instead felt weightless and free. It also helped that I was wrapped in Olly's strong arms and could bury my face against his chest, the smell of cookies filling my nose. I was grateful he wasn't addicted to something like broccoli or asparagus.

We landed at the edge of a field filled with dead weeds and littered with trash. We quickly followed Asher and Tobias who had landed before us. I wished I had gotten a picture of Asher being carried by Tobias, but I heard that pictures of an angel with wings out came out blank.

"Won't they sense us or something if we get too close?" I whispered as we scooted along the side of a brick building with half of its windows busted out. My boots crunched on the broken shards of glass and debris littering the ground.

"Not with me here," Tobias said glancing back at me. He didn't elaborate and the look on his face told me he would tell me later. Knowing me, I'd probably forget to ask. I needed to spend some time in the library reading about angels because there was way more to them than just having a pair of wings.

As we walked, we looked in the windows of the building. It showed signs that, at some point, people had squatted in it, but it was currently lifeless besides the faint sound of scuttling feet on the concrete floor I could hear through the broken windows. Gross.

We moved around the side of the building to an access road where large tractor trailers could have access to loading docks. A chill ran up my spine as we made our way to the next building. I felt like something was going to jump out and attack us.

"This is like looking for a needle in a haystack. It's going to take forever to check all of these buildings. Can't we split up?" I felt restless, even though we were moving. The thought of having to look in each and every building was daunting.

"If we split up then two of us won't have Tobias's suppression skills," Olly explained.

"I can extend it, but every angel in the bubble will have it and they will notice when they can't sense each other."

"Unless they have an angel that can suppress too. I can't sense any angels in any of these buildings," Olly said, stopping and shutting his eyes.

We turned towards him, curiosity on our faces. He shook his head and opened his eyes again.

"How far can you do that and why didn't you mention anything before now?" Asher let out a heavy breath of air like he was trying to suppress the need to wring his neck.

He shrugged. "No one seemed interested in what I had to say. Besides, I really wanted to fly with Danica in my arms."

Tobias squeezed the bridge of his nose and Asher started walking back the way we had just come. I felt bad for Olly and I was tempted to wrap my arms around him and tell him I was interested in what he had to say. Even if sometimes what he said was off by a mile.

"To answer your first question, I haven't really tried to see how far I can see. Michael is supposed to train me on how to use the sight fully."

"What is the sight? Is there an 'Angels for Dummies' book somewhere?" I was really feeling out of the loop. It was possible that I missed all of the information I needed to understand angels in the first semester of the year.

"I can focus on something and locate it. The location will flare in my mind. If I've been close to the person then I just know the little flare is them. Not sure how that works. That's how we found you last week. All angels have some sensing ability but it usually only expands a short distance."

"You could sense her from campus all the way here?"

"Yes."

"And you're just now telling us this."

Olly looked down and kicked at the ground. "What would I even look for? There are angels and Fallen all over the Los Angeles area. It's a giant speckled map of light."

"If you look for a large group of Fallen or even a few together... remember Fallen usually aren't with other Fallen," Asher suggested.

We were back at the edge of the field we had landed in and stood in a small semicircle around Olly. He shut his eyes and took a deep breath. I could see his eyes moving under his eyelids, like he was dreaming. What other special abilities did these angels have that I didn't know about?

"No large groups. There's a group of four Fallen moving in downtown like they're in a vehicle. No, wait. Three Fallen and an angel. It's..." He gasped and his eyes popped open. "We have to go! They have Levi."

He grabbed me and his wings extended. "Wait! You need to see where they go. If we go in there with guns blazing then we might not figure out where they're taking them," I said, pulling away from him.

"So we just *let* him get taken? That's ridic-"

"She's right. Plus, if he's stupid enough to get abducted twice, I have no problem using him as a sacrificial lamb," Asher said, putting his hand around my waist and pulling me to him.

Olly narrowed his eyes at Asher, for what seemed like the hundredth time, and then shut his eyes again. Asher drummed his fingers on my hip before sliding his hand in my back pocket and squeezing my ass. Tobias watched us and licked his bottom lip before turning his attention back to Olly.

Asher put his lips to my ear, his warm breath tickling my ear as he said, "He likes to watch."

My eyes went wide and I turned my head to look at Asher, our faces inches apart. He glanced down at my lips and then lowered his to hover over mine.

"If you're interested in that kind of thing," he said.

"They vanished!" Olly said. I pushed away from the trance Asher had me in and tried to look innocent. "That must be where they're taking them, but I thought Fallen didn't have any of their abilities?"

All eyes went to Asher who said, "We don't."

"Let's go," Olly said, scooping me up, causing me to let out a small squeal.

Tobias picked up Asher the same way as he grumbled under his breath about feeling like a damsel in distress. I shut my eyes as we took off from the ground. I was still too scared to watch but as soon as we were in the air, it felt like we were in a pneumatic tube, like in the bank drive-thru.

We landed softly and my feet touched the ground. I blinked my eyes open and stared up at a five-story white building with a domed roof in the center, a cross reaching into the night sky. Chills ran up my arms and I rubbed them through my leather jacket.

"What is this place?"

"It's an abandoned hospital," Tobias said, taking my hand as we jogged to the building to stay out of plain sight. "What's the plan?" He looked at Asher.

"Figure out what they're doing, how many angels they have. No heroics, at least not tonight." Asher looked at me and then at Olly. "No matter who or what you might see. There are going to be more than just three Fallen in there."

"Let's split up. Now, I know you aren't going to like this, Asher, but you and Olly pair up. I'll be with Danica. That way there's experience plus someone with wings."

Asher grumbled something under his breath but then nodded.

"Let's do this." I tried to sound confident but wasn't so sure.

CHAPTER 15

OLIVER

*A*sher Thorne. His last name fit him to a T because one thing was for certain, he was a thorn in my side. Not only was he Fallen but he also looked at and touched Danica like she was a piece of meat.

They both did. Tobias and Asher were predators and she was their prey. When I had walked in after she and Tobias had done who knows what on his desk, it took everything in me not to sling her over my shoulder and get her away from him. I may have been naive and inexperienced, but having sex on a desk, in a classroom, is no way to treat a lady of her caliber.

Too bad Tobias knows too much. Could you imagine if it got out that I lost the Holy Grail? Everyone already laughs at me because I'm quirky. Yeah, we'll go with that. I'm a quirky guy.

It was Tobias's idea to split up to check out the abandoned hospital that probably had ghosts. Or zombies. Or a nest of vampires. Or the Gargoyle King. I wasn't nervous, not one bit. I could take on any of those.

I followed Asher just far enough away from him to be out of reach. We did not get along and I wouldn't put it past him to choke me or snap my neck. Neither of those would kill me, but they wouldn't feel pleasant.

As we moved around the front of the hospital we looked in windows and saw nothing except the faint glow of exit signs and a few dim lights running down the length of the hallways. Why did it still have power?

"It still has power," I commented.

"Thank you, Captain Obvious."

God, he was such an asshole. What Danica saw in him was beyond my comprehension. Well, maybe not completely beyond my comprehension. He wasn't ugly, at least on the outside. Also, it seemed, at least from what I had watched, that women seemed to forgive a man for being an asshole if he had abs and a big dick. Asher probably had the biggest dick known to man to make up for how much of an asshole he was.

Why was I thinking about Asher's dick?

We rounded the side of the building and ended up in a partially closed off area. Parked in a neat row were five gray vans, the same as the one that had tried to take me. Asher put his arm out and stopped me from moving forward and we moved behind a dumpster. He pulled out his phone and sent a text to Tobias.

What we needed were walkie talkies or those ear communication devices the secret service used. I would want my name to be Golden Cherub. It has a nice ring to it.

"We need to find a way in. Stay close." He crouched down and I rolled my eyes at his back before following him.

I didn't really agree with this plan of theirs, to just check things out. Levi was in there, and probably Brooklyn too. We needed to act fast. Angels couldn't exactly die again, so whatever was going on with them was something I didn't even want to think about, but I couldn't help it. Was it like a torture chamber in there? I shuddered. Danica was right; I needed to stop watching so much on television.

Asher stopped at a window and tried it. Locked. I shoved him out of the way and put my hand near the lock and then slid the window open.

"Wipe that smug look off your face, angel baby." Asher moved me out of the way with his shoulder and climbed through the window first.

I followed and resisted the urge to slam him against the wall. That would make too much noise. He opened the door leading out of the abandoned office we were in and peeked out.

"You are damn lucky they didn't get you and your friends the other night." I knew it was only a matter of time before he yet again made me feel like a complete fool. I knew I was lucky, both me and Levi. If Asher hadn't rescued us, I would probably be living out a real-life horror movie. Except now, Levi was.

"That stupid idiot. He can't even go two days without checking in on his record. I bet that's why he was in the city."

"What do you mean?" Asher turned back to look at me.

"He has the top score for some arcade game in the mall. He's obsessed with it."

Asher's frown deepened as he studied my face. He then made a gesture with his head for me to follow. It wasn't like I could argue with him. We crept down the hall, the silence in the abandoned halls deafening. We stepped lightly, trying to keep the sounds of our foot-steps to a minimum. There were so many hallways it was going to be difficult to remember where we came in, if that even mattered. Asher cut across a large open area that looked like a former emergency room and started going up the stairs.

"Is that a good idea?" I whisper screamed. They could come down at any minute.

He shrugged but continued up, with me hot on his heels. I might be safe from dying, but Fallen could die. Did this guy have some kind of death wish? Fallen lost their wings, their healing ability, and their sanity.

We reached the top of the stairs and Asher grabbed my arm and yanked me behind a large desk in a crouch. The faint sounds of voices came from down a corridor, but we were still too far away to see what was going on or to hear what they were saying.

He pulled out his phone again and texted Tobias, then we were on the move down the hall, ducking in a few rooms to make sure no one was coming. If I could sweat, I'm sure I'd have been sweating bullets. We made it to the last room before a large open area and Asher put his index finger over his lips.

Did he think I was a complete idiot and was going to talk? He crouched low again and we darted behind another large circular desk and then into a dark storage room. We couldn't see much, but could see the backs of a few men.

"Any problems tonight?"

"None. The kid says the academy has told the students to stay on campus. He was able to get us that sweet little thing last night, but tonight we were unsuccessful. Maybe we should go back to finding guardians."

"The guardians suppress their signatures most of the time, that's why we switched to the academy punks. When do you twerps learn suppression? Back in my day they didn't have a fancy training academy."

"Third year."

My eyes went wide at the sound of Levi's voice and Asher's eyes met mine. He shook his head at me and then turned back to watch out the door.

"She says we're taking too long. We need to recruit more. After those nine were killed, we need all the help we can get. The last thing we want to do is piss *her* off."

I was about to mouth something to Asher when the sound of squeaky wheels and weeping drew my attention back to the large open room. Judging from the signs still hanging on the walls, it was the holding room for the operation room.

I strained to see and caught a glimpse of a rolling cage of sorts and a head of brown curly hair that was tangled but sat in a distinctive bun on the top of her head. I was so focused on looking that I didn't notice my foot was right next to a fire extinguisher on the floor. When I moved back, my leg knocked it over, the clang of metal on linoleum loud in the mostly silent emptiness.

"Who's there?" Quick footsteps made their way towards our hiding spot, but there was nowhere to go.

My wings extended, quickly folding forward and grabbing Asher. I moved us toward the back of the storage room, Asher tripping over something in his backwards movement, sending us falling to the floor.

"Wha-" I put my hand over his mouth and shook my head, pleading with my eyes for him to stay quiet. He tried moving out from underneath me, but I had several inches on him, plus my wings helped hold him still.

It was dark, but I could make out the white of Asher's wide eyes before they clenched shut and his body trembled underneath mine. What the hell was he so scared for? He could snap necks like it was his job.

A light flicked on overhead and I breathed slow, even breaths as a few sets of heavy shoes walked into the room. Someone moved the fire extinguisher.

"Maybe it was a ghost."

"They do say this place is haunted. I don't see anything. Let's go."

The light was flicked off and the footsteps retreated but the men stopped outside the door to talk with two other men. Asher continued to shake. Moisture soaked into the side of my hand, which was still against his mouth. I wanted to take my hand away but knew that would be a bad idea.

I heard the men move a little farther away, but not far enough for comfort.

I lowered my mouth next to his ear and whispered, "Are you okay?" He shook his head. "I can help but I need to move my hand off your mouth. Can you stay quiet?"

One of his hands clutched the back of my shirt. He nodded. I took my hand off his mouth, ready to put it back if he made any noise. I placed my hands on his cheeks; the wetness felt like tears. I wiped them away with my thumbs.

I could feel his heart hammering into my chest. I'd only tried this once with Abby when she had a memory from her past and freaked out. I hadn't even known what I was doing at the time, but when I had grabbed her face in my hands to get her to stop screaming, she calmed.

I stroked Asher's cheeks with my thumbs until I felt his body relax and a sigh left his lips. As much as he was a complete asshole, the sound of relief in his sigh made a warmness fill inside of me. I made one last swipe with my thumbs and went to move my hands but his hands went over mine, stopping me.

"Don't stop until you get off of me." His voice was barely a whisper.

Those damn Fallen were still too close by so I relaxed on top of Asher, keeping my thumbs lightly stroking his slightly rough cheek. He needed a shave. I was glad I didn't have to deal with facial hair.

I shifted on top of him and he let out a grunt as my dick rubbed against his erection. His erection? I froze and my hands stilled on his face. Did Asher Thorne have a boner for me? He despised me, but my own dick didn't care and I let out a frustrated noise as it twitched to life.

"Fuck." Asher gritted out.

I wasn't even entirely sure I liked men sexually. I knew I liked women, but a man? That night Levi had kissed me and I had kissed him back, it hadn't excited me like I thought it would.

"There! Go, go, go!" Shouts and loud feet snapped me out of trying to figure out what I was feeling.

My wings snapped back and I jumped up, holding my hand out to Asher. He glanced at it briefly before getting to his feet on his own and adjusting himself.

The men had taken off down a different hallway so we retraced our steps until we were outside the building. We heard shouting from a distance and moved back around to the front of the building.

"Fuck. They were probably after Toby and Danica."

"Thank you, Captain Obvious." I couldn't keep the snark out of my voice.

He grabbed my arm. "Thanks for that back there. Sometimes I can't stop my brain from freezing up." Then he narrowed his eyes. "And not a word about my dick getting hard."

"I make no promises." I went to walk back towards the lawn in front of the building but he pulled me back and pinned me against the wall, the bumpy surface digging into my elbows.

"Don't fuck with me, angel baby. It won't be pretty." He sounded like he was half beast with his growly voice.

"It felt to me like that's exactly what you wanted. To fuck me." I inwardly cringed at my words.

"The only ass I'll be fucking is Danica's." He shoved himself away from me and took out his phone, cursing at the cracked screen. "They're back at my place. Let's go."

I grabbed him and lifted him with a grunt and took off. He stared at my face until we landed on his roof.

"That's the problem, Danica, you didn't think and you almost got us killed or even worse, captured!"

"I wasn't going to just stand there and watch them take her into that... that... that room!"

Asher and I exchanged glances and rushed to where Danica was jabbing her finger into Tobias's chest. I took Danica's elbow as gently as I could and steered her away before she took a swing at him.

"What happened?"

Danica shook her head and sat on a chair, crossing her arms over her chest. Tobias had his hands on his hips and was shooting daggers at her.

"The plan was to see what they were doing in the operating rooms. They roll them in and out in cages and drain their blood on those grated tables they use in morgues." He shuddered. "And of course, after the angel they drained, they brought in Brooklyn and *she* decided to be a fucking hero." He turned his eyes back to Danica. "Well, I hate to break it to you, but heroes end up dead!"

"I said I was sorry!" Her voice cracked with a sob and she covered her face with her hands.

"Dude, calm down," Asher said, putting his hand on Tobias's shoulder, which he aggressively shoved off.

"It's late. Let's get back to campus. We can meet tomorrow about what we're going to do," I suggested.

"You two go ahead, Toby and I will contact Michael and fill him in."

Danica stood from the chair, keeping her eyes on the ground, and walked to the door leading into Asher's house. I looked back at Asher and I swear he winked at me.

CHAPTER 16

DANICA

I woke up to the sound of my alarm and a grunt in my ear from Olly. Damn, last night had sucked. I hated confrontation and put myself right smack dab in the middle of one with Tobias. Tobias, who was fairly non-confrontational, at least until I started spending more time with him. That was a tough pill to swallow.

I hit the button on my phone and wiggled out of Olly's arms, looking down just as a small smile spread across his lips. He was a beautiful man and if he was a human he would break hearts all over the Los Angeles area.

"Good morning, beautiful," he said, slowly opening his sparkling blue eyes and staring up at me. I could stare into their sparkling depths all day if we didn't have more important things to do like go to class. Oh, and saving Brooklyn and the other angels held captive with her.

He reached for my face and brushed his thumb over my lips. I sighed and stood, adjusting my clothes that had gotten twisted during the night. After driving back last night and crying all over again, I hadn't even bothered changing before falling asleep against Olly's chest.

Olly said nothing as I made my way into the bathroom and shut the door. At least one of us had the ability to stop ourselves from saying or doing something stupid. That's exactly what had happened last night, I was stupid and almost got us caught. Tobias didn't have to yell at me though. I felt bad enough without the raised voice and the looks of irritation.

I looked at myself in the mirror and touched under my eyes. The skin was slightly swollen from not being able to hold anything back anymore. Olly had glued the pieces back together.

I showered quickly and walked back into my room with a towel wrapped around me. Olly was gone, so I dropped my towel and got dressed in my dreaded uniform. I wanted to curl back up in bed and come up with a plan to rescue Brooklyn and the others. That was a pipe dream though. I was not equipped to take on a large group of Fallen. I didn't have immortality on my side.

How was I going to face Cora and Ethan, knowing I had Brooklyn within sight but couldn't rescue her? She had looked really bad when they had rolled her into that room. Not as bad as the angel they had wheeled out before her, but after they drained her she would have looked worse.

I didn't know what I was going to do when I saw Levi. If I had it my way, I would kill him with my bare hands. Except angels were already dead so how to kill one was a mystery to me. Maybe they could be killed the same way as a vampire; heart removal or decapitation. I needed to ask Olly. I would not be asking Tobias. He'd scold me again like I was a child.

Tobias. My chest hurt thinking about last night.

I grabbed my phone and checked my messages. The only one was a group text from Asher telling Olly and I to stay away from Levi and to tell no one what we saw since we didn't know who else was involved.

There was a soft knock on my door as I grabbed my bag. My heart rate increased and I took a deep breath. I wasn't ready to see Tobias, but at least if it happened now, I could rip the Band-Aid off before class and it would be over and done with.

I looked out the peephole and sighed with relief as Olly smiled on the other side. That angel always seemed to be happy. I opened the door and he stepped in the doorway and gave me a hug. I could get lost in his hugs; they felt like a warm blanket fresh out of the dryer.

"How do you already smell like cookies?" I craned my neck to look up at him. "Don't tell me you bought cookie scented cologne."

"I had cookies for breakfast. Decided to mix it up a little today. Ready to go?"

After trekking across campus together, him holding my hand as we walked, we sat together in class. Today there weren't even any stares or hushed voices discussing what that meant.

I looked at the time on my phone; class should have started five minutes ago, but still no Tobias. A few students had already left, mumbling about him never being late and that they hoped he was okay.

Olly and I were just about to put our stuff away when Dean Whittaker walked in. My favorite person.

"Class is canceled today. Mr. Armstrong is stuck in a meeting. He did want me to tell you that tomorrow there will be a quiz on dream demons and it would behoof you to stay anyway and familiarize yourself with them in your book. You might also use it as an opportunity to ask your classmate about them." She nodded in my direction and then left the room.

I turned to Olly who was running his hand over the cover of the book. "What are you doing?" My question was answered when he moved his hand and the book flopped open to dream demons, my eyes going wide. "Since when did you get all these abilities?"

"I've always had them. Just haven't had a reason to use them until recently. I don't want to be a show off since the Class IIs and IIIs only have a few things they can do." He looked over at me and gave me a tight smile before his eyes went back to his book. "Sometimes I don't even know that I have an ability until it just happens..."

"What?" I could tell he wanted to say something else.

"Nothing," he said reaching up and touching his hair. "Just learned a little about myself yesterday is all."

"Tell me about it." I opened my book and skimmed the introduction information on dream demons.

Dream demons, also known as night mares, are a highly prevalent psychological demon of hell. The mare is said to be humanoid in form and terrorizes the mind when it enters each REM cycle. It has been rumored, but not confirmed, that these demons walk the Earth unbeknownst to both humans and angels due to its ability to stay hidden.

"Does your dad really have demons here on Earth?" Olly spoke so no one could hear him except me. After yesterday's conversation with him, I'm sure he wasn't the only one that had more questions and probably a plethora of concerns.

"He wouldn't have just made it up. This is probably one of them. He doesn't tell me about *which* demons he has hanging around here."

Olly shuddered and closed his book, putting it in his bag. Most of the other students had already left. I guess they didn't want my expertise, not that I was an expert. I only knew what my father offered.

After hanging out for a while, Olly walked me to PE. Ah, yes, my favorite class. After the snake debacle, Brooklyn's disappearance, and Levi being in the class, I considered going to the library and studying. Most instructors would notice I was missing, since they always seemed to keep an eye on me, so I sucked it up and changed.

Walking into the gym, I scanned and easily found Coach Ferguson talking with Levi. I squared my shoulders and walked towards them. Coach Ferguson had an extreme dislike for me, and Levi, well, I would have said he was working for the devil, but that wasn't true.

"Deville. Wright has offered to work with you today." Before I could protest, he turned and walked away. I clenched my hands, digging my nails into my palms to keep from popping off some comment.

I could do this. I could get through an hour with a monster. Or not. I started making my way back towards the locker room but he grabbed my arm and steered me towards the training room. I yanked my arm away and rubbed where he grabbed. It hadn't exactly been a loving touch.

"Don't touch me again," I warned as we entered the room.

I suddenly felt very vulnerable being somewhat alone with him.

We could still see the rest of the class, but there were also several spots in the room where the rest of the gym was out of sight. I'd avoid those like the plague.

"Or what, Dee? You'll sic your angel boyfriends on me?" he taunted, walking to a cabinet and pulling out two focus mitts and slipping them onto his hands. "Now let's see what you got before I kick your ass."

I scoffed and crossed my arms. "Don't call me Dee, and if you think I'm going to fight with you then-" In a quick jab, he knocked me over the side of the head with his mitt. "You fucking asshole."

I could have just turned around and left the room, but the opportunity was too great to let it slip through my fingers. I had half expected him not to show his face on campus again, yet here he was, acting as if he wasn't a traitor.

"My beef isn't with you, *Dee*." He hit me again, this time hard enough to make me stumble back.

I positioned my body to strike back and he held up the mitts with a satisfied smirk on his face. I took several punches and dodged several of his swipes.

"Who is your beef with then?" *Punch, punch, duck.*

"Angels." He kicked out with his foot and tripped me. I grunted as my ass hit the mat. "Get up."

"You're an angel. Why?" *Punch, punch, duck, jump back.*

We ran through several more combinations before he answered. "Do you know how I died?"

I stopped mid-punch and his mitt slammed into my face. It stung and I rubbed my nose. "How?"

"I was texting and speeding." He swept out and knocked me down again. "Two lane road."

I stood up again and backed up as he took another swipe at me. He had a determined glint in his eyes, like he wanted to take out all of his anger on me.

"How do you know that? I thought they just told you in general how you died, like a car crash." I backed up, avoiding his increasingly aggressive kicks and jabs. I took a deep breath as he stopped in front of me.

"I'm not an idiot. I used Google." I flinched as he punched the wall at the side of my head. That would have hurt.

"And what did Google tell you?" I whispered.

"I was going over a hundred. What do you think it told me?" he asked through clenched teeth. He punched the wall on the other side of my head, with a lot less force, but now I was trapped between his arms.

I shut my eyes for a brief moment before opening them and searching his tormented green eyes. "Did you crash into another car?"

Nod.

"Were there people inside?"

Nod.

"Did they survive?"

Shake.

The only sounds in the room were his deep breathing, my heartbeat, and Coach Ferguson's booming voice shouting directions.

"I deserve to be in hell." He backed away from me and threw the mitts off to the side. "And now I'll get what I deserve. And with what I've done, they won't even bother making me a Fallen. They will send me straight to hell like they should have done in the first place."

My heart was thudding wildly in my chest. I felt a twinge of sympathy, but also a whole lot of anger that he would betray angels just to give himself a punishment. "How did you even get involved with them?"

"A few months ago, they took me when I was at the arcade. They offer all the angels they take the opportunity to work with them or be drained daily." He shrugged, like it was no big deal. "It was a win-win. They'd get their insider and eventually I'd get a one-way ticket to hell."

"Do you know what they're planning on doing with all the blood?" As soon as the words left my mouth, he laughed. It wasn't a normal laugh, but the laugh of a crazy person; a broken person. Maybe at some point he had been sane, but now he had gotten himself in too deep, let his past eat away at his future.

"Danica." Tobias's voice came from the doorway and I turned to see him, the dean, and Michael standing there. He stared at me for a moment, not showing an ounce of emotion and then turned and walked towards Levi. "Levi, you need to come with us."

"Nice talk, Dee. Tell Oliver I'm sorry for leading him on," he said, following Tobias with his head hanging.

I stood in the doorway and watched them exit out of the gym.

~

By the time school was done, I was mentally exhausted. It was hard keeping it together on a normal day, but trying to focus and have everything else in my life going on? Impossible.

A group text came shortly after dinner from Tobias. *Meet us at Asher's. Oliver, fly with her.*

Butterflies filled my stomach at the thought of having to face Tobias. He had consumed my thoughts all day. Maybe he'd be over it by now and we could just move on. I had fucked up and he had acted like a dickwad about it.

We landed on the roof to find Asher and Tobias roasting marshmallows over the fire pit like they were boy scouts on a camping trip. I smiled to myself. They had the whole bromance vibe going on and I hoped they would start including Olly more. He needed it.

I flopped down in one of the empty chairs next to Tobias and stared into the fire. It was the perfect night for sitting around a fire outside. Not too cold, but just cold enough to need something other than a jacket.

"Angel baby, have you ever had a s'more?" Asher asked, turning the metal rod he had speared through a marshmallow in the flames. He pulled the marshmallow out and blew out the flame, the white covered in bumpy brown and black.

"Can't say I have," he responded, his eyes lighting up as he watched Asher with curiosity.

"Well, first you take the graham, stick the chocolate on the graham." Asher already had the marshmallow cooked so he smooshed it all together and handed to Olly. "Tada, a s'more."

We watched as Olly took a bite and a grin lit up his face. It would be nice to feel that kind of wonder again, like every moment of the day was a new gift being unwrapped. I bet he'd never been to Disneyland and my list of fun places to go and things to do was slowly growing inside my head. We needed an Olly bucket list.

"Drinks?" Asher asked, standing and wiping his hands on his jeans, leaving graham cracker crumbs behind.

"I'll take a water," I said, staring back into the fire, getting lost in the mesmerizing flicker of colors.

Tobias's eyes darted over to me with a questioning look. It seemed like every time I was drinking something, it was Diet Dr. Pepper. It was a problem, but everyone seemed to have their vice.

"I was doing some research online about natural remedies to my inattentive impulsivity issue. Drinking a six pack of diet soda a day is probably not helping any." I propped my chin up on my fist and looked at Tobias. "Right?"

"I'll join you to get the drinks," Olly said, standing and following Asher inside. I just hoped they didn't kill each other in there without supervision.

Tobias took a drink of his beer before leaning forward to assemble a s'more and offering it to me without a word. I shook my head.

"So... the silent treatment? Never took you for the silent treatment type. Seems below you." I grabbed a marshmallow and stabbed it with the metal roasting fork.

"I think I said enough last night." Tobias bit into his s'more, getting some marshmallow on his beard. I wanted to reach over and wipe it off but refrained. The last thing I wanted was for him to pull away from my touch.

I nodded and slowly turned the marshmallow just out of reach of the flames. I liked my marshmallows golden brown, not burned to a crisp. Despite my less-than-traditional upbringing, my dad did still teach me a thing or two. Like how to not burn a marshmallow.

"You yelled at me like I was your child instead of your girlfriend."

I brought the marshmallow to my lips and blew on it, the sweetness filling my nose and making my mouth water. I could feel him watching me as I bit into it and then had to use my fingers to break the sticky strings holding onto the other half. I licked my fingers and sighed.

"I know you were pissed and scared, and I respect that was how you felt, but yelling at me? I couldn't just stand there and watch them hurt my friend, or anyone for that matter. I know it was stupid, and reckless, and horribly impulsive. I already feel like enough of a fuck up. I don't need you to remind me of it by yelling at me or giving me the silent treatment." I popped the other half of the marshmallow in my mouth.

"You aren't a fuck up." He moved his chair closer to me, the sound of the metal legs scraping on the roof. He grabbed my wrist and brought my sticky fingers to his lips. "I just really like you and you could have been hurt or killed."

I shut my eyes as he put my fingers in his mouth and swirled his tongue around them. He pulled them out with a pop and yanked my arm towards him, pulling me onto his lap. I laced my fingers behind his neck and put my forehead against his.

"If you ever yell at me again, I *will* spank you." He made a noise in his throat and slid his hand under my shirt to rest on my side.

"The only one that will be doing any spanking is me." I shivered as his cold hand moved up my stomach and traced the band of my bra. "What color is it?"

"Black." He made a satisfied noise in his throat at my answer and kissed my neck.

We heard the door to the roof open and Olly and Asher sat back down. I looked over at them and sighed as Tobias continued to pepper my neck with kisses. I pulled away, but stayed in his lap. I wasn't sure what the etiquette was for PDA in front of your other boyfriends.

"So, what are our next steps with the Fallen?"

"For you two?" Asher pointed at me and Olly with his beer. "Nothing. We went with a few of the archangels and Michael's soldiers last night back to St. Luke and they had already moved their entire operation. They must have an older angel working with them because no one could get a read on them."

I went to move off Tobias's lap, but he held me in place, his fingers digging into my waist.

"They've been recruiting on the streets. Now that Levi isn't going to be interfering and none of them saw Asher, he's going to go under-cover and find out where they are. We don't know how long it's going to take for him to infiltrate. They're probably going to be very cautious now."

"What about your business?" What I really wanted to say was, 'what about me.?' It was a selfish thing to think, but the idea of him joining them made me sick to my stomach.

"I have foremen who will run things while I'm gone. I won't be able to come back here until this is all over. I won't risk them ruining this part of my life." Asher swirled the beer that was left in his bottle and drank it down. "Let's go inside. I'm getting cold."

I should have known when we all sat on the couch that things were going to take an interesting turn. Especially when Asher turned off the lights, the only light coming from a lamp by the bed and the television.

It started with Asher's hand rubbing my leg in slow circles. He had a slight smirk on his face, like he knew exactly what he was doing. I felt the tips of my ears burn slightly at the thought of him touching me in front of the others. My legs parted slightly and I saw Tobias glance over at the movement and watch Asher as he trailed his hand up and down my inner thigh along the seam of my jeans. I could already feel the wetness building between my legs.

He raised his eyebrows at Asher and then put his hand on my other thigh, massaging it with firm squeezes. I just about let out a moan at the thought of both of them touching my naked body. Would they even want to do something like that? I was down for anything, but we hadn't exactly discussed how it was going to work when we were all together and they all wanted me.

"Boys, behave," I whispered, looking over at Olly. Now I really wished I hadn't been taking things slow with him because I was pretty sure by the way the other two were touching me that they were in the mood and didn't care if they had to share.

It's not like we could go into another room. I mean there was the bathroom, but I didn't want my first threesome to be in a bathroom.

Olly was so engrossed in watching the Marvel action flick he picked, he wasn't even paying us any attention. At least not yet.

Asher turned his body towards me and kissed my neck, trailing his hand to cup me between the legs. I bit my lip and tried to focus on the movie. Tobias took my hand and kissed my wrist before slowly moving up my arm with his lips. I squirmed slightly, feeling the tickling between my legs increase, the need to be touched already reaching a point of discomfort.

"What are you doing?" I sighed and slid on the couch so I could rest my neck on the back cushion.

"Are you complaining?" Asher kissed under my ear before moving his hand to unbutton my jeans.

My breath got louder and I sank into the couch as Tobias's hand moved up my shirt and Asher slipped his hand into my pants, cupping my wet panties.

"How long do you think it will take for angel baby over there to notice anything is going on?" Asher said once Tobias had moved his lips to the other side of my neck.

"I think the bigger question is what is he going to do when he does look over here," Tobias said, glancing in his direction.

"Pull your pants down a little. They're too tight," Asher mumbled against my neck, his fingers tracing around my belly button.

A hand slipped back under my shirt and pushed my bra up over my breasts, giving easy access to my nipples. I lifted my ass and slid my pants and panties down. Asher's hand found my clit and leisurely moved his fingers across it. I stifled my moan and glanced over at Olly.

I half expected him not to notice, but his eyes met mine. He put a finger to his lips to tell me to be quiet. The gesture had me closing my eyes and putting my head back on the couch.

"Do you want him to see?" Tobias kissed down my jaw. "We can stop."

"Don't stop," I moaned, finally giving in to the sounds my body wanted to make.

Tobias moved off the couch and knelt in front of me, taking off my pants the rest of the way and spreading my legs. Asher took care of my shirt and bra. Olly took in an audible gulp of air and my eyes went back to him. His eyes were locked on my exposed pussy as Tobias kneaded my inner thighs and then pulled me to the edge of the couch and buried his face between my legs.

"Fuck..." My hips bucked as his tongue dived into me, his thumb circling my clit. His mouth devoured me like I was his last supper.

Asher moved his lips to mine and pulled my lip between his teeth as I moved my hand to his pants and unbuttoned them. Out of the corner of my eye I watched Olly unbutton his own pants and pull out his cock. The thought of all three of them at once sent the first wave of pleasure crashing through my body, my legs trying to squeeze shut and my body shaking.

Asher stood and took off his pants, grabbing the base of his dick and pumping it a few times. "How do we want to do this?"

I couldn't help it, I giggled. Maybe it was all the endorphins from my orgasm or the sheer fact we were about to have a very awkward conversation.

"Smooth man, real smooth." Tobias rolled his eyes and leisurely moved his thumb over my clit, sending lightning bolt jolts up my spine. He looked over at Olly who sat quietly stroking himself. "Are you going to join in?"

"I just want to watch tonight. If that's okay with Danica." He looked at me with an almost embarrassed look on his face. I gave him a nod of approval.

I pulled myself up so I was sitting and clamped my legs shut, my clit needing a brief break from the assault Tobias had rained down upon it. I looked up at the men in front of me, in various states of undress.

I grabbed Asher's hand and tugged him down so he was on top of me, my legs wrapping around his waist. He moaned against my lips as he grinded into me, his dick moving across my folds. He pulled back and put my calves over his shoulders before slowly sinking into me with a groan.

"Fuck, this will never get old," he said, kissing one of my calves and moving slowly, almost obnoxiously slow, like he was savoring every thrust. Tobias watched us, dick in hand, like he was trying to figure out what his next move was.

"Come here. I want you in my mouth." I licked my lips and waited for him to take the two steps to the couch. I couldn't exactly reach him from my spot. "Kneel behind my head, then you can watch."

Asher moved one of my legs to drape on the back of the couch, giving an unobstructed view to both me and Tobias. Tobias climbed on the couch on his knees, his dick hanging in front of my lips. I took him in my mouth, one of my hands wrapping firmly around the base.

The room filled with moans as Asher's pace increased and my mouth sucked and licked Tobias. I heard a sharp inhale of breath from the other end of the couch and then a shaky exhale. I had almost forgotten that Olly was watching and the thought of him coming all over his hand as he got off on seeing the three of us was almost too much.

"Harder," I mumbled around Tobias's cock. He groaned and leaned forward on one hand, the other going to my clit. His hips were slowly thrusting his cock deeper in my throat, stifling my moans.

"I'm going to fucking come if you do that," Asher growled as his thrusts became harder and more erratic. I knew exactly what he was talking about when I felt Tobias's mouth close around my clit and suck it between his teeth.

My entire body seemed to combust as Asher thrust into me hard and spilled himself in my clenching pussy. I cried out around Tobias's cock, moving one of my hands to his balls and massaging them. He came with a curse, spilling into my mouth.

I swallowed and pulled him out of my mouth, my heart beating wildly, my breaths short and deep. My ears were ringing and my toes felt like they had just woken up from falling asleep.

Tobias plopped back next to my head and smoothed his fingers across my forehead. "I'm glad I wasn't a stubborn asshole about this whole concept."

Asher pulled out of me, the emptiness without him making me shiver. He pulled a blanket from the back of the couch and threw it over me. "That was fucking mind-blowing." He pulled my legs into his lap and ran his hands over my blanketed calves. We sat in comfortable silence for a few minutes, catching our breaths.

"How is it going to work with three of us?" Olly was buttoning up his pants and didn't look up. If blushing had a sound, it would have been the sound of his voice.

"We'll make it work, angel baby. When you're ready to join, we'll take care of you," Asher said, surprising the shit out of me. I looked at Asher who was looking at Olly with a small smile turning up the corners of his lips.

"So about that name... angel baby. It's not very creative. Last night I thought it would be cool if we had walkie talkies or those secret service ear pieces. Then we could have those nicknames people say on them. Danica's could be something with sexy in it. Tobias could be Dirty Teach or something. Asher, you could be Whiskey Dick. What do you guys think of Golden Cherub for me?"

The perfect way to end the night was wiping tears off my face from laughing so hard.

CHAPTER 17

ASHER

The name Danica means 'the morning star' which I discovered when I Googled her after we first met. I might not have known her for very long, but she was the first thing I thought about in the morning. She was *my* morning star. Which made it that much harder that I couldn't see her, talk to her, or even fucking text her.

I groaned as I rolled over on the crappy mattress in a crappy motel just on the outskirts of downtown Los Angeles. Five years ago I wouldn't have given a shit about a lumpy mattress with questionable stains on the bedspread, but now I cared. I could never go back to that life; the life of a lost Fallen.

With my third day undercover behind me, it seemed this mission was futile. I never thought I'd be on another mission, but here I was, following Michael's orders yet again. It better be fucking worth it.

I sat up and cradled my head in my hands, rubbing my temples. The last few weeks had reopened wounds I had thought were mostly behind me. I had a routine with familiar places, people, sounds, smells. Now the mild comfort it had given me had vanished and was replaced by a tightness in my gut that only disappeared when Danica was around. Or when Oliver touched me.

. . .

I TOSSED *and turned on the couch, willing myself to sleep. I hadn't wanted to try to infiltrate the Fallen. There were too many unknown variables, but Michael had convinced me that if I helped then he would personally escort me to another review board hearing.*

On the eve of uncertainty, I found myself back in the trenches, gunfire whizzing past my ears, blood soaking my clothing. I let out a frustrated grunt and made my way to the bathroom. I glanced in the direction of the bed where three forms were sleeping peacefully. Lucky bastards.

I shut the door and looked at myself in the mirror. I looked like shit and gripped the edge of the counter in frustration. Why couldn't it all just fucking stop?

The bathroom door slid open and my head snapped in that direction, my heartrate increasing. Another unknown variable taunting me. Oliver slid in, sliding the door shut behind him.

"Are you okay?" He looked and sounded half asleep, his eyes squinting at the bright light in the bathroom.

"Not your problem," I said between clenched teeth. I just wanted to be alone and I most certainly didn't want to be bothered by Oliver, who half the time used my last slivers of patience.

He walked farther into the large bathroom and leaned his hip against the vanity. I felt his eyes on me and looked at him again.

"Do you need to take a piss or what?" I let go of the counter and crossed my arms over my bare chest, feeling exposed, which was interesting considering he had just watched Toby and I have sex with Danica.

"I heard you on the couch and was worried. You could come sleep with us in the bed." He moved away from the vanity and blocked my path out of the bathroom.

I stared at him. Man, he had some cojones coming into the bathroom like this. I moved forward to step around him and he grabbed my arm. My knees nearly gave out as a wave of calmness washed over me.

"I'll sleep right next to you. You don't have to sleep alone anymore," he said softly.

I felt my eyes burning with tears and kept my eyes glued to his hand on my forearm. I cleared my throat. "Can't risk it. I'd never forgive myself if I did something in my sleep."

"Then let me sleep with you on the couch." His hand squeezed my arm and he started moving towards the door, not letting go.

I followed him, unable to resist whatever comfort he was giving me. It was more intense than it had been back at the hospital when he had fallen on top of me.

He laid down on the couch on his side and looked up at me. I glanced at the bottle of whiskey sitting open on the coffee table and then back at him. He shook his head and patted the couch. Fuck.

I sat down and felt his hand touch the middle of my back. I took a deep breath and laid down, his chest against my back, his arms wrapping around me.

THE MEMORY of the best night's sleep I had ever had plagued me as I grabbed my wrinkled clothes off the chair and put them on. Oliver was now on my mind almost as frequently as Danica and I didn't know if I liked it or not.

For the past three nights I had wandered the streets and nothing came of it. I was sleep deprived and I smelled like something the cat dragged in. I don't know what Michael really expected, for them to just come up to me and recruit me?

It was just before sunrise and traffic was virtually nonexistent in this area. I passed a few shops and bars as I made my way away from the motel and turned down an alley. I had been frequenting this alley since it had large painted angel wings on the brick. That had to mean something, right?

I leaned against the wall, my back right in the center of those damn wings, and waited. There was no way that someone would paint these down a narrow alley unless they meant something, at least that was what I kept telling myself.

I waited for an hour and then pushed off the wall, shuffling the rest of the way down the alley. It was fucking depressing here. Years ago I was living this way, moving around aimlessly, sleeping in doorways, sleeping on sidewalks.

I exited the alley and made my way past makeshift tents made of ripped blue tarps, sleeping figures in sleeping bags, countless shopping carts. Where were the guardian angels when these people needed them? Clearly their own damn people didn't care enough to have a shred of humanity. And here I was being a hypocrite because I didn't help them myself.

I took a seat on the curb and ran my hands through my tangled and greasy hair. I had only encountered a few Fallen the past few nights, but they were all solo and high or drunk out of their minds. I might have been out here for weeks before I even encountered the Fallen I was after.

I'm not one that really believes that things happen because you're thinking about them, but sure as shit, not a minute after wallowing in the idea of spending more time out here, a gray van turned down the street and slowly made its way in my direction. I could sense two of them in the van. They were going slow because they could sense me too.

The van pulled in just past where I was and then stopped. I kept my eyes fixed on the ground until a pair of black combat boots came into my line of sight.

"Hey, man. You look like you could use a warm meal and a shower. Interested?"

I looked up and squinted at the Fallen in front of me. He needed to work on his delivery because that sounded like a fucking proposition. Literally.

"What's the price? I'm not into dicks."

The guy held his hands up in front of himself in defense. "Woah, man. Not like that. Just trying to help out a brother who's down on his luck."

"I'm not your brother," I said, standing and nodding my chin towards the van. "You and your buddy murdering homeless Fallen?"

He laughed and put out his hand. I could see why this guy was the one to approach me; he was charming in a serial killer type of way.

"Name's Paul. If you'll come to breakfast, I might have a job opportunity for you."

I eyed his hand warily. I had to make this shit believable because if I was too eager then they might question my sanity. The goal was to get in and get close fast.

"I don't know, man. My mom told me to never get into a van with a stranger." I grabbed his hand and shook it. "But I guess since my mom is dead and I am too, what else do I have to lose?"

"That's the spirit." He smacked me on the arm and then made his way to the van, opening the back door. "What's your name?"

"Tom," I lied. Although it wasn't a complete lie since my middle name was Thomas. There was no fucking way I was giving those idiots my real name.

I climbed in the back of the van and he shut the door behind me. It was clean and smelled faintly of bleach. Always a good sign when getting into a creepy ass van with complete strangers.

The van took off and I reached down and pressed the button on the inside tongue of my boot. It was a one-way communication and tracking device that would record my location and anything that was said.

"Where are we going? I'm claustrophobic as fuck, man!" I shouted, hoping they'd hear me.

I didn't get a reply so I just sat back and tried to calm myself down. Wherever they were taking me, they didn't want me to know.

I WAS IN. After some convincing on their part, I agreed to join them. The only problem was that to actually beat them, I was going to have to do some morally questionable things, like help capture angels.

Coming into this whole thing, Michael had warned me that they would probably have me prove myself before I even learned where they were holed up. I just hadn't expected it to be so quickly, but I guess they were desperate.

Paul fed me, made me shower, convinced me to be a part of his team, and twelve hours later I was riding with him and another Fallen named Jimmy. They were desperate for more angels, saying their supply in Pasadena dried up.

"What do you do, just drive around all night?" I was in the passenger seat with Jimmy, sitting in the middle of the bench seat. "Seems a little unorganized."

"We were organized in Pasadena, were doing well capturing angels for a while but then three of our teams got taken out."

I grunted a response and looked out the window at the passing buildings. "Have you tried hospitals?"

"Too risky. We know they're there a lot, but we can never sense them."

"What about a trap where we don't necessarily need to sense them?" I was actually surprised they flew by the seats of their pants most of the time. From my understanding they had been abducting angels for over two months and had two dozen somewhere.

"What kind of trap? We try not to draw human attention." I could hear the concern in Jimmy's voice.

"What's the first rule of Fight Club?" I crossed my arms over my chest and turned slightly towards them.

"You do not talk about Fight Club. What's your point? You got a hard-on for Pitt?" Jimmy rolled his eyes and looked moderately annoyed.

"I did a rotation during my guardian days as a security guard. The security guards are always guardians. No special medical skills needed, and no one questions why they wander the floor and go in rooms. There's typically only one guardian per department. I'll just go in there and start screaming about angels. Lure one out." I was surprised at how calm my voice sounded with the lies spewing out of it.

"And if the security isn't a guardian?" Paul was tapping one of his hands on the steering wheel. I could tell the idea excited him.

I shrugged. "We'll know as soon as we spray him with that shit you have and we can either take him anyway and dump him or just let him go. If this works we can hit several hospitals."

"Where should we start?" Paul asked, pulling over and getting out his phone. He was the only one of us that had one. I didn't bother bringing mine since I knew they would have taken it.

"Nearest hospital." It didn't matter where we went, the guardians would be ready and make a show of it.

Ten minutes later, Jimmy sat in the driver's seat and I made my way to the emergency room doors after letting Paul take several swings at me. With blood pouring out of my nose, I walked in the sliding door and went right up to the reception desk.

"I need to see an angel." The man and woman that were sitting at the desk had already started to rise as I had approached the desk.

"Sir, we'll have a nurse to get the bleeding to stop and it will be a couple of hours to see a doctor."

I laughed at the woman's words and slammed my fists down on the desk, leaving blood smeared on the counter.

"I said I want to see a fucking angel. So either go find one or I will-"

"I got this," the security guard said from behind me.

I spun around and took a swing at him, but he stopped my fist with his hand and wrenched my arm behind my back, a little too hard for my liking. He shoved me forward and we stepped out of the sliding doors.

Everything happened in a blur then. I twisted away from him, Paul sprayed him with demon blood serum, and then I snapped his neck. Completely not part of the plan, but shit, my shoulder still stung from him twisting it.

Paul stared at me and shook his head as Jimmy pulled up beside us. We secured the angel's arms and legs and tossed him in the back.

We hit three more hospitals, resulting in a total of four angels with snapped necks. They were easier to deal with being incapacitated completely, but would heal in a day or two. Paul dropped Jimmy off and we were on the I-110 South headed towards the Port of Los Angeles, straight to the heart of the beast.

CHAPTER 18

DANICA

*O*ver two weeks had passed since Asher went undercover with the Fallen. Whatever was happening, we weren't privy to it, not even Tobias. It was completely understandable since we had gone rogue in our attempts to find out what the Fallen were doing. Classes continued, weird stares and hushed comments followed me, and a small feeling of normalcy crept back into my life.

"I want to drive your car," Olly announced after a movie finished. I should have known something like this would happen after watching *The Fast and the Furious*.

Olly and I had fallen into a comfortable pattern of movie watching before dinner and studying. Sometimes we would even watch the entire movie instead of making out the whole time.

"Excuse me? You want to drive *my* car?" I laughed at the absurdity. "Do you even know how to drive?"

"It can't be that hard, can it?"

Laughter bubbled out of me at the vision of him trying to drive a car. I mulled over his words and shrugged my shoulders. Everyone has to start somewhere.

"We aren't supposed to leave campus."

He made a dismissive sound. "It's the middle of the day and I'm starting to feel claustrophobic being stuck here, kind of like I used to feel when I was in heaven. If we don't go then I'm bound to do something stupid." He poked my ribs and stood up, offering me his hand. "Maybe when we're done we can park somewhere and make out."

I grinned up at him and let him pull me to my feet. I could totally get on board with a make out session in the car, especially with him. We hadn't slept together yet, but we had certainly been having fun building up to it.

I drove to a high school parking lot and let him slide behind the wheel of my baby. I explained the basics and made sure he understood what each pedal did before I let him put it into drive. This was either going to go surprisingly well or I would finally understand how parents feel when teaching their kids to drive.

He caught on quickly and after a solid thirty minutes of driving at a snail's pace around the parking lot we switched back. No lives were lost in the parking lot during our lesson, although I felt like I might have a bit of whiplash from all the stopping and starting we did in the beginning. Next time he'd probably be ready to drive around a housing tract with extra wide streets. Maybe. If it wasn't trash day.

I slid back behind the wheel and smiled over at Olly before leaning over and giving him a kiss. He grinned ear to ear and I matched his glee. The closer I got to him, the more I realized how hard his short life had been. Small experiences that so many other angels had as human or angel just weren't in his schema of the world.

We pulled out onto the road and then the highway, heading back towards campus. The sun was setting, making the sky glow a beautiful blend of coral, pink, and purple. Olly put his hand on my thigh as I drove, a comfortable silence falling between us, with the radio playing in the background.

Angeles Crest Highway finally wound its way into the rocky hills and the Angeles National Forest sign greeted us as we started winding our way along the two-lane highway. On the driver's side was the opposite lane and the rock face, and on the passenger side were the slopes of hills and mountains and splattering of guard rails when needed. I enjoyed this drive, feeling like I was on a rollercoaster. Even if I had wings, I wouldn't give up the feel of asphalt against my tires and the relaxing lull of controlling a beautiful piece of machinery.

"I don't think I'll be ready to drive like this for a while," Olly said with a laugh.

"You learned quickly today. I half expected to yell at you or slam my foot on the invisible brake pedal on the passenger side. I was lucky I had already driven plenty of go karts before actually driving a car."

"Is that something we can do too? Drive go karts?"

"We can do anything you want. I'm sure Asher and Tobias would like to tag along too."

We passed a turnout that had a viewpoint looking out over the hills with the city in the distance. Olly moved his hand off my leg and turned in his seat to look out the passenger window as we passed and then twisted towards me to look out the back window.

"A gray van and a truck just pulled out after us." I clenched the steering wheel at his words and looked in the rearview mirror. The truck was about four car lengths behind. Olly had his eyes shut. "There are three Fallen in the van and three in the truck."

"Call Tobias." Olly had his phone out and to his ear before I finished speaking.

We were approaching another viewpoint, and just as we were at the entrance, the truck gunned its engine, moved into the other lane, and sent me spinning into the lot for the viewpoint. I could hear Tobias yelling on the other end of the phone as it flew out of Olly's hand on impact and landed somewhere on the floor.

Everything was a blur as the car came to a screeching halt. I must have slammed on the brakes at some point because the smell of burned rubber filled my nose and made me gag. We had no time before they were on us. The van, the truck, another van that had been waiting.

The doors ripped open and both of us were pulled from the seats and thrown to the ground. I caught a brief flash of white as Olly's wings extended but saw him on the ground with a net over him. Our eyes met, the fear in his matching my own.

I managed to stagger to my feet. Most of the men were

surrounding Olly now, his fight fierce, but no match for the net that was more than likely doused in demon blood. One of the Fallen grabbed Olly's head and gave it a sharp twist, snapping it.

Rough hands picked me up and slammed me back into the cement and a steel-toe boot kicked me in the ribs. Pain filled my body and I coughed as my chest got tight. I felt like a thousand pounds were sitting on my chest. I could taste blood in my mouth and a cry lodged in my throat as my hands were jerked behind me and metal clicked around my wrists.

"Get them in the vans," a rough voice commanded as I was yanked to my feet by my hair, a wet cry leaving my throat.

My ears rang with a high-pitched fuzziness as I was dragged to one of the vans. My vision sparked with pops of color before going black. I was jolted awake as my body was slammed onto the cold metal of the van before I was knocked out again.

HANDS WERE UNDER MY ARMPITS. The hands set me on something cold and hard. I couldn't see or even really hear, but I could feel. Drops of something warm hit my face. There were two blurry blobs off to the side of me. The voices were muffled for a while and then I heard an agonizing cry before the pain took me back to darkness.

PAIN. So much pain. *Just let me die already.* Every bone in my body had to be broken. It felt like my eyeballs were ripped to shreds. Was my skin on fire? A scream ripped out of my throat causing me to cough and splutter. Everything went numb and I felt my body floating upwards. *Finally.*

Awareness returned to me before my body was fully awake. Cold concrete. The smell of blood. *Fuck.* I was in hell. I think. I never asked my dad what happened when you got sent to hell. Where was he?

Drip. Drip. Drip. The sound echoed in my skull and I jerked awake, my eyes going to a sink in the corner. On the other side of thick medal bars. What in the hell?

I moved my eyes around the room, everything clear in the dim light filtering down from a single lightbulb at the top of the staircase. Nothing good ever came from a basement with a single light bulb.

I was in a cage against a far wall, all four sides being reinforced with two-inch diameter steel rods. Chains were bolted to the floor. Four. One for each limb. Luckily, they weren't attached to me.

I ran my hands over my body; it was perfectly intact but caked with blood and dirt, among other things. This was some next level shit I was in. I reached through the bars and grabbed a water bottle that sat just within my reach. I ripped open the bottle, chugging the entire contents in one gulp. My throat was so raw it felt like I had swallowed shards of glass, or maybe that had been from my screams.

The basement was the size of a small apartment with a staircase leading up to a door, and another door on the far side of the room. There was also a table with slats in it and a basin off the side of it. It was an autopsy table.

Bile rose in my throat and I swallowed it down as I racked my brain for what had happened. The Fallen had captured us. They snapped Olly's neck. Then there was lots and lots of pain. The thought of the pain made me wretch, sending the water I had just gulped out onto the floor. My stomach felt like it was in a million knots, twisting tighter by the minute.

The click of a lock at the top of the stairs ripped me from my agony and I felt panic rising in my chest. I quickly laid down and curled in a ball facing the wall. Maybe they would leave me alone if they thought I was still passed out.

Three sets of footsteps made their way down the stairs. Oh God, where was Olly?

One set of feet sounded heavy, as if the person didn't really give a shit, another was a pair of heels, and the last was firm and sure.

I tried to control my breathing as they approached. They stopped what sounded like a few feet from the bars. Several long minutes passed, and I wondered why they were so quiet.

"How long has she been out? He healed her. She should be awake by now." A woman spoke, her voice sending a slight shiver through my body.

"Just over twenty-four hours. Do you want us to try to wake her?" a gruff voice asked, stepping closer as he spoke.

"Wait until I'm gone. What is the status of our supply?"

"We are at eighty percent of what is needed. The archangel has been an added benefit, but if we drain *him* too much he can't heal the rest."

The woman made a sound of annoyance in her throat and then her heels moved back towards the stairs. "Make sure she's fed and cleaned."

Her heel taps faded as she climbed the stairs and exited the door. I trembled slightly, feeling their eyes boring into my back. A set of keys jingled and the sound of the metal lock clicking made me whimper.

"Do you need help?" The gruff voice spoke again from the same spot he had been in. "I don't think I can stomach this shit, man. She's not even a fucking angel. You clean her up. I'll lock the door just in case and go get some food for her."

"You do that." Asher's voice nearly caused me to jump up and fling myself at him, but I bit down on my knuckle instead, holding back the sob that was threatening to spill out.

He was here.

He was going to save me. Save Olly.

The heavy feet retreated up the stairs and the lock slid into place after the door was closed. Asher let out a shaky breath and opened my prison, kneeling next to me.

"Hun... I'm so fucking sorry." He pulled me into his arms, my body shaking with sobs and fear. "I need to hurry and get you cleaned up before he comes back."

He scooped me in his arms, not caring how completely nasty I was, and walked past the autopsy table and to the door on the other side. Inside was a bathroom, a gross looking bathroom, but it had a shower, toilet, and sink.

He set me down on the toilet lid and went back into the room. I heard him opening a cabinet and then he came back with a towel, washcloth, and what looked like scrubs. He turned on the shower and pulled me up.

"Where are we?" My words left my lips, my teeth chattering. I wasn't cold, but my body was reacting to the bone deep fear coursing through my body.

I had thought fear was sitting outside the principal's office waiting for my dad. Watching horror movies with the lights off at night. Having to talk to the police about the joint in my locker. I was wrong about what fear felt like.

"Port of Los Angeles. They plan on taking a ship with the angel blood out into the Pacific and creating another gate to hell." I let him take off my clothes as he talked. "This has been in the works for a long time, Danica. Years. That woman and some fucker named Adamson are the masterminds behind it all."

My hands gripped Asher's forearms. "John Adamson?" My heart had already been beating fast, now it was reaching its peak. Could a heart explode? I was pretty sure mine was about to.

"You know him? Or them? There's two of them, although the kid was only here once." I loosened my grip and he moved me into the warm water of the shower. He grabbed a washcloth and began cleaning me. I let him because my mind couldn't even handle what was happening.

"I punched that fucker in the nose because he was trying to get me to join his 'church' to be a dealer."

Asher silently cleaned my body and hair without speaking. He was processing that new information. Hell, I was processing that information. He shut off the water and started to dry me off.

"So this goes even deeper than we thought. Your dad is going to lose his shit even more than he already is. It took four angels to

193

restrain him and keep him from coming to get you. I think that's what they want."

"John Adamson Senior was my doctor. He delivered me. He's known this whole time."

I stepped into the scrub bottoms Asher held open for me, balancing myself by putting my hands on his shoulders. "Who's the woman?"

Asher pulled the scrub top over my head and ran his hands over my arms.

"She says she has no name like we're in *Game of Thrones* or some shit. She wears a scarf around her head and sunglasses even inside so I don't even really know what she looks like. Listen, we don't have much time before Paul gets back."

He pulled me to him and hugged me, raking his fingers over my tangled wet hair. He lowered his voice to a whisper. "After sunset tonight all hell is going to break loose on this place. I'm going to pretend to lock the cell and then unlock the door upstairs later. You can't try to escape until you hear all the noise. Okay?" He pulled back and looked in my face. "I will be freeing the others and you need to run. Take a right at the top of the stairs and just run. No matter what you hear or see. Do you understand?"

I nodded.

"No. I need to hear that you understand." Tears were in his eyes. "What's out there... promise me you will turn right and run."

"I promise I'll turn right and run, no matter what."

He let out a sigh of relief and scooped me back into his arms to carry me back to my cage. Just as he was shutting the door, the lock turned at the top of the stairs.

"I love you, Danica."

I wish I could have said it back to him before Paul came down the stairs.

CHAPTER 19

DANICA

I loved him. I loved *them*. I don't know how it happened so quickly, but I knew in my heart that I loved all three of them.

Sitting on the cold concrete floor in scrubs that were made for a man, probably the same doctor who had delivered me eighteen years ago, suddenly all the stupid shit didn't seem so important anymore. What mattered was that I hadn't even gotten to say 'I love you' to the three men who had swooped in and captured my heart.

I didn't want to sleep for fear of passing out so hard that I might not hear anything upstairs. I could occasionally hear voices, but since Paul and Asher there had been no one.

I was losing my battle, fighting to keep my eyes open when I heard the lock slide in the door. It didn't open. I stood from my place on the floor, my ass stinging with pain from sitting in one place for so long. I wished I had shoes, but they were nowhere to be seen. I opened the metal door and crept up the stairs towards the door, listening intently.

Turn right. Run.

I played his words over and over in my head as I waited for chaos to erupt outside the door. I don't know what I expected, but it wasn't to hear gunfire erupt suddenly. I nearly fell but managed to hold onto the door handle to regain my balance.

Turn right. Run.

No matter what.

Turn right.

Run.

I took a deep breath, the tears already pouring down my cheeks like hot reminders that this wasn't a movie. This was real. I opened the door and tried not to look at what was ahead of me, because I was supposed to turn right and run.

Cages. Rows and rows of cages with angels. Turn right. Run.

My eyes scanned the sea of cages and Olly's bloodshot blue eyes met mine. I couldn't hear over all the noise but one word came from his mouth. *Run.*

I snapped my head to the right and took off, staying close to the wall. The gunfire was behind me now. My feet hurt from unknown debris digging into them, but I ran. There was a metal door straight ahead.

"Stop her!" Boots pounded on the cement behind me as I flung open the door and ran into the night.

The lights were on outside, the sky a deep blue color. My eyes scanned quickly, trying to figure out where I was supposed to go. Where I could hide. To my left was dark water, glittering in the artificial lights. Straight ahead were rows and rows of metal shipping containers with cranes towering over them, ready to put them on ships. To the right was chain link fencing, and beyond that, another building.

Hide. I needed to hide.

I ran as fast as I could and darted between the first two containers. The containers were arranged in groups of two with two groups in each row. They were stacked four containers high. The spaces between were narrow. I went towards the water and ran straight along the small strip of concrete between the containers and water. I would jump in if I needed to.

196

My lungs burned and I felt my airway not wanting to cooperate. I slowed slightly until I heard gunshots and shouts.

Where was I supposed to go? He said run. Run, run, run. That was what I did but now I was reaching the end of the area I was in and would run straight into the water. I turned at the last row, the chain link fence now in front of me. It went straight to the edge where the port met the water, but maybe I could hold onto the pole and slip around it? I definitely couldn't climb it since there was barbed wire at the top.

I ran towards the fence and slipped around the edge of it before stopping in my tracks. A black SUV was idling outside the building I was just in, and two large men were ushering a woman wearing a scarf around her head and sunglasses into the backseat. Before she climbed in she looked over at me.

"Danica! Run!" I heard Asher's yell, but didn't see him. I ran; there was not much cover between the fence and the next building over.

The sounds of boots on the pavement behind me was a reminder that I was being chased. A bullet hit the ground next to me and in a panic I lost my footing and fell onto the cement, my hands and knees scraping along the rough surface. I scrambled, trying to get up, to get farther away from the men, the bullets, the noise.

I managed to get up, but then was knocked back by a body tackling me, bullets hitting the ground, a scream of pain. Shouts. Curses. I struggled under the weight, the feel of warm blood seeping into the blue scrubs.

The body rolled over, the person gasping for air. I rose to my knees to run.

No.

The scream left my throat with so much force that I fell back, the world going silent around me before rushing back into my ears all at once.

No.

There was so much blood I didn't know where to put my hands to stop the flow of it. I pushed his blond hair out of his eyes and he stared back at me with sad slate blue eyes. Two blinks. A tear slid down his cheek.

No.

The gunfire had stopped. No more pounding feet. No more shouts. A ship's horn blew in the distance. The lulling sound of water filled my ears.

I put my lips against Asher's, his breath shuddering against them as I kissed him. "I love you, Asher." His hand gripped mine. He tried to speak but all that came from his mouth were gurgles.

Footsteps beside me. Silence.

Dad. He kneeled on the other side of Asher, his glowing hands hovering over his torso. He shook his head.

My sobs filled the night, the stars just making their appearance as Asher took a ragged breath. Seconds turned into minutes. No more breaths.

"Danica... they have to take him. They're being summoned."

I looked up at my father. He hadn't left his spot, but glanced to the side. I looked. Tobias. Olly. Tear-stained faces. Wings extended. Glazed eyes.

"They can't control it. They have to take him."

No.

Tobias walked forward, his wings folding back, but not away, and he scooped Asher in his arms. He backed away and they shot into the sky. Shooting stars.

CHAPTER 20

DANICA

*D*ad took me home and said he was staying a while, taking a vacation. Last time I checked, moping around on the couch with your daughter was not much of a vacation. He said that he left three of his most trusted demons in charge. I couldn't tell if he was serious or joking since he wasn't one to joke around.

It was the first time in recent memory where he stuck around longer than a day. The first time *ever*, at least that I could remember, that I had seen him out of a suit. He was a man who would arrive in a suit, go into the bedroom at night in a suit, and then come down the next morning in a suit. I guess it was just his way of expressing himself and showing he was in charge.

It was also the first time he watched more than the news and business channel. He binged on Netflix to humor his broken-hearted daughter.

"I find it rather peculiar that this Lucifer not only wears a suit constantly, but bears a striking resemblance to me. I'm going to have to figure out who is involved in making this show," he said, taking a bite out of a slice of pizza. I had talked him into watching *Lucifer*, curious to see his reaction. "I bet a dream demon planted that in someone's head."

I picked a piece of sausage off my plate and popped it in my mouth. I held myself back from shoving the entire extra-large pizza we had ordered into my face and devouring it like a pig. My appetite had been non-existent the last few days, but now it greeted me like a greedy child who wanted to take all the Halloween candy in the bowl.

"Do you think they're coming back?" I asked absently as I ate my crust, leaving the rest of the pizza. I had this thing with my pizza; I liked to eat my least favorite parts first, starting with the crust and ending with a small pile of sausage I picked off beforehand.

I had asked my father countless questions over the past few days, including what I was asking him now. Sometimes he didn't know the answer, sometimes he did. He would slip away into his office he never used, and talk on the phone to whoever was on the other end. Sometimes his answers would change the next time I circled back to them.

He put his plate on the coffee table and turned towards me. I focused on my pizza, folding it and biting into it. I probably shouldn't have been asking questions I didn't want the answers to while I was eating, but it was hard to resist. I needed to know, and if that meant crying into my pizza, then so be it.

"Ham says they are but there isn't a timeline. He doesn't know what's going on. No one does."

I met my father's eyes; he was serious. I let out a shaky breath and continued to eat. His answer meant it could be days, weeks, months, maybe even years. It had been three days since Tobias and Oliver had flown off into the night with Asher's lifeless body. Three days of radio silence from them and three days where I peppered my father with so many questions he probably wished he would have spent more years in my youth explaining celestial life to me.

The first day, I learned that the soul could only be restored once. Fallen that died, died for good. The second day, I learned that when an angel was summoned to heaven like Tobias and Olly were, that it was forced in dire circumstances, which is why they had glazed-over eyes. At least the third day brought me a little peace of mind, but just barely. They'd be back at some point. Tobias and Olly.

"Do you think they'll be Fallen?" I asked casually, like it wasn't a big deal. It was a very big deal. Olly might still have his mental state intact after, but Tobias would remember his death.

"Why would they be Fallen? They did nothing wrong." He gave me a serious look, a concerned look. A look you give your child when they say something outlandish.

I shrugged, trying to show him I wasn't certain in my answer. "Because of me."

His face softened, a look I wasn't used to seeing often. Especially not with sweatpants and a t-shirt on. He almost looked like a normal dad. Almost.

"Love is not damning, Danica. It lightens the soul, puts it at ease, destroys the darkness. The souls that end up in hell, they don't love. They destroy it in themselves and those around them. Those that fall, fall because they hate more than they love. I fell because I hated more than loved." He paused and squeezed the bridge of his nose. "But love... love for you and for your mother..." His voice cracked as if he was holding back tears. "That love is what let me be free again."

"Does that mean your devil days are over?"

He chuckled and grabbed another slice of pizza, his emotions now tucked tightly away. I wish I could fold up my emotions and tuck them away just as easily.

"No. I am still going to run hell, at least for now, until this threat of opening another gate to hell is gone. I will be delegating a little more, something I should have done a long time ago."

"I don't understand how someone can open a gate to hell when you're right there."

"I only take up a small portion of hell. Heaven and hell both run in infinitely expanding planes of existence. If someone decided to just keep walking straight in heaven or hell they will never find an end, it will continue to expand. There are some demons not under my control but they have always kept to themselves. My blood is the only key to hell so I don't know what they expect to do with all that angel blood they collected. I don't think it can create a gate by itself."

That was what worried me the most. None of us knew what their endgame was.

~

I HADN'T REALIZED how much I had missed Ava until she was lying next to me on my queen-sized bed. I had to tell her something about what had happened, but also couldn't tell her everything. She thought I was at an academy for troubled youth and we were being trained to go into the military. That was completely plausible given my track record and my dad's fortune. He could afford to send me to a top-secret military academy.

The reason for my tears was a little more difficult to explain. When I told her I had three boyfriends, she blinked at me for at least a minute, running it through her head. She was fairly innocent, only having made-out with a boyfriend, so the fact that I was with them all was a shocker for her. An even bigger shocker was that my dad didn't have anything bad to say about three men being in my life. I couldn't explain to her that he had been around so long that me having a harem of men wouldn't faze him. In fact, I think he was happy I had men around to protect me.

Well, now two men. Or maybe none if heaven didn't send them back to me.

"Are you sure you want to go back to that school? It sounds like torture. You should punch those bitches."

"I'm not doing too horribly in the classes. Mostly Cs. Plus, they might get out soon." I had told Ava that Olly and Tobias were taken by the court-martial since it was a military matter and I didn't know when or if they would come back.

I had decided that I couldn't just stay here and mope for the rest of my life. It had been almost a week. I could very well have moped back at school, where at least I'd have something to do to keep my mind off the overwhelming pain I felt inside.

Loud voices, one being my father, came from downstairs and we both sat up and looked at each other. Ava was up and out the door before I could stop her. It was so out of character for her that I quickly ran after her and grabbed her arm at the top of the stairs.

"You can't go down there! What are you doing?" I whisper shouted, yanking on her arm like it was the pull to a lawnmower. My dad had told me to stay upstairs with Ava until he came and got us.

"That voice..." she said on a sigh, still trying to descend down the steps.

I couldn't hear what the other voice was saying but it had a very seductive quality to it, like fine wine and dark chocolate if they could talk. I was certain it belonged to a demon, because why else would my best friend be in some kind of weird lust-filled trance trying to run to it.

The voices cut off and there was silence, except for Ava's deep breathing. She managed to snake her arm away and took the steps two at a time, holding onto the banister. Fuck my life, I couldn't even keep my best friend from throwing herself in harm's way.

I ran after her and collided into her back at the bottom of the stairs, nearly knocking her over. She was openly ogling a very attractive man who was leaning with his hip propped against the kitchen island. His skin was very tan, military shaved dark hair, and the most striking green eyes I had ever seen.

"Ricky, you didn't tell me you kept humans here. I would have turned it off had I known," he said, his eyes locked on Ava before glancing at me and then settling back on Ava. "I didn't take you for someone who has pets."

"I don't," Lucifer said, a slight tremor in his voice that probably only I could detect. Crap, this was bad. Why was there even a demon in our house?

"And I certainly didn't know you liked them so young."

"Well, I definitely can't have prostitutes that have been used. Ladies, why don't you head back upstairs? I was just about done." He stepped in between us and gave me a very serious look that told me to go with it.

Ava shook her head and looked back and forth between me and him. I grabbed her arm and yanked her back upstairs before she could get a word out.

"You're no fun, Ricky." I could almost imagine the pout on the man's face. It sounded like he was throwing out his bottom lip.

"Stop calling me that."

"Fine, you're no fun, *Lucy.*"

I heard a smack and a laugh as I shut my door and leaned up against it. Ava slowly sank on the bed, still seeming out of it. I had no clue what kind of demon that was but I was certain it couldn't be anything good.

"Are you okay?" I stayed in front of the door, not sure if she was going to take off out of it again.

She put her hand over her heart and took several deep breaths. I could see her trembling from my spot against the door. She met my eyes and a huge smile spread across her face. Oh, no. I knew that face. That was the same face she made when her beloved Nick Jonas came on the screen or radio.

"I know this is crazy, but I think I'm in love with that man." She stood and went to the window.

Shit, was she going to climb out the window now? I rushed over to her and grabbed her biceps. I sighed in relief when all she did was pull the curtains back and stare outside into the darkness. Although, maybe that should have concerned me even more.

"What did he do to you?" I still kept my hand on her arm and she turned her head to look at me.

"Stole my heart, that's what he did."

I MANAGED to convince Ava that she had been dreaming and that my dad never had business associates over to the house or anyone else for that matter. Crisis averted.

I decided it was time to attempt to get back to school. I was already behind, but surprisingly not as far behind as I was in human school. Everyone at school knew what happened and instead of looking at me like I would murder them, they looked at me with indifference and maybe a touch of curiosity.

Rumors of my scream had spread fast since several third-year students were part of the rescue mission. When I screamed with everything that was in my heart and soul, something had happened. Something that I had already tried to replicate countless times once my dad finally spilled the beans about it. At the time it happened, I hadn't even noticed because I was so distraught.

But when I had screamed, the Fallen dropped to their knees and dropped their weapons. It made no sense to me. It made no sense to anyone. The Fallen hadn't even known what had come over them, but described it as a compulsion to surrender.

We learned nothing more than we already knew from the Fallen. Someone wanted to open a gate to hell and needed angel blood to do it. My role in it all was still unclear. Maybe I was the sacrificial lamb or leverage. All we knew was that the mystery woman and John Adamson Sr. were nowhere to be found. John Jr. was back at school; apparently the charges against him and his father for drug trafficking, distribution, and coercion were dropped.

I spent my nights off campus at Asher's place because I needed to be close to him, to them, and the only place I felt that way was in his bed or on his roof. Since the weather was getting a smidgen warmer, I'd pull his duvet off his bed and sleep on a reclining lounge chair under the stars.

The stars, the moon, the faint sounds of revelers down the street always relaxed me enough to fall asleep, even though sleep was painful. The scene played on repeat night after night. Me turning right and running, running, running. Until Asher threw himself on me and died.

My nightmares seemed to suddenly stop and I could finally get decent sleep. In fact, I found myself looking forward to sleeping every night, where I'd get lost in a dream so vivid and enjoyable that it made me feel guilty considering Tobias and Oliver were still missing.

Two weeks had passed since returning to school, three since my world imploded. It was early for me to sleep, barely nine, but I'd had a long day dealing with the sneers and under-their-breath comments from the Divine 7. They had been so quiet that it surprised and saddened me to hear their demeaning remarks yet again.

To make the day worse, now Spring had decided to bring a shower with it, the sprinkles hitting the duvet I had just gotten comfortable under. I grumbled curses at the sky and trudged my way to the door, the duvet trailing after me.

"Danica?" My hand was on the door knob and I froze at the sound of my name on Tobias's lips. My heart sped up and I dropped the duvet as I turned around.

Tobias and Oliver stood in the middle of the roof, their wings still extended. They were dressed in white cotton pants, no shoes. I stepped forward, over the duvet. Was I dreaming?

They both turned their heads and looked at each other and their wings folded back and away. My heart stopped and I reached out and grabbed onto the back of the chair near me.

Asher.

His eyes met mine and a grin spread across his face as he moved his wings in the smallest of movements. I couldn't move, the shock and awe too much. Olly and Tobias passed by me, hugging me tightly, but my eyes stayed glued to Asher. They laughed and went inside, leaving me on the roof with him.

"Are you going to fuckin' stand there and stare or come here?"

"Are angels allowed to cuss like that?" I finally regained my composure and met him halfway.

He brought his hand to my cheek and wiped away the tears that I hadn't even felt falling with the raindrops that were hitting my face. Then he pulled me into him, wrapping his arms and wings around me.

"I'm sorry we couldn't come back sooner. They had to go find my soul," he said as if it was the most normal thing in the world to have his buddies go track down his lost soul. "Let's get inside."

It was an out of body experience being reunited with my angels. I had almost come to terms with the fact that not even the two I thought were alive were coming back.

Shock. That's what I felt. After spending weeks in a steady state of grief that had numbed me, the onslaught of feelings ripped my heart out of my chest, put it in a blender, then shoved it all back in my chest cavity creating a gooey mess.

We sat on the couch, draped over each other like a pile of puppies. There was so much I wanted to say, so much I needed to know. They had been gone for practically a month and it had felt like an essential part of me was missing.

"Asher is the first of his kind. Never has a soul been plucked out of the pit of lost souls," Olly explained, stuffing a cookie in his mouth. In heaven, the need for food was nonexistent so he was eating enough cookies to make up for the lost time.

"How? Why?"

"Angel baby and Toby went to the outskirts of heaven where the lost souls are sent. It's kind of like a prison but the souls just float around like jellyfish in the ocean, can't communicate, no corporeal form, just there in solitude and silence. Probably a couple of weeks passed and I felt them getting closer but I couldn't yell for them. The next thing I know, they were standing buck naked in front of my soul. I'd never been so happy to see two limp dicks before in my life." Asher twirled my hair around his finger as he spoke.

"Why were you naked" I asked Olly and Tobias.

"Couldn't risk a soul getting their hands on something they can attach to," Tobias explained. "A soul by itself can't escape that part of heaven, but if it attaches itself to an item it can."

"So they got me out and here I am. My job wasn't done yet." Asher looked at Tobias and Olly and they nodded before he continued. "There is a prophecy that was delivered to Michael by Nostradamus that when the darkness overshadowed the light, a baby would be born to the creator's two greatest regrets. That baby would grow into a woman and save the light from the dark with her four guardians."

"When did the darkness overshadow the light?" My heart was beating wildly in my chest, knowing what they were going to tell me. Why else would they be telling me about some prophecy from Nostradamus? I was always under the impression that Nostradamus was a quack job who just had a way with words that could fit multiple situations.

"January 20, 2001."

My birthday. I shut my eyes and took a deep breath. *Crap.* That was a lot to take in. "It makes sense Lucifer was a regret, but my mother? She was just a human who ran a coffee shop." I watched as the three faces around me fell into contemplative frowns. "Right?"

Suddenly, I wasn't so sure, unless the human race was a regret. That would be much more depressing than finding out I was half swamp creature or something. I opened my eyes and Olly took my hand, rubbing his thumb in small circles in the palm. I felt myself relax slightly but not nearly enough to stop the slight panic welling up inside of me. My mom *had* to be a human. She had to be.

"Your mom is Lilith."

EPILOGUE

REVE

ONE WEEK AGO

She was curled up on the rooftop chair again, a blanket covering her, her brown hair fanning around her face and shoulders. She was a fragile-looking thing. If I dropped her she would shatter into shards that would pierce the skin deep. Striking. Deadly. Beautiful.

I wanted her shards to pierce me.

I ignored my other assignments and decided to take this detour; one night would not set me back in my work. Besides, the bossman was surprisingly distracted and he would never know. He'd never know that I was about to do something that was forbidden. Something based on a feeling that I'm not even capable of.

Her cries were just too tempting to ignore. She was vulnerable. Broken. Delectable. I needed a taste of her.

I descended and landed in a crouch at the foot of the chair. No one was ever up there with her, she was always alone. It was just her and her sorrows that filled the night with her cries for what she'd lost. I wanted to feel her pain as badly as a root wants to touch water during a drought.

My body hovered over hers, my breath causing a single strand of her hair to move. I wanted to take her hair in my hands and let it cascade between my fingers like a waterfall. I traced my finger along her jawline, not touching the skin. I wondered what her skin might feel like under my fingertips. Would I taint it with my touch?

I stifled back a groan. I shouldn't have been doing this. I should have been down the street giving Mr. Campbell the nightmare he deserved. But I was too close now. I shut my eyes and pushed my way into her dream.

SHE WAS RUNNING, *gunshots all around. Feet pounding the pavement behind her.*

She was tackled, shielded by a man's body, who took the gunshots aimed at her.

She screamed.

An endless cycle of pain.

She was running, gunshots all around. Feet pounding the pavement behind her.

I grabbed her and took off into the night.

I SHOULDN'T HAVE DONE it. I should have left her there in her misery and feasted on it. I am the bringer of nightmares, not an eradicator of terrors. If anything, I should have made it worse by having all of the men she loved fall to their deaths.

Her scream was what did it. I had heard my fair share of screams, usually feasting on the fear and pain in them, fueling myself. Her scream made my skin crawl and my heart sputter like it was running out of fuel.

So I grabbed her and plopped her into a new dream.

· · ·

SHE WAS GORGEOUS, *standing at the top of the wide staircase, her hair in loose curls around her face. Her dress was red with a lace-up corset bodice and mermaid bottom. My choice. She smoothed her hands down her hips, unsure of herself. She was a princess tonight; my princess.*

Eyes were drawn to her and a blush creeped up to her cheeks, turning them slightly pink. She slowly made her way down the steps in her heels, which were probably an inch too high for her. I'd remember to make them shorter next time I put her in heels. Three inches instead of four.

She reached the bottom of the staircase and moved into the crowd. I let her have some control of the dream, but still held the strings tightly in my grasp. A group of three approached her, two young women and a young man. They greeted her with hugs and laughter.

I watched from afar, taking her in. Her smile. Her lips. The curve of her shoulders. My mouth watered for the taste of her, the smile on her lips, the feeling of her skin against mine.

If this was a nightmare I would have killed her three friends right then and there. I would have made her watch as I peeled back their skin. I would have feasted on her screams.

I walked towards her, tipping my head back to drink the last of my champagne. It went down smoothly. I passed a server and put the flute on the silver tray. I adjusted my cuff links and straightened my bow tie.

She was only a few feet away. I approached, touching her elbow gently, the touch sending a jolt through my body like a lightning bolt.

She turned towards me, her eyebrows raised in curiosity, a smile still on her face. She didn't pull her arm away and I didn't pull my hand away.

Nothing Else Matters *by Metallica began playing as couples took to the large dance floor under the sparkling chandeliers to waltz.*

I bent at the waist, keeping my eyes locked on hers, and offered her my hand. "May I have this dance?"

MAYA NICOLE

DESCEND

CELESTIAL ACADEMY BOOK 2

PROLOGUE

LUCIFER

18 Years Ago

$\mathcal{I}$ stood next to the gaping hole in the ground, the mahogany casket staring back at me. It was an inanimate object, but somehow I felt it was mocking me for opening my heart.

Opening my heart only to have it shattered to pieces.

The casket was the color of her hair; rich brown with a million other shades woven intricately in the strands. It was the reason I chose it.

I had walked into the funeral home with a pearlescent white casket in mind, but when I spotted the glistening mahogany, I knew it was the one.

I never thought instead of picking out an engagement ring, I'd be picking out a casket. I had the engagement all planned out. I would fill her coffee shop with a thousand lilies.

It didn't escape me now that lilies were also a funeral flower. The florist informed me they represented innocence being restored to the soul. Everyone ordered lilies for funerals.

Was that fact supposed to bring me peace?

It didn't.

I ordered them because they were her favorite flower. They were her namesake, Lily. Several wreaths of them lay atop the closed casket.

I stared at them, willing for this to be a twisted nightmare I was stuck in. It wouldn't be the first time I was stuck in a nightmare.

My whole existence had been one.

I looked to my left, and several feet away, stood John Adamson with his pregnant wife. She was due any day now. The two women had bonded over pregnancy stories and the excitement bringing a baby into the world brought.

I had wanted to kill John when he came into the waiting room, covered in blood, to tell me she was gone.

My Lily. Gone.

In that moment, it had taken every ounce of my being not to rip his throat out. I had wanted to be in the operating room, just in case.

I could have healed her.

He had said there was nothing to worry about. That the baby was showing no signs of having wings in the womb. That she was just a healthy baby girl and the birth would be standard.

A standard pregnancy. A standard birth. And it was, until it wasn't.

The umbilical cord was wrapped around her neck. She was in distress. Cesarean section or she would die. He told me to let him do his job.

Now Lily lay dead in a casket. She didn't even get to hold our daughter.

My chest tightened and my eyes burned with unshed tears. I wasn't a crier. At least until five days ago.

I brought the sleeping bundle in my arms closer to my body. She was a quiet newborn. She only cried when I cried. Somehow, I think she knew.

"Sir? Are you ready?"

My eyes snapped to the priest who looked at me with concern and pity. I was too tired and broken to care how he looked at me.

I nodded. I wasn't ready.

He pressed a button and the casket began to lower into the ground, taking my heart with it. I had given her my heart completely.

I was a fool for believing I'd ever find happiness.

My daughter made a small noise and I looked away from the scene in front of me and down at her tiny face. She had Lily's nose.

How was I going to do this? Raise a baby, alone, without Lily?

Her eyes opened for a moment and then shut, her tiny fists coming up near her chin and a smile forming on her face. My own lips twitched as I looked down at her.

I felt someone next to me and looked to find John and his wife. The small service was over. I had wanted to be alone for this, but John had convinced me to let them attend.

"Have you decided on a name for her yet?" He reached over and touched her little fist.

She would be a fighter, I could tell. She would have to be.

I looked back down at her, her mouth still curved in a smile as she slept. She was my world now. The one I would fight for, give my heart to, bleed for. Without her light, I would be lost in darkness.

"Her name is Danica."

CHAPTER 1

DANICA

I sat straight up, my heart pounding, my mind not quite sure where I was. I sprung from the bed, my legs getting twisted in my sheets. The floor met my face and a sharp pain went through my nose.

"Fuck!" I rolled over onto my back and pounded my fists on the floor. I stared at the ceiling, wondering if the nightmares would ever end.

My nose felt like it had been hit by a soccer ball and I brought my hand up to rub it. Luckily, it didn't bleed from its intimate acquaintance with the hardwood floor.

My nightmares seemed to be getting worse as the days went on. My only reprieve from them was on the weekends when I was with Asher.

On Sunday nights they would start and be manageable, but by Thursday, they were enough to make me want to bash my head against the wall. Now they were, apparently, enough to almost break my nose.

Oliver's comfort superpower didn't help. Tobias just worried too much with his never-ending questions. The only comfort from the nightly terrors was to sleep at Asher's house. It was like when I was near him, my body knew he was safe and not lost forever.

It had been three weeks since Olly and Tobias returned with a newly unfallen Asher. Three weeks since they told me I was part of a cryptic prophecy delivered by a psychic. Three weeks since finding out my mother was possibly *the* Lilith.

"Your mom is Lilith."

The name played over and over in my head. What was I supposed to do with *that*?

I felt like I was on an episode of some prank show where at any moment a camera crew would jump out and scream "gotcha!" It had to be a sick, twisted joke.

I wasn't well versed in the Bible or even stories surrounding the Bible. But what I did know from television and fiction was that Lilith was not one of the good guys. There had to be a reason for that.

I held hope that it was all wrong. What I thought I knew about angels was certainly all wrong.

As soon as I had been alone after her name was uttered, I had done the worst thing possible. I had internet searched the hell out of her. It was very similar to looking up medical symptoms. One minute it was just a name, and the next it was like a flesh-eating amoeba was gnawing at my insides and I only had three minutes to live.

There were so many stories about Lilith and none of them left me with a warm fuzzy feeling.

To add insult to injury, it was highly probable that the mysterious woman behind the angel abductions was *her*. John Adamson was involved. It couldn't purely be coincidence that the doctor who birthed me just happened to also be involved in an elaborate scheme to steal angel blood to open a gate to hell.

Everything had returned to normal. Most of the abducted angels that hadn't been part of the rescue operation were in heaven, healing mentally from their torture. Angels might not be able to die, but draining their blood day after day did a number on them.

Olly and I were back to school, Tobias resumed teaching his classes, and Asher continued to run his business.

Their guardian duties? *Me.*

Everything *seemed* normal, but it wasn't. I was freaking out.

I sat up from my place on the floor and glanced at the clock. It was only six. I had barely fallen asleep at two. I was exhausted and knew trying to sleep for another hour would be pointless.

I trudged to the bathroom and turned on the shower before peeling my damp pajamas off. I felt like I had run a marathon in my sleep, and looking in the mirror, I looked like it too.

Today was the last day before Spring break and most angels had guardian assignments to protect drunken college students partying it up in exotic locations. Warm waters and sandy beaches sounded like just the reprieve I needed.

I wasn't invited to the party because I wasn't an angel.

I showered quickly and attempted to cover up the dark circles under my eyes. They had progressively gotten worse throughout the week. I didn't need Tobias or Olly hovering over me because I looked like hell.

I had Spring break plans of my own and didn't need them worrying about me.

I dressed in my uniform and sat at my desk, opening my laptop. Most of my morning had become ritualistic lately. I would wake from a nightmare, shower and get dressed, then research Lilith and John Adamson.

I needed to know more about Lilith. It had become an addiction and scenarios ran through my brain constantly throughout the day. Someone had answers and that someone was John Adamson.

So, like any completely rational person, I decided to go to the man who had overseen my birth. The same man who was behind draining angels of their blood. Completely a good idea, if I do say so myself.

I pulled up my password protected folder and opened a screenshot of the party invitation Ava sent me.

Every year, John Junior had a Spring break kick-off party. It was the party of the year, and even though I was still pissed as hell about what had gone down between us, I was going. I had a mission to accomplish, and since John Senior was seldom around, it would be easy to accomplish.

At least I hoped so.

The movies always made it look like a piece of cake to break into an office. If nothing else, I would snoop to try to figure out why John Senior would involve himself in such nefarious activities.

I closed the image of the party invitation and opened a document containing my mother's obituary. From what little my dad had told me growing up, she had no family. I thought nothing of it before, but now those little details raised red flags.

Lily Judith Gardener, age 25, passed away quietly on January 20, 2001. She was born April 30, 1975. She owned and operated Viva La Vida Coffee, a Montecito award winning coffee establishment. Lily was strong in spirit and brought light into the lives of those she met. She is survived by her life partner and newborn daughter.

I had read it at least a million times, and each time my heart ached at the words "life partner." She had been my father's life. Had everything been a lie?

The obituary was short and simple, which was Lucifer's style. It didn't give me much information, other than she was not very creative with her name if she really was Lilith.

I had scoured the internet for her, but besides the coffee shop, there were no traces of her. These days it was hard to remain anonymous in the world, so it seemed she had sprung up out of nowhere.

That was the exact reason I was going to John's party. To find information on a person that was buried over eighteen years ago.

LYING IS INFINITELY EASIER when you use Lucifer as your alibi. Not even Tobias, Asher, and Olly, would dare call him to verify that we were going on a father-daughter vacation. They *had* given me a slightly skeptical look though.

On a scale of one to ten, this lie was right in the middle at a five or six. My lie wasn't hurting anyone but it would certainly piss Tobias off. Asher would be frustrated but then move on. Olly would see my point of view.

I pulled my car into the garage and breathed a sigh of relief. So far, operation *Who's My Mommy?* was off to a great start. Who doesn't love lying to the men they love?

After turning off the alarm, I walked into the dark house, turning on lights. Besides the impromptu stay when I thought Asher was gone forever, I'd been gone for almost three months. I missed the freedom the house gave me, especially when Lucifer wasn't around. It might sometimes be lonely with a semi-absent father, but it was better than living with the staff members of your school.

This week away was just what I needed to refresh and try to regain my sanity. *Alone.* The word felt wrong somehow as it echoed in my head. Or maybe that was just my guilt.

I pulled out my phone and messaged my angels that I had made it. They were under the assumption that my dad was flying us to Hawaii. The thought of flying over the ocean angel-style gave me the heebie-jeebies and that should have been their first clue that I was pulling the wool over their eyes.

Asher was the first to respond. *Make sure to send us plenty of pictures of you in a bikini.*

I rolled my eyes. I should have said we were going somewhere cold instead of to Hawaii. I wasn't sure what they were going to do when they found out I deceived them. They cut me too much slack most of the time, but this might push them over the edge.

I needed to do this on my own, and they would just complicate matters. Walking into a party with three men, two of which were well into their twenties appearance-wise, would raise a lot of eyebrows. The attention would complicate my stealth-mode operation. At least that was what I kept telling myself.

Maybe this *was* a bad idea.

I carried my bag up to my old room and plopped down on the bed. Ava would arrive soon to get ready for the party. I was a bit nervous about John Junior and how much he knew about me. Had he been in Los Angeles when I was abducted and brought to the port?

I would soon find out just how much he knew when I showed up at his house uninvited. It wasn't like I could hide out once I was there. I had lots of friends and acquaintances, and word would spread through the party like wildfire.

My phone buzzed with a text from Ava and I practically flew down the stairs to let her in. It had only been three weeks since I last saw her, but when I opened the door it felt like it had been a lifetime. How can someone change so much in less than a month?

"Ava! What the hell?" I grabbed her arm and yanked her in the house, looking behind her. Clearly she'd been body snatched and it was possible the culprit was right behind her.

She let out a frustrated sigh and put her hands on her hips. I shut the door and turned to stare at her.

Ava had always been unassuming, wearing her long blond hair in a braid or ponytail. She dressed modestly by today's standards. Now she was sporting royal blue hair, styled in large curls that fell down her back. Her makeup was thick and her eyes rimmed with eyeliner and fake eyelashes. I had never once been able to get her to try them and here she was with falsies.

Her clothes were what concerned me most. Typically, for a party, she would wear jeans and a blouse. Maybe a dress if she wanted to dress up. But now, my best friend had on booty shorts over fishnet stockings and a corset-like top. Her boots looked like something a stripper might wear.

"You look great, but seriously, what the hell?" I was pretty sure it was April and not October. Maybe Halloween had moved to the Spring? In my sleep deprived state, I was tempted to pull out my phone to double check the date.

"It was time for a change. That's not what you're wearing, is it?" She scrunched up her nose at my pajama bottoms and hoodie I had changed into after class.

"Of course not. Time for a change? *Some* change." I moved towards the stairs, my mind still reeling over her drastic change in appearance. "So, who's the boy?"

"Why do you assume it's a boy?" She followed me, her heeled knee-high boots echoing in the empty room.

"A girl?" It had to be someone or something because she just wouldn't make that drastic a change to her appearance for no reason. None of her texts over the past three weeks said anything about dying her hair blue or going all hoochy mama. Her outfit was something *I* would wear.

"It's just because. Do I need a reason to dye my hair?" We entered my room and she sat in my desk chair. "While you're here, we should dye your hair. You'd look really good with red."

I snorted and pulled a pair of skinny jeans and a red crop top out of my bag. "I think my boyfriends would kill me."

"Even more reason to change your hair, spice things up a little. Not that they aren't spicy enough as it is. I mean, there are three of them." She propped her legs up on the desk and turned her head towards me. "Have you had two in you at once yet? You've had anal right?" She spewed questions like it was the Spanish Inquisition.

My eyes widened at the abrupt change in subject from her hair to my sex life. I changed into my clothes while considering my answer, although I wasn't sure I wanted to even go there with her. I told Ava almost everything, but had been keeping my sexual exploits with three men more private because I didn't think she'd want to hear anything about it.

She had barely had her first kiss, and now she was asking me about anal sex? I was sure she knew all about the birds and the bees, she was too smart not to, but she had never asked me details before.

"They haven't asked, so I haven't brought it up. It's not that I'm opposed to it though." Sleeping with multiple guys at once was still something so foreign to me. I felt like I was dreaming every time we were together.

Once Olly decided to join the mix, things would get even more interesting. Especially if my observation of the tiny spark between him and Asher was correct. I was anxiously awaiting that moment.

I walked into my bathroom and left the door open while I put on more make-up than I'd worn in months. Fake eyelashes felt incredibly strange after not wearing them for a while. I finished my look with a bright red lip.

"It's good to be back," I said, flipping the light off and grabbing my purse and jacket. "Let's roll."

"Heck yes! Are you drinking or smoking tonight? I kind of want to have a drink." Ava stood and headed for the door.

I grabbed her arm and stopped her. Ava never drank. What had happened to my best friend?

"Spill it. Now. Or I swear I will tie you to my bed until you tell me what's going on." I frowned at her and really examined her face. She didn't look like she was in pain or sad, but even I knew how easy it was to hide the pain within.

She bit her lip and seemed to be thinking about what she wanted to tell me. My heart dropped. I was losing my best friend by not being here. Maybe this change had started even earlier than the three weeks I'd been gone.

"Stanford rescinded my scholarship. I'm still waiting for them to decide if they're going to revoke my admissions." Tears formed in her eyes and she took a deep breath. "I was arrested."

I dropped her arm. "When? How? Holy shit, Ava." I sat down on the edge of my bed and looked up at her.

If anyone should have been arrested by this point in their life, it was me. They hadn't even arrested me for the joint in my locker. What had she done? Robbed a bank? Stolen all the blue hair dye from Sally's Beauty Supply?

She sat down next to me and put her face in her hands. I put my arm around her and tried to think of what to say. What do you say to someone who literally *never* got into trouble?

"Right after you went back to school. It's so embarrassing." She took her hands off her face and I grabbed her hand in support. "I broke into a house, but I don't even know why I did it. The whole night was kind of a blur. One second I was in my bedroom, studying, and the next I felt this overwhelming pull. So I followed where it led."

My eyebrows drew together at this odd story she was delivering. The last time she was at my house she had felt a strong pull towards a demon in my kitchen. I never did ask my dad what type of demon he was. Did he have something to do with this?

"I broke in through a window of the house but no one was there. There must have been a silent alarm because the next thing I knew I was being handcuffed and put in the back of a police car."

That still didn't explain why Ava decided to go all Clementine from *Eternal Sunshine of a Spotless Mind* and dye her hair blue. Her new look screamed 'look at me!'

"You didn't steal anything, did you?" I stood, keeping her hand clasped in mine and pulled her up from the bed.

"No, but it was a celebrity's house. I don't know how I got close enough to even break in. There were security guards and the gate was pretty tall. My parents are so disappointed in me and are making me help pay for my lawyer. I had to get a job and this," she gestured to herself, "is part of it. Let's just go. I don't want to talk about it anymore."

Ignoring her plea to drop the subject, I probed. "What job? You're not a stripper are you?"

She laughed. "No. There's this new bar and restaurant in downtown Santa Barbara called Blue Wave and it has a giant mermaid aquarium. I'm a mermaid. I get amazing tips."

I let out a sigh of relief that she wasn't taking off her clothes, at least not in the way I had thought, and hugged her before we left for John's house.

THE THING about high school parties in Montecito is that they are typically thrown by the most popular, richest of teenagers. Everyone who is anyone in the immediate area shows up and it is one big booze, drug, and fuck fest. Case in point, John Adamson's parties.

I parked my car in the lot next to John's estate. There were already dozens of cars parked in the dirt lot next door that had forever been vacant land. In fact, vacant lots surrounded all four sides of the house. I'd never thought much of it before, but now it piqued my curiosity.

We made our way through the side gate and into the backyard that already had drunken chicken fighting going on in the heated pool. The steam from the water made it look like something straight out of a horror movie right before someone gets killed.

"Danica fucking Deville, how the hell have you been? Heard you were sent to a military school or some bullshit. Rough," a guy named Brad said, slinging his arm around my shoulders. "John has some sweet ass devil's lettuce in the game room. You should check it out."

A grin spread across my face. I missed this crowd and how much they made me smile. Being surrounded by people that actually liked me, and at the very least tolerated me, was such a stark difference from being at the academy.

I followed Ava into the house where music was blaring from speakers and people were jumping around with their arms in the air. We made it to the kitchen and Ava grabbed a cup of some concoction that looked like punch but surely packed a punch of its own. I just grabbed a cup and filled it with water.

I was still reeling from what she had shared with me. It still wasn't clear what happened leading up to breaking into the house. Surely it couldn't have been so cut and dry. I'd have to probe her more once she had some alcohol in her.

My first order of business was to figure out where John was. I left Ava with a few friends and told her I was going to go mingle. Instead, I made my way to the game room where I knew John usually congregated with his inner circle and slipped inside.

The musky smell of Santa Barbara's finest weed hit my nostrils. I didn't love or hate the smell, but was glad the French doors leading outside were open to help dissipate the pungent odor. There were a few dozen people inside, lounging on couches and bar stools. A few people were using the single lane bowling alley and several were gathered around the pool table.

I glanced around and spotted John at the same time he spotted me. A large grin spread across his face and he rose from his spot on the couch and made his way over to me.

The last time I saw him he had blood running through his fingers as he held his broken nose. His nose looked better than it had before. Maybe a career in nose jobs was in my future.

"Dee! I'm surprised you have the balls to show your face in my house. I hope you're here to apologize for fucking up my nose." He grabbed my hips and put his lips against my ear to whisper. "We can go somewhere more private, unless you prefer an audience."

I shoved him away and resisted the urge to wrinkle my nose in disgust. He might be a stereotypical rich pretty boy, but he was sorely lacking in the personality department. It made him ugly.

"Why would I apologize when your nose looks so much better now?" I smirked and turned to walk away but he grabbed my arm. I stopped and turned back to face him.

"You're lucky you moved away," he said, his mouth in a tight line instead of the smile he was previously wearing. The sound of his voice held a threat. He let go of my arm with a shove. "Enjoy the party."

I watched as he made his way back to the couch and didn't spare me another glance. *Perfect.*

I left the room and made my way to the staircase leading upstairs. It was strictly off-limits but it was doubtful anyone would say anything if they saw me slip up the stairs.

I tried several doors, finding guest rooms and bathrooms. The room I assumed was John Senior's office had an electronic lock on it. It was the only door on the hall that had it and it was the only one locked.

I slipped into the guest room next to it and made my way to the French door leading out onto the upstairs terrace that spanned the entire back of the house. I was hoping what I thought was the office had a similar door.

It seemed a bit ridiculous that someone would have a state-of-the-art lock on an inner door, but then ignore the fact that the outer door was covered in glass panes. The lack of outer stair access gave a false sense of security.

I examined the door and pulled the lock picking tools I had bought on Amazon out of my purse. I had practiced on my own door at the academy, and after several YouTube videos, I was efficient as a burglar. You really could learn to do anything on the Internet. Why did I need school?

It was almost too easy to pop the locks on the door and I waited for twenty knives to fly at me or an alarm to sound. When nothing happened, I moved inside the room that was all wood accents. It smelled faintly of sweet cigar smoke. I pulled out my cell phone and turned on the flashlight.

I started at the bookshelves and skimmed the titles. Most were medical books with one shelf devoted to Stephen King. Of course he would be a Stephen King fan. He had Stephen King vibes written all over him.

I wasn't sure what I was looking for. I just knew that if he had something, it was going to be in his office. All bad guys kept important information in their office. It was in the rule book of being a bad guy.

I opened a few drawers and cabinets at the bottom of the built-in bookcases and found old medical instruments in boxes, but not much else. He probably had a safe hidden behind a picture. I looked around but the walls were bare.

Where would he keep information about private patients?

I went to the desk and tried the drawers. The only one that opened was the center one which just had a bunch of junk in it. I sifted through it and then turned my attention to the drawer that was the size of a file cabinet drawer. I picked the lock and pulled it open. All the files were labeled with initials. I wasn't sure he would have files on any of us, but one could hope.

I located them easily, all three the same colored red folders right next to each other. I quickly checked inside to make sure I had the correct ones before shoving them into the waistband of my jeans and zipping up my leather jacket.

It was so tempting to look at them right then and there, but I was already pushing my luck being in the office for so long.

I exited the same way I'd entered and turned the bottom lock so at least then it wouldn't seem too obvious the room had been broken into. I made my way back through the guest room and down the stairs into the fray of the party.

I found Ava in a group of people, her eyes glossy from drinking.

"Hey, I forgot something in my car. I'm going to run out and grab it." She hugged me and kissed my cheek. She was definitely feeling the effects of whatever was in the punch. When I got back from my car I was going to have to cut her off and then interrogate her to find out more about her break-in and her new job. Something was fishy about it, and not just because she was moonlighting as a mermaid.

Out in the lot there were a few people making out against the sides of cars, but otherwise it was quiet besides the faint sound of the ocean. I slid the files out from my jacket and locked them in the glove box. It was tempting to sit in the car and go through them, but Ava probably was in need of a babysitter.

I somehow felt responsible for whatever was going on with her.

I shut the door and turned around, only to bump right into some-one's chest. I stepped back to meet the angry eyes of John, with two of his friends flanking his sides. I turned to run but his two friends grabbed me by the arms and shoved me against my car. John stepped close to me. I could smell the stench of weed coming off his clothes.

"You shouldn't have come back. You know the drill, right? Nothing personal." He spoke in a low voice that sent shivers down my spine and a few small drops of his saliva landed on my face. There was no amount of washing that would ever get the feeling off.

"Fuck you, you piece of-" My words were cut off as his fist connected with my gut, causing me to double over as far as the two goons holding me would allow.

I tried to kick out at him, but his friends shifted their bodies to hold my legs against my car with theirs. I let out a scream, but it was useless. Everyone knew that if John invited you to be a part of his band of merry drug dealers and you refused, he'd beat the shit out of you. I really had been hoping it was an urban legend, but who was I kidding? He'd probably kick an infant if it refused. I'd made it ten times worse by turning him down publicly and punching the fucker in the nose.

He sent another punch to my side and my eyes blurred as tears filled them. I spat at him, my saliva landing on his jawline. He wiped it off with a disgusted look on his face.

"Bitch." He slapped my face. The shape of his hand burned into my cheek.

"You aren't going to get away with this," I managed to get out through clenched teeth.

John threw his head back and laughed like Jack Nicholson in *The Shining*. I may have pissed my pants a little at the menacing sound.

"What do you guys think? Should I fuck up her face like she did mine? It's really too bad. She's such a gorgeous girl." He trailed his index finger down the side of my face and bopped my nose with it. I shivered in revulsion at his touch. This was going to hurt.

His fist connected with the center of my face, snapping my head back. My eyes slammed shut and warm liquid filled my nose and started seeping out. He then threw a punch at my chest that left me gasping for breath.

The two men that had ahold of my arms let me go and I fell to the ground, my palms scraping on the rough surface of the dirt. With one last kick to my stomach, John stepped away, laughing.

"I'm taking it easy on you, Dee. I hope you appreciate my leniency. If it were anyone else, it'd be so much worse." He squatted down next to me and patted my head. "I do hope you enjoyed my party. Don't let me see you at my house again."

With that, they turned and left me bleeding next to my car.

CHAPTER 2

DANICA

The mission had gone smashingly. A fist smashing right into my face. It had to be karma for keeping this from those who were supposed to be guarding me.

Guarding me from what exactly was still up for debate. I didn't need babysitters to steal harmless files, did I?

I had considered calling the police, but what would I tell them? Hell, he and his father had been arrested and gotten off scot-free. They probably had the cops on a leash.

This was the second time in my life I had the shit beaten out of me. The first time was when the Fallen kidnapped me. I didn't really remember much because I was in and out of consciousness. Olly healed me before I could fully wake up and process the pain.

The pain from John's beating still had me feeling intensely sorry for myself on Sunday. My face and bruises hadn't looked that bad on Friday night, but now everything was blue and dark purple. It was going to be hard to hide the evidence.

Ava stayed with me Friday and Saturday. I had been unable to get anything else out of her about her new look and job. I hoped she wasn't headed down the same path of bad decisions I had been down.

I was alone again. In hindsight, going to the party was a mistake. I hadn't thought he'd actually beat me, maybe just give me shit about breaking his nose. I should've known he had no moral compass. What a jackass.

I hadn't even bothered getting the files out of my car. It took too much effort to go up and down the stairs. With Ava being gone, I had to hobble down the stairs to get food. I made sure to grab the files out of my glovebox.

Taking them back to my room, I sat on my bed and stared at the blood red folders. None of them were thick, with only a few documents in each. I ran my hand over one of the folders. It was Lucifer's.

I lifted the corner. There was only one piece of paper inside. I stood and stared down at the folder. If I looked in the files, I would know more about myself, hopefully. I might also find out things I *didn't* want to know about myself. It was hard enough being the daughter of the devil, but now there was a great probability my mother was right up there on the list of most hated too.

No one ever talked about *the* Lilith. She was mysterious. She was deadly. Some internet websites said she stole babies. Some said she was a demon. Movies and TV shows often portrayed her as an evil vampire queen. A few sources proclaimed she was the representation of the independent woman and should be revered.

It was possible the prophecy wasn't even true and all of my worrying was for nothing. It did seem a bit ridiculous on second thought, but archangels didn't make shit up. Tobias confirmed that Michael had, in fact, said that Lilith and Lucifer were the creator's biggest regrets.

What did that make me then? A double regret?

I lowered to my knees on the floor next to the bed and lay my chin on crossed arms. Lucifer's file would be the easiest to start with. He was an angel, of that I was sure.

I pulled the folder towards me and opened it, revealing a simple document.

Name: Lucifer
Alias: Michael Deville

Blood type: Nonhuman; Celestial 100%
Date of birth: Unknown

Under his vital information was a paragraph explaining his blood's reactions to introduced antigens and substances. Most of what was listed was written in code. There was one that had a plus sign next to it but the series of letters and numbers didn't reveal what it was.

How John even got a sample of my father's blood was beyond me. My dad guarded his blood like the Queen's Guard guards Buckingham Palace.

I closed the file and set it to the side. I grabbed my mother's file next and stared at it. What if she was human and died a normal death during childbirth? What if she wasn't even my mother and she had baby-snatched me from a real human and implanted me into her womb?

Now, that was a Syfy movie waiting to happen.

Name: Lilith
Alias: Lilith Judith Gardner
Blood type: Nonhuman; Demonoid 100%
Date of birth: Unknown
Alias DOB: April 30, 1975

The first paper in the file was similar to Lucifer's, several codes for antigens were listed. One had a plus sign next to it. I wish I knew what it meant.

I stared at the page for a long time before turning to the next where an autopsy report done by Doctor Adamson detailed the date of death and the unknown cause of massive blood loss during a routine cesarean section.

I shut the folder and sat it on top of my father's. My chin trembled and tears blurred my vision. My father had been duped into loving a demon.

I sucked in a breath of air and let it out slowly. My file was staring back at me. It had more than just two papers in it.

How could this even happen? How could my mother be a demon?

I opened the file.

Name: Danica Marie Deville
Blood type: Nonhuman; Inconclusive Celestial, Inconclusive Demonoid
Date of birth: January 20, 2001

The same tests were run on my blood, with several having plus signs. I flipped the page to a detailed list of tests run on my blood to determine the percentages of my lineage, but every test repeated the same word "inconclusive." It figured that even my blood couldn't pass a test.

I grumbled in frustration. Leaving the folder open on my bed, I made my way downstairs again to watch television. My brain couldn't handle anymore digging into my mother or into what I was. My brain certainly didn't want to let go of the fact that I might be half demon though.

Is that why I didn't have angel wings?

Is that why I was such a fuck up at everything I did?

I fell asleep on the couch, my nightmares worse than ever. When I woke, I didn't feel rested. In fact, I felt like I hadn't slept at all, and my breast hurt and my nose throbbed.

I trudged upstairs, my feet dragging on the ground and hopped in the shower. The hot water did little to ease my mind or the aches from being beaten. There was a weariness that came with the exhaustion that had slowly been building in my body over the past few weeks.

I should have been happy. I should have been excited for this next phase in my life with my three angels. Instead, I was petrified that I would sprout horns or go ape-shit and kill someone. Demons were not the soft and cuddly type. What if it was like in the movies with werewolves and one day I just woke up growly and lusting after blood?

I had so many questions that I didn't know who to ask. Lucifer would probably know a lot of the answers, but how could I tell him that Lily was Lilith? At least, that's what all signs were pointing to.

Hell, maybe he already knew.

I threw on my purple terry cloth robe and opened the bathroom door. I nearly jumped out of my skin seeing my father sitting on the side of my bed looking through the papers I had left there. He was lucky I hadn't decided to walk out of my bathroom naked.

"Dad, what are you doing here?" I asked, rushing over to the bed and starting to gather the papers and folders.

He didn't look up from the papers he was examining. He just sat there and stared at them in his hand in silence. I gathered what he didn't have in his hands and plopped next to him. I didn't know if I was more anxious about him seeing the papers or seeing the bruises that covered my face. At least he couldn't see the ones covering my torso.

"Please say something." My hands were shaking and I felt my eyes burning.

This was not how I wanted to tell him that Lily might have been a lie. Had she even loved him? He didn't talk about her often, but when he did it was evident he had loved her so damn much. When he did talk to me about her, he always had a wistful look in his eyes, which was always odd to see on his typically stoic face.

The possibility of her deceiving him was inconceivable. It would break his heart all over again. How do you mend the devil's heart? It was impossible. It would ruin him.

"Oliver called me last night. He wanted to know if on the last night in Hawaii I would be okay with them coming to join us. He said they wanted it to be a surprise. Why did you tell your boyfriends that you're in Hawaii? They're supposed to protect you. How can they protect you when you're putting your nose in places it doesn't belong?" He lifted his head to look at me then, his expression changing immediately from sad to angry.

He lifted his hand to my face and ran his fingers along my swollen nose, busted lip, and the dark bruise around my eye. I looked down at my hands as a tear slid down my cheek.

"Who did this to you?" His voice held a note of violence. He was pissed and he hadn't even seen the rest of my body.

"Just let it be. It's done and over with." I stood, wincing at the pain in my side with the quick movement. "It's my own fault."

I made my way to my bag that Ava had kindly placed on my desk and dug out some comfortable clothes. I went into the bathroom and changed, coming back out in pajama pants and one of Asher's T-shirts.

"Let me see your stomach." Lucifer was still sitting on my bed, papers in his hand. He must have remained in that same position while I changed.

I twisted my mouth in concern. He paid too much attention. Of course he would know that my face was not the only thing that had been beaten to a pulp.

I sighed and stood in front of him, lifting my shirt to reveal my stomach. He took a sharp inhale of breath and my head swam as the room filled with anger. He was going to murder John, I was sure of it. Maybe he deserved it.

"Danica Marie. I'm going to ask you again, who did this?" The initial swell of his anger receded a bit and he stared up at me.

I pulled my shirt back down and gingerly sat back down next to him. All the movement was starting to make me feel stiff. Instead of telling him directly who had beaten the shit out of me, I changed the subject back to the files.

"I needed to do this on my own," I said gesturing to the files on the bed. "I had to know, to confirm it. Did you know?"

He placed the papers he had been holding for an eternity behind him and then ran a hand through his hair. "I did not. How did you get these files? Is that how you were beaten?"

"I broke into John Adamson's office while John Junior was having his annual Spring break party." I played with the hem of my shirt. "Are you mad?"

"I'm not mad. I'm disappointed in you. You should've told me this sooner. How long have you known?" He stood from the bed and walked over to my dresser, flipping open my jewelry box.

"About three weeks. Michael told Tobias that we couldn't tell you. Something about it might make you go crazy," I said softly. It had seemed like logical reasoning at the time, but now I wasn't so sure.

He made an annoyed noise in his throat. He and Michael weren't the best of friends.

He returned to sit next to me with a necklace in his hand. It was a pendant necklace he had given my mother that had a lily encrusted with the tiniest of diamonds. He gazed down at it in the palm of his hand as if he were trudging through a memory.

"The papers in my file say I'm angel and demon but then say it's all inconclusive. What does that mean?" My voice was shaking.

"It means nothing. You're still you. Just because you know this new information about yourself doesn't change who you are in your heart. Does it?" He held out the necklace and I opened my palm for him to drop it into. I wrapped my fist around it, my knuckles turning white, the pendant digging into my skin.

My tears were falling freely now. My dad pulled me into a hug as gently as possible, his hand rubbing my back. I hadn't wanted it to happen this way, him finding out about Lilith. Now I was glad it had because it was just us. The both of us would deal with the deceit together.

After several minutes of silence, he finally spoke. "What should I tell your boyfriends? I told Oliver I'd get back to him. If you won't tell me who beat you up, maybe you'll tell them."

Shit. I almost forgot about that. What was I going to tell them? Now there was no hiding the fact that Hawaii had been a fabrication. Maybe my dad could heal my bruises. They would never have to know. I was too scared to ask him to add to the lie.

"I should just let you take care of it. Anything else going on that I should know about?" He raised his eyebrows.

"Well, now that you mention it, Ava got arrested for breaking into a house." A small smile turned up the corners of Lucifer's lips. "She told me she was at home and she felt the overwhelming urge to go there, but doesn't really remember much."

Lucifer's face fell and he stood abruptly. "I need to go."

"What is it? Is it that demon that was in our kitchen three weeks ago? Ava thought she was in love with him. What kind of demon is he?" I spewed my questions out in quick succession, already sensing he was about to take off.

Whatever it was, it wasn't good. He seemed panicked.

He grabbed the stack of papers and folders, and without another word, he vanished. I wished he would have healed me before he left.

THEY SAY honesty is the best policy, but I'm not so sure about that. Did I really need to tell them that I lied to them or what I had found out? Maybe I'd just tell them some of the truth. I didn't plan on telling them I was half demon. I could barely tell myself.

I took a deep breath and pressed the green call button on Olly's contact information. He'd probably take the news the best. He could have the honor of telling the other two.

"Dani! How's paradise?" Olly answered, his voice full of excitement.

Now I really felt like my demon blood was at work inside of me. Why did I think going all secret agent was a good idea? I was fine, up until Olly's cheerful voice smacked me back to reality, and the fact that they were angels and I wasn't hit me across the face.

Fuck. I needed a drink. Maybe ten drinks.

"Hey there. What are you up to?" I laid back on my bed and stared at the ceiling fan as it slowly spun round and round.

My stomach muscles pulled tight and I twisted my face to keep a sound from escaping. I needed to go get my ice packs out of the freezer. The hopes of my dad coming back and healing me were diminishing. My calls and texts to him sat unanswered.

"Just up here on the roof with Tobias, helping Asher with his garden. Here, let me put you on speaker." Before I could object, I heard fumbling. "I've never planted anything before. It's pretty neat, but dirty."

"I'll show you dirty," I heard Asher say in the background. "Hey,

Danica! Where are those bikini pics? Ow!" He grunted like he had been hit.

"Excuse him, he has no respect. How are you doing? Getting lots of rest I hope." Tobias, always the concerned one. He had good reasons to always be concerned about me. I acted first, thought later. Story of my life.

"I want to preface this conversation by saying that I'm sorry. Lucifer told me Olly called." I pulled up my shirt as I spoke and looked at the bruises.

"Damn. Who would have thought the devil wouldn't be able to keep a secret," Olly said.

"I'm not in Hawaii." I flinched before I could even hear their reactions.

In my mind, I could see them react. Tobias would stop whatever he was doing and stare at the phone in disbelief before putting his hands on his hips. He'd then give the phone his 'teacher' look. The one that sends chills to the very depths of souls.

Asher would hesitate for a second before continuing whatever he was doing, avoiding the anxiety a confrontation might bring.

Olly, well he was the wildcard of the group, more of a Switzerland type. That was the reason I had called him and not the other two.

"Where are you then?" Olly asked, uncertainty in his voice.

"My house. There was never a Hawaii trip." Silence. Complete silence. "There was something I needed to take care of."

"You lied to us? Why would you do that?" I was surprised that Olly was the one who spoke, hurt evident in his voice. He was supposed to be my Switzerland.

I let out a sigh and winced as I sat up against my headboard, the bruises on my torso protesting. "I couldn't exactly take three angels to a high school party, could I? Plus if John saw Asher, he might have known I was up to something."

"What do you mean if John saw me? What did you do?" Asher was closer to the phone now, his voice coming through the speaker loud and clear.

"I think the more important question is why she lied just to go to a high school party by herself," Tobias said.

"I broke into John Senior's office and helped myself to some medical files." I bit my lip and held the phone slightly away from my ear, already knowing by now that I was going to get a reaction.

"You did what?" Tobias's raised voice sounded like he was about to have a heart attack. "I thought we had all agreed to wait for Michael to give us directions on our next steps."

"Plans change," I mumbled into the phone. My life had certainly changed.

"We're coming," Tobias said and then the line went dead before I could protest.

My heart thudded in my chest, making my bruises ache even more. John didn't kill me, but I was pretty sure I was about to die at the hands of Tobias.

Twenty minutes later, they knocked on the door. Having angel wings had its perks, like lightning fast travel.

I slid off the barstool I had been waiting on and walked to the door like I was marching to my reckoning. Or more like hobbling towards it.

When I opened the door, they stood there with bags in hand. I met their gazes head on, because there was no hiding my swollen nose and the bruised flesh on my face.

They didn't look happy to begin with, and as they took in my face, their eyes widened. The frowns on their faces grew deeper the longer they stared.

I moved out of the way and they walked in without a word.

I shut the door behind them, then made my way to the couch and sat down gingerly. I felt like I had done one thousand sit-ups. Maybe if I had, I would have had abs of steel and John would have been the one in pain.

Their silence was killing me. Asher sat on my left and Olly on my right. Tobias sat in the armchair.

"What the hell happened?" Tobias finally asked. It was hard to tell what he was feeling. My guess was that there was anger simmering under the surface, along with concern.

"To make a long story short, this was three months in the making," I said, gesturing to my face with a sigh. I looked at the coffee table in front of me, wishing it was a portal away from the scrutinizing gazes.

Olly brought his hands to my face and they began to glow. Warmness spread across my cheeks, nose, and around my eyes. The dull ache that had settled across it slowly ebbed and my face was left feeling like I had just had a relaxing facial at a spa.

"Did that John kid do this?" Asher asked, balling his fists in his lap.

His eyes kept darting around the room, as if he was looking for something. The last thing I needed was for any of them to kill John. We all knew that killing a human without an order would mean falling as an angel.

I nodded. "You don't need to go and defend my honor."

I lifted my shirt and Asher's eyes widened. He clenched his jaw. Olly frowned down at me and placed his hands over my bruised ribs, healing them. I bit my lip and raised my shirt to expose my breast.

"I'm going to kill that motherfucker." Asher stood and walked out of the house, slamming the door behind him. I didn't know where he thought he was going; it wasn't like he knew where John lived.

I looked back at the door. I hadn't meant to set off Asher. He had been doing so well lately. Just another fuck up to add to my ever-growing list.

Tobias moved to the couch next to me, taking my hand. Olly healed the bruise on my breast before placing a kiss on it. Thank God it was healed; it had been the worst of them all.

"I'll go make sure he's all right," Olly said, standing and walking out the door.

"He could've killed you, and for what? Was risking your life really worth what you were after?" Tobias's eyes searched mine as if trying to understand me and my less than stellar choices.

Sometimes I didn't even understand my choices, and I was the one who made them.

I leaned back on the cushions and shut my eyes. Was it worth it to reveal myself? It was, but it wasn't. I was torn into a million little pieces. I was inconclusive, whatever that meant.

"My dad took the files." I left it at that. No need to get into specifics until I knew more.

I felt Tobias shift next to me and then he pulled me towards him. I kept my eyes shut because I didn't want to see the disappointment on his face. He ran his fingers through my hair and kissed my forehead.

"So Lucifer knows now? Michael warned us not to tell him. At least not yet."

"There was an autopsy report for her. My dad buried her, or at least he thinks he did. I wonder..." I stopped speaking as the thought came to my mind. I must be more demon than angel, because no angel would consider digging up a grave.

Would they?

"If you're thinking about what I think you're thinking about... No," Tobias said firmly, reading my mind. Or maybe he read the look on my face.

"We'd know for sure. Well, at least that she really isn't dead. Lilith or not, I need to know. Wouldn't you want to know if it was your mother?" I opened my eyes and his brown eyes stared sparkling back at me.

He leaned forward and brushed his lips over mine. I pulled him closer and deepened the kiss, my mouth opening and allowing his tongue to explore. His lips moved to my jaw and slowly kissed their way to my ear.

"I think that, later, a spanking is in order," he said before sucking the skin right under my ear. My nipples hardened and rubbed against my T-shirt. He sure talked a big spanking game, but had yet to bend me over his lap. I wasn't opposed to the idea; the thought mostly made me giggly.

Tobias moved back to my lips and stood, placing a knee on the couch and then straddled me. I moaned into his mouth. The weight of his body on top of mine increased the wetness already forming between my legs.

There was something so intimate about him being on top of me like he was. No wonder guys liked to be straddled; it was fucking hot.

My hands slipped under his shirt and ran up and down his spine. He made a noise in his throat and moved his lips to my neck, suckling the skin just shy of leaving a hickey.

"We're gone for five minutes and he's already trying to get in her pants," I heard Asher mumble as the front door clicked shut. Olly chuckled in response.

Tobias continued to kiss my neck and moved a hand under my shirt, cupping a breast in his hand. He moved his thumb across the hard nipple and I shuddered with pleasure. I glanced over as Asher and Olly sat down as if we weren't dry humping in front of them.

It still blew my mind that they were content with sharing me. I wouldn't be able to share them with another woman, that was for sure. Did that make me a hypocrite?

"Olly and I have decided that John deserves to get his ass kicked. He'll do the ass kicking part since I can't risk being sent back to the high court. Are you two in or are you going to stay and suck each other's faces off?" Asher had an amused lilt to his voice. It was nice to hear considering he had left the room in a murderous rage not long ago.

I groaned as Tobias pulled his hand away and looked over at Asher. "Can't it wait?"

"Can it *wait*? I am vengeance," Asher said in a lower register. He stood back up from his place on the couch.

Tobias made a strangled noise in his throat and moved off of me. "Well, now I have to go since you think you're Batman and just ruined the mood. I sometimes feel like a babysitter to grown ass men." I really felt like he should have added "and a woman."

"Well, if you really feel that way, then I guess you can be my Alfred, Olly can be my Robin, and Danica can be my Catwoman."

"I don't know about that." I scrunched my nose.

Asher grabbed my hand and pulled me off the couch. He planted a wet kiss on my lips that I had to wipe off with my hand. I both loved and hated when he did that. "Alfred, why don't you make us some dinner? We need sustenance for all the ass kicking and fucking we're going to do tonight."

I lightly smacked Asher's chest and squirmed out of his arms. He had been very playful lately and the troubled look that was usually in his eyes had lessened. It was definitely still there though, like when he walked in and saw me beaten.

"There's no food in the house, unless you want hot pockets or a sandwich." I was slightly embarrassed by my food selection. It wasn't like I'd had time to go to the grocery store. What I had was what Ava picked up.

"Then what have you been eating?" Tobias sounded concerned. If he didn't mellow out he was going to give himself a coronary or a head of gray hair.

"Hot pockets, cereal, sandwiches, and takeout. The usual."

Olly jumped up and faced Tobias. "Let's go out to eat then. Please, *Dad*, we never go out to eat!"

Tobias lunged for him and put him in a headlock. "Take it back or I'll spank your ass too." Tobias made a move to try to smack him on the ass and he twisted to avoid his hand, laughing hysterically.

Were they all on something? They were supposed to be mad at me for going rogue and getting my ass kicked, not acting like teenage boys. I half expected to get a lecture on the finer points of thinking and using common sense.

"So you guys aren't mad at me?" My question caused Tobias to finally let Olly go.

"There's no use in being mad. It's done and over with," Asher said, sitting on the arm of the couch. "Now go get changed so we can go eat."

CHAPTER 3

ASHER

I knew the second my feelings escalated with Oliver. I had just damn near had a panic attack over Danica's bruised body. I loved the girl to pieces, would give my life for her again if necessary, but she was going to give me an ulcer.

Not that I could get an ulcer now.

The result of the exposé of her bruises was that I had badly wanted to punch or destroy something. My heart had been pounding at an uncomfortable level and my body was thrumming for a release, and not a sexual one. Shit would be so much simpler if *that* was the case.

My eyes had darted from the television, to the decorative bowl in the center of the coffee table, and then to the lamp on the end table. All prime stock for smashing to pieces.

Instead of destroying the living room, I had rushed out of the house and punched the shit out of the brick siding. I hadn't been able to stop myself. I'd needed to feel something other than the panic in my chest.

The impact had brought me back to reality, but in the process it also did a number on my hand. My skin was ripped to shreds, blood seeping out of my knuckles. It fucking hurt like it had gone through a meat grinder.

I was cradling my hand, trying to calm myself down, when I felt Oliver touch my shoulder to alert me to his presence. He was as silent as a ninja when he wanted to be.

His touch was gentle, just like *all* his touches were.

Fuck him and his gentle touches.

They did something to me, and not just ease my anxiety. Every time he touched me it was like he was touching my soul or some shit. My soul was already confused as it was. He just made it worse.

His touching had increasingly gotten more and more frequent and definitely not just at night when he was keeping away my anxiety. He'd touch me anytime he was near. His favorite move was brushing his arm against me as he passed or as he stood at my side.

And damn if I didn't start touching him too. I found myself moving closer to him when we were in the same room. Purposefully placing myself next to him on a couch or at a table.

I never really considered a relationship with a man before. Hell, I never considered being part of a polyamorous relationship either. Yet here we all were. There was a strange connection between us, where we felt drawn to each other.

Oliver was not my type at all. He was all doe-eyed and virginal, while I had the experience of at least ten men. I didn't know how to be gentle or take things slow. Hell, I would have slept with Danica on our first date if he and his idiot friend hadn't interrupted us.

"Let me see your hand." The fucker didn't even wait for my response but took it anyway, making my pulse speed up. He was supposed to ease my anxiety, not increase it.

I had my self-healing ability back, but it didn't exactly work like it was supposed to. I could heal a hangnail and that was my limit. Healing took complete mental and physical awareness, which I was running low on. I might have gotten my wings back, but normalcy still eluded me.

But at least I could fly again.

His hands started glowing the color of a setting sun, and I watched as my skin knitted back together and the bruising faded away. It was a handy trick to be able to heal others. Archangels were born to do it;

the rest of us could only heal ourselves unless we went through years of study. It involved a lot of inner peace and positive thoughts. No wonder I couldn't even heal myself.

He kept ahold of my hand and pulled me towards the water hose attached to the house. He turned on the spicket and grabbed the end of the hose, running the cold water over my hand to rinse the blood off.

I didn't speak as he held my hand in his palm and rubbed his thumb over my knuckles, working the blood out of the creases. He was so focused, his blue eyes sparkling as he worked.

I felt like a fucking chick with hearts in my eyes when I was around him. When he and Tobias showed up on my rooftop earlier in the afternoon, I had seriously looked down at myself and regretted the ripped and dirty work clothes I was wearing. It was similar to how I had felt the first time I had Danica over to my house. The need to make a good impression was strong.

Punching a wall was probably not making a good impression, but he continued to come to me, to lock the demons back in their cages.

It was taking an awfully long time for him to clean my hand. I should have helped, but was content with him touching my hand in such an intimate way.

Where the fuck did this guy come from anyways? He had been a complete bastard to Danica and then did an abrupt one-eighty, seemingly overnight. If it had been anyone else I would have questioned their intentions, but Oliver was horribly naïve.

That was why I decided that it wasn't just Danica who needed protection, but him too. I would protect him from the world. However, I wasn't willing to protect him from the true threat. *Me.*

"I want to kick that guy's ass," I finally said. I had been wracking my brain for what to say after my epic meltdown of bloody proportions. "Who beats the shit out of a woman like that?"

A beaten woman was what had caused me to fall in the first place. I had snapped at the sight of her in the hallway of an apartment building I was a security guard at. My mission was explicit: get her to a battered women's shelter, file a police report. Instead, when the man had come out of the apartment after her, I had beaten the shit out of him. That wouldn't have been a problem but then I threw him off the fifth-floor balcony.

I can't say I regretted my decision.

Olly made a non-committal noise in his throat, never taking his eyes off my hand. "You can't beat him up, it's too risky. I'll do it."

I snorted and pulled my hand away, drying it on my jeans. He wasn't a violent person. His words surprised me.

Olly rinsed his own hands off then turned off the water, hanging the hose back up.

"Do you even know how to fight?" I teased. He was much more of a lover than a fighter. He saved cockroaches for God's sake. Who saves *those?*

"I'm more into using a sword." He met my eyes and winked. What the hell was the wink for? Was he joking about his dick?

"Let me see your hand again just to make sure I healed it all the way," he said, reaching towards me again. I was pretty sure he knew he had, it was just another instance of him wanting to touch me.

I complied and he took my hand in his, gently probing the knuckles before turning my hand over and rubbing his thumb across the palm.

Fuck, that felt good. And fuck if I didn't want to kiss the motherfucker, but instead, I pulled my hand away.

"We should get back inside," I said, turning towards the door before he could touch me again.

AFTER CHANGING, we decided on a seafood restaurant on the water in Santa Barbara, since Oliver had never had seafood before. The four of us had never all gone out together, at least not to relax, and it was long overdue. With everything that had been happening, going on dates was pretty low on our priorities list.

Besides, we were long past what I would consider dating. We were right in the trenches of a committed relationship. All four of us.

We'd been through a lot. Danica and Oliver getting abducted. Oliver being forced to heal angels so they could be drained more frequently. Then there was the whole situation of my soul floating around like a jellyfish in a never-ending black abyss.

I thought being Fallen was bad, but being a lost soul was infinitely worse. There I was, for weeks, just floating in a dark void with only my thoughts as company. I thought my memories were bad now, but with no outlet like alcohol, violence, or sex, I had been a fucking mess.

Now that I had my angel wings back, things weren't much better. It's not like my memories could be erased because now they were so intertwined with who I was. Really, the only benefit was the wings; who wouldn't want to be able to fly? Traffic sucked a pair of hairy balls.

I slid into a chair next to a plexiglass wall, the sandy beach and ocean on the other side. The sun was just starting to go down and the waiters were lighting the outdoor heaters spread around the eating area.

Oliver slid into the seat next to me and placed the placemat and crayons he had grabbed at the hostess station in front of him. His old friends must have never taken him off campus much, judging by the way he was enthralled with every new experience. Coloring included.

We all watched as he emptied out the small box of four crayons and then looked up at us.

"You guys sure you don't want to color? I can go get you some. The hostess said adults can color too." He made me smile. Hell, he made us all smile.

I nudged his arm. "I'll pass, but make sure you bring that back with us and I'll hang it on my fridge, right beside your finger painting."

Oliver narrowed his eyes at me as the other two laughed. It was fun to tease him. I bet he would be fun to tease in the bedroom too. Not that I was thinking about it. Not at all.

"They sell adult coloring books. It's no different than me doodling," Danica said, shrugging. Oliver smiled at her and she winked.

"You and your doodles. You don't even need to put your name on your papers anymore, I just know which one belongs to you." Tobias opened his menu and took a drink of his water. "I want some oysters."

"Yuck. Aren't those raw?" I watched as Oliver started to shade in the pineapple in the picture. It was some kind of house for cartoon characters.

"Angel baby, can I order for you?" I asked, looking right at Oliver, who wasn't even looking at his menu yet. Knowing him, he had somehow already read the menu without even opening it. "You order the weirdest crap."

He'd probably order a plate of lemon wedges or some shit. He put the crayon down and cocked his head to the side with an incredulous look on his face.

"I do not. Food is food. Who cares what I eat?"

Last week when we ordered Chinese takeout, he had ordered brown rice. Who just eats brown rice? Brown rice tastes like cardboard.

The guy was as tall as the Jolly Green Giant and was built like an Adonis. He needed more than just rice, cantaloupe, and cookies. Sure he'd eat other things on occasion, but the list of Oliver approved foods was shorter than my dick. It was like he was scared of food, which was a shame. Seafood was going to really test his taste buds.

The restaurant did have a kids' selection, but damn if I was going to let him order macaroni and cheese and a corn dog.

The waitress arrived and raised her eyebrows at Oliver, who had just picked his crayon back up after staring me down. I couldn't blame her for the inquisitive look she was giving him, but I wanted to ask her what she was staring at. I was allowed to judge and tease him; he had seen my ass naked.

Danica and Tobias placed their orders.

"And for you, sir?" She looked down at me and made a show of running her eyes down what she could see of me before they landed back on my face.

Danica cleared her throat and was glaring daggers at the waitress. I hadn't even paid attention to the waitress up until this point, but judging by the smirk on Tobias's face, she had done the same to him.

"We'll both have the seafood pasta." I handed her the menus.

"She just openly eye-fucked all three of you," Danica said as soon as the waitress was out of earshot.

"You sound jealous," Tobias teased. "Women—or men—are allowed to check us out, aren't they?"

She made a strangled noise. "Not when they look like her."

I put my chin on my fist and stared across the table at her. Something was off about her tonight. I couldn't read people very well, but she seemed suddenly self-conscious. She was slightly hunched in her seat and had a frown across her face.

She was like that before the waitress even ogled us. It was unlike her and I didn't like it.

"She's got nothing on you. So what, she checked us out? You should see it as a compliment of your fine taste in men." I reached across the table and she took my hand. "What's going on with you?"

"Nothing," she answered quickly and squeezed my hand. "I guess I'm just PMSing."

I decided to drop it because I didn't want to touch *that* with a ten-foot pole. Tobias changed the subject and started rambling about the Dodgers.

When our appetizer arrived, Oliver's eyes nearly bugged out of his head as he examined the grand seafood platter Tobias had ordered to share. It was a sight to behold with oysters, shrimp, lobster, and crab.

"It looks like snot." He held a raw oyster in a half shell in his hand and the cocktail fork in the other. "You want me to *eat* this? What if I vomit or die? It could have worms in it."

"Have you been looking at a lot of snot lately? *Jesus*. You aren't going to vomit or die. I doubt an oyster is going to take you out. Look, Dani isn't vomiting *or* dying." I showed him how to make sure the oyster was sliding around in the shell and then tipped it into my mouth. "See? Easy."

"Can I put ketchup on it?" He eyed the oyster with uncertainty. A few people at another table were looking at him with amusement. He wasn't exactly being quiet. I was struggling not to grab his jaw and force the damn thing down his throat like he was a dog in need of his medicine.

"That's cocktail sauce, genius. Kind of defeats the purpose of having an oyster. An oyster is supposed to taste like eating the ocean. Like poetry in your mouth." Tobias ate his own oyster and then grabbed a shrimp and dipped it in the cocktail sauce. "Just try it. Be a man. You should have your man card revoked for coloring anyway."

I leaned over and whispered in Oliver's ear, "I bet watching you eat an oyster will make Dani extra horny for you."

A blush creeped up his face and the tips of his ears turned the color of the cocktail sauce. He looked over at Danica and then ate his oyster without another complaint. The table next to us clapped and I scowled at their intrusion. Oliver didn't seem to notice or he just didn't care.

He narrowed his eyes in contemplation and then grabbed another.

"What'd you say to him?" Danica asked, lifting her water and taking a drink.

"I told him that if you saw him suck down an oyster it would make you horny for him." I shrugged and took a bite of crab.

She turned her head to the side and started coughing as she choked on the water. Her eyes teared up. Tobias, who was next to her, patted her back. She continued to cough and splutter.

"Excuse me, I'm a mess," she barely managed to say. She stood and headed inside the restaurant.

"I should go make sure she's okay. After all we've been through, can't have her die choking on her damn water," I said before following her inside the noisy restaurant.

I turned the corner to the hall with the bathrooms and pushed the women's bathroom door open.

"Are you okay?" I asked, peeking my head inside. She was in an open stall and there was no one else inside.

I walked in and flipped the lock on the door. Women tended to freak out finding men in their bathrooms. Not that I had any experience with that. Nope, none at all.

I heard the toilet paper dispenser and she walked out of the stall wiping her eyes and nose.

"I swallowed wrong," she said clearing her throat several times.

I bit my lip, trying to hold back the comment I wanted to make. I had been binge watching too much of *The Office* and really wanted to say, "that's what she said."

She threw the toilet paper in the trash and then washed her hands, watching me in the mirror. She had a contemplative look on her face but said nothing as she turned around to face me.

"I just wanted to make sure you're okay. We're your guardians and all. Can you imagine us calling Lucifer and telling him you died from choking on ice water?"

"Is that why you followed me into the women's restroom and *locked* the door?" She closed the distance between us and put her hands on my chest. "My hero, saving me from the evil ice cubes."

I chuckled and put my hands over hers, moving them down to my growing erection. I had honestly followed her to check on her, but now that she brought it up, my dick was pretty happy to have her in a locked bathroom.

She stared back at me and raised her eyebrows as her hand began stroking me through my jeans. The bathroom wasn't the most appropriate place to get it on, but my dick didn't seem to care and neither did Danica.

Our lips met in a fevered kiss that left my brain feeling like mush. It was hard to put into words what kissing her was like. Whatever had been on my mind was forgotten and my sole focus was on her.

She deserved more than a quick bathroom fuck and I was about to pull away, but she was already unbuttoning my pants. We needed to be quick, but my brain wanted to kiss her for days.

I unbuttoned her pants and pulled them and her panties down past her ass. She insisted on wearing skin tight jeans so I moved her towards the sink and bent her over with her hands on the edge.

"Next time wear a dress or a skirt when we go out." I ran my hand over the smooth, milky skin of her ass and gave it a little pinch. Her breath hitched and she looked in the mirror and met my eyes.

"Next time don't follow me into the bathroom and my pants wouldn't be a problem." She cocked an eyebrow at me. She looked so damn sexy looking at me in the mirror, bent over, that I damn near came before I even got my dick out.

I pulled down my pants just enough so my cock sprung free. I put the tip against her ass, just to gauge her reaction. I hadn't broached the subject with her yet, but Toby and I had discussed it at length. She didn't need to know that though.

"I think we need some lube and foreplay for that." She bit her lip and reached her hand back to grip my cock.

I moved my dick to its intended destination and pushed the tip in. Fuck, she was tight from not being able to spread her legs wide. On second thought, she should always wear tight jeans.

"And how would you know that?" I teased her pussy by barely pushing the tip in. I gritted my teeth and felt like my eyes wanted to roll back in my head.

"I've had anal a few times," she said with a shrug.

I thrust into her with a groan and bit down on the inside of my cheek. Her words alone were enough to make me come. I wanted to question her about her experiences with that, but our time was running out.

She gripped the edge of the counter as I increased my pace. The only sounds in the bathroom were our heated breaths, the smacking of our skin, and the bustling restaurant on the other side of the door.

I was so turned on and so into what we were doing, my brain just ignored the knocks on the door. I felt my orgasm creeping up on me. I slid my hand to Danica's clit, and worked it in quick strokes until her mouth opened in a quiet scream.

As her legs went weak and her body shook with release, I came inside her, her pussy milking every last drop from me.

I leaned into her to keep myself from falling over, because God damn that was good. Whatever worries had been on Danica's mind earlier, seemed to disappear.

"People keep knocking, we better get out of here before they start peeing themselves," she managed to say between breaths.

I pulled out of her and she went into a stall to clean herself up. I heard her zip up her pants and took that as my cue to leave the bathroom. Luckily no one was standing there as I exited. It was doubtful they would say anything anyways.

When I got back to the table, Tobias raised his eyebrows and then shook his head. I bet he wished he had been the one to follow her to the bathroom.

"Is Danica okay? You were gone an awfully long time," Oliver asked, seeming to have no clue what had just gone down.

"She's definitely okay, angel baby." I slapped him on the shoulder and then left my hand there for a few seconds longer than necessary.

I was pretty certain I was going to corrupt him.

CHAPTER 4

DANICA

*G*roup dates needed to happen more often, and not just because of the impromptu bathroom sex Asher and I had. It was unexpected and quite the rush. Experiencing life like a normal person made me forget about everything else.

At least for that moment.

On the way back to Montecito, I let Tobias drive my car. Somehow, I managed to talk the angels into driving instead of flying. Olly insisted on sitting in the back with Asher, even though there wasn't much space for his legs. When I picked out my Nissan GTR, I never imagined I'd be cramming three full-sized men inside of it.

"Are we just going to go over to John's house and beat him up? Or should I text him and get him to meet us somewhere?" I asked as we drew closer to Montecito. My stomach was in knots thinking about seeing John again. If I had it my way, I'd never see him again.

"I don't think going to his house with three angels is a good idea. Maybe your old high school's parking lot? It'll be deserted," Asher suggested. I could hear him popping his knuckles in the back.

I turned and gave him a pointed look. "You aren't fighting so stop that."

"None of us should be fighting," Tobias warned as he merged onto the highway.

"How about this. You guys hold him and I'll throw the punches." It was a fair compromise. I had been the one beaten to shit by him; I should be the one to deliver the blows. Plus, I had no wings to lose.

I took my phone out and hesitated after pulling up John's contact information. Talking about kicking his ass was one thing, but actually doing it? I wasn't so sure if it was even worth it.

"What if he brings other people with him?" It was highly unlikely he'd just show up to meet me without backup. He wasn't an idiot.

"Then we kick all their asses," Asher replied and Olly agreed. I was surprised Olly was on board with the idea.

"Maybe this is a stupid idea." I closed out of the contact and put my phone in the cupholder.

So many things could go wrong. John could recognize Asher and then would know I was involved in angel business. If he already knew, he did a good job of hiding it. I couldn't risk him finding out.

"It is," Tobias mumbled under his breath.

The last thing I needed was to look over my shoulder every time I was at home. If we beat up John, he would continue to come at me. Who knew what he was capable of since he was raised by a deranged doctor.

I turned and looked at Olly and Asher in the backseat. They both jerked their hands into their laps at the same time. I raised my eyebrows and smiled at them. They really weren't fooling anyone. We saw them touching all the time. It was subtle, but it was hard to miss. Plus, Olly looked at Asher the same way he looked at me.

"I appreciate that you two want to deliver justice, but if we beat him up, then he's going to come at me worse the next time I see him. This is a small suburb. I'll probably see him on occasion." I shuddered at the thought of always wondering when John would strike next.

Asher grunted and crossed his arms over his chest, but nodded in agreement.

"What are we going to do then? It's not even close to nine yet." Olly had a point; it was too early to go back to my house.

I looked over at Tobias. "Home Depot is still open."

"No. We aren't going to do that!" Tobias sounded like he was reaching his limit of bad ideas on my part. I couldn't help it. My mind was stuck on it. I had to know if everything was true.

I turned and looked at Asher and Olly again. "How do you feel about digging up my mother's grave?"

~

I SAT cross-legged on the damp grass watching three shirtless men as they shoveled dirt over the side of the hole they were in. Angels might not sweat, but apparently they got hot. Or maybe they just wanted to give me a show. I wasn't complaining in either case.

They were all covered in dirt thanks to Olly's inability to consistently get the dirt outside the three foot by seven-foot hole they were digging. They were only about four feet deep and they'd been digging for an hour.

Of course all of this would have been easier had we told my dad about it. He could have signed paperwork to exhume the body and they would have used a backhoe to get the casket out. Going down the legal route would take way too long though, and I had a feeling he wouldn't be onboard with us digging up the love of his life.

So naturally, instead, here we were in the darkness of night digging up my mother's grave.

Totally normal activities to pass the time.

I looked over at the black granite headstone.

Lily Judith Gardner

April 30, 1975 - January 20, 2001

Viva La Vida

On both sides of her name were Viva La Vida lilies. 'Long live life' was rather fitting considering my father was practically immortal. She might even be immortal too.

"I think I'm getting a side cramp. I knew those oysters were a bad idea," Olly moaned, snapping me out of my trance. I had been doing a lot of that lately, zoning out more than usual, my mind thinking of a million different scenarios. Not something I needed more of in my life.

"I'll give you a side cramp," Asher mumbled under his breath as he dug his shovel into the dirt and flung a pile out of the hole.

I laughed at their exchange and pulled my knees to my chest, resting my chin on my folded arms. How had I gotten so lucky to have three men in my life that would do anything for me? I thought I had lost them for good, but now that they were back I didn't plan on letting them go ever again.

Unless they wanted to go.

My head was still spinning from the information they came back from heaven with. All signs pointed to my mother being *the* Lilith. If her casket was empty, I would be ninety-five percent sure of it. The only true confirmation would have to come from the woman herself. If she were still alive, did I even want to meet her?

The fact that this was all part of some end of the world prophecy made things a little bleaker. At least that's what I *assumed* "saving the light from the dark" meant. Whoever decided it might be up to me, had to be on some serious crack.

"I don't think I was made for manual labor," Olly said, flopping down next to me and leaning back on his forearms. I hadn't even noticed he had climbed out.

"The hole wasn't big enough for three of us anyways." Tobias had his back to us but I could imagine him rolling his eyes.

"That's what she said." Asher laughed like it was the funniest thing in the world. I sincerely hoped he wasn't going to start saying that phrase all the time.

Olly sat up and put his arm around my waist, pulling me closer to him. I leaned back and tried to relax.

A lot was riding on this little field trip to the cemetery. The files were one thing, but verifying if she was in her grave was the real proof I needed. It would also mean my father was duped twenty years ago into falling in love and having me. I was pretty sure hell would implode if it were true.

Lucifer adored Lily. Her betrayal would most likely break him in a way I didn't want to be near him for.

"I'm worried about you Dani." Olly put his lips to my temple. "I wish what I gave you was enough." He was referring to his ability to calm people's nerves with his touch. It worked for Asher, but not for me, at least not as much as I needed it to.

Before I was expelled from Montecito High and sent to the Angel Academy, I was blissfully unaware of what the true hardships in life were. All along I thought hardship was homework, suspensions and detentions, and a seldom seen father. Those were the hardships teenagers *should* have to face.

Now I felt the weight of the world on my shoulders and I didn't quite know what to do with that. I didn't even know what the weight of the world entailed just yet.

"We hit something," Tobias called out, his head the only thing visible. "Did you want us to look first?"

I nodded in response and then realized he couldn't see me. "Yeah." It was eerily silent besides the sounds of scraping and prying coming from the hole.

"Holy shit," Asher said. "Oliver, get her back to the house."

My heart seemed to stop for a few beats before beating wildly in my chest. I jumped up, but Olly grabbed me around the waist and started leading me towards my car. He had an unfair advantage of height, weight, and angel strength. He easily pulled me away.

"It's my mother's grave. I deserve to see whatever it is that's in there!" I yanked away from him when we got to the car, which was a short distance away.

Olly reached forward and I stepped back. I was acting unreasonable considering I didn't even know what was in the casket. They wouldn't have just sent me away unless it was serious, but at the same time it better be a damn bomb.

He ran his hand over his face and frowned back at me, an uncommon sight from him. He stepped forward and put his hands on either side of me against the car, trapping me.

"Sometimes we don't like what's best for us." I narrowed my eyes at his serious tone. "Sometimes what's best for us can end up changing our lives forever. Now let's do what Asher asked."

I looked up into his blue eyes which seemed a shade darker than their usual ocean blue color. I bit my lip and looked down at his lips, his bottom slightly bigger than the top, just begging to be kissed. Now wasn't the time or the place.

I pushed him away and opened the door, sliding into the driver's seat. Olly walked around and climbed in, sliding the seat back so he'd have more leg room. He hadn't asked to drive my car again; I think he was nervous after our run-in with a truck full of Fallen.

We rode to my house in silence. When we got inside he followed me upstairs to my room.

"How long do you think they're going to be gone?" Olly asked, looking around my room and walking over to a large bookshelf. He picked up a few pictures on the shelf and examined them.

"Probably a while. They aren't just going to leave an open hole." I sat down on the edge of my bed and watched as he squatted down and pulled a box from the bottom shelf. "You sure are nosy. What if I have top secret love letters from past boyfriends in there?"

He shrugged. "Your past boyfriends have nothing on your current boyfriends. Did you save notes from your boyfriends?"

"Of course I did. They're in my closet somewhere though. A well written note is something to be cherished. People just don't write each other notes anymore." It was true, I had saved every note ever passed between not only me and Ava, but anyone else too. It was fun to look back at them to see what ridiculous things they wrote.

"I know I've been in your room at school before, but that doesn't count. This is your actual room. The one you grew up in, right?" I nodded in response as he lifted the lid off the box and his face lit up. He emptied the box on the floor and grabbed a Ken doll.

How embarrassing.

"Just so we're clear, these are from when I was a kid." I sat on the floor next to him and grabbed a naked Barbie I had given a bad haircut to. "Poor Jessica. No one told me the hair on these things didn't grow back."

"Jessica? They have names? Are you sure they're from when you were a kid? You still have them," he teased.

"It's hard to get rid of something you spent a lot of time playing with. And yes, I named them all. You are holding Jessica's super rich, trust fund boyfriend, Trent. He likes long walks on the beach, working out, and kissing Jessica under the stars."

He raised an eyebrow, his eyes twinkling in amusement, and looked at me. "Kissing? That's it? With these abs, you'd think she'd be in his pants." He slid the board shorts that were on the doll off and laughed. "Although he doesn't have much to work with."

"I remember the first time I saw a penis, I freaked out. I thought everyone had vaginas because Trent looked just like Jessica. They still had the Barbie equivalent of sex though. Face smashing." I grabbed his doll and smashed his face into the Barbie. If they were real people there would have been lost teeth and bruised faces. Maybe a concussion or brain bleed too. "Trent really knew how to give it to her."

Olly laughed and laid back on the carpet, lacing his fingers behind his head. "I feel like I missed out on pivotal developmental things, like toys and coloring. Going to school. Other things. Instead I just woke up one day."

I set the dolls down and swiveled towards him. "I think that makes you intriguing. I know we poke fun at you a lot, but I hope you know it's because we love you."

"I know that. I just feel like I have all this knowledge about my world, but when it comes to this one, I'm an idiot. I'm a virgin in every sense of the word." He was avoiding my eyes, a faint blush blooming on his freckled cheeks.

"You aren't an idiot and there's nothing wrong with being a virgin." There was a long silence and my mind started to wander back to the cemetery.

"Do you want to have sex?" He cleared his throat. "With me?"

Him asking was a shocker. I thought it would just kind of happen one day. I did want to have sex with him, every time I saw him. Despite having frequent sex with Asher and Tobias both separate and together, Olly was the missing piece of the puzzle. We had waited long enough.

Originally I hadn't made any moves because a small part of me didn't trust him. But now, it was hard not to trust him with every fiber of my being. If he happened to be playing a long game of deceit for the Divine then I'd cut off his dick.

With a butter knife.

Making out and dry humping each other was driving me mad. I wanted to be respectful of him and his need to "research enough so I know what I'm doing" (his words, not mine), but being left in a constant state of arousal by him was frustrating. I was glad we were finally on the same page.

I crawled over to him and sat on his thighs. I was more than ready after the little sex-capade with Asher.

He sat up and looked at me with a serious expression before placing his hands on my thighs and capturing my lips with his. It was the type of kiss that made me want to live attached to his mouth. Sweet and gentle.

That was short-lived though. He grabbed my hips as he pulled my bottom lip between his. His mouth began working against mine in a rush of hormones and need. I could feel his hard length straining against his pants.

"This is really happening," he whispered as his mouth slid to the sensitive skin below my ear. It was my favorite spot to be kissed and all three of them knew it opened up my floodgates. I moaned and grinded my hips against him.

His hands slid under my shirt and I grabbed the hem and pulled it over my head. He reached behind me, unclasping my bra before ripping it off and flinging it across the room. He pushed me back a little on his thighs and stared down at my exposed breasts.

This was only the second time he had been up close and personal with them, and this time he was sober. The last time was months ago after we made the poor decision to play Never Have I Ever. Since then he had only seen them if he was watching me with the others. Which had only been a few times.

"You're perfect." He slid his thumbs over my nipples and pulled me back towards him, lowering his mouth and biting one gently.

"Oliver," I breathed, my eyes closing and my fingers gripping onto his hair. We had months of foreplay leading up to this moment, which made every touch of his hands or lips that much more potent.

I just hoped that if Asher and Tobias came back in the middle of this distraction from real life, that they wouldn't interrupt us from our moment together. This was his moment.

I fumbled to get his pants undone and my fingertips connected with the head of his cock.

"Fuck, that feels so good," he mumbled around my nipple. I let out a breathy laugh at his sudden use of the word fuck. We needed to start a swear jar for Asher; he was a bad influence.

Olly grabbed the back of my legs and stood up with me wrapped around his middle. He walked towards the bed, setting me down. He took off his shirt and slid his pants and boxers down as he kicked off his shoes.

"How is your cock just as beautiful as you are?" I gripped him at his base and pumped him a few times before he pushed me back on the bed and took off my jeans.

He kissed his way down my stomach, occasionally scraping his teeth across the skin. His hands slid under the waistband of my panties and pulled them off. All I really wanted was for him to be inside of me, where I had been yearning for him for so long. I trusted him completely. He may have been a teensy bit of an asshole when we first met, but he had more than redeemed himself.

He was about to redeem himself even more by putting his mouth between my legs.

He planted kisses on my thighs and along my slit before his tongue dipped into the wet heat begging to be tasted. I arched into him and let out a satisfied sigh. He licked the length of me from bottom to top before swirling his tongue over my clit.

I threaded my fingers in his hair as he brought me closer and closer to an orgasm. I gripped my comforter as he slid two fingers into me and began pumping them at the same pace as the flick of his tongue. *Good lord.* How was he so good at this already?

My climax crashed into me with such force that my ears rang and there was a rush of wet heat between my legs. I pushed at Olly's head before he killed me and managed to push him on his back to straddle him, his dick nestled in my folds.

I cupped his cheek. "Are you sure you're ready for this? It's a big step."

"This is perfect. You're perfect." He turned his head and kissed my palm.

I leaned forward and kissed him gently as I lined him up with my opening and slowly lowered onto his length. He let out all the air in his lungs with a groan. In one swift movement, he flipped us and nestled himself between my legs.

He moved with long, slow strokes that left me yearning for more. How we had managed to wait this long was still baffling to me. It sure had taken every ounce of *my* willpower not to throw myself at him every chance I got.

He buried his face in the crook of my neck as his thrusts gradually increased in urgency. I dug my nails into his shoulder blades where his wings usually appeared.

He growled deep in his throat. "Again."

I felt another orgasm building at the sounds of his grunts and growls. The sounds were so primal coming from him. I arched my back, my clit rubbing against his pelvis every time he thrust.

"Oh, Oliver." I dug my nails into him as my orgasm hit me hard, my pussy clenching around him.

He gave one last thrust, spilling himself inside of me. His lips brushed over mine as he came down from his high.

"I love you." He put his forehead against my sweaty one.

"I love you too." I ran my fingers up and down his spine.

Once he'd regained his breath, he rolled off of me and pulled me towards him, tucking me into his side. I put my hand on his chest and threw a leg over his thigh.

"That was amazing. Are you doing okay?" I lightly patted his chest.

"Yes. That was better than chocolate chip cookies if I'm being honest."

I let out a half moan, half laugh. "Nice to know how I rank against cookies."

After a few more minutes of recovery, Olly put his hand over mine. "Would you tell me if it was bad?"

What kind of question was that? I'd clearly had two orgasms, which was a testament to whatever research he had performed. Maybe he had a blow-up sex doll for practice. I wouldn't have been surprised.

I propped myself up on my elbow and looked down at him. "I would. You aren't though. It's only going to get even more amazing."

We heard footsteps on the stairs but didn't move. A rap of knuckles knocked on the door and then the door slowly opened. Both Tobias and Asher stopped in their tracks when they saw Olly and I buck naked on top of the covers. Neither of us moved to cover up, although after finding my dad in my room after a shower, I probably should have been more concerned at who was at my bedroom door.

"It's about damn time," Asher said, a grin spreading across his dirt-smeared face.

I rolled my eyes and got up from the bed. I felt their eyes watching me as I walked into the bathroom and shut the door. I was still trying to figure out how having three boyfriends was supposed to work. Would one of them get jealous one of these days and just leave?

I cleaned up and walked back into the room, finding all three men lounging on my bed. Olly had put his pants back on. Their eyes were on me again as I purposely swung my hips a little more than usual and bent over to grab my clothes off the floor.

"That ass deserves an award," Tobias murmured. "Hurry up and put some clothes on before I come over there and have my turn with it."

After pulling on my clothes, I joined them on the bed, letting Tobias pull me into his lap. He still had dirt on him, but I wasn't about to complain.

"What was in the grave?" I asked, turning so I could look at Tobias. I usually deferred my questions to him because he was most likely to know the answers. Plus, he was kind of the leader of our group. I wouldn't be caught dead telling him that though.

I fiddled with my hands, nervous about what his answer would be. I had a sickening feeling in my stomach. Olly had distracted me for a while, but now the unease was back.

Asher looked at Tobias in some kind of silent communication. It seemed they were deciding who was going to tell me what they had found. Their silence spoke volumes.

"Was it empty or was she in it?" I sighed and ran my hand through my hair. Where had my hair tie gone?

"The grave was empty except for a symbol painted with blood. At least we think it was blood." Asher handed over his cell phone that had a picture pulled up. I took it gingerly in my hands as if it might break. I frowned at the image of the letter C.

"Why a C? What does it mean?" I handed the phone to Olly. His eyes widened and he zoomed in and then back out.

"It's not a C, it's a crescent moon. There are many rumors and beliefs here on Earth about the origins and location of Lilith. Almost all of them in some way incorporate the night or darkness. A crescent moon is a common symbol that humans use for her. Interesting she would choose to use it like that," Olly said. He looked over at me and handed the phone back to Asher. "But she can't be Lilith. You're half human. Besides, a demon and an archangel having a baby? I don't think so."

My eyes widened and I looked down at my lap. They thought I was half human because that's what my father and I always thought. Now, it seemed I wasn't. I should tell them about the medical files, but I was scared of what they might say or do. I wasn't sure they'd take well to knowing they'd been fucking a demon.

"What is it Dani?" Asher asked softly.

"Nothing, just a lot to process. I don't think we'll ever know the whole story unless we actually talk to her. It's probably not safe though, considering she's also most likely behind whatever was planned with the angel blood." I finally looked up and met his eyes. He didn't look worried often, but a small crease had appeared between his brows.

"What was in the medical files you stole?" *Crap.* I never had told them what was in the files, just that I had stolen them.

I looked back down again and silence filled the room for several awkward minutes. They were waiting for me to talk. What if I never talked? Would we sit there in silence for eternity?

"Danica." Tobias squeezed my hip and put his chin on my shoulder. "We're in this together. No secrets."

I sighed and cleared my throat, as if that would give me some magical ability to find my voice. "My dad is obviously an angel. My blood work was inconclusive."

I shut my eyes briefly and opened them, hoping by chance that we'd moved on from our conversation and the next question would never come.

"And your mother?" Tobias asked gently, his thumb moving reassuringly back and forth across my hip.

"There was only her autopsy results."

"You're not telling us everything." Asher looked straight at me, frowning.

Yeah, I was omitting some facts.

"Everything pointed to her being human. Whether or not that was a fabrication, well, we'd have to find Dr. Adamson and ask." I snapped my mouth shut and wiggled out of Tobias's lap, causing him to grunt as my ass hit his dick. "I'm tired. Can we just go to sleep?"

No one argued with me, thankfully sensing that the conversation was over and I wasn't going to say more. I just wasn't ready to let that tiny piece of information out into the world yet.

CHAPTER 5

DANICA

I wasn't supposed to have any nightmares with Asher around. I had gone to sleep feeling relief that he was around, sleeping on an air mattress with Olly in my bedroom. As soon as I woke, my hair plastered to my head with sweat, my heart beating wildly, I knew that it wasn't Asher keeping the nightmares away.

It was something else.

I just wasn't ready to admit it to myself yet.

I stared up at the ceiling; something that seemed to be becoming a new hobby of mine. The deep sounds of breathing filled my ears and taunted me.

I rolled over. Faint light coming through the curtains. The sun was just starting to rise and I could hear a few birds starting their incessant chattering in the nearby trees.

I wiggled out of Tobias's arms and slipped into the bathroom to wash my face and brush my teeth. I felt dirty, like I was somehow tainted by the knowledge that my mother might have faked her own death. Why would she do something like that to her own flesh and blood? To someone who had loved her with all his heart?

I pulled on my robe and headed downstairs to the smell of bacon frying. I got to the bottom of the stairs. My father was in the kitchen cooking. It was an odd sight, seeing him preparing breakfast in jeans and a t-shirt.

He cursed as a piece of bacon popped. I laughed at his reaction and slid onto a barstool at the island.

"Good morning." He turned and looked at me, the smile he wore not reaching his eyes. He looked like he hadn't slept well. Something we had in common. "I see Oliver was able to heal you. Sorry I rushed out of here like that."

He turned back to the stove and I reached across the counter to grab a glass and the carton of orange juice sitting out. I was almost tempted to drink coffee to wake myself up, but even the smell made me want to vomit.

"Yeah, about that. Why did you rush out of here?" I took a sip and scrunched my face having taken a drink too soon after brushing my teeth.

He turned around again and let out a chuckle. "You would think by now you'd learn not to do that."

I shrugged in response. I never remembered until it was too late. He walked over to the refrigerator and got out a bottle of water to hand to me.

"I left so abruptly because when you told me about Ava, I knew exactly who had caused it. You remember that night I called you two girls prostitutes?"

I snorted. Of course I remembered that night. Who could forget the moment their dad acted like his daughter and her best friend were working girls and sent them back up to his room? It had all been a cover to keep the demon that had been in the kitchen from knowing I was his daughter.

"Well, that *was* one of my most trusted demons that I leave in charge when I'm not there. He took his new liberties the job gave him, to come here and torment people. Ava caught his eye." He shook his head and ran a hand through his hair. I noticed he wasn't wearing one of his fancy watches today.

"What about Ava? Is she in danger?" I took a steadying breath. It seemed everything I touched was in danger these days.

"Not anymore, I kicked him out of my territory in hell and took away his ability to come here. I will have one of my lawyers look into her case." He put the tongs he had been flipping bacon with down and turned to look at me.

I nodded and played with the water bottle cap on the counter.

"What's on your mind? Besides Ava," he said, breaking the silence that had settled around us.

"She really was Lilith wasn't she?" I didn't look up, fearing what his answer would be.

Several long moments passed. He cleared his throat and I looked up, meeting his stormy eyes. The intelligence in them always amazed me and also unnerved me. He had lived a long time. Would I live just as long?

"Michael is having some of his soldiers look for John to get answers. He seems to have dropped off the radar. We think the woman behind all of this is Lilith. We just can't rely on a prophecy to identify your mother." He ran a hand over his face and then through his hair. He had been doing that a lot. I never knew he had a nervous tick.

"Dad, I need to tell you something. Last night we-"

Olly appeared in the kitchen, somehow getting down the stairs and several feet into the room without being heard. I snapped my mouth shut, not wanting to discuss the potential of me being some demon-angel hybrid freak in front of the others.

It always amazed me how the largest of the three angels could appear in a room so quietly. He was so stealthy he put all superheroes to shame. And right now he was standing in only his boxers, sporting morning wood in front of my father.

"Morning." He was rubbing his eyes as he made his way to the refrigerator and stood with the door open, staring inside. He didn't seem to process the fact that the man in the kitchen was Lucifer. Maybe it was because he was dressed so casually he was unrecognizable.

My dad made a coughing noise and Olly shut the door slowly. He still looked half asleep.

"Son, you need to go upstairs and put some clothes on. Now." He raised his eyebrows and then looked down at Olly's crotch.

I couldn't help but laugh as Olly finally zeroed in on my father and his eyes widened. Now he was awake.

He left as quickly as he had arrived and my dad cracked a smile. "Why is he so easy to torment? Maybe he wasn't created for you, but for me to torment the hell out of." As if realizing what he just said, he closed his mouth and his jaw ticked.

"Created for me?" I put my chin on my fists.

He looked thoughtful for a few moments before opening his mouth again. "I think the more appropriate explanation is he was sent to you. You know how each archangel has a purpose? " I nodded. "Well, his purpose is to act as a balance."

"A balance of what?" I furrowed my brows.

"Light and dark, good and evil, love and hate. That's why he is so even in temperament."

I considered his words. "So him being an asshole when I first met him was a balance?"

"He's not perfect. All angels have a learning curve." He laughed and took a tray of biscuits out of the oven. "His just took an interesting turn."

"Since when do you cook?" The buttery scent hit my nose and my mouth watered.

"I've always been able to cook, I just haven't had the desire." He turned off all the burners on the stove. "Go get all of your boyfriends up. The food is ready."

It still amazed me that he was fine with me having more than one boyfriend. He hadn't even batted an eyelid. He had seen and heard it all apparently.

After waking up Tobias and Asher, and convincing Olly that my dad wasn't going to kill him for having a boner in the kitchen, we gathered around the dining room table. Everyone was impressed by the biscuits and gravy and the perfectly cooked bacon that was crispy but not burnt.

"What did you four do last night? Danica was about to tell me when Woody wandered into the kitchen." My dad put his fork down on his empty plate and leaned back in his chair.

Olly's cheeks turned pink and I suppressed a laugh. My dad had made it his mission to give Olly as much shit as possible and he didn't need any more ammo. He never teased or tormented Asher and Tobias.

They all looked at me, waiting for me to answer the question. I didn't think the breakfast table, where we were all still in our pajamas, was the place to tell Lucifer that we had dug up his love's grave because I was a neurotic mess.

"Danica." The warning in his voice was clear. It was that tone parents got when they knew you were hiding something and they wanted the truth, or *else*.

"Why don't you guys go upstairs and change?" I was pretty sure that my dad was going to have a less than favorable reaction to what we did last night and didn't want them to bear any of the fallout.

"What did you do?" He narrowed his eyes at me and I felt hot. How the hell did he do that? It was like he had turned up my internal thermostat a few degrees.

Tobias, Asher, and Olly stood to leave.

"Sit."

Their asses hit their chairs and they kept their eyes averted from us. They looked like scolded puppies who had been caught tearing up the house. All they needed were the shame signs.

"Dad, I don't think... let's talk alone." I stood and gave him a pleading look. I didn't know how he was going to react.

"If they were with you, then they are just as responsible. And my guess is from how all four of you are acting, that it wasn't something good." His voice was neutral, which was the scariest of all because that meant he was holding back his emotions.

I put my hands on the edge of the table and braced myself. I should have considered this last night, but I also had been hopefully optimistic that the casket wouldn't be empty and we would just pretend it never happened.

For once in my life, I went over my words in my head. I needed all the blame to fall on me, not the others.

"I made them dig up Mom's grave. It was empty and had a crescent symbol drawn in blood."

My heart was beating so hard I was certain it was about to stop working from overuse. Hearing my own words come from my mouth, made me feel sick. *We dug up a grave last night.*

The silence was deafening. My dad's jaw ticked and then he stood abruptly. I gripped the table, my knuckles turning white.

"Get out."

"What?" My voice was shaking. What did he mean, get out? Was he talking to me?

"Get. Out," he repeated, his words coming out between his clenched teeth.

I stared at him, not completely comprehending his words. I felt a hand on my arm and was led out of the dining room and upstairs. My bedroom door wasn't even shut all the way when we heard a large crash from downstairs.

WE SAT on the roof in a tight circle around the unlit fire pit. My cheeks were stained from tears. I had fucked up royally this time.

Once the noise from downstairs had stopped, we had taken our bags and gone downstairs. My dad was gone, but the dining room and living room were trashed. The table was flipped, the television was cracked with a broken lamp laying under it, and glass was everywhere. There were even singe marks marring the couch and chairs. I hadn't even known my dad was capable of producing flames.

No one had said a word. Instead, Tobias drove me back in my car, while Asher and Olly stayed to clean up a bit before flying back to Asher's place.

"He hates me." It had been hours since any of us had spoken. My voice sounded foreign to my ears.

"He doesn't hate you. He's hurt. I don't think it had anything to do with you." I was surprised at Olly's insight. "You just told him that the woman he loved was not who he thought she was."

I looked down at my nails that were almost bitten down to the quick. I never bit my nails. Until today. I frowned down at them. Wasn't I doing the same thing to them as my mother had done to my father?

"He's your father, he could never hate you. Give him some time." Tobias ran his hand over his beard and then reached for my hand. I let him take it and he ran his thumb over the ends of my fingers.

The rooftop went silent again, the only sound the noise from the street below. It was overcast, the sun hidden behind a blanket of clouds. It was fitting considering the mood.

"We should do something to take our minds off things," Olly suggested.

I looked up at him and examined his face and demeanor. Now that I knew more about him, I was going to pay closer attention. He was the least affected by what had happened. His body was relaxed and his face was content.

"Now is not the time for sex, angel baby. I know that now you popped your cherry you're going to want it all the time, but now is not that time." Asher had his chin in his hand and he looked over at Olly as he spoke.

Olly just smiled in response and then turned his attention to me. "Let's go do something."

"What did you have in mind?" I pulled out my phone and opened the document I had started listing all the things Olly hadn't experienced. It was fairly long and I started listing off all that was on the list.

"Universal Studios!" His eyes lit up and he moved to the edge of his seat. "That will cheer us right up."

"I'm not sure I'm up for faking a good time." I put my phone away and Olly's face fell. "You guys can go."

"I know you probably don't want to hear any advice right now, but keeping busy will help you keep your mind off of it. There's no point in sitting here and marinating in your unhappiness. Trust me on that."

Asher stood and stretched his arms over his head. My eyes fell on the sliver of stomach showing as his shirt lifted. So did Olly's.

I sighed and squinted up at him, the day still bright despite the overcast skies. "Are *you* going to be all right going to a place like that?"

He shrugged his shoulders and looked at Olly. "I think I'll be fine."

I'LL ADMIT IT. I was having fun, especially after my dad texted me back after I sent numerous apology texts. He said he was fine and we'd talk later. I tried to push the negative thoughts that had been running through my head away for the time being.

We walked through the gates of Hogwarts School of Witchcraft and Wizardry, and made our way along the path. I felt like I was walking up to Hogwarts itself.

We walked through a stone archway and into a dark and damp tunnel. Asher and Olly walked in front and Asher stepped closer to Olly, their arms connecting as they walked.

Once we were back outside again under the frosted glass of the greenhouse, Asher's shoulders relaxed. I had been worried about him coming to a theme park because the sheer amount of people and the noises were overwhelming at times. Whatever Olly was doing, seemed to be keeping him, well, balanced.

We walked back inside after the winding pathway ended and into the halls of Hogwarts. Tobias and I followed Asher and Olly, who were chatting animatedly.

"What do you think is going on with them?" Tobias said in my ear so they wouldn't hear.

"Something special." I didn't quite know how to respond to his question. There were moments between them that transcended the boundaries between friends and more than friends.

Although, I guess that would be the case in a relationship like we had. Tobias wasn't like that with either of them though. He was closest to Asher, but they didn't walk around touching arms or hold hands secretly. At least, not that I had seen.

After the ride, we exited back outside and made our way towards the bathrooms. It had taken almost an hour for the ride and before that we had all drank butterbeers.

I stood in the line for the women's restroom. Someone tapped on my shoulder and I turned. The woman looked familiar, but I couldn't quite place her. Her hair was pulled back through a baseball cap. Half her face was covered in a large pair of sunglasses.

"Can I help you?" I turned my body to the side so I could still watch the line moving in front of me.

"I couldn't help but notice outside that you are with three very gorgeous men." Her voice was seductive and I felt myself leaning towards her slightly, drawn into the sound.

"I am." I wasn't sure what else to say. I didn't know if this woman was about to compliment me for having three boyfriends or give me her opinion about how wrong it was.

"You're with them all? Romantically?" Her voice sounded curious but I narrowed my eyes anyway. She noticed and held up a hand. "There's nothing wrong with it, I was just wondering."

I looked past her and outside but couldn't see the men in question anywhere. I looked back at the woman and looked at where her eyes were. I hated not seeing people's eyes.

"We are, yes." She smiled broadly at my response and then tapped her bottom lip with her pristinely manicured nail.

"My daughter is in a similar relationship, but with four men. Do you have more or just the three?"

I felt myself flush. Four boyfriends? How would I handle that? This woman had some balls talking to me about my relationship.

"Nope, just the three." I turned back around and moved forward in line. I was almost at the front.

I turned back to tell the woman she should consider minding her own business in the future but she was gone. The woman now behind me raised her eyebrows at my confused face and took hold of her little girl's hand.

"What happened to the woman that was right behind me?"

"What? I've been behind you the entire time." The woman backed up a step.

"I was talking to a woman, she had on a baseball cap, big glasses." I knew I was freaking the woman out, especially because she had her little girl with her.

"You haven't said anything until just now when you turned around. It's your turn."

I turned back around and walked to the open stall.

What the hell had just happened?

CHAPTER 6

REVE

*W*atching them together was killing me. For weeks I had endured these men that kept her from me. I hadn't seen Danica in days. It was the weekend, when she was typically at Asher's, but this weekend she was gone and so was Asher.

I sat in the dark room, waiting. I felt like a damn stalker.

In a way, I suppose I was.

It was a Sunday and there were unpacked bags in the living room. Wherever they had gone, they were back, just not here. The weekends were the only times she was here and the only time she was accessible to me.

I had followed her on my bike one evening and most of the time she was hidden away at some kind of angel military fortress. I couldn't even get within ten feet of the boundary without feeling intense pain.

This never should have happened, me falling for a woman inside of her dreams. I needed her more than she needed me. She had woken me up from my own nightmare that I lived day after day, night after night.

After my first night with her, I had tried to replicate what had happened with her, with others. It never worked and my hunger for fear would overwhelm me. I could only produce nightmares with everyone except her.

The door to the roof opened and the four I had become way too familiar with came down the stairs. They had flown wherever they had disappeared to. I watched as they sat down around the kitchen table, a pizza box placed in the middle.

I moved to the kitchen and hopped up on the countertop to be closer. No one looked in my direction. They were talking about a flood, an earthquake, and a shark.

"I wish I had recorded him screaming when that shark came out of the water. It was so plastic-looking and fake that I'm actually surprised I was the one that had to calm *you* down." Asher laughed as Oliver narrowed his eyes at him.

I watched them as they finished eating and chatted. They all seemed to be in great moods, except for Danica. She did have a smile on her face, but something was wrong. It was a fake smile.

She kept taking her hair out of her ponytail, running her fingers through it, and putting it back up. It took everything in me not to waltz over to her and bury my face in the soft strands. It was probably just as I had imagined it, soft and silky.

Tobias reached over and took her hand. He must have noticed her mood before the other two. The other two had increasingly become more and more infatuated with each other over the last several weeks. It was subtle when they were around Danica and Tobias, but I was certain they held flames for each other.

Jealousy surged in me as Tobias stood and wrapped his arms around Danica from behind. They all touched her entirely too much for my liking and I considered ripping their throats out while they slept on a nightly basis.

Weren't they supposed to be angels? What they did to her on the regular was not very holy at all. The only thing holy about them was that they stuck their dicks in her holes.

If anyone should have been shoving things inside her, it was me.

"What am I going to do if Lilith really is my mother?" she asked out of nowhere. "We need to find her. I need to know for sure."

I hopped off the counter and paced the length of the kitchen. It couldn't be that they were looking for Lilith, could it? The rumor was she disappeared from Inferna decades ago and hadn't been seen since. Thank fuck for that.

I shuddered at the thought of the woman who had caused me and my family so much pain. She needed to be put down. If that was even remotely possible.

"I don't think that's a good idea considering she likes to drain angels of their blood," Tobias said, his chin resting on the top of her head.

It was no secret that Lilith had a few screws loose. The entire demon population of Inferna had suffered at her hands. Many of us, including me, escaped her rule centuries ago and swore fealty to Lucifer. Some disappeared into the vast emptiness beyond the cities or remained loyal to her crazy delusions of grandeur.

If Lilith really was here on Earth, Earth was screwed.

"Excuse me." Danica stood and walked towards the bathroom. Oliver stood to follow her but Asher grabbed his arm, stopping him.

The bathroom door slid shut behind her and I heard the lock slide into place. I frowned at the three men around the table. Here they were making her suffer again. Her suffering should have fueled me; instead it seemed to drain me. This should be enough to make me stay far away, but I was a glutton for punishment, even if it was my own.

"I think we need to consider telling Michael to fuck off about this whole prophecy thing. She's still dealing with everything that's happened. It's too soon to expect her to handle all of this well." Asher stood and walked past me to pour himself a glass of whiskey.

It figured the drunken tormented one was the one with any sense. I would have given anything to get in his dreams and feast on his pain. Too bad I couldn't access angel brains.

"You know we can't do that. We need to talk to Lucifer about this once he's calmed down and find out more about Lilith. If Michael is right about this prophecy then Danica is the key to saving us all," Tobias said, raising his eyebrows as he watched Asher drink the entire glass of whiskey.

"The prophecy said 'save the light from the dark' not the end of the world. Besides, the prophecy might not even be about her, there are only three of us." Olly put his chin in his hand and watched as Asher poured another glass.

"The other guardian could be her father. It didn't say all of her guardians needed to be in a relationship with her." Asher returned to the table and sat down. "Michael seems to think it is about us though."

"You could be right, Lucifer has been around more lately," Tobias said.

My stomach dropped and I almost lost control of my phantom form. Lucifer was her father. *Crap.* I unconsciously put my hands over my crotch. He would lop off my balls if he knew what I was doing in her dreams.

My attention went to the bathroom door, where I could hear her crying on the other side. I made my way to the door and walked through it, finding her sitting on the floor against the cabinets. She had her knees drawn up and her face buried in her arms.

I wanted to give her comfort but couldn't until she fell asleep. I sat on the floor across from her, leaning against the clear glass of the shower. Would it be so bad if I revealed myself to her? Would she run away screaming knowing I was the one she dreamed about?

She looked up and right at where I was sitting. I knew she couldn't see me, but it didn't stop my heart from spluttering in my chest.

A soft knock came at the door, snapping us both out of our stare off. If it could be called that.

"Dani, are you okay?" Tobias asked, concern in his voice.

"Yeah. I'll be out in a second." She stood and splashed her face with cold water before exiting the bathroom.

They were getting ready for bed finally. Asher went to the couch and Oliver and Tobias sandwiched Danica in between them in the bed. It was an interesting setup they had going.

As soon as Tobias and Danica were asleep, Oliver slid from the bed and made his way to the couch. He had done this every time they all slept over on the weekends. He would slip out of bed after the other two were asleep and then slip back in before they woke.

Oliver and Asher were much *friendlier* with each other now. Tonight they were practically intertwined facing each other. Asher was always stiff at first before relaxing and drifting off to sleep, usually while Oliver stroked his hair or back. I wondered what Danica would think of their secret night time couch rendezvous?

I made my way to the bed and hovered just over it. Tobias was behind her, wrapped around her in his typical protective manner. He couldn't protect her from me though, no one could.

I shut my eyes and pushed into her dream.

BLACKNESS ENGULFED her as she stood over four rectangular holes in the ground. She stood unmoving, except for her eyes which landed on each of the four headstones at the top of the graves.

Tobias Armstrong.

Asher Thorne.

Oliver Morgan.

The Fourth.

I approached and stood by her side, taking her hand in mine. The holes were empty. She looked over at me and then back at the empty graves, except now they weren't empty. Each of the men stared blankly up at the black sky.

Danica let go of my hand and a shovel appeared. She began shoveling dirt into each of the graves, burying the bodies. The last hole held a faceless body.

I grabbed her hand and pulled her away.

"Where are we going?" she asked, sadness seeping out of her voice. Her dream tonight was a new one. Typically she dreamed of Asher's death or her imprisonment.

"Have you ever been to Capri, Italy?" I flashed her my award-winning smile before the landscape around us changed and we were on a terrace at La Terrazza di Lucullo restaurant at the Caesar Augustus Hotel, overlooking the Bay of Naples.

She needed more tonight and I was pulling out all the stops.

She gasped and rushed to the railing as she took in the sunset that made the water appear purple. I joined her and put my arm around her, resting my hand on her hip.

"Do you like it? We can go somewhere else if it's not to your liking."

She shook her head and turned her head to look up at me. "You're crazy. It's perfect."

I took her hand and led her to the single table on the terrace. Several candles were lit and a champagne bucket sat with ice and a bottle of vintage Dom Perignon.

I poured her a glass and sat back in my chair, watching as she took a sip and scrunched up her nose. Every time I gave her champagne she'd do the same.

"What's your name?" she asked as she took a bite of our seared tuna appetizer. Food wasn't necessary, but was something she enjoyed.

"You know I can't tell you that."

She asked me in every dream, and every time my answer was the same. I was already breaking all the rules by showing her my face.

"Not even a hint?" She set her fork down and put her hand on my wrist, tracing the edge of my tattoo peeking out of my shirt.

I watched as her index finger traced the inked chain links circling my wrist. The same chain that was tattooed around my other wrist, my ankles, and the base of my neck. I shut my eyes and cleared my throat, her touch sending a foreign sensation up my arm.

"It's French in origin, but I'm not from France." I opened my eyes and she was staring back at me, a small smile on her lips.

"Then where are you from?" She threaded her fingers through mine and brought them to her lips, placing a kiss on my fingers. Why was she so perfect?

"Here and there." I stood and grabbed the bottle of champagne and my glass. "Let's go."

She grabbed her own glass and I changed the scene to inside a cliff-side suite overlooking the bay. I hadn't brought her to a room yet, but tonight I felt bold. I wanted her, even if it was just in a dream.

DESCEND

She glanced around the room, taking in the canopy bed and the views before turning towards me. "Are you seducing me, Frenchie?"

Her nickname sent shivers down my spine. "Depends. Are you seducible?"

She drank the rest of her champagne before spotting the rose petals on the floor and narrowing her eyes at me.

"I am if you tell me your name."

Giving her some freedoms in these dreams was blowing up in my face. Her knowing my name would put me at risk of Lucifer finding out about this. Dream demons did not duplicate names and if she happened to say it in conversation, he'd know.

Trying to distract her from my name, I grabbed her hand and led her to the bathroom that had a jacuzzi tub filled with bubbles. It was surrounded by candles and rose petals.

"Let me bathe you." I took her glass and set it on the side of the tub with mine and the bottle of champagne.

I began unbuttoning my shirt as she watched, licking her lips as it fell open, revealing my heavily tattooed torso. My blue dress shirt fell to the ground and I unhooked my belt, smiling as she took a loud inhale of breath as I pulled it out of the loops and it dropped with a clink to the marble floor.

I popped the button on my slacks and slowly pulled down the zipper, keeping my eyes locked on hers. Her eyes widened and then darkened in anticipation as I pushed my slacks and boxers down slightly, stopping at the base of my dick. It was already hardening as her eyes perused my body.

I pushed them down the rest of the way and stepped out of them, kicking them to the side and standing in front of her in all my glory. She took in a deep breath and then turned around, pulling her hair to the side so I could unzip her dress.

She shivered as I took my time sliding the zipper down and then lowered the thin spaghetti straps down her shoulders. She wasn't wearing a bra or panties, so as soon as her dress slid off her body I was treated with a view that was better than anything Italy had to offer.

"You're exquisite," I whispered into her neck. "The most beautiful woman I've had the pleasure of laying my eyes on."

Goosebumps spread across her skin and I ran my hands up and down her arms. She turned and I scanned her body, taking in her full breasts that would fit perfectly in my hands, the slight flair of her hips that were perfect for grabbing onto, and her delicious looking pussy. It was going to be difficult to control myself tonight.

Taking her hand, I helped her into the tub before joining her and pulling her to rest against my chest. I knew she could feel how hard I was, my erection was pressed up against her lower back.

"Do you not trust me?"

And there it was, we were back to my name.

I grabbed a washcloth and dipped it into the water before I ran it along her upper back. I didn't speak, hoping she would lose her mind and just stick to calling me Frenchie. I could live with that.

She sighed as I moved my hands around to her front, starting with her stomach, before moving up to her breasts. I took my time rubbing the cloth over her erect nipples. I dropped the cloth and took both her breasts in my hands, massaging them gently.

"Whose name am I supposed to moan?" She scooted up against me and wiggled her ass into my erection, causing me to groan. "Whose name am I supposed to scream when I come?"

I ran my lips along her shoulder and placed them under her ear, sucking the skin and then taking her earlobe between my teeth. I pinched her nipples and she let out a whimper.

My resolve to keep my name from her was thinning quickly, as she covered my hands with hers and then moved one of them down her body to her clit. I rubbed the sensitive nub between my fingers, drawing shaky breaths from her.

"Please."

I buried my face in her neck and willed myself not to speak as she began undulating her hips against my hand, the water starting to slosh against the sides of the tub. I moved my hand further down and slid a finger inside of her tight heat. She was going to let me bury myself there tonight if I gave her my name.

I slid in a second finger. "Reve."

"Reve," she moaned, my name sounding so sweet coming from her parted lips.

I moved her to the other side of the tub, lifting her onto the edge where the wall and window met. She gasped as I spread her apart and dove into her with my tongue. One of her hands gripped my head and the other went to the window, bracing herself as she moved against my mouth.

I slid my tongue up to her clit and swirled my tongue around it, making sure to hit it with my tongue ring. She gasped and her fingers nearly ripped the hair out of my scalp.

"Take me to bed," she breathed.

I whisked us to the bed and settled between her legs, my fingers threading through her hair. Tonight I would do things her way, but I couldn't wait to tie her up and shatter everything she thought she knew about pleasure.

I took her lips with mine and explored her mouth with my tongue, my tongue ring gently hitting her teeth. She gasped at the sensation and I pulled away to stare down at her. Her brown eyes sparkled with desire.

She reached between us and grabbed my cock, guiding it to her entrance and thrusting her hips up to take me inside of her. Fuck, maybe she'd be the one tying me up.

I took over and pulled out so only the head of my cock was inside of her and slammed back into her. Her hands went to the sheets and fisted them as I drove inside of her again and again. Our skin slapped together with heat and sweat.

"Reve, I need more."

I wasn't sure how to give her more without turning this from a fantasy to a nightmare.

I pulled out and flipped her over, taking her from behind. She buried her face in the pillows to muffle her screams. I grabbed her around the waist and pulled her up, her back against my chest. I wanted to hear her scream my name more than anything in the world.

"You wanted to know my name. Let me hear it," I ground out

between clenched teeth as I moved her forward and put her hands on the headboard.

"Reve," she moaned, my fingers working against her clit. "Oh God, yes!"

She clenched around me so hard as she came. I exploded inside of her not being able to help myself. If dream sex was this good with her, I couldn't fathom what sex with her awake would be like.

We collapsed into a heap on the mattress, her head resting on my heaving chest. She sighed in satisfaction and traced my screaming skull tattoo with her fingertip.

"You have interesting tattoos. I don't know whether to be scared of them or intrigued by them," she commented, moving a finger over one of my nipple rings. It sent a jolt straight to my dick. We didn't have time for a round two so I willed it to behave.

I kissed her forehead. "We have to leave soon."

"I don't want you to leave." She sat up and looked down at me, her hair falling over her shoulder. I brushed it out of the way, my knuckles light touching her soft skin.

I didn't want to leave either.

I pulled her back onto my chest and smoothed her hair until she fell asleep.

A SMALL, satisfied smile graced her lips as I watched her sleep in Tobias's arms. I would give anything to be able to hold her as he was. But I knew we could never have what they had.

CHAPTER 7

DANICA

$\mathcal{M}$y eyes felt heavy as I opened them at the sound of my alarm clock. I had such a restful Spring break, but last night was torture trying to sleep. Every time my eyes closed I saw death. Except when I dreamed about Reve, but those dreams didn't seem to happen nearly enough.

I pulled myself out of bed and dragged myself to the shower to try to wake myself up. I could really go for a Diet Dr. Pepper but I was almost two months sober.

As the warm water cascaded over my body, I couldn't help but think of Reve. Several nights in a row I had dreamed of Capri, Italy. The first night was mind blowing sex with an orgasm that was so powerful it could really only happen in a dream. Then we had spent the day on a yacht in the Bay of Naples, laying naked in the sunshine.

A pang of guilt surged through me and I opened my eyes. I shouldn't have been fantasizing about another man, even if imaginary, when I already had three almost perfect ones. Almost being that they currently treated me like a fragile fucking porcelain doll. I guess in a way I was.

I stepped out of the shower and dried off. I might need to give coffee another shot if I wanted to survive my current state of sleep deprivation. Asher's assholishness suddenly made perfect sense to me, although lately he had been more cheerful. More alive than I'd ever seen him. I guess getting your angel wings back had that effect. More likely it was Olly's doing though.

I slid into my uniform and shoved a granola bar in my mouth as I exited my room. I was running late. I made it to class with minutes to spare and slid in next to Olly who was scrolling through his phone.

"Good morning," he mumbled, not looking up from the screen.

I leaned over and tried glancing at what had captivated his attention. He was never glued to his phone and he put it away quickly. I narrowed my eyes at him as he looked up with an innocent expression on his face, but his eyes looked worried.

"What is it?" I couldn't help but let the concern creep into my voice. We had just gotten back some semblance of normalcy if you ignored the fact that I was part of a prophecy and my mother was apparently Lilith.

"After class," he mumbled as Tobias entered the room looking pissed off.

Now I was really concerned. Class passed in a blur of information. Tobias didn't even glance in our direction. Why did I get the feeling that I had done something somehow?

After the class emptied, Tobias leaned against the edge of his desk in front of us and crossed his arms over his chest. I could feel the tension radiating from him, similar to the tension when I had almost gotten us captured at the abandoned hospital.

"What did I do?" For once in my life I literally had no clue what I had done.

Tobias shook his head and then ran a hand over his face before pushing off his desk to stand fully. "You didn't do anything, Danica. Several pictures of us returning to campus last night were taken and posted."

My stomach clenched and I felt nausea swirl in my gut. Olly and I weren't that big of a deal, but Tobias and I? A big fucking deal. Especially since last night he had been carrying me when we returned from Asher's.

"Dean Whittaker has requested a meeting with the three of us this afternoon after classes are over. Until then, please try to keep a low profile. Both of you." Tobias looked between me and Olly, his eyes all business.

"What if I say we got drunk and I called you because I couldn't carry her? Asher made that suggestion," Olly said furrowing his eyebrows.

I turned towards him and gave him a pointed look. "How did Asher know about this before I even did?"

Olly shrugged and pulled his bag over his shoulder. "I texted him."

I shook my head and turned back to Tobias who was regarding Olly with a look of curiosity.

"Let's just see what she says first before we go down that route. You two better get going before you're late for your next class." Tobias moved around to the other side of his desk and plopped down in the chair.

He didn't glance up as we left the room.

On my way out of Uriel Hall, I stopped at the bathroom. Our meeting with the dean was one more thing to add to the shit storm that seemed to be my life. All because I punched John in his nose like he deserved.

After using the restroom, I stepped out of the stall, washed my hands, and then splashed cold water on my face. I heard the door open and glanced in the direction of the sound, water dripping from my face as I grabbed a paper towel from the dispenser. Of course the damn thing got stuck and I had to nearly break off a finger turning the knob on the side.

"Danica Deville, what a pleasant surprise running into you," Betty, the newest Divine, sneered as she came to a stop in front of me. "Cleaning Mr. Armstrong's cum off your face?"

Betty was even bitchier than the rest of the female Divine 7. The men had at least called a cease fire in their attempts at squashing my spirit. They must have been hard pressed for guardian angels to let them stick around. Or their inner bitch hadn't overshadowed what-ever light they possessed.

If they expected perfection, there would literally be no angels.

I rolled my eyes at her and moved towards the door, but she stepped in my way. I frowned and she pulled out her phone and flashed a picture of Olly kissing me goodnight while I was still in Tobias's arms.

I remembered the moment. Tobias's eyes had flared with heat as he watched us kiss. I was glad you couldn't see that in that particular picture.

"I don't know what sick game you're playing, Eve, but angels are off limits to your kind." She put her phone away before I could think of snatching it from her, which was probably a good thing.

"Sounds like you're jealous. By the way, jealousy isn't a good look on you, *Beatriz*." I pushed past her and heard her make a noise in her throat as I left the bathroom. Someone needed to knock the Divine down a peg or two.

In most of my classes I was met with stares, but nothing unusual. I was already regarded as some kind of exotic animal on display, now the pictures just added a new layer of intrigue for the masses.

With the warmer weather, Cora, Ethan, Olly, and I ate outside under a tree to avoid any run-ins with the Divine 7.

"How was Cabo?" I asked Cora. Ethan and Olly were engaged in a heated debate about who the Gargoyle King was on *Riverdale*.

"It was great. We pretty much got to party. We had to stay sober, but it was still a blast. I wish you could have come." She picked a blade of grass and rubbed it between her fingers. "I wish Brooklyn would have been able to too."

I know it was a ludicrous thought, but I somehow felt responsible for what had happened to Brooklyn. If only I had stopped her from going out with Levi. She would have hated me, but at least she wouldn't have been tortured at the hands of the Fallen.

And my mother.

When I walked into the library at the end of the day, Olly was already situated in our corner. I smiled and sat in the leather chair next to him, pulling out my binder. We were almost done reviewing the ins and outs of Los Angeles Celestial Academy.

I could have easily read the binder in a day and taken the test that was specially created just for me, but studying with Olly was quite enjoyable.

"Ready for a fun filled hour?" I kicked his leg because he was on his phone again. "Are you addicted to that now or something?"

He put his phone away with a smile on his face and looked at me. "Was just texting Asher."

"Oh really? What's going on with you two? Did I miss something?" I asked, pulling out my notebook and Flair pens. I was glad I had remembered to put them in my bag today; usually I left them in my room.

Olly shrugged. "I've been sleeping on the couch with him. He thinks he's ready to try the bed with us."

My eyes widened and then teared up. Asher never slept in the bed when any of us were over out of fear of having a nightmare and hurting one of us in his sleep. If Olly could help him with his magical soothing touch, I was all for it. "That's really sweet of you. So, you two cuddle?"

Olly let out a laugh and opened his binder to the section we were on. "I guess you could call it that. Why? Does that bother you?"

"No. It's kind of hot thinking of you together like that." I leaned over and looked at what page he opened to and opened my binder. "And if you two wanted to take things further or whatever, I wouldn't be opposed."

"I'm not sure Asher likes me like that." Olly cleared his throat and looked at his binder. "We're onto the good stuff in the binder now. Before the end of this school year, you'll take an aptitude test to see which guardian path best suits you. Healer, warrior, intellectual, or spiritual. Asher and Tobias were both warrior guardians, but when Asher fell, Tobias requested a transfer to intellectual."

"What kind do you think you are?" I was trying to stop the worry from eating me alive. I was really more curious at what the test would say about me since I wasn't an angel. I felt like I was just biding my time at the academy until they figured out what to do with me.

"I don't take the test since I'm an archangel; I'm all of them.

Although sometimes I don't feel like it." A flash of sadness passed over his eyes. "Everyone is disappointed in me because I lost that stupid cup."

I suppressed a smile that threatened to come out at the mental image of a wave crashing into him and sending the Holy Grail to the depths of the Pacific Ocean. It was a harsh punishment to be cast out of heaven for such a trivial occurrence. After the conversation with my dad about him being some kind of balance, I wondered if the cup was the only thing that led to his arrival on Earth.

We finished up the section on different types of guardians and packed up our belongings. It was time to face Dean Whittaker, who'd had it out for me from the beginning.

We arrived at the administration offices before Tobias and waited in chairs outside the dean's office. Olly seemed calm and collected, while I was a nervous wreck. If I hadn't just painted my nails, I'd have been chewing on them again.

Tobias walked in right as the minute hand clicked straight up and sat down on the other side of Olly. None of us spoke and Tobias was bouncing his knee. He was just as nervous as I was. It occurred to me he might lose his job over this. Then what would he do? Work on Asher's construction crew gutting kitchens?

"Dean Whittaker will see you now," the secretary said from her desk, gesturing to the closed door.

We stood in unison and I opened the door, walking inside first. Sue Whittaker sat at her desk, pen tapping on the surface, frown on her face. She was not a very inviting person to say the least.

The three of us sat down in chairs in front of her desk and waited for her to strike. If I had learned anything over the past several months, it was to bite my tongue, especially with people like her.

"I'm sure you are all aware of the pictures that surfaced overnight of your clandestine rendezvous outside the staff living quarters. Care to explain?"

"I-" Tobias started to speak but Olly cut him off.

"It's my fault, ma'am. I asked Danica to go to a party with me and we got drunk. I couldn't fly back with her and I called Mr. Armstrong to come get us."

"Are you and Ms. Deville seeing each other now?" She set her pen on her desk and crossed her arms over her ample chest.

"I really don't think that's of your concern, Sue." Tobias crossed his arms over his chest to match her posture and looked between Olly and me. "What they do with their personal time is their own business."

She laughed, but not because it was funny. It was a pissed off laugh. "There is no 'personal time' as you put it, when it comes to being a guardian. Need I remind you that Ms. Deville is not even technically an angel and that relationships with humans are strictly forbidden. Not to mention that she herself is a product of a human and angel indiscretion."

"If you'd like to discuss this further, I suggest you speak with Michael." Tobias stood and looked at us. "We're done here. Let's go."

I was grateful he was taking the lead because I was bound to say something stupid and get myself into trouble. I stood and followed Olly out the door with Tobias trailing behind. He slammed the door behind him and I flinched.

We walked in silence out of Ariel Hall and Olly split away from us, heading back to his room to study.

"Why don't you go change and then come to my room. I'll help you study and cook dinner so you don't have to eat in the dining hall." Tobias finally spoke when we were mere feet from the staff's building.

The longer I lived in the staff building, the more I hated it. At first I liked living down the hall from Tobias, but now I felt I was always sneaking around in order to not be seen by the other staff members. When I did run into them, they weren't exactly friendly, instead pretending I was invisible. Well, all except Tobias.

"I'm really tired. I think I might just call it a day." I walked ahead of him to the door and he grabbed my wrist, stopping me. I turned back towards him and looked around, hoping no one was looking. "What?"

"It's barely four o'clock. You're coming over." His head tilted slightly to the side and the smallest of smiles turned up the corners of his mouth.

"You aren't the boss of me, Mr. Armstrong." I had the impulse to stick my tongue out at him and run, but held it in. I was eighteen years old, not eight.

He yanked my arm and pulled me to his chest. He bent his head so his mouth was right next to my ear. My heart was hammering from such a public display of affection, especially after the picture fiasco.

"What did you call me?" His lips barely brushed my ear and a zing went straight to my clit.

"Mr. Armstrong. Ow!" He bit my earlobe before pulling it into his mouth. "You're naughty. I need to find my ruler to keep you off me."

He pulled away, his eyes simmering with an unspoken promise of what was to come.

"Is that a threat?" he asked, taking his keys out and opening the door. "Because I'm the only one who will be doing any spanking."

We walked quietly through the common room together, my face heating up as a few sets of eyes landed on us. Tobias was a well-liked teacher among students and other staff. I doubted any of them would say anything even if they did see something. Or maybe they would since it was me.

I changed quickly, throwing on a pair of pajama bottoms and a tank top. Only the best for Tobias. I grabbed my bag and headed down the hall to his room, letting myself in.

Tobias was already in a pair of gray sweats with no shirt and was watching the Dodgers. I dropped my bag on his coffee table and sat next to him.

"Why do you like the Dodgers so much?" I looked over at him and resisted the urge to run my fingers along his muscular stomach. His abs were just barely peeking through his skin. And those sweatpants. Good god, a man in gray sweats was sexy as hell.

He put his hand between my thighs, resting it there. "My dad took me to games at Ebbets Field. Used to cost about a dollar. I was never able to take my sons to a game."

"Tell me about them," I said softly. "You never talk about your past."

He grunted and looked over at me before turning back to the game. He was quiet for several minutes before deciding to speak.

"I don't talk about my past because it hurts. Unlike Asher who willingly enlisted, I didn't. I ended up being one of the unlucky twenty-percent of those in the draft and left a wife and three small children behind." He looked down at his right arm. He pointed to the woman. "Margaret, everyone called her Margie. I called her Sugar Hips. It drove her crazy, especially when we were out in public. We were high school sweethearts, got married the summer after we graduated."

I ran my finger along her portrait. "She's beautiful. You were a lucky man."

He smiled and pointed to the twins. "Jeffrey and Charlie. They were both precocious and kept us on our toes. I think I got a few gray hairs because of them. Jeffrey became a lawyer and Charlie a history teacher."

"Like you."

"Like me." He cleared his throat and moved his hand down to stroke the portrait of the baby girl. "Sarah. She was the sweetest baby. I wish I would have had more time with her."

I put my head on his shoulder. I wanted to know more but could hear a slight tremor in Tobias's normally steady voice. I was surprised he told me as much as he had.

"Are you going to study?" He leaned forward and grabbed my bag off the table, changing the subject and breaking the tension. "You're doing decent in your classes. A very reliable source says you have an A in Demonology."

"The only A I've ever gotten was in PE. I hope I earned it." I didn't mean for it to come out like it did. I hoped he graded me just like he did everyone else.

"You've earned your A. You know more than I do. I'm starting to feel a little concerned about my job. You should be the one teaching Demonology."

If he only knew just how close I was to the demon world, he'd probably have re-thought his comment about me teaching at an angel school.

CHAPTER 8

DANICA

By Wednesday, I was beyond exhausted. I texted Asher before he got off work and told him I was staying with him that night. Since I had a key, I drove the thirty minutes to his place with music blaring. I shouldn't have been driving, but I was desperate.

Pulling into the small lot next to the building, there was a motorcycle parked in the spot I usually pulled into. It was one of those crotch rockets that thought they owned the road. I made a face at the bike. They scared the crap out of me when they came zooming between stopped traffic.

It wasn't that I owned that spot, but when you get used to always parking in the same space, you do kind of feel like someone stole it. I pulled into the next available spot, although I was very tempted to park where Asher parked his truck. I'd never hear the end of it though.

I slung my duffel bag over my shoulder and made my way to the stairs. I stopped short at the 'For Rent' sign in the window of the front unit. I backed up and peeked into the slightly open blinds of the window.

From what I could see, it held the same industrial look as Asher's place, but was more of an apartment style with separate living and sleeping spaces. It was the perfect space for a young woman.

An ill-formed plan took hold in my head. I didn't really need to think about it. I took out my phone and dialed the administrative offices at the academy.

"Judy speaking, how may I help you?" I cringed at the secretary's nasally voice.

"Hi Judy. This is Danica Deville. I have a question for you. Am I allowed to live off campus?" I bit my lip and pleaded with heaven above that it was possible. This was too perfect being right downstairs from Asher. I practically lived here anyway.

"Let me speak with Dean Whittaker. Just a moment." She put me on hold. The music playing sounded like it was composed in heaven and I rolled my eyes.

It wouldn't be so bad driving to campus every day and I would finally feel a bit of relief from always being under a microscope. Tobias and Olly wouldn't be happy, but they had wings and could get here in no time.

"Danica?" The secretary came back on the line. "She said she will approve it. She thinks it is a great idea." Of course Sue Whittaker would think it was a great idea, she hated my guts. She'd have hated me even more if she knew I had demon blood in me. They probably wouldn't even let me attend the academy.

I hung up and then dialed the number for the rental agency that was listed on the window sign. The woman that answered was enthusiastic and said she had just rented out the other unit the day before. That explained the motorcycle.

She arranged to meet me in an hour for a tour and I let out a squeal after hanging up with her. It would be amazing to have a place of my own where I didn't have to worry about eyes being on me.

As I turned and headed for the stairs, I saw the curtains next door fall back into place and stopped short. I guess I had been a little loud.

An hour later I was touring the downstairs unit with the rental broker. It was one bedroom with a large open concept living space. It was a beautiful space, which I knew it would be since Asher had remodeled it.

I filled out paperwork, gave her a deposit, and headed back upstairs. Asher's truck was parked in his spot. He was probably wondering where I was.

I opened the door and smelled the familiar scent of his shampoo—pineapple and coconut—wafting through the air. He was standing at his dresser, his towel in a heap on the floor at his feet. Asher after a shower was always too much for my libido. It was an instant turn on, the small droplets of water were still sitting on his skin. I wanted to lick them off.

"There you are. Where were you? You missed out on a shower." He pulled a pair of basketball shorts out of a drawer and slid them on.

I licked my lips and kept my eyes on his chest as he pulled a shirt over his head. With a body like that, he shouldn't be allowed to wear a shirt, ever.

"When you look at me like that, it's like you've never seen me naked before." He picked up his towel and made his way towards me. "Are you going to answer me or just stand there and stare?"

"What's wrong with staring? I'm making up for lost time." I sometimes found myself staring at him, still not believing he was actually back and alive.

He pulled me in for a quick kiss before hanging up his towel in the bathroom. I followed him into the kitchen where he got out a beer.

"I was downstairs getting a tour and filling out papers for the front rental," I finally said, answering the question he had asked me when I first walked in.

He paused with the bottle halfway to his lips and stared at me for a moment before taking a drink. "And why is that?"

I rolled my eyes and took the beer out of his hand, putting it on the counter. I stepped into him and put my hands on his chest.

"I can't stay on campus anymore. Please support me in this because Tobias is going to flip the fuck out."

"As he should. Did you even think this through all the way?" His expression was neutral as he examined my face, his eyes lingering on the dark circles under my eyes. "We are all worried about you. I don't think it's a good idea for you to be on your own."

I stepped away from him and gathered my hair in a pony tail, wrapping the elastic that had been on my wrist around the handful of hair. In a way he was right, but what if being alone was exactly what I needed?

"I'm eighteen years old, and I've had plenty of experience being on my own. Summer break is only a few weeks away anyways and I don't plan on staying on campus or in Montecito all summer by myself. This is the best move for me." I folded my arms across my chest.

"You can stay here. With me." He put his hands on my hips and looked at me seriously.

I raised my eyebrows. "You can't just sleep on the couch all the time. Besides, you have no walls. I need walls."

"Walls are overrated. So you're saying you wouldn't want to live here with me?" He stuck out his bottom lip in a mock pout. "You wound me."

I was shocked he would even suggest me moving in with him. That would completely change the group dynamic if I decided to live with one over the others. Plus, even though I loved him, I still needed privacy.

"What about Olly?" I propped my hip against the counter and watched as his face twisted in surprise at my question.

"What about him?" Asher grabbed his beer and took a long drink.

"Don't you want him to move in too?" He tensed up slightly and walked over to get another beer, even though he wasn't completely done with the first.

"Do you want something to drink?" he asked, avoiding my question. I shook my head and watched him open another beer. He had been drinking less lately, but still drank more than he probably should.

"I fully support anything you and Olly feel towards each other. Or do with each other."

He leaned against the counter and examined the label on his beer bottle. "It just kind of snuck up on me. I don't want to be unfaithful to you. Not that I'd have sex with him or anything."

I furrowed my brows. "You wouldn't be unfaithful. You don't feel I'm cheating when I'm with Olly or Tobias, do you?" He shook his head, a chunk of his hair falling in his face. I brushed it behind his ear. "I'd be okay with any of you hooking up with each other. No one else though. Makes me feel like a hypocrite since I'm with three men."

"Really what it makes you is one hell of a lucky woman." He held his beer bottle by the stem and traced his index finger around the rim, his eyes focusing on his movement. "What has Oliver said to you?"

"Maybe you need to talk to him. Figure things out. Life's too short to have regrets," I suggested, placing my hand on his arm.

"It might make things complicated between us. We have a good thing going right now. Why add *that* into the mix?"

"Because it's what you both want. If you're worried about whether you're top or bottom, I'm sure you're a top." I couldn't help the smile that spread across my face at the mental image. "Just make sure you stretch him out beforehand."

I pushed it too far and watched as he visibly shut down, his hand gripping his beer. "Jesus Christ, Dani," he bit out, moving towards the stairs leading to the roof. "This is a big deal and you're joking about anal."

I watched his retreating back as he made his way up the metal stairs and stopped at the door, his hand on the handle. I can't say I was surprised our conversation had led to him escaping. It was what he did when his feelings got too intense or uncomfortable. It was as if he had reached his quota on intense emotions and couldn't stomach anymore.

It had to be a lot to process, the idea of being with a man when for so long he had only been with women.

"Are you coming?" He looked down at me.

"I didn't think I was invited. You're acting all butt hurt. No pun intended." I bit my lip and stifled a laugh. I was evil, I was sure.

He rolled his eyes and left the door open for me to follow.

FALLING asleep was easy when you knew your dreams would be sweet instead of torturous. Despite how much I loved my *good* dreams, I was getting more and more suspicious of their source. It didn't stop me from wanting to spend all my time in the only place I could have them.

I stood on the rooftop, the wind blowing my hair into my face. Dark gray storm clouds rolled overhead. The faint rumble of thunder in the distance matched the intensity of my thudding heart.

Tobias, Asher, and Oliver stood before me, their backs ramrod straight, their faces devoid of emotion. Except their eyes. Their eyes stared back at me with hate and disgust.

"Please, don't do this. It shouldn't matter!" I pleaded with them, taking a step forward. They met my advance with a step back. "I love you!"

"We don't love you. Not anymore." Tobias's lip curled off his teeth in a sneer. He was disgusted by me.

This couldn't be happening. They said they loved me and now they were going to leave me. I needed to wake up, I needed to get out of this before my heart shattered.

Their wings snapped open as I sank to my knees on the wet surface of the roof. The rain had started to fall, soaking my clothes, covering the tears streaming down my face. I shivered, but I wasn't sure if it was from the chill seeping into my body from the rain or from my heart breaking.

"I could never love a demon. You disgust me." Asher clenched his fists at his side. "Let's go before she ruins us."

A sob shook my body and my hands braced against the rough surface of the roof. My heart felt as if it was being ripped from my chest.

"Wait." Oliver stepped towards me and kneeled next to me. I knew I could rely on him to see the good in this situation. He was my bright light in the darkness.

I sat back on my heels and he leaned forward, close to my ear. "You're nothing to me."

His words cut like a knife and he backed away before the three angels shot into the sky. The sky lit up with lightening and the thunder shook the roof.

I screamed into the sky, my throat burning with the force. Flames erupted around me as I stood and tilted my head towards the darkened sky.

"Danica." The soft voice came from behind me.

I spun around, the flames intensifying around us. It felt like I had set the whole world on fire. "Where have you been?" I choked out through my tears.

"I'm sorry I'm late, I was..." He didn't complete his thought and he reached forward. I backed away.

"No. You don't get to touch me. Not anymore."

"Danica." His voice held a warning as I backed away another step, closer to the flames.

"Why are you here, Reve?" The flames began swirling up into the sky, like mini tornados.

"I'm here because I love you."

I tilted my head back and laughed and then choked on the sound. I clutched my chest as the gaping hole opened wider.

"You aren't even real. I don't want you here anymore. I don't need you! Leave!" I yelled as the sound of the flames made my voice difficult to hear.

"Danica." My body shook as my name left his lips, sadness in his eyes.

"Danica." A hand was shaking my shoulder. "Baby, wake up."

I sat up abruptly, my head smashing into Asher's. The sharp pain in my forehead ripped me back to reality. I gasped in air, trying to clear my lungs of the empty sensation that had taken hold.

My eyes burned with tears and sweat, blurring my vision and leaving me wondering if I was still in the nightmare. Asher didn't touch me, but sat close to me, ready to comfort me. My vision was starting to clear and I caught a flash of a retreating back in my peripheral vision.

Dark green eyes stared at me from across the railing surrounding the bedroom. He kept his eyes locked on mine as he slowly backed away. My eyes went wide as his legs disappeared, then his torso, and right before Asher swung his head in that direction, his face.

"Reve." The name left my lips as I crawled off the bed and stumbled in the direction he had disappeared. I stood in the spot and wrapped my arms around myself as if that would help me hold myself together.

"Reve? Like an engine?" Asher came to stand in front of me, concern wrinkling his features. "Did you have a nightmare about the Fallen taking you?"

I took a step back from him and shook my head. Had I been screaming in my sleep? My throat felt scratchy and dry. I brushed past him and walked into the kitchen. I grabbed a bottle of water out of the refrigerator and gulped it down, staring at the *SpongeBob SquarePants* picture hanging by a magnet.

"Do you want to talk about it?" Asher asked, standing near the table.

I threw the empty water bottle into the sink and turned to face him, leaning against the counter. My heart rate was returning to normal and the air chilled my sweaty skin. I shivered and Asher stepped forward. I let him.

"I thought your nightmares were under control when you were here." I let Asher wrap his arms around me and lead me over to the couch. He pulled his blanket around me and sat next to me, tucking me under his arm.

I shook my head and let out a shaky breath. *Reve.* Reve was the one keeping the nightmares away. It made so much sense now that I thought about it. He couldn't get onto campus without permission (which he would *never* get) and he didn't know about Montecito. The thought had first snuck into the corner of my mind when Asher was in Montecito but I still had nightmares.

"I dreamed that I was a demon and you all left me." I put my head against his chest as his hand rubbed my arm through the blanket. "And then the whole world was burning around me."

"Hey," he said softly, tilting my chin up to meet his eyes. "Nothing would make me leave you. Nothing."

I nodded, not believing his words but not wanting to explain to him my insecurities. People said those things all the time, yet there was always *something* that would cause a person to leave.

I leaned into him and shut my eyes.

"I think there's been a dream demon in my dreams," I mumbled, barely audible even to myself. I felt his hand tighten on my arm before continuing to rub slowly back and forth. "He has been taking me out of the nightmares, but he was too late this time. I got mad at him."

"A dream demon?" Asher sounded confused. "What do you mean he takes you out of them? Aren't they supposed to cause nightmares or make them worse?"

My hand found his free one and intertwined our fingers before I continued. "He pulls me from my nightmares and takes me to all kinds of places like fancy parties, Disneyland, the beach, Italy. I thought I had just made it all up in my head as an escape. It made no sense until I saw him when I woke up just now." I didn't mention the part about him taking me to bed in some of the most lavish hotels I had ever seen in the past few dreams.

Asher stiffened behind me. "You need to tell your father."

My heart sped up. "You can't say a word about this, Asher. He doesn't hurt me. My dad will kill him if he finds out. I need him."

"He's a demon." Asher sighed and leaned back on the couch, examining my face. "What if he comes back and hurts you?"

That was a good question and one I didn't have an answer to. I didn't know why Reve was around. All I knew was that I needed him.

CHAPTER 9

DANICA

I was sure Asher thought I was losing my mind when I decided to just up and practically move in with him until my lease started in the space downstairs. One week of cohabitating with a man that hadn't lived with anyone in decades was something akin to intruding on a bear's den.

Sure, we usually stayed with Asher on the weekends, but an entire week, seven days, was asking the man who preferred to be alone, a lot.

Typically on the weekends Asher had his place cleaned up. It quickly became apparent to me that Asher was a slob.

A sexy slob, but the pile of dirty clothes he left in the bathroom on a daily basis was a constant reminder that being around me, Tobias, and Olly was a chore for him.

He was fine at first, but as the days passed, it became clear to me that Asher needed his space. It probably didn't help that I wanted to binge watch *Gilmore Girls* and he wanted to binge *The Office*. Naked. With a drink in his hand.

His naked binge watching made it rather difficult to study for my finals which were the following week. I would be taking notes and hear him laugh, which always caused me to look up. Even though I knew he was sitting there naked, it still surprised me every damn time my eyes glimpsed the sight and I would spend several minutes gawking.

After a week of sharing his space and existing on takeout I decided to cook. My history with cooking was sketchy. Ramen and frozen foods were about all I could manage. I never had a reason to cook growing up, my caregivers always cooked for me.

They should really make Home Economics a mandatory class in high school. Learning how to cut an onion is much more useful than learning the parts of a cell or the Pythagorean theorem. If there was a zombie apocalypse neither of those things would help me survive. Cooking would though. Well, unless there was nothing left to cook.

After classes ended for the day, I hustled to the grocery store on the way home, since home did not include an all you can eat smorgasbord of food. I could still eat in the dining hall if I wanted, but I didn't particularly want to hang around campus until they served dinner.

I walked through the sliding doors of the grocery store and grabbed a cart. I came prepared with a list after watching YouTube videos the night before when I couldn't sleep. I was also going to cheat a bit by not actually making anything from scratch.

My goal wasn't to kill my boyfriends.

I stopped in front of the packaged salad and scanned the thirty different mixes. Clearly other people were just as lazy as I was and couldn't even cut their own lettuce. Why else would they have so many? I grabbed a Caesar salad kit, considered who I was feeding, then grabbed a second.

I was feeling pretty good with my two bags of salad until I turned down the pasta aisle. It had to be at least twenty feet of shelving filled top to bottom. And that was just the actual pasta, not the sauce choices.

I'd been in a grocery store before, but it had been a while since I'd been shopping anywhere besides the frozen food section and cereal aisle. I couldn't be the only eighteen-year old to feel lost in a grocery store.

"What the hell am I supposed to do? Eeny meeny miny moe?" I

mumbled to myself as I grabbed a bag of rigatoni and examined the back.

"If I may make a suggestion," a woman said from behind me.

I turned and raised my eyebrows at her intrusion on my pasta selection activities.

"Do I know you?" She was dressed in a red power suit, heels that screamed "fuck me," and had long dark hair that left me feeling hair envy.

"I don't think so. Are you cooking for someone special?" I nodded. She glanced at the pasta box I was holding before plucking it from my hands and putting it back on the shelf. "In the refrigerated section they have pasta and sauces that are far superior to anything you can find down this aisle. I'll help you."

She grabbed my cart and started pushing it in the opposite direction. Who did this woman think she was? I frowned but followed behind her, feeling drawn to her chipper demeanor. Maybe she was just in a good mood and paying it forward.

We stopped in front of the section with prepared pasta and she grabbed the family sized three cheese tortellini and a container of alfredo sauce.

"This is the way to a man's heart, or at the very least, a simple way into his pants." Her red stained lips pulled up into a smile showing her shockingly white, perfect teeth. This woman was walking, talking sex.

"Thanks," I said, watching her as she put them in my cart. "What else should I get? I made a list but I could use all the help I can get."

"Definitely garlic bread, a nice Chardonnay, and something sweet for dessert." She took off again and I followed her.

"I can't buy alcohol," I informed her as we turned down the wine aisle. She grabbed two bottles and put them in her empty hand basket she had been toting around. She winked at me, her blue eyes sparkling.

After gathering the rest of the meal I followed her to the checkout line and purchased my pretty epic date night meal. I hoped I wouldn't burn it. Boiling water couldn't be that hard, could it?

Once in the parking lot the woman handed me the two bottles of wine and refused the cash I tried to give her.

"Consider it a gift."

"Thanks, I really appreciate your help."

She smiled brightly and walked away, her heels clicking on the pavement.

I loaded my car and made it to Asher's with thirty minutes to spare before my dinner dates arrived.

I placed everything on the counter and snapped a quick photo. I sent it to my dad with a text. *Look, I'm going to actually cook something for other people. Supposedly this meal is the way to a man's heart and into his pants.*

I snickered after hitting send, imagining my dad's face as he read it. He almost immediately texted me back. *What made you decide on that particular meal?*

A woman at the store. She was nice, even bought the wine for me.

The typing bubbles appeared and disappeared several times. I put the phone down and preheated the oven for the bread. Preheating an oven was my jam.

The front door opened and slammed shut as I turned on the stove to boil water. I heard Asher drop his keys in the metal bowl by the door and make a grunt as he took off his boots. I didn't need to turn to see him do it, it was the same every day.

"Are you *cooking?*" He seemed to have stopped in his tracks across the room.

I turned after placing the lid on the pot of water just in time to see Asher pull off his shirt and toss it near the wall by the bathroom. He walked towards me and I put my hands up.

"I want it to be a surprise. Go shower. Olly and Tobias will be here in a bit." My eyes moved from his abs up to his face where his eyebrows were raised.

"I need a drink." He started forward again and I met him halfway, stopping him. "At least give me a beer or my bottle of whiskey."

"It will ruin your palate for my meal. We're having wine." I put a hand on his chest and he covered it with his before yanking me the rest of the way towards him and kissing me.

He hadn't even eaten the meal yet and I was halfway into his pants. Not that I needed a reason to ever sleep with any of them. One or more was always willing. But tonight wasn't about that. Tonight was about repaying them for always putting up with my crap.

"You do remember that time you decided to make toast, don't you? There were flames." He traced my bottom lip with his finger and his eyes twinkled. My face started to burn as I recalled my failed attempt at toasting bread.

There weren't flames. There definitely was a lot of smoke that set off the smoke detectors though.

He let me go and opened the cabinet under the sink, grabbing a fire extinguisher from inside.

I frowned as he set the red canister on the counter. "Don't burn down my kitchen."

Smart ass.

He turned and headed towards the bathroom. I grabbed a potholder and chucked it at him. It sailed past him and he turned and smirked. "You missed. I hope your cooking is better than your aim."

I rolled my eyes and turned back to watch the water pot. He was distracting to say the least.

By some miracle I didn't burn anything and the food tasted great. Maybe I could get on board the cooking train if it was really that easy.

"THAT WAS amazing and you know how picky I am," Olly said, putting his fork down on his empty plate and sitting back. He took a sip of his Chardonnay and frowned into the glass. "I don't think I like *this* though."

"It was perfect. What's the special occasion?" Tobias asked, swirling his wine before taking a sip.

I shrugged. "No reason. Just felt like cooking you guys dinner. I was also sick of eating takeout and frozen pizza."

Tobias ran his finger around the rim of his wine glass. "I don't think you should move off campus."

I sighed. This conversation was a daily occurrence in some shape or form. Olly was also not a fan of me moving off campus, but neither man really had a clue what living there was like for me.

"She'll be perfectly fine downstairs. We can even get walkie talkies if it would make you two get off her back." Asher stood and started piling plates to take to the sink. "You can't expect her to stay somewhere that makes her stay in the same building with her teachers."

"They might be willing to let you move to a student building. Let me talk to Sue." I frowned at Tobias and stood to help Asher. Living in a student building would be even worse than living with the teachers.

"Sit. We'll do the dishes," Olly said, standing to help Asher.

"I knew I could count on you, angel baby." Asher grabbed the plates from Olly's hands and took them to the sink. "Unlike Toby. See him sitting over there pretending like we aren't doing the dishes? That's why he approved of this whole harem business, now he has three maids."

I laughed as Tobias ignored Asher's dig. It was true though. Tobias tended to sit back after eating, even when everyone else jumped up to clean.

"I've already signed papers and ordered furniture. I'm not even sure I'm going to continue next year now that I have my GED. The fact that I'm going to have to make up the first semester over the summer is not appealing at all."

"We told you we'd help you with that. You can't just quit, Danica." Tobias frowned and finished his drink.

"Why not? No one there likes me, plus being an angel just isn't in my cards." I turned my attention to Olly and Asher cleaning up the kitchen. Every time Asher handed Olly a plate to put in the dishwasher, their fingers would brush. I wasn't sure who they thought they were fooling, but something special was brewing between them. Maybe they just needed a little push.

"I like you. Oliver likes you. Ethan and Cora like you. Screw the rest of them." He stood and moved behind me, putting his hands on my shoulders and starting to massage them. "I'll miss you."

"Now you guys will know how I felt all these months with her so far away. Imagine how I felt not even able to go to her on campus. You two can at least fly and be here in a few minutes." Asher dried his hands and he and Olly sat on the sectional next to each other.

Tobias moved my hair off my shoulders and leaned down to kiss my neck. He trailed his lips to my ear and moved his mouth so it was only touching when he spoke. "No more early morning visits."

"You can still visit me in the mornings," I breathed as he flicked his tongue against my ear.

"Not the same." He kissed my temple and pulled me after him to the couch.

I turned back towards the kitchen when my phone buzzed on the countertop. I picked it up, finally seeing a reply from my dad. *Your mother cooked me that same exact meal the night she told me she was pregnant.*

My phone slipped from my hand.

~

I HAD CONVINCED myself that the woman from the grocery store couldn't have been Lilith. That would mean she was following me. I didn't say a word about it to the guys; they didn't need any reason to try to stop me from moving off campus.

I made my way across the lush campus of Los Angeles Celestial Academy towards the staff building. The grounds were mostly deserted since it was class time and all first years were taking their guardian placement assessment.

I had been the first one done. Whether that was a good sign or a bad sign would be known soon. Would I be a healer, warrior, intellectual, or a spiritual guardian angel?

The test was a joke, at least for me. I was no angel. I couldn't heal. I wasn't a fighter. I definitely didn't have the brains to be an intellectual. And well, my spiritual beliefs were shaky at best. The test was supposed to determine which courses angels took from second year forward.

I smiled to myself, thinking of the test. It had some ridiculous questions on it. It was mostly multiple choice that tried to gauge interest and personality. My favorite questions were the open-ended ones. In particular the question: *Two people are in a room and you are told one of them has to die. What five questions would you ask to decide who lives and who dies?*

I was certain my response was not what they were looking for at all. I wrote:

What is this, the movie Saw? First off, I would never be in a room where one of two people has to die. In what world would this happen? I will humor you though. This is assuming the two people don't know that one of them is going to die.

1. *How would you describe the one person in your life you would die for?*
2. *If you had one day left to live, what would you do?*
3. *Diet Dr. Pepper or Diet Pepsi?*
4. *Dogs or cats?*
5. *Dark chocolate or white chocolate?*

Clearly anyone that answers Diet Pepsi, cats, or white chocolate is a prime candidate for death. Asking who deserves to live or die in any situation is a ridiculous question. I expect better from angels.

MOST OF MY answers were filled with snark. I was sure Olly came up with something that transcended the fine line between morality and immorality.

I changed into jeans and an old shirt once back in my room. I texted Asher that I was done with my test. He had taken half the day off to help me and Olly pack my life and move it to my new place.

Thirty minutes later, I went downstairs to let Asher into the building and to help him carry boxes in. The building was mostly empty since all of the teachers were teaching or scoring the placement assessments.

"You got finished with your test pretty quickly," Asher commented, following me up the stairs. He had to stop halfway to adjust the grip on the stack of boxes he held. "Did it go okay?"

"Everyone stared at me like I was crazy for being done so fast, so probably not. I thought it was better to just answer with my immediate thoughts. I bet I'm in Slytherin." I walked into my room and dropped the broken-down boxes on my bed.

"Slytherin?" I turned and saw the confused look on his face. Was he kidding? He had to be kidding. He must not have paid any attention at Universal Studios.

I grabbed a box and taped it up. The déjà vu was strong as I pulled the tape gun across the bottom.

"What do you want me to help with?" He grabbed the tape gun from me and taped another box.

I was just about to answer when Olly burst into the room, panting. The door banged against the counter. Asher dropped the tape gun he was holding and cursed.

"Fuck, man! Don't do shit like that!" Asher shook his head and went into the bathroom, slamming the door behind him.

I frowned and put my hands on my hips.

"I didn't know he'd be here yet." He had to take two breaths to get his words out.

"Why are you panting? Did something happen?" I went back to taping boxes. I wanted to check on Asher, but the lock had clicked, meaning he wanted to be left alone.

"Just wanted to see you." He made his way to the bathroom door and knocked gently. "I'm sorry."

There were grumbles in return and Olly turned back to me with a frown. I just shrugged. I was used to the mood swings from Asher. Sometimes they were for a reason, like when something unpredictable happened, but they were also seemingly for no reason.

"Here, why don't you put the crap in my nightstands in this box." I handed him a box and then started emptying my dresser drawers.

"I'm sure none of your stuff is crap," he said as Asher finally came out of the bathroom.

Olly was bent at the waist, his hand starting to open the nightstand when he looked over his shoulder. Asher's eyes were heated as he stared back at Olly. His eyes slid briefly to his ass before turning back to the box he had dropped.

The sexual tension between the two of them was getting worse every time we were together. I didn't know what was holding them back. I had been pretty clear that I wanted them to explore their feelings for each other, but maybe I hadn't been clear enough.

Olly started putting the contents of my nightstand into the box. It mostly contained cords and old notes from Ava.

"What is this?" He held up my purple clit stimulator with an amused look on his face. My face heated as both their eyes landed on me.

He pushed the button and it started buzzing, causing him to drop it on the bed. Asher grabbed it and turned it off.

"What would you even need this for?" Asher asked, his eyes widening and glimmering with mischief. "Are the three of us just not doing it for you anymore? We can remedy that pretty quickly."

"When was the last time you jacked off?" I grabbed it from him and he grabbed my wrist, tugging me towards him.

"In the shower before coming here. I don't see what that has to do with you having a toy." His eyes went to my lips.

"So you can get off without me, but I can't without you?" I laughed and pulled away from him before he could move in to kiss me.

We had packing to do. Not that there was much, but I was more than ready to leave this place in the dust.

"Do you use it often?"

"Lately, no. Now, say two really hot male angels walked in my room and started making out and touching each other. I wouldn't even hesitate to use it." I couldn't stop the smirk that spread across my face as Asher's eyes widened further and Olly made a sound that was half gasp, half choke.

"Do you often get hot angels coming to your room and making

out?" Asher moved back to the dresser he was emptying. He grabbed a handful of clothes and put them in a box, avoiding Olly, who was staring at him.

I sat down against my headboard and turned on the toy, the sound filling the quiet room. "Not as often as I'd like."

"Let's say two hot angels did come to your room. Wouldn't you just use *them* instead of that hunk of plastic?" Asher shut the empty drawer and turned to look straight at me, his lips in a tight-line, his eyes darkened by his dilated pupils.

"Maybe, but sometimes it's fun to watch. Especially when they've been eye-fucking each other." I unbuttoned my pants and looked between the two of them. "I don't know what's been holding them back."

The tension in the room escalated, the lust so palpable I could almost reach out and dip my fingers in it. Olly took a step towards Asher who backed against the dresser. This was one of those moments that it felt like the world stopped spinning for everyone except the two men in front of me.

Olly cupped the back of his neck, pulling him closer. His move surprised me, but then again Olly seemed to have turned over a new leaf.

"I don't know if this is-" He didn't even let Asher get the words out before he kissed him hard.

In my head I had imagined their first kiss being a little softer, very PG. I thought it would be Hallmark Channel gentle with U2's *With or Without You* playing in the background. Instead, what I got was stormy, forceful, and enough to melt my panties right off.

Asher put his hands on Olly's shoulders and pushed him slightly. Olly didn't budge, having a few inches and pounds of muscle on him. Asher was stiff as a board, and when Olly finally pulled away, they were both breathing hard.

"Sorry, I-" Olly started, but Asher grabbed him and spun him so he was pressed against the dresser. The dresser hit the wall and he stared at Olly, one hand bunched in his shirt, the other braced on the edge of the dresser.

I couldn't take my eyes off the two of them, my toy forgotten for the moment. It was like two pit bulls circling each other, waiting to go in for the kill. Olly's eyes landed on me but Asher let go of his shirt and grabbed his chin, bringing his eyes back to him.

They stared at each other for what felt like an eternity, having a silent conversation with their eyes. I knew Olly was open to being with a man, but Asher was a closed book when it was brought up. My stomach dropped as my brain finally processed the fallout that this might cause between all of us.

I shouldn't have pushed them so hard. They weren't ready and I had forced their hand with my flirting and teasing.

I was just about to get off the bed to make sure Asher didn't turn violent when he leaned forward and kissed Olly. My heart thumped hard in my chest as their lips moved against each other, Olly's hand settling on Asher's waist.

Asher pulled away and cleared his throat. "We should finish packing her stuff."

Words must have escaped Olly because he nodded before both he and Asher looked at me on the bed. There was uncertainty written in their eyes, like maybe they thought I'd have an issue with what they just did.

"That was... wow." I stood on shaky legs and threw my vibrator in the box.

They probably didn't need me masturbating to their first kiss, although the wetness between my legs was hard to ignore.

CHAPTER 10

DANICA

I didn't think it would be too different living in my own place, but somehow, it was. Living on campus never felt right and being in my dad's house never came with the responsibility of taking care of things on my own.

Now I was on my own.

The space was quite large for being a one-bedroom apartment, with an open concept living room and kitchen. The ceilings were high and the windows were the same old factory style as Asher's. The bedroom was probably my favorite because it was large enough to fit a gigantic bed that could easily fit all of us.

The guys hadn't seen the bed yet, and I'm sure their reactions would be priceless.

I plopped down on my couch and hugged a pillow to my chest. Things were finally starting to look up for me. School was almost out and I was going to pass all of my classes. The only problem was that I didn't see what purpose they would serve.

Did the academy offer a course on dealing with your tainted blood?

Did they offer a class on not turning evil?

I stared at my reflection in the blank television screen. The angels at the academy weren't wrong that I had evil blood. They just thought it was my father's. Boy, were they wrong.

I still had to figure out how to tell Tobias, Asher, and Olly about what I knew about my mother and about my own blood. I didn't know who would have a worse reaction.

I pulled myself from the couch, which was absurdly comfortable and had to have some kind of tranquilizing properties, and walked around the island into the kitchen. I was about to start pulling out ingredients to cook when a knock came at my door.

The guys weren't supposed to come over for another hour. I was cooking for them again. The only way to learn is to actually do it. This time I was doing more than boiling water and dumping sauce on pasta.

I walked to the door and looked out the peephole. A delivery driver stood outside, a van with 'Beautiful Blossoms' written on the side was behind him. My stomach fluttered and I opened the door. No one had sent me flowers before.

"Danica? I have a delivery here for you." My eyes went wide as I took in the vase of roses in his hands and the open back door of his delivery van. "Forty-two roses."

"Forty-two?" I took the vase and he turned to grab two more vases.

"He was very specific."

I didn't see a card and twisted my face in thought. "Is there not a card? Who are they from?"

"He was very specific about that too. There isn't a card and I can't give you his name." The man smiled and then got into the van to leave.

I didn't know rose buying protocol, but with crazy stalkers I would have thought a buyer would have to give more information to the recipient. I set the vases on the counter and stared at the roses. Who would send me such a random number?

Maybe he had meant forty-eight. That made more sense. I started counting them. Forty-one. I counted again.

I picked up my phone and sent a group text. *Thanks for the roses, whoever sent them.*

I pulled out the ingredients to make chicken enchiladas. The website I got the recipe off of said only an idiot would mess up the recipe that pretty much was tortillas, canned chicken, sour cream, canned sauce, and cheese. As long as I remembered to set the timer, I was confident I wouldn't be an idiot.

I emptied the cans of chicken in a bowl and added the sour cream. It would probably be better with fresh chicken but there was no way I was risking giving everyone salmonella poisoning due to my poor cooking skills. Plus raw chicken grossed me out.

I checked my phone and frowned down at the responses to my thank you. None of them had sent me roses. Maybe my dad had sent them, although that certainly didn't make any sense.

I laid a flour tortilla on a cutting board and was about to scoop the chicken mixture inside when there was another knock on the door. I wiped my hands on a towel and looked out the peephole.

My heart stopped.

Reve's head was down, but I'd recognize his slicked back hair anywhere. How had he even known where I lived? I gulped down the lump that had suddenly worked its way into my throat and put my shaking hand on the door handle.

When I had told him to leave, he hadn't been back. I didn't quite know how to feel about him standing on the other side of my door in the flesh. Would he be the same as he was in my dreams?

He knocked again and I took a steadying breath before opening the door a crack. He had a hand behind his back, and the other tucked in his front pocket, his thumb in the belt loop of his distressed jeans.

"Hi." His voice was just as soothing as it had always been.

I ran my eyes down his body before meeting his moss-colored eyes twinkling back at me. He pulled his hand out from behind his back.

"You sent me the roses?" I still hadn't opened the door fully, trying to decide if it was safe. He was a demon.

My shoulders slumped as my own thoughts hit me like a ton of bricks. *I* was a demon too. His slight smile suddenly dropped and his eyes glistened with concern. He could read me like a book. Of course he could; he had been inside my head.

"Yes, I did. Are you okay? You're pale."

I put my hand against my cheek. I stepped out of the way and opened the door.

"It's just, you're real. You're a demon. You were inside my dreams."

Were all demons so attractive?

He blinked a few times and cleared his throat. "Are you going to let me in or should I go?"

I moved to the side and he stepped into the foyer, handing me the rose in his hand. I didn't know what to make of him. He tortured people in their dreams, turning them into nightmares. Yet, here he was, sending me roses.

We stood awkwardly facing each other, the rose acting as a barrier between us. I probably shouldn't just go opening my door to strangers and then letting them inside. He wasn't a stranger though. He knew me more intimately than my boyfriends even did. He knew my worries and fears. He knew my desires.

Besides, he could probably get inside without me even opening the door.

"Do you want something to drink? Do demons eat and drink?" I bit my lip as I stepped back into the kitchen. I didn't know what to say to him.

He stopped at the edge of the counter and propped his hip against it, his legs crossed at the ankles, and folded his arms crossed over his chest. The fabric of his black cotton t-shirt stretched and his biceps poked out from the sleeves.

His arms were covered in tattoos, just like they were in my dreams. The most noticeable tattoos being the chains around his neck and wrists. I hadn't had the balls to ask him about them yet.

"I don't *have* to eat or drink."

I nodded and went back to putting the chicken and sour cream mixture in a tortilla with cheese as if I hadn't just let a demon into my apartment. I could feel his eyes watching me and braved another glance at him.

"Are you cooking for them?" His voice had a hint of jealousy to it. "Maybe I should go."

I shook my head. I finished the last enchilada and dumped the can of green sauce over them and sprinkled grated cheese on top. I was considering what I wanted to say to him as I preheated the oven.

"Why were you in my dreams? Was I even in control? I felt like I was." It really had felt like my feelings and actions were my own.

He hopped up on my counter like he owned the place and his hands wrapped around the edge. I kept my distance, not trusting myself to be closer to him. I was drawn to him, just like I had been in my dreams.

"Forty-two days ago I was over the roof and was drawn to your pain. I couldn't resist a taste since pain and suffering feed me. But when I was in your own nightmare it made me sick. That was the night I asked you to dance." His eyes darkened slightly as he looked at me. "You've always had free will. Well except when you wanted your three boyfriends there. I blocked that."

His expression turned into a smile and my breath caught in my throat. His smile was enough to bring me to my knees. Even here in the flesh, I wanted him.

"We are a package deal." What was I saying? I couldn't just make a decision without making sure the other three were fine with it. My heart stuttered at the thought of them rejecting Reve.

"Toby will be the hardest to convince of my intentions. He is very protective of you." I gave him a confused look and he continued. "Sometimes you are all still awake when I come to you. I observe your interactions. If anyone is going to try to kill me, it will be him. The other two are too caught up in each other that they probably won't care. Toby though, you're his end game."

"Let me take care of Tobias." I looked down at my hands. "Stay for dinner. Let's see what happens."

What could possibly go wrong? It would be so simple to introduce him as the dream demon who had been wooing me with romantic gestures in dreams. They would totally be on board with me wanting to explore him in the flesh. Totally.

"There's another small problem. Your father can't know about this.

If I would have known he was your father I wouldn't have..." He sighed and ran his hand through his hair. "Now I'm in too deep."

"I can't guarantee that." I really couldn't. Sometimes my dad just showed up unannounced. Besides, if I didn't tell him then someone else would, I was sure.

I grabbed my phone. It was better that they were prepared for Reve and not entering blindly. *A dream demon will be at dinner. You better be on your best behavior.*

Reve slid off the counter and walked around the island into the living room. He picked up a few pictures I had and looked at them.

I watched him as he moved around the room before he sat down on the couch, crossing his ankle onto his knee. His movement was much smoother than a human's or even an angel's.

"Do you fly?" I asked. Of course everyone had super powers except me.

"Something like that. It's more of a float and only when I'm in phantom form." He patted the couch cushion. "Come sit. You set the timer on the oven. You don't have to watch it."

"You cook?"

"No, but I've been around long enough that I know how things work. Like timers." He grinned at me. He was a little bit of a smart ass, something he hadn't been in my head.

I needed to keep him away from Asher.

"How long have you been alive?" I was starting to realize that this question didn't matter much anymore. Not when those around you lived seemingly forever.

"Do you really want the answer to that? It's much longer than your angels." I stood off to the side of the couch and his eyes moved from my face, down my body, and back up. I did the same to him.

"You look twenty." If I had to hazard a real guess, he was much older than twenty. Tobias and Asher were one hundred. He couldn't be that much older.

"In Inferna, we don't measure time. It's hard to say how long I've been alive, if I'm being honest. Are you going to sit? I don't bite.

Unless you want me to." He ran his hand over the cushion next to him and then folded his hands in his lap.

I sat down next to him and turned my body towards him. "Inferna?"

"The part that your father runs is referred to as hell, but that's in Inferna. Could you imagine someone saying, 'go to Inferna' instead of 'go to hell?'" He chuckled and shook his head. "Inferna doesn't flow off the tongue like hell does."

"You never said how old you are."

He rubbed his chin, thinking. He looked up at the ceiling and then did some elaborate counting on his fingers, mouthing things to himself. "Maybe around two thousand."

My eyes widened. "We're talking weeks, right?"

"Years. It's an approximation, give or take a century or two."

My mouth opened in disbelief. I didn't even have time to completely process his age, when there was a knock at the door. He went to stand and I put my hand across his chest, stopping him like when you slam the brakes in a car and put your hand out to stop the passenger from flying forward.

This was about to be a car crash.

"I'll get it. Wouldn't want you to fall and break a hip." I stood as he laughed. What else do you say to a demon that is so old?

I felt like puking as I went to the door. They wouldn't try to *kill* Reve, would they? Could Reve even die? Jesus, he was practically older *than* Jesus. Perhaps he *was* older than him.

I opened the door to three concerned faces. At least this time I wasn't covered in bruises. It's the small victories.

"A dream demon sent you roses and is now in your apartment to join us for dinner?" Tobias wasted no time brushing past me and walking right into my living room. He had connected all the dots quickly, although Asher had most likely told him everything already.

Asher followed close behind him, but Olly stopped in front of me as I shut the door. "Did he hurt you?"

My mouth had opened to respond but then I heard a grunt and

turned to see Tobias had pinned Reve to the brick wall. Of course, at that moment, the timer for the oven went off.

"Let him go." I stopped several feet away, not knowing if they were going to come to blows. Reve had his hands up in surrender and had an amused look on his face. "Now."

Tobias let him go and stepped back, a scowl on his face. "I think it's time for you to leave."

"*You* can leave, but Reve isn't." I gave him a pointed look and then went to turn off the oven and take out the enchiladas. It was a risky move taking out a hot pan with shaky hands, but somehow I managed to get the Pyrex dish onto the stovetop without burning myself.

"What if he tries to kill us or something?" Olly whispered, suddenly appearing right beside me. I jumped at his sudden appearance next to me. Somehow he managed to move like a tiger going in for the kill.

I slammed the spatula I had in my hand down and turned towards him. "No one is going to kill anyone. Actually, you know what? I take that statement back. I will kill each and every one of you assholes if you don't sit your asses down at the table and shut up."

Olly's eyes went wide before he turned and marched his ass to the table and sat down. I watched as the rest of them sat down silently.

I was tired and irritable and just wanted to enjoy the dinner I cooked, not listen to them berate Reve about being a demon. It was the last thing I wanted to hear.

I let out a shaky breath and dumped a bag of tortilla chips in a bowl, grabbed the premade salsa and guacamole, and put them in the middle of the table. No one said a word but there was still a lot of distrustful looks going on.

How would they react when they knew about me? I shuddered at the thought as I placed the pan of enchiladas on the table and sat down.

We ate in silence, besides the grunts that acknowledged that what I had cooked was actually decent. Maybe there was a future for me in the culinary arts, although all it would take was one squirrel and I would be distracted enough to burn a house down.

I was munching on a chip when Tobias put his fork down and looked between me and Reve. "Have you two slept together?"

The tortilla chip lodged in my throat and I damn near felt like I was going to die. I gulped down half the glass of water in front of me as the chip went down like a knife.

"I don't know how best to answer that question." Reve pushed his plate slightly forward on the table and folded his hands in front of him. "Technically speaking, no."

Tobias's eyes narrowed on Reve. "Either you have or you haven't."

"Well, I have never physically touched her." Reve looked over at me.

"What does that even mean? You've touched her, just not with your hands? I don't speak demon, so you're going to have to clarify." I was a little shocked at how Tobias was speaking to Reve. He was protective of me, but this was a whole new level.

"Aren't you some hotshot teacher? I'd expect a little more from a man that teaches Demonology. You must be one of those that they can't shake because of tenure." My eyes went wide as Reve blasted Tobias. "It means I haven't *physically* touched her. I'm a dream demon. I'm sure you are smart enough to figure out the rest."

My head swiveled back and forth between the two. Reve looked smug and Tobias's face had turned red.

"So you took advantage of her in her dreams?" Tobias put his hands on the table like he was about to stand up. I didn't want him to stand up.

Asher and Olly just sat in silence. They seemed amused at the back and forth between the two men. At least they weren't attacking Reve too.

"I can assure you that her subconscious made all the decisions to proceed with any sex that was had. Right Danica?"

"Sex that wouldn't have happened if you weren't in her head to begin with."

"Guys, can you please stop." I let out a sigh. "Even in the dreams, I feel the same way as I do with any of you. Protected, loved."

"You think *he's* the fourth guardian?" Tobias scrunched up his nose in disgust. "It's highly unlikely-"

"It actually makes sense. An archangel, a Fallen, a turned angel, a demon." Olly brought his hand to his chin.

"Do they all walk into a bar?" Asher seemed to be the least interested in the whole conversation of sex with Reve. He had the most time to process the whole situation, which gave me hope that Tobias would come around too.

"What?" Olly looked at Asher, shook his head in confusion and turned back to me. "The prophecy never said anything about your guardians being angels."

"I'm not sure why she needs guardians. She is powerful enough to protect herself." Reve looked confused and then turned thoughtful and looked at me. "Must be the angel part of you. Angels have always been the weaker ones."

My eyes widened and my heart stopped for a fraction of a second. Did he know I was part demon? He winked before turning his attention back to a disgruntled Tobias.

"I just don't foresee this working with a demon. We are all angels, and you are most certainly not." Tobias crossed his arms over his chest as if his word was final.

"You love me, don't you?" I asked softly.

"Of course I do." He seemed shocked that I would even ask.

"And you know I love you?" He nodded in reply. "When we started this, *you* were the one that said being with the others was fine. You said you'd be with me no matter what."

"He's a demon, Danica."

"So what? He's taken care of me. Why do you think I always wanted to sleep at Asher's? He was the reason. I just didn't understand that what was happening in my dreams was an actual person."

"You slept with him." Hurt passed over Tobias's eyes.

Should I feel guilty about having sex in a dream? I wasn't sure. "In a dream. I haven't touched him awake, but I think I will now, because we've discussed and I've decided."

There was a moment of silence and Tobias shut his eyes briefly, as if to gather his thoughts and emotions. "So you want this? To have him be a part of our... thing?"

"I believe it's called a harem." Olly was staring at Reve as if trying to get a read on him. I wouldn't be surprised if that was in his skillset too.

"Whatever it's called, I do want to have him be a part of it. The same way I wanted to be close to all three of you. For whatever reason, he's here, with us. I know it seems sudden, but hasn't everything been a bit sudden?" I couldn't help the way I felt. To an outsider, everything was unconventional, but to me it was my normal.

People meet and fall in love quickly all the time. For me, it was just with four men. Four men I was incredibly sexually attracted to as well.

"Would it help if I let you take a swing at me? Violence seems to help alpha males such as yourself move past any hang-ups." Reve smirked across the table at Tobias.

"I'm not an alpha male!" I would have laughed at Tobias's defensiveness if it hadn't been such a serious conversation.

"Dude. You are. Maybe not a loud one or one that pisses all over the place, but you *do* get a bit mental over her." Asher chuckled and ran a hand through his wavy locks. "Olly told me about you freaking out that you couldn't come back to Earth right away when you were summoned to heaven."

"I agree. You are a quiet, brooding dick at times when it comes to her. It's fucking annoying," Olly mumbled.

My eyes widened. "Asher is rubbing off on you."

"They haven't done that yet, have they? Rubbed each other off?" Reve asked, clearly misconstruing my words as a sexual reference. Or maybe he wasn't and he just wanted to instigate a confrontation.

Now that I had seen him interact with others, I was certain it was the latter.

"You *told* him about us?" Asher sighed and looked at me for an answer.

"No." It had only been a day, why would I tell Reve of all people?

"What do you mean *us*?" Tobias seemed to forget about Reve for the moment. He gestured between Olly and Asher. "As in you two... together?"

"It's complicated," Asher responded. "We're still working on the details of what we are."

Olly frowned at Asher's words, but still kept his eyes locked on the side of Asher's head. I didn't know what details needed to be worked out, but it was pretty clear after their kiss the day before that they were about to combust.

I stood and grabbed Tobias's arm because the conversation was headed down the toilet.

"Let's talk in the bedroom." I turned to Reve. "Maybe you can explain yourself to them."

Tobias followed me into the bedroom and I shut the door. His eyes immediately went to the bed.

"Really? They make a bed *this* big? I guess we kind of need it now that Asher and Oliver are doing whatever and you seem to be convinced that a demon could be one of your guardians. Have you told your dad about this yet?"

"No, and you aren't going to. I will tell him." He made a noise in his throat. "What's going through your head?"

"Well, let's see. You've been abducted and almost died in a basement used for bleeding out angels. Then you decide to steal medical files and get the shit beat out of you. You irrationally move off campus. And now there's Reve, a demon. What is supposed to be going through my head? I love you, and I want to protect you, but you are making it so fucking hard."

Tears sprung to my eyes. When he said all the facts in a nice succinct way, he had a point. I sat on the edge of the bed.

"Are you breaking up with me?" I wouldn't blame him if he was. Out of all of them, he was the one I worried would leave the most. We were an unlikely pair, and despite it feeling so natural between us, sometimes I wondered if he felt the same.

"No. Why would you even jump to that conclusion?" He sat down next to me and ran his fingers through his hair and then rested his elbows on his legs, his face in his hands. "The thought of something happening to you terrifies me." He shook his head slightly. "I can't lose another family."

I put my hand on his back and let out a shaky sigh. "You aren't going to lose me, or Asher, or Olly. I'm sure eventually you will feel better about Reve."

He turned his head towards me, his hands resting on one side of his face. The eye that I could see was swimming with tears and one dripped out and onto his jeans. I bit my lip to keep my own tears from spilling over.

"You can't know that for sure. We all know something is coming. When it does, what if..."

"That's why I have guardians, right? There's no use in worrying about it when instead we could be spending that time loving each other. I mean, look at this bed," I joked.

He snorted and rubbed his eyes with the palms of his hands before sitting up straight and pulling me towards him into a hug. "I don't trust him." He kissed my temple and stood, taking my hand. "I think you should have one of us with you for a while if you plan on hanging around with him."

The logical part of my brain, the part that actually took the time to think things through all the way, knew he had a point. I wasn't about to admit that to him though. Mainly because that would give his alpha complex even more of a boost.

"Are you going to be nice? I'm not as worried about Asher and Olly." I followed him to the door where we stopped.

"I'll try my best." That was a non-answer if I'd ever heard one.

We went back into the living area and Reve, Olly, and Asher were cleaning up the dinner mess. I turned to look over my shoulder at Tobias and give him a 'see, they can get along with him' look.

"Olly wants to go see a movie." Asher flung a dishtowel over his shoulder and turned towards us. He leaned back against the counter and I about had an orgasm from how hot he looked in my kitchen. I guess a man doing the dishes was a turn on.

Naked dishes would be even better.

"I don't do well in crowds." Reve put the last dish in the dishwasher and shut it.

"You two should go." I looked between Olly and Asher. They both looked at each other before Asher shrugged his shoulders and put the dishtowel on the counter.

"I know what you're doing Dani." Asher pulled me into a hug and put his lips near my ear so only I could hear his words. "And thank you."

He pulled back and kissed me before heading to the door, Olly doing the same.

After the door clicked shut, the tension between Reve and Tobias was palpable. It was tempting to send them both on their way, but instead, I plopped down on the center cushion of the couch and patted the cushions on each side of me.

"Mind if I check the game? Then we can watch a movie or something." Tobias grabbed the remote, not waiting for my answer, and turned on the television. I didn't know much about baseball, but what I did know bored me to tears.

Reve sat down and put his arm across the back of the couch, purposely brushing his fingers against my neck. I shivered and my nipples hardened. It was the first time he'd touched me outside of a dream.

"Please don't tell me you're a Dodger's fan," Reve groaned as soon as the game was on. "No wonder you have a stick up your ass."

He twirled the end of my ponytail in his fingers as he shook his head at the screen showing the Dodgers up two runs against the Nationals. They were in the top of the eighth inning and the bases were loaded with red jerseys. I had picked up a few things about baseball from Tobias but was no expert.

"We only root for the Dodger's in this harem," Tobias said, not looking away from the television. He was leaning forward with his forearms on his legs.

I snorted. "You're the only one who watches baseball. I thought you were just checking the score."

"He's nervous, the bases are loaded." Reve was watching the screen now too.

I got bored quickly and leaned into Reve, fitting like a puzzle piece in the crook of his arm. His light touches on my skin as he played with my hair were so relaxing I felt my eyes grow heavy.

My head jerked as Reve started laughing and Tobias let out a slew of curses. Someone hit a homerun with the bases loaded.

"The Giants will always be superior to the Dodgers, by the way."

"Funny. Dodgers are at the top of the league right now. Where are the Giants? Oh, that's right, near the bottom."

I didn't know much about team rivalries in sports, but living in California for your entire life, it is well known that Dodgers fans and Giants fans did not see eye to eye.

"Can you two please stop. There's only so much of this back and forth I can take." I put my head on Reve's shoulder as Tobias looked over at me with a frown on his face.

"If he tells me he's a Raider's fan, I don't think I can deal. Raider's fans are crazy." Was he being serious? I didn't understand the obsessive nature of liking a sports team. Maybe there was a sports demon that had hold of Tobias's brain.

"Raider Nation, baby."

"You two have a lot in common after all. Both of you are sports fans and you both love me." I leaned over and grabbed the controller that Tobias was still gripping. "And you both want to make me happy by turning to something else."

"I think maybe it's time for Tobias to head home for the night."

"I'm going nowhere if you're still here."

"So, what you're saying is that if I wanted to have sex with Danica this evening, you'd want to supervise?"

"You aren't having sex with her."

"Shouldn't that be her decision? You have all had sex with her. Two of you at a time. Watching each other. Why can't I have sex with her?"

"Guys, I'm sitting right here." I couldn't believe they were still at each other's throats. Was this how parents felt when their two children bickered with each other?

"You're probably into all kinds of BDSM shit. That's not Danica's style."

"I can assure you that shit is never part of the equation. Maybe Danica has some secret fantasies you are unaware of. Did you ever think of that?"

"Like what?"

My face must have been fifty shades of red when both men turned their heads to look at me.

"Danica?" Tobias raised his eyebrows.

"I might be a little interested in trying some things out. You always threaten to spank me and you haven't yet. Being tied up appeals to me." I bit my lip because I didn't want to sound like I was unsatisfied with the sex because, hell yes, I was very satisfied. "And I definitely would be turned on if I could boss Olly and Asher around with each other."

"See? I know her better than you think." A cocky grin spread across Reve's face.

"Only because you hijacked her dreams. We could tie you up and torture you a bit. That sounds right up your alley."

The smile slid from Reve's face and he cleared his throat before turning his attention back to me. "I should get going. I have night-mares to create."

He stood and I jumped up after him as he started walking away. I grabbed his wrist and he froze. I let go quickly.

"Reve-"

"It's fine."

I followed him to the door. Once he stepped outside, he turned towards me and gave me a small reassuring smile. It wasn't very reas-suring at all.

My eyes dropped to the chain tattoo around his neck then down to the chains on his wrists. I looked back at his face.

"It was a long time ago, I just haven't been reminded of it in a while. I really do need to get to work." He put his hands in his pockets and I heard a set of keys move.

"Will you be visiting me tonight? It's been a while." I bit my lip. I missed him taking me out of my own nightmares.

"I will." Then he turned and unlocked the door to the apartment right next door.

I should have been shocked or upset with the fact that he was a level ten stalker by a human's standards, but I wasn't. I was starting to come to terms with the fact that nothing in my life was quite human anymore.

CHAPTER 11

DANICA

*M*onday mornings were such a drag, but first thing when I opened my door to leave, I found another bouquet of roses sitting on my doorstep. Reve might be a demon, but he certainly was a charmer.

I quickly unwrapped the cellophane and cut off the ends. I ended up poking myself about a dozen times and wondered why floral shops didn't take more care to cut off the thorns. I emptied the packet of flower preserver in water and stuck the roses in a vase.

I drove to school and walked into class excited for once. There were only two more days of classes before three days of finals. Half of my excitement was from classes being done and half was from not having to wear the atrocious sailor's uniform anymore. Every time I looked in the mirror I thought about how easy it would be to sneak on a yacht and steal it without looking suspicious.

If I didn't need them for next year, I'd have burned them. I *really* wanted to burn them. The temptation to not return was strong.

I put my bag down on the table and approached Tobias's desk where he was staring at his computer screen with an intensity that made him sexier than usual.

"Good morning, Mr. Armstrong. How are you this marvelous Monday?"

He grunted without looking up from his computer screen. I stood there for another moment, hoping he was just in the middle of reading an email, but then he closed his computer and shuffled some papers.

I swear sometimes Tobias had mood swings like he was the one that had to deal with a bleeding vagina. Yesterday we had all, with the exception of Reve, hung out all day. Tobias even helped me study.

"You need to take a seat Ms. Deville." He looked up at me, his eyes pleading.

I tilted my head a bit, trying to figure him out. He hadn't called me Ms. Deville in what felt like forever. It was a warning.

I rolled my eyes at him and sat down in my seat just as other students began trickling in. They were talking in hushed whispers and kept sneaking glances in Tobias's direction. I picked up bits and pieces of the conversation and my eyes widened and my gut clenched.

"She moved off campus."

"He was on call Saturday night and Sunday, but he wasn't here."

"I heard Dean Whittaker got a report that our wards were compromised for a short time because he wasn't here when he was supposed to be."

"Oliver is never around anymore either."

"She must have them under some kind of spell. Do you think they even know?"

"I hope he doesn't get fired. He's my favorite teacher."

The sudden urge to vomit hit me and I tried to busy myself by getting out my notebook. This was my fault. I was the one who moved off campus. I was the one who had a demon love interest that made Tobias uncomfortable enough to shirk his duties.

I braved a glance up in Tobias's direction. He was holding it together pretty well considering what was being said about him. Well, besides the slight tremor in his hands and the frown on his face.

When Olly entered the room, the whispering stopped and more staring happened as he strode over to the seat next to me and sat down. Whispers started again and he turned to look around the room and then to look at me.

"What happened?" he asked under his breath.

"I'm not sure but they're whispering about us. *All* of us. I think Tobias is in trouble." I worked my bottom lip between my teeth and took a calming breath, not that it helped much. "What if he gets fired?"

Olly made a noise somewhere between a grunt and a snort. "Michael assigned him here. He isn't going anywhere."

I considered his words, allowing myself to calm down a bit. "But he'll have some kind of consequence, won't he?"

"Stop worrying. You have enough on your plate. We've all made our choice to be with you. He's known that people might find out at some point." Olly put his hand on my thigh and squeezed.

Class started and Tobias went through what we would be covering over the next two days. Our final was on Friday so we would spend time reviewing the most important takeaways from the semester.

I tried to pay attention to his words, but my mind had other ideas and instead played through the events from the weekend. Tobias had built himself as a well-respected and competent instructor, and here I was ruining it for him.

CLASSES WERE over for the day. I was glad I no longer had to study for my GED or meet Olly to review the absurd amount of expectations at the academy. I had passed both the GED test and the bullshit made-up test with flying colors.

I walked across campus to the faculty building and let myself in. Tobias hadn't taken my keys yet. I made my way to his room and let myself in with the key he had given me. He wasn't back yet, so I planted myself on his futon.

I pulled my phone out of my bag and was surprised to see a text from my dad. He had been fairly silent lately and we hadn't been talking much. He knew I had moved, had been opposed to it as any father would, but he hadn't stopped me.

I would like to see your new place. Thursday evening?

Despite knowing that he hadn't wanted me to move off campus, I was excited to show him I was adulting. I knew he just worried about me being on my own, but I had Asher right upstairs and apparently Reve had slyly leased the apartment next door.

It was like the building was made for the three of us rejects. The ex-Fallen, the demon, and the freak.

I put my phone on the table and picked up a large, leather-covered photo album I had never seen before. Tobias didn't have pictures lying around. I flipped open the cover and smiled. These were probably the pictures Asher had gotten from Tobias's family and scanned into his computer.

The photos were black and white, but in a way that made them even more vibrant with life. You notice other things in black and white photos. The first several pages were of Tobias and his wife, Margie. In every picture of them, they were glued at the hip with smiles on their faces. There were pictures of their wedding day, them posing on a beach, and them in front of a house.

They were a beautiful couple. Tobias looked exactly the same with his trimmed beard, broad shoulders, and narrow waist. Margie was what I'm sure was considered a bombshell back during that time; a classic beauty. She had long blond hair, the softest eyes, and Marilyn Monroe-like curves.

I turned the pages and watched his children grow up before my eyes. He had done the same, watched them grow in photographs. It broke my heart to know he only had memories up until the time he left for war.

He had missed everything. Their first days of school, their first lost teeth, graduations, marriages. I wiped at my face to stop the tears from dripping onto the plastic protected pages.

I heard the door open behind me, but continued to look through the pictures. I wasn't sure if he'd be upset that I was looking at them, but I couldn't hide the fact that I had seen them. I had taken an intimate tour of his past life and a life that could have been.

"Hey." I heard his bag hit the kitchen table and his keys follow shortly behind. I could tell by the sounds that he was kicking his shoes off. First his left, then his right. It was always the same.

I didn't say anything and instead shut the album and placed it back on the table. I heard him let out a sigh as he walked towards me.

"I'm assuming you've heard the rumors?" He sat down next to me and reached forward to run his hand over the cover of the album.

"It's all anyone talked about today. No one seemed to care that I could hear every word they said." I fiddled with the hem of my button-down shirt, which I had untucked earlier. "Are you in trouble?"

He grabbed one of my hands to stop me from fiddling and laced his fingers through mine. His head landed on my shoulder and my heart nearly burst out of my chest.

"Michael is coming tomorrow after classes to meet with me and Sue." He ran his thumb back and forth across the length of my thumb. "I'm sorry about this morning. There was a pretty scathing email sent to me and Michael about it. You know how Whittaker is."

"I do. Maybe we should cool things off for a bit. Until you clear this mess up." The words felt wrong coming out of my mouth. I hadn't wanted to say them, but I also couldn't sit by and watch Tobias let his life spiral out of control because of me.

Especially not when I was harboring such a large secret that I was certain would change things.

His head popped up from my shoulder, and with his other hand, he grabbed my chin and turned my face towards him. His eyes searched mine.

"We're not running away from this. I won't run away from it." His eyes were glossy and I bit the inside of my lip, trying to keep my own tears at bay.

I nodded my head and he pulled me against him, taking the hair band out of my hair and running his fingers lightly through it.

"Don't say shit like that. It hurts." I could barely hear his voice against my hair. "I don't care what anyone says. I haven't since the moment I touched you. I love you and I'm never letting you go."

I couldn't stop the tears from falling. He said that now, but I wasn't so sure. I needed to tell them, all of them.

"Make love to me," I mumbled into his shirt.

He pulled back and looked at me, swiping his thumbs under my eyes to wipe the tears away.

"Are *you* okay?"

I nodded my response and he brushed his wet thumb over my bottom lip, my salty tears spreading over it.

"I'm fine." I shifted so I was straddling him. I really wasn't fine, and I hadn't been in a while, but telling him now would just make matters worse.

I lowered my lips to his neck and kissed my way down as I unbuttoned his shirt. Right now, what I needed was him in my mouth.

His lids grew heavy as I reached the final button and slid from his lap onto the floor in front of him. He parted his knees and I kept my eyes on his as I unbuckled his belt.

"Danica, you don't have to-" His head tilted back onto the cushion and he let out a hiss of breath as I palmed his length through his slacks.

He came to life against my hand, and despite the somber mood, I couldn't keep the smile off my face. I loved the effect I had on these men, time and time again. No matter what I said or did, they always seemed to have an eternal flame burning for me. I could only hope that it would remain.

I pulled his zipper down and tugged his pants down and off. I ran my hands up his thighs before gripping him at the base of his cock. He was fully aroused now, a bead of pre-cum already at the tip, waiting for my tongue to lap it up.

I gave him a few firm pumps before blowing air gently on the tip.

"Fucking hell." His voice was raspy with desire.

He threaded his fingers through my hair as I flicked my tongue across the head, taking a taste of him. He rolled his hips up, urging me to take him into my mouth. As much as I wanted to, I also wanted to savor him, to worship him.

I tilted my head and sucked the sensitive skin at the base, my tongue darting out to tease his balls.

His breaths became short and fast as I slowly moved my lips back to the tip and took him in my mouth. I watched his face as I took him all the way in until he hit the back of my throat.

I hummed as I worked him with my mouth, his hips moving in shallow thrusts, attempting to get deeper.

Once he was thoroughly worked up and panting, I stood up and made slow work of taking off my blazer, shirt, and skirt. He eyed me hungrily, but didn't move from his spot.

As much as he enjoyed taking charge in the bedroom, he also enjoyed torturing himself by watching. I unclasped my bra, letting it fall as I took an extra-long time sliding my panties off. I dropped them on top of his pants, the message clear. He could keep them.

I watched as he stroked himself before I lowered onto his lap, my knees on either side of him. I braced my hands on the back of the futon as he helped guide himself into me until we were completely connected.

Our lips touched in a gentle kiss that left my toes curling as I began rolling my hips. This was my favorite position, the downward movement always hitting my clit just the right way.

Tobias buried his face in my neck, sucking the skin lightly as I increased my pace. His hands slid to my ass and palmed my flesh.

"Spank me," I breathed, barely managing to get the words out as my body prepared itself to erupt. I gripped the back of the futon and felt my body tense as one of his hands moved and then sent a sharp slap to my cheek.

"Jesus, Danica," he growled, rubbing the spot. His hips began working under mine, pushing himself deeper.

"Again." I'd never been spanked before, and now I wondered why I had waited so long to request it. When his flattened palm hit my ass again, my muscles clenched around him and my orgasm hit with such force that I ceased to exist. My bones turned to jelly and I could barely move.

Taking that as his cue to take over, he lifted me and laid me on the futon, settling between my legs. I arched my body into his and brought his lips back to mine.

He moved in slow, torturous strokes with his face buried in the crook of my neck. I clung to him like he was the anchor keeping me from floating away.

As his pace increased, I felt another orgasm building deep inside of me. My skin felt feverish from the friction of our bodies and the prolonged love making that was making my head feel fuzzy.

Tobias came in a final deep thrust that sent me over the edge with him, our bodies shuddering as they rode out the waves of pleasure.

"That was..." I couldn't find the words to describe it. I loved sex, but this transcended sex. It was a declaration.

"I love you." He kissed my cheek and then pulled back, concern in his eyes. "You're burning up."

I raised a hand to my cheek and shrugged. "Fantastic sex will do that to a person."

"I don't have a thermometer." Tobias pulled out, leaving me feeling empty, and stood. I gazed up at him. "You look really flushed."

"I'm fine." I sat up and my head spun. That was some orgasm. "Really. Don't worry so much. I'm sure in a few minutes my body will realize the orgasms are done with. At least for now."

He went into his bathroom and returned with a washcloth and folded it in fourths. He put it across my forehead. I sighed and leaned my head back to keep it from falling off.

He sat down, still naked, next to me. "Have you been sleeping at all?"

"Yes, better than I have in months thanks to Reve." I shut my eyes and let the cool washcloth work its magic. I felt Tobias's hands stroking the hair back from my face.

He made a noise in his throat and I cracked an eye open to see him staring intently at me. I shut it again and focused on the feel of his fingers smoothing back my hair.

"What if one night he decides to torment you in your dreams?"

"He won't."

"You don't know that."

I was quiet for several minutes before responding. "I do know that. Just like I know that all of you have my best interests at heart, even when you drive me nuts sometimes."

"He's a-"

I cut him off, not wanting to hear him say the five-letter word again. "I don't care. My dad is the devil. My mom is Lilith. Asher used to be Fallen. You're being close-minded and not thinking about how much he's helping me or about how much I-" I opened my eyes and stared at the ceiling fan. There was something soothing about watching the blades spin. "How much I love him. I haven't been doing well, Tobias. You know it. I know it. Everyone knows it. Let me have the peace he brings me, please."

I sounded desperate. I *was* desperate. I hated feeling like my life was spiraling out of control. For once I wanted to be in control of my own destiny, even if that meant pissing off some people along the way.

"Okay."

"Okay?" I cocked an eyebrow and the washcloth slid off and plopped onto my chest. Tobias ran his fingers over my moist forehead. "Just like that you're okay with me and Reve?"

"Just like that." He placed his lips against my cheek. "I love you. If you think Reve will help you in a way we can't... I don't want you to resent me."

I brought my hand to his cheek. "I could never resent you. I love you."

"The biggest issue is he likes the Giants *and* the Raiders. It's completely unacceptable. I don't see how it's going to work."

I groaned and couldn't keep the smile from spreading across my face.

CHAPTER 12

DANICA

I could taste the sweet flavors of freedom. One more final left on Friday and I was home free, or at least academy free for the summer. Well, besides the independent study classes I had to complete from semester one.

I sat with my feet propped on my ottoman and stared at the blank television screen. I didn't need to study for my Demonology final so I was left with nothing to do but wait for my dad to show up.

I hadn't seen him since I told him we dug up Lily's grave and had barely spoken to him. He was preoccupied, and I couldn't blame him. I didn't even want to imagine what he was going through.

First he finds out his partner was lying to him, then that his daughter is half demon, and then to top it all off, that the casket was empty. It was a lot for me to handle with the support of my angels. He was dealing with the shitstorm alone.

I knew I needed to tell my angels I was half demon. The thing was, I didn't feel like a demon, not that I would know what that felt like. I didn't feel like an angel either though.

I must have fallen asleep on the couch because I was jolted awake by a sharp knock on the door. I rubbed my eyes and went to the door.

I opened it, finding my father standing outside, dressed in a charcoal gray suit. He looked tired. He never looked tired. I moved out of the way for him to enter and shut the door.

"Dad," I greeted him, standing there awkwardly. The last time we had been in the same room with each other he had told me to get out.

"Give me a tour?" He walked into the kitchen and I followed, biting my lip. I guess he was still upset. He looked around, but didn't say another word.

"Well, obviously this is the kitchen. That's the living room." He followed me, nodding his head in what I hoped was approval until we got to the bedroom. "The bedroom."

I stepped inside and did a sweeping motion with my hand. His eyebrows nearly shot off his face as he took in the bed that nearly took up the entire space.

"Danica Marie. What in the hell do you need a bed this big for?" He must have realized he didn't really want the answer to that question. "Never mind. Some things fathers don't need to know."

He followed me back into the living room and we sat on the couch. Several awkward moments of silence passed before we both started talking at once.

"I'm sorry I dug up Mom's grave."

"I shouldn't have snapped like I did."

He ran a hand over his face before continuing. "You shouldn't be prying into this, Danica. Clearly she is up to something if she felt the need to have a child then fake her own death. Then almost two decades later start abducting angels for their blood."

"Are you sure it's her?" I asked in a whisper.

"We're positive it's her. She was here and we think she's been following you. Michael was able to get the security footage from the grocery store. She looks different than she did eighteen years ago." He cleared his throat. "We think she and John are in Shanghai, China, right now. There have been angel disappearances there. We just can't figure out what role John plays in all of this, unless he's under her spell."

"She can put a spell on people?" I drew my eyebrows together, considering his words. I was fairly certain the woman behind me in the bathroom line at Universal Studios had been her too. What other explanation was there for her disappearing suddenly and the woman behind me saying there had been no one?

"She is certainly manipulative. With humans she might be able to sway their thoughts. I honestly don't know what she's capable of. If she's capable of having a child and then faking her own death, well..." He adjusted the watch on his wrist. I had never seen him so antsy in my life.

"I haven't told the guys about what this all means for me." I tried to keep the tears that were filling my eyes from spilling over, but a few escaped and trailed down my cheeks.

He scooted over on the couch and pulled me into a hug. "It doesn't mean anything. You're the same girl you were before we knew she was Lilith."

I shook my head and let the tears soak his suit jacket. "I don't know who I am anymore."

He rubbed my back in small circles and I felt the tension leaving my shoulders. I hadn't even realized they'd been so tense.

"You need to tell them. You shouldn't have to carry the weight of this on your shoulders. They love you. They know that your blood isn't what defines you."

"But it does. They-" I stopped short, realizing he didn't know about Reve. Their reactions to Reve said enough about what their reaction to me would be.

"They what?" He pulled back and looked at me, worry plaguing his face.

"They don't like demons."

"They've never even met a demon. And you're forgetting something very important. You aren't a demon." He brushed the tears from my cheeks.

"I'm not an angel either then. So what am I, Dad? Just a freak?"

He took a sharp inhale of breath and searched my eyes like he was seeing me for the first time. Seeing the woman who was confused about who she was and what that meant.

"You're-"

"Danica, you home?" Reve's head came through the brick wall separating his apartment from mine. He really had the worst timing.

When his eyes landed on Lucifer they went wide and I could tell he tried to retreat but something in the air shifted. He was frozen in place, stuck with his head through the wall.

"Sir," Reve said in a strangled voice. "I can't breathe."

Lucifer stood and walked over to the wall where Reve was trapped. I stood too, but stayed where I was. I could feel the air pulsating with the threat of violence.

"Reve." His voice was rough and angry. He grabbed a handful of Reve's hair and yanked him through the wall the rest of the way before slamming him up against the brick so hard the mounted television shook.

"Sir, I can explain." Lucifer's hand was around his throat, Reve's feet hanging a foot above the ground.

"How do you know Danica?"

A choking sound came from Reve and his face turned bright red. He was trying to speak but Lucifer's grip was crushing his throat.

"Dad. Stop." I was frozen in place, watching the train that was my life speed down the mountain, ready to wreck.

He turned his head towards me and his face made me back up a step. He was barely containing his anger and I knew if I didn't calm him down, it would be a repeat of when I told him about Lily's grave.

"He's... I'm in love with him." My voice was shaking as I said the words and his head snapped back around to look at Reve.

"How is she in love with a demon whose sole purpose on this Earth is to punish people with nightmares?" Reve's feet kicked against the wall as he struggled to get air. "Are you what's been causing her to lose sleep?"

He shook his head vigorously, his eyes wide.

Finally, my feet started working and I rushed to them. I grabbed the arm that was holding Reve hostage.

This was why I was scared to tell Tobias, Asher, and Olly I was a demon. Even my own father wasn't immune to the disgust towards them. I could see it in his eyes.

I choked on a sob and yanked his arm again. He relented and dropped Reve who took such a large gasp of air, I thought he might suck all of the air out of the room.

"How can you say that me having demon blood means nothing when you... when you..." I couldn't get the words out so instead I just punched him in the arm in frustration. I might as well have punched the brick wall.

He grabbed my fist as I was about to punch him again. "You know that's not-"

"It *is* the same thing!" I yelled, and tried to yank my arm away. "Where does this leave me? I'm not angel enough to be an angel, I have no wings, my mother is some kind of demon, and now my father is looking at me like he doesn't even know me." I managed to get my arm free and turned away from the two men who were staring at me with what looked very much like pity. "My own mother didn't even want me."

I was spiraling. I knew that. I was never one for self-loathing, but that was until the world seemed out to take me down. Other eighteen-year olds didn't have to wonder if they were going to suddenly sprout ten heads or tentacles. With my luck, I'd morph into a fingernail demon and be condemned to a life of munching on fingernails.

Reve appeared in front of me and I looked away.

"Look at me." His voice was raspy, probably from being almost choked to death by the devil.

I shook my head and he took my chin and forced my eyes to meet his.

"Am I evil?" I shook my head. "Then what makes you think you are? You are the farthest from evil I have ever seen. Your heart and soul are so overflowing with love and light that you could never be evil."

"But they... does it matter how I feel?" I might not feel like anything other than a plain old human, but when people treated you differently, it made you feel like less of one.

"I think to them, it does matter how you feel. They didn't kill me. Your father hasn't killed me."

"Yet."

Reve rolled his eyes and I started to laugh. I was standing in a room with a devil and a demon who just rolled his eyes at him. Sometimes I wondered if I would one day wake up in a mental institution in a straitjacket and padded room, having imagined it all.

He pulled me towards him and wrapped his arms around me. I heard my dad grumbling and braved a look over my shoulder to see him running his fingers through his hair and shaking his head.

"Dad?" I pulled away and stepped around Reve. "What's wrong?"

"The prophecy. It's true. Of course it's true. Lucifer and Lilith, his greatest regrets have a daughter that has to save us all." He started laughing and Reve let me go. I backed up a step. "Is this my redemption?" He spread his arms out and spoke to the ceiling. "Really fucking funny! Isn't a life in hell enough?"

Reve grabbed my hand. "Sir, from what I've overheard about the prophecy, it sounds like a load of crap. It is well known in the dream demon community that Nostradamus was plagued by a rogue dream demon for many years."

"Like you're plaguing my daughter?" He turned and his eyes went straight to our connected hands. "Reve. This is-"

"I know what it seems like, Sir, but I can assure you that I've only brought happiness to Danica's dreams."

I didn't know whether to fear for him or be in awe of him for interrupting and standing up to my father. When my father looked over at me, I nodded.

"I need to contact Michael. Damn it. I'm going to have to admit that he was right." He stared at Reve for a moment. "If you hurt her, I will rescind my protection."

Protection? I opened my mouth to ask but Reve answered, "I can assure you, I won't."

With one last look, Lucifer vanished.

∼

I SENT A GROUP TEXT. *Meet me on the roof.*

I was already a mess, might as well rip the Band-Aid clean off the wound and bleed out if necessary.

Reve was by my side, holding my hand, when Olly, Asher, and Tobias landed on the roof together. Had they all been off doing something together? I guess it made sense, since I told them my dad and I were going to hang out.

Although I'd hardly call the events downstairs hanging out.

We met in the middle of the roof and I shut my eyes for a brief moment. I was experiencing an extreme case of déjà vu from the recurring nightmare I'd been having, except this time, Reve was right next to me.

"I need to talk to you all about something." Reve gave my hand a reassuring squeeze as I spoke. Three sets of eyes tracked his movements.

I looked between them before letting go of Reve's hand. I moved to stand in front of each of them, looking them in the eye one by one. I needed to tell them.

What do I say? How do I say it?

My breathing felt irregular as I stopped in front of Olly. If anyone was going to accept the fact that I was of diabolical origins, it was him.

"Dani?" Olly's voice was laced with concern.

"My mother, Lily, is Lilith. She is a demon." I shut my eyes and let the setting sun hit my face, the warmth doing nothing to ease the chill that had come over me. "I'm not half human. I'm part angel, part demon."

Complete silence fell on the roof, it seemed even the traffic and noise on the street below had been muted for this moment. My words sounded completely crazy, even to my own ears.

"I figured as much," Tobias said.

"Me too," Asher confirmed.

I looked at Olly who was staring at me, hurt in his eyes. It was a look that wasn't common on his face and it broke my heart.

"You've known this since Spring break?" I nodded in reply. "And you kept it from us?"

I reached forward to grab his hand but he backed up a step. "Olly, I was-"

"You were what, Danica? Scared of how we'd react? Scared we would up and leave?" Both Asher and Tobias stood with wide eyes as Olly showed an emotion we hadn't seen before: anger. "I can't be here right now."

Before anyone could say anything to stop him, his wings extended and he shot into the sky like a blur.

"I'm going to go after him," Asher said. He cupped my cheek and then followed Olly.

I brought one of my hands to my mouth to contain the sob that was threatening to spill out. Tobias stepped forward and wrapped his arms around me.

"He'll come around. He's just been really worried about you these past few weeks. I think he knew too, but you just hadn't confirmed it." He kissed my temple and then looked over at Reve who was standing back, observing.

"I'm not going anywhere," Reve said.

Tobias sighed and walked over to stand in front of him. "We're not going anywhere either."

"So where does that leave us, angel? I don't intend to hurt anyone. If I do, Lucifer will have my head." Reve stuck out his hand. "Truce?"

Tobias eyed his hand and finally took it, the two shaking.

~

My HAND SHOOK SLIGHTLY as I stared down at the unopened text message from Olly. Out of the three, I never expected him to be as upset as he was.

Tobias and Reve were oblivious to the world. They had somehow managed to settle on watching a baseball game and wanted the same team to win. I was glad for the time being they were at least making an attempt to get along.

I finally clicked the text open. *I'm sorry I flew off like that. It's not because you have demon blood, it's because you kept it from us and were suffering because of it. I'll see you tomorrow for our final.*

I let out a shaky breath of air and Tobias's and Reve's heads turned towards me.

"Olly texted me. Everything's fine, I think." I slumped down in the chair and put my head on the cushion. "I should come with the warning label 'requires patience.'"

Tobias snorted.

"Am I missing something?" Reve asked.

"Just as she said. She sometimes requires patience. I'm working on having more of it myself," Tobias answered with a chuckle.

"I've been getting a little better. Making a conscious effort," I defended myself. Unfortunately, I could think of several things in the past month where a little more thought would have been advantageous.

"It makes things interesting. I think we all should be a little more spur of the moment."

I heard the television go silent and then movement. I popped open an eye to see Tobias standing next to the chair. He had a look in his eye.

"I have *your* final tomorrow," I warned, sitting up all the way and glancing at Reve who appeared to be in deep thought. "Stop looking at me like that."

"How am I looking at you?" A smirk formed on his face as he grabbed me and threw me over his shoulder.

I reached down and swatted his ass. "Put me down. We should be going to sleep soon."

"It's barely nine. If anyone should be worried about what time they're going to be sleeping, it's Reve since he's ancient." Tobias smoothed a hand over my ass and walked towards the bedroom.

I lifted my head to look to Reve for help but he just stood and followed silently.

"Reve, aren't you going to say anything back to that? He just called you an old man."

Reve looked directly in my eyes and slowly shook his head.

His lack of words was making my heartbeat go straight to my clit. Tobias dumped me on the bed and lay down next to me. I made a move to roll towards him but he pinned my wrists as he moved to hover over me.

"Tobias, what do you think you're doing?" I looked up at him and licked my lips, ready for him to come in for the kill.

"I'm being spur of the moment. Plus keeping your mind occupied. You've been thinking too much lately." He let go of one of my wrists and trailed a finger down my cheek, causing me to shiver with pleasure. He lowered his lips to my ear. "The whole time, I'll be watching to make sure he behaves himself."

He wasn't even touching me and I felt a jolt of electricity between my legs. He pushed up off the bed and I looked past him, but Reve was nowhere to be seen. Had I missed how this had even transpired?

"He left!" I sat up on my forearms. "Maybe he's not into-"

"I'm into it." I heard his voice next to me on the bed and turned.

Tobias let me go and sat on the other side of the bed. I turned back to the direction Reve's voice had come from.

"Show yourself." My heart was thudding in my chest as I watched his hand appear and move towards the hem of my shirt. "Reve, what are you doing?"

"Am I scaring you?" His voice was like a caress.

"No, but-" His finger came to my lip to hush me. He ran it along my bottom lip before trailing it down to lift my shirt off. "You didn't hear a thing Tobias and I talked about while you stared at your phone, did you?"

"Well, no. Weren't you talking about RBIs and pinch hitters? Hardly anything I want to listen to." His finger appeared and traced along the edge of my bra before disappearing again. It was like being blindfolded, but not. My breath came in small gasps as his fingers touched my skin and then disappeared again.

"I told him I was going to have sex with you and asked him if he had a problem with that."

"And what did he say?" I breathed as his hand unclasped my bra and pulled it off.

His mouth appeared above my breast and he swirled his tongue around the rosy bud that was so hard it almost hurt. I arched off the bed and tried to grab him but he disappeared.

"Can't try to touch me when I'm doing this." He ran a finger down my stomach to my pants and unbuttoned them.

"Tobias said he still didn't trust me, but that if you wanted this then he was going to have to be fine with it. But he wants to watch." He put his mouth next to my ear. "Do you want him to watch? Because I don't mind. Maybe he'll learn a thing or two."

I let out a moan that was answer enough and Reve reappeared, completely naked. He was exactly as he was in my dreams; muscled and tattooed from his neck to his feet. He was magnificent.

He wasted no time removing my pants and panties. He sat back on his heels and stared down at me with hooded eyes before a wicked grin spread across his face. Then he faded from sight.

I looked over at Tobias, who hadn't moved from the other end of the bed, but was watching intently. I always thought it would be weird to have someone watch me have sex, but since these men came into my life, it was nothing but a turn-on. The self-control it must have taken to just sit back and watch was something I couldn't do. I had struggled just watching Asher and Olly kiss.

He rubbed a palm over his erection through his pants. I felt lips on my inner thigh and gripped the sheets to avoid trying to grab at Reve.

"Holy shit." The lips moved up and brushed along the outer folds of my pussy. It was killing me not being able to see him or anticipate what he was going to do next. "Reve, please."

I don't know what I was begging for, but I was begging for *something*. A finger ran along my slit, spreading my slickness with it. It wasn't something new I had never experienced before, but when you couldn't see anything that was happening but could still *see*, it was something else entirely.

"Oh my God. Are you going to fuck me while you're like this?" The thought made me jack my hips towards him. "Reve!" Two fingers thrust into me and I heard Tobias chuckle.

I turned my head towards him and watched as he stroked himself, his cock pulled free of his pants. I bit my lip and he tightened his fist.

"I've never heard you so vocal." His voice was low and he groaned as Reve appeared again and met my lips.

"If this makes you uncomfortable, I'll stop." Reve slid his erection along my pussy and put the tip at my entrance.

"It doesn't." I traced his cheek with my finger and then he vanished again and then thrust into me in one smooth move. "Oh, God damn."

My voice seemed to fail me as he thrust in and out of me with such even and smooth thrusts that I wondered if he was some kind of sex robot. I could hear his grunts and breaths, but not seeing him was driving me crazy and we'd barely even started.

"I'm going to come," I said through clenched teeth. "Reve!" His name left me in a rush as my orgasm shook my body.

Reve reappeared and I dug my nails into his back. He groaned and pulled me to my hands and knees, facing Tobias who was working his cock with such force, I thought he might break it off.

He thrust back into me from behind and pulled me back against him, one arm going across my chest, holding me in place, and the other going to my clit and matching Tobias's speed.

A chorus of "fucks" filled the room as we all fell head first into orgasms. I fell onto the bed, still convulsing with pleasure as Reve pulled me to his chest and lay behind me.

And to think I had wondered how I'd ever please four men.

CHAPTER 13

DANICA

My last final was Demonology. I was more than ready to ace it, but of course I woke up with a splitting headache. I stopped on the way to campus and got a Diet Dr. Pepper, hoping it would help.

When I had first quit soda cold turkey, I had gotten similar headaches that had taken me a solid week to shake. I was probably just stressed or stayed up too late with Tobias and Reve.

I made my way across campus, the bright morning sun making me shield my eyes with my hand. I loved the sun, but today I wanted it to hide behind some clouds.

I trudged my way up the two flights of stairs, feeling my pulse behind my eyes with each step I took. If an archangel could heal bruises, maybe they could also heal a headache.

I took my seat next to Olly and pulled out a pen. I had barely made it in time.

"Can you heal a headache?" I glanced over at Olly, who was folding a piece of paper into an intricate design.

He didn't look up from his paper folding. "I don't know. Let me finish this and I'll try."

"Settle down and we'll get started," Tobias said, standing from his desk with a stack of booklets in his hand. "It's been a pleasure teaching you this semester. Good luck and have a great summer."

"I bet he did have a lot of pleasure this semester," I heard someone mumble a few rows back. Several students snickered and Tobias cleared his throat.

While he was passing out our finals, I felt Oliver slide his hand into the pocket of my blazer. I looked at the two of him and then rubbed my eyes. Jesus, I had never seen double before, not even high or drunk.

"Read that later." He put his cool hand on my forehead and I flinched at how cold it felt. "You're really hot."

"Uhm, thanks?" I felt a tingling sensation but nothing else. He removed his hand.

"I mean your forehead. It's burning up. Maybe you should go to the-"

"The final is out. No talking," Tobias warned.

Olly gave me a concerned look but I just shook my head and opened my booklet. I stared down at the first question. I knew my shit. I had this one in the bag. I put my name on the top and answered the first question.

The room was silent besides the soft whir of the air conditioner, pens moving across pages, and my heartbeat that seemed to be beating in my ears.

I pinched the bridge of my nose and turned the page. I rested my chin on my fist that I had placed on the table. My eyes felt like they were about to pop out of my head and my vision blurred again.

Crap. Was this what a migraine felt like? I'd never had one, but this was far more than any headache. I stood abruptly as nausea surged in my belly. It felt like the room was spinning. My stomach felt like it was stuck in the spin cycle of the washing machine.

"Danica?" I wasn't sure who said it; the voice was hard to make out behind the ringing in my ears.

I stumbled out from behind the table and headed for the door. I needed air. I needed to get outside. I felt warm liquid on my face and reached up to wipe at it. I pulled my hand away and stared down at the bright red liquid. I quickly put my hand back up to cup my nose.

I could feel the blood oozing through my fingers. I made it to the door and lowered my hand to grip the door handle. There was so much blood; where was it all coming from? Had my brain exploded?

The classroom behind me had erupted in chatter and several chairs scraped across the floor. I couldn't hear what the voices were saying as I managed to get the door open.

I stumbled into the empty hall and fell.

A FAINT TICKING PULLED me out of the darkness that had taken me under. I wasn't dreaming. I wasn't having a nightmare. It was just an emptiness staring back at me, black and infinite.

My eyelids felt heavy, and after several attempts at opening them, I gave up. Instead, I tapped into my other senses that did seem to be working. My skin felt clammy and cold, goosebumps slowly moving across my skin as my body registered that it was cold in the room. What the fuck had happened to me?

I heard voices behind a closed door drawing nearer. The sound of a door opening.

"How is she?" It was Tobias.

"We think we have the fever and bleeding under control," my dad responded. His voice had an edge to it.

"What are you doing here?" Tobias said, not sounding happy at all. It was hard to see who he was talking to. My eyes seemed to be stuck shut.

"I called him," Olly said. "He is just as much a part of this as we are."

Tobias made a noise in his throat. "A part of this? Ever since he's been around she's been a mess. Can't sleep, her focus is even worse, and now she's sick. Interesting it happened right after she slept with him."

"Tobias," Asher warned.

"Did you ever stop to consider that *you* three are the cause of this?

Her nightmares only have you in them. When Asher died, it changed her. Plus, you have stressed her out beyond belief because I'm a demon." I heard several footsteps and then Reve warned, "Get your hand off me, angel."

"Stop." My voice sounded foreign in my ears, like it was laced with gravel. I managed to pry my eyes open just a fraction, enough that when the light seeped in, I clenched them shut again.

A hand took mine. "Danica, sweetie. How are you feeling?" My dad put two hands around mine. They were cold against my skin. "She has a fever again. Damn it. Where are they?"

Where was who? Where was I?

"Folks, let's clear the room so we can check her vitals," a male voice I didn't recognize said. "Lucifer can stay. Maybe you four can try to find out where Michael is and the ETA for Raphael."

I heard grumbles and feet retreating before the door was shut.

"Danica? I'm Dr. Hughes and this is my assistant, Diane. Can you open your eyes for me?"

"Bright." I managed to say. My throat and mouth felt like the Sahara desert. I needed water. Stat.

I heard a lamp switch being turned and slowly opened my eyes. It wasn't as bright as before. The overhead light was turned off and a bedside lamp was switched on. I looked around. I was in my own room, on my giant bed.

"Very good. How is your head feeling? Oliver said you complained of a headache before passing out."

I looked at the doctor who was dressed in normal street clothes and his assistant who was dressed similarly. Then I turned my head to see my father standing a few feet back, his brows furrowed in worry. He was wearing part of his normal attire. Not only was his hair a mess, but his jacket and tie were missing. The top two buttons of his shirt were unbuttoned and the hem was untucked. He looked about as good as I felt.

"Water." I could tell my throat was only going to handle one-word answers until I had some water. I was parched.

Lucifer went over to a chair that had been dragged into the room from the kitchen table and grabbed a water bottle off the floor. The doctor and his assistant moved out of the way and he sat on the side of the bed. He put his arm under me, helping me to sit up halfway.

I winced, my muscles not liking the movement, and stopped once I was elevated enough not to choke. I took the bottle in my hands and he helped me raise it to my lips. The cool liquid slid down my throat and I felt immediate relief.

He helped me lie back down and put the bottle on the nightstand. He stayed next to me and took my hand, his own shaking slightly.

"I feel funny." I didn't quite know how to describe how I felt. I didn't feel like I had my own body. Almost like my brain had been transplanted into someone else.

The doctor crossed his arms and then brought one of his hands to his chin in thought. "Your blood sample seems to indicate some kind of autoimmune response. We were unable to pinpoint the exact cause. Mr. Armstrong mentioned you had intercourse last night with a demon?"

Well, now my body felt like it was back. My face heated up and I avoided looking at my dad. Instead, I looked down at where he held my hand, stroking it with his thumb.

"I don't see how that has anything to do with this." My voice shook as I spoke.

"Danica, this is important." I looked up at my dad; his eyes were pleading.

I sighed and let my head sink farther into the pillow. "I did."

"Was anything abnormal? Did you use protection?" The doctor sounded so clinical. I wondered if he was an angel or just a regular person that somehow was privy to angels and demons.

"No. I have a birth control implant. There was nothing abnormal about it. It was better than usual." I thought back to last night. The details were a little fuzzy at the moment, but the way he had touched me had been far from abnormal.

My heart stopped as my brain played through last night. The mirror. My eyes. "My eyes."

"What about your eyes?"

"When we were done, I went into the bathroom to clean up and my eyes were weird. The pupils were so dilated that the iris color was practically gone. I splashed water on my face and they were normal again. I thought it was just from, you know... the orgasms."

My dad made a strangled noise and I wanted to go back to the black void I had been asleep in.

"Besides intercourse, was there anything else abnormal you did last night? Anything new you ate or drank?"

"I had a glass of wine." I shrugged. If it was the wine, then damn, this was some hangover.

"Thank you. We'll let you rest now and be back in later to check on you." The doctor and assistant left the room.

"Dad, you don't think this is from sleeping with Reve, do you? What even happened?"

"I'm not sure what to think." He ran his free hand through his hair. "You passed out in the hall at the academy. Your nose was bleeding so badly the blood was also coming out of your mouth. They were going to take you to a human hospital but your temperature reached one hundred and ten degrees."

A tear escaped his eye and he wiped it away. I'd never seen him shed a tear in my entire life.

"Shouldn't I be dead?" I whispered. "Why am I not dead?"

"I don't know. Both Oliver and I tried healing you, but it only seems to help for a bit before your fever spikes again. We're trying to get in contact with Raphael. He's the best healer there is."

There was a soft knock on the door and Olly entered the room. He looked tired with dark circles under his eyes.

"Michael says that Raphael is in the Congo dealing with an Ebola outbreak. He's having trouble getting into contact with him." He sat down in the chair at the end of the bed. "He's headed there now to find him."

A cell phone buzzed and my dad stood and walked around to the other side of the bed where his jacket and tie were. He dug his phone out of the pocket and looked at the screen before cursing under his breath and answering.

"This better be an emergency... Now is not the time for jokes... How?... What do you mean you don't know how?... I'm the only one who can open it... That's impossible!... Where?" He jammed his finger onto the screen and I could see the tension in his shoulders and the deep breaths he was taking.

"What's wrong?" Olly was brave asking when he was clearly trying to calm down.

My dad turned and looked at me then at Olly. "Demons got through." He held up his hand when Olly's mouth opened to speak. "I don't know how. It's an impossibility. The only demons that can go through the gate are the ones I personally escort."

I blinked several times, trying to process the information. Demons were through the gate? What did that even mean?

Olly hopped to his feet. "We need to call Michael."

"Michael needs to find Raphael. We'll go."

"Dad? What's happening?" I was confused. Maybe it was partly the fever's fault, or partly just because I missed parts of the conversation.

"Danica, we have to take care of this before they terrorize Los Angeles. There's at least half a dozen. We'll be back. Dr. Hughes and Diane will be here. They're both angels." He leaned down and kissed my forehead, the gesture bringing tears to my eyes.

Somehow, over the past several months, instead of growing further apart than we already had been, we had become closer. Sure, I always had a decent relationship with him, but since losing my shit when Asher died, he had become increasingly present. I didn't want him to leave my side. I felt a little like a five-year old that wanted her daddy when she was sick.

"Get some rest. We'll be back before you wake up." Olly gave me a small smile and followed my dad out of the room.

I let my tears fall. My cheeks felt warm to the touch as I wiped them away. I pulled the covers up around me and shut my eyes.

～

I'M NOT sure how long I slept, but I felt a presence in the room as I came out of a foggy, dreamless sleep. My eyes opened much easier this time and landed on a woman sitting in a chair next to my bed.

As my eyes focused, I took in a sharp breath. It was her.

It was the woman from the grocery store. She was still dressed to the nines. She stared back at me as our eyes met. In the grocery store, hers had been blue, but in hindsight they had been so blue that they had to have been contacts.

"You're awake."

I just blinked back at her, trying to make sense of her black eyes. The entire iris was black. They were larger than normal irises, but still had the white surrounding them.

I brought a shaking hand to my mouth as everything started to click together. The sunglasses perched on her head. The eyes. The hair that was the same shade of brown as mine. The nose.

"You." It was the only word I could manage. I squinted, trying to imagine her with a scarf around her head. I had only caught a glimpse. But those heels. That voice. It all came rushing back.

"Me." She reached forward and tried to take the hand lying at my side but I pulled it onto my chest. I clutched the blanket to me.

She let out a small laugh. "I don't blame you." She stood and walked to the end of the bed and then back to the chair. She sat down, crossed her legs, moved her leg a few times, then stood again.

A tear slid down my cheek. Now was not the time to cry. But God damn it, this had to be Lily, Lilith, my mother. I wasn't sure what to label her. I took in several deep breaths. Where was my dad? My guardians?

"Are you scared of your own mother?"

It had seemed like an eternity since I had been awake. My eyes felt heavy.

I couldn't find words so I just stared back at her. Stared at how similar we were. I gripped the blanket tighter.

"You have no reason to be scared." She sat again and leaned forward. "I'm the one who's going to save you."

"You abandoned me." I stared back at her, even though her eyes were freaking me out. I wouldn't let this woman intimidate me. "I'll take my chances with the angels."

She laughed again and leaned back in the chair. She stared at me for several moments and then her face softened and she almost appeared to not look like a psychopath.

"Leaving you behind was one of the hardest things I ever had to do."

I narrowed my eyes and made a disbelieving noise in my throat. "Is that why you kidnapped me and put me in a cage? Is that why you're here now?" My teeth chattered as I spoke.

I was sure my fever was spiking again. Where had the doctor and his assistant gone? How did Lilith even get into my place?

"You were an added bonus to snagging the archangel. John only put you in the basement because he wasn't sure what was going to happen to you. You are the first of your kind, after all." She stood. She certainly was antsy, like she had bottled energy trying to escape. "Your fever is increasing again and your angels are currently occupied dealing with my soldiers. They won't return for a while, if they return at all. The choice is yours."

"How did you..." I shook my head, not believing a word from her lips.

"You do know the 'gate' just refers to the ability to pass through the barrier between Earth and Inferna, don't you?" I shook my head. What was I supposed to think? A gate is a fucking gate. "Let's just say that I have figured out how to get demons through. Now," her voice lilted higher in excitement. "We need to leave."

"I'm not going anywhere with you."

"You can stay here and always be mediocre, or you can join me and become the queen you are." Queen? Was this woman on something? It was possible she was tripping out on something.

"I have everything I need here."

"You don't need them. Why do you think four men are in love with you?" I couldn't stop my face from displaying my shock at her words. "It's in your blood. It's the same way I sucked your father in. The same way I sucked John in. You can have as many men or women as your heart and body desires."

I shifted in the bed, my muscles protesting at the small movement. "I'd rather die."

A phone rang from a leather handbag sitting next to the chair. Her grin broadened and she reached inside it and pulled out her cell phone.

"Perfect timing." She pressed a button on the screen and held it away from her to video chat. "Are your tasks complete?"

"They are. I sent four of my best to meet up with the others with enough demon serum to take down an army of angels. I'm also ready to move in on the girl at your command, my queen." The voice was gruff.

"Let us see the girl." Lilith waited for a moment before turning the phone towards me.

It was a dark blur of people and blue lights before whoever was holding the phone adjusted the angle and it was pointing at a large tank behind a bar. Inside were women with mermaid tails and shockingly blue hair.

"Don't," I managed to choke out, a sob lodged in my throat.

"I'll call off my men if you come with me. Otherwise, I'm afraid there's nothing that will help them."

I shut my eyes. I didn't have a choice. I couldn't just let everyone I loved die or be gravely injured. "Call them off and I'll go."

"You heard the girl. Stay on standby though, just in case she tries anything," she said into the phone before hanging up. What would I try? I was sick and could barely throw a punch. "Get dressed. I will wait for you in the living room."

She exited the room, leaving the door open behind her. I slid from the bed, and on shaky legs, changed out of the pajamas I was in. I pulled on a pair of loose jeans and a t-shirt. I spotted my blazer in a heap on the floor and picked it up, feeling the weight of my cell phone in the pocket.

I took it out and my fingers brushed a folded piece of paper. The note Olly slid in my pocket during the final stared back at me and I slipped it into my bra before tapping open my cell phone. I figured that Lilith was going to take my phone or search me at some point, so I quickly typed out a message to my dad.

It was a trap. Lilith is here. This is all my fault. I'm sorry. I love you. Tell Tobias, Asher, Olly, and Reve that I love them too.

I hit send and then deleted the message from the thread just as Lilith came back in the room. She narrowed her eyes and snatched the phone from me. She threw it across the room, hitting the brick wall, causing it to shatter.

I flinched and she grabbed my arm, her nails digging into my skin. "Let's go."

"But I need my shoes!" Before I could even move to grab them, she was pulling me towards the door.

As we entered the living space, my eyes immediately landed on Dr. Hughes and Diane sprawled out on the floor. I yanked my arm, but despite her petite size, she was stronger than ten men.

The front door opened and two abnormally large men stepped in and one picked me up. They looked like those men that flipped logs and pulled airplanes. Lilith went back into my apartment as I was loaded into a black SUV with limo tinting on the windows. I stopped struggling, my head hurting again. It was no use anyways.

I had made my decision to save the ones I loved.

CHAPTER 14

TOBIAS

The day had been a complete and utter disaster. There had been a lot of disastrous days lately. I could really go for a vacation from it all.

The night before, I watched Danica have sex with Reve. Really good sex with Reve.

Yeah, it bothered me, but watching them together turned me on. If he made her happy, it seemed I was going to have to accept it or, well, I wasn't sure what other choice I had. She was headstrong about what she wanted.

The demon seemed to be normal, if that was even possible for a demon. If we didn't know he was a full-fledged demon, I would have never guessed. Instead, he struck me as some overly inked biker. The part that bothered me the most was he could go invisible. Who knows how many times he'd watched us with Danica.

I was a bit jealous.

On top of the Reve situation, Danica was in a funk over what she was. I can't say I blamed her. I had wondered about it for months and so had Asher. The only one who seemed to push the idea of Lilith being her mother out of his head was Oliver. He'd much rather see the glass half full than half empty.

We landed in the middle of a loading dock outside an abandoned mall and stood in a line, looking at the dark building in front of us. I felt a chill sweep over me as a breeze gently blew.

I hoped Danica was all right without us with her. I had never been so scared in my life as she had stumbled out of my classroom, her nose gushing blood. When we got to her, she was already lying face down in a pool of red. When we had touched her, she felt like she was on fire.

Not how you want to see your girlfriend.

Oliver and I had taken her to the infirmary. We were told to go back to class to complete the final. I had refused to leave her side. Sue was already pissed that Michael had firmly told her that I was allowed to have a relationship with Danica. But me refusing to go back to my classroom to finish the final? That had tipped her over the edge.

I'd worry about my suspension later.

"What should we be looking for?" Oliver broke the silence that had descended over our small group.

"Depends what we're up against," Reve answered from somewhere near Lucifer. Before we left, he decided to stay invisible as an element of surprise.

I still didn't completely trust him. He could have done something to Danica without us knowing. He could have been working for Lilith.

"Are we all clear on how to kill demons?" We all said yes in some shape or form. None of us had been specifically trained in killing demons. Apparently the risk of demons coming through the barrier to Earth was an impossibility.

Or so everyone thought.

Lucifer was scanning the area. For what, I wasn't sure. "This way. They came through over here." He was all business as he marched towards a chain link fence surrounding the building.

We followed like well-trained soldiers. We all carried swords we had grabbed from a weapons cache angels kept in the city. It hadn't been used in centuries.

To incapacitate a demon we needed to behead them or rip out

their heart, then burn the body. The problem was that different demons had multiple heads or hearts in weird places. They might also be heavily shielded.

We squeezed through a hole cut in the chain link and made our way to a side door off a loading dock. The place was completely deserted and quiet, with graffiti covering the walls and trash thrown about.

The light was fading fast; it was nearly seven in the evening. We entered a large room that looked like a gutted section of the mall. The light coming in through skylights overhead cast eerie shadows across the floor. In the middle of the room were giant holes leading to the bottom floor of the mall. At some point, there had been a railing around them.

"Should we wait for the others?" I asked as we looked down into the darkness of the first level. Lucifer had called in reinforcements; they would be arriving soon.

Just as he started to answer, a low growl came from the darkness. My eyes searched in the direction of the sound and six beady red eyes looked back. The growl came again and this time a few more joined.

My heart rate quickened. I wasn't sure what was growling. I had a clue but didn't want to admit to myself what it was. I studied demons, but I certainly wasn't an expert.

"Is that a dog?" Oliver took a step closer to the edge. "Nope, definitely not a-"

The cement beneath his feet gave way and he dropped like a sack of potatoes. I saw a flash of white as he fell and then all hell literally broke loose.

Those six red eyes? It was a fucking hellhound, except it was so unlike anything I'd studied that I was doubting if I had any business even being a Demonology teacher. It looked more like some kind of prehistoric dinosaur with spikes running along its three spines. Its three tails lit up with fire, sending light around the darkened recesses of the lower level. Then the thing split and formed three separate hounds.

Reading about demons is one thing, but seeing them in person is something else entirely. It felt like an out of body experience staring at a beast that had just split itself into three.

We all jumped down to the bottom level to find Oliver already fending off a humanoid-looking demon. It opened its mouth to reveal a circular ring of sharp teeth and a long tongue that lashed out to grab his wrist. It looked similar to a Demogorgon from *Stranger Things*.

He let out a scream and Asher swung his sword, cutting the tongue off, sending black blood across the floor. With one swift move, he took off its head. The loud, high-pitched screeching sound it made had me wanting to cover my ears.

"Stay close, these are some of the worst," Lucifer warned us. We were standing in a tight half-circle. "If one of them gets you alone... well, just don't let it get you alone. Stay in pairs. Don't let them surround us."

"We need to take care of this hellhound first. If it stays separated long enough each hound will form three bodies again and continue to split. It's a multiplier." Reve took his sword that Lucifer was holding for him. All I could see of him was the sword he was holding and his hand.

We made quick work of the hounds, taking their heads off. It was more difficult than I thought to remove a head. The movies made it seem so easy. We had no time to rest though because several other creatures zeroed in on us.

I glanced over at Lucifer, Olly, and Asher who were stabbing the ground. It looked like a million spiders were descending upon them. Lucifer's wings came out and he flew towards a woman that looked like a normal woman, except for her black eyes and the spiders pouring from her skin. She managed to jump at the last minute before his sword could connect with her. She disappeared into the darkness.

I managed to take down a demon that had the head of a man and body of a scorpion, but as the head flew, something from its tail hit my right arm, right in the middle of Charlie's face. At first, I just thought it was a splatter of dark demon blood it left behind, but then it started to burn and smoke. I wiped at it with my left hand, which was stupid, and I dropped to my knees as a burning sensation spread up my arms. It was eating away at my flesh.

Flashes of white from up above caught my eye as other angels arrived to help. The screeches from dying demons hit my ears, but I was struggling to move out of the way of the melee.

Arms took hold of me from behind and I was dragged backwards. It was Reve.

He stopped on the other side of an old set of escalators and sat me against the wall. The action was happening out of eyesight. If Reve was on the other team, I was a dead man.

"I have to cut it off." My eyes went wide at his words and I vehemently shook my head, words refusing to come out. "Just the flesh that has been touched. If I don't, it will spread and we'll have to cut off both your arms. If I don't do this you will die."

I looked at him pleadingly and then down at my arm where my tattoo was already destroyed by whatever the black substance was.

I shut my eyes and then nodded.

"I'm sorry I have to do this." He sounded pained at the thought of cutting into my flesh.

I could hear the shouts and sounds of demons on the other side of where he had dragged me. I kept my eyes shut and then he began to cut.

I woke as my body was jostled against a muscular chest. The smell of sulfur and ash was in the air and I opened my eyes to find Reve's face staring down at me.

I lifted my arm that had been cradled against my chest. Whatever it had looked like when he carved off the decaying flesh was now healed to a flawless new patch of skin. I could only see part of Margie's face. My children were gone.

The sense of loss was overwhelming and I clenched my eyes shut.

"Oliver was able to heal your arm. I'm sorry about your tattoo. I know how much they can mean." He spoke low, so only I could hear. I knew the others were near from the sounds of their feet shuffling on the floor as he made his way across the dark mall. "I'll fix it for you."

"How?" I managed to get the word out and a hiccup came after. I looked at my arm again. It might have been healed, but the whole thing looked like a layer of smooth scar tissue.

Angel tattoos were a complicated and painful process that involved several passes with a tattoo gun. When I had gotten mine back in the sixties the wait list for the one angel tattoo artist was several years long.

"I'll do it, if you'll let me." I grunted as he stopped and set me down. He took my elbow to steady me.

I glanced around at the twenty or so angels. Some looked worse for wear, but it seemed there were no casualties on our end. Asher and Oliver were walking several feet ahead of us with Lucifer in between them.

Lucifer reached into his pocket and pulled out his cell phone. He stopped abruptly and stood staring at his phone for several seconds before he took off running towards the exit.

Danica.

We took off after him, seeing him launch into the sky just as we came out of the door. As soon as we were far enough outside, Asher grabbed me and we shot into the sky too. He was a perceptive bastard, knowing I was still recovering from whatever that demon had hit me with.

We landed outside Asher's building and rushed into Danica's open door, nearly falling over each other in our haste. The first sight that greeted us was the doctor and assistant laying sprawled out on the floor. Oliver rushed to them.

Both of his hands lit up as he put one hand on the doctor and one on the assistant.

"Don't overdo it, angel baby," Asher said, stepping into the hallway leading to Danica's room.

I followed, with Reve behind me. Asher braced his hands on the doorframe, stopping us from rushing forward. Lucifer was on his knees by the side of the bed, his hands on the empty mattress.

"Lily... Lilith took her." Lucifer's voice shook. He gripped the sheets in his hand.

Asher stepped into the room so we could take in the scene. The room looked how we had left it, except instead of Danica on the bed, there was a crescent burned into the sheets.

Lucifer stood, clenching his fists next to his sides. Asher and I looked at each other and backed up towards the door. We felt the temperature jump at least ten degrees in the room.

"We'll find her." Reve was one brave motherfucker for speaking. He even took a step farther into the room. Although, I guess if things really got heated, he could just ghost-out.

"This is my fucking fault." We ducked as a lamp was thrown across the room and shattered, sending shards of glass flying in our direction.

He moved so fast we barely had time to track his movements. First the lamp. Then the nightstand. Then the sheets on the bed.

Oliver shoved his way through us and tackled Lucifer onto the floor. I was starting to think whatever demon poison had eaten my skin had somehow made it to my brain. I had to have just imagined Oliver taking Lucifer down and pinning him to the ground.

"Calm down!" He flipped him and twisted his arm behind him while putting his knee on his back. Was Oliver a police officer in a previous life? *Jesus.*

Lucifer struggled but then went limp under him, his shoulders shaking with sobs. Oliver let out a tired sounding sigh and we watched in awe, as we always did, as his hands glowed and spread to Lucifer.

"You know we can't locate her if we aren't calm." Oliver's voice was shaking. He had healed too much.

He finally let Lucifer go and sat back on his ass against the side of the bed. He put his face in his hands and took deep breaths.

"She's not within a three-hundred-mile radius of here. That's as far as I can search. That, or she's being hidden."

Lucifer rolled over, staying on the floor, and stared up at the ceiling. He looked like shit, but I'm sure we all did. I certainly felt like it. A numbness had settled over me. I was sure I was going to wake up and this would be some nightmare Reve had somehow decided to torment us with.

I sat down in a chair that hadn't been destroyed and felt the weight of the day slam down on me. My job might as well be gone. My tattoo was gone. Danica was gone.

"She's not being hidden." Lucifer had his eyes shut, but his eyes were moving under his eyelids. "This was a message to me to come get her."

"What do you mean a message?" Asher lowered himself next to Oliver, their arms touching.

"She doesn't want Danica. She wants me." He stood then and walked over to the other side of the bed where his suit jacket was. He slid his arms into it, resolve in his movements. "They're in Shanghai."

"China?" Reve asked, sounding as confused as we all felt. "Why would she take her there? How did they get there so fast? Lilith can't fly, can she?"

"I don't know how. My guess is she has demon transport, but maybe she can fly. Are you coming with me or not?" He stopped in front of us and gave each of us a look. "She's going to need you four."

I stared up at him. At one point in time I had thought the angel was this untouchable, unbreakable king of the underworld. Now, staring up at him, he was much, much more than that. He was a worried father who loved his daughter and would do anything to get her back.

"We can rest once we get there. Regroup. Contact the others." He had quickly switched back to all business. "There are only three places we can land in the city."

We all got to our feet. I didn't even know if I could make it all the way to China with how exhausted I was. We walked outside to the small parking lot. It was the middle of the night and the street was quiet.

Lucifer took my hand and I raised an eyebrow at him.

"Don't want you to fall in the Pacific."

Our wings extended and we took off into the night sky.

CHAPTER 15

DANICA

Originally, I thought we were going to be taking a private plane or helicopter to wherever it was Lilith was taking me. Boy, was I wrong.

We didn't drive far from my apartment, but the area we were at was deserted. Waiting for us was a crazy-looking creature the size of a school bus.

"What is it?" Despite being scared shitless, I couldn't help but ask.

"What does it look like? I know you didn't do well in school, but you aren't stupid." The two men, who I assumed were her guards, laughed, and I deepened my frown.

"Maybe if I'd had a mother to help me, I would have done better in school."

She let out an exasperated sigh and turned towards me. "You've always been destined for something greater than any human education could give you." She gestured towards the creature. "This is a fire dragon."

"Versus what? A water dragon?" I spat.

A dragon. A motherfucking dragon in a field. I felt like this was a setup for a joke you might find on a popsicle stick, or from some creeper at a bar.

"Exactly." The men laughed again and she started walking towards it. I kept my feet firmly planted on the ground.

"Can't we teleport there or something?" My brain was telling me to run but my body wasn't cooperating. I had a slight headache again too.

"Teleporting isn't a thing. If you're referring to how your father just seemingly appears and disappears, that is only him going through the barrier between Earth and Inferna. Now, let's go."

I already felt dizzy enough, I didn't need to ride on a... *oh my God*. I was looking at a dragon. Was it really a dragon? I squinted in its direction and confirmed. Yes, it was a dragon of some sort. It was solid black like tar and seemed to be bonier than the typical type. It was more of a snake with wings.

Was my mother the Mad Queen? She wasn't the Queen of England, that was for sure. I was hallucinating. My father was Lucifer and my mother was Lilith, but a dragon? The line had to be drawn somewhere and a motherfucking dragon was that line.

I took a step forward and stumbled, one of the bodyguards catching me. My vision was blurring again. That was the last thing I remembered.

I WOKE to the smell of something delicious. Thank fuck. It had all been one of my nightmares again. I'd seriously have to reconsider my concept of reality if I had actually ridden on a dragon.

I lengthened my body under the soft sheets and looked around the room. I sat straight up and took in the decor. It was modern and clean. Gray light was filtering in under the closed curtains.

It wasn't a nightmare, I was living it. I wasn't in *my* bed or any other bed I knew.

I stood and stretched, my body feeling refreshed. I felt completely fine with no signs of a fever or headache.

Someone, hopefully my mother and not one of the demon men, had changed me into a pair of black pajamas. Silk? I could never tell the difference between fabrics, but these pajamas felt like heaven against my skin.

I went to the window and pulled the curtains back. I was surprised to see trees outside the window, a window that had a key lock to prevent it from being opened. That was totally up to fire code.

I made my way to the bedroom door and put my ear against it to see if I could hear anything. I could hear sounds down the hall but nothing else. I tried the door and the handle turned.

Poking my head out, I took in the shiny dark wood running down the length of the hall where there were several closed doors. I walked down the hall towards the sounds and smells. Someone was cooking.

I entered a large living area and my eyes landed on my mother, who was sitting at a large dining room table, sipping coffee and staring at the screen of a laptop. Her eyes darted to me when I stepped into the room.

"Danica, please join me. John was just cooking us breakfast." She looked towards the kitchen and smiled.

I tentatively walked towards her and could finally see the man in the kitchen. John Senior looked older than the last time I had seen him, gray hairs peppering his dark hair. He turned his head towards me and gave me a smile.

"Where are we?" I stayed where I was. "And did we really ride a dragon here?"

She threw her head back and laughed. We even had the same laugh and I cringed. I wanted to be nothing like this woman. She had threatened the only family I had. They must be out of their minds with worry wondering where I was.

"It wasn't a dragon, but your reaction when I told you it was, was priceless. It was a hell serpent. Please join me." She gestured to the chair to her right.

A hell serpent? As if that was any better than a dragon. Where was this so-called hell serpent now? I would have felt much better if it had been a dragon.

I moved towards the table but sat with one chair in between us, which only caused her to smile even more. I looked around the room.

I could tell from the kitchen that wherever we were, we weren't in the United States anymore. Everything was more compact here and everything had a gloss to it. Not your typical American-style choices.

"We are in Shanghai. We have business here tomorrow night. John, bring her some coffee." She tapped her nails on the table. The more I watched her, the more similarities I was finding between us. I didn't like it.

"I don't drink coffee." A cup was set in front of me anyways, but I didn't touch it.

"You look much better this morning," John said as he stepped back after putting the coffee down. "I was afraid we'd made an error in our serum calculations."

"What serum?" I looked from him to Lilith. "Why is he even here?"

Lilith steepled her finger under her chin and then nodded her head back to the kitchen in a gesture to get John to leave.

"A serum with my blood. It was how we stopped the reaction you were having."

"Reaction?"

"It's been going on for quite some time, actually. Ever since you had such grievous injuries when we first took you. But with all the stress you've been under, the introduction of a demon into your sex life, and some poison, your angel blood couldn't keep the demon part of you locked away any longer."

"I don't understand." I scrunched my forehead in thought. I needed something to do with my hands so I picked up the coffee cup and drank down the bitter liquid. I cringed and shuddered at the taste.

"The roses. That really threw your angel blood off balance. Now the question is, just how much your demon blood was able to take hold. How do you feel? John will take a blood sample from you once we eat."

I gripped the edge of my chair to stop my hands from shaking and from throwing objects at her. I was so stupid coming here with her, but what choice did I have? I couldn't let everyone die because of my fear.

"I feel fine. What did you do to me? Blood doesn't work like that." I brought my hands to rest on the table and examined them, as if the skin would give me an answer.

John spoke from the kitchen. "*Human* blood doesn't work like that, but you aren't human. Your blood was fifty percent angel and fifty percent demon. Since you are here on Earth, your angel blood is stronger. Giving you Lilith's blood should have decreased the angel blood significantly, especially with the stress you were under and the viruses I put on those thorns and roses."

I clenched my teeth to keep from whimpering.

"We've been running experiments on some of the blood we've collected from angels, and Lilith's blood destroys angel blood at a rate twice as fast as regular demon blood."

I felt sick and stood. "Excuse me. I need to use the restroom."

I took off down the hall and slammed the door shut behind me. I rushed into the bathroom and looked in the mirror. I looked just as I always had. I leaned forward on the counter and pulled my eyelids further apart to examine my eyes. Normal.

I let out a shaky breath and turned to lock the bathroom door. I needed a shower and a plan. My duffel bag was sitting on the bathmat and I picked it up. She had packed a bag for me. I shook my head in disbelief.

Lilith was a monster, but somewhere deep inside of her she at least had the heart to pack me a bag. I didn't know how to feel about that, because what could I feel? I hated her.

I stripped out of the pajamas that weren't mine and took my bra off, the note I had stuffed in it falling to the floor. I picked it up and unfolded the heart shaped note. It was cute and I cracked a smile despite the dire situation I was in.

DEAR DANICA,

I've never written a note to someone before. I'm sorry for acting like a "complete fucking asshole dick" last night (that's what Asher called me and I agree). I may have overreacted, but I was hurt that you would keep something like that from me. Now that I'm thinking about it, maybe I did deserve that. You don't owe me anything with how I once treated you.

I honestly don't care what you are. You are Danica Deville, my girlfriend, my love, my everything. As corny as that sounds, it's true. Even if you sprouted horns and a tail, I'd love you.

Please forgive me for acting like an idiot. I will make it up to you with orgasms. Asher tells me that orgasms are a great apology. So how many will it take?

Love and cookies,

Olly

I STARED down at the note written in flawless handwriting. It was simple, yet in that moment it was exactly what I needed to read. I refolded the note and buried it in my duffel bag. Hopefully it would make it back to California.

Would I ever get to go home?

I turned on the shower and stepped under the hot water, my thoughts drifting to the angels I had left behind. Where were they right now? Had they survived the demons that made it through? Would they be able to find me?

I needed to make a plan to escape. Shanghai was a big city and it would be easy to slip away and hide among the throngs of people. But then what? I couldn't go to the police because I didn't even have my passport with me. What would I tell them? My evil, demon mother, *the* Lilith took me on a magical hell serpent ride?

That would get me a one-way ticket into China's finest mental institution.

Once showered and dressed, I walked down the hall and entered the living space where John was sitting, staring off into nothingness. I approached slowly and sat in a chair across from him.

"Why are you helping her?" The woman in question was nowhere to be seen and I needed to find out information.

The more I knew, the better I could plan an escape. The house we were in was like a fortress and I had yet to see the hell serpent or the two burly men anywhere. They were probably right outside, just waiting for me to attempt an escape.

"Why would I not help her?" He straightened in his seat and looked at me. "You're going to help her now, are you not?"

I chose my words carefully. "Not because I want to. What do you gain from helping her?"

He looked down the hall and then leaned forward on the couch, as if the few inches were going to give us privacy for what he was planning on saying.

"Freedom for my son." I stared back at him and raised my eyebrows, urging him to continue. "I am the closest in blood to the original Adam. It was a story that I thought was made up by my grandfather, so when I jokingly told my fraternity brothers about it, they dared me to try to summon Lilith. One of them had read a story about her being a demon that could be summoned."

"So you summoned her as a drunken frat boy, she showed up, and she forced you to be her little bitch?"

"Yes. I know it seems crazy, but it happened. Isn't all of it a bit crazy? I have pledged myself to her. Those were her terms. Pledge myself to her or she'd take my first born." He seemed defeated, like he'd rather be anywhere but here. "Whatever you do, don't pledge yourself to her."

Just as he finished speaking, Lilith's heels could be heard down the hall and his eyes widened. He sat back in his chair and returned to staring off into space.

"Danica. I'm glad to see you've rejoined us. We have business to discuss." She sauntered into the room, her eyes locked on John.

It was unclear if she had heard what he had said, but if she had, well, I wasn't going to wish him the best.

"What business?" I kept my feet firmly planted on the ground, ready to run if I needed to. I wasn't sure where I'd run, but I'd find a way out if I needed to.

"You of course." She perched on the arm of the couch, right next to John, and jabbed her fingers into his hair before fisting it and pulling his head to the side. "Go check on our guests."

She shoved his head away and John stood; he looked like he was about to cry. I watched as he retreated from the room and wondered who she was referring to as guests.

"Now. It's time to talk about your future at my side." She turned her body towards me and I shifted in my seat, trying to make the distance between us wider.

"I don't want to be at your side." She frowned at my response. "I want nothing to do with you."

"I have big plans for Earth. Inferna is getting a little stuffy and my demons are getting restless." She stood and started to pace behind the couch. "You'll want to be by my side when I get them through the barrier."

"Why? Why are you doing this?" I watched her back and forth movements. I wanted to stand and pace too, but stayed glued to the seat. I wouldn't let her see just how similar we were. She'd use it against me.

"It's all part of a bigger plan, years and years in the making. Now all the stars have aligned and I'll be able to take back what is mine." She stopped pacing and looked at me. "What's yours."

"And what's that?" I had an uneasy feeling in my belly. She really was batshit crazy.

"Everything."

I let out an uncomfortable laugh and then smacked my hand over my mouth. I hadn't meant to laugh, but I was starting to think this was some kind of elaborate prank. Maybe this woman was a former Divine 7 and it was all a setup.

"How many people do you think live in Shanghai?"

I frowned and lowered my hand from my mouth. I shrugged because I honestly had no clue.

"Twenty-four million." She smiled and resumed her trot behind the couch. I was glad there was a barrier between us. "Now, imagine a hell serpent being let loose." She paused. "Are you imagining it?"

"You wouldn't." I knew she was evil, but she wasn't *that* evil, was she?

"My demons do as I ask." She snapped her fingers. "I could level this city with a simple command. You could too, with the right training."

My eyes widened and I felt all the blood drain from my face. I swallowed the lump in my throat.

"Those angels and humans can offer you nothing. How do you think four men seemingly fell in love with you at first sight?" I wanted her to stop talking, so I covered my ears with my hands. She just spoke louder. "Once they find out that you can control them, manipulate their minds, they'll run for the hills."

"No. I never manipulated them!" I let my hands fall to my lap.

"Oh, but you did. You just didn't realize it. Do you really think they would love you otherwise? You are nothing more than a silly girl. Even your father can't stand to be around you. Why do you think he was never around when you were growing up?"

I took in her words and looked down at my hands. Part of me didn't believe a word she said, but the other part of me knew it made sense.

"Don't hurt them. Anyone, please." A calmness spread over my body. I didn't want to play into her plans, but I also couldn't let her kill millions of people.

"Very well. Tomorrow night we will be attending a gala where a very precious artifact will be on display. You are going to steal it for me."

"What artifact? Why can't you steal it yourself?" I spoke cautiously.

"I can't touch it, but I'm pretty sure since you can get onto academy grounds that you can." She laughed and sat down on the couch, crossing her legs. "You're going to steal the Holy Grail."

Holy shit.

CHAPTER 16

OLIVER

I felt the change in the air a few miles from the border of China. The air was thick and muggy, like an old house that had been closed up for too long. I was exhausted, but Asher had hold of me the entire flight, although it was all of a few minutes.

There were a few places in the city we could land. Shanghai had strict flying rules due to the population density and the vast amount of street cameras. The camera system was so good, it was rumored that if someone stole something, the cameras would track them all the way to where they lived.

We landed on top of the Peninsula Hotel. No one could see us when we were flying, but if you were on the street and suddenly someone seemed to magically appear in front of you, you'd start asking questions. Or freak out. In large cities, landing was tricky.

We took the elevator down to the ground floor and Lucifer worked his magic at the front desk. They seemed to immediately know who he was, greeting him as Mr. Deville.

"How many rooms do I need to get?" He turned his head towards Asher and me. We were standing next to each other. Why did everyone keep looking at us like that? It wasn't like we had announced to the world that we had shared a kiss or two.

"We can share two rooms. I don't mind sharing with Reve, as long as he doesn't snore." Tobias surprised the heck out of me sometimes. One minute he hated Reve, the next he seemed to be buddies with him.

"I can afford separate rooms, son. Don't feel you need to share just because I'm footing the bill." Lucifer's voice lacked its normal vibrato. He was letting his guard down around us.

Tobias's face softened. "It's fine. We probably should bond or whatever it is we're supposed to do when we share a..." He didn't finish his sentence.

"I'm fine sharing a room. I don't sleep anyways." Reve had his arms cross over his chest and was tapping his foot on the marble floor. His eyes were dark and he didn't make eye contact with any of us. "I need to go hunt."

Hunt? What the hell was he talking about? I looked at Asher and he shrugged.

Lucifer nodded and turned back to the counter to book three rooms. He hadn't even waited for a response from me or Asher.

"What do you mean by hunt? Like a vampire?" I couldn't help but ask, my curiosity probably my most well-developed trait. Although it was also the trait that got me in the most trouble.

"I feed off the fear in nightmares I create or enter into. I haven't had to feed in a while because of Danica." He stopped and frowned. "I should go."

He walked away and turned down a hall. I didn't think I wanted to find out what happened when a demon was starving.

Lucifer handed us our keycards. We were given river-view rooms, which brightened my mood just a tad. I had seen pictures of Pudong, which was the part of Shanghai across the river with all of the tall skyscrapers, and was curious to see how glorious it was in person.

The hotel staff was going to send clothing to our rooms. We hadn't bothered packing anything. We must have been a sight with disheveled clothing, messy hair, and faces pinched tight with worry. We looked like bedraggled travelers who had been mugged. If they only knew what we had been up to.

"Let's get some rest. I'll make some calls. There's not much we can do right now. I know she's here. There are too many angels packed together and I'm too tired to directly pinpoint her." He walked towards the elevators and we followed.

He scratched at his arm while we waited for the elevator and pulled back the sleeve of his shirt. One of those damn spiders from the mall must have bit him. I reached forward and healed it.

"Thanks, Oliver. I didn't even know it was there." I shuddered, remembering the large spiders that had crawled out of the demon's skin. It was the creepiest thing I had ever seen. Luckily, one of the other angels had caught her, ripped out her heart, and burned her body.

It was gruesome, images that would haunt me for a while, but killing a demon was no easy feat. I just hoped we got them all and the clean-up crew had disposed of them before humans found the evidence of our battle.

We rode the elevator up to our floor in silence and went our separate ways. Asher opened the door to the room we would share and I walked down the hallway entrance, past the closet and bathroom, to the main room. It had floor to ceiling windows and a view of across the river.

There was one bed.

I had never seen anything quite like the skyline. Los Angeles was a big city but had nothing on this.

I felt Asher move across the room towards me, my neck prickling with his approach. He was so unpredictable. So volatile. I didn't quite know what to do half the time. Which is why I always touched him, hoping to curb whatever storm he had brewing.

The thing was, I also touched him when I knew he was fine. Touching always seemed to put him in a better head space. It took the edge off, but lately it only amped up the intensity between us.

He pretended it didn't affect him, but I could see it in his eyes. I could feel it in the way he'd touch my arm. In the way he'd put a hand on my lower back for a mere second when he passed by.

And then there was that kiss.

We had been avoiding being alone with each other since the hot kiss we shared. Well, *he* had. I wanted nothing more than to be close to him. To explore what Danica had set in motion.

I shuddered at the thought that I had once mistreated her. She was more divine in spirit than any of the angels. She had brought us together and been nothing but accepting of whatever was to be.

"Are you doing all right?" I asked as he stopped next to me.

"It comes and goes. I'm glad you're here." He stared out the window and put his hand against it. "Where do you think she is?"

"She could be anywhere. I mean, look at this place. It's like finding a needle in a haystack. If anyone is going to be able to find her though, it's Lucifer." I tried to sound sure. I could locate people I knew well with ease, but when angels were in mass, it was difficult, at least for me being so new.

"What are you seeing?"

"It's just a sea of white light. There are too many angels in such close proximity." I sighed and leaned my forehead against the window. "I can't even do that right."

"What are you talking about? Lucifer is even struggling to locate her now that we're here."

"Everything I touch seems to get messed up. The Holy Grail, Levi, Dani, you."

"I hardly think you had anything to do with Levi being fucked up. He was fucked up to begin with. As for Dani, how is her being taken by her own mother your fault?"

"I was so angry with her for not telling us about what was going on. I'm supposed to protect her. What if..." I banged my head lightly on the window. My brain hurt. I was second guessing every decision I'd ever made.

"What if what?" Asher prompted, turning and propping his shoulder against the window.

I was distracted by his nearness. Whenever he was near me, I couldn't resist the urge to reach out and touch him. The last thing I needed to be thinking about at the moment was all the ways I wanted to touch him. We were having a serious discussion. We'd never talked like *this* before.

"What if the whole reason I was created was for this moment? I was never given a purpose in heaven and all angels are given a purpose. But here I am, Oliver Morgan. First archangel since the originals, and I was just left to roam the Great City in heaven? Doesn't sound quite right. No direction. No reason. No purpose. Then one day I just felt this pull towards the religious artifacts and the cup caught my eye. The need to come to Earth and try it out was so strong I couldn't resist. What if that happened for a reason? So I'd be at the academy. So I'd meet Danica. So I'd meet Tobias." I took a breath. "So I'd meet you."

"I guess that's plausible." Asher brought his hand to his jaw and rubbed his stubble. I tracked the movement, my forehead turned slightly so I could watch him.

"My existence didn't make sense. Nothing around me made sense. Until Danica and now you. You make sense to me."

Asher's face softened and his hands dropped to his sides. It was a look I was only used to seeing when he looked at Danica. His stormy eyes looked back into mine, searching for something.

"You sure do know how to sweet talk someone, don't you?" His voice was gentle. "I don't know what to do with these thoughts and feelings I have towards you. With Danica, it's so natural, but with you..."

My heart sank and I turned my eyes back to the Oriental Pearl Tower across the Huangpu River.

He was quiet for a few moments before speaking again. "With you, it's so new. Definitely unexpected and unfamiliar territory. Being intimate with a man is not something I know how to do. Hell, it's new to you too. It's like I'm an innocent virgin all over again." He paused. "Would you even want to explore that side of things?"

I could feel his eyes on me as my face and ears felt like they were on fire. If he only knew how I'd fantasized about him and the things he would do to me and the things I would do to him. The thoughts I'd

391

had of him were sinful enough to make me wonder if a trip to hell was in my future.

"Have you thought about it? Being with me?" I bit my lip and watched as a barge that had tires around the entire edge made its way slowly down the river. A yacht was not far behind.

"I have. I've thought a little too much about it. What it would be like to have a man's mouth, your mouth, on mine, wrapped around me, your hands on me." His voice was raspy.

My cock twitched at his words and I shut my eyes. "Have you thought about what you'd do to me?"

I felt him move closer and he trailed a finger down my arm and grabbed my hand. He held it in his and started drawing shapes in the palm, just like I always did with him. I couldn't keep back the small noise that escaped my mouth.

He spoke almost in a whisper, despite us being the only ones in the room. Not quite next to my ear, but close enough that when he let out a breath, I could feel it.

"There's so much I want to do to you, angel baby. I'd start by kissing the fuck out of you like that first time. I'd lay you on the bed and grind my dick against yours. I imagine that would feel amazing. Don't you think so?"

I grunted and let out a breath of air as he put his lips against my palm and swirled his tongue in the center.

"Then I'd take your hand and put it right here." He moved my hand down to his erection and pressed my hand onto it. "So you'd know just how turned on the thought of being with you makes me."

He moved his hips against our joined hands and groaned in the back of his throat. "Fuck, Oliver. I've never wanted a man before."

I moved my hand away from him and turned so I was facing him. I was slightly taller than him and his eyes landed directly on my mouth. I licked my bottom lip and that was all the invitation he needed to cup both of my cheeks and take my lips in a blistering kiss.

This was more urgent than our first, needier. We both needed each other in this moment. Needed the comfort. Needed the passion. Needed the distraction.

"Asher." His lips left mine and his teeth scraped down my jawline.

There was nothing soft or gentle about his mouth and teeth as they grazed across my skin. He was greedy and took me with his lips and teeth. He trailed his tongue along my Adam's apple and I put my hand against the window to steady myself.

"Are we going to do this? For real?" he mumbled against my neck. "Because I think I'm about to reach the point of no turning back. So if you don't want this, you need to tell me." He kissed under my ear and bit down on my earlobe, causing me to gasp. "Because if you don't stop me, I'm about to fucking take you, Oliver Morgan."

I moaned and grabbed a fist full of his hair and pulled his lips back to mine. He took my bottom lip in his teeth and then sucked it into his mouth. I had always imagined this happening so gently, but screw that. This was what I needed. What I wanted.

We stumbled towards the bed in the center of the room and fell onto the mattress on our sides, our lips never breaking contact. In a way it felt wrong to be doing this with Asher while Danica was out there somewhere.

"Maybe this isn't the right time to be doing this," I managed to get out as we broke for air. "With everything that's going on."

Asher looked back at me and his eyes dropped to my mouth where he took a finger and pressed it into my bottom lip.

"When is the right time?" His finger trailed down the front of my shirt and then hooked into the front of my jeans. I almost forgot about what I had asked.

Words were failing me as he popped the button and slid down the zipper. My breath came in heavy inhales and exhales. I was surprised I even remembered to breathe. I had wanted this for so long. Not just with Asher. I had wanted to explore this side of my sexuality.

"That's quite the answer." He was amused at my lack of words.

His hand dipped inside my pants and his fingers gripped me through my boxer briefs. I couldn't help but thrust my hips.

What was I so worried about?

He pushed at my shoulder so I'd roll onto my back and hovered over me, his lips close to mine, but not touching.

"You know, when I first met you, I didn't like you." His hand slid into my boxers and pulled my cock out. I shut my eyes as he gripped it in his hand. "But then, I don't know. You just started fucking caring about me too much."

"Do you care about me?" The question had crossed my mind several times. He didn't exactly give off warm and fuzzy vibes. Plus, before Danica, he was a notorious womanizer. He said so himself one night on the couch. I would hope I wasn't just going to be another notch on his belt.

"Yes." He ran his thumb up the underside of my cock and swiped his finger over the head. "If I didn't, I wouldn't be willing to try this."

I had no coherent words left, so I gripped the back of his head and pulled his lips back to mine. He parted his lips and I moved my tongue inside, tangling with his. His hips moved and he thrust his dick against my leg as he slid his hand up and down my shaft.

He pulled away and sat back on his heels, staring down at me, my erect dick pointing straight at him. His eyes moved downward and took me in.

"Danica always complains that blowjobs make her jaw hurt. I wonder if it's true. What do you think?" He moved his hands up and down my thighs a few times before his hands gripped my pants and boxers and pulled them down.

"Maybe it's like a muscle and you just have to use it enough," I said, somehow managing to get words to come out of my mouth in a complete, coherent thought.

Asher threw his head back and laughed. Things had been so tense lately, it was a pleasant sight to see. "Please say that to Dani and make sure I'm around when you do."

"I can't say anything to her until we've run some experiments." I looked at his lips. "And since you've received the most blowjobs out of the two of us, it's only scientifically appropriate for your mouth to be the first test subject."

"Is that so?" Asher ran his finger over the bead of pre-cum at my slit.

He was slowly killing me with his torture. I had noticed he had two extreme versions in the bedroom. Hard and fast, or slow and teasing. There was no in between with him.

"Are you going to suck my dick or not?" The words left my mouth before I could stop them. He had wound me up tight like a rubber band stretched between two fingers. I was about ready to snap and make a mess and he had barely even touched me.

He smirked down at me. "I was thinking that maybe we should shower. I need to relax a little and you seem to have forgotten that you had a tongue that wasn't mine wrapped around your arm earlier."

I groaned and pushed myself up on my forearms. "You're a tease."

He stood up and offered me his hand, which I begrudgingly took. I followed him to the bathroom, shedding my clothes as I went, since I already had my pants down anyways.

Asher turned on the shower and then looked at me in the mirror. He might have been taking charge a minute ago, but now he looked nervous. I had no misgivings about us, whatever it was that we were now.

He turned towards me as I stepped closer. He shut his eyes as I unbuttoned his pants. I was so used to him taking charge of situations, that this new dynamic felt strange. A good strange; definitely a strange that made my dick even harder.

He pulled off his shirt as I pushed his pants down his well-defined legs. I always thought I'd be turned on by abdominal muscles or even strong shoulders on a man, but Asher's legs were perfect.

We climbed into the shower that had two showerheads. I moaned as the warm water hit my body. I guess I did need a shower. We didn't speak as we washed ourselves.

I finished before Asher and leaned back against the shower wall, the steam enclosed in the shower, making it feel like a sauna.

I shut my eyes and brought my hand down to my dick. Asher made a noise and I opened my eyes as he stepped forward and pressed against me, our dicks touching.

"What are you doing to me?" He reached over and squirted body wash in his hand. He buried his face in my neck and took the both of us in his slick hand. "Fuck."

His grip was strong, and as he slid his hand up and down our joined cocks, I felt my balls tingle. I wasn't going to last long with his hands *and* dick on me.

My hands slid down his chest and I put my hand over his on our dicks. We moaned into each other as his hand tightened and our hips thrust together. I bit his bottom lip and then sucked it into my mouth.

He pushed closer to me and his other hand reached around me and gripped my ass, his nails digging into the sensitive flesh. My body shook and my knees felt unsteady as my orgasm crashed into me, spilling onto us. Asher let out a curse as he came.

We stood panting against the shower wall, coming down from the high of our releases.

"I'm exhausted." The sound of the water hitting the tiles was lulling me to sleep.

We cleaned off and then climbed into bed. The sun was barely rising as our heads hit the pillows and we drifted off to sleep in each other's arms.

CHAPTER 17

DANICA

I stood in front of the mirror and stared back at a woman I didn't recognize. My hair was pulled into a chignon and my makeup was simple with a bright red lip. My dress was a floor length, black lace gown with cap sleeves and a plunging neckline.

I guess if I was going to have to steal the Holy Grail, I was going to do it in style.

I shouldn't be going through with it, but how could I not? I didn't want to be at fault for millions of people dying. I knew that, regardless of my choice, she would steal the artifact anyways. Might as well save some people while I was at it.

What she even wanted with the Holy Grail was beyond me.

Maybe she had a wine drinking problem.

I had decided to detach myself from the situation. I was a robot, going through the motions. I could run, but she'd find me. Or she'd just kill everyone. She was a psychopath.

I dug in the duffle bag and found the letter from Olly. I had a feeling I wouldn't be coming back after this, so I shoved it in my bra.

I slid on the heels left by the door and walked out of the bedroom. My palms were sweaty and I wiped them down my lace covered thighs. It really was a gorgeous gown. Too bad it was tainted by the one who had given it to me.

I walked into the living room to find Lilith dressed in a burgundy velvet trumpet-style gown. The sleeves were long and the deep V neckline accentuated the necklace she wore. I took several steps closer to her and realized it was the lily necklace that had been in my jewelry box.

"You stole it," I said flatly, stopping several feet from her.

She brought her hand to the pendant and brought it away from her skin to look down at it. "You're insinuating that it wasn't mine to begin with."

I rolled my eyes. "Where's John?" I had assumed he'd be joining us.

"He has more pressing things to deal with." She sauntered over to me and looped her arm through mine. I tried to pull away but her grip on my arm was strong. "Are you clear on the plan? My sources tell me that we will be in good company tonight. I don't want you to get any grand ideas in that head of yours. My hell serpent is ready to go if you do."

I nodded, not trusting myself to speak. If I did, I would give her a piece of my mind and what I had to say wasn't nice.

We exited into the garage where a black SUV was waiting with the two goons from before. They were dressed in tuxedos, and had they not manhandled and laughed at me back in California, I would have said they were handsome.

One climbed into the driver's seat, with Lilith taking the passenger side. I climbed into the back. The door locks engaged and we backed out of the garage.

"Those are childproof, so don't get any ideas," the goon with me in the back said. His voice was smooth as silk and I wondered what kind of demon he was.

I stayed silent as we pulled out of the housing development and onto a highway. We crossed over a river that had a bridge that looked like it had giant wishbones holding it up. I just stared out the window, in awe at the massive city that was outside.

After about thirty minutes, we pulled up to a hotel and waited in a long line of taxis and vehicles to be let out at the entrance.

"What kind of event is this?" I asked, finally breaking the silence.

"It's a gala auction," Lilith said as her door was opened and she got out of the SUV.

"No funny business in there, you got that? Hell serpents are hungry as fuck. Remember that," the goon next to me warned. He got out and I followed.

We entered into a ballroom that was already packed with people dressed to the nines in tuxedos and gowns. We blended in perfectly, except for the stolen glances towards Lilith.

As much as I didn't want to admit it, she was striking and had a commanding presence about her. There was a large dance floor set up in the front of the ballroom with a stage on the other side of it. Couples floated across the floor, looking as if they were part of a royal court.

It reminded me of Reve.

Where were my guardians right now? They had so quickly become engrained in my life and being away from them made me anxious.

We sat down at a table near the edge of the dance floor and a glass of wine was shoved in front of my face by Lilith.

"You're fidgeting. Follow the plan and everything will be fine." When I didn't take the wine glass from her, she set it down on the table. "Think of it this way. You are righting a wrong that happened long ago."

I made a noise in my throat. "And what wrong is that? Didn't you get pissed off that you couldn't be on top? Seems kind of childish to throw this big a tantrum."

The smile she had fell and she narrowed her eyes. "The internet is the worst invention known to man. Do you believe everything you read?" I shook my head. "I was created from nothing and promised everything. I stood up for myself as a woman and what did that get me?"

"Bitterness?"

She laughed and stood. She looked across the dance floor and a smile lit up her face. "Right on time. Your father always did have perfect timing."

I followed her gaze and saw my father standing alone on the other edge of the dance floor. He was staring right at Lilith, his gaze unwavering. His eyes then landed on me before quickly rising back to follow Lilith, who was moving around the perimeter of the floor towards him.

"I don't know if I believe that this goblet they have is the Holy Grail." I turned my head towards the voice, surprised to hear English. My eyes widened at the table full of businessmen at the next table over. A few of them were well known in the United States.

"Supposedly, a deep-sea fishing boat caught it in their cage. They said it was buoyant, which is odd, wouldn't you say?"

"Only a fool would spend their money on something like that."

I lost track of Lilith and my dad. I stood, searching for them and found them on the dance floor. Together.

My heart jumped into my throat taking in the sight. Lucifer looked tense. I stepped forward to the edge, keeping my eyes on them. They moved in sync with each other as they glided across the floor.

Why was he not coming to rescue me? Maybe he knew what was at stake.

"Danica." I nearly jumped out of my skin as Olly appeared beside me. Damn him and his sneaky ways. "We have to go while she's distracted."

"I can't." I spoke low enough that the goons a few feet away couldn't hear. "She's going to kill a lot of people if I don't do what she asks."

He took my hand and I relaxed the tiniest amount. I wanted to run away with him, but too much was on the line.

"And what about you?" he whispered. I could feel his hand shaking in mine.

"She won't kill me. She wants me to rule with her." Hearing it come from my lips made me cringe.

"Rule what? You can't seriously be considering-" Just then, the fire alarm went off.

The two goons grabbed Olly and yanked him away from me. I gave him a look that I hope conveyed how sorry I was, then dashed across the dance floor through the throngs of people moving towards the exits.

I made my way around to the back of the stage and walked right up to the two security guards who were making no move to leave.

I took a deep breath and balled my fists at my sides. Lilith had given me my first lessons on being her daughter. With the right motivation, I could control anyone or anything with darkness in them. John and the security guards hadn't enjoyed my training.

"I'm going to need for you to leave." I had the motivation and they had the darkness.

At first they seemed confused, and I wondered if they knew English, but then they walked past me, leaving me alone.

The auction items were behind the stage curtain, displayed in cases that could be rolled out when needed. I climbed up and stood in front of the Holy Grail. It's gold and silver design gleamed unnaturally and I felt a strong pull towards it.

It wanted me to take it.

I lifted the cover and grabbed it, the cool metal sending goosebumps up my arms. It felt powerful in my hands and I quickly made my way towards the side exit. Lilith was going to meet me just outside.

As soon as I was through the fire exit door, I knew something was wrong. Screams erupted from around the corner and I rushed down the sidewalk to peek around the edge of the building.

At the front of the hotel were swarms of evacuated people, and right in the middle was a large brawl that had my heart stopping. Right in the middle of it were the goons, Lucifer, Tobias, Asher, and Olly.

I took a step around the corner when a hand clamped on my arm and pulled me back, the nails of the owner digging into my arm. Lilith snatched the cup away from me and wrapped it in a cloth napkin.

"Let's go." She was pulling me across the crosswalk. Sirens could be heard in the distance, but were still far away.

"I got you what you wanted. Let me go!" I knew the plan wasn't for her to set me free, but it was worth a shot. When we were on the sidewalk, I planted my feet firmly.

"Let her go, Lilith." Reve's voice came from the side and Lilith stopped in her tracks, her head tilting to the side and the grin I was becoming all too familiar with spreading across her face.

"Show yourself, *Reve*." I did not like the tone her voice had. It was guttural and threatening.

Reve appeared, dressed in a tuxedo. He took a step forward and I begged him with my eyes to turn and run away.

"You have some balls coming here tonight. Does Danica know about us? About how you once pledged yourself to me?" She sounded amused.

My eyes widened and I watched Reve back up a step. "That's in my past. I'm no longer your slave."

"I beg to differ. Come here." I watched in horror as Reve obeyed her command and stopped in front of us. "How long has it been since you gave someone a vision?"

Reve paled. A small drop of blood escaped his mouth. He was biting himself to keep from answering.

"Answer me." I heard a noise behind me and a knife appeared in front of me. "Or I'll ruin her pretty little face."

I nearly went cross-eyed looking down at the knife now pressed against my chest. This was not part of the plan she had laid out for us. She wouldn't really cut my face, would she?

Who was I kidding? She would if it meant she got what she wanted.

"I haven't. Not for centuries." As he spoke, I could see the blood on his teeth. My knees trembled at the sight.

"I think tonight is a good night to rekindle that part of you. We'll start with all the people at the front of the hotel. You're to give them a vision of their worst nightmare come to life."

"There are hundreds! It will kill me!" His body was shaking and he backed up a step towards the hotel. He seemed to be fighting the compulsion. "Don't do this, Lilith."

"It's already done." The knife pressed a little harder against my chest. "And Reve? I am not Lilith to you."

"Your highness." His words came out stuttered as he bowed to her. Then he turned and walked towards the front of the hotel.

"What have you done?" I whispered. She lowered the knife and pulled me down the sidewalk towards a waiting black SUV.

She didn't answer me. We were feet away from the vehicle when my dad landed in front of it, blocking the doors.

"Lilith." His wings retracted and he took a step forward.

Lilith's arm tightened around me and she backed up several steps, dragging me along with her. I stumbled in my shoes but managed to stay upright.

She brought her other arm back and threw the goblet towards the SUV. My eyes followed it as it landed in John's hands. He slid into the passenger seat as three men got out of the back. They were different from the two that had been with us earlier.

"Lilith, give me my daughter." His voice held no emotion, but his eyes told a different story. He was pissed and scared.

She held the sharp blade to my throat, the edge digging into my skin. I could feel the blood trickle down my neck.

My dad held his hands up and stayed where he was. His eyes were troubled, and his mouth was drawn in a tight line.

Lilith laughed behind me, the movement causing the knife to dig into my skin. All it would take was one good swipe and I'd be a goner.

"I can't be beat, Lucifer. Danica really was the best thing I could have done for myself. I was able to give myself at least another thousand years. To think all it takes to have immortality is a cup and some of your own offspring's blood. I have no use for her now."

My eyes teared up. A few tears escaped the corners and slid down my cheeks.

"If she's of no use to you now, why not let her go? What do you want? Just don't hurt her." He took a step towards us and she backed up, closer to the railing separating us from the river.

"Dad." I pleaded with my eyes. He had a determined look on his face.

His eyes met mine and his lip trembled as Lilith answered him.

"You know what I want. You've known since I had her the first time."

He let out a shaky breath and a tear slid down his cheek. He nodded and I knew she had wanted more than just the Holy Grail tonight.

"Don't, please!" I wanted to run to him and beg him not to play into her plan, whatever it was. The three men flanked him, two to the sides and one behind him.

"I love you, Danica. Whatever happens, know that."

The men grabbed him and one stabbed a needle into his neck, plunging a black substance into his vein. His eyes went glossy and his knees gave out.

"You fool." Lilith laughed and then plunged the knife into my chest.

His eyes went wide and his mouth opened in a silent scream as I reached my shaking hands to the knife. I looked at it in disbelief and then back at my father.

I stumbled backwards as I watched them drag my dad by his arms to a waiting van and throw him in the back.

"He's always thought too much with his heart. Not so much with his brain." Lilith stood in front of me, her eyes devoid of any human emotion. "I had hoped for you to be by my side, but now that you have bonded with all four of those guardians of yours, I can't risk you getting in the way of my plans."

"I'm just a girl. I..." The pain in my chest prevented me from saying more.

"You aren't just a girl. I think you know that." With those words, she placed her hands on my cheeks. "My beautiful daughter. If only..."

If only what? But I never got my answer, because her hands lowered to my shoulders and shoved me over the railing and into the river.

CHAPTER 18

DANICA

ater filled my lungs as the initial impact of the water sent me under. I struggled to move towards the surface. The knife was still lodged in my chest and I was too afraid to pull it out. My head finally surfaced and I coughed violently, the taste of copper and dirt in my mouth.

The shore seemed so far away and my vision blurred. My ears didn't seem to be working, no sound reaching them. They felt numb. I felt numb.

I didn't want to die in a river.

I felt myself sinking again. My head had just gone back under when arms wrapped around me and I shot into the sky. We landed on the sidewalk and I was laid on the cement.

Asher stared down at me, his hair dripping water onto my face.

"Fuck, fuck, fuck!" I couldn't hear him completely, but that certainly sounded like what he was saying.

I opened my mouth to speak and coughed. I realized how difficult it was to breathe as I tried to inhale and felt like I was getting no air. My hands went to the knife and Asher grabbed my wrists, stopping me.

I was starting to panic, air not getting inside like I needed it to.

Olly appeared next to Asher and his hands went to my chest. He shook his head and Asher yelled something at him. My eyes fluttered shut.

~

"Danica."

My eyes popped open at the sound. I was in a large room with a single bed in the middle of it. Everything was white. Chinese hospitals were strange. Sterile.

My hands went to my chest, but the only thing I found was the white fabric of a top. I sat up and scanned the room. I definitely wasn't in Kansas anymore.

"Hello?" My voice echoed in the room and made me shudder. *Shit.* Was I dead?

This wouldn't be the first time I thought I was dead, but I also hadn't been in a white room with nothing but myself and a bed.

"You have to wake up. Your job is not done yet." The voice came from nowhere and sounded an awful lot like Morgan Freeman.

"You have got to be kidding me. Reve, if this is you playing a prank, I'm going to cut you." I swung my legs over the side of the bed and eyed the door on the other side. It gleamed like it was made from a thousand diamonds.

"This is not a prank, child. You just had surgery. Your blood can't heal you from your injuries."

"Why do you sound like Morgan Freeman? That's a little cliché, don't you think?"

The voice chuckled. "Or is he the cliché?"

I stood and walked towards the door. "Why can't I heal? Am I a demon now?"

He laughed again, the deep baritone sound making me want to smile. I reached for the handle of the door but it wouldn't turn.

"The angel part of your blood has always been stronger and has fought off the demon blood from taking over. Lilith attempted to disrupt that balance. She was unsuccessful."

"So what am I?" I looked at the ceiling as if it held all the answers. It seemed to be speaking, so maybe it actually did.

"When it's your time, the door will open for you."

"That doesn't answer my question." I rolled my eyes at the ceiling and the voice laughed again.

"You are your father's daughter."

Dad. Where was he? I opened my mouth to ask but the room started to spin.

∿

A DISTANT PHONE ringing woke me. My eyes adjusted to the dim light. Asher and Olly were on a bench seat by the window, Olly with his head in Asher's lap. Tobias was in a chair next to the bed, his cheek resting on his hand.

My tongue darted to my dry lips and I raised a hand to them. I stared at the heart rate monitor clamped onto my finger and then at the IV taped to the top of my hand.

"You had surgery," Reve's quiet voice said from right next to the bed.

I startled and my hand went to my chest where I could feel thick bandages through the rough material of the hospital gown. I turned my head in the direction of his voice.

I had thought he had gone off to die.

"Tobias saved me. He claims he owed me for saving him." He was whispering and his voice came closer. "The short time I projected visions weakened me quite a bit though. I won't be able to get out of this form until I go feed. I wanted to wait until you woke up."

"Reve." My word came out more as air. I cleared my throat and tried again. "Reve."

My brain felt a bit foggy and I didn't understand what he meant by feed. I shifted in the bed and winced and sucked in air as pain radiated from my chest down to the tips of my fingers.

Tobias stirred in the chair and his eyes slowly cracked open. He blinked several times and then sat up straight and leaned forward, taking my hand.

"You're awake." I just nodded in reply and looked back to the other side of the bed where Reve was. Or at least where I thought he was.

"I'll be back," Reve said. "I love you, Danica."

I felt the stirring of air near my face and knew it was him. *I love you too.*

Tobias stood and walked around the end of the bed to a rolling tray that had a pitcher and cup. He poured water in the cup and put a straw in it.

He pushed a button on a controller and my bed moved so I was sitting up a little. It hurt, but I was desperate for water. After a few sips, I let out a sigh and cleared my throat again.

"My dad."

Tobias put the cup back and sat back down heavily. He looked over at Asher and Olly, still sleeping and oblivious.

"I should wake them up." He stood again and shook Asher's shoulder.

Asher jerked awake, jostling Olly's head, almost causing him to fall off the window seat they were on.

"My dad," I repeated. His face was the last thing I remembered.

Tobias sat back down and took my hand again. Asher and Olly both stood behind him.

"Where is he?" I felt a tear slip down my cheek. It was a feeling I was becoming well acquainted with.

"Dani." Olly sat on the edge of my bed and took my other hand. "We don't know where he is. The other archangels have been looking for him, but he vanished."

"Is he dead?" I felt my chest tightening as the words left my lips.

"Reve thinks she took him to Inferna." Asher stayed behind Tobias and looked at all the wires and tubes hooked up to me.

I wanted him to come to me, to touch me, but didn't know if I trusted myself to make any requests. What if everything they felt and did was because I had somehow manipulated them into it.

I didn't want to be like my mother.

"We have to go find him." I shifted again and tried to sit up but Olly put his arm out to stop me. "Please. We have to."

"I know, but we don't know where he is exactly and you need to heal."

"Heal me then," I said, grabbing his hand and putting it on my chest. "Heal me now."

The motivation was there. The command was there. His eyes softened and he brought my hand to his lips and kissed my knuckles.

"She used some kind of demon bone knife. I can't heal the wound. Rafael can't either. You lost a lot of blood. They had to give you a transfusion of angel blood. That seemed to stop whatever autoimmune response you were having too because your temperature is back to normal."

I hadn't even been aware it was abnormal since it spiked to crazy high levels. How long ago was that? What day was it?

"Does the creator, or God, or whatever he's called, sound a bit like Morgan Freeman?" I wasn't going to say anything about my dream, but it was out of my mouth before I could stop myself.

Asher snorted and I looked at him. A smile crossed his face. "He sounds like whatever you want him to sound like."

"It felt so real. I-"

A loud rumble came from outside and the ground started to shake, the bed and machines moving. Olly and Tobias jumped up and rushed to the window with Asher.

"What is it?" I gripped the sheets and the shaking subsided fairly quickly.

The three angels stood at the window, staring out. A loud siren started blaring in the distance. At first it sounded like someone was lying on a car horn but then the sound became familiar. A sound that I had only heard in movies.

"An air raid?" Maybe this was another part of the dream I was having.

"Is that a motherfucking *dragon*?" Asher backed away from the window. "Holy shit, it's a fucking dragon. Dragons are real?"

My heart stopped. "It's a hell serpent. She said she wouldn't use it. I have to stop it!"

I didn't know how I'd stop it, but if I could command it to stop, maybe it would.

Tobias turned and he and Asher made their way to me, stopping me from getting out of the bed and yanking off all the wires and tubes.

"Uhh, guys!" Olly was still looking out the window. "It's headed this way."

The hospital room door slammed open and a man with quite the head of long blond hair pulled into a braid rushed in. He had a sword at his hip and looked all business. His eyes landed on me then went to Olly.

"Michael, what's-" Tobias started.

"Get her back to the academy. She'll be safe there." He was looking directly at Olly. "Do you understand, boy?"

"Yes, sir."

"She can't die. Not yet." With that, he turned and left as quickly as he'd appeared.

Not yet? What the actual fuck did that mean? I didn't have much time to think on it because my machines started beeping as things were unhooked. Olly scooped me into his arms and I winced.

Was the hell serpent coming for me? I shuddered as we entered the hall where there was a flurry of activity with doctors, nurses, and patients rushing around. The building shook again and I flinched as a plastic light cover fell from the ceiling in front of us.

I'd like to think I could have stopped the creature with a command, but who was I kidding? The only experience I had was practicing on John and commanding the two human security guards. A bus-sized hell serpent was something else entirely.

Asher, who was somehow keeping his shit together, opened the stairwell door and we followed Tobias up the stairs to the roof. It was for helicopters, but tonight it would be our launching pad.

A screech filled the night sky along with all of the sounds you'd expect when a giant, dragon-like creature was ravaging a city.

We had to be over thirty stories high. I clung to Olly's shirt. His wings came out just as the head of the serpent came into view. It was either smart as fuck or somehow was tracking us.

We took off from the roof just as it let out a screech and fire poured from its mouth. The entire top of the building went up in flames.

I knew this was just the beginning.

MAYA NICOLE

TRANSCEND

CELESTIAL ACADEMY BOOK 3

CHAPTER 1

DANICA

Breathe in. Breathe out.

The words played on repeat in my head as I focused on the movement of my chest. My skin felt sticky and hot. I could feel the scar knitted together on my chest as each breath stretched the scar tissue. The scar that had closed over the wound that had taken part of my heart.

It had been over a month since my mother stabbed me in the chest and then sent a hell serpent to finish the job. The hell serpent had failed. Lilith had not.

It had been over a month since she took my dad.

I desperately wanted to find him. Lilith was beyond psychotic, and the longer she had him, the worse off we would all be. No one knew where they were exactly. Hell, probably. None of the archangels wanted to go on an expedition into an unknown realm. Especially when there had been no sign of Lilith since that night.

Where else would she have taken him?

I gripped the sides of the lounge chair. *We have to find him.*

"Cannonball!" My eyes popped open behind my sunglasses as Olly ran past me and jumped into the pool. Water splashed over the sides and onto me. I jumped up from my chair.

We really needed to have a talk about mimicking movies. It was all fun and games until someone got hurt. Like he was about to.

"Damn it, Olly!" I wiped the water from my skin that had just started baking at the level I wanted it. I walked to the edge of the pool and put my hands on my hips. "You're going to pay for that!"

Asher's laugh grabbed my attention, and I looked over at him laying a towel on the chair next to mine. He had his hair pulled back in a small bun at the nape of his neck and his aviator sunglasses shielded his eyes. I'm sure they were twinkling with glee over Olly's assault.

"Did he get you all wet?" He cocked an eyebrow as he pulled his shirt off.

I bit my lip and perused his well-defined chest as he threw his shirt on the chair and pulled his sunglasses off. What was I mad about again?

"Someone got me wet." I plopped back down on my chair and watched as Asher walked to the edge of the pool.

He looked over his shoulder at me and gave me a shit-eating grin before jumping into the pool, sending more water in my direction.

Dick.

I couldn't stop a smile from turning up my mouth. Smiling made me feel guilty, but Asher, Olly, Tobias, and Reve had made it their mission to get me smiling again.

I let out a sigh and laid back again, the moment of glee over as quickly as it began. How could I pretend to be happy when my dad was missing and so many had died?

The hell serpent might have been dead, but that wouldn't bring back the hundreds that were in its path to get to me. Media coverage of the incident had been sparse in the days following the attack.

Chinese President Calls for Investigation into Military Mishap

Shanghai, China - An investigation is underway in Shanghai, two days after an experimental drone killed 243 people and injured hundreds more. China's armed forces are taking responsibility for the jetliner-sized aircraft that malfunctioned during a test flight, entering a densely populated area of Shanghai.

Ironically, most structural damage is to the Changzheng Hospital, which is affiliated with the military. Losses are estimated in the billions.

How many other incidents had the angels been able to cover up over the years? If they could cover up a giant monster flying through the air, who knows what else they were hiding.

Water splashed over the side of the pool, ripping me from my thoughts. Asher was trying to dunk Olly under the water. When his attempts failed, they both put their arms over the side and looked up at me.

"Why don't you join us?" Olly ran a hand through his wet hair, making the brown strands stand on end. "I don't see how laying in the sun is relaxing."

"The weather is perfect for sunbathing. Besides, I jumped in a while ago." It really was perfect. Mid-eighties was excellent summer weather. I had been spending too much time indoors.

"You're going to get wrinkles," Asher teased. I watched as Olly turned towards him, grabbed him around the waist, and then flung him back into the water.

I shut my eyes again and let the sounds of Asher and Olly horsing around fade into the background. I was just starting to feel the much-needed burning sensation of the sun again when I felt the sun disappear.

I cracked an eye open to find Tobias and Reve standing above me. They both had intense expressions on their faces.

"Like I was saying, the Dodgers are taking it all the way this season." Tobias pulled off his shirt and folded it neatly. "And when they do, it'll be time to pay up."

"They'll make it to the postseason, but then choke like they usually do."

Both my eyes were open to watch the display in front of me as Reve removed his shirt. All four of them were a sight to behold when shirtless. It was like I had my very own *Magic Mike* cast. I was sure they'd have stripped if I'd asked.

I definitely needed to ask.

I still didn't quite understand how they were all mine. This summer was giving me man overload though.

"Isn't there anywhere on this damn campus where I can get some peace and quiet?" I grumbled.

I loved them, but I was sick of hearing about baseball all the damn time. Some women might join their significant others in their love of the game. I just didn't see the appeal besides it being a nice way to fall asleep quickly.

Los Angeles Celestial Academy might be situated on twenty acres, but they never strayed farther than twenty feet from me it seemed, despite there being hardly anyone on campus for the summer.

Silence met my ears and a small smile formed on my lips as they got the hint that I wanted them to shut up about baseball. Finally, some peace.

It was short-lived.

"Reve, there's really only one solution to this problem we're having." My eyes popped open and I watched as Tobias and Reve reached over me and shook hands. "Count of three?"

I let out a shriek as their hands reached for me. I tried to scramble off the chair, but Tobias took my left side, and Reve took my right. They lifted me like I weighed nothing and walked in sync to the pool.

They needed to stop ganging up on me. Unless it was in the bedroom. I was all for that.

"I'm going to kill-" They tossed me into the pool, the water gliding over my sun-kissed skin. I sank below the surface and came up spluttering.

"What was that, Dani?" Reve laughed before jumping in. He came up and slicked his dark hair back. "Want to see a neat party trick?"

Tobias sat on the edge and dangled his feet in as I swam over to the side. "If the party trick includes kicking your asses, then sure."

I turned to face Reve, but he was gone. Or at least his body was. I could make out his head by the water droplets floating in the air. He moved towards us, the water drops moving with him. It looked like a movie special effect where the rain stopped mid-air.

If the dream demon thing stopped working for him, he could always start a career in Hollywood.

"You promised not to use any of your abilities on campus," Tobias warned. They had gotten into it several times over the past few weeks over the same issue.

Reve let out a grunt and reappeared. "There is no one here. Even if there was, how would they know if they can't see me?" He rolled his eyes and then smirked. He grabbed Tobias's legs and yanked him into the pool with us.

"Reve has a point," Olly said, appearing right next to us. "There's no one here to see anything."

He grabbed me around the waist and turned me towards him. On instinct, my legs wrapped around his waist, and I rested my arms around his neck.

"Do you think of anything else these days?" I gasped as he lifted me enough for my breasts to be out of the water. He planted a kiss right on the top of my cleavage.

"He has a one-track mind." Asher swam up behind me and put his hands on my waist and his mouth next to my ear. "And right now, this bikini is not helping."

I arched back into Asher as Olly moved his mouth to mine and parted my lips with his tongue. This was definitely my preferred way of keeping my mind off things. I wasn't going to complain about being sandwiched between two hot, wet men.

Asher's lips trailed down my neck to my shoulders as I moaned into Olly's mouth. Our tongues tangled in a hot kiss that made my skin heat more than the sun. I was surprised the water around us wasn't boiling from the amount of heat in the kiss.

"Danica, your phone is ringing," Tobias's voice snuck into my lust-filled ears where the only sound I could hear was my heart beating, not the incessant bells of my phone alarm.

"Crap," I moaned, pushing away from Olly and Asher. I swam to the pool ladder and climbed out, feeling like I weighed three times what I usually did. Leave it to gravity to remind me that I had the weight of the world on my shoulders.

I grabbed my phone and turned off the alarm. I had a meeting with Sue Whittaker to discuss my options since my guardian placement exam showed what she called "a complete incompatibility" with being a guardian angel.

I wasn't surprised. I wasn't an angel. In fact, I was precisely fifty percent angel and fifty percent demon. Despite Rafael experimenting with angel blood transfusions, it always went right back to fifty-fifty.

"Want me to go with you?" Tobias hoisted himself out of the pool and made his way towards me. I licked my lips as water droplets skated down his skin.

After toweling myself off and sliding on my shorts, I looked over at Tobias again before pulling on my tank top. His brows were drawn together. I let out a puff of air and slid my feet into my flip flops.

"It'll be fine. I don't think it's a good idea for you to poke the bear any more than you already have." I slid my phone into my back pocket and put my sunglasses on the top of my head.

"I'll go," Olly shouted from the pool. "We can hold hands the entire time. She'll love that!"

"I can go in my phantom form and mess around with her a bit." Reve sat down on my empty chair. "But that might give away that I've been the one fucking around with her shit the last few weeks."

I put my hands on my hips and looked down at him. "Michael told you to knock that off because he didn't want to have to listen to her screeching at him."

He grinned and shrugged. "That wench insulted all of us. Plus, she's taking out all of her insecurities on poor Tobias here. Think of it as repentance for her sins. If it makes it easier."

When we had returned from Shanghai, Michael sequestered me to the campus. As unhappy as I had been, the dean had been even more so. Sue had been livid with having not only me back but also Tobias and Asher. To top it off, Michael had given special permission to Reve to be on campus.

I had thought Sue's head was going to explode with how red she turned at the news that a demon would be staying until further notice.

"I'm sure I can handle myself. If I can survive a knife to the chest, I think I can survive a tongue lashing from a bitter old woman." I touched my scar through my shirt and plastered a smile on my face. "Be ready with alcohol and pizza, just in case."

I made my way across campus to Ariel Hall and up to the second-floor administrative offices. It would have been faster to get a ride with one of the guys, but sometimes it was good to walk instead of flying everywhere.

It was quiet since there were only a few staff members on campus for the summer. I turned the corner leading to the dean's office and nearly collided with a mountain of a man with long blond hair. Michael had a phone plastered to his ear and a pensive look on his face. He held up his hand in silent greeting before stalking back down the hall.

The dean's office door was closed, so I sat in one of the chairs outside the door and watched Michael pace back and forth down the hall.

I felt sick. If the archangel was here, it couldn't be good. The meeting was supposed to be just Dean Whittaker and me.

"Next time, please try not to kill them... Well, obviously if it is spitting fire, kill those... You should be able to handle one of those, Ham... They torture souls, so what if we torture them?... Don't give me a lecture about my moral compass!" He ended the call and then turned to look at me. "Sorry about that. Chamuel can be a pill."

I nodded. Anytime Michael was around, I felt like I was in the presence of a major celebrity and could hardly find words. It might also have been the fact that he was one scary-ass angel that looked like he could remove someone's head with his bare hands.

"More demon attacks?" I managed to ask as he raised his fist and knocked on Sue's door.

I stood as he opened the door to the office. He looked back at me and gave me a curt nod.

Demons had been coming through the barrier to Earth more and more frequently over the last month. Usually, it was only a few and nothing like the attack at the abandoned mall. Still, demons coming to Earth had disaster written all over it.

Just ask the two hundred and forty-three people who died in Shanghai.

"Michael, what a pleasant surprise," Sue said as we walked into her office. She didn't sound like it was a pleasant surprise at all.

"Well, as you know, I receive notifications of all meetings and interactions logged in the system for Danica now." He sat down in a chair and crossed his legs. "So imagine my surprise when I get a notification on my phone that you've scheduled a meeting without my consent or notifying me personally."

Sue opened her mouth to speak, but Michael held up his hand. She sat down in her chair and moved some papers around on her desk. I took a seat next to Michael.

What was he, my Heaven-appointed advocate now?

"You said you want to speak to me about incompatibility with being a guardian angel?" I couldn't help but smile as she shifted uncomfortably in her seat.

She let out a strained laugh and pulled out a sheet of paper. "Well, yes. It seems your test results yielded no results for the four guardian angel paths we have here."

"Oliver doesn't have a path, either." I folded my hands in my lap. He was an archangel. All the paths were his. "I will just take whatever classes he is taking."

"Oliver Morgan is an archangel, Ms. Deville. This is hardly the same thing. It will be rather difficult for you to participate in the Advanced Healing Techniques course when you have no healing powers."

She looked at Michael to gauge his reaction. He sat silently next to me. She took his silence as permission to continue.

She looked back at me and picked up her pen. "You are not an angel. It's time for us to all acknowledge that your attendance here is at a detriment to angels who earned the right to call themselves guardian angels."

I looked over at Michael, who looked bored with this entire exchange. Shouldn't he be saying something? It was his idea for me to stay here in the first place. No wonder Lucifer didn't like him. My dad would never let someone speak to me the way Sue was.

"Earned their right? Maybe at some point they did. I think you're fooling yourself if you think some of the students here are any better than I am." I crossed my arms over my chest. "Besides, I'm half-angel. My blood tests confirm that."

She didn't need to know that the other half was demon or that my mother was Lilith. If she knew, the entire academy would know. I could only imagine the torment that would happen if that piece of information came out.

She made a strangled noise in her throat. "Even so, you have no abilities. Not to mention the company you seem to keep. Angels do not befriend or date demons. Him being on campus poses great danger to us all. It's bad enough it's being requested that Tobias Armstrong stay here when he's been suspended. Don't even get me started on that Fallen drunk that walks around half-dressed."

I wanted to laugh but bit my inner cheek. I couldn't deny the fact that Asher drank too much. He also had the tendency to walk around without a shirt. It didn't help that one day, Sue had entered the staff building and found him naked on the common room couch.

That had gone over *real* well.

A silence fell over the room. I willed myself to not break eye contact with the woman who had hated me before she had even known me. Her pen started to tap as the silence in the room lengthened.

"Sue." Michael cleared his throat. "Were you aware that Danica visited the white room?"

Michael had his eyes locked on Sue. She bristled at the mention of the room I had woken up in while dying of a stab wound. I was only half-surprised that Michael knew I had been knocking on Heaven's diamond-encrusted door.

It just wouldn't open for me.

"But how? There are only two ways for a person to get out of that room." Her pen dropped to the desk. She looked back and forth between us. I furrowed my brows because there had just been one door. Plus swirling. Lots and lots of swirling. "By going to Heaven or going to hell."

"It seems there are more important things in store for Danica. We don't know exactly what yet, but when the time comes, we want her as prepared as possible. You will enroll her in the warrior courses." He stood and crossed his arms. "And Sue? Need I remind you that you are easily replaceable. I can think of one perfectly suitable candidate that is unoccupied this next semester. I'm sure he would be willing to pick up the slack."

Her jaw nearly hit her desk. I stood and followed Michael out of the office. I looked back at Sue and gave her a sticky sweet smile before shutting the door.

"What exactly does being a warrior entail?" Sure, I could throw a punch, but being some kind of fighter?

"Hard work." He turned and put his hands on my shoulders. It was a very fatherly move, and my eyes teared up as he looked down at me. "Hard work and passion."

"Do you think we'll find him?" I broke eye contact with him and stared at the center of his chest.

He sighed. "We will."

"Do you think he'll be okay?" I looked back up again and saw sadness in his eyes. He let go of my shoulders.

"He'll live." His phone vibrated in his pocket, but he didn't move to answer it. "We are getting closer to finding him. We'd be closer if Chamuel stopped killing the demons we can get information from."

He'd live. That didn't ease the dread swirling in my gut. He'd live, but he probably would never be the same.

CHAPTER 2

DANICA

*J*une had come and gone. With nothing but an empty campus and time on my hands, I had already caught up on the coursework from the first semester that I hadn't been in attendance. I had also been working on perfecting my cooking skills in the large academy kitchen.

Me. Danica Marie Deville. Cooking. It was newsworthy and should have been taken to the press. They'd have a field day and warn the masses of impending doom.

The campus had taken on a whole new look and feel with it empty. I had always been so focused on avoiding the haters that I had never stopped to appreciate its beauty or what it had to offer. I hadn't even known there was a pool or state of the art fitness facility.

Not that I used the fitness facility. Although, maybe I should since I was a warrior now. The idea made me laugh.

I jumped onto the stainless-steel workstation in the kitchen and pulled out my phone. Tobias was supposed to be teaching me how to make pasta from scratch. *Where are you?*

Sorry! On my way, there was an extra inning.

I rolled my eyes and pulled up a list of ingredients for pasta. It seemed easy enough. If I messed it up and it tasted like cardboard, I would just blame Tobias and his baseball obsession.

I slid off the counter and pulled out the flour, eggs, and olive oil. It would have been easier to just use boxed pasta, but Tobias insisted on fresh since we had use of an actual kitchen.

I missed my own kitchen. Not that I had used it much, but the few times I did cook in it, the food had been a hit. Or at least I thought it was. No one had died.

The kitchen door swung open. Tobias rushed in, out of breath. He was dressed in jeans, a Dodgers shirt, and a backward baseball cap. I'd much rather have had him for dinner.

"Did they at least win?" I asked as he came around the counter. He stepped behind me and wrapped his arms around my waist.

"Of course they won." He kissed my neck, his beard tickling the sensitive skin below my ear. I tilted my head to the side and shut my eyes as he peppered kisses across my neck. "You ready?"

"I'm always ready," I breathed. Tobias chuckled and stepped around me to lean against the counter. "Oh, you meant to make pasta."

"What else would I have been talking about?" He opened a cabinet and pulled out a pasta maker contraption. It looked like some kind of medieval torture device.

"I'll remember that later." I hip bumped him as he grabbed the measuring cup I was holding out of my hand and dumped a pile of flour on the counter. "The recipe says-"

"Pasta making is an art form. Recipes are for noobs." He grabbed a second type of flour from the pantry and dumped it on top of the pile. "I'm no noob."

"You aren't Italian, are you?"

"My best friend growing up was Italian." He created a well to act as a bowl for the eggs in the center of the flour. "Want to crack four eggs in the center?"

We fell into a comfortable silence as we made the pasta and started the sauce. I popped a pan of meatballs in the oven and turned to find Tobias watching me.

"Were you checking out my ass?" I pulled him into a hug, burying my face in his shirt. He wrapped his arms around me, and his hand ran up and down my spine.

"Just worrying, as usual," he said into my hair. "I can't help it."

"I'm fine." I pulled back slightly so I could look at him. "What's there to worry about?"

He pushed a lock of hair out of my face and behind my ear, leaving his hand on the side of my neck. His thumb stroked my jaw. I shut my eyes and sighed.

"What if I somehow manipulated you into falling in love with me?" I whispered. It had been on my mind for weeks.

His thumb stilled for a moment before continuing to stroke in soothing swipes across my skin.

"I don't think that's possible. My love runs pretty deep." His thumb brushed over my bottom lip. "You aren't your mother."

I pulled away from him and went to the stove, checking on the sauce. I stirred it for longer than necessary before turning back to him.

"I am, though. At least fifty percent of me." I turned off the burner and put a lid on the pan. "I can manipulate demons and humans. It wouldn't be such a stretch to think that I had somehow coerced you guys into being with me. I mean, there *are* four of you. That's a bit abnormal." I crossed my arms over my chest and leaned against the opposite counter.

We had talked about my newly discovered ability after returning from China but hadn't discussed it as much as we should have. Every time I was around them, I wondered if I had somehow duped them into being with me.

"Let's test it." He placed his arms on either side of me, trapping me against the counter. "Make me bark like a dog or kiss your feet."

His eyes danced in amusement. I didn't think it was funny that everything I thought we had might be one-sided. I did want to test it, but the thought made me want to throw up. What if he barked like a dog?

"You don't need anything else to worry about. Just give it a try so it'll be one less thing to think about." He stepped back. "I'm ready."

I sighed and stood up straight. I balled my fists at my side, which somehow helped. If I had been somehow controlling them all, what would we do? Would they leave me?

"Bark like a dog." Nothing. "Tobias, bark like a dog."

"Is this some kind of new sex foreplay you two are into?" Reve's voice came from the doorway just before the door opened. Olly and Asher walked in. "If so, I'm not sure I'm going to be into it."

"Kitchen foreplay? That sounds like fun. Where's the whipped cream?" Asher went to the stove and lifted the lid. "It smells good in here. What's on the menu besides foreplay?"

"Danica thinks she made us fall in love with her." Tobias kissed my cheek in reassurance.

"Well, she kind of did, didn't she? I mean, I'm in love with her. I don't know about you fools." Asher pulled me in for a kiss before passing me off to Olly, who did the same.

Reve appeared and took my hand, kissing the top of it like a gallant suitor from a different century. My heart fluttered and my face flushed.

My heart always felt unstable when all four were around me.

"Show off," Tobias coughed into his hand. "What I meant was, she thinks she can control us like Lilith can control demons."

Reve paled and cleared his throat. "You think you forced us into this?" He shook his head. "It doesn't feel like it. When someone is controlling you, you feel it right here." He put his hand over my chest, right over my heart. "It's like someone is pulling strings and constricting the blood flow."

The timer for the meatballs went off, saving me from the uncomfortable conversation. I pulled them out of the oven, and the scent of meaty goodness filled the air. My stomach growled, despite the knot that sat in it.

"Maybe Tobias is right. I should test it out on all of you. After we eat. I'm starved."

After making our plates, we headed out to the empty dining room. There was a circular table that was the perfect size for the five of us and gave a view to the outside courtyard.

"I have to go check in on my guys tomorrow. We're almost finished with a refurb, and I need to make sure they haven't fucked up my design." Asher took a drink of his wine. "So, if you need anything from your place, just text me a list and where to find it."

I sighed. I hated not being able to be at my apartment. I had barely even moved in before shit hit the fan with Lilith. Now I was sequestered back where I was trying to escape from. "I still don't see why I can't go home. Tobias can just suppress my aura or whatever it is you can do."

"I could, but we aren't going to take that chance. That hell serpent still found you, and I was actively hiding you. It could be the demon side of you."

I nearly choked on a meatball. We didn't often talk about me being a demon. Mostly because it made me freak out and cry. I was still waiting for the day I sprouted an extra head or grew tentacles.

"It might be good to test things out. If demons come our way, we can just fly back here. I know Michael said to stay here, but it's my birthday." Olly shoved half a meatball into his mouth and made a noise of approval. His days of eating the same foods were long gone.

"What do you mean it's your *birthday*?" Asher put his fork down and folded his arms on the table. "*Tomorrow* is your birthday?"

Olly shrugged. "I kind of forgot about it until earlier today. I don't know the exact date, but it was before July Fourth."

"Angel baby, you can't just spring something like this on us on such short notice. This is your first birthday!" Asher finished his wine and reached for the bottle to pour himself more. Olly watched him with raised eyebrows. "Don't give me that look. I've had one glass tonight."

"I didn't say anything." Olly's voice was monotone.

I frowned at their tense exchange. Now that we practically all lived together, Asher's drinking problem had become glaringly obvious. Olly was the most vocal about it.

"Are you finally cutting back?" Tobias set his fork down and let out a content sigh as he leaned back in his chair.

"Trying to, but then my boyfriend drops surprise birthday news. Now I'm forced to have another glass." He filled his glass and took a drink from the bottle. "And don't start." He pointed the top of the bottle at Reve.

Reve held up his hands before grinning at the two of them. He was an instigator and liked to stir the pot as much as possible. He didn't sleep and had too much time on his hands to plot.

"I wasn't going to say anything." Reve stood and walked over to the window overlooking a courtyard. "I'm just glad he dropped birthday news and not a bar of soap. Some things I do *not* want to see."

I threw my head back and laughed along with Tobias as Asher jumped up from the table and darted towards Reve. Reve disappeared but started whistling as he moved around the dining room.

"You filthy son of a bitch. It's a good thing you don't sleep." Asher swatted at the air where the laughing was coming from. "Or you'd need to sleep with one eye open."

Reve reappeared, sitting cross-legged on a table on the other side of the room. "Is that a threat, angel? Because if it is, *you* do sleep."

"Can't we all just get along?" Olly rested his cheek on his fist. "Why would I have a bar of soap at dinner, anyway? Sometimes you make absolutely no sense."

"Maybe next time you two shower together, Asher can drop a bar of soap and show you what I was referring to." Reve climbed off the table after Asher returned to his seat.

"We have to do something off-campus for his birthday. I vote we go on a field trip tomorrow," I said, returning their attention back to what we had been discussing. The mental image of them in the shower was still playing on repeat in my head.

"It's not worth the risk." Tobias sighed and ran a hand over his beard.

"I'm with Dani on this one. We can't just keep her here indefinitely. There's three of us that can fly her back here if we need to." Asher looked over at Olly, who nodded in agreement.

"Fine." Tobias stood and started stacking plates. I was surprised he was clearing off the table. "But don't say I didn't warn you."

After cleaning up our dinner mess, we headed to the gymnasium to test my theory about controlling them. Tobias was immune, but the others might not be.

The gymnasium was the safest place to test out my ability without the risk of prying eyes seeing us. The campus was mostly empty, but Sue Whittaker was on campus at times, and so were a few other teachers who were on rotation to keep the wards intact.

"So, how are we going to do this? Are you just going to tell us to do shit and then see if we do it?" Asher had his arms folded across his chest. "Wouldn't this be more interesting done in a bedroom?"

"Are you always such a horny bastard?" Reve had his hands shoved in the pockets of his jeans. He looked nervous. I can't say I blamed him since the last time someone commanded him to do something, it was meant to kill him.

We hadn't talked about that night in Shanghai when Lilith had told him to give visions to a crowd full of people. He had tried resisting her request but had done her bidding. Tobias had flown him away before he had drained himself completely.

None of us knew what Reve was fully capable of. Apparently, being a dream demon didn't just mean he could invade a person's dreams. He could send terrifying images while a person was awake.

"If you two don't knock it off, I'm going to make you sit with your arms around each other," Tobias warned. At times, the fatherly side of him came out. Dealing with the three other men did feel like wrangling a group of unruly children.

I was a handful myself.

I stood in front of Asher. He used to be Fallen, and I wondered if at first, I had swayed his opinion of me. He had been a notorious womanizer before meeting me, or at least that's what I assumed from the stories he shared.

"Fly." He raised his eyebrows at my command, but stayed in front of me. I tried a few other commands, but he stood firmly in place, a smug look on his face.

"See. No fake love here." He leaned forward and kissed me.

I tried Olly next, who yielded the same results. Maybe I was overthinking everything that had happened in Shanghai. These men loved me without strings attached. I knew that deep in my heart, but I'm sure my dad also felt some things deep in his heart for Lilith. Look how that turned out.

I stood in front of Reve. His eyes were wider than usual. He looked to be in pain. Not the physical kind, but the kind that ripped your heart to shreds. I brought my hand to his face.

"I'm going to do whatever you tell me to do. I can tell you for certain that you didn't brainwash me into falling in love with you." He spoke so only I could hear him. There was an edge to his voice like he was holding back what he really wanted to say.

I searched his eyes, trying to understand how he was feeling. Reve might have been the newest addition to my group of guardians, but he was the one I had come to rely on the most. Without him, I'd have been walking around like a zombie.

"Kiss me." He complied, taking my lips with his. His lips trembled against mine before pulling away.

I took a sharp inhale of air. I didn't want to start questioning every single thing between us.

His hands fell to his sides, and he backed up a few steps. "Something other than kiss you or touch you. It's not like I can resist that command."

I sucked my bottom lip in between my teeth to keep the whimper in my throat from coming out. Tobias stepped forward to stand beside me, placing his hand on my lower back.

"Do a backflip." He nodded. I watched in fascination and sadness as he landed a perfect backflip.

"Again."

"Reve, we don't-"

"Again."

"Lay on the floor."

As Reve laid down on the floor, Asher stood on the other side of me. "Have him do something ridiculous like waddle like a duck or crawl around like a dog."

Reve stood and glared at Asher, clenching and unclenching his fists. "I know that you walk around drunk half the time, but you do realize that I was controlled by Lilith for centuries, don't you?"

A silence fell over the gym as they stared each other down. Asher finally broke the silence. "I didn't know besides that one time. We don't read minds, Reve."

Reve ran a hand through his hair and then shook his head. "This was a shitty idea. I'm going back to the room."

We followed him out of the gym in silence. I knew Lilith had controlled him, but not that it had lasted centuries. Not that any time under Lilith's control would have been a good thing.

Once back at our building, Reve sat down heavily on the leather couch in the common room. He grabbed the television remote from the coffee table and turned on the television. I sat down next to him with the rest of the guys spreading out on other couches.

The common room was quickly becoming one of my favorite places on campus. The tall ceilings, stone fireplace, and comfortable couches made it feel like the lodge of a ski resort.

The building was empty, with the few other staff members opting to stay in a different building because of Reve. It would have pissed me off, but it ended up working out because we had privacy.

The giant flat-screen television came to life, and Reve started flipping through the endless list of movies we had on the 'to be watched' list.

"When I was younger, in my teenage years by demon standards, I snuck out one night to smoke in the woods next to our castle." Reve's eyes didn't leave the television screen, but all four of us had our eyes glued on him as he spoke. "To smoke the Inferna equivalent of what weed is here on Earth. I took my guard, Alaric, who was more of my best friend than anyone that would enforce my parents' rules. The Black Woods weren't dangerous at the time, but there were definitely stories the elders liked to tell about children being kidnapped, men being gutted, and women being taken." He sighed and put the remote on the arm of the couch. He stared off into space as if he remembered the night perfectly.

"Ric and I met up with a few buddies from the village next to the castle, and we settled into this little clearing in the trees. They came out of nowhere, the vampire demons."

"Vampires?" I took his hand, and he squeezed it tightly. There had been no mention of vampire demons in any of the books I'd read. "Blood-sucking vampires?"

"What else would they drink?" He shrugged. "I was grabbed as soon as we were aware of them. I hadn't developed my phantom form yet, so I couldn't get away."

There was a solid minute of silence before he continued. "We were outnumbered. My two other friends were killed instantly. Ric ran off into the woods with his tail between his legs."

"I'm sorry." I stroked the side of our clasped hands with my thumb. He still didn't make eye contact.

"Then, she appeared. She was the most gorgeous woman I had ever laid eyes on at the time. I stopped fighting to get away because I was so enamored by her. The vampires held me. She just walked right up to me and told me to go kill my parents and then chain myself in our dungeons."

A tear slid down my cheek as I looked down at his wrist, tattooed with a chain.

"So I killed them. I tried to stop myself, because even when Lilith is controlling you, you still have an awareness of what you're doing." He let out a shaky breath and ran a hand over his face. He shut his eyes and pinched the bridge of his nose.

I had so many questions, but the pain in his voice and face stopped me from asking them. I put my hand on his arm and squeezed.

"Why would she want you to kill your parents?" Olly was sitting on the edge of his seat and leaning forward slightly.

Reve let out a sharp laugh before standing. "She wanted the throne."

Then, he disappeared and left us to pick our jaws up off the floor.

CHAPTER 3

OLIVER

$\mathcal{B}$irthdays seemed to be a big deal on Earth, at least to those still alive. I was an adult who had never had a birthday. Never felt the swirl of excitement in my belly over what the day had in store for me. I hadn't thought it would be a big deal to just skip it, but no one else felt that way.

After Reve revealed he was the prince of hell the night before, we had tried to occupy ourselves with making birthday plans. I wasn't a hundred percent sure of when my birthday was. The days all blended together in Heaven. What I did know was that it was in July but before the Fourth of July.

Asher decided we needed to celebrate for three days to ensure we had the right day. I wasn't going to complain if the people I loved wanted to put all of their attention on me for seventy-two hours.

I lengthened my body under the covers, letting out a small moan as I stretched from a restful sleep. My hand fell on the empty spot next to me. Asher had to check in with his business and left before the sun had even peeked over the horizon.

The five of us had fallen into a comfortable living arrangement considering we were holed up at the academy. Most nights Asher and

I slept in Tobias's room while he and Reve slept in Danica's room. Well, at least, Tobias slept.

We had talked about moving two beds into one room, but even I knew that too much testosterone in one small space would spell disaster. Danica loved us, but being around us twenty-four seven had to be a lot at times.

Especially when Reve decided to stir up drama. It kept things lively, to say the least.

I sat up, and my eyes quickly adjusted to the darkened room. Dark blobs floated around the ceiling. I switched on the lamp.

Balloons of various colors floated around the ceiling with a giant 'happy birthday' balloon tied to the back of a chair. How they had even managed to get balloons in the room without waking me up was a mystery.

There was a cupcake that sat on the table with a '1' candle on the top. I grabbed the card next to it and opened it.

Happy birthday, angel baby! Sorry, I couldn't be there for your birthday blowjob. I'll make it up to you later.

I grinned and set the card down. I would definitely collect on that later.

I was one lucky angel. After Shanghai, Asher and I decided that there was too much uncertainty to not embrace what had developed between us. We both were still crazy about Danica, but now we were also crazy about each other.

Still not crazy enough to go all the way with each other, though. I wanted it more than anything. I always thought about it, which was probably why I walked around with a hard-on most of the time now.

I got dressed and made my way to Danica's room. Some nights she would sleep with me and Asher, but until we had a bigger space or it was safe to sleep off-campus, we had to be okay with separate beds.

Reve was sitting on the floor outside the door with his back against the wall. His knees were drawn up to his chest. I put my hand on the doorknob but then backed up a few steps to look at him.

"What's wrong?" He looked distant and tired. Reve never looked tired.

It was a loaded question given what he had shared with us the night before. Everything was not right with Reve. Did he even have a last name? There were so many things we still didn't know about the demon. Thinking back on our interactions, I realized most centered around Danica. Never about him as a demon.

He was the type of demon that survived on the pain and fear he caused others. Or recently, the joy and pleasure he brought Danica in her sleep. No one wanted to admit it, but that was deep fucking soul-mate level shit.

Shit. Now my thoughts were starting to sound like Asher too.

"Last night brought up a lot of memories." His voice held no emotion.

I sat down on the other side of him. Reve was the hardest one in our group to get along with. Not because he was a bad person, but he was the new guy. Plus, I think all of us were envious of his relationship with Danica.

We didn't mind sharing, but he got her all to himself for hours with no interruptions. They at least didn't rub our faces in their dream galivanting. Although I did make Danica tell me the hot air balloon dream in which he had eaten her out high up in the sky.

How did he even come up with such romantic gestures? My romantic ideas were about as creative as my pinky toe.

"Do you want to talk about it?" I touched his arm and sent a wave of calmness to him. I hadn't tried anything with him yet. I didn't even know if my abilities would work on a demon.

He looked down at my hand that was covering a tattoo of a wolf and then looked up at me. He sighed and put his head against the wall.

"No wonder Asher fell in love with you." He shut his eyes. If I didn't know he didn't sleep, I would have thought he had fallen asleep. His breaths evened out, and his face relaxed. "No offense, but you're not my type."

I moved my hand from his arm. "Why do you always have to be like that?"

"Be like what?" One of his eyes popped open. He looked back at me before shutting it again. "I'm just letting you know."

"Make everything some kind of joke."

"When you've lived for as long as me and have done the things I have, finding a way to laugh is the only way to stop yourself from self-destructing. Asher is the same way."

I grunted and stood up. It was different coming from Reve.

"Well, if you need to talk or need me to send some good vibes your way, let me know." I stepped around him and turned the doorknob, cracking the door open.

"Olly." I looked down at him, his eyes still shut. "Happy birthday."

I walked into Danica's room and shut the door gently behind me. She and Tobias were still asleep.

I slipped my shoes off and slid in next to Danica. Tobias must have been awake because he moved his arms from around her, and I slid mine into place.

"Mmm." She turned over so that her head was in the crook of my neck. "Good morning, birthday boy."

Her hand slid around to my ass and gave it a squeeze. We really needed to resolve our sleeping situation so I could wake up with her squeezing my ass daily. She slipped her hand into my back pocket.

"Is there such a thing as a birthday blowjob?" I whispered over Danica's head to Tobias, who was staring right at me.

Danica made a noise and pinched my cheek through my jeans. "Let me guess, Asher told you there was? There's birthday sex. Can't say I've ever heard of a birthday blowjob. I wouldn't be opposed to there being such a thing. January needs to hurry up and get here."

Tobias slid out of bed, and his bare ass greeted me. He did have a pretty spectacular ass.

"I'll let you two have a few minutes. That's all it'll take, right?" He chuckled as he pulled on a pair of athletic shorts and turned to smirk at me.

I frowned at him. I lasted way longer than a few minutes. In fact, I had more stamina than all three of them. Archangel perk.

"Don't be mean to the birthday boy," Danica said, removing her hand from my back pocket and unbuttoning my jeans. My dick instantly sprang to life, straining against the zipper she had yet to unzip.

"Did you see Reve?" Tobias pulled on a shirt and grabbed a can of some coffee beverage from the refrigerator.

"He's in the hall. He isn't in the best of moods." I was having a hard time with my words since Danica had unzipped my pants and reached her hand inside to stroke me through my boxers.

"I'm going to the gym. You two have fun." He shut the door behind himself, and I let out the moan I had been holding in.

"I'm surprised... oh God, Dani. Don't stop." I rolled onto my back and tugged my pants down to my thighs.

"Surprised?" Her hand slipped into my boxers, and her fingers wrapped around my length. Her other hand slid my shirt up so she could kiss my stomach.

Surprised? What was I going to say? "Surprised he didn't stay to watch."

She laughed against my stomach, the sound the best birthday present she could give me. Seeing her happy again was the only thing I wanted.

I WAS an advocate for birthday blowjobs. I had tried to reciprocate, but Danica said there'd be time for that later. The day was about me.

We spent the morning hanging out and then took one of the academy's SUVs into the city. Tobias was on edge, but I knew if something did happen while we were off-campus, we'd be able to protect Danica.

I was practically bouncing off the walls with excitement as we waited on Asher to get home. We were on his rooftop deck under the shade of the gazebo. Reve had decided I needed to learn to play poker.

"How are you so good at this game already?" Reve complained as I gathered the chips in the center of the table and arranged them in front of me.

I shrugged and watched Tobias shuffle the cards. I wasn't about to tell them that I could see their cards. Not when the mention of strip poker in the future was on the table.

Danica narrowed her eyes at me; I couldn't stop the smile that spread across my face. So much for having a poker face.

"You're cheating." She picked up the cards Tobias had put in front of her, glanced at them quickly and put them face down. It was cute that she thought that would stop me from seeing them.

I had tried not to see through the cards, but my brain couldn't help itself.

"I'm not. Maybe I am just really that good."

We played until Asher came home. I purposely lost a few hands just to keep things interesting. Maybe a trip to Vegas was in the near future.

We headed to the bowling alley that I had decided on the night before. Danica had a list in her phone that she added to often. It had to have at least a hundred experiences on it by now. All of which she said were necessary.

I don't know if playing hide and go seek was a necessity, but I wasn't about to argue with her.

The bowling alley was noisy, with blaring music and the sounds of balls knocking down pins. I looked over at Asher as we waited in line to borrow shoes and pay for our games. Every so often, he would flinch. I took his hand.

"Just got to get used to the sound." I squeezed his hand in reply. His eyes darted around, taking in the surroundings. He zeroed in on the bar. "Get me a size ten. You guys want anything from the bar?"

There appeared to be waitresses walking around with drink orders, but his need to escape was written clearly on his face. I let his hand go and watched him walk quickly towards the bar area.

Danica stepped up beside me and looped her arm through mine. "You worry about him too much."

"I worry about a lot of things too much," I said, looking down at her. I was worried about her. Worried about Lucifer. Worried about Reve. Even Tobias had been looking worse for wear lately.

"Remember that you need to take care of yourself too." She rubbed my arm, and we stepped up to the counter.

I didn't want to deal with my own issues. Taking care of everyone else and making sure they weren't losing their minds helped me keep my mind off of the fact that everything was my fault.

I lost the Holy Grail.

Lilith wanted it.

She got what she wanted, and in the process almost killed her own daughter and Reve. And now Lucifer was missing.

We grabbed our shoes and went to our lane. I scrunched my nose at the shoes before sliding my feet into them. They smelled like other people's feet, which made me want to gag. I saw the guy at the counter spraying shoes people brought back, but that didn't help ease my mind any.

Asher was back with a glass of something dark brown. It was most likely whiskey, his drink of choice. I thought it tasted like battery acid.

"Let's go find our balls." Asher snorted and took a sip of his drink.

"I think the blue ones are just the right weight for you three." Reve was already holding a purple bowling ball. He put it in the ball rack.

"The only person whose balls will be blue tonight will be yours when I hand your ass to you." Tobias took off in search of a ball, a cocky grin on his face.

"He must really be good at handling balls," Asher said, chuckling and taking my hand.

We followed Tobias, and all three of us ended up with blue balls after all.

After the first few frames, the rivalry between Reve and Tobias became a sideshow. Both had only bowled strikes so far.

Reve lined himself up in front of the lane and stepped forward to release the ball.

"Gutter ball!" Tobias yelled right before he released it, causing Reve to curse as it stayed on course, but split the pins.

"Your victory is going to be marred by foul play." Reve waited for the pins to reset and his ball to return.

He couldn't knock both pins down and cursed as he returned to his seat. When it was Tobias's turn, Reve grinned. He was up to something, as usual.

"Oh. My. God. Is that Justin Timberlake?" A girl shrieked from halfway across the bowling alley. We all turned in her direction to see several women making their way toward us.

Tobias was oblivious as he stood on the hardwood and set himself up to bowl another strike. I watched in sheer fascination as the small group of women entered into our area and walked right up to Tobias, who was already bringing his arm forward. He didn't look anything like the pop star.

There's a reason you're supposed to wait for the player on the lane next to you to throw their ball. Tobias released it, which made a thud on the lane and rolled into the gutter.

"Can we get a selfie? I can't believe this is happening! Where's your wife? Are these your friends? I can't believe I'm meeting you!" The questions and comments were fired off at him as they pulled out their phones.

"What? I look nothing like Timberlake." Tobias backed up and then turned to glare at Reve. "You! I'm going to kill you!"

I was slightly surprised that Reve would send a vision, but I guess it was harmless. It made me wonder how often he used that ability.

After a lot of back and forth between Reve and Tobias, we took a break and ordered food. I wasn't too sure about eating greasy food from the bowling alley, but Danica said it was the best.

"What are we going to do for the Fourth of July?" Danica asked while we waited for our burgers to arrive. "Fireworks are out, right?"

Asher grunted and finished his second drink of the evening. "I'm glad I can come on campus now. There aren't any fireworks in the area, are there?"

"Nope. We can watch them from the top of Ariel Hall, without the loud noise."

"My dad's favorite holiday was... is July Fourth. He liked to light shit on fire," Danica said softly. She looked down at the table and then swiped at her eyes.

My breath caught in my throat. She hurt because of me. Because I was an idiot that thought trying to turn ocean water into wine was a good way to pass the time.

I stood and headed in the direction of the bathrooms. I slammed open the door and braced my hands on the counter. My heart was racing. I shut my eyes and tried to catch my breath. It felt like I had just sprinted.

The door opened behind me, and I looked in the mirror, seeing Asher slip in. He flipped the lock on the door and stepped towards me.

I straightened and turned to face him. "I don't want to talk about it."

"From the looks of it, you do need to talk about it." He leaned against the counter. "What's eating at you, Oliver?"

I put my hands in my hair, clenching the strands in my fists. "This is my fault."

He grunted and stepped towards me, grabbing my arms and pulling them until my hands were in his. "This isn't your fault."

"But I-" He shut me up with his mouth. I moaned into it before shoving him away. "Not everything can be fixed with sex."

"There's something wrong with that cup, Olly. Danica said it practically sang to her when she took it. Stop blaming yourself." Asher leaned back against the counter.

I knew all of that already, but it didn't change the fact that it had happened. I dropped it. It was safe in Heaven, and now it was with a psychotic woman who was using it for who knows what.

I doubted she was drinking wine with it.

"I don't like seeing you like this. I'm supposed to be the deeply disturbed one, not you." Asher's face softened. He reached out a hand towards me. I took it and laced our fingers together. "Now, let's go eat. You can drown your woes in a greasy burger and a drink. I'll even throw in a wartime story."

Asher didn't talk about the war often, but when he did, it was either a hilarious anecdote or a gut-wrenching tale. I followed him back to the table where our burgers and fries were already waiting for us. My stomach growled in anticipation.

I had missed out on almost an entire year of delicious food because I didn't have the right people in my corner. Now I did, and I trusted them. So whenever they put food in front of me, I ate it. My days of cantaloupe and brown rice were over. I still couldn't resist cookies.

"This food is much better than what I got for my twenty-third birthday in 1944." Asher took the last bite of his burger and then wiped his mouth on his napkin. We all looked at him in interest. "We were on the move between towns and were eating a diet of field rations. When I came back from being on patrol, Toby here had concocted a culinary masterpiece for me. He and the guys took their biscuits from their C-Rats and ground them up, added sugar, and made a makeshift cake. They put melted lime-flavored hard candies as the frosting. Stuck a cigarette in the top and sang *Happy Birthday* to me."

"That sounds like something I'd do. How'd it taste?" Tobias smiled at the memory he couldn't remember himself.

Asher laughed. "Like shit. I ate it though, couldn't waste precious calories." He rubbed the side of his face. "I wish I could say the rest of the day was as great as that moment, but we at least had a little fun."

"I wish I could remember some of those things," Tobias said, a wistful look passing over his eyes.

"No, you don't. For every good memory, there are ten times as many bad memories. Several members of our platoon were sniped later that day on patrol."

The table fell silent for a moment before a waitress brought out a plate with vanilla ice cream smooshed between two chocolate chip cookies.

"We ordered it for you while you were gone." Danica rubbed her hands together. "Try it."

I had tried my fair share of ice cream but never sandwiched between my favorite food. I picked it up and took a bite. If food could cause an orgasm, I would have had one.

I looked around the table at Danica, Asher, Tobias, and Reve. They were my family now, and I wouldn't trade them for anything in the world.

CHAPTER 4

DANICA

I was not ready for classes to start. Summer had seemed to drag on forever, but as soon as the calendar rolled over to August, I didn't want it to end.

The summer brought no new news on the whereabouts of my dad. None of the captured demons knew where he was. I assumed he had to be with Lilith in Inferna, because how else were demons getting through the barrier?

I pulled my uniform out of my closet and put it on. I was going to brave the cafeteria for the sheer fact that I really had a craving for bacon.

I grabbed my bag and walked into the hall. Olly was leaning against the wall waiting for me. He grinned when he saw me. His eyes traveled down to my legs and then back up, stopping briefly on my chest before settling on my lips.

I kissed him and took his hand. Olly would be in all of my classes this semester except Weaponry since he was already skilled in that area.

It wasn't fair that he was just born one day and could wield a sword like a knight and throw daggers like a ninja. I should have been able to do at least half of those things since I was half-angel.

Things didn't quite work that way.

We made our way to the cafeteria and joined Cora and Ethan at our usual table. My eyes couldn't help but fall on the table in the corner. Several of the Divine 7 had finished the academy and moved on. It was unfortunate that Betty and Abby were still there. They saw me looking and sneered.

"I'm so excited for this year!" Cora could hardly contain her happiness. She and Ethan were doing well and had spent the summer in South America.

As much as I was opposed to being a guardian angel myself, a pang of jealousy ran through me anytime they mentioned the missions they had been on. My only mission for the summer was staying on campus. I hadn't even gotten to visit Ava. It wasn't like my best friend could come to the academy and visit me. Plus she seemed to always be working.

"I'm only excited because we have training in the evenings." Ethan slung his arm over the back of Cora's chair. "I heard there's a demon teaching us how to kill other demons."

Both Cora and Ethan looked at me. I munched on a piece of bacon. I knew what their looks were for. I was the obvious connection to the demon.

"He's a dream demon. He's decent." Olly moved his eggs around on his plate before scooping some onto his fork. He scrunched up his nose before taking a bite. "These don't taste as good as yours."

"That's because I put love in mine." I sat up a little straighter, hearing that Olly thought my cooking was better than the cooks in the back. Well, at least my eggs were.

"So this demon, how do you two know him?" Ethan asked.

"Why does everyone assume I know him because he's a demon?" I rolled my eyes.

As if on cue, Abby and her posse walked past the table, overhearing me. She stopped, several of them almost bumping into her.

"Eve, you are the spawn of Satan. Of course you'd know him. Is he one of your boyfriends now too?" A few people at the table next to us sniggered.

"Go away, Abby." Olly scooped a spoonful of oatmeal and blew on it. "No one wants to hear your nasally voice. It's ruining my appetite."

She made a noise in her throat and narrowed her eyes at him. "I see you're still slumming it with the rejects."

Olly finally looked at her and smiled. "I think you've forgotten that you were the reject back in the first semester. If I recall, you tried to cop a feel."

Her face turned red, and she opened and closed her mouth. She let out a huff and stomped off. In her previous life, she must have been a spoiled brat who threw tantrums to get what she wanted. How she became an angel was beyond my comprehension.

"Did she really?" I laughed, piling my silverware and napkin on my empty plate.

"More than once." He shrugged as Ethan gave him a fist bump. "I think she figured since the other guys let her have her way with them, that I'd be the same."

After we finished eating, we walked together to our first class: Crisis Intervention. Cora and Ethan both tested as intellectual guardian angels, but all students were required to take it.

Just like all second and third-year students were required to attend training in the evenings. You know, in case all hell broke loose.

After Crisis Intervention, which had my name written all over it, I had Weaponry without any moral support. At least it didn't involve flying.

What it did involve was Coach Ferguson and Betty. Betty didn't strike me as the type to be a warrior, but I didn't feel like a warrior myself, so I couldn't really judge.

"It's nice to see a good crop of angels for once," the coach said once class started. He paused when he saw me and raised his eyebrows. "Besides training with common weapons you might use out in the field, this evening, you will strengthen your fighting skills and swordsmanship."

Most of class time was spent with Coach Ferguson showing us different weapons: knives, clubs, tasers, handguns. I felt I was on even ground with the rest of the class for once since no one had fired a gun or wielded a taser before. At least that's what everyone said.

Betty seemed to know an awful lot about weapons.

After dinner, we were required to go to the football field for extra training. There were three rotations lasting thirty minutes each. Asher was teaching hand to hand combat with Tobias as his assistant. When Asher had shared the news, Tobias had looked furious. He was still suspended, but Michael was running the show after school hours.

Olly was with Coach Ferguson teaching swordsmanship. Despite his short time using a sword, Olly was as skilled as Michael. It must have been an archangel thing.

Then there was Reve. Reve had been all the buzz during the day, especially when word got around that he would be training us on how to kill specific demons.

I started in the group training with Asher and Tobias. Tobias was off to the side, reading a book. He wasn't taking the whole situation in his stride. Can't say I blamed him.

"Combat is no joke. When you're out there in the trenches, anything can fucking happen. You can get a limb blown off. Lose your sight. Lose your hearing. Fucking die." Asher paced back and forth in front of us and stopped and looked right at me when he mentioned dying.

Was his speech meant to instill confidence in us? It scared the crap out of me.

"Where did they find this nut job? This isn't Vietnam," a guy behind me mumbled to another student. A few laughs broke the tension in the group.

Asher glared over my shoulder. "You're right. This isn't fucking Vietnam or World War II. This is worse. Heaven versus hell. Good versus evil. When you are staring frozen at a mother fucking Widow demon that just sent hundreds of spiders to eat your ass, are you going to be more concerned about how to kill her and her spiders or where the fuck they found this quack job?"

I cringed as he referred to himself in the third person. He wasn't helping his case any. I knew he wasn't insane but had I never met him before, I'd probably have some serious questions about him.

"This semester, we're going to push you hard because the demons are only increasing in number. We will need all hands on deck when the time comes." Tobias spoke without looking up from his book, annoyance dripping from his voice.

"The time comes for what?" Someone in the back spoke loudly, their voice shaking slightly.

"War. The apocalypse. We don't fucking know yet, but when it does happen, we'll be prepared." Asher blew his whistle for us to line up.

After running through some drills, he paired us up to practice what he called "ram and run." He paired me with Cora.

"Listen up! When I blow my whistle, partner A is going to run straight at partner B. Hit them just like we practiced, right in the midsection. Then sprint to the other set of cones."

There were lots of grumbles as we lined up on the line. I was more nervous about my lack of healing than anything else. The angels could knock each other out with no problem. I had a lot more to risk.

"Drop and give me ten burpees for that!" Fuck, he was a hardass. "You too, Danica!"

I glared at him. "I didn't complain!" I crossed my arms, and a few others joined my resistance.

"Make it twenty!" My jaw dropped. I wanted to punch him in the face. Instead, I dropped to the ground to start the burpees.

The thirty minutes seemed more like two hours. We rotated next to Olly, who was holding a pool noodle. I had only glanced in the direction of his station once when I heard the group before us laughing

I wiped the sweat from my forehead with the hem of my tank top. I had been worried about taking hits, but all along, I should have been concerned about Asher going drill sergeant on us. Tobias had just sat by, glancing up from his book occasionally, his expression unreadable

Coach Ferguson stood on a chair and blew his whistle to quiet us down. "We don't typically teach swordsmanship here at the academy since it is not common to carry a sword around on duty. A sword is the best way to incapacitate a demon long enough to take them out. Oliver will be doing most of the training with you since he is highly skilled."

I wondered how they knew a sword was best. Had demons come through before? That had to be the case.

He jumped down, and Olly took his place. "Thanks, Coach. Tonight we're going to start with our reactions to stimuli. Wielding a sword requires confidence and the ability to hold your ground, even when something is trying to take you out." He waved a pool noodle that had been cut in half in front of us. "With the same partner you just had in the last rotation, you'll act like this is a sword."

"When do we get to use a real sword?" someone in the middle shouted.

"When I feel no one is going to take someone's head off. The objective tonight is to stop your partner from hitting you with the pool noodle and to not flinch."

"This is stupid," Betty said. A few other students agreed. Betty was worse than the other six Divine combined.

"Feel free to go back to the last station since you find this activity stupid." The comment didn't even faze Olly.

After grabbing our pool noodles, Cora and I faced off.

"On guard!" I jabbed the noodle at her, and she laughed.

"This isn't fencing, Danica." She blocked me.

By the end of the half-hour, my arms were burning, My face hurt from smiling and laughing so much. Using a light object only made me realize that a real sword was going to be impossible to swing around.

Our last rotation was with Reve in a room on the side of the gym. Chairs were set up, and a projector displayed a photograph of a normal-looking man. I was pretty sure it wasn't a man. We were learning how to kill demons.

I sat in the front row with Cora and Ethan. I could feel the tension in the room as the others sat down, leaving the front row empty besides the three of us. A few teachers stood off to the sides, swords on their hips.

"Do you think they really think he's going to attack, or is it just to placate everyone?" Ethan leaned forward to ask me.

"If they are scared of a dream demon, I don't know how they expect them to fight much more frightening demons. Reve is a big teddy bear. Most of the teachers have at least been civil towards Reve. He's pretty charismatic."

Reve cleared his throat. "Let's start out with getting all of your questions out of the way. We have a lot of ground to cover, and I won't have time to answer your questions later."

Almost every hand went up except mine, Cora's, and Ethan's. Before he called on anyone, he gave a brief introduction, which eliminated about half of the hands.

"Why are you helping us?"

Reve looked at me, then at the student asking the question. "Earth has become my home. I don't think humans deserve to be terrorized by crazed demons that get through the barrier."

"Don't you terrorize humans?"

"I had a job to do here. Several of the souls I visited made it to Heaven instead of hell. The power of a well-composed nightmare is underrated."

The questioning went on for a solid fifteen minutes. Not once did Reve lose his cool or waver in his confidence. Once all questions were answered, he went on to show drawings of demons and discussed how to identify and kill them. He had drawn the pictures himself.

The time flew by, and before I knew it, the rotation was over.

"I'll see you guys tomorrow," I said, waving goodbye to Cora and Ethan.

I hung back as the room emptied. Reve was packing up his laptop.

"I think they were impressed." I tilted back in my chair and nearly fell backward. Reve laughed.

I felt my face flush and stood instead. I picked up a few water bottles left on the floor and put them in the recycling bin.

"I think they were all in shock that I didn't kill them." He slung his bag over his shoulder and led me out of the room.

It was dark outside, but the lights from the football field lit the area.

"We have a quick staff debriefing. Are you okay to walk back alone?"

"It's an angel academy, Reve." He kissed my cheek and headed off towards Ariel Hall.

I walked along the path towards the staff building. I was just about past the second student dorm building when I heard loud laughter coming from a courtyard. I moved closer to the building, so I'd be out of sight.

"Can you believe they have those idiots training us to fight demons?" One of the male Divine 7 was speaking. I couldn't remember his name, but he was a third-year, like most of them.

"Asher is fucking hot. I'd hit that. I bet he likes it rough." A girl spoke, one of the new ones.

"Gross, girl. You know that they are all in some kind of freakish relationship with devil girl, right?"

"What a slut," one of the guys said. "She's like a sex doll."

A lump formed in my throat, and I put my hand over my mouth to silence my shocked gasp. I'd talked plenty of shit about people before, but never so loudly and in such an open area.

"I think I'm going to try to hit that. Do you think she charges?"

Laughter followed.

I couldn't stop the tears from sliding down my cheeks. I should have stepped around the corner and given them a piece of my mind, but a group of assholes versus one person wasn't good odds.

I slipped around the other side of the building so they wouldn't see me and made my way towards my room.

I knew I wasn't a slut, despite what others thought. So what I was having sex with four different men? We loved each other and supported each other.

I opened my door and walked into my room, throwing my bag

down and giving it a solid kick. That didn't feel like enough, so I kicked it again.

"What the hell are you doing?" Tobias popped up on the futon, running his hand over his face.

I jumped and let out a squeal.

"Aren't you supposed to be at some kind of staff meeting?" I put my hand over my heart. "Jesus, that scared me."

"Attending the staff meeting would mean I qualified as a staff member." He laid back down. "I was only helping tonight because Asher is a little bit of a loose cannon."

I snorted. "That's an understatement."

I kicked my shoes off and walked over to the futon. I lifted his legs and sat down, putting them back down in my lap.

"You've been crying." He had his hands behind his head and was staring at me.

I patted his leg and looked at the ceiling. "I'm not just the princess of hell, Eve, or demon spawn anymore. Just call me Danica, the slutty sex doll who has four boyfriends."

"You aren't a slut." He shut his eyes. "They're just jealous."

"Being jealous isn't an excuse to sit around and talk about someone like they are an insignificant piece of trash. You know, if this was reversed and I was a man with four women, no one would say a word. If I were a boy and the son of Lucifer, everyone would think I was badass."

He snorted. "I think you're badass."

"You don't count." I looked at him and waited for him to open his eyes, but he didn't. "Are you all right?"

He sighed and opened his eyes, choosing to look at the ceiling instead of at me. I could see the worry etched on his features.

"I just want all of this to be over so we can move on with our lives. Together. Somewhere away from here." He sat up, his legs falling to the floor. "We should all just escape somewhere."

I shut my eyes as he pulled me towards him. "That would be nice."

"Somewhere tropical." He kissed my neck. "We can find an uninhabited island. Maybe build a treehouse like they did in *The Swiss Family Robinson.*"

"Mmm." I tilted my head to the side, giving him better access to my neck. "Don't know who they are, but keep going."

"We can run around naked all day. Make love all night." His hand slipped under the back of my tank.

"I need a shower. I was all sweaty earlier." His lips hovered over mine. "I could use some help getting out of these clothes."

He ran his finger across the neckline of my top, sending shivers down my spine and a jolt of desire through my core.

I half expected to have steamy shower sex, but Tobias undressed me then left the bathroom to let me shower. I considered using the showerhead because he had left me hanging, but decided against it.

If Tobias wasn't in the mood, someone surely would be.

I brushed out my hair and secured the towel around my body before stepping out of the bathroom. Tobias sat shirtless on the edge of my bed, a box next to him.

"What's that?" I made my way to the bed and peeked into the box. "Holy shit."

"Reve and I stashed it under the bed. I feel like tonight is a good night to try some of it out. Might be a nice distraction for us both." Tobias reached into the box and pulled out a pair of black leather cuffs that were fuzzy on the inside. They were attached together with another piece of leather.

I clenched my thighs together as desire raced through my body. Talking about it was one thing, but knowing it was about to happen was something else entirely.

"You and Reve..." I gulped. "You bought this stuff? Together?"

I reached into the box and pulled out an eye mask and a stick with feathers on the end.

"Reve has an online shopping problem. He told me he had purchased some fun things for us to try." He moved the box off the bed and grabbed my hips, pulling me towards him.

I stepped in between his legs. "Do you two talk about sex with me or something?"

He shrugged. "Things do take a little bit of communication between the four of us. Especially since we aren't all living together." He yanked my towel, and it fell to the ground. His eyes devoured me hungrily, and he ran his hands down my sides to rest on my hips.

I gasped as he leaned forward and kissed near my belly button. "So you guys..." He pulled me to straddle his lap and trailed his lips over my breasts. "You decide who gets me when?"

He chuckled against my sensitive skin, his beard tickling. "I wouldn't put it that way. It's just better if we're all on the same page."

I jabbed my fingers through his hair as he took a nipple in his mouth, swirling his tongue around and then biting gently. They could put a schedule up on the refrigerator for all I cared.

"Dodgers," he mumbled, pulling away and looking at me. I raised my eyebrows. "That will be your safe word."

I rolled my eyes. "I don't need a safe word."

He put me on the bed and reached into the box and pulled out the cuffs, eye mask, and a pair of headphones. My eyes widened, and I held out my wrists. He laughed at my eagerness and secured them, moving them so they were on the pillow above my head.

I was shivering with anticipation as he slipped the blindfold over my eyes and then the headphones. I'd never even thought about a lack of sound during sex, but as I laid there completely incapacitated, I saw the appeal.

I could hear and feel my heart beating in my ears. He wasn't touching me yet, but somehow, I could feel his nearness on my skin. It felt as if electrical currents were jumping between our bodies.

I moaned as minutes went by. I couldn't even tell how loud I was because I couldn't hear a damn thing.

After what felt like an eternity, I felt something on my foot. It had to be a finger trailing up from the heel. I couldn't be sure. It was soft and warm, and then hands wrapped around my ankles and pulled me down the bed.

"Tobias, you're killing me here." The only response I got was a finger trailing up my leg to my inner thigh, where it stopped and made circles.

The desire between my legs blossomed, and I slammed my thighs shut on his hand. If I could hear or see him, I bet he would have been laughing.

He pushed my legs open, and his finger was replaced by his tongue. I whimpered as it moved closer and closer to my apex. Just a little farther, and he'd be right where I wanted him.

Nothing. The fucker stopped. I let out a curse and squirmed on the covers, the fabric of the comforter soft as silk on my skin. I had never stopped to appreciate how good the sheets felt.

One side of the headphones was pulled from my ear, and a pair of lips came close. "Can I join in?"

Reve.

I nodded, words lodged in my throat. I heard both Tobias and Reve laugh as the headphones were put back in place.

I was about to orgasm at the thought of not knowing who was touching me. Would I be able to tell who was who? I would have liked to think that I would be able to tell the difference between the two men.

Hands touched my body. Mouths tasted my skin. Were they taking turns, or were both of them driving me mad with lust at the same time? They always took turns with me.

"I can't take this anymore. Please." I was desperate for something to take away the ache between my legs.

I was about to flip over and dry hump the damn sheets when a finger ran across my slit. Or at least it felt like a finger. For all I could tell, it could have been the tip of a penis. It definitely wasn't a tongue.

It worked back and forth, and then a second finger was added. They dove into my wet heat and curled against that sweet spot that made my toes curl. Over and over, the fingers brushed the sensitive place inside my pussy, driving me mad.

My body spasmed as my orgasm ripped through me like a freight train. I couldn't hear myself, but I'm sure someone standing outside would have been able to hear me.

A tongue flicked my clit, and my legs closed on instinct, the sensations of my climax still shaking my body. Could orgasms kill someone? I already felt another one about to split me in two.

A body shifted over me. The tip of a dick touched my lips, and I opened my mouth to take it inside. I slid my tongue over the head. I couldn't tell who it was. I should have been able to since they had different dicks. I needed to pay more attention.

My body trembled as he worked his length in and out of my mouth. I spread my legs, hoping whoever was unoccupied would get the hint.

Teeth scraped across my thigh, and I cried out around the cock in my mouth. A tongue ran up the length of me.

"Dodgers." I really couldn't take any more. I needed my senses back.

The headphones came off first.

"Really, you made the safe word Dodgers?" Reve's voice was amused, and as the eye mask was removed, his smiling face came into view.

After my hands were freed, I rubbed my eyes.

"You did well for your first time." Reve laid on his side next to me. He trailed a hand between my breasts and then rested it on my pubic bone.

Tobias was sitting on the end of the bed, his eyes hooded with desire. I bit my lip and looked between the two of them. Tobias never minded a little group action, but Reve had never seemed too interested.

I pushed Reve onto his back and lowered myself onto him, my thighs already quivering with the onset of another orgasm. I looked over my shoulder at Tobias, who was fisting his dick.

"I have lube in the top drawer."

His hand stopped, and his mouth opened a bit like he wanted to say something. Instead, he stood and opened my drawer, pulling out the bottle.

Reve started moving his hips in slow rolls underneath me. I leaned forward, resting my forearms next to his head. Tobias's hand moved down my spine, and he trailed a finger between my cheeks.

I buried my face in Reve's inked neck as Tobias squirted lube on his fingers and began stretching me. I wasn't an expert in backdoor play, but after the initial shock wore off, I found myself wanting more.

His fingers left me, and the bed dipped as he positioned himself behind me.

"Relax." Reve brought his hands to my face and moved my hair behind my ears. He stopped moving underneath me as Tobias slowly worked his way into my tight hole.

"Fuck," I gasped. My entire body burned at the intrusion. It felt way better than the last time I had tried it but still was a foreign feeling.

He took it slow; his breath was strained as he held back.

"Oh, fuck," Reve moaned as Tobias began rocking his hips.

My eyes felt like they were going to roll back into my head. Reve started moving under me, matching the pace Tobias was setting. The tips of my ears and my toes felt like they had pins and needles. I felt so full and safe between them.

We should have done this sooner.

Our bodies moved together like a boat rocking gently over waves. I dug my hands into the pillow under Reve's head.

"More. Give me more," I gritted out, as my body loosened up more and what was already pretty amazing became magnificent.

Tobias grunted behind me and increased his pace. My skin was damp with sweat as our skin smacked against each other with the driving of his hips.

"Oh, God." Tobias thrust into me one last time before his body shook, and he spilled inside of me. He stayed in place as Reve dove into me harder than before.

My hand went to my clit, my orgasm mounting from what felt like fifty different directions. Tobias's hand joined mine as I pressed into it.

The orgasm, if it could even be called that because it was so much more, crashed into me with such force that I screamed out as all of my muscles seized up around Reve and Tobias.

Reve cursed and joined me, my body collapsing on top of his.

Tobias pulled out of me, the emptiness making me feel a longing to have him buried back inside me.

Reve let out a laugh and ran his fingers through my hair before gathering it over one of my shoulders. I was still lying on top of him, spent from the orgasm that went into my own personal *Guinness Book of World Records*.

"I might be old as fuck, but that was a first for me."

I slid off of him and laid on my stomach next to him. "I find that hard to believe. All those centuries and never once did you get curious?"

"Dream demons are monogamous even when dating someone. If we are lucky to find our mate, we get our strength from them."

I was about to ask him more about that when Tobias reappeared with a washcloth. He cleaned me up and then laid on the other side of me, placing his hand on the small of my back.

"Your ass okay?" He was so serious that I couldn't hold back the giggle.

"It'll be fine." I moved to lay my head on Reve's chest. "Do you think I'm your mate?"

Reve played with my hair. My eyes fluttered shut as my body relaxed.

"I think that's the only explanation. I never had the chance to ask my father and mother how it worked. My father didn't often go hunting. I just assumed he kept prisoners and fed off them."

"We should call it something else other than feeding." Tobias kissed my shoulder. "What you two have is so much more."

"We could say he eats me. That's not inaccurate."

Reve groaned and tugged my hair a little. "The way everyone acts around you, I'm beginning to think we are all your mates. I know that's not proper human lingo, but there isn't a word for it here, is there?"

I drew a circle in the center of his chest around the tattoo of two skulls with crowns on the top of their heads. It made sense now.

"And here I thought all I was, was a sex doll."

Tobias squeezed my hip. "Stop saying that. Their opinions shouldn't matter."

"I can mess with them a bit if you want me to. Really scare the shit out of them." Reve sounded like he meant business. The allure of having him fuck with those idiots was strong.

I shook my head. As much as I wanted Reve to screw with them, I didn't want him to get kicked off-campus. We had been lucky enough as it was that he'd been permitted to be around. Besides, two wrongs don't make a right.

"I love you two." I sighed. "What would I do without you?"

I fell asleep for the first time in a long time, feeling like I was right where I should be.

CHAPTER 5

DANICA

I stood on the sidewalk, the skyline on the other side of the river lighting the night sky.

"Why do you keep doing this to yourself?" Reve appeared next to me and leaned on the railing. A railing that didn't protect someone's mother from throwing them over it and into the river below.

"I can't control it."

I turned towards the street, where a dark SUV sat idling at the curb. My father appeared with three goons surrounding him. Lilith's laugh filled the night sky.

I looked up, the sky dark with clouds. Lilith laughed again, this time from right next to me.

"Foolish girl. Did you really think everything was going to work out at the end of this?"

Just as my father reached forward, I was standing in the middle of a lush green field with mountains all around.

Reve gestured to a blanket and picnic basket laid out. "My lady."

I sat down, my mind now on what lay before me. For being a demon, Reve certainly was romantic. I guess he did have a lot of years of practice. How many women had he even been with?

"Where are we?" I opened the lid of the basket and pulled out a bottle of champagne. He took it from me and popped the cork.

"A figment of my imagination." He chuckled. "Also, a merging of different locations I've seen in movies."

"You have quite the imagination."

He pulled out two silver flutes from the basket and filled them. He could never go wrong with champagne. He pulled out a container of strawberries and melted chocolate. I wasn't sure how the chocolate remained melted, but it was a dream, of that much I was sure.

"I wish the others could be here with us." I took a sip of the crisp champagne and scrunched my nose as the bubbles fizzed in my mouth.

"They can be if you really want them to." It was the first time Reve had agreed to let me have them. I knew it wouldn't be the same as them in real life. "I'll have complete control of them." His grin grew as he watched my eyes widen. "Remember, you asked for it."

"Reve," I warned.

In the distance, three figures approached. I squinted my eyes because they were all the way across the field. As they got closer, a peal of laughter shot out of me. They were dressed in yodeler outfits, sans the shirts.

"I think it's a good look for them, don't you?"

I held my stomach as they got closer. They didn't speak at first, but then Tobias opened his mouth, and a yodeling noise came out.

"Oh my God, make it stop." I fell back onto the blanket and covered my ears.

The yodeling stopped, and Asher, Tobias, and Olly disappeared. Reve appeared over me, grinning from ear to ear.

"You think you're so funny, don't you?" I lowered my arms from my ears to his chest. "You just have to have me all to yourself."

"I do. Can you really blame me?" He lowered his lips to mine. "If we could stay this way forever, I would."

I sighed and kissed him, wrapping my arms around him and pulling him closer. It would be so simple to stay in the dream world for eternity. Life would be easier.

I felt the pull of my consciousness and pulled away from him. I didn't want him to go.

He faded away.

WE FELL into a comfortable pattern of classes, training, and pretending the world wasn't about to face an unknown threat. Weeks passed, and Michael still didn't have a plan on how to get Lucifer back.

He was avoiding us. Well, mostly avoiding me. Every time he visited campus, he steered clear of my questioning gaze. No one else seemed to be as worried about the passage of time as much as I was.

I guess when you are practically immortal, a few months feels like a few days. For me, it felt like years.

I walked into the gym for Weaponry class. It seemed like a waste of time since I would never be allowed to see any action, even if demons were pouring into the city.

Reve had shown us enough demon sketches that my mind was overwhelmed with what lurked on the other side of some invisible magical barrier. I wouldn't fight those things. Instead, I would do the smart thing and run.

My brain almost couldn't process it all.

I walked into weaponry class, wondering how the world was going to handle bug-eyed cat creatures that had nails as sharp as knives when Betty stepped into my path.

"Beatriz. Did you need something?" I crossed my arms and propped my hip to the side. It felt like the appropriate thing to do since I was in the angel version of some teen movie.

"Thanks to you, they are getting rid of divinity points." She spoke from her throat in the way only a bitch could.

"Oh. I'm sorry." I stuck my bottom lip out in a mock pout. "Did that make your self-worth go down?"

She smirked and examined her nails before looking at me again. "Just means that now we have nothing to lose."

"Is that a threat?" I stood my ground, even as she took a step closer. She smelled like she had on one too many squirts of perfume. I resisted the urge to gag. "Because that certainly sounded like a threat to me."

She shrugged and dropped her voice low. "I overheard a conversation about your mother."

My eyes widened, but I quickly schooled my expression. No one was supposed to know that Lilith was my mother. "About how she is Lilith, and how she has your father." She put her hand on my crossed arm. I looked down at it and then at her, narrowing my eyes. "Part of a guardian's duties is to protect from any and all threats. Michael doesn't seem to be doing his job anymore."

She patted my arm and stepped back, a smile on her face. Did she have some kind of God complex now? If these were the angels accepted into the academy, what were the angels who were rejected like?

"Are you sure you're an angel? I find it kind of hard to believe how you are even here. You have an ugly soul."

She laughed. "You aren't even an angel. I paid my dues."

"Is that how it works now? Blow jobs in exchange for wings?"

She was just about to step forward, probably to smack me, when Coach Ferguson blew his whistle.

She turned on her heel, and I followed to join the group of students already gathered around the coach. We had been practicing throwing knives at targets over the week. I managed to hit the target about half of the time. I wasn't the worst in the class, at least.

"Betty, why don't you demonstrate again for us how you angle your body to set up for the perfect throw." Coach Ferguson did not need to boost her ego any more than it already was.

Betty sashayed to the setup area. Of course, she had to be good at throwing knives. It seemed to fit her personality perfectly. She demonstrated by throwing two knives in quick succession at the targets. They hit the practice dummy right in the center of the chest.

"Perfect! Today I'm partnering everyone up! If you have mastered knife throwing, be prepared to help someone who hasn't." Great. Another opportunity to feel inferior to everyone else.

He started partnering us up. As the pairs split off, I stifled a groan. He paired up the two men that were left, leaving Betty and me.

"Betty, I trust that you understand the importance of getting Danica up to par with you."

He walked away, leaving me and public enemy number one to train together.

She made a face at the coach's back and then grabbed a set of knives. The knife-throwing dummies were set up around the perimeter of the gym so that no one would get nailed with a knife retrieving them from their dummy.

"Let's see what you've got." She handed me a knife and moved to the side. I threw the knife and barely hit the dummy's leg.

"It doesn't seem to help if I pretend it's you." I sighed and then smirked at her.

She snorted. "You have to pretend it's your worst enemy. I doubt I'm your worst enemy."

"Who's your worst enemy?" I watched as she balanced the blade on a finger. I had tried to do the same earlier in the week and damn near cut off a toe when I dropped it.

Lightning fast, she popped the blade in the air, caught it buy its hilt, and threw it at the dummy, hitting it right in the center of the forehead.

"My father." She walked to the dummy and pulled out the knives lodged in it.

I sometimes forgot that angels had once had lives that had led to their deaths. It was easy to forget when they were assholes to you. Case in point, Betty.

"Picture someone you despise more than anyone else in the world. Someone that hurt you so deeply that nothing can ever undo the pain." She handed me a knife. "You already have the proper form. Now you just need the right motivation to hit your target."

We practiced in silence until the coach blew his whistle that time was up. I made my way to the dummy and yanked out the three knives lodged in its chest. Where the hell did the fourth go?

I felt a sharp sting on my cheek and then the clang of metal onto the gym floor. I reached for my cheek. The second I touched it, the sting of the slice caught up with me. It felt like a nasty paper cut from a thick piece of paper.

That fucking bitch cut me.

I charged at her before she even realized I was coming and tackled her to the ground. All of the training was paying off. I climbed on top of her and grabbed a fist full of hair. I brought my fist back to punch her. Before I could, a hand grabbed my arm and yanked me off.

"What the flying fuck is going on here?" Coach Ferguson yelled.

"Ask her! She threw a knife at me!" I gestured to my face that was dripping blood.

I never did understand how I could be half angel and half demon and still have no healing ability. One would think with the short end of the stick, there'd be some benefits.

He turned to glare down at Betty, who sat up and was rubbing her head like I had bashed it into the hardwood floor. I'd give her something to really rub her head about. I moved towards her again, and Coach Ferguson stopped me by putting out his arm.

"It was an accident." She made herself sound so innocent. She looked up at the coach with tears in her eyes. "I tried to stop the throw, but she was already in its path. She must not have been counting the knives as we threw them."

I made one last move to attack her again, but he got in between us with his entire body.

"That's enough, Danica! Betty, apologize. Now." He should have sounded firm and angry that a student had been injured. Instead, he just seemed annoyed he had to deal with our brawl.

"That's it? Just an apology? She could have killed me! Or taken an eye out!" I could feel my face turning red as my anger bubbled up inside of me. "If this were any other school, she'd be expelled, or the police would be called. In fact, you know what! I'm pressing charges!"

Coach Ferguson put a hand on my shoulder. The move was meant to calm me down, possibly to get a grip on me in case I attacked, but all it did was piss me off more. I stepped back, shrugging off his hand.

"I'm sorry, Danica. Honestly, it was a mistake." She stood, and since the coach was focused on stopping me from wringing her neck, he didn't see her grin behind his back.

And to think, I had just been about to thank her for helping me.

~

I LOVED ASHER, I really did. But the second he found out about what happened with Betty, he decided that he would pair us up in a collaborative partnership during evening training.

As if forcing us to work together, would solve the more significant issue of her being a raging bitch. Rookie teacher mistake.

"When you're out there in battle, with bullets whizzing past your-" Asher was explaining the training we would be doing.

"We're going to have bullets flying at us?" Someone smarted off from the back of the group. A chorus of groans went up. Typically, that meant burpees for all.

Asher must have been in a good mood because he just rolled his eyes in response. "Hypothetically speaking. When you are being attacked, it's not going to matter who the person standing next to you is. You're a soldier. You're a unit. You are one."

I side-eyed Betty, who had a pout on her face. I was just as unhappy about being partnered with her as she was with me.

Asher rubbed his hands together like a mad scientist who thinks he has a good idea. Whether it was an evil gesture or an excited one was still up for debate.

"I've paired you up. Half of the pairs will be team A, and half will be team B." He held up touch-football mesh jerseys in two colors. "The objective is to make it to the other side of the field together as a pair. If your partner is knocked out, your job is to pick their ass up and carry them. Also, please remember not all of your classmates can heal."

After handing out the jerseys, we took our positions on the field. Those on team A were the "demons" and running through the field, and those on team B were angels trying to stop them.

This activity had disaster written all over it, especially for me.

"Maybe I should sit this one out," I said to Asher as he handed me and Betty blue jerseys. We would be pretending to be demons.

"You'll be fine. Betty should be taking the brunt of it." He nodded at Betty and then walked off.

I turned and looked at Betty, who had a smirk on her face. Great. Fantastic. I was going to end up in a wheelchair by the end of the activity.

We lined up on the edge of the field while team B spread out. When Asher blew the whistle, we took off at a jog. Other pairs seemed to be communicating, but Betty just headed straight through the center. I followed and kept up with her because I didn't have much choice. It reminded me of playing sharks and minnows in elementary school. Except instead of being frozen when you were caught, you were tackled.

We were doing great until a third-year, who used to be a line-backer for his high school football team, barreled towards us. Betty was in position next to me to take the hit. He had even aimed himself at her.

Right as he was about to plow into her, Betty shoved me in front.

I fell to the ground with the behemoth of a man on top of me, and a sharp pain ripped through my knee. Why did men play tackle foot-ball? There was nothing fun about being hit by a wall of muscle.

"Shit, Danica! I'm sorry," Joseph said, scrambling up and holding out his hand.

I reached for it, and he pulled me to my feet. Pain radiated from my knee, and tears stung my eyes. I'd been injured more times in the past months living the life of an angel than in my entire existence.

"Fuck." I tried to put weight on my leg but almost fell.

Since my partner was already on the other side of the field, and I didn't want to risk getting hit again, I just plopped my ass down right in the center of the field and crossed my arms.

I saw red. Betty was a bitch. Asher was incompetent. Linebackers were way too strong for their own good.

"What the hell are you sitting in the middle of the field for?" Asher shouted from down the field. He was in the middle of the mayhem with angels tackling each other right and left. He clearly hadn't seen what happened.

Joseph jogged over to Asher and was speaking to him animatedly. Asher's eyes widened. He jogged over and squatted beside me. I glared nice and hard at him.

"Where does it hurt?" He touched my knee, and I hissed in pain. Tears were already streaming down my cheeks. They were a combination of anger and pain.

"Where does it hurt?" I couldn't believe him. "Don't touch me! I need to be healed. Since you aren't capable of that, get me someone who can." It was a harsh comment, but my knee was about to explode. I could see that it was twice the size it was supposed to be under the fabric of my capris.

He frowned and stood. He barked at Joseph to go get Olly, and then he stalked over to the other side of the field where Betty stood chatting with friends.

I could hear him yelling, but couldn't quite make out what he said. The end result was Betty bursting into tears, her wings extending, and her flying off towards her building.

Tobias, who had been on the sidelines reading his damn book again, made his way to me and scooped me in his arms.

"Maybe pay a little more attention instead of reading, Mr. Armstrong," I gritted out. "What's even the point of this bull shit? Are demons going to be tackling angels?"

"We don't know what's in store for us." Tobias set me down on a chair just as Olly jogged over to us.

"What happened?" He knelt in front of me, and then ripped the fabric of my capris up past my knee. I cried even more because they were my favorite Lululemon capris. "It's dislocated."

"Your fucking boyfriend wouldn't let me sit out." I winced as he put his hand over the knee. His hand glowed, and the pain receded instantly.

"Look at Tobias for me." He waited for me to look away, and then I heard a pop. "You're good to go. It might still feel a little tender."

Without waiting for a reply, he took off, jogging towards his section of the field. He seemed to be in his element with the teaching thing. I had even heard several students making comments on how he should become a teacher at the academy.

He did have the patience of a saint.

Tobias helped me stand and put his arm around my waist. "Let's get you back to the room. I think you need to rest that knee."

By the time we were back in the room, my knee felt perfectly fine. The walking seemed to have stretched out whatever remaining discomfort there was.

"Shouldn't you go supervise Asher?" I stripped my shirt off and threw it in the laundry basket.

"Are you going to be okay?" Tobias didn't just mean my knee.

"I'm fine *now*." I was only talking about my knee. I wouldn't be fine if we never made a move to rescue my dad. It seemed everything we were training for was to protect Earth, not save my father.

How could we just leave him with Lilith? There should be more urgency in finding him. His blood was powerful. *He* was powerful.

Tobias watched me as I took off the rest of my clothes. He cleared his throat as I walked into the bathroom.

"I'll see you later, then, after training." He turned and left, leaving me to fume.

Smart man.

"Danica. Can we talk?" Asher poked his head inside the room about two hours later. I had managed to take my mind off Betty but still found my mind drifting to thoughts of my dad.

I looked up from my studying and narrowed my eyes at him. Now I was reminded of my knee and the gash on my face. Both healed to perfection by Olly.

Asher slid into the room with Olly behind him.

"Where are Tobias and Reve?" I turned back to my notes.

"Where do you think? The game is on."

I grunted and tried to focus on my notes. I could feel both of them watching me. I imagined they were having a silent conversation behind my back with hand gestures and faces. I'd caught them once when I was in a particularly bad mood one day.

"Danica." Asher sighed.

I dropped my pen and swiveled in my chair to face him. "*What?*"

"I'm sorry."

I crossed my arms and stood. "You knew she had it out for me, and you deliberately paired us up. I told you I should have sat out."

He frowned and looked at Olly like he would fix the problem. Olly shrugged his shoulders.

"I thought-"

"Well, clearly, you thought wrong. What if he had broken my neck instead of dislocating my knee? What if Betty had shanked me in the kidney?"

I caught Olly smiling and leveled a glare at him. His smiled dropped.

"I'm serious. She is just the type to carry a shank on her. One second she'll be smiling and flipping that hair of hers, the next she'll be gutting me like a fish. Is that what you want? Fillet of Danica?"

He stepped towards me. "I said I was sorry. I thought it might help your dislike for each other if you had to work together towards a common goal."

I let him pull me towards him, and he wrapped his arms around me. He kissed my temple and then looked at me with a serious expression. "All right, how many orgasms is this going to take? At least three?"

"You can't just give me orgasms and expect me to-" His lips collided with mine, and I moaned.

Maybe my forgiveness could be bought with a kiss as good as the one he was giving me. His tongue probed, and I opened my lips for him. I really wanted to stay mad. When everything was falling apart, being angry felt right.

I was backing towards the bed when the door burst open, causing all three of us to nearly come out of our skin. For once, it wasn't just Asher on edge.

"A large group of demons has gotten through at Griffith Observatory. Let's go!" Tobias was frantic. "There are already civilian casualties."

"Shit!" Asher and Olly moved towards the door. I grabbed my shoes and sat down on the bed to put them on.

"You aren't going." Tobias shut the door because there was a lot of commotion in the hall as staff members grabbed their gear from their rooms.

"Why not? I could help!" I dropped my shoes and grabbed my boots instead. "I could stop them."

"Only staff are going. You'd just be a distraction."

The comment burned in my gut, and I crossed my arms over my chest.

"You aren't ready yet, Danica. We would be worried about your safety the entire time. Please don't take it personally. No students are coming this time." Tobias kissed my cheek, and then the three of them left without me.

CHAPTER 6

ASHER

I felt like I was back at war again. Rushing around, grabbing gear, leaving the one I loved behind to protect others.

I thought I'd be fine since we didn't use guns or explosives. Demons didn't either.

That didn't stop the dread from welling up in my gut as we gathered in the parking lot of the academy. Other guardians from throughout the Los Angeles area were meeting us at the observatory, which as of five minutes ago, was being infiltrated by several dozen demons.

Demons that had somehow gotten through the barrier between Inferna and Earth. Lilith was making her move, and we were far from prepared. The academy students sorely lacked combat skills.

The angels in charge of coverups were going to have quite the task keeping a hoard of demons attacking a tourist trap under wraps.

We landed on the side of the observatory and joined the other angels already gathered. A few looked in my direction and then narrowed their eyes. Word on the street was that I had been nicknamed Snap.

"Thorne, are you going to be able to follow orders tonight?" one of the angels said, jabbing me in the shoulder with his finger. I resisted the urge to grab that finger and snap it in half.

"Fuck off, man. I said I was sorry for snapping your neck." I was still getting shit for snapping necks when we infiltrated the angel blood draining operation. "Look at the bright side, it meant one less draining since you had to heal."

"I still wake up with a crick in my neck every morning."

Michael landed in the center of our group, and everyone fell silent. "We have at least three dozen demons we're dealing with. Several are inside. We'll first take care of the ones outside. There will most likely be casualties tonight, but if we have each other's backs, we won't see as many as they do." Michael looked around the group. "Now, let's go kill some demons!"

He took off around the side of the building and into a grassy area at the front. The others followed.

"Fuck, fuck, fuck." My feet seemed to be cemented to the ground. Everyone else was headed out there with swords raised, and I was frozen.

"Deep breaths." Toby appeared in front of me and put his hands on my shoulders.

Toby didn't realize it, but he did the exact same thing back in the war on multiple occasions.

I shut my eyes and took several deep breaths before opening them again. I was a little calmer, but the feeling of dread still coursed through my veins. I don't know why I thought I would be suited to fight.

"You good?" He stepped away and unsheathed his sword.

"I'm never good." I pulled out my own sword and met Olly's concerned eyes. "Don't you dare look at me like that. Take care of yourself, angel baby. The second you worry about me out there, we're both dead men. Well, angels."

I took off after Toby. I was fairly certain that Reve was nearby, but he was incognito. It was a minor comfort that the demon we had grown to trust had our backs.

The area at the front of the building was already pure chaos.

Demons that looked human, but clearly weren't judging from their fangs and blood running down their chins, were dodging our swords faster than humanly possible.

Angels were fast, but they weren't vampire fast.

I shouldn't have been surprised there were vampire demons. After all, I was an angel. Still, seeing one up close and personal was a mind fuck.

I rammed my sword into the gut of a nasty looking demon that looked like a science experiment gone horribly wrong. It had the body of a wolf, the tail of a serpent, and the head of a raven. It fell to the ground, and I swung my sword to take off its head.

Danica had wanted to come along for this shit show, yet the woman couldn't even kill a spider without squealing. She'd lose it seeing some of these demons.

"Ugh, guys?" Olly shouted over the sounds of dying demons and swords slicing through flesh and bone.

I turned in his direction. It was just like in the movies. The moment some crazy-ass monster appears, and everyone pauses because, holy fuck.

It was at least ten feet tall and looked like one of the rhinos from *Ninja Turtles*. Angels and demons alike dove out of the way as it barreled straight towards the Astronomers Monument. It must have thought the six astronomers depicted on it were actually people because it began punching Galileo in the face.

While it was occupied, Ferguson and Michael tried to incapacitate it. It wheeled around and sent them flying. With a roar mightier than any lion, it took off, charging after Ferguson. It seemed to set its sight on him like a missile aimed at a moving target.

Several of us joined Michael in following as Ferguson ran into the observatory, trying to get away from the beast of a demon. The doorway didn't stop it, it just ran straight through the metal and bronze doorway.

It roared as a piece of metal stuck from its arm. It pulled it out and threw it, knocking over anyone and anything in its path.

It was like a bull in a china shop. Things that weren't even in the rhino demon's way were somehow broken and sent crashing to the ground. Ferguson was running around the Foucault Pendulum in the center of the room.

The rhino motherfucker had his sights set on goring him up the ass. Every time he'd get close, he would lower his single horn and surge forward.

It was only a matter of time before the rhino figured out it could jump across the giant circular hole housing the ball of the pendulum.

"I'm going to jump on it," Olly shouted over the noise and moved closer.

I wanted to tell him to use some common sense. Jumping on the back of a pissed-off demon was idiotic, but just as I opened my mouth, the side door burst open, and more demons poured in.

Was this it? Was this how I was going to die for the third time? It was doubtful I'd be given another chance. Angels weren't like cats. We didn't get nine lives.

I took a few more demons out when I heard a man scream. Nothing was worse than hearing agony pour out of a fellow soldier's mouth. It was the antecedent of something really fucking bad.

I was on the far side of the room by the doors leading into the main planetarium. The irony of angels and demons fighting in a place that studied the sky was not lost on me.

The last demon near me went down with a thud, and I rushed forward towards the pendulum. What looked like gremlins were swarming over the sides and into the hole. More screams, this time frantic, erupted from inside of it. Someone was down there.

I backed up against the wall, my arms and legs not wanting to cooperate any longer. The sounds bombarded my ears until the only thing I could hear were the screams of agony. I slid down the wall to the ground and put my hands over my ears. I watched as Michael flew over the hole, trying to get into it and save whoever was down there.

My eyes darted around the room. I hadn't seen Toby or Reve since Galileo's head went flying and shattered into hundreds of plaster pieces. A panic set into my chest as I scanned the room for Olly.

Headless demon bodies were scattered around, as well as a few downed angels.

"Stand back!" Michael's voice echoed through the rotunda. The hole the Foucault Pendulum was in lit up like a bonfire.

The shrieking of the gremlin-looking demons was deafening, and I covered my ears. I tried to get to my feet but was frozen with an unrelenting dread.

Demon heads and bodies were thrown in the fire.

"Asher? You doing all right?" Reve's voice came from next to me, and then he appeared. He looked fresh as a daisy.

"Olly," I managed to grit out. My mind was telling me to run away from this hell we had been thrown into, but my body wouldn't cooperate. I hadn't shut down like this since the day my lieutenant had his brains blown out right next to me during the liberation of a small town in Belgium.

"He's outside. The Behemoth took him for a little ride, but Olly killed it. You should have seen it! It was-"

A door burst open, and several vampires poured in. At least that's what they appeared to be.

Reve vanished and took one out from behind in a swift move that sent the head flying clear across the room. I hadn't seen Reve in action before, and it was something to behold. It was like the blades he was wielding were an extension of him as he sliced and diced the small cluster of vampires.

"Prince Reve?" A vampire stopped in its tracks, and its eyes went wide in recognition. He fell to his knees and lowered himself down in a submissive position in front of Reve.

What the actual fuck?

He hadn't told us outright that he was a prince, we just assumed. Hearing it from a demon's mouth was just another cluster fuck to add to the ever-growing pile.

"We thought you were dead."

Reve needed to kill the fucker before he jumped up and ripped out his throat.

"Why are you here?" Reve still had his knives ready but had relaxed slightly. I looked between him and the vampire.

I managed to pull myself to my feet and put myself behind Reve. If he wasn't going to take out the vampire yet, I didn't want to be anywhere near it.

"She ordered us to." He looked up but avoided making eye contact with Reve. Instead, his eyes landed on me, and a chill ran up my spine.

"Why?"

Instead of answering, the vampire got a pained look on his face. He then dug into his chest with some kind of crazy hand strength and ripped out his heart. It was almost like he had been compelled to kill himself if captured. A cyanide pill would have done the trick. But then again, these were demons we were talking about.

I cringed as the body fell with a thud, and the heart, still beating, landed near Reve's boot.

"Fuck." Reve stabbed the heart, and blood pooled around it.

I was going to be sick.

I turned to find somewhere to vomit in peace. The fighting was over. Angels were scattered around the room. Some grabbed the limp bodies of other angels and went out the doors with them.

The smell of burning flesh hit me in the face as I staggered past the fire. Michael gave me a concerned look as I passed by him but didn't stop me.

I managed to make it outside the doors before hurling the contents of my stomach into a bush. Besides my retching, there was silence.

I braced my hand on the side of the building and turned my head to look for the others. Reve had stayed inside with Michael, but I hadn't spotted Toby or Olly yet.

Stumbling down the stone steps, I stopped to put my hands on my knees. Maybe I wasn't cut out for this job anymore and should hang up my wings. Heaven was one of the best retirement communities.

A pair of boots came into my line of vision. They had splatters of blood on them.

"Asher." Olly's voice was like music to my ears.

He grabbed my arm and pulled me up to my full height. He looked like he had taken a ride on a massive demon. His cuts and bruises were healing before my eyes.

He cupped my cheek, and I felt the familiar warmth spread through my body. I didn't know how he fucking did it. He was a miracle worker, keeping me sane when I should very well have been rocking myself back and forth in a padded room.

"You're going to drain yourself," I warned, clasping his wrist and trying to pull his hand away.

He grunted and slid his thumb over my bottom lip. "I'll be fine."

"You shouldn't have done that. That was stupid." I took in the sight outside. It was like a war zone. Piles of demons were being prepared to be burned.

"Where's Toby?"

"Making sure humans don't see what's going on here. He's fine."

I breathed a sigh of relief.

A cleanup crew arrived, and I watched in fascination as they made quick work of cleaning up the evidence that anything crazy had happened. Galileo was a goner, but vandals were always destroying shit; it wouldn't be entirely out of the ordinary.

"Gather round," Michael bellowed from the top of the steps.

Everyone looked worse for wear, with several angels missing. I couldn't quite figure out who. Toby came to stand on the side of me that Olly wasn't on and put a hand on my shoulder.

"We lost five tonight. Moore, Reed, Sullivan, Nguyen, and Ferguson." He paused and looked up at the sky. "We're going to need to step up the training at the academy. The attacks are only going to get worse."

THE LAST PLACE I wanted to be was at the academy. I desperately needed to take the edge off. So, instead of heading back right away, we went to my building to shower and change. Reve went to his place, Tobias to Danica's, and Olly and me to mine.

What I really wanted to do at some point was knock a hole in the floor and build stairs. It wouldn't be too difficult of a remodel.

I texted Danica that we were safe. She was probably still pissed that she didn't get to join in on the action. She could be mad all she wanted. Our job was to keep her safe.

"Are you sure you're okay?" Olly asked as the door shut behind Reve and Tobias. Three bathrooms was the perfect number for our family of five. I was determined to make the three separate living spaces one mega space.

"I said I was fine." I went to my liquor cabinet and pulled out a new bottle of whiskey. I heard Olly sigh from behind me.

I was trying to cut back, but it was hard. Life just kept throwing curve balls my way. And now, with being on that damned academy campus all the time, I was struggling to maintain my calm persona.

I laughed as I thought about describing myself as calm. I poured the whiskey into a glass, and the smell filled my nostrils. Even the smell was a comfort.

I felt him move close behind me as I braced one of my hands on the counter. He slid his arm around me and worked my belt buckle loose.

"You don't need to drink." His mouth was on my neck before I could pull away, and I shifted my head to the side.

I let out a breath and then brought the glass to my lips and took a sip. "Tell me what I need then."

My belt was undone, and then he was unbuttoning my pants. His breath was hot against my neck as he worked the zipper down. We were supposed to be showering, not messing around.

An image of him taking me against the counter flashed through my mind, and I shuddered as my dick gave a happy little jerk and came to life.

"People died tonight, Oliver." I groaned as he worked my pants down past my ass and pressed against me.

I could feel his hard length and braced my other hand on the counter, forgetting my drink for the time being.

"I know." He rubbed against me. One of his hands went over the top of mine, and he reached the other around and grabbed my cock. "I need a reminder that you're still here."

I turned my head to the side, and he kissed the corner of my mouth. My dick slid through his fist as I rocked my hips.

"Get on the counter."

I loved when he got bossy with me. He saved that side of himself for me, and it made my heart flutter. Yeah, he had me dick whipped. If there was such a thing.

I turned and jumped up. I kicked my boots off as he yanked his shirt over his head. My pants fell down my legs and gathered at my ankles. He slid his hands down to where the pants were stuck on my heels and took them off the rest of the way, along with my socks.

"Take off your shirt." I complied and sat bare on the cold counter with him looking at me with a hunger I hadn't seen in a while.

He took me in his mouth without any teasing and gripped me at the base. I groaned and buried my fingers in his hair. I had urged him to grow it out a little more so I would have more to hold onto, but he liked it short.

"Jesus, angel baby." I was nearly at the back of his throat and felt my balls tighten. He was sucking on me like it would be the last time he'd have a taste.

I leaned my head back against the shelf and willed myself to hold onto my load.

My dick popped out of his mouth, and he pulled me towards him as his wings spread. I may have squealed like a little girl as he flew us to the bed and dropped me in the center.

He removed his pants and settled between my legs.

"I want inside of you." His lips crashed into mine, and he rubbed against me. I slid my hands to his ass and dug my nails in.

"Not ready for *that*." I groaned as he lowered his lips to my nipple and swirled his tongue around it. "Are *you* ready?"

"You just want to be first." He bit my nipple, and I smacked the side of his head. "Ow!"

"You know I have really sensitive nipples."

He smirked and leaned down and kissed it before his hand gripped us both. "If you can handle my fingers, you can handle my dick."

I was pretty sure his dick was substantially bigger than his damn fingers. I bucked my hips against him then rolled us so I was on top. "Let me fuck you, Oliver."

"Such a nice way of phrasing that. Let me roll right over." He rolled his eyes and groaned as I reached down and stroked him between his balls and his tight hole.

He sure had gotten mouthy. Danica liked to give me a hard time about how I was corrupting innocent little Olly, but I was convinced he was never that innocent to begin with.

"What would you prefer I say? Dearest Oliver. Let me make sweet man love to your ass?"

He chuckled and pinched my ass cheek. "Get the lube."

I reeled back and narrowed my eyes in suspicion. We always joked about going all the way but never ended up going through with it. It was a big step. It made me feel like such a virgin. Well, at least an ass virgin.

"You're serious?" I raised an eyebrow.

He cupped my cheek. "Either you're going to be inside me, or I'm going to be inside you."

"Fuck." I rolled off him and grabbed the lube from the bedside drawer. "Spread your legs."

He bit his lip and spread open for me. This was really fucking happening. My dick twitched in anticipation, and I damn near told it to calm the fuck down.

I worked my lubed finger inside of him and stroked his prostate. I could hardly wait until I could stroke it with my dick. I worked in a second finger and rolled him onto his side.

"Give it to me, Asher."

I was about to come from just his words.

I grabbed the bottle of lube and covered my dick in it before squirting some down his crack.

I scooted behind him and slowly eased in. He was so fucking tight, and I bit the inside of my cheek to stop myself from crying out. Once his ass hit my thighs, I stopped and reached around to grip his dick.

"Is it okay?" The urge to pound him into the mattress was strong.

"It's amazing." He pushed back against me, and I took that as my cue to start moving.

I tried to take it slow, but before I knew it, I had him on his knees, my fingers digging into his hips to hold him in place.

He took over working his cock, his hand pumping faster than I had ever seen it move. We had waited too long for this.

The grunts coming out of his sweet little mouth sent me over the edge, and my balls tightened as my release slammed into me. Olly came with a grunt, and then we collapsed next to each other. I buried my face in between his shoulder blades.

Olly's shoulders started to shake, and my stomach dropped. "Did I hurt you?"

A laugh ripped out of him. "I landed in my own cum."

I groaned a laugh and sat up, looking down at him. "I love you. You know that, right?"

His laughter faded, and he pushed himself up to take my face in his hands. "I do." He kissed me gently. "I love you too."

We made our way into the bathroom. My chest felt tight, and for once, it wasn't because I was about to have a panic attack. It was because my heart was fuller than it had ever been.

CHAPTER 7

DANICA

I felt useless staying behind while everyone went to kick demon butt. Yes, I had just been angry about being included and then injured in a training exercise, but this was different. This was real. People's lives were at risk.

Wasn't I supposed to save the light from the dark? How could I do that if I was sitting on my ass at the academy? I should have been fighting. I could have possibly incapacitated a demon enough for a more capable angel to kill. Hell, maybe I could have even brought them all to their knees.

I scrolled through my phone, scouring the internet for any mention of demons or monsters attacking in the area. I even scanned the police logs.

There was nothing. It was probably for the best. People would lose their shit if they knew what existed on the other side of some magical barrier.

A magical barrier that could easily be manipulated with angel blood and opened completely with my father's blood. Supposedly.

If it was so simple, wouldn't Lilith have blown the barrier wide open by now?

I sent Ava a text. She was working, but usually, she called me on her breaks. Never in a million years did I think I'd be the one still in school, and she'd be the one with a full-time job.

The charges in her breaking and entering case had been dropped, but the damage was already done. Stanford hadn't rescinded her admissions, but Ava had decided to take a gap year.

My best friend, the one who had straight As and perfect attendance, had decided to have a quarter-life crisis.

I couldn't say I blamed her. I was on the verge of one myself. I needed a year off. Or maybe ten.

Fifteen minutes later, my phone rang with an incoming call from Ava.

"Girl, you will not believe the juicy piece of gossip floating around Blue Wave," Ava said as soon as the call connected.

"Hi to you too." I laughed.

Blue Wave was the hottest restaurant and bar in Santa Barbara. It was also the reason Ava was taking a break from school. She said it made her feel alive. I wasn't sure how swimming around in a tank all evening with men gawking at her seashell bikini top made her feel alive.

"I'd like to think we're past the stage of pleasantries." I heard a beep, and then the sounds of the restaurant disappeared. "So, do you want to hear what is making the rounds tonight at the bar?"

Gossip was just what I needed to distract myself from the fact that my guardians were somewhere fighting a hoard of demons without me.

"Sure, go for it." I sat in my chair and propped my feet on my desk.

"So get this, they found Dr. Adamson's body in some abandoned warehouse in Asia. He had a giant crescent or something carved on his chest."

I gripped the phone in my hand. "What?"

"He had been dead a few months. Isn't that crazy? I guess karma got ahold of him for all that weed he sold to high schoolers."

My heart was pounding so hard that I wondered if Ava could hear it on the other end of the phone. My feet slid off the desk, and I damn near fell out of the chair.

"Dani, you there?" She sounded concerned. I had gone radio silent.

"Yeah. It's just, that was it? They just found his body?" I stood and started pacing. Hadn't Lilith been using him to run her experiments on blood? Why would she kill him? Unless she had gotten what she wanted and didn't need him to experiment anymore.

"That's all the information anyone has. I feel a little bad for John. He was already pretty fucked up, and now with his dad being murdered..." She sighed.

While I understood her bleeding heart, I wouldn't go as far as to say I was sorry for John. I didn't know if that made me a horrible person or one that just saw things for what they really were.

I cleared my throat, still processing the fact that Lilith had killed John. Had she killed my father? Would she?

"I miss you. I can't believe your school wouldn't let you leave for the summer. See, this is why you should have taken a gap year too." I was grateful she changed the subject before I had more time to think about Lilith killing the doctor and leaving him to rot in an empty building.

"I feel like my entire life has been a big giant gap year." I sat back down in my desk chair and spun a few times. "I actually like my classes. Maybe I just needed to find something I was interested in. Math and studying poetry were definitely not my thing."

"Sir, you aren't supposed to be back here." Ava's voice was muffled like she was holding her phone against her shirt. "What are you-" Her scream pierced my eardrum, and I nearly dropped the phone.

"Ava?" I jumped out of my chair, sending it toppling onto its side.

There was scuffling, and a grunt before the line went dead.

With shaking fingers, I called her phone back. It went to voicemail. I tried calling again.

Damn it.

I quickly slid my feet into my shoes and took off out of my room like a bat out of hell. The building was empty since most of the staff were off fighting.

I ran as fast as my hybrid ass could to the first student building, which was where Cora and Ethan lived.

No one answered when I pounded on Ethan's door. I took the stairs to the next floor and banged on Cora's door. Where the fuck were they?

Panicking, I called their phones. Wings would come in handy right now.

I was pacing in front of Cora's door, trying them again and again when the elevator slid open, and Betty sauntered down the hall. You know, because my night wasn't shitty enough already.

"Eve. What an unpleasant surprise. Please tell me you aren't stalking me now." She looked me up and down with a scrunched-up nose.

"Have you seen Cora or Ethan?" I bit out. I was half tempted to call one of the guys but knew they wouldn't answer either.

"Do I look like your personal surveillance?" She rolled her eyes and stopped at her door with her keys in her hand.

"Goddamn it! Can't you for one second not be such a bitch?" I shoved past her but didn't make it very far before she grabbed my arm. "Don't touch me."

"What's wrong?" She wasn't sarcastic or condescending for once. "You aren't normally so... neurotic."

"What isn't wrong? I don't need this right now. What I need is a pair of goddamned wings!" I flung open the door to the stairs and ran down to the bottom floor.

Once outside, I tried to calm myself down. Good decisions weren't made when I was panicking. I called Ava again, her phone going straight to voicemail instead of ringing.

Maybe I could just ask a random student to take me to Blue Wave. Not every angel hated my guts. I would say that most tolerated my presence now.

The door to the building opened, and Betty stepped out. "Where do you need to go?"

I spun around and narrowed my eyes. There was no way she was about to offer to take me somewhere without some kind of strings being attached or a prank involved.

She would probably drop me and laugh as I splattered.

"What's your angle?"

"I'll take you where you need to go to make up for the injuries I caused earlier." She shrugged her shoulders as if what was happening wasn't a big deal.

It was a big deal. Betty did a complete one-eighty out of nowhere.

To say I was shocked by her offer to take me to Blue Wave was an understatement. I only hesitated for a second before accepting her offer. Beggars can't be choosers.

She wrapped an arm around my waist, and we shot into the sky. I kept my eyes closed and prayed she wouldn't let me go.

We landed and I breathed a sigh of relief. I was lucky she hadn't taken me somewhere and left me to find my own way back.

I rushed inside the restaurant, which was packed. There was no way anyone inside would have heard Ava scream. It had only been ten minutes; maybe everything was fine.

I should have called the police or the manager, but in my panic, I had only had one thought: get to Ava.

"Table for two?" The hostess asked as I approached the hostess station.

I looked over my shoulder to find Betty right behind me. I told her when we landed that she could go. I hadn't expected her to stay. She was probably collecting information to use against me.

"Ava. I need to find her."

The woman raised her eyebrows and took a better assessment of me. I'm sure I looked like hell after the day I had.

"She's on her break. Do you want a table in the bar area? Otherwise, we have about an hour wait for a table."

"She was outside, and she screamed. Please, where's a security guard or the manager or someone!" I gripped the edge of the counter, and Betty stepped next to me.

"We aren't allowed outside on our breaks. Especially not the mermaids."

Did this hostess not understand simple English?

I was about to lose my shit when Betty slammed her hand down on the counter. "Get the fucking manager."

My eyes widened, and I looked over at her. She looked back and shrugged as if she did this all the time.

The hostess backed up several steps and then pressed a button on the phone. Less than a minute passed when a burly man joined the hostess.

"What seems to be the problem?" He looked confused as he took us in. At first glance, we looked like college coeds out for dinner.

Before the hostess could even get a word in, I repeated what I had already said.

"Come with me." He turned and headed towards a set of stairs. I looked at Betty, and she nodded before we followed the man with the word 'Security' on the back of his blue tee-shirt.

Upstairs appeared to be the VIP section. The mermaid tank extended up into the area, with a platform where they could get in and out of it.

"Wait here." The security guard was a man of few words. He opened a door that led down a hall and disappeared.

"I've heard they are going to open one of these places in the Los Angeles area soon." Betty was attempting to make small talk while we waited. "I wonder how much a gig like this pays."

"Thirty an hour plus tips for the mermaids." I nearly jumped out of my skin at the voice behind me.

I turned, and the security guard was back with a man that looked like his suit cost more than my car. I knew a quality suit when I saw one. My heart ached at the thought of my father.

"My friend, Ava. She was on her break and-" I felt like I had been repeating myself for hours.

"She's fine." He looked between Betty and me. "She's in my office."

Betty gripped my arm, but I ignored her.

"I want to see her."

He nodded and then opened the door to the hall.

"Danica," Betty whispered. "He's Fallen."

I didn't care what he was, as long as my best friend was in one piece. His office door was open, and when Ava saw me, she jumped up as fast as her mermaid costume would allow and threw her arms around me.

"How'd you get here so fast? Danica, you're squeezing me a little too hard." Ava pulled away from the hug. She had been crying but didn't look like she was hurt.

"Doesn't matter. What happened?" I should have planned a better response to her question. Ava was smart. There was no way she would let go of the fact that it had been barely twenty minutes since we talked on the phone.

Santa Barbara was almost two hours away. Maybe she'd believe we took a helicopter?

She sighed and sat back down. She looked over at the man who had brought us in to see her as he sat down at his desk.

"A man attacked her." He folded his hands over his stomach and leaned back in his chair. "I took care of the situation."

I looked at Ava, and she bit her lip. There was more to this than they were saying.

"Where's the man?" Betty asked from behind me. I had almost forgotten she was there.

"He's locked in a room downstairs until he can be taken care of." I looked back at who I assumed was Ava's boss.

"You mean until the cops arrive?" I raised my eyebrows.

I examined the man in front of me. He was slender but had broad shoulders under his suit jacket. His hair was black. He looked dangerous in a low-key kind of way.

"We can't call the cops on this one."

Ava made a whimpering sound from her chair, and I sat down next to her, taking her hand. She looked pale and was trembling.

"He... he... he had fangs." She gulped and gripped my hand. "It was *him*."

I stared at her, and then my eyes widened. "What do you mean it was him?"

"The man from your house," she whispered. "That one I thought I was in love with."

Fuck. I thought my dad had banished him back to hell. Had he been able to get through the barrier?

"What does she mean the man from your house?" Ava's boss narrowed his eyes at me. "Who are you?" He looked from me to Ava. He should have been able to tell we weren't human.

"Who are *you*?" I demanded.

His hands were folded on his desk, and he was leaning forward slightly. "Kai Matsui. I'm the owner." He shook his head. "Stop doing that."

"Stop doing what?" As soon as I finished asking the question, it occurred to me that I was commanding him to answer my question.

He didn't answer and instead got up from his chair. Betty shifted uncomfortably from her spot by the door.

"If a vampire is visiting your house and then tracking down a girl like Ava, I want to know why." He moved his suit jacket back a bit, and I saw he had on a holster with a gun and knife.

"You aren't supposed to be carrying weapons." Betty stepped forward as if she was going to disarm him.

I'd give it to her. She had some balls.

Kai snorted. "And I'm pretty sure you shouldn't be here right now." He looked at me. "Your signature doesn't look the same as hers. Why?"

Ava was looking between us with confusion written all over her face. I was going to have to tell her something. There was no way she wouldn't remember every detail of the conversation we were having in front of her.

"She doesn't need to answer to you. Should I give Michael a call? I'm sure he'd love to hear about the heat you're packing." Betty surprised me again. Mere hours ago, she was trying to get me killed. What had Asher said to her?

"That won't be necessary. I was only curious. Would you like to see her attacker before we dispose of him?"

From the corner of my eye, I saw Ava's face pale even further. I was surprised she hadn't dwelled on how quickly I had gotten to Santa Barbara. Or maybe she hadn't completely processed it yet.

Trauma could really do a number on the brain.

We followed Kai downstairs and through the bar area to the kitchen. He took a set of keys out of his pocket and unlocked a door off of a hallway.

As soon as we entered the storage room, the hairs on my arms stood on end. The vampire was sitting against a far wall with chains wrapped around his ankles and wrists.

"Chains will hold him?" I looked to Kai, who had just locked us in with the vampire.

"They do if they are from Heaven." I raised my eyebrows and then looked at the vampire.

He was definitely the one from my house. As soon as he recognized me, he let out a laugh that almost made me piss myself.

"Danica Deville. And to think I once thought you were a prostitute." He shook his head. "How is your daddy doing? Oh, wait..."

I regretted that I hadn't made Betty stay behind with Ava upstairs. She certainly didn't need any more ammo to use against me.

"Why are you here? How are you here?" I stepped closer, and his eyes seemed to look right through me. "Answer me."

He met my eyes. "I'm sworn to Lilith. You shouldn't be able to control me." He laughed. "But apparently you can."

"Do you know where she has him?"

"You are all screwed." He blinked a few times. "She's in the castle. In Inferna. That's where she has him."

I shut my eyes for a moment, and when I reopened them, he had his head cocked to the side. "You can stop her." I narrowed my eyes at him. "She's using Lucifer's blood to put a hole in the barrier. It won't be long before Inferna comes to Earth."

"What the hell is he talking about?" I ignored Kai's question.

"How is she doing it? I thought she was giving demons angel blood."

"She is. But our bodies fight it and eliminate it pretty quickly. When we have an injection, we have a minute to get through to Earth if we're strong enough. The same with his blood. Plus, a little dark magic." He shifted on the floor like he was trying to move his hands up, but the chains were wrapped too tightly around him. "I'm telling you too much."

"Why are you after Ava?"

He coughed, and a trickle of blood ran out of the side of his mouth. "Pure... so pure." He toppled over onto his side and looked to be in pain. "You have to kill her." When my eyes went wide, he shook his head. "Lilith. Kill her before..."

"Before what?"

He passed out before he could answer.

Kai cleared his throat. "Is he serious?"

I looked down at the vampire and then turned towards the door. Shit was getting way too strange. It wasn't like I hadn't heard Michael or Reve talk about vampires, but seeing one was something else entirely. They looked human, well besides their pointy teeth. But the one laying on the ground didn't even have those out.

We had been learning about all kinds of demons in Reve's training. Many of the myths humans believed in were a reality to some extent.

At some point, I needed to tell Ava about me. Her life had changed because of me. I at least owed her the truth. Maybe just after I saved the world from my mother.

I hesitated at the door and then turned back to face Kai. "Tell Ava I had to go. You'll make sure she gets home all right?"

He nodded, and Betty and I left Blue Wave.

WE LANDED outside the faculty building sometime well after midnight. The vampire wasn't dead but was close enough to death that there was no use in waiting around to see if he'd wake up again.

Betty started walking towards her building after we landed. I was still surprised she hadn't ditched me at Blue Wave.

"Betty." She turned back. "Thanks for helping me."

She sighed and took a step back in my direction. "Lilith is your mom, isn't she?"

She was smart, I'd give her that. I probably wouldn't have been able to connect the dots if it was me in her position.

I didn't answer.

"I wish I would have had the strength to kill my father before he killed me." She swallowed hard. "Don't let us down."

I made my way into the building, mulling over her words. I wasn't a killer. Even if my mother needed to die, the thought of having to end her life made me feel sick to my stomach.

The faculty building was eerily quiet. Everyone should have been back by now. I ran up the stairs and down the hall to my room.

The room was dark, but I could make out forms lying on the floor. I turned on my cell phone screen for light and smiled, seeing they had pushed furniture against the walls and dragged the mattress to the floor. It looked like a second mattress was right next to mine.

I took off my clothes, leaving only my panties on, and slid in the middle. Arms wrapped around me.

"Where were you?" Reve's voice came from the end of the mattresses, and I felt the mattress dip by my feet.

I rolled onto my back, and he moved one of my legs so he could settle between them. He rested his head on my stomach.

"Ava needed help. A vampire attacked her."

"Vampire?" Asher mumbled next to me. He grabbed my hand. "How'd you get there?"

"Betty. What'd you say to her?"

"I told her to stop being a fucking bitch because you were about to save the world." He kissed my shoulder and snuggled closer to me. "I may have said a few other things that don't need repeating."

"How did everything go?"

I felt Tobias's beard against my other shoulder as he moved in closer. He and Olly had been quiet so far. Olly sounded like he was sleeping.

"We lost five. Ferguson and Nguyen are gone." Tobias's voice was sad, and I felt a tear hit my shoulder.

"Coach Ferguson?" There was no other Ferguson that I knew of. Sadness washed over me. Sure he hadn't been the nicest in the world to me, but over the past several weeks, he had been indifferent towards me.

I felt Tobias nod. I slid my hand into his and gave it a squeeze. I didn't quite know what to say to ease his grief, so I just laid there quietly, letting him rub his beard against my skin and squeeze my hand.

Sometimes just being there for someone was enough.

CHAPTER 8

DANICA

*W*hen an angel dies, their body is taken back to Heaven so their soul can be saved. No one was quite clear on the details when I had asked. Did the souls just float around like Asher's had? Did they get a second chance at being an angel?

There was a memorial on the football field the next night. The entire school plus several angels from outside the school showed up to light candles and tell stories about the angels that died.

I stood at the back of the crowd with Reve, both of us feeling out of place among the angels. He held my hand as we looked on.

Since I had woken up that morning, a feeling of dread had encompassed my every move. One of the dead angels could have been one of my angels. Every time there was a demon attack, the risk of losing one of them increased.

I couldn't handle the thought of one of them dying.

Asher's death had shaken me to my core. I couldn't go through that again.

After the service, we decided to take a case of beer to one of our favorite spots on campus. On the other side of the parking lot was a copse of trees that had a small clearing in the middle. Over the summer, we had set up Adirondack chairs and a fire-pit.

Tobias started up the fire while I passed beers around. I downed half the bottle before the others had even opened theirs.

"Whoa there, fish lips." Asher chuckled, popping the cap off of his. He took a long pull from it before setting it on the arm of his chair. "You've been quiet all day."

"Just have a lot on my mind." I finished the bottle and burped. A small price to pay for drinking it so fast.

I felt my cheeks flush with heat as the fire sprang to life in front of me, and the beer hit my blood. I reached forward and grabbed another bottle.

"Tell me about it." He watched as I took a much more reasonable swig.

"Did you know that John Adamson's body was found in an abandoned warehouse?" I tapped my finger on the side of the bottle and then started to pick at the label.

Olly sat down on the arm of Asher's chair. Asher looked up at him and then back at me. "We heard about it."

"You didn't tell me." A long strip of the beer label came off. I rolled it into a ball and then threw it into the fire. "What else haven't you told me?"

"There was no point in telling you." Tobias grabbed my hand and yanked me up before sitting in my seat. He pulled me into his lap.

I protested with a grunt, but he had already secured an arm around my waist.

"What happened to no secrets?" I frowned at him as he grabbed my beer and took a drink. "That's mine."

I snatched it from him. John dying seemed like a mighty big secret to keep from me. What else weren't they telling me?

"You're stressed enough as it is." Reve joined us and grabbed a beer. "Your nightmares are just now starting to lessen. We felt it was in your best interest to keep it to ourselves."

"My whole life is a nightmare, Reve." I leaned back against Tobias. I was still mad, but not enough to deny myself the comfort he brought me. "What else?"

They hadn't answered it the first time I asked. Maybe they thought I would forget..

They all went silent, the only sounds the crackling of the fire and the chirps of crickets.

"Tobias?"

He sighed. "Michael is planning a mission to Inferna. He wants us to go. You included."

"I can't go to hell. My body can't handle it." The thought had already crossed my mind. How were we supposed to save my father if he was there and we were here?

"Rafael thinks that was because you went before you had matured. He thinks you could handle it now." He cleared his throat. "He also already took a blood sample there to see how it would react."

I made a disapproving sound in my throat. Everyone was always fucking with my blood. I was one big walking, talking science experiment.

"Then what are we waiting for?" I looked amongst them. "If we don't stop her, we're all going to die."

"That's an overly dramatic way of looking at it." Asher finished his beer, and Olly grabbed him another. We all needed the booze after the last two days we'd had.

I looked down at my beer bottle. "What if one of you dies trying to protect me?"

Tobias put his chin on my shoulder. "We know what we signed up for. As guardian angels, it's our job to protect and defend from the darkness."

"And my job as a has-been prince is to keep my people at peace." We all looked over at him. It was the first time he had referred to himself as a prince. "Plus, to protect you."

"I don't know if I can live with myself if one of you..." I choked on my words and squeezed my eyes shut.

"Dani. Our job is to make sure you're safe. We know what might be in store for us. If we weren't willing to make that sacrifice, we wouldn't be here with you." Asher reached across the gap in the chairs and took my free hand.

A tear slid down my cheek, and I wiped it away. No one spoke again for several minutes.

"I let Asher stick it in my ass," Olly said nonchalantly.

My eyes popped open and went wide. Reve choked on his beer and spit it out onto the dirt. A laugh bubbled out of me. It shouldn't have been funny, but Olly's delivery was perfect timing. For a moment, I forgot what I was so sad about.

"Jesus Christ. That was information I didn't need to know." Tobias's chest shook against me as he laughed. "Not that I think there's anything wrong with it."

"You should try it." Olly grinned as Tobias shook his head vigorously. "Come on. I'm sure Reve is willing."

"Reve is not willing." Reve stood and dumped the rest of his beer in the fire. He wasn't that big of a drinker. He looked at Tobias. "Want to finish up your tattoo tonight, since we might be going to hell soon?"

Tobias moved me off his lap. "Let's do it."

"Danica, want a tattoo? I brought all my stuff." Reve looked down at me from next to the fire. The flames behind him made him look scary as fuck, and my heart sped up a little. He looked like he was going to eat me alive.

I scrunched my nose. I had no desire to get stabbed repeatedly by a needle. I didn't know how Tobias could tolerate the pain of repeated tattooing sessions.

We stayed outside a little longer and then went back to my room. It was a tight squeeze having two mattresses on the floor, but with tomorrow being a big fat question mark, we all wanted to be near each other.

I really couldn't explain the desire to be close. It was what it was. Now, it felt even more vital.

Reve set up his tattoo equipment and ink on the kitchen table, and Tobias sat in a chair. He already had most of his tattoo redone, but still needed to have Margie's face tattooed. The process required Reve to go over the same spot several times.

Olly hooked up his gaming system, and he and Asher started

playing some game involving zombies. I was just glad they hadn't put on Fortnite.

"Do you think with everything going on, they're going to lessen our workload?" I pulled one of my notebooks out that was filled with notes. I had to review what I wrote after classes because I tended to mindlessly take notes.

"Probably." Tobias took his shirt off and nodded to the chair opposite him. I moved from my desk to the table with my notebook. "Not that I would know."

"I'm sorry." Guilt twisted in my stomach. I felt partly to blame for his suspension. If it had been any other student, Sue Whittaker wouldn't have come down so harshly on him.

"You don't need to apologize." Tobias winced as Reve started working on his tattoo. "Maybe it's time for a change."

"You can come work for me." Asher somehow managed to pay attention to our conversation and stab a zombie without looking away from the screen.

Tobias grunted and shook his head. "I was thinking of writing a book."

I opened my notebook and looked down at my chicken-scratch handwriting. Half the battle was reading my notes. The teachers talked so fast I had to sacrifice legibility for something that looked like a doctor wrote it.

"A book would take you like what? A week?" I started underlining and circling parts of my notes with a Flair pen. I'd rewrite what was most important.

"I think a book takes a little longer than that to write. What would you write a book about?" Reve didn't take his eyes from the face he was drawing onto Tobias's skin.

"Love. Loss. Friendship. I don't know. It was just an idea. It's not like I'm doing anything else at the moment."

I looked up, and Tobias was watching me. I smiled and put down my pen. "You could be my professional tutor."

"Tutors are paid good money. When I was a kid, my parents paid for tutors since going to school was out of the question." Reve put his tattoo gun down and swapped out the ink.

"There are schools in hell?" I wanted to know so much more about it but had never felt it was the right time to bring it up. "Like here?"

"Similar to here for the most part. Most demons live in villages with demons similar to them. Some don't go to school at all. The more human-like the demon, the more human things they do." Reve started to work again, never glancing up. "It's a little crazy how similar Inferna is to Earth. Well, at least for some things."

"Were you really a prince?" Leave it to Asher to ask the uncomfortable question. We had all been wondering if he was just yanking our chains.

"Yes. I suppose now, I am the king. Not that I would even want that job if I had the chance. I never wanted to be a king." He went back to tattooing.

"What about your siblings?"

"Even if they were willing, the first-born male heir to the throne always develops the gift of visions and a phantom form. The females have no special abilities, not even to produce nightmares. Dream demons have exclusively been the sole demon race on the throne because we can control others to an extent. Having a phantom form also prevents assassinations." He cleared his throat. "That is until Lilith."

Reve finished Tobias's tattoo and wrapped his arm in plastic wrap. The portrait of his family looked even better than it had before.

"Thanks, man. Maybe I will stop giving you so much shit about the Giants and Raiders."

"No problem. I definitely won't stop giving you shit over your teams." Reve put his gear away.

My phone rang, and I flipped it over to see who was calling. Why on earth would Michael be calling me? He never called me, opting to go through Tobias.

"It's Michael." I accepted the call. "Hello?"

"Danica." His voice was serious, not that he had any other tone. "I have some news about your father."

I gripped the table with my free hand and tried not to let the pounding of my heart consume me. Michael was quiet on the other end, waiting for me to respond. "Tell me."

"I was able to have a talk with that demon at Blue Wave. He told me much of the same information he told you." I wished he would get to the point. "Lilith is using the Holy Grail to perform a ritual with your father's blood and weaken the barrier."

"What are we going to do? How long can he...." Live. I didn't let myself speak it out loud. He could live forever, couldn't he? But what if one time she took too much?

"We leave tomorrow at sunrise."

"We?" The others gathered around the table.

"You five. I'll take you there, but then you'll have to go find him. We can't risk Lilith capturing any other original archangels or a large group of angels."

That left me with even more questions, but I was starting to realize that sometimes I didn't need an explanation for every single little thing. Some things were better left without an answer.

I let the phone drop to the table after ending the call and looked up. "I'm going to hell to look for my dad. I'll understand if you don't want to-"

"We're in this together." Tobias took my hand and then pulled me to him. "Stop questioning our devotion to you. We're all still here, aren't we?"

I bit my lip and searched his eyes. It's not that I was insecure, but I still had a hard time believing I had four men in my corner.

"We'll find him." Reve moved behind me and brushed my hair over my shoulder. "Even if it's the last thing we do."

I shut my eyes as he kissed the back of my neck. It's like they knew when I was about to freak out and how to distract me from my thoughts.

"Let's take your mind off things for a bit." Tobias leaned forward and brushed his lips over mine. "I know exactly what will help us have a good night's sleep tonight."

My lips parted as Reve's hands slid around to the clasp on my jeans. Tobias's beard scraped along my jaw, and his lips brushed against my ear. My knees felt like they were about to give out on me.

I moaned as Reve popped the button on my jeans and pulled down the zipper. His hand slid into my jeans and found my clit through my panties. I whimpered.

I opened my eyes just in time to see Olly grab Asher by the belt loops and pull him towards him. He looked over at me and winked.

So this was actually going to happen. The night before we might all die. We were going to finally all have sex. Together. At least I thought that's what was about to happen.

I'd be lying if I said I hadn't done an internet search for how to be with four men at once. The results had left me wishing I would have brought my box of Barbies. You know, to see if it was actually possible.

Tobias grabbed my chin and brought my gaze back to his. He looked at my lips, and then kissed me. It was a kiss that told me to stop overthinking things and let myself go.

Reve was working my pants and panties down my legs while Tobias lifted my shirt over my head and unclasped my bra. I stood before them, baring everything. Four sets of eyes took me in. I shivered with desire, and my nipples tightened.

"Get on the bed." Tobias's voice had dropped a considerable amount. It was the lowest I'd heard it, laced with desire.

I crawled onto the mattress and laid on my back, sitting up slightly on my forearms. "Are you just going to stand there and stare at me or are you going to take your clothes off?" I looked at each of them, and they looked at each other.

I bit my lip and moved my hand down my body and spread my legs. Something about being naked in front of them all made me feel empowered. Like I could take on the world.

"I mean, you don't have to." I slid my hand between my legs. "I think I have my vibrator somewhere."

Clothes went flying, and I laughed at their haste. I wasn't sure what was about to happen, but the wetness and heat between my legs told me it could only work out favorably for me.

Asher was the first to make it to me and kissed me hard before moving his mouth to a nipple. He swirled his tongue around the tight bud and moaned as Olly moved behind him to kiss his shoulders.

I shut my eyes and turned off my brain. I arched into Asher as Olly leaned over him to kiss me. A pair of lips trailed up my leg until they reached the apex and flicked my clit. I wasn't going to last long with four of them touching me at once.

I opened my eyes as the bed dipped, and Tobias laid on the other side of me. He stroked my hair and then ran the back of his hand up and down my side. Goosebumps spread across my skin, and he smirked.

"Want to know something funny?" Tobias's finger drew circles around the nipple that Asher wasn't flicking with his tongue.

I moaned, and my mouth opened in a pant. I didn't think it was the time or place to be talking but nodded my head anyway. It was hard to stay focused on any of them when Reve was swirling his tongue in the most sinful way.

"Olly went to Ikea and bought those little wooden artist dolls. He glued our faces on them and has been showing us different positions."

My laugh morphed into a moan. I moved my hips up to meet Reve's tongue as the pressure continued to build. I heard a bottle open, and then Asher moaned against my skin. Whatever Olly was doing behind him, he was enjoying, if his erection working against my leg was any indication.

Two fingers slid into my pussy as Tobias kissed me. He silenced my cry as my orgasm ripped through my body. Tobias rolled me on top of him and slid into me in one swift movement that made my core clench.

Reve moved to the front of me and stood over Tobias's head. "I hope you enjoy the view down there." He chuckled and moved forward for me to take him in my mouth. His hands went to my hair.

I was so blissed out that my mind wasn't even on the other two. It was hard keeping track of where everyone was when I could barely keep my eyes from closing.

Wet fingers slid between my cheeks, and I slid my mouth off Reve and looked back over my shoulder. Asher had his eyes on my ass as he slid a finger between the cheeks.

I groaned as he probed the tight hole and then slowly worked his finger inside. Olly was behind him doing the same. I raised an eyebrow.

"Don't even say anything, Dani." He shut his eyes for a moment then opened them. "I can't believe I'm about to lose my ass virginity."

I stifled a laugh and turned back to Reve, who was slowly stroking his dick. Asher slid into me, and Tobias grunted a curse under me. I took Reve in my mouth and flicked my tongue over the head.

It took a few minutes to find a rhythm, but soon the sounds that filled the room sent another orgasm crashing through my body. I dug my nails into Reve's ass cheeks, and he thrust deeper into my mouth, nearly hitting the back of my throat.

Asher's thrusts behind me got more erratic, and he bit into my shoulder. I felt like I might float away as my entire body tightened again.

"Fuck," Reve grunted as he came. I swallowed all of him as another orgasm rocketed through me. That seemed to set off a flurry of cursing and grunts as a chain reaction of orgasms rolled through everyone.

Reve moved, and I collapsed forward on Tobias.

"I love you guys." I gasped. Tobias's chest shook as he laughed. "Don't laugh at me."

They could laugh at me all they wanted if they kept giving me orgasms. I just hoped it wasn't the last time I got to experience all of them at once.

After cleaning up, we fell asleep ready for whatever hell was going to throw at us.

CHAPTER 9

DANICA

*W*e were supposed to leave at sunrise, but instead, we were jolted awake as the earth shook. I dove under the table like the well-trained Californian I was. Earthquakes and California went hand in hand. Earthquake drills were the norm in school.

The guys joined me under the table, with Olly looking the most disturbed by what was happening. When we were in Shanghai, the hospital had shaken slightly as the massive demon serpent flew towards it, but this was ten times worse.

This earthquake was much different than what I had experienced before. I wondered if the building was going to collapse. It lasted twice as long as a typical earthquake.

As soon as the shaking stopped, we climbed out from under the table and threw on our clothes. None of us spoke, because what do you say to each other when it's pretty apparent something substantial just happened?

Nothing.

You say nothing.

"It's demons." Reve appeared just before our phones started pinging with messages. He was out of breath and bent over with his hands on his knees.

I had gotten so used to him being invisible that I hadn't even realized he was missing when the earthquake started.

I grabbed my phone off the charger and swiped open the messages. Tobias came to look over my shoulder and then snatched the phone from me.

"Seriously?" I glared at him and tried to take the phone back.

"It's an emergency message from Michael." As if that gave him an excuse to be grabby with my phone. He pushed a few buttons. "A mass amount of demons came through at the same time."

"Through the ground?"

"The ground just happened to get in the way." Reve had finally caught his breath and was pacing while we finished putting on clothes and shoes.

I snatched my phone from Tobias's fingers and looked at the messages. It was a mass push message.

Over a hundred demons have broken through on the Griffith Observatory's grounds. More arrive every few minutes. All capable angels, including academy students, are requested immediately. Weapons will be available upon arrival.

My heart felt like it was coming up through my throat. Had a hole been ripped through the barrier? Was hell about to come to Earth? Were we all going to die?

I tugged on my boots and jumped up once they were on. Four sets of eyes were watching me, then they looked at each other. I knew what they were thinking, and I wasn't about to let them leave without me.

"I'm *not* staying behind this time. What if I can control them? Isn't this the perfect opportunity for me to see what I'm capable of?" I crossed my arms over my chest.

Olly ran his hands over his head. It was a nervous movement I hadn't seen him do before. He looked at the guys again before stepping towards me and taking my hands in his.

"We don't want to-"

I pulled my hands away and backed up a step. "Don't give me that shit. I want to fight."

"You aren't ready, Dani." He made a move to grab my hands again, and I put them in my pockets. "We decided to keep you out of this for as long as possible."

I narrowed my eyes and saw Asher shift from one foot to the other. His unease was definitely warranted in this case. I was tired of being stuck on the fine line between fragile and badass. It was time for me to spread my hypothetical wings and fly.

"Let's just go. She'll get over it," Reve said.

Oh no, he didn't.

"I'm a grown-ass woman. Reve, you will take me." I cringed as I said the words, and saw the hurt on his face but then threw his words back at him. "You'll get over it."

Tobias cleared his throat from where he was watching the exchange between us. "Let's go. Reve. Go ahead and take her like she's requested. I'm sure your bike will get you two there in no time."

Shit, shit, shit.

My jaw dropped a bit as Asher, Tobias, and Olly walked past me and planted kisses on my cheek. They walked quickly out the door, leaving Reve and me in the room.

"What just happened?" I looked at the closed door and then to Reve, who had an amused look on his face.

"I certainly will take you." He pulled his keys out of his pocket. "We should get going, it will take us almost an hour to get there."

I followed him downstairs and out of the building, where angels were taking off in groups. Reve couldn't fly with me. It had been an oversight on my part. A foolish one.

Reve walked in front of me as we made our way to the parking lot. There was no way in hell I was going to sit for almost an hour on his crotch rocket. We were supposed to stick together. Save the light from the dark and all that bull shit.

How could we if I wasn't even included?

Before I could question my sanity, and before Reve realized the wheels in my mind were spinning, I turned and ran towards the student dorm buildings.

Someone would take me. Even if I had to beg and offer them my first-born child or my car, I'd get someone to fly me to hell on Earth.

I heard Reve shout my name, but I was already closing in on the large clusters of students readying to take off from between the dorm buildings.

Spotting Ethan and Cora, I plowed through a few groups and nearly ran straight into them in my haste.

"Let's go now!" I looked over my shoulder and saw all the students I had just moved through part like the Red Sea for Reve.

Ethan's eyes widened, and he looked at Cora for direction. See, that's what the men were supposed to do; look to the woman for direction.

"You heard the lady! Let's go." Cora's wings snapped out with Ethan's following quickly behind.

Ethan grabbed me around the waist, and we shot into the sky. I was getting used to flying, finally, but still couldn't keep my eyes open. I'd rather not see how far my potential death lay.

We landed in a large parking lot. It was chaos as angels dashed around in search of weapons, which were piled on the asphalt. I managed to find a sword that was lightweight, and we ran towards the mayhem.

The noise level intensified as we got closer to the actual observatory, or what was left of it. I had only seen it once on a field trip and remembered how amazing the building was.

Now, it was starting to look like a pile of rubble.

Angels were carrying other angels back towards the parking lot, while others flew past us right into the melee. My ears were ringing as screams and shrieks pierced them.

Several fires were spread out on the lawn, bonfire style. The smell made bile rise in my throat.

"Holy shit." Cora seemed to be frozen in place as her mind processed the scene before her.

I wanted to be frozen too, but a demon that looked like a science experiment gone wrong was headed straight for us.

Practicing with each other and on practice dummies was nothing compared to having a horse-sized demon that had the head of some kind of bird and the body of a dog, come barreling towards you. I certainly wasn't going to stay standing in its way. I grabbed Cora's arm and pulled her with me out of its path.

It was headed towards the parking lot, but just before it reached where the grass and cement met, two knives landed in its throat, sending it falling onto its side. Betty landed next to it and stabbed it in its heart before another angel came along to take its head.

She retrieved her bloody knives and then shot back into the sky. I still didn't like her much, but that was a badass move she had just pulled.

"Where'd Ethan go?" Cora looked around frantically as we stayed glued to each other's sides.

We were out of our element. Coming here was a stupid idea. The amount of capability we had in us was about the size of our pinkies. At least that was the case when things were so crazy all around us.

Had there just been one demon, we would have been fine.

There were hundreds.

I needed to find my angels. I might not have known what the hell I was doing, but they'd help guide me. Or at least have my back.

A gremlin-looking creature seemed to come out of nowhere and attached itself to my boot. Thank fuck for knee-high boots because the little bugger couldn't bite through the leather, despite his best efforts.

Cora kicked him off and then brought her sword down on him, slicing him in two. Green goop coated her sword, and it suddenly smelled like cotton candy.

I couldn't resist the urge to take in the sweet scent and breathed in deeply. The world suddenly became much more vibrant and seemed to streak with rainbow colors. I looked over at Cora, who had dropped her sword and was examining her hand in fascination.

She had such gorgeous hair. It looked like a unicorn had painted it with all the colors of the rainbow. I dropped my sword and reached out my hand to pet it. It was so soft, like the fur of a chinchilla.

How did I even know what the fur of a chinchilla felt like?

"You're so pretty, Cora."

She touched my hair and nodded, her eyes glazed over and shiny in the light coming from the moon and fires. "No. You're the pretty one, Danica. You have four boyfriends. Four!" She burst into giggles, and so did I.

We wrapped our arms around each other in a hug.

"Fuck! You spilled its blood!" There Ethan was. Cora's face lit up like a Christmas tree. Really, like an actual Christmas tree.

Ethan rushed over to us and picked up my sword. He grabbed us and tried to pull us away from the cotton candy scent that made everything so lovely.

"No, Big E." Cora twisted out of his grasp and linked her arm with mine. "It's so perfectly lovely right here. Dani, I think you should leave your four boyfriends, and we can go get married."

I giggled, and both of us burst into laughter again. In the back of my mind, I knew that this wasn't the time or place to laugh like two cackling hyenas. I felt so free. So alive.

"You killed a Dulcis Fiend!" Cora cocked her head as Ethan chastised us. I didn't know what the hell he was talking about. "Oh my God, we need to move now!"

I didn't know what all the fuss was over. I was perfectly content where I was. We struggled with Ethan as he attempted to push us away from the really gross-looking animal on the ground. Where had that come from?

"Dulcis Fiends?" Cora shook her head and rubbed her eyes. "I killed... oh! Oh, my God!"

I glanced where her eyes were glued. I didn't see what the big deal was. They were kind of cute. There were about ten headed straight towards us.

Cora picked up her sword and pushed me behind her. "Damn it. Is this all of them?"

"How much did she inhale?" Just as the question left Ethan's lips, the demons made it to us and spread in a semi-circle.

Cora had a tight grip on my arm because I tried to walk forward to pet one. They looked like little old green grandpas. They were adorable.

"We have to burn them!" Ethan shouted as the sounds around us escalated. "Fuck!"

One of the demons was on Ethan's leg. He started shaking his leg to get it off. Just when it went flying, another one lunged for him.

"What's happening?" My mind was foggy, and I looked around. "What in the fresh hell are these things?"

I grabbed my sword out of Ethan's hand.

"Don't kill them with a sword!" Cora was attempting to get two off Ethan's leg.

"Hey!" I shouted. "Get off him!"

Ten sets of beady little eyes turned to look at me. My eyes went wide, and I backed up a step. This was like the scene out of Jurassic Park when the Dilophosaurus stares at the nerdy guy right before it kills his ass.

"Send them home," Reve said from next to me.

"Go home!" They hesitated for only a moment before they ran towards the observatory.

"Fuck, my leg." Ethan was now on the ground holding his leg. "It's not healing. Why isn't it healing?"

He was panicking. Two angels jogged over to us and picked him up. Cora looked torn between going with him and staying with me. Hell, I wanted to go with her.

"Go, I'll be fine."

Would I be fine? Would Ethan be fine?

She gave my arm a squeeze and then ran after the angels and Ethan towards the parking lot.

"Let's go." I looked in the direction of Reve's voice. He was pissed. "Now."

"But I can help! You saw me! I can send them home!" I turned back towards the observatory.

"Danica." His hand wrapped around my arm. "You think you're helping? You just signed Ethan's death certificate. Now, let's go before-"

"What do you mean I signed his death certificate?" I turned to where I knew he was. His hand was still on my arm.

"Dulcis Fiends have venom that is so potent that one drop of it can kill two thousand people."

"He'll be fine. The healers will take care of it." Reve didn't reply, and I bit my lip to stop from bursting into tears. "Let me go, Reve."

Reve's hand disappeared, and I turned and ran towards the first demon I spotted. I told him to go home. He ran in the same direction I had seen the others run. This would work. I could send them all back to where they came from.

Things became a blur then. I had to clamp down on my fear every time I got close to a demon.

I had sent at least ten back when my command didn't work. The demon was humanoid and killed another angel right in front of me.

"What was that, little girl?" He cocked his head to the side and then lunged for me, grabbing me around the neck.

I felt my throat being squeezed as he lifted me off the ground and then threw me. A body caught my fall, and we landed in a heap.

The demon stalked towards me again, a murderous look in his eyes. Why hadn't my command worked?

"Go home! Kill yourself!" I sounded desperate. Was this it? Was I about to die because I was stubborn?

The body under me shifted and jumped to his feet. I looked up to see Reve. He grabbed two knives from somewhere on his body and met the demon head-on.

They were a blur of motion as they fought. I scrambled back a little farther, and then a head rolled towards me.

I shut my eyes, and for the first time in forever, I said a little prayer to the man upstairs to not let it be Reve.

Arms lifted me, and my eyes snapped open. Reve looked back at me. I was shaking and felt the overwhelming urge to cry.

Things hadn't processed up until that point. I slowly turned my head and looked around. There were so many bodies in the grass that the grass was no longer green. It was painted a dark brown color with both angel blood and demon blood mixing.

"We need to go, Danica. I know you want to help, but this is why we didn't want you here."

My eyes were drawn to a spot near the Astronomers Monument. Or at least what was left of it. The ground and air were rippling.

"Do you see that?" I pointed and stepped around Reve, heading towards it.

"See what?"

As I got closer, I could feel the change in the air. It was warmer and smelled like the inside of a drawer that hadn't been opened in years.

I was about ten feet away when several demons came out of it and ran straight towards us. I raised my sword, but before I could get a swing in, Asher, Olly, and Tobias landed in front of us and killed the demons.

"How the fuck did she get here?" Asher moved towards Reve with a murderous look on his face. "We had a plan."

"She ran." Reve ghosted just before Asher got to him.

He turned towards me. "Let's go."

Olly and Tobias were fighting off another few demons that just came through the ripple.

"Is that a present?" Asher let go of my hand that he had just taken and approached a beautifully wrapped box near one of the beheaded demons. "Jesus. It has your name on it, Dani."

I stepped up beside him and looked at it. I squatted down and then snatched it from the ground. Asher made a noise, and I looked over at him.

"How do you know it's not a bomb?" I rolled my eyes at his question and ran a thumb over the name tag.

It was my father's handwriting, I was sure of it. I ripped it open and dropped the box as my fingers clasped the watch that was inside. It was one of his favorites that he always wore.

He was probably wearing it the night he was taken.

I gripped it in my hand, and before Asher could grab me, I darted towards the rippling that was growing smaller.

When I had first spotted it, it had been the size of a garage door. Now it was no bigger than a regular door.

"Dani, no!" Olly jumped in front of me, right before I got to the doorway.

He pushed me backwards as arms came from the ripple, grabbed him, and pulled him back into it.

He vanished, and a loud pop shook the ground as the ripples seemed to close in on themselves.

I fell to the ground where it had been and ran my hands over the grass frantically. It had just been here. Where had it gone?

"Olly?" Asher yelled. He was standing in front of me and turned around in a circle with a confused look on his face. "Where the fuck did he go?"

"It was... I think it was where the demons were getting through." I grabbed grass in my hands and ripped it from the soil. "Fuck!"

"What do you mean?" Asher knelt next to me. "Is he..." He grabbed me by the arms and made me look at him. "Where is he?"

"He was pulled into Inferna." Reve appeared and bent down to pick up my father's watch I had dropped. "You two get back to the academy. Tobias and I will find Michael."

My eyes stung, and I wiped at them with my forearm. I just kept fucking things up. I should have been the one pulled into Inferna, not Olly. It had all happened so fast.

The fighting seemed to be winding down as Asher silently scooped me into his arms. He was staring straight ahead, unblinking. I put my head against his shoulder as we shot into the sky.

CHAPTER 10

DANICA

We landed back on campus in the empty parking lot next to our building. It was deafeningly quiet, especially compared to all the noises of fighting.

My stomach rolled, and I bent over with my hands on my knees. Asher put his hand in the center of my back and stood silent next to me. I dry heaved a few times and let the tears fall to the asphalt.

Ethan might be dead. Olly might be dead. It was all my fault.

Asher grabbed my elbow and pulled me up from being hunched over. He cupped my cheek with worry in his eyes and then headed for the door without a word.

I wanted to speak but didn't know the words to say.

I needed to be strong. I needed to hold myself together.

We got back to my room, our room, and I sat down on one of the mattresses on the floor. My resolve to stay strong was crumbling quickly as I watched Asher grab his bottle of whiskey. He took a very long drink from it and stood still, the bottle gripped in his hand.

I pulled my knees to my chest. I needed to say something. Do something.

Before I came into their lives, they had normal problems to deal with. Now, it seemed every time I turned around, I was causing another catastrophic problem.

I bet my dad wished he would have just let me fail at life. Now the entire angel population of Los Angeles was risking their second lives because I had been too eager to be away from the academy.

Reaching into my pocket, I pulled out my dad's watch. I rubbed my thumb over the face of it. It wasn't even working anymore. I set it on my knee and stared at it.

"Asher-"

"Fuck!" He hurled the bottle across the room. The thick glass of the bottle fell with a hard clunk to the floor.

I flinched, the watch falling off my knee and onto the mattress.

Asher went into the bathroom, slamming the door behind him. I heard the shower turning on and got up off the mattress to pick up the bottle that was lying on its side. With shaking hands, I put it upright on the table. A small puddle of whiskey lay on the hardwood.

I pulled my shirt over my head and mopped up the mess. I grabbed the bottle, walked to the sink in the kitchenette, and dumped the rest of the liquid down the drain.

I swiped at my face, wiping the tears that had fallen without me even realizing it, from my cheeks. I was so tired. Not just from lack of sleep, but life.

Looking at the room, I took in the mess that was my life now. Duffel bags lined a wall with clothes spilling out of them. The two mattresses lay in the center of the room, taking up most of the floor space. The sheets and blankets were crumpled and tangled.

I walked towards the bathroom, unhooking my bra and letting it fall to the floor. What was another piece of clothing left lying in the middle of the room? I didn't care. None of us seemed to care much for cleanliness these days.

After I pulled off my boots and jeans and left them by the bathroom door, I stepped inside. The door had at least been left unlocked.

I shut the door gently behind me and pulled the shower curtain open a bit. Asher was standing with his head bent, his arms leaning against the shower wall. His shoulders shook, and choked sobs escaped his mouth.

"Ash," I whispered, letting him know I was behind him.

I gulped back my own tears and stepped into the shower. Asher didn't move or look in my direction. I placed a hand in the middle of his back and put my chin on his shoulder.

He took several deep inhales and exhales. "We have to get him back, Dani."

"It's my fault. I didn't listen." I put my cheek against his back and wrapped my arms around him. "I'm always fucking up."

Asher didn't say anything as we stood there. He moved one of his hands to cover mine.

"When this is all over, I'll understand if you and the others want to-"

"Don't." He shook his head and then turned, so my head was on his chest. "None of this is your fault. You did what any of us would have done."

"But-"

"But nothing, Dani." He rubbed my back in small circles. "Olly has this theory that everything that happens is fated to happen."

I looked up at him. His eyes were blood-shot, and sadness was evident on his face, but his lips quirked a bit as he spoke about Olly.

"He thinks the cup is sentient, and it's pissed that the world is going to shit." He laughed a little. "Like it's seeking vengeance or something. I think it's a load of crap."

If Olly thought the cup had a mind of its own, maybe it did. When I had stolen it for Lilith, it had seemed to be egging me on, daring me to take it. It could have just all been in my imagination.

"It's not that hard to believe that an inanimate object might be alive or something. There are demons, and hell is some sort of parallel realm. Plus, Reve is the rightful king of hell." A giggle burst out of me. It was crazy hearing it out loud. "You don't think he'll make us bow to him, do you?"

Asher kissed my forehead. "I'd like to see him try to make us. I'll make him kiss my left nut before I ever bow to his ass."

"Why the left one?" I looked down at the nuts in question. They both looked the same to me. "Is it the inferior nut?"

"The right is only for you." He kissed me gently and then grabbed the loofah and body wash.

We stayed in the shower for several more minutes before climbing out. Reve was sitting on the counter.

"Michael is here." He lifted his chin towards a stack of clothes on the closed toilet seat. "Figured since he already saw your bra and panties lying around, we shouldn't make him feel even more awkward."

"How long have you been sitting there? Is Toby all right?" Asher dried off and grabbed his jeans.

"He's fine." He hopped off the counter. "How do you know I haven't already kissed *both* your nuts? All those hands and mouths. The passion."

Asher paused in the middle of pulling on a tee-shirt. Reve grinned and then disappeared.

"Can you believe that fucker?" Asher finished pulling on his shirt and watched me as I got dressed.

"He's just trying to provoke you." They were all getting along better with Reve, but things still weren't perfect. Especially since Reve purposely said off the wall things to them.

I took a deep breath and then opened the bathroom door. It was time to deal with reality.

Michael and Tobias were sitting at the table. Both looked exhausted and a little worse for wear. Asher and I sat down in the other two chairs. Reve was sitting on the counter. That seemed to be his seat of choice.

"Is Ethan okay?" I looked at Tobias, who had a grim look on his face. He shook his head in the smallest of movements. "He's... he died?"

Michael sighed. "He no longer has his human form. A soul can only return to it once. He's with all the other souls."

My heart ripped in two. I didn't know how much more death I could handle. My heart hurt for Cora.

"A guardian angel knows the risks they sign up for when they make the decision to come back to Earth." Michael seemed to read my mind and gave me a sympathetic look. His words did nothing to ease the pain of losing a friend.

My gaze fell to my dad's watch that sat in front of Michael. I went to grab it, and he stopped me.

"It's a message. The date on it is set for two weeks from now." He rubbed his hands over his face and then picked up the watch. "But that was before Oliver got pulled through."

"What does Olly have to do with the date on the watch?" Asher leaned forward on his arms.

"If Lilith figures out that it's not just Lucifer's blood that can create a gate, so to speak, but any archangel..." He took a sharp inhale of breath. "It's probably more like a week."

"Wait. What?" I snatched the watch before he could stop me again and put it on my wrist.

"The whole concept of hell as a punishment for darkened souls was meant to be shared among the archangels. That was until Lucifer made one too many mistakes." Michael sat back in his chair. "Once we have him back with us, some things are going to change. They're going to be how they should have been all along."

"What if we can't save him before..." I choked on my words, and Reve came behind me and put his hands on my shoulders.

Michael was quiet for a few moments before he spoke. "Let's not think about that. You will. Archangels can never die, but grave injuries can take years to heal. The longest I've been down is two years."

My eyes went wide.

"Partial decapitation." His words were not helping at all. If anything, they made my anxiety over my dad and Olly being at the mercy of a deranged madwoman worse.

"So, what do we do now?" I cleared my throat and looked up at the four men staring back at me.

"We go to hell. They are expecting us."

Of course there was a welcoming party waiting for us.

~

I F MY FATHER had the choice, it would have been for me to never visit hell.

My visit when I was nine years old, wasn't because he *wanted* me in hell with him. What father would want his daughter to go to hell?

I had begged and begged for him to take me. I had an intense curiosity and didn't care if it was literal hell. Plus, when it's Christmas Eve, it's hard to say no to your nine-year-old.

I had been excited to finally see where my dad disappeared to all the time. As soon as my feet hit the ground in the foyer, a wave of pain washed over me. It had felt like my skin was being ripped off. Then I vomited all over my dad's expensive suit.

Needless to say, I didn't see much of hell.

As we stood in the backyard of my house in Montecito, I wondered why my dad never tried to take me again. Was it because I had gotten sick? Was it because he had a wife and a houseful of little demon angel babies running around?

We all held hands like we were about to go on a field trip some-where. There was popping in my ears, and then we were standing in a courtyard of what looked like a medieval manor.

My house was lined up directly with where Lucifer stayed in hell.

The sound of water trickling in a fountain nearby and birds chirping greeted us. Right along with the smell of a distant burning fire.

I looked around, taking in the large outdoor area we were in. Everything seemed darker here. Dark stones, dark sky, dark trees. There was at least a large moon to give some light to the landscape.

I squinted in the direction of the trees. "Are those birds?"

"Don't look at them! They will attack you." Reve stepped in front of me. "Let's just all not look at or touch anything."

"So, just assume everything is going to kill us?" Tobias took a step towards the fountain. "Jesus Christ, is this blood?"

"It's water. There are algae in the water here that turns it red. It's safe to drink." While I trusted Reve, I wasn't too keen on drinking water that looked like freshly spilled blood.

A man stepped into the courtyard from an outdoor hallway. He came to a stop in front of Michael and bowed his head. "Archangel Michael. It is lovely to see you again. Are these the guests you spoke of?"

"They are. I trust that you have prepared for them?" Michael was all business. I wondered if he ever let his hair down and had a laugh.

"Indeed, we have."

The man looked up, and I had to bite my lip to stop a gasp from escaping. His eyes were almost entirely black, but other than that tiny little detail, he appeared human. His eyes landed on me first.

He took a step forward and held out his hand. I looked at Michael with raised eyebrows, and he nodded. The man took my hand and clasped it in between both of his.

"Not many know of your existence. It is an honor to meet you." He let my hand go, and then he spotted Reve. His eyes went wide, and he opened and shut his mouth like he was going to say something, but couldn't quite get the words out.

"Alex. It is good to see you again." Reve stuck out his hand, but instead of taking it, Alex dropped to a knee.

"We did not think you would ever return, my king."

Tobias snorted, and Alex looked up and narrowed his eyes as if he was offended at the noise.

"Please stand. There's no need for formalities." Reve shifted uncomfortably and looked at me.

I just smiled. What else was I supposed to do? Information overload was a thing, and I was currently experiencing it.

A loud crack of thunder sounded in the distance, and Asher grabbed onto Tobias's arm. I was worried about what this was going to do to him. I didn't want my need for him to be at the detriment of what sanity he had regained. Without Olly around to soothe him, it was going to take all of us to help him hold it together.

He had refused to stay behind. I couldn't blame him.

"Let's get you inside and settled. We have many things to discuss." Alex rose from the ground and turned on his heel.

"Is he a servant?" Tobias whispered to Reve.

Michael cleared his throat. "Alex is an Incubi demon. He is currently in charge of our part of Inferna in Lucifer's absence."

Incubi demons feed off of having sex and the sexual desire they create. I looked at Alex with entirely different eyes now. Sometimes I wondered if I was the female version, a Succubus. I seemed to really like sex.

"What kind of demon is Lilith?" I wondered aloud.

We followed Alex through two massive iron doors and into a large living room. It looked unused. I doubt the devil ever had company. But maybe he did. I mean, how much did I *really* know about my dad? Would I ever get to know him?

"She doesn't have a classification. She slowly evolved into whatever she is. She was human at first." Alex stopped and turned towards us.

I stopped in front of the giant black stone fireplace and looked at my pictures lining the mantle. I had only just started to really get to know my dad. I blinked back tears as I felt a hand on my lower back.

"You were a cute kid." Asher pulled me towards him. "What happened?"

I spun and smacked his chest. "Thanks."

"I will show you to your rooms now."

Alex put us in two rooms that adjoined with a Jack and Jill bathroom. He said he would send for us in an hour.

I plopped down on the large four-poster bed and pulled off my boots. I needed a nap, especially if we were going to be traipsing through hell looking for my dad.

"Why does he even have a house like this?" I laid back and moved my arms like I was making a snow angel. It was the softest material I had ever felt. "Seems a bit excessive for just one man. Our house in Montecito isn't even *this* big, and it's pretty big."

"It's a symbol of his status." Reve walked to the velvet-covered windows and pulled the curtains back. The sky was a dark shade of blue, like it couldn't make up its mind if it were night or day.

"Didn't you mention a castle?" Asher was looking through drawers. He was antsy, and I couldn't blame him.

"I did. It's much bigger than this place." He left the drapes open and moved towards the bed. "There's a storm coming. We'll have to wait until it passes to make our way towards where Lilith has your father."

I moved up to the pillow and shut my eyes. Reve settled in next to me and pulled me against him.

"How'd my dad save you?" I ran my fingers along his arm. He made a noise in his throat. "You said you locked yourself in your castle's dungeons."

"I did." He cleared his throat, and Tobias and Asher sat on the edge of the bed. "My powers were useless against her, and I still hadn't developed my phantom form yet. She sent me to kill him."

I stopped moving my hand and gripped his forearm.

"Clearly, I didn't succeed. Your father is strong. I don't think Lilith realized just how strong he is. He was going to kill me until Alex told him I was royalty. He gave me a drop of his blood, which broke whatever hold Lilith held over me and then took me to Earth. He saved me."

We lay in silence for several minutes before I let out a frustrated grunt and sat up. "Let's explore."

I felt like a little kid as we creeped out of the room and down the hall to the first door we came to. It was just another guest room. Most rooms off the hallway we were in were guest rooms with large four-poster beds.

"Did he ever have visitors?" I just assumed he existed a lonely life in hell. "He didn't have any friends on Earth."

"I'm not sure."

I crossed over into another wing of the house and opened the first door. It was a library. Finally, something other than beds.

Books lined the walls, and chairs were scattered throughout the room that was double the size of the large bedrooms. I walked over to an armchair that had a large book sitting on it.

"Widows?" I grabbed the book and flipped through it, stopping on a picture of a large group of women.

They looked human, but on the next page was a close up of one of them. Her eyes were nearly black, and her skin looked like it had spiders crawling under the surface. I scrunched my nose and goose-bumps broke out across my skin. I hated spiders.

Reve grabbed the book and let out a small laugh. "Widows are the definition of female empowerment. They kill men that wrong women. I was actually surprised there was one in that mall the first time demons got through. They usually stick to themselves."

"There are only women Widows?" I made my way across the room to a shelf and scanned the titles. It seemed each type of demon had a book. Who had written all of them?

"Yes. Well, no. There are men, but they always wrong the women in some way and end up dead. They are a dwindling population... or at least they were the last I heard."

We set off down the hall and found where my father kept his watches. It was rather loud inside, with all the ticking.

"You know what this reminds me of?" Asher ran his finger along the top of a case. It looked like a jewelry store in the room. "That movie, *Hook*, where Captain Hook keeps all the clocks."

I slid the watch from my wrist and placed it in an empty slot in a case. Tobias put his arm around me and tucked me against him.

"I think I'm ready for a nap now." I leaned against Tobias.

What if we couldn't find him or get him back? I wasn't ready to lose my dad.

CHAPTER 11

REVE

*W*atching Danica try to hold herself together was painful. She put on a brave face, but we all saw through it. She was scared shitless.

We all were.

After she was asleep, we made our way downstairs. Michael had wanted to meet with us to come up with a plan. I didn't know how much of a plan was needed.

"Alex is preparing supplies for your journey. He says you won't be able to leave until after the storm passes." Michael laid out a paper map in front of us. I didn't want to tell him that we didn't need it because I knew exactly where we were headed.

"So the plan is to walk to this castle where they are keeping Olly and Lucifer, break in, and take them back? That seems a little too easy." Asher sounded skeptical as he looked at the map. He traced his finger over the path that was drawn from where we were located to the castle.

"Reve will do most of the breaking in. He knows the castle well."

I grunted. There was a secret entrance I could get us through, although Lilith might have changed the place in the centuries I had been gone.

"Lilith needs to be taken out." Michael looked at each of us. "At all costs. Can you handle that burden?"

"Do you mean..." Tobias stood up straight and crossed his arms. "I thought our job was to protect Danica."

"Yes." Michael looked sad. "I know you are willing to risk your own lives, but sometimes protecting the ones you love means letting them go."

"Fuck." Asher put his face in his hands. "She should be part of this conversation."

It was quiet for several minutes. Danica should have been here, but I was grateful she wasn't. She didn't need to know we were discussing killing her mother and the possibility of one or all of us dying in the process.

Or the possibility that she might die too.

"She'd go to Heaven. Right?" I looked at Michael, who now wore an impassive expression.

"Yes." His expression was grim, and he looked at Tobias. "It will be similar to dying in war. She'll remember that she fought in one, but not the specifics."

Tobias sat down in a chair and looked at Asher. "So, she won't remember us?"

"It's hard to say how much will be blocked from her memory. I'm not privy to that information."

We couldn't let her die.

~

MORNING CAME TOO QUICKLY. We made our way downstairs to the dining room for breakfast. This might be the last regular meal we'd get for a while.

Food in Inferna was similar to Earth, except the animals and plants were a bit different. Several servants brought out our food and drinks.

"Your Highness, if the food and beverages are not to your liking, we can get you something else." A servant placed a plate with eggs, bacon, and toast in front of me.

I didn't need to eat, but it was something to occupy my time and to feel more a part of the group. Danica was already devouring her eggs.

"Good?" I took a bite of bacon.

Everything here had richer flavors. It might be home to demons, but they took care of the land and its resources.

"It's delicious. There are chickens here?"

"They are similar to chickens." I wasn't about to tell her they had ten eyes and ate the males.

Inferna was savage like that.

But the bacon was top notch.

"Your Highness, would you like more bacon?" I looked up at the servant, and she bowed deeply.

"I'm fine. Thank you."

"Your Highness." Asher set his fork down and took a drink of his coffee. "I just don't see it. Toby is more kingly than you."

Danica sniggered and hit Asher's arm. "He's kingly in the bedroom."

"So, what you're saying is that he's a better lay than us?"

Danica nearly choked on her juice. "You are all kingly in the bedroom."

"There is only one king. Asher is more of a princess." I smirked.

Tobias cleared his throat. "Are you planning on reclaiming your throne?"

I picked at my eggs. If we were able to take care of Lilith, the throne would be up for grabs. Did I want it? I couldn't see myself staying in Inferna where the sun never shines, and the air always smells faintly of burning wood.

"I've been on Earth for so long because I never wanted the throne to begin with." I set my fork down. "I might have to settle things, but I plan on returning to Earth. That's where my home is."

After breakfast, we gathered the packs Alex prepared for us and headed out to where a carriage was waiting for us. It was too risky to fly and way too risky to take air transport. Lilith would see us coming from a mile away.

We climbed into the horse-drawn carriage, settling in for the first part of our journey. The carriage would take us to the edge of the Black Forest, and then we would go the rest of the way on foot.

As soon as we started rolling along the dirt path, I solidified.

"What if we get there and she controls you again?" Danica was peeking out the window. She looked in awe of what she was seeing, which was a whole lot of dark landscape.

"It will be more difficult for her here. She could do it before because I was young. In Shanghai, she could because I am weaker on Earth."

I had kept many things from them. Including the fact that Lucifer had offered to help me get my throne back, and I had opted to live on Earth.

"What can you do now that we're here?" Tobias had been quiet since we left Earth. I could tell he was worried.

"At the height of my father's power, he could cause visions in entire villages. Lilith used me to do the same, but on a much smaller scale since I was still developing my skills."

"Can you give Lilith visions and dreams?" Danica looked at me and frowned. "If so, you should give her a vision of me cutting off each finger one by one and then shoving it down her throat."

My eyes widened at the violence in her voice. Surely she was joking. I shook my head in response. Lilith's brain was utterly inaccessible to me. Whatever kind of demon she had evolved into over the centuries was a strong one.

She would have to be if she was able to get back and forth to Earth. I thought only archangels were capable of such feats. That and a dose of dark magic and angel blood.

We fell into a comfortable silence. The first leg of our journey would be smooth. This part of Inferna wasn't very populated, which was why the angels had set up their prison of souls here.

The carriage came to a stop after several hours. I went to my phantom form before the door was opened. Lilith probably thought I was dead, and I intended to keep it that way.

We climbed out, and Asher, Tobias, and Danica took their packs from the demon that had driven the carriage.

We walked through the Black Forest at a snail's pace. Any faster and we would attract attention. The Black Forest lived up to its name. The trees were black, and the low light that was ever-present in Inferna made everything look dark blue.

It looked like it should be freezing, but the temperature was warm. At night, the air became chilly, which was the only way to distinguish night from day.

It was approaching nightfall when a pack of creatures came at us from the side. I sent a vision at them, but they continued forward. They relied on their other senses instead of sight.

"What the fuck are they?" Asher had ahold of Danica's hand and let it go to unsheathe his sword.

All of the creatures' heads turned in his direction at the sound.

"They're like zombies." They weren't exactly zombies. You couldn't turn into one from a bite, but they did enjoy feasting on the flesh.

"Can I try to get them to go away?" Danica looked to Tobias.

I don't know why she was asking permission all of a sudden. She tended to do what she wanted. Not that I could blame her. Tobias nodded.

"Leave us alone."

They stopped and then turned around and headed back the way they had come. It was an amazing thing to watch but it made me shudder.

We continued on. About an hour later, we came to a small group of tents surrounding a campfire. If demons had set up camp, they were most likely humanoid.

"Stay here." I didn't know if whoever was living in the woods were friend or foe. My family had a lot of pull in Inferna, but there were a lot of demons that hated our power.

The campsite was occupied but whoever was living there wasn't there at the moment. I turned back towards the group and froze. They were walking towards me with their hands in the air and a group of about ten men behind them.

"Let us go." Danica was attempting to control them. From this far away, they looked humanoid, which seemed to be harder for her to control since demons that took human-like forms usually had much more complicated brains.

"They don't smell right," one of the men said.

I floated around the group. I breathed a sigh of relief that they were shifters. I could deal with shifters.

I landed in front of them and revealed myself.

"Holy shit. Is that-"

"It can't be."

"Wait until-"

They all started talking at once, and Asher, Tobias, and Danica darted behind me while they were distracted.

"Enough!" I yelled.

They fell silent but kept their knives and clubs raised. None of them looked familiar.

"Are you back to save us from Lilith?" One of the men took a step forward, and one of his buddies put out his arm and stopped him from getting any closer.

"Something like that."

"Please join us tonight. It would be an honor to host you and your party," one of the men offered with a slight bow of his head.

I looked over the men and decided they seemed sane enough. Shifters struggled to hold back their emotions, so if they meant to harm us, they would have already.

We set up our own tent next to theirs and gathered around the campfire. They had just been out hunting when they came across us.

"You don't live in your village?" I asked as I watched Danica bite into the leg of the boar they had killed. She let out a small, satisfied groan.

"She kicked us out centuries ago. Instead, demons who do her bidding live there. Anytime we set up somewhere new, she takes that from us too. Many packs moved North."

Leaves crunched behind us, drawing everyone's attention. The shifters sniffed the air and then went back to eating and drinking. Someone was coming, but they didn't seem to think it was a threat.

"Reve?" The feet stopped behind us.

I stood and turned to look. I'd recognize Alaric's voice anywhere. He was just as I remembered. Short dark hair, scruff on his face, shockingly green eyes. The eyes of an alpha.

The eyes of the man who was supposed to be my guard.

I walked towards him and stopped before him. My heart wanted to leap out of my chest, and I swallowed down the lump that had worked its way into my throat.

Then I punched him.

"REVE?" Danica unzipped the tent and crawled inside.

She laid next to me on her side and reached for my bruised hand. She ran her fingers across the knuckles.

I turned my head and looked at her. "He was supposed to protect me. Instead, he ran."

"He would have died." She brought my knuckles to her lips and kissed them. They would heal all the way soon.

I shut my eyes. "I thought I was over it. I guess I was wrong."

"Did he really have a choice? I mean, he would have been killed."

I looked back at the top of the tent and sighed. She was right. Of course she was right. But Alaric had taken a vow to protect me until his last breath. Running from his own last breath didn't exactly show his loyalty.

"He was your best friend, right?" I grumbled my response. "You haven't seen him in practically forever. He could help us."

"I don't trust him."

"I didn't say you had to trust him." She kissed me lightly on the lips and stood.

I followed her out of the tent and sat next to her and Asher around the fire. It was starting to get cooler, and the warmth felt nice.

I looked at Alaric across the fire, and he stared back at me with a bruised cheek. He hadn't dared to take a swing back at me, although I had seen the desire to strike me back in his eyes.

He stood and sat on the ground in front of us, his back to the fire.

"I'm sorry. I was young and scared and-" A small squeaking noise interrupted him, and he looked down at the pocket of his jacket.

The tiniest head poked out.

"What's his name?" Danica leaned forward to get a better look at the monkey. If it could even be considered one. It could fit in the palm of Alaric's hand.

"Picard Rupert Ferdinand the Fifth."

"That's a fucked-up name for a tiny little pipsqueak." Asher snorted and reached his hand out to pet the little guy. "Ow! Fuck!"

Asher shook his hand and examined the small bite.

"He doesn't like being called names." Alaric held the monkey in his palm and stroked the top of his head. "Isn't that right, Picard?"

The monkey rubbed its little head, which was no bigger than a golf ball, into his finger. It made a tiny squeaking noise as if it were talking to him.

"I thought those things hated wolves."

I watched as it jumped off his hand and scurried across the fallen leaves to my pant leg. It scampered up and sat on my thigh, looking at me with a cocked head and glossy eyes. I held out my hand, and it climbed onto it and then curled into the tiniest ball. It was the cutest thing I'd ever seen.

"I'm not most wolves."

"Wait. You turn into a wolf?" Asher was leaning forward with his forearms on his knees. "There are vampires *and* werewolves? I'll be damned."

"Don't mention those bloodsuckers in the same sentence as wolves." He let out a growl. "But, yes. All of us turn into something. Some of us are wolves. Foxes. A squirrel."

He gestured to the other men.

"How does that work? Being a squirrel shifter? Is your monkey a shifter too?" Danica was fascinated with the new information. I could see the wonder in her eyes.

"We recognize each other as pack. Picard is not a shifter. He is the last of his kind, unfortunately."

The conversation died down after a bit, and Danica stifled a yawn.

I could tell she wanted to stay awake and learn more about this realm, but we all needed to recharge for what lay ahead.

We made our way to the tent, and the three situated themselves in the sleeping bags.

I first noticed that Tobias and Asher were weakening when we woke up after our first night in Inferna. I'm not sure they realized it themselves. There was a reason that archangels were the only angels that could get in and out.

Inferna drained turned angels.

Eventually, they would weaken to the point where they wouldn't be able to fly, heal, or whatever else it was they could do.

I sat at their feet in the tent. It had taken Asher a while, but he had finally stopped tossing and turning.

I licked my lips as I watched his eyes move under his eyelids. I could feel his unease. His restlessness. I looked over at Tobias and Danica entwined together. Tobias never showed signs of nightmares. Recently, Danica had less severe nightmares.

I knew that with their weakened states, I could push into both of their brains and into their dreams. But did I want to?

Asher kicked out a leg, and I flinched as he came close to kicking Danica. Maybe just once wouldn't hurt.

I moved to hover over him and pushed into his dream.

"If I never have to eat another damn K-ration again, I'll be a happy man. I don't even need pussy ever again. Just give me some damn meatloaf and mashed potatoes!"

Laughter went up around Asher in what looked like an abandoned warehouse.

Tobias was next to him and stuck a cigarette in his mouth, lighting it up. "I can't wait to eat my wife when I get back."

More laughter. I looked around the group of men. They looked ragged, like they had just gotten done on the battlefield.

All of a sudden, a loud explosion rocked the building, and a mortar shell crashed through the center of the roof, exploding on impact.

Panic ensued, and Tobias and Asher jumped to their feet. The men on either side of them were wounded.

"Go get litters!" Tobias had jumped into action and was applying pressure to someone's leg that had nearly been blown off.

Asher took off out of the building and down the hill. I followed. He ran to a medic camp and collected stretchers. I could feel his panic and fear, but like Danica, instead of feeling energized by it, I felt drained.

Tobias was coming down the hill towards Asher, and someone yelled, "Watch out!"

Asher dove over Tobias and a mortar shell hit the ground and exploded, sending debris everywhere.

I made my way up the hill and grabbed Asher's hand, yanking him out of the hell he was living in.

We landed at a miniature golf course. As soon as I released his hand, he shoved me.

"Where's Toby?" He looked around frantically. "Toby!"

"He's fine. He's safe."

Asher grabbed the front of my shirt and shoved me against a large, decorative boulder.

"We have to go back and get him! We can't just leave him there! He'll die!"

I'd never experienced this before with Danica. He was still freaking the fuck out. I tried to reign the control of him, but it wasn't working.

"Calm down, man! I'll go get him, okay?" I didn't know what the fuck I was saying.

I tried to make Tobias appear, but Asher had taken over the dream himself. His pupils were pinpricks in his irises as he looked around again. His grip loosened a bit.

"You'll bring him here too?" His hands shook as he held onto my shirt.

"I'll get Danica too. Just... stay here and don't freak out."

I walked away from him and took several deep breaths. I had never attempted to merge people into dreams together before. I knew my father could do it, but before he could train me on the finer points of it, I had killed him.

I floated above them in the tent. Asher had rolled away from Danica and curled into a tight ball, fisting the sleeping bag covering him. I didn't want to move him, so I laid down in the small space between them. I put my hand over hers and a hand on Asher's back.

She stirred but didn't wake. Tobias snored softly and tightened his grip on her. I focused on all three brains and pushed in.

My head spun as I grabbed Tobias out of his dream, which had an awful lot of sex going on, and Danica out of hers, which had her lying on a beach somewhere. I was somewhat surprised she was having a good dream for once.

At least, that's how it appeared. Knowing her dreams, some kind of monster would come out of the water and try to eat her.

I landed with Tobias and Danica at the miniature golf course again to find Asher sitting against the boulder he had shoved me into with his knees drawn to his chest.

"I brought them. See?" I approached him, and he looked up. He looked like hell, with bloodshot eyes.

I offered him my hand, and he took it.

"What is this, Reve?" Danica stepped towards Asher with concern etched on her features and then took him in her arms. He buried his face in her neck.

"Regular angels are weakened in Inferna. I could get into his nightmare. I had no clue they were that bad."

"Toby?" Asher finally pulled away from Danica and looked at Tobias. "Are you okay?"

"I'm fine." Tobias grabbed Asher and pulled him into a hug, smacking him on the back. "Which one was it this time?"

"The warehouse."

"Damn." Tobias sighed and put his hands on Asher's shoulders. "I'm sorry."

Danica disappeared and then reappeared with putters and golf balls. "Let's knock some balls around."

I kept a close eye on Asher as we moved through the golf course. He seemed to relax more and more, but I still felt like he was in control of the dream instead of me.

"You're staring at me." Asher turned towards me after taking a putt through a moving obstacle. "I'm fine now."

"Are you? If you were, you'd loosen up a bit more." I set my ball on the tee

and hit it through the spinning blades of the windmill. It sailed through with no problem. "We need to wake up soon."

I was nervous that I wouldn't be able to wake the three of them up with Asher in control. I didn't even know how he was holding onto control like he was.

"Maybe we shouldn't wake up." We walked along the path behind Tobias and Danica. He had his hand in the back pocket of her jeans. "At least here we're safe."

"Our minds are safe. Our bodies are lying in a tent in the middle of Inferna with a crazy-ass demon woman sitting in power."

"Then why don't you go and take care of her. I'm sure you can get the drop on her with your invisibility. You watched us for over a month, and we never even knew."

"You make me sound like a creeper."

He turned and grinned at me. "You are a creeper."

"Fuck you, Asher." I shoved his arm and caught up to Tobias and Danica. "We need to get him out of here."

"But he's so relaxed now. A little longer?" Danica slid her arm around my waist, and I shut my eyes.

"If we stay any longer, you might get stuck here. Like, be in a coma kind of stuck."

"That wouldn't be a bad thing, would it?"

Fuck, they were all spiraling now.

This had been a mistake. The only way I could think to get them out was to turn the dream into a nightmare. The little control I had still only extended to the environment.

I stood in the center of the path and looked at them. "I'm sorry."

The ground exploded around us.

CHAPTER 12

DANICA

I woke with a scream and nearly butted heads with Tobias, who was breathing heavily. Everything had been fine, and then the explosion happened. It had felt so real.

Asher.

Sobs shook his body. I placed a tentative hand on his back, and he jerked away from the touch.

"Asher... sweetie. It's okay. We're okay." I tried a hand again, and this time he didn't cringe at my touch.

"I'm sorry. I'm so sorry." Reve was standing up, slightly hunched over so his head wouldn't hit the ceiling of the tent. "I thought-"

"Get out, Reve." Tobias sat up and glared at him. "What the fuck were you thinking? He isn't Danica!"

"I thought-"

"Get out before I throw you out."

Reve looked at me with pleading eyes. I wasn't sure how to feel about the whole thing. On one hand, he had really fucked. On the other, he had been trying to help Asher, not hurt him.

But that explosion.

He disappeared before I could say anything. Tobias ran a hand over his face and let out a shaky breath.

"Jesus Christ. What the fuck?" Tobias moved closer to Asher and me. "Are you okay?"

I nodded and moved my hand in small circles on Asher's back. He was still shaking, but his sobs had stopped. What *had* Reve been thinking?

"He shouldn't have been able to do that." Tobias put his hand on Asher's shoulder.

"We wouldn't let him end the dream." Asher shook his head. "The fucker didn't have to make an explosion, though."

"I'll go talk to him." I ran my fingers through my hair the best I could, and then pulled my hair back into a ponytail. "Is it even daytime? I can't tell."

The sky was still dark, but it was slightly warmer than before we went to sleep. I climbed out of the tent and spotted Alaric stirring something in a pot over the fire.

"Have you seen Reve?" I joined him next to the fire and held my hands out over the flames. For being hell, it was a little on the cold side.

Alaric looked at me with furrowed brows and then laughed. "I doubt he'd show himself around me."

"We need to leave soon, and he disappeared." I hugged my arms around myself.

"I was talking to a few of my men last night. We'd like to help you." He scooped some of what looked like oatmeal into a bowl and handed it to me. "At least until you get to the castle."

"I don't see why not. You know your way around here better than we do."

"Plus, your angels are weakening."

"Excuse me?" I paused halfway to my mouth with a spoonful of oatmeal. "What do you mean they're weakening?"

"I'm a predator. I can sense a weakened animal. Even last night, I could smell them weakening." He started eating his food while walking away. "Let them know they can help themselves to breakfast."

I turned and walked back to the tent. At least now I understood how Reve could get into their dreams.

We set off about an hour later. Alaric and three of his men joined us. Reve hadn't returned, no matter how much we called out for him. He had to be staying invisible to avoid us. There was no way he would leave us.

"It should take a few hours to get to the castle. Once we're there, there's a secret entrance we can use to get you inside." It was hard to take anything Alaric said seriously because he had a miniature monkey on his shoulder.

"We appreciate you helping us since Reve left us high and dry." Tobias was holding my hand as we walked.

Asher grunted from the other side of me and looked straight ahead. "I just want this all to be over."

I sighed. I wanted it all to be over too. For so long, I had wanted to experience hell for myself, but now that I was here, I missed Earth.

Alaric stopped suddenly, and Picard made a small squeaking noise. Before Alaric even had time to react, a dart hit him in the neck. He turned slowly towards us before his eyes rolled back, and he collapsed in a heap.

The other three men were hit with darts and fell as well. Picard was jumping up and down on Alaric's chest, making really loud screeching noises for such a small creature.

Tobias and Asher pulled their swords and put me in between them. We looked into the trees but didn't see anyone or anything.

It would have been a good time for Reve to appear. Just as I had the thought, ten men dropped from the trees in front of us. We backed up several steps as they fanned out into the forest.

I pulled a knife from my belt and threw it at one of the men. It hit him in the shoulder, and even from the distance, I could see his eyes turn black.

"Oh, shit." My body was screaming at me to run, but instead, I pulled out another knife and prepared to fight.

Darts came whizzing towards us, and Tobias spread his wings and took them in his left one. He winced and fell to the forest floor, his wings retracting as he fell.

"I'll fight them off. Run." Asher took a step forward and dodged a dart.

I hesitated for only an instant before I took off back towards the campsite. I could only hope that none of the demons had managed to circle around. I zig-zagged to avoid any darts aimed my way and felt like I was making progress when arms went around my waist.

I screamed as I was lifted off the ground and thrown over a shoulder. My knife was still in my hand, so I swung my arm and stabbed the demon in the back. He laughed and turned back in the direction I had just come from.

"Bring them all." He spoke sternly to the other men as we passed through the area where Alaric and his men, Asher, and Tobias were lying on the ground.

"Where are you taking us?" I grabbed onto the knife and pulled it out. There was no blood, and his wound closed instantly.

"Your knife does nothing to me, young one." I stabbed him again. "You can stab me all you want."

"Where. Are. You. Taking. Us." I made sure to annunciate each word in case he didn't understand me. I squirmed, and his hand pressed more firmly into me as he carried me in the direction of the castle.

"There's a bounty on your head. Her Highness said you'd be in this direction. She wasn't wrong."

A motherfucking bounty? How had she even known we were here? Did Tobias's suppression not work anymore?

"Whatever she's offering you, I can pay double." I tried to pull the knife out again, but it was stuck in his back as if he was holding it in.

I really couldn't pay this demon, but he didn't need to know that. It seemed like the thing to say. I didn't know how smart these demons were.

He grunted, and the knife fell out of his back and to the ground before I could catch it. "My whole life, I have dreamed of having a place at the castle. I don't think you can top that."

"I don't understand."

His deep baritone laugh shook me as we walked. "You really are from Earth, aren't you? I didn't believe it when I heard it. Queen Lilith's daughter, a human."

"I'm not a-" I stopped as we came out of the trees, and a castle rose up in front of us. "There really *is* a castle. Holy shit."

Sometimes when someone tells you something exists, you don't believe it until you see it with your very own two eyes. The castle seemed to rise out of the ground and looked exactly like a castle straight out of a fairytale.

This was no fairytale, though.

I should have been fighting more, trying to escape, not gawking at the castle. We entered what appeared to be a small village until we came to a stone building with bars for windows.

"You will stay here until she fulfills her end of the bargain." We entered into what was definitely a jail.

He set me down in a cell, and the others put Asher and Tobias in with me. They were still knocked out cold from whatever was in the darts. Alaric and his men were placed in a cell next to us.

"Let us go."

He laughed again and shook his head. "We aren't idiots, young one. Your tricks don't work on us."

The demon who had carried me and one of the others stopped at the entrance of the jail and stood facing each other. They were having a hushed conversation, and then, all of a sudden, they turned to stone.

"What the fuck?" I squinted, trying to see better. There was some light in the cell, but not much.

The stone figure slowly turned its head in my direction, and its eyes turned red. I backed up, and it swiveled its head back towards the other.

I was going crazy. I sat down against the stone wall and shut my eyes, hoping that when I reopened them, I'd be back to reality, and two gargoyles wouldn't be holding us hostage.

$\sim$

I STOOD outside Reve's door and knocked for the fifth time. Where was he?

I moved to the window and peeked in. I could see the pristine white coun-tertop of the kitchen, and that was it. He was ignoring me or wasn't home.

"I'm going to steal your bike! You better open up!" I knocked one last time before making my way to his crotch rocket. He could fly. It seemed like a useless toy.

I threw my leg over it and sat on the leather seat. It was a sexy-looking bike.

"That's a good look for you." Reve appeared next to me and gave me a small smile. "I like to see you with your legs spread."

I grinned and leaned forward. "I bet they'd look even better wrapped around you."

He made a noise in his throat and moved onto the bike seat behind me. His lips brushed the shell of my ear. "I'm going to get you out of here, Dani. I promise."

"You left." I sighed as his lips moved down to my neck, and he breathed a sigh against my skin. "Why'd you leave?"

"I was scared you wouldn't forgive me."

He placed his hand on my thigh, and I covered it with mine. "I'm sure Tobias would have kicked your ass, but then they would have forgiven you. Eventually."

He pulled me back against him and wrapped both arms around me. "I have to go get reinforcements. My abilities don't work against the demons in this village. They are using a rare herb called Tutela. That also means they are even more dangerous because they are truly Lilith's followers."

"Please hurry."

"I love you, Dani."

I turned, and he kissed my cheek before vanishing.

~

MY EYES FLUTTERED OPEN to find Asher staring at me. His eyes were bloodshot, and a crease had formed between his eyebrows as if he had been thinking too hard.

"Reve?" he whispered.

I shifted on the floor and winced as my tailbone protested sitting on the hard ground. I nodded.

"I can tell when he's in your head. You get this look on your face like you're... home." He looked at me thoughtfully. "I think that's how I felt when he was in my head. That's why I didn't want to leave the dream."

I scooted closer to him and wrapped my arms around him, putting my chin on his arm and looking up at him. "It can be addictive. Escaping in the dreams."

"What did he say?" Tobias stretched his arms over his head and then stood. He was looking around the cell as if it was suddenly going to have a weakness in the bars.

"He's going for reinforcements," I whispered. "Alaric said you two are weakened here. That's why Reve could get in your head and how Lilith knew where we were."

"Fuck." Asher ran a hand over his face and shook his head as if he couldn't believe it.

"Do you think Olly is weaker here too?" Tobias sat down on the other side of me.

I shrugged. "My dad isn't. At least I don't think he is. If he was, how could he have so much control over the demons he works with?"

"They used to be human." Alaric's sleep-filled voice came from the other side of the bars. "Humans are weak from what I know of them."

Picard climbed out of his jacket and scurried over to our cell. As if to prove Alaric's point, it jumped up onto Asher's thigh and then chomped down on his finger.

Asher was about ready to whack it clear back to Earth. Before he could, I picked it up between my thumb and forefinger.

It let out a flurry of squeaks as I held it by the back of its neck like it was a cat. "You are a bad monkey!"

Its little eyes welled with tears, and its tiny lip quivered. Jesus, why was he so cute?

I put him back down, and he ran to Alaric's open palm on the ground.

"Can't that little shit break us out of here or something?" Asher glared at Picard. Picard turned around and spit his tongue out. "He has a fucking piss-poor attitude."

"The last man that spoke poorly of Mr. Ferdinand had his dick bitten off in his sleep." Alaric scratched Picard behind the ear. I laughed as Asher put his hands over his dick.

"I can't believe I'm sitting here watching a demon wolf shifter talk to his pet monkey." Tobias ran his fingers through his hair and rubbed the back of his neck.

A silence fell over us as the reality of our situation grew bleaker. Alaric confirmed that the two stone men at the entrance were gargoyles. Even if we could make it out of the cells, the gargoyles would stop us from leaving.

I leaned against Asher and ran through the last several months. When I had punched John in the face, I would have never thought my actions would lead me to being stuck in a musty and damp cell in hell.

"What if it's one big giant nightmare?" I was playing with Asher's fingers. His head was back against the stone wall.

"Not all of it has been a nightmare. Has it?" I felt Tobias shift next to me. His hand slid behind me to rest on my hip.

Alaric looked over at us with curiosity written in his eyes. He hadn't said anything in a while. None of his men had.

"For everything bad that has happened, there has been twice as much good." Asher looked down at me then shut his eyes. "The bad has just been really fucking bad. You think we're all a dream in your head?"

I made a noise in my throat. The thought had crossed my mind several times, especially when shit got pretty dicey. If it was a dream, it was pretty elaborate. Maybe I was in a coma?

"Reve wouldn't do that," Alaric practically growled.

Tobias leaned forward and looked at him. "He exploded our dream the other night. He tortures people in their dreams. Or at least he did before Danica."

Alaric moved closer to the bars and wrapped his hands around them. "She's his mate."

Asher's eyes popped open, and he rolled his eyes. "We don't believe in that kind of shit on Earth."

"That's a shame." His face became thoughtful. "You're all mates. How does that work with three men?"

"There's four," I said. "It works how you think it would."

He let out a whistle. "They just share you? Don't they fight?"

I laughed, and Tobias squeezed my hip. "They fight, but over time it's become less frequent. I don't think that sharing me is an appropriate explanation of what we have together."

"She's always protected and feels loved. But we also feel the same way from her and each other. I'm pretty lucky. I not only get Danica but also three best friends." Tobias kissed my temple.

My heart swelled, and a smile tugged at my lips. The feeling was short-lived.

The two gargoyles at the entrance transformed back into men and stepped to the side. Tobias jumped to his feet and stood in front of me.

I peered around his legs as the two goons that seemed to be Lilith's right-hand men, came and stood in front of our cell.

"Mark. Sam. I see you still don't know how to think for yourselves." Alaric stood, and one of the goons stepped over to his cell.

They stared at each other before a growl ripped from Alaric's throat, and the goons looked away. Alaric and his men laughed at whatever had just transpired.

"You're the one locked in a cell right now. What do you think, Mark? Will Lilith let me be the one to take his head?"

"Sure. As long as I can eat his monkey in front of him first." He gestured for one of the gargoyles to unlock our cell. "She wants the girl only."

Tobias hadn't budged from his spot in front of me. Asher rose to his feet as well, and together they stood as a united front.

"Are we going to do this the easy way or the hard way?" one of the men said, stepping into the cell.

Tobias brought his fist back and swung at him. He moved faster than I could track and grabbed Tobias's fist before it connected with his face. A grin spread across his face, and his fist connected with the side of Tobias's head, sending him to the hard stone floor.

I rushed to Tobias, who was unconscious on the ground. Asher stood clenching his fists at his sides but didn't strike.

"Now, are you going to come with us, or do we need to knock this one out too?"

I stood and squared my shoulders. "Go away."

They both threw their heads back and laughed. "That shit doesn't work on us, princess."

I would have taken his name for me as an insult, but I guess I literally was a princess. I looked at Asher. I couldn't get a read on what he was thinking, but there was a tick in his jaw.

"What will happen to them?" My voice was surprisingly even considering how scared I felt at the prospect of seeing my mother again.

The last time I had seen her, she had poisoned me and then stabbed me in the chest. She wasn't exactly mother of the year material.

"They stay here. Lilith will decide. You think you have a choice in this matter? You don't." Sam or Mark, I'd already forgotten which one was which, stepped forward and grabbed my elbow.

Alaric and his three friends growled from the other cell. Picard was on Alaric's shoulder and let out a screech.

"Get your hands off her," Asher warned. I had never heard him sound so menacing before.

"Asher." I put my hand on his arm and looked at him. "There's no use in you getting hurt too."

I looked down at Tobias, who had rolled over and let out a pained groan. I knew I didn't have a choice. I just had to hope that Reve would come through for them.

"She's a smart one, this one." They laughed again and stepped back out of the cell.

I turned to Asher and wrapped my arms around him. "It will be okay. Reve is coming." I didn't think anyone except him heard me. The goons were back to glaring at Alaric.

I knelt down next to Tobias and put my hand on his cheek. His eyes cracked open before shutting again. I hoped he could still heal himself.

Before I lost my courage, I stood and walked out of the cell.

CHAPTER 13

DANICA

*J*t crossed my mind several times to run. Now that I was walking on my own two feet and not slung over a gargoyle's shoulder, that plan was quickly squashed.

We were in a small village near the castle. The houses were made of stone, and the streets were dirt in some places and cobblestone in others. I felt like I was walking through medieval London.

Many demons came to their doorways or stopped in the streets to gawk at me. Most looked human. *If* I ignored their eyes and the extra appendages some had.

"Do all demons live in towns?" I was walking between Tweedledee and Tweedledum. Had I tried to run, their big meaty hands would have stopped me in an instant. I'd given up trying to remember their actual names. It didn't deserve the extra mental effort.

"No. Only the civilized ones." I didn't even want to know what uncivilized demons were like.

I snorted at his answer, and he turned his head to glare at me, his eyes seeming to glow. "And what are you?"

"Civilized."

"No. I mean, what type of demons." I scanned the surroundings, looking for a place to escape to. Nothing looked promising.

"Bear shifters." He grunted and grabbed my elbow, steering me towards a paved set of stairs leading up a hill.

I hated stairs. I also hated hell and demons. Except for Reve. Unless Reve really had ditched us. I hoped he was just laying low until the time was right.

"I don't understand how Inferna and Earth are so similar." I was thinking out loud because I was trying to ease the panic churning inside my gut.

"Inferna was a fuck up. He took what he liked and started over on Earth."

"God?" I was half-angel, and most of the time, I doubted one man was behind creating everything. It would certainly explain how eerily similar I was finding certain aspects of Inferna, though.

"Is that what he calls himself?" They laughed, and one of them prodded my shoulder. "Speed up. We don't have all day."

We came to a large iron gate that slowly opened to let us into a courtyard. The gate shut with a clang, and I felt my freedom slowly getting farther and farther away.

My dad was inside the castle. At least if I were going to be held against my will, it would be with my father. Hopefully, Olly was inside too.

I couldn't think about what state I would find them in.

I followed the two men up to a large iron door, and we waited. A small piece of the door slid open, and an eye peered out at us. It felt very much like *The Wizard of Oz*, except I wasn't going to be going back to Kansas.

The door opened, and a tall man stood to the side in a suit. He bowed his head slightly and gestured with his arm to enter. I looked to my two captors, and they pushed me forward and into the dark foyer.

If it could be called a foyer. It was big enough to house a family of four and had a large chandelier hanging in the center that sparkled unnaturally.

"We'll show you to your room. You will have a few hours to bathe yourself and dress for dinner." One of them took the lead and went to a large staircase that took my breath away.

"So you aren't sticking me in the dungeons? How kind of you. Can I also find my father and boyfriend up here?" Tweedledum stopped on a stair and looked down at me. Maybe it had come out a little too snarky.

I couldn't exactly fight two bear shifters with my fists, so my words were my next best weapon. Except that all of my words were mostly just nervous banter to keep from losing my shit.

"You have quite the mouth on you for being in the situation you're in."

"Well, I am the daughter of the evil demon queen and the devil. What did you expect?"

He made a noise and continued up the stairs while Tweedledee followed. We entered a long hallway and stopped in front of a pair of double doors.

"This will be your room. We will be right here outside the door. The windows are locked." He opened the door and waited for me to walk inside before shutting the door behind me.

I heard the lock turn and immediately ran to one of the windows. I checked them all, but they were all locked with bars covering them. Of course, escaping couldn't be as easy as they made it in the movies.

My attention was drawn to a chair where a flowing pale blue gown was laid out. There was a card on top.

MY PRINCESS,

At last, we can be together as a family. Please wear this dress to dinner. You can find the accompanying accessories on the dresser.

Love,

Mom

· · ·

I THREW up a little in my mouth and chucked the card across the room. The dress had way too much taffeta and far too many embroidered flowers for my liking.

I looked down at my dirty clothes and lifted an arm to sniff. I didn't seem to have a choice about what I was going to wear. I'd have to suck it up and dress like I was going to prom.

～

I MUST HAVE ALREADY BEEN EXPERIENCING Stockholm syndrome because I had no problem pampering myself in the large bathtub. I dressed like the princess Lilith wanted me to be and completed my look with a thin crown of diamonds on the top of my head.

At least I thought they were diamonds. For all I knew, they could be melted together souls of kidnapped puppies.

I looked at myself in the floor-length mirror and tried to put on a fake smile. I was going to have to get Lilith to believe I was all for being a happy little family.

A fist pounded on my door before the lock was undone, and the door opened. I followed the bear shifters down to the main floor, where we entered the dining room.

I stopped in my tracks.

"Danica. So glad you could join us." Lilith stood at the head of a long table. She gestured to the seat to her right.

My breath caught in my throat as I looked at my dad. He had cuffs around his wrists and neck. It didn't appear they were attached to anything.

I made my way to the seat to her right and sat down. I didn't take my eyes off my father, who was now staring at me from across the table. Lilith sat down and tapped her nails on the table. I looked at her.

She looked exactly as she had in Shanghai. Her mahogany hair was pulled into a chignon with tendrils of hair framing her face. Her eyes shined with mirth, or maybe that was just the crazy in her leaking out.

"Tomorrow evening, there will be a ceremony to reunite our family." She took a sip of her wine and then grinned at me. "You, my dear, will be bound to me as my one and only heir."

A lump formed in my throat. "And my dad?" I choked out.

"We are already bound. We were sorry that you had to miss it. It really was the party of the century, wasn't it, sweetheart?" She patted his hand that was balled in a fist on the top of the table. "Now that we are bound together, if anyone hurts or attacks me, he feels everything." She laughed in that way that sent chills down my spine. "Isn't blood magic wonderful? I can't wait to teach you!"

I'm pretty sure if I had a mirror, I would have been pale as a ghost.

I looked at my dad, who sat to the left of Lilith. He stared straight ahead, his jaw set in stone.

"Your father already made the mistake of trying to kill me after the ceremony while I slept. He won't dare make that mistake again. Isn't that right, sweetie?" She put her hand over his and squeezed.

"Right," he bit out through his teeth.

She cleared her throat. "Honey. I don't think I like the tone you are taking in front of our daughter."

I bit my tongue to stop myself from saying something utterly stupid. The whole exchange made me want to vomit. She was fucking crazy. How was it that I had come from her womb? Would I eventually end up like her?

She stood from her seat and snapped her fingers. The two goons approached the table carrying a knife and the Holy Grail. My eyes nearly popped out of my head, seeing it.

I pushed back from the table, and my dad looked at me and shook his head. I grabbed onto the edge of the table as Lilith took my dad's hand, swiped the knife across his wrist just above the cuff he had on, and let his blood fall into the cup.

"It will be any day now when the barrier will finally give way and stay open permanently." She tapped a nail on the side of the cup as it filled with his blood. "It's unfortunate that your boyfriend seemed to have skin of steel this time around."

"Olly? Where is he?" I choked out.

She threw her head back and laughed. "In the dungeons. He's a fighter, that one. If only John were still around to make his special serum to weaken him." She made a noise like she regretted killing the doctor. She lowered the cup to the table and wrapped a cloth napkin around my dad's wrist.

"How can you touch it?" I nodded towards the Holy Grail.

"It bends to my will now. If an angel tried to touch it while here, it would burn them." At my confused expression, she continued, "It pulls its power from whatever power source is greatest. Here in Inferna, it is an object of great darkness."

The servants returned to the table and cleared our plates. Lilith remained standing and grabbed the goblet.

"I will leave you two for a few moments while I take care of this blood." She sauntered out of the room with the goon squad behind her.

The doors shut, and I heard a lock click into place. I stood and rushed to my dad.

"Dad-"

"You shouldn't have come." He put his palms on the table and stood, the bloody napkin falling to the floor. His cut was nearly healed but should have closed already.

"We can't let demons get through. We have to stop her."

"There's only one way to stop her, Dani." He ran his hand through his hair, and I noticed the puckered skin of scars running across his forearm.

I grabbed his arm and pulled it towards me, running my thumb over the pink, raised skin. "What has she done to you?"

He sighed and looked forlorn. "She weakened me and then bound us together. You can't let her do it to you. These cuffs prevent me from breaking free. You need to find a way out of here. Where are your guardians?"

"In a jail." I whimpered and brought the back of my hand to my mouth to stop a sob from escaping. "I don't think they're coming."

He shook his head and then sat back down in his chair. I sat in the chair next to him.

"You have to kill one of us." He spoke in a barely audible voice. He straightened in his chair and then turned towards me.

My eyes widened. "What?"

"Our lives are tied together. Kill one of us, you kill the other."

Did he even hear what he was asking me to do? I couldn't kill someone. I couldn't even kill a spider.

"There has to be another way. I can't just-" I felt myself starting to panic and wanted to jump up and run from the room.

"Yes, you can."

Tears slid down my cheeks, and I shook my head. He took my face between his hands.

"You can. You must, or she's going to permanently open a way to Earth. She already managed to get the barrier open for a substantial amount of time. And if I did manage to escape, she would go back to kidnapping angels. In large quantities, their blood can get a single demon through."

A sob left me. He pulled me towards him, smoothing my hair back.

"Find something sharp. Stab it through my heart. Right here." He took my hand and put it over his chest. "Stabbing me is your best bet."

"Dad. You can't die. I can't-"

"This is the only way. She thought binding us together would protect her. She won't see this coming."

No words were coming from my mouth. Instead, I was inhaling sharp gasps of air. Kill my father? I couldn't. I wouldn't. There had to be another way.

He brought my hand to his cheek, and I looked back at the dull gray eyes that should have been smoldering. He was weak. I was no genius when it came to reading angels, but the power that once coursed through my father had significantly diminished.

"Tobias, Reve, Asher, and Oliver." He let out a shaky breath. "They will protect you and keep you safe." I opened my mouth to argue with him, but he shook his head. "Sometimes, life isn't fair, Danica. I can think of no other way to go than saving you." His voice cracked, and a tear slid down his cheek.

"I can't."

He leaned forward and kissed my forehead. "You can. Tomorrow at the ceremony before she performs the ritual."

I was about to respond when the doors opened, and Lilith strode back in, looking smug.

"I love you, Danica," my dad whispered.

"I love you, too." I hugged him tightly before the goons took me back to my room for the night.

CHAPTER 14

TOBIAS

*M*y head was throbbing from the blow I took to the side of the head. It should have been healed in less than five minutes. Inferna really was weakening us. How could we protect Danica if we were completely drained of what strength and abilities we had?

I turned on my side and curled into a ball. I was a poor excuse for a man. They took Danica. They took Oliver. Now we were locked in some musty smelling cell with gargoyles guarding us.

My job was to protect, and I failed. It wasn't the first time I hadn't protected my loved ones. I allowed a moan to pass through my lips. My vision grew fuzzy, and I passed out for what seemed like the hundredth time.

"Margie." I stood at the entrance to the kitchen, my hands shaking.

She had been cooking my favorite meal: pot roast with mashed potatoes and green beans. I shut my eyes and breathed in. The aromas usually caused my mouth to water and my stomach to growl, but tonight it just made bile rise in my throat.

We knew it might happen, with the news of Pearl Harbor and the president calling for war. But I thought, no, I prayed, that there'd be enough voluntary enlistments to stop the ever-present fear of my serial number being called.

"Dinner's just about ready. Can you get the boys washed up?" She didn't turn around. She was busy mashing potatoes.

"Margaret."

She stilled over the stove, the potato masher dropping into the pan. I never used her full name. The last time I had used it, I had been down on one knee, asking her to marry me.

She turned slowly, bringing her hand to her mouth as she took in what I could only assume was my scared-shitless expression.

"We'll hide." A tear slid down her cheek, and she came to me, grabbing my face between her hands. They were warm and smelled of potatoes. "We'll pack up the car and head to Canada."

I shook my head and put my hands over hers. A sob left her, and I put my forehead against hers.

"I have to do my duty. Even if I don't want to." The words felt foreign. As much as I loved being an American, I wasn't sure the price for that was worth it now that I had the choice to fight ripped away from me.

I had thought about enlisting with the news of the attack, but I had a family. Now that I had been one of the unlucky ones selected, I didn't have a choice.

My wife was well off. Old money. She didn't need me to support her. There was no way they were letting me out of it.

"What if-"

"No what-ifs. I probably won't even leave American soil." I cupped her face and searched her eyes for the strength I knew was there. "It will all be fine."

I jolted awake as something wet ran up my face. Picard was licking my tears. I batted him away.

Who the hell has a pet monkey? PETA would have a field day over it. As if seeming to know that's what I was thinking, Picard spat his tongue out at me and ran back to Alaric.

I didn't know what to make of the wolf shifter. He seemed decent enough, but he had also left Reve to be captured by Lilith. I didn't trust him.

I pulled myself up and leaned against the wall next to Asher. He looked like shit. I'm sure I did too.

"When you enlisted, how did your wife react?" I tried to steer clear of war talk with Asher. It was hit or miss whether it would cause him to spiral. Lately, he had been sharing a lot more of his memories.

He shrugged. "How do you think she reacted? She called me a selfish asshole, smacked me, and then let me fuck her on the kitchen table. Why are you asking?"

"Why does everything have to be so crass with you?"

"What would you prefer I say, Toby? That I made love to her on the kitchen table?" He made a noise in his throat. "It is what it is. I'm not going to sugarcoat the terminology because you're a pansy-ass."

I rolled my eyes and looked over at him. He was clenching his jaw.

"I remembered when I told Margie I had been drafted. It's the last memory I have before leaving." I sighed. It must have been painful for me to leave if I couldn't even remember the day I left.

He grunted and turned his head to look at me. "We weren't the only ones that fought in that war, were we?"

I shook my head. Our families might not have been in the line of fire, but every time the mail came or a knock sounded on the door, I'm sure they felt like they were in a battle of their own. I shuddered, thinking about Margie opening the letter announcing my death.

"I honestly try not to think about Lena. It hurts too much." I was surprised he mentioned her by name. He rarely spoke of her. Even when we served together, he didn't talk about her.

"Did you ever find out what happened after we... you know..."

He shook his head in response. I had always assumed he had taken it upon himself to track her down and find out what she did after his death.

"It might help to know."

"I don't want to know if another man was sticking it in her, Toby. You might be into that shit, but I would have probably killed the fucker, even though it was my fault I died."

I decided to keep my mouth shut. He was getting agitated, and the last thing we needed was to come to blows.

"I think Reve is here," Asher whispered after several minutes of silence. "Don't ask me how I know that, but I've started being able to feel the fucker lately."

I looked around the cell, and my eyes stopped in the corner. I could sense him too if I really focused. I wondered how recently that had started happening.

He wasn't saying anything. I didn't exactly trust him at the moment, what with the whole dream fiasco and him up and leaving. It was a shame because I had started to actually like him enough to want to hang out.

Alaric grunted and stood along with his men. They were a relatively quiet bunch. I half expected shifters to be loud.

"They're coming." Alaric scooped Picard off the floor and put him in his pocket. I should have asked what kind of demon he was. Surely he was something other than just a miniature monkey.

"Who's-" Asher's question was interrupted by loud thumps outside.

I looked in the direction of the gargoyles who had just started to transform back into men when two massive fists came smashing down on top of them.

Not going to lie. Asher and I ended up clutching each other like two little girls watching a horror movie. The building we were in shook and rubble fell from the ceiling. Asher was shaking, so I kept hold of him.

"Tony. That's enough!" Reve's voice was coming from outside the bars now. "Stand guard."

An eye appeared in the doorway and looked in at us. Its pupil was big enough that I could walk into it. Jesus Christ. I was about to pass out.

"I'm surprised you found Tony. He and Miles have been MIA for centuries." Alaric was at the bars with his hands wrapped around them. Hair was sprouting from them like he was mid-shift.

I was an angel, but seeing different types of demons I had only read about was making me question everything I knew about the world. I mean, hell, we were in another realm that literally meant hell in Latin.

Reve appeared and grabbed a set of keys among the remains for the gargoyles. I guess with strong enough fists, even gargoyles could be defeated.

He unlocked our cells. "Invitations have been sent out to the elite demons, requesting their presence at a coronation ceremony this evening."

"What?" I knew I sounded stupid asking the question, but I was still mind-fucked over the giant that was still staring at us with its eye in the doorway.

"There was a coronation months ago for Lucifer. She's going to bind Danica to them and make her the heir to the throne."

"But you're the rightful heir." Alaric stepped out of the cell and took several breaths. The hair, or fur, on his hands disappeared.

Reve ignored his comment and looked at me. "I'm sorry."

"You're late." I led Asher out of the cell and eyed the giant. "Can you move your friend here."

"I have an army waiting in the forest."

I stopped and blinked at him. How he had managed to round up an army of demons in less than twenty-four hours was beyond my comprehension. But then again, he was King Reve, not just pain in the ass Reve.

"I have a plan." Reve stepped in front of us to stop us from leaving out the door. The giant had luckily understood my comment and moved.

"And what's that?" Asher was pale, but at least he was talking. "If it involves any more explosions, I'm out."

"We'll sneak in through the secret entrance that appears to have been abandoned since my days in the castle. It will easily give us access to the dungeons."

"What if they aren't in the dungeons?"

"Then, tonight, we'll go to the coronation."

"Lilith is going to know we're up to something. You can't miss a big ass giant and an even bigger hell serpent." Alaric stepped beside Reve.

"She doesn't have as many demons on her side as she thinks." He got a faraway look in his eyes as if he remembered something from the past. He had quite the history to remember. "I will need to stay invisible. Someone from inside the castle told me that she thinks I'm dead."

"Why would she think that? You're indestructible." Alaric seemed shocked that Reve would think he wasn't immortal.

"Not on Earth."

We left the building, and the sight greeting us was destruction. It was as if the giant had just barreled right on through the center of town. Waiting on a pile of rubble from a building was a hell serpent that was twice the size of the one we had seen in Shanghai.

"This way." Reve was invisible again. He was headed to the right of the castle. In fact, we were moving farther away from it.

We walked in silence. Alaric was in front. He seemed to know exactly where Reve was. He had to be smelling him or something. I tried to sense Reve like we had in the cell, but there were too many other stimuli to distract me.

We ended up at the edge of the Black Forest and went into the tree line. I was starting to wonder where this secret entrance was when we came to a rock formation. It was covered in black moss, but if I stared long enough, I could see the opening.

"I'm not going in there." Asher had stopped and crossed his arms.

I honestly didn't want to go into the dark cavern either, but we didn't have a choice. I put my hand on Asher's shoulder and gave it a reassuring squeeze.

"Do we have any lights?" Our cellphones had already died, so using their flashlights was out of the question.

Alaric's men slipped through the opening, and he stopped, reaching into his pocket for Picard.

"We don't need light to see in the dark. Here. Take Picard. He will help." I put my hand out, and Picard jumped onto my hand and then up my arm to my shoulder.

"How is a monkey going to help?" Asher rolled his eyes. He just didn't like the little guy because he bit him. I would have bitten him too if he had made fun of my name.

Alaric shook his head and followed his men.

"Picard is a luminous demon monkey. If you want him to, he will light up." Reve's voice came from just inside the entrance.

I looked at Picard on my shoulder and raised my eyebrows. A monkey that lit up? I didn't know whether to be scared or in awe. I slid through the entrance, and Picard made several noises before his entire body lit up like a magical orb.

"It's possible we are going crazy." Asher stood next to me, and we looked around the cave we were standing in.

The cave wasn't large but sloped downward towards a corridor.

"Reve, why are you still invisible?" I made my way carefully to the passageway where Alaric and his men had stopped to wait for us.

"She might have spies down here," Alaric answered for him.

A chill ran down my spine. We made a single file line and walked for what felt like ten minutes. One of the men at the front of the line held up his hand to stop us.

Before I even knew what was happening, Alaric and his men hunched and then dropped down out of the passageway. I caught a flash of fur and sharp teeth before several thuds and groans.

Picard seemed to vibrate on my shoulder before the light he was giving off disappeared, and we could only see a very faint sliver of light in front of us.

"It's a small drop, and then you need to crawl." Reve's voice came from behind us. "They will have taken care of any guards."

I could see Asher's eyes watching me as I crept forward and then jumped down into the hole. It wasn't as deep as I expected. What I wasn't expecting was to have to army crawl under rocks that looked like they could come crashing down at any second.

I made it through and stood in a dim hallway that was lit by torches. I felt like I was in the middle ages.

I put my hand out to help Asher up. He was holding it together well, all things considered. We took off in the direction of growls and turned the corner to find a large room with cells lining the sides and wolves dismembering demons.

As soon as I saw the pile of white, silver-flecked feathers in one of the cells, my heart stopped beating. The only thing that brought me back to the present was Asher grabbing onto my arm and squeezing it so tight that I thought he was going to rip it off.

"Do you feel it?" Asher whispered.

I looked at him, still frozen in place. Oliver was curled in a ball in the corner of the cell. His wings were wrapped around him, but there were large patches of feathers missing. One wing seemed to be at an odd angle.

"Feel what?" I grabbed onto his fingers that were digging into me and peeled them off.

"I have to take him."

Asher moved forward, stepping over an arm then a torso. The cell was locked, and I looked around for a set of keys. I grimaced, finding them clutched in a ripped off hand.

I grabbed them before I had time to talk myself out of it and unlocked the cell. Asher rushed in and scooped Oliver into his arms.

"I have to take him home." He blinked a few times and then looked at me. "It's like I'm being summoned, but it's a fuzzy connection. How am I supposed to get back to Earth?"

I looked down at Oliver, who had cracked his eyes open. Dirt caked his face, and his lips were drawn in a grimace of pain.

"Wouldn't let them take my blood," he mumbled. "They rebreak them every thirty minutes. They'll be back soon."

My stomach was in knots as his eyes closed again, and Asher looked at me with panic written in his eyes.

"Have to stop her." Oliver's head fell against Asher's chest.

"I'll help them get out of here," said one of Alaric's men, who had shifted back to looking like a man and not a beast.

"I can't just-"

"Go, Asher. If you are being summoned back to Heaven, you can't fight it." I looked down at Oliver's limp body, then back at him. "If you're with him, I think you can just fly straight through. Let the summons happen; it will guide you home."

He blinked a few times, and then his eyes glossed over. Danica had described to us what it looked like when Oliver and I had been summoned to take Asher back to Heaven. It was a chilling effect to see the blank stare on Asher's face now.

I watched them exit the room, feathers falling from Oliver's wings. I gritted my teeth and turned around in a circle, taking in the room. I wanted to vomit.

"This way." Reve's arm appeared and grabbed my elbow. "We'll go up through the servants' quarters and hide in a room there."

We made it into an empty servant's room, and Reve shut the door behind us.

"Some of the servants are going to get us tuxedos for tonight. It's the easiest way to have access to both Lucifer and Danica at the same time." He started pacing in front of us and looked out of sorts. "I tried to go find them the other night, but as soon as I get to a certain spot, my invisibility doesn't work anymore."

"Dark magic," Alaric grumbled from his spot on the floor. He had one of his men with him; the other two had gone with Asher and Oliver.

"That's an actual thing?" I sat down on a chair and put my elbows on the table, running my hands over my hair. I was ready to go back to Earth.

"How do you think you exist with all your special abilities? That's light magic. Inferna once was full of light magic." Alaric seemed annoyed to have to explain things to me. "It's only a matter of time before your precious Earth turns into another Inferna."

I looked at Reve with raised eyebrows. He just nodded and sat down on the mattress. It made a horrible squeaking sound underneath him.

"Me making an appearance will cause an uproar. Lilith will be distracted, and so will her guards. That's when you need to get Lucifer and Danica out." Reve looked between Alaric and me. "I don't know if Lilith will be able to control me. So be quick."

"What about you?" I frowned at him from across the small room. "She'll kill you."

Reve shut his eyes for a brief moment before opening them. His jaw ticked. "She'll die trying."

CHAPTER 15

DANICA

*M*y day had been a blur of preparations for my coronation, or whatever it was that Lilith was calling it. To me, it felt more like I was heading to my execution.

I had been massaged, waxed, primped, and put in my room to select my gown. I stared at the ten dresses in front of me. I was not a gown person, but I couldn't help but drool over the beautiful fabrics and colors.

I grabbed a champagne-colored halter that was an A-line style and had intricate beadwork. I needed to be able to move in it. I also grabbed a pink ballgown that had a lot of tulle under the cupcake-like skirt. I hung both on the back of the bathroom door.

I hummed to myself and grabbed a lamp off the nightstand, and took it into the bathroom. I needed a weapon, and since there was absolutely nothing around I could shank someone with, I was going to have to improvise.

I shut the bathroom door and shoved a towel in front of it. I wasn't sure how good bear shifter hearing was, but I wasn't going to take any chances.

I turned on the shower and the faucet to drown out any noise.

Grabbing a hand towel and the lamp, I looked at the mirror. My best bet was probably a corner.

I held the towel the best I could and then slammed the bottom of the lamp repeatedly into the glass. Pieces fell onto the counter.

I turned off the faucet and shower and listened at the bathroom door. All was quiet on the other side.

I smiled to myself. My plan might actually work.

I took one of the shards of glass and wrapped it in toilet paper and began ripping long lengths of tulle from the pink dress. I then tied the pieces together.

I wrapped the pointiest piece of glass I could find in the tulle and then tied it to my shin. It felt awkward, but that was the only place I could think of that had easy access and no body parts that would accidentally be stabbed.

Satisfied with my concealed shank, I slipped on the champagne-colored dress. It was time to save the light from the dark. At least, I hoped this would be it.

I STOOD at the top of the staircase leading into the ballroom. I had been here before during my first dream with Reve. I looked around the room of sharply-dressed demons. Most looked human. I wasn't one to be fooled.

Several heads turned in my direction as I wiped my hands on the sides of the dress, smoothing out unseen wrinkles. I could feel the weapon strapped to my leg. Hopefully, it was secure and wouldn't fall off before it was time for me to make my move.

I moved down the stairs, feeling like I was on display. I suppose I was, being the daughter of their crazy queen. Were all these demons on her side freely, or had they been brainwashed into supporting Lilith?

I reached the bottom, and my dad stepped beside me.

"You look beautiful." He took my hand and set it in the crook of his arm. "Just remember to breathe."

I nodded and let him lead me onto the dance floor. He took my hand in his, and I put my head on his shoulder. Now would be the perfect opportunity to do what he asked and kill him.

"I'm proud of you, Danica Marie. I don't think I've ever told you that." I could only hear his voice, despite the room that was filled with music and chatter. We were in our own little bubble. "I should have been around more."

I shut my eyes and willed myself not to cry. "I love you, Dad."

When the song ended, he wiped the few tears that had escaped away from my face. Then he led me to a dais at the front of the room. Lilith was already sitting in one of the chairs, a crown perched on her head.

"My daughter, how beautiful you are tonight." She gestured to a chair to her right.

I took my seat and looked around the room. If I didn't know we were in Inferna, I would have never guessed the room was full of demons.

I was just about to excuse myself to the restroom so I could get ready to attack when I saw Tobias at the perimeter of the room. I grabbed onto the arms of the chair.

Lilith noticed him as well. She snapped her fingers, and two men grabbed him by the elbows and dragged him across the room.

I looked wide-eyed at my dad, and he shook his head. Lilith stood and walked down the five steps where the men with Tobias stopped and shoved him to the ground.

"Where are the rest of you?" She sounded angrier than I had ever heard her sound.

With all attention on Lilith and Tobias, I reached down and took the piece of glass out of the makeshift holster I had made. I held it next to my leg, waiting for the perfect moment.

I knew that whatever I did to Lilith would hurt Lucifer, but it surely couldn't kill him. He was an archangel. Archangels were indestructible. At least, that's what I kept telling myself.

I continued to reassure myself as the guests parted with hushed murmurs and gasps. Reve was walking towards us, and the room went silent.

No one moved to stop him, not even Lilith's guards. They all seemed to be in some kind of trance. Where were Olly and Asher?

"Boy, what do you think you are doing? Stop this madness immediately." She pulled a long dagger from one of the guards near her when her command didn't work.

"What's wrong, Lilith?" Reve had a deadly glint in his eye.

She straightened her back and stepped back up the steps. I stood and prepared myself. She was so focused on Reve that she wasn't paying my dad or me any attention.

I glanced over at my dad, and he nodded his head. He mouthed, "I love you."

I didn't want to do it.

I lunged towards Lilith, just like I had practiced in training at the academy. At the same time my shard of glass dug into her neck, she turned, and the dagger she was holding went into my side.

I'm sure a scream came from my lips, but I was in shock. The room suddenly came to life as Reve lost control of whatever he was doing to the demons.

I fell to my knees as Lilith pulled the dagger out and stabbed me again. My dad was on his knees, crawling in our direction. A flash of black fur flew over us and took out one of the goons that had been going for my dad.

My entire body felt like it was on fire as the dagger was pulled out for a second time. Or maybe it was a third time. She reared back again to stab me, but then her face froze in a scream as something hit her from behind.

She fell down the stairs as her body was engulfed in flames so hot that it felt like my own skin was burning.

My eyes landed on my dad. His hands still had tiny flames on them as he collapsed forward.

"No!" I scrambled as fast as I could on the blood-covered marble floor to him. "Dad!"

I rolled him over and put my ear near his mouth. He wasn't

breathing. I collapsed back on my ass. The rest of the room was in chaos.

Bring him to me. The voice entered my head, and I looked around, thinking someone was talking to me. I was hallucinating from the blood loss. And the grief. The grief was making it hard to breathe.

I coughed and felt like I was about to pass out. I had been stabbed way too many times in my short life.

I barely even felt the pain anymore. I was going numb. It was the end of the road for me.

Bring him to me. The voice was more commanding this time. I looked up at the ceiling. It sounded an awful lot like Morgan Freeman.

I needed help.

I pushed myself to my feet and stumbled a little. How was I supposed to get my dad somewhere when he weighed way more than me?

I looked down at my wounds. My dress was now crimson. A laugh bubbled out of me at the sight.

I fell forward as a sense of peace washed over me. I caught myself on my hands and knees and felt the air stir around me. I turned my head.

Wings. One of my angels was here to take us. I smiled as the wings moved.

Bring him to me.

I looked at my dad and wrapped my arms around him.

"Danica! Wait!" I could hear Tobias, but I couldn't bring myself to pay attention to him.

My sole focus was on my dad.

The wings beat with more force, and I felt myself being lifted into the air. My dad felt abnormally light for being a grown-ass man, and I wrapped my arms around him tighter just in case.

I shut my eyes as we flew towards a window and broke through. I don't know where my angel was taking us, but wherever it was, I knew I'd be safe.

CHAPTER 16

DANICA

"*D*anica." The deep voice sounded in my ears, and I groaned. *Not again.* "It's time for you to wake up."

My eyes fluttered open, and I took in the white room that was the last place I wanted to be. What had happened? Was I actually dead this time?

"Where am I?" I sat up and took in my crisp white gown. I knew exactly where I was.

"Judgment."

I stood and looked at the ceiling. If this was judgment, then I was screwed. I had just played a part in killing my own mother. My eyes went to the diamond-encrusted door.

"So, this is it? If it opens, then I'm an angel, and if it doesn't..."

"It will open. You've always been an angel. Your father's angel."

I laughed and wanted to cry at the same time. *My father.*

"Is he... alive?" A tear slid down my cheek, and I sat back down on the bed. "He did this fireball thing, and then he stopped breathing."

The voice made a sound in his throat and then cleared it. "He threw most of the light he had left at her. He is recovering at the celestial hospital."

"Aren't I supposed to lose all my painful memories?"

"Do you want to lose them?"

I walked towards the door and put my hand on the handle. "I don't want to forget all the good."

The room went silent, and I bit my lip as I turned the handle. I half expected it not to turn, but it did, and the door opened into a very brightly lit hallway. I stepped out, and the door slammed shut behind me.

The hallway was long, with several doors. I walked towards what looked like an elevator. I tried a few doors along the way out of sheer curiosity, but they were all locked. Were there dead people inside? What happened if they died and the door didn't open?

I pushed the up button since there was no down button. The doors slid open, and I stepped inside. Every surface, including the floor, was encrusted in what looked like diamonds.

This was not what I had expected. I actually wasn't sure what I expected, but everything covered in diamond-looking stones wasn't it.

I pushed the only button and looked closer. I wasn't a diamond expert, but they sure did look real. That or someone had too much fun with a Bedazzler.

The elevator ride seemed to go on forever. I couldn't help but giggle over the fact that the elevator was going up. Did the hell elevator go down?

The door dinged and slid open to a large white room that was filled with chairs and people. As soon as I stepped out of the elevator, there was a ticket dispenser.

"You have got to be kidding me." I pulled one out.

B102.

I looked up at the ceiling where a number was displayed. They were on A24.

Maybe they would be faster than the DMV. One would hope, with it being Heaven and all.

I made my way to an empty seat next to a little old man, who immediately turned to me.

"Oh, dear." He shook his head and clucked his tongue. "Too young. Too young, I tell ya."

I raised my eyebrows. "It was for a good cause."

"You remember? I don't remember a lick past my ninetieth birthday." His eyes went wide, and he shook his head again. "Whoooooeeee. I can't believe I made it to the pearly gates."

"You had pearly gates? I had a diamond-encrusted elevator."

In response, he burst into laughter and slapped his leg. Why had I never spent more time talking to senior citizens? They were hilarious.

I smiled, and his face softened. "You remind me of my great-granddaughter."

My smile fell, and I looked away. I had never experienced an actual family before. No doting grandma that let me eat popsicles before breakfast. No grandpa to take me on adventures in the backyard.

He reached for my hand, and I let him take it in his soft wrinkled one. "It'll be all right, dear."

I sure hoped so, because my heart was bruised and battered enough.

~

I'M NOT sure how long the wait was. Time seemed to function differently in Heaven. Not once did I feel hungry or that I had to pee.

B098 flashed on the ceiling, and my kind-hearted old man of a seatmate, whose name was Jack, stood.

"That would be me. Take care of yourself now, you hear?"

I smiled and then bit my lip nervously, waiting for my number to flash on the ceiling. Was this the part where they told me how much darkness my soul had and how long it would take to get my wings? I needed to get back to Earth.

I tried to look back over my shoulder at my shoulder blades but wasn't flexible enough. They had been slightly tingly since I sat down. I figured it was all in my head.

This whole thing might have been all in my head.

B101 flashed overhead, and I shut my eyes and took a steadying breath before standing. There was a single white door on the far side of the room where people had been knocking and gaining entrance.

What if this was some kind of social experiment to see who were followers?

I glanced around the room, and there were no other entrances. The elevator even had disappeared and just was a giant glowing area on the wall that people walked out of.

I approached the door and knocked softly. It opened, and I walked inside to find a desk and two chairs. I sat down and waited.

And waited some more.

There was a whole lot of waiting going on. My stomach should have been doing somersaults or churning up some bile, but instead, I felt oddly at peace. I could see why so many chose to stay in Heaven.

The door opened, and I turned. *Holy shit.*

"Brooklyn?" I stood, and she smiled back at me. "Holy shit!" I smacked a hand over my mouth. "Crap, I don't think I'm supposed to say that here."

She laughed and sat down across from me, opening up a laptop she had. I didn't know whether to be in awe over the fact that she was sitting across from me looking better than ever or the fact that laptops seemed to work in Heaven.

I guess if cell phones worked from Inferna, then MacBook Air having a stronghold in Heaven wasn't so much of a stretch.

"I would say I'm happy to see you, but I'm not." She reached her hand across the desk, and I took it. "I mean, I'm glad you're *here* and not *elsewhere.*"

I laughed. "I had my doubts."

She typed on the laptop, and her eyes widened. "It says here you already have your wings. But that can't be right."

She typed lightning fast and then looked at me, her eyes wide.

"What?" I looked over both my shoulders. "I think I'd know if I had wings. Wouldn't I?"

"I would think so. But this definitely says you are an archangel. Your trajectory is Los Angeles Celestial Academy, Class I, year two." She turned the laptop so I could see the screen.

"Bull shit." I pulled the laptop towards me and stared at the screen that had my picture, date of birth, date of death, and the information that said I was an archangel.

"What am I an archangel of? Fucking up? Surely this is just Morgan Freeman's way of playing a joke on me."

Brooklyn gave me a confused look and then pulled the laptop back towards her. "There is a flag on here." She double-clicked on something, and I waited as her eyes scanned the screen. "It says instead of sending you to the Earth entry point, that I am to take you to the hospital to see your dad, Oliver, and Asher."

I gripped the arms of the chair and fought off the panic that was churning in my gut. "What's wrong with Olly and Asher?"

She shook her head and shut the laptop. "It doesn't say. If they're in the hospital, that's a good thing. That means they're healing."

She stood, and I jumped up. She walked around the desk to the same door we had entered and opened it. It led right outside.

I shouldn't have been surprised, but I was. I could deal with glowing monkeys, cotton candy-smelling gremlin-lookalikes, and even shapeshifters. Throw a door that opened to somewhere different than before, and I was flabbergasted.

"I'm not tripping out on acid, am I?" I followed her out the door and stopped. "The ground. Is it clouds?"

She laughed and looped her arm through mine. It looked like Earth, except everything was clean and shiny. The ground felt a little like the recycled rubber they put on playgrounds.

"Welcome to the Great City."

I looked up in awe at the tall skyscrapers that appeared to go on for miles and miles into the sky. I had no concept of what Heaven would be like, but it definitely wasn't what I was seeing. Where were the cute little cherubs floating on clouds?

Walking with Brooklyn, a sense of peace washed over me again. There weren't many angels walking or flying around, so it was quiet. We didn't walk far before we were at one of the giant skyscrapers, and I followed Brooklyn inside.

"This is where I leave you." She gave me a hug and pressed the button for the elevator. "It will take you straight to the floor the hospital is on."

I hugged her. "Will you ever come back to Earth?"

She gave me a sad smile and shrugged. "I don't think so. Take care of yourself. Tell Cora I said hi."

The elevator doors slid shut and began its ascent. Soft harp music played over the speakers, and I snorted. I shouldn't have been laughing. I was dead. My dad and boyfriends were in the hospital.

The door opened, and I stepped out to a reception area. "I'm here to see Lucifer, Asher Thorne, and Oliver Morgan."

The woman at the desk looked up from her computer and smiled brightly at me. "Ms. Deville! It is such an honor to meet you!"

She stood and took my hand in hers. I raised a brow but followed her down the hall. She opened a door and led me inside.

"How is he?"

"He isn't well. He is healing very slowly, and the other archangels are dealing with the aftermath of demons on Earth. Only they can heal him." She patted my arm and then shut the door softly behind me.

The room was quiet and dim. In a bed in the center was my father. He wasn't hooked to any machines, but he didn't look good at all. His skin was pale, and the age lines on his face showed prominently.

Not that he had a lot of age lines to begin with.

I approached the bed and sat down in a chair. He looked so frail under the covers. I took his hand and squeezed.

"Dad?" He showed no signs of waking up. "I've seen Heaven and hell within a few days. I really need a hug right about now." I squeezed his hand and moved the chair closer. "Please be okay."

I put my head on the side of the bed, my hand still holding his. Suddenly, the gravity of the situation hit me like a ton of bricks. *I'm dead.*

My tears fell in a never-ending stream that had me turning my head into the sheet. Would this mean I could never return to my normal life again? Was my body on Earth or down in hell where it had died?

The intake in Heaven really needed to amp up their explanations.

"Please, Dad. Wake up."

A tingling sensation shot up my arm, and I sat up. With my free hand, I scrubbed the tears blurring my vision.

Oh, fuck. My hand was glowing.

My dad's eyes fluttered like they were trying to open. "Dad?"

He let out a pained moan, and his hand squeezed mine. "Healing."

"What?"

"You're healing me." His voice was raspy.

"I'm what?" My voice went up a solid octave, and I looked at our hands again. My hand was definitely glowing, but I didn't feel anything besides a slight tingle, which I thought was an effect of being dead and all. "How is that even possible? I don't know what the fuck I'm doing!"

"Language." He tried to laugh and ended up groaning instead.

I looked at my father lying in the hospital bed and choked on a sob. I had almost lost everything. I *had* lost everything. I wasn't even alive anymore.

"It's all over now." He sighed and squeezed my hand. "She can't hurt us anymore."

I looked at him and tried to control the tears swimming in my eyes. They fell anyway. "Are you-"

"I'll be fine. You should go find your boyfriends. You haven't seen them yet, have you?" Here he was lying in a hospital bed needing his newly turned angel of a daughter to heal him, and he was worried about me seeing my four lovers.

I shook my head and looked down at my hands. "What if this changes things?"

He looked thoughtful and pushed himself up to sit against the headboard. He patted the spot next to him.

My father wasn't the most affectionate, and I stared at him blankly before he patted the bed again. I crawled onto the bed and settled in next to him. I leaned my head against his shoulder.

"Things *will* be different now. You'll have duties that you need to fulfill, but those four will always be a part of your life. Unless you don't want them to be."

"I died."

He squeezed my arm and put his cheek on top of my head. My heart squeezed in my chest. It was surprising I could still feel it beating.

We sat there in silence for several minutes before he pulled away and pulled me to look at him.

"You saved the light from the dark."

I rolled my eyes, and then we both started to laugh. It wasn't a laugh because it was funny, but a laugh because *what the fuck*. It ended with him clearing his throat.

"Are you okay?" I'd never had to ask my dad that before. He had a faraway look in his eyes.

"You're okay. That's all that matters." He put his hand on my cheek and gave me a weak smile.

I settled back into the crook of his arm. He didn't seem fine at all.

I MISSED Olly and Asher by half an hour. They had been released from the hospital and went back to Earth to wait for me. I had no clue where my cell phone had ended up, so it wasn't like I could call them.

It was probably lost in the depths of hell. Were there roaming charges if a demon decided to make some calls with it?

"So tell me again, how am I supposed to get back there?" I really didn't believe the woman, who had led me to the Earth entry point.

"You are making it more difficult than it needs to be. You just step off the side. Think of where you want to go. Your wings will do all the work." She was getting annoyed. I could tell from the way she pursed her lips together.

"Why aren't they coming out now? I'm telling them to."

The woman laughed and shook her head. "They will once you jump. Think of it as the maiden voyage."

"What if they don't come out?"

"They will." She let out a sigh and backed up. "This is why new angels stay here for a while. Are you sure you don't want to stay?"

"Michael said-"

"I know. I know. He said you are an *exception* to the rule."

I let out a frustrated sigh and looked over the edge of the platform I was standing on. We were at the edge of the city, and there was a hole through the surface that looked like it fell right into an abyss of white swirling clouds.

This woman expected me to just jump and hope for the best. Could I die twice? I wasn't too keen on having my soul be lost.

"When's the next flight back?"

"There isn't. Would you prefer if I pushed you?" She had reached her limit.

"What? Hell no! I mean, sorry. Thanks for the offer."

I had my feet at the edge. Where would they be? Earth was safe now. At least as far as I knew.

I shut my eyes and stepped off.

CHAPTER 17

REVE

I had never been one to believe that a heart could actually break. That was until blood-covered Danica had wings burst from her back. Then she flew through the stained-glass window in the ballroom, with her father in her arms.

My heart shattered right along with the window.

Toby looked at me, fear in his eyes. They seemed to ask the same questions as I was wondering. Did that mean Danica was dead?

"Go." I turned back towards the chaos that had erupted in the ballroom.

"What about you? You can't get through."

I clenched my jaw. "I have to take care of this mess. I'll go back to Lucifer's house once I get things sorted out here."

I hoped I wasn't making a poor decision. It was possible that whoever was in charge might decide to cut Inferna off completely. If I were in charge, I would.

Inferna and Earth had no business mingling.

Toby pulled me into a hug and clapped me on the back. I pulled back and looked at him, surprised by his gesture.

"You still have piss-poor taste in sports teams." With those words, he spread his wings and flew out the window. Hopefully, he could catch up with Danica and make it through with them.

I have never been one to get overly emotional, but standing on the steps to the dais, my chosen family gone, I felt an emptiness spread throughout my body.

Shaking off the feeling, I walked up the steps and looked out across the large room where my family once hosted extravagant parties monthly.

"Enough!" I shouted, my voice naturally projecting across the room.

Hundreds of pairs of eyes landed on me, and I felt a heat moving up my neck. It had been a long time since I had to stand in front of such a large crowd.

"Lilith is dead." I looked over at the pile of ashes. That had taken some serious power to light her up like that.

The room remained silent, and then the first demon took a knee and bowed their head. I balled my hands into fists, controlling my urge to flee.

I didn't want to be King. I had never wanted the throne.

We sat at the large dining table, a feast laid before us. It was a joyous occasion for our family. I was turning half a century old, which meant my full capabilities would soon start to develop.

My father stood with his wine glass in hand. "To Reve, future King of Inferna." He looked at me at the opposite end of the table. "Son, it's time to take your place as my protege."

"Must he be so corny?" my sister, Sammy, complained from next to me.

"Samara," my mother warned from her place next to my father.

I hid my chuckle with my hand over my mouth. My younger sister was not scared of our father. She would make a great Queen if it were allowed.

We raised our glasses and drank. I gulped mine down.

"What if I don't want the throne?"

Silence fell over the room; not even a breath could be heard. My mother looked like she was going to cry. My father's face flamed red.

"Why would you reject your heritage? Your birthright?" My father's voice

was dangerously low. If I didn't choose my words carefully, he was liable to snap my neck.

"Lucas is just as suitable a successor. And he wants it. I don't."

My sister shifted uncomfortably next to me. "I'll do it."

My dad made a noise in his throat. "They would kill you before you even had the crown upon your head."

I looked to my sister, who was twisting her napkin in her lap. Unlike my brother and me, she had been born with no special abilities. It was impossible for women to be dream demons since only males developed those traits. But she hadn't even developed my mother's ability to lull someone asleep with a simple touch.

"Lucas does not have the skill set required to rule. He will start a civil war among the demon races." My mother spoke quietly and then reached for her wine glass. "Your father is getting older, Reve. It is your duty as firstborn to take his place. Marry a nice demon girl. Have lots of demon babies."

I rolled my eyes. It wasn't the first time my love life had been brought to the table. I had no interest in the high-born demon girls they paraded in front of me at our monthly gatherings.

I wanted someone real. Someone to make me laugh. Someone to challenge me. Someone that wasn't afraid to be herself around me.

I looked out across the crowd of bowing forms. I found Alaric with his men, surrounding a group of other shifters that had decided it was a good idea to follow Lilith.

"Take them to the dungeons." I sounded just like my father. I had a no-nonsense edge to my voice that I hadn't known I possessed.

The room was silent as Alaric and his men led the group of demons out.

"You've freed us," a woman near the steps, still on her knee, cried out. "Long live the king!"

I *almost* laughed, but then a series of shouts repeating the phrase went up around the room. I wondered if they would still be shouting the words if they knew I was the one that killed my father and mother.

I held up my hands to signal them to stop. "I do not wish to be your king."

If there had been fans in the ballroom, the shit would have hit them. The noise hit a crescendo as the elite among the demons began talking all at once.

"Blasphemy! He can't renounce the throne!"

"There will be a civil war!"

"Where has he been all this time?"

The comments felt like a knife through my chest. These were my people. But at the same time, they weren't my people anymore.

"Quiet!" I bellowed. Jesus, I really did sound just like my father. The room fell silent. "I will meet with the Infernal Council, at least those that are present. We will decide on a plan of action. In the meantime, return to your villages and clean up the mess Lilith caused. Any demons that fought with free will for her should be handled accordingly."

With that, I turned and exited out the door behind the dais. It led to a large meeting room. Growing up, Alaric had nicknamed it "sticks" because the council members always seemed to have sticks up their asses.

I sat down at the head of the table and waited for the council members to trickle in. Many of them were familiar faces and others were new. It had been centuries upon centuries since they met in this room.

Alaric slipped in the room with three of his men, and they spread out along the perimeter. I hadn't requested his presence, but he naturally fell back into a protective role.

Once it seemed no one else was going to join the ten demons around the table, I cleared my throat and folded my hands on the table. I looked at each of them.

"Our people haven't been free in centuries. With Lilith's control over, we need to act fast to stop civil wars from breaking out among the less civilized of us."

"No offense, Your Highness, but where have you been all these years? Last I heard you were sent on a mission by Lilith to kill Lucifer and take back that section of our land."

I heard Alaric shift behind me as if to tell me he could take the council member out if I needed him to.

"It is true, I was sent to kill him. Instead, he broke the hold Lilith had over me. He gave me a choice. Die or be sent to Earth to work for him."

"And now you wish to go back to Earth?"

"Yes. My mate is there." I shut my eyes briefly to stop the tears that had suddenly felt like they were pooling somewhere behind them.

Several of the council members made noises of approval. Finding your fated mate was a big deal in Inferna.

"Who will lead us then?"

Historically, the alpha dream demon had always been King. There was no other demon that matched the capabilities and could bring all the other demons to their knees. Only the alpha had a phantom form and could push daydreams.

"We can vote, or the council can make decisions." It sounded like a good plan. Except that the democratic method wasn't even working out for Earth.

The door slammed open, and the guards moved towards the intruder.

"Get your bloody paws away from me!"

I stood and leaned against the table. My sister had fled when I told her to. Right before I killed our mother and father. I assumed she was dead or far away in the outer territories of Inferna.

"Samara?" It was somewhat of a stupid question, stemming from the shock of seeing her.

She was just like she had always been, besides her purple hair. She scrunched her nose at me and brushed her hair from her face.

"Reve, you know I hate that name." She strode towards me and stopped. Her face softened, and then she pulled me into a hug.

"Sammy. I thought you-"

"Yeah, yeah. The rumors of angels flitting around, and the rightful king, brought me back. Word traveled fast."

I pulled back and looked at her. Wherever she had been in Inferna, she had been treated well. The guilt I felt for leaving her behind lessened.

She sat down in an empty chair, and the all-male council looked like they were about to implode. She just smiled at them.

"We are discussing serious realm business, young lady. You can wait outside." A vampire demon looked at her in disgust. "You are not welcome here with your... with your purple hair and inappropriate attire."

Sammy slowly swiveled her chair in the direction of the vampire. "You have got to be kidding me. All this time, and we still oppress women? Where I've been-"

"We know where you've been. You can go right back." The vampire was asking for it and not from me. My sister looked murderous.

I furrowed my brows and had so many questions about what my sister had been up to over the past several centuries. Now didn't seem like the appropriate time to ask.

"My people are requesting a place on the council."

Her people? I cleared my throat and took a serious look at her. Her skin seemed to glow with a power she hadn't had before. It wasn't unheard of that demons could morph into a different type of demon with time.

Lilith was an example of that if there was ever an example.

"Absolutely not!" Another man, who had been one of my father's most trusted advisors, said with a raised voice. "The gypsies are criminals! Parading around with their bright colors and debauchery!"

My sister's laugh echoed in the room. She was enjoying the drama she was causing. Or at least she was pretending she was.

"That's enough. With me stepping down, Sammy can step in for me until a solution is reached." I pushed in my chair. "Good luck."

Before they could stop me, I went phantom and left the room.

∾

I HONESTLY DIDN'T CARE if the council bit each other's heads off. As much as I wanted to stay and catch up with my sister, I'd have to at another time.

Inferna was no longer my home. My home was where my heart was, as corny as the idea was.

Alaric was quiet most of the way back to Lucifer's territory. He had insisted he come along to protect me. I didn't need protection when I could simply vanish, but I let him accompany me anyway. Maybe he felt like he was making up for all those years ago when he left me.

"You're really going back to Earth?" He finally spoke once the iron gates of hell rose before us.

It was a vast territory of Inferna, entirely surrounded by iron bars that rose at least twenty feet in the air. Not that the gates would keep some kinds of demons out, but it would certainly keep some things in.

At first glance, it looked like a run-of-the-mill Inferna estate, but once close enough, you could sense the power behind the gates.

"I am. Once I make sure Danica is in one piece, I'll come back to see Sammy."

Alaric grunted and stopped at the main entrance of the property. There was a call box off to the side, and he pressed the button.

The gates opened immediately. Not creepy at all.

"Do you think I could come back with you?"

I stopped and turned to look at him. He had a hopeful look on his face. So did Picard, who sat on his shoulder.

"I don't get to make that decision. I'm not even sure how I'm getting back."

We walked towards the house, and Alex was waiting at the open door as if he was expecting us. A shiver ran down my spine at his gaze.

I didn't love or hate Incubus demons. We were similar in nature. I fed off fear, and they fed off sexual desire. He seemed way too proper to be an incubus. His kind were usually outlandish and flaunted their heritage around.

"This is hell?" Alaric followed me inside and looked around. "It's just a house."

Alex laughed and led us into the kitchen. "It's underground. Would you like a tour?"

"I think I'll pass." Alaric slid onto a barstool, and Picard jumped onto the counter to sniff a pile of pastries on a plate. He dragged one off and started eating it.

"Chamuel will be up in a few minutes." Alex bowed and then left us in the kitchen.

Several minutes later, Chamuel walked into the kitchen. I was surprised the angel known for peace and love was in Inferna.

"Is Danica...?" I couldn't say it. I wouldn't say it.

"She's an angel now."

I didn't know how I felt about that. I was the odd man out now. At least with her as half-demon, I hadn't felt so alone. Would she even still want me now that she was a full-fledged angel?

It was selfish of me to even have the thoughts, considering the fact she was an angel meant she had died.

Chamuel's gaze fell on me, and his face softened. "Do not fret, son. Just because she's an angel, doesn't mean her feelings are going to change."

I nodded. I didn't feel that reassured. "Why are you here in Inferna?"

He sighed. "Things are changing. Lucifer will no longer bear this burden alone. The archangels will rotate. I volunteered to go first."

"That's very noble of you." Alaric was such a kiss-ass when he needed to be. "So, Reve and I were wondering if I could also go back to Earth."

Chamuel looked from him to Picard, then at me. He raised his eyebrows. "For what purpose? We are still tracking down demons that escaped. Why would we want to let more through?"

"I am a hunter by nature. I can help with that. I'm one of the good ones." Alaric sat up a little straighter and looked at me. "A little help here, Reve."

"He might be of use. He did help save Lucifer."

He looked at Picard, who was sitting like a meerkat, giving him puppy-dog eyes. "Very well. Let me get you back to Earth."

～

TIME IN HEAVEN apparently passed slowly.

When I returned from Inferna, I hadn't returned to the academy's campus. It was doubtful that would be the first place any of them would return to. Instead, I set up Alaric in my apartment and stayed at Asher's.

Toby, Asher, and Oliver returned about a week after I had gotten home. Asher and Toby forgave me for exploding the dream I had pulled them into, on the promise that I would never go into their heads again.

The days and nights passed, and we still weren't given a date on when Danica would return. Michael said that she had a choice to stay there, plus, Lucifer was bedridden. He had drained himself almost completely of angelic power.

I didn't even know there was such a thing.

"Let's play Cards Against Humanity." Asher finished clearing off the table from dinner and grabbed us all another round of beers.

Most of our days and nights followed the same pattern. Asher went to work, Oliver went to school, Toby and I waited in case Danica returned. At night we, ate together and then played games or watched movies.

Oliver was big on learning all the games that he had no clue how to play. I was glad it wasn't his turn to pick because there was only so much of Uno and Checkers that I could take. I was pretty sure he could see through cards.

We each took seven white cards from the stack.

Asher read the first black card. "Just got dumped! Retweet #dumpedbecauseof...?"

I looked through my stack of white cards and snorted. I selected and put it face down. Oliver took the longest, staring at his very seriously. He often won because his choices made us laugh.

Asher picked the cards up and read them. "Dumped because 'jerking off into a pool of unicorn tears.' Dumped because 'Oprah.' Dumped because 'the past.' As much as I love the unicorn tears, I'm going to go with Oprah."

"Yes!" Oliver grabbed the card and did a little celebratory dance in his seat.

"Do you even know who Oprah is?" Toby took a drink of his beer and couldn't stop himself from smiling.

That's why we had game or movie night. We needed to smile. The thought of Danica never coming back or her not remembering us was too much to handle.

"Of course I know who she is."

We continued on for several more rounds until Oliver suddenly sprang from his chair, his eyes going wide and then looking at the door to the roof.

"She's back."

CHAPTER 18

DANICA

*I*t turned out the woman who had been tasked to get me out of Heaven hadn't been wrong. As soon as I was through the opening, my wings came out of my back.

It wasn't painful like I had thought. Instead, they tingled where they connected to my back. I didn't even quite understand how two appendages so substantial could hide mysteriously inside my body.

I wasn't a believer in magic before. Now, I definitely was.

At first, everything was a foggy white as I glided down, but then land came into view. Then the city. The wings seemed to do what I wanted them to and steered me towards the old factory building in Pasadena.

I shut my eyes as my body was torpedoed towards the roof. My body righted itself, and my feet touched down gently.

"Jesus." My wings shook like a dog shaking water off after a bath and snapped away. I had at least managed to keep my eyes open most of the flight. It was easier when I was the one doing the navigating.

I looked down at my white dress and cringed. I was not a fan of dresses or the color white. It made me feel innocent.

The door leading inside burst open, and I let out a squeal of surprise. I put my hand over my heart and could feel it beating wildly.

I stood dumbstruck as Oliver stood in the doorway, a big grin on his face. I felt like I hadn't seen him in ages. Maybe I hadn't.

"Danica!" Oliver ran across the short distance and scooped me into his arms. I felt the air being squeezed out of me as he spun me around.

I was passed off to another set of arms. Asher skipped the spinning and took my face in his hands. "You remember us?" His voice shook.

I laughed and kissed him. His fingers went to my hair and pulled me closer. How scared must they have been, thinking that I had forgotten them?

"I'd never forget you." I breathed deeply, catching my breath from the spinning and kissing.

Lips brushed against my neck, and I turned towards Tobias. He had tears in his eyes. I cupped his cheek, and he leaned into it.

"I was starting to worry you stayed there." He kissed me gently and pulled me into a hug.

Just past him, standing back from the group was Reve. His face was expressionless. Would he still want me now that I was an angel?

I pulled away from Tobias and stood in front of Reve. "Say something." I searched his eyes, hoping I could get a read on him.

"What took you so long?" He pulled me into a fierce hug that made me gasp. "Don't ever die again."

I laughed and buried my face in his shirt. I tried not to let the tears in my eyes escape. I had cried too much over the past several months. These tears were different, though. They were happy tears.

THAT NIGHT, I couldn't sleep. I shimmied out from between Olly and Tobias and made my way to the roof. I pulled the throw blanket I grabbed off the couch around my shoulders as I stepped out into the chilly November air.

I sat down on a lounge chair and stared up at the sky.

Everything in my world had changed. I was dead but was never really a human to begin with. That didn't ease the finality of what had happened.

"Can't sleep?" Reve appeared next to me and made me scoot over so he could lay next to me on his side. We barely fit on the lounger. "I can't sleep either."

I laughed and turned on my side to look at him. "What are you going to do to feed now?"

His brows furrowed together in thought. "I think I can still get into your dreams. You haven't been asleep yet, so I haven't tried." He moved hair out of my eyes. "You're my mate. Can't you feel it?"

He took my hand and put it over my chest, where my heart was beating. I shut my eyes and focused. I had always felt a pull and connection towards all four of them, but just thought it was normal when falling in love.

It had become such a normal sensation that I never gave it a second thought. I shrugged and opened my eyes.

"It feels like love. Like my heart could crack open in an instant." He brought my hand to his mouth and kissed the palm.

"Exactly." He pulled me closer and tucked me into his chest. "My father didn't have to hunt anymore once he found my mother."

I snorted back a laugh because talking about feeding off of a mate was a weird conversation. I put my ear against Reve's chest and listened to his heartbeat.

"Do you think my dad is going to be all right?" He was still up in Heaven healing. My healing could only wake him.

"I think that your dad went through a lot. He loved that crazy bitch at one point. It's not going to be easy for him to get over something like that."

I nodded and let out a sigh.

"What else is on your mind?"

"Life. I thought I would want to be an angel, but now everything seems so final. I'm a guardian now. I could be called back to Heaven at any time. Before, when I thought I was at least half a human... I did have things I wanted out of life."

Reve stroked my back, urging me to continue.

"Like a family. One like I never had growing up. It was just my dad and me. I wanted a husband who had a big family. Maybe kids. Now though..."

He pulled away and looked at me. "You can still have all those things. With us."

I snorted. "It's illegal to marry four men. Not that we could anyways with you four not even having paperwork or whatever."

"It doesn't have to be legal. It can be just for us. As for babies... your father had you."

"But who knows how. For all we know, Lilith could have used dark magic to get pregnant." I winced at the thought of being conceived in such a way. "She used me."

He sighed and pulled me close again. "Why don't you get some sleep? It's all over now. We can finally breathe."

CHAPTER 19

DANICA

 $\mathcal{I}$ stood in the empty living room of the house I had grown up in. After being released to come home, my dad decided to sell the house. He said he had bought it for Lily.

I couldn't say I blamed him. It still hurt to leave it behind.

"Are you sure you want to sell it?" I asked, turning towards him.

He had been sitting at the kitchen island, signing paperwork for the real estate agent.

"I'm sure." He stood and met me at the door. "It was a good house. At least when I was here."

We walked out the door for the last time, and he locked it behind us. "I'll see you tomorrow, bright and early?"

"Is it normal to feel nervous?" I couldn't stop the fluttering of butterflies in my stomach. Or maybe that was the tacos I had for lunch.

My dad pulled me into a hug and kissed my forehead. "I think so. I wouldn't know. I've never been married."

He unlocked his car and took off down the driveway. We had come separately because there was something I needed to do before leaving Montecito behind for good. I hadn't told my dad about it because it was against angel protocol.

I was never one for following rules.

I took one last look at the house before getting in my own car. Wings were cool and all, but I still couldn't resist driving.

I pulled up outside Ava's house and walked to the door. We still had been talking and texting occasionally, but I hadn't seen her since the night she was attacked by a vampire at Blue Wave.

She opened the door before I could even ring the doorbell. Her hair wasn't blue any longer. Now it was a dark blonde.

"What happened to your blue hair?" I walked in as she stepped out of the way, and then we hugged. "You didn't get fired, did you?"

She laughed and shook her head. "Promotion. I'm a manager now. With Kai opening the new location, he needed another manager to run the show."

"That's great, Ava!" I gave her another hug, and we sat down on the couch. "Are you still going to go to school?"

"Eventually."

An awkward silence fell over the room, and I shifted on the couch. I didn't know where to start and opened my mouth to speak several times before thinking twice.

"You're one of them. Aren't you?" She finally broke the tension. "Some kind of supernatural."

"It's a little more than that." I cleared my throat and took her hand. "You can't ever breathe a word of this."

"You know I won't. Kai explained to me that there are different types of demons after that vampire incident."

"I'm not a demon. I'm an angel." With my admission, she narrowed her eyes and then laughed. "Are you seriously laughing about me being an angel?"

"Yes. No. I don't know." She pulled her hand away and ran her fingers through her hair. "What do you mean, you're an angel?"

I gave her the short version of the past several months of my life. Her mouth was wide open by the end of it.

"You died?" Tears welled in her eyes, and I took her hand again. She looked down, and then she looked up and glared at me. "Is that a fucking engagement ring on your finger?"

I bit my lip. I should have known she would eventually notice the rock on my left ring finger. "Yes."

"Which one did you choose?" She stood and started pacing. "You aren't eloping, are you?"

I laughed. "It happened at Thanksgiving. They-"

"They? So you didn't pick one?" She stopped and looked down at me, her hands on her hips. "Isn't it against the law to have more than one husband?"

"It is. I don't quite understand why. This isn't the eighteen-hundreds. We're doing it just for us." I looked down at my hands. "I wanted you to come, but if the other angels knew that you were aware of our existence because of me. Well..."

She sighed. "You'd get in trouble."

I nodded, and she sat back down.

"I'm sorry for keeping everything from you."

"I'll get over it. You're happy, though?"

"Happier than I ever thought I could be."

"You just about ready?" my dad asked from the other side of the bathroom door.

I looked in the mirror at myself. I had gone with a simple white wedding dress that had an empire waist and flowing lace. I may not have liked white, but this day wasn't just about me. It was about four others too.

I pulled out the folded piece of paper I had shoved in my bra. I hoped my words were enough to convey my feelings towards the four of them. I scanned it one last time and put it back in my bra. There was probably a better place to stick it, but no one would be surprised when I reached in and pulled it out.

I should have gotten a dress with pockets.

I slid open the bathroom door and smiled at my dad. "How do I look?"

His eyes glistened as he took me in. He was wearing one of his best black three-piece suits. I hadn't seen him in a suit in a long time. It was nice to see he was trying to get back to normal.

"You look beautiful." He kissed my cheek and walked me to the metal stairs leading to the roof.

My stomach was in knots. If my hands were able to sweat, they would have been. Sweat wasn't something I missed. It was quite possibly the best thing about being an angel so far.

We stopped at the top of the stairs, and he opened the door. "Ready?"

"More than ready."

There was no music. No flowers. No wedding parties. It was just Tobias, Asher, Olly, Reve, and me in front of the select few that we invited. Chamuel was officiating.

They stood at the edge of the roof in a row. My heart stuttered as we approached them dressed in their suits. I had seen Reve in a suit, but not the other three.

I was ready for our honeymoon to start immediately.

Most of the ceremony followed the standard wedding script. When we got to the vows, I pulled my folded-up piece of paper from my bra. Everyone laughed.

I cleared my throat and unfolded the paper. I had wanted to memorize what I had written but was glad I had written it down. I was an emotional mess and couldn't remember what I wrote.

"For most of my life, I've been lost. I was never really sure where I fit in. Was I an angel? Was I good enough to be an angel? Until I met you, I didn't know that being good meant more than just being perfect. Tobias, you've taught me that it means loving with your entire heart and being patient." I wiped a tear from my cheek. "Asher, you've taught me that it means not taking everything so seriously and leaning on others. Oliver, from you, I've learned that it means to let go of the past and be forgiving. And Reve, I've learned that being good means not being afraid of being different, and that keeping the darkness away means playing for the same team. Just not the Giants or the Raiders."

"Hey now." He laughed. "Those are some pretty loaded words."

I grinned. "Each of you keeps my darkness away. I can't wait to spend all of eternity with you. We might sometimes drive each other crazy, but there's no one else I'd rather go crazy with than you four."

I finally looked up then to find four pairs of eyes looking at me with all the love in the world. Maybe my words weren't the most poetic, but they were honest and how I truly felt about each of them.

Tobias spoke next. "When we first met you, none of us knew we were missing an essential part of our hearts and souls. I love that you feel so intensely and do so unapologetically. I love that you never give up and fight for what you want. I promise to protect you and love you forever."

Asher cleared his throat and pulled a card out of his pocket. I was glad I wasn't the only one that couldn't memorize a few hundred words. "I knew I was in love with you that night on the roof when you told me to stop running. I took a chance and opened my heart to you. What I got in return was a woman who allows me to breathe again. A woman who allows me to love again. A woman who makes me want to be better. I not only gained a pretty spectacular lover, but four best friends."

My dad made a coughing sound, and we all laughed.

Oliver smiled brightly at me. "I was a complete idiot when I first met you. I was lost and didn't know my purpose. But a miracle happened, and you forgave me when I wasn't sure I should be forgiven. You've opened my eyes to the world and allowed me to love with my entire heart and soul."

Hearing them say such heartfelt words to me made me want to ugly cry. Tears were already pouring down my cheeks at an alarming rate. I was a mess.

Reve stepped forward and handed me the handkerchief that was in his jacket pocket. I mouthed "thank you," and he stepped back.

"Where I'm from, they say that mates are hard to find. That only the most connected of souls will find each other during their greatest times of need. I didn't know what I was missing in my life until I found you. You saved me from a darkness that I didn't know existed in me. I walked for two thousand years without you, and it was two thousand years too long."

The ceremony came to a close, and champagne was passed around. I was giddy with excitement about going on a vacation. Alone. Just me and my four men.

"Are you going to be okay? I feel bad taking off on Christmas Eve." I hugged my dad tightly as we prepared to leave.

"I'll be fine."

"Yeah. He'll be fine." Alaric slung his arm around his shoulder. "We're going to hit Blue Wave. Pick up some fine ladies."

I rolled my eyes. "Please do not talk about my dad and picking up fine ladies in the same sentence ever again."

Picard let out a series of squeaks. It sounded like he was laughing, but I couldn't be sure. Alaric and my father had oddly become friends over the past several weeks. Alaric had also killed a goon that had been aiming his sword at my father's head.

Asher and Olly each took one of my hands. I didn't know where we were going, but wherever it was, we'd be together.

Forever.

EPILOGUE

DANICA

*W*e landed on the soft sand of a beach. The sun was rising, and the sky was a gorgeous array of shades of orange. It was quiet; the only sound was the waves crashing along the shore.

Where were we? Hawaii?

"I bet you think we're in Hawaii." Tobias came behind me and slid his arms around to rest on my waist, pulling me back against him. He could never seem to keep his hands off me. It was like he thought I wasn't real and had to touch me to ensure I was there.

Now that we were married, he was never going to let me go. I wasn't complaining.

"Just because there's a beach doesn't mean I automatically assume we're in Hawaii," I lied.

He laughed and buried his face in my neck, his beard tickling my skin. Reve stepped beside us and looked out at the waves.

"I'm still amazed at the colors in this world. Even if I have been here for centuries now." He took one of my hands and gave it a gentle squeeze.

I couldn't believe how much my life had changed in less than a year.

. . .

"You want me to put my hand where?" I looked down at the turkey in front of me. Its legs were spread wide open, and it was ready to be violated.

Tobias had to be kidding me. I knew I should have been more adamant about buying an already prepared feast. I was getting better at cooking, but not enough to want to stick my hand in a turkey's hoo-ha.

"In the cavity. It's all in a bag, Dani. All you have to do is pull it out." Tobias leaned his hip against the counter. He had an amused smirk on his face that he would pay for later.

"So, you're telling me that someone already violated this bird, put all of its guts in a bag, and then shoved it back inside? Why?" I scrunched my nose. Raw poultry gave me the willies.

"Because some people like gravy not out of a can."

I made a gagging noise. "You do it."

"I told you she wouldn't be able to do it. You owe me twenty." Reve was sitting on the end of the counter swinging his legs as he watched us fuss over the turkey.

"Can you not kick the cabinets? I'm already going to have enough to repair once I knock holes down into the units below." Asher had just walked in from the roof where he had set up a turkey fryer.

Construction on the building would start soon, combining the three units together. We could have just moved somewhere else, but where was the fun in that?

Tobias elbowed me out of the way and took the bag of giblets out of the turkey. I cringed and went to stand between Reve's legs. He wrapped his arms around me and kissed my forehead.

"Saves the world, yet can't clean a turkey out." He laughed and slid off the counter. "You excited about your dad coming home?"

My dad had been recovering in Heaven for what felt like forever. He could have come back sooner, but he wanted to be at full health. Plus, he was supposedly creating a 'How to Guide' for running Hell since he was no longer in charge of soul redemption and torture.

Olly and I would have our turns once I was done at the academy. It wasn't something I was looking forward to.

"I am. He was wearing a suit again when I saw him last week. That's major progress."

Olly burst in through the front door, his arms weighed down by several bags. I met him halfway and took a few.

"Whose idea was it to teach Ric to drive? If I wasn't an angel, I'm pretty sure my life would have flashed before my eyes." Olly put the rest of the bags he was carrying on the table.

"You could learn how to drive." I started pulling the rest of our Thanksgiving dinner out of the bags. Apparently, it was fine to order all the sides but not the turkey.

Men.

"I don't like cars. You know that."

I wrapped my arms around his neck and stood on my tiptoes to kiss his cheek. He bent his head down and kissed me. His lips were soft as they brushed against mine. He gently pulled my bottom lip between his teeth.

"Get a room." Alaric grumbled from behind us.

"This is our room." I pulled away from Olly and turned toward the wolf shifter, who had become somewhat of a fixture in our lives.

We were responsible for him until my dad got back. He had volunteered to make sure he didn't get into any trouble while he was on Earth. He had saved my dad from being beheaded after all.

"Where's Picard?" Asher had an irrational fear of the little guy. Whenever Alaric was around and Picard wasn't anywhere to be seen, Asher had to know where he was. He feared a sneak attack from the monkey.

"Why? Do you miss him?" Alaric laughed. *"He's napping in the cupholder of the car."* He made himself at home and went to the refrigerator to grab himself a beer.

The door to the roof opened, and we all turned as my dad walked in, dressed in a dark gray suit and an orange tie.

I spread my wings, not caring what I knocked over, and flew up to the landing. I threw myself into his arms and he wrapped his arms around me in a tight hug.

"I see you're getting used to those wings of yours." He laughed and pulled back to look at me. *"You look beautiful."*

Tears stung my eyes, and I swallowed the lump in my throat. I still randomly burst into tears thinking about all that had transpired.

"Thank you. You're looking pretty good yourself."

We joined the others, and hugs and handshakes were exchanged.

"Alaric." My dad stuck out his hand. "Thank you."

They shook firmly before Alaric pulled him into a hug and slapped his back like they had known each other for their entire lives.

Once dinner was ready, we all headed to the roof where the guys had set up a large table. Lights were strung up all around the rooftop, and there were a few patio heaters set up near the table.

My heart felt like it would burst as we all gathered around. Thanksgiving was usually just my dad and me, but now my family had grown.

The basket of rolls was handed my way, and I folded back the cloth napkin that was covering them. My breath caught in my throat.

I must have stared in the basket for a solid minute as everyone at the table sat silently watching me. I finally reached in and took out the small velvet box.

I flipped the box open and brought my hand to my mouth to stop myself from making an embarrassing sound. The ring was beautiful, with one large diamond surrounded by four smaller diamonds.

"Will you marry us?" Olly turned toward me and took my hand. "We love you and want you to have everything you've ever wanted."

I looked at each of their hopeful faces as tears slid down my cheeks. I was completely caught off guard.

I looked at my dad, who I swore swiped at his eye. He gave me a slight nod of the head. Not that I would have changed my mind had he shaken it.

"Yes." A laugh burst out of me, the same way you see in the movies. I inwardly cringed and swore to never make fun of women's reactions at proposals again.

Olly grinned and slid the ring onto my finger.

I smiled at the memory of how they had asked me to marry them. There had definitely been a lot of shitty moments in the past several months, but the last month made up for those tenfold.

"Are you going to tell me where we are?" It had been the middle of the day back in California. We were clearly somewhere on the other side of the world.

"We are near Fuck It, Thailand." Olly kicked his dress shoes off and peeled his socks off his feet.

"We've told you a million times, angel baby, it's Phuket." Asher laughed and put his arm around Olly's neck, yanking him to his side. "There will be a lot of fucking going on, though."

"This is a private island. It's a wedding gift from your dad." Tobias unwrapped himself from around me and took my other hand.

I followed them down the shoreline and then away from the shore to the stretch of large trees. "Where are we staying?" I hadn't seen a house when we landed.

Hands covered my eyes, and I nearly tripped over my feet. They laughed, and we continued walking.

"You guys aren't going to kill me, are you?" Laughter filled my ears.

We stopped, and the hands left my eyes.

It took a minute for my brain to process what I was seeing. Up in the trees, half-hidden, was the largest treehouse I had ever seen.

There was a large wraparound deck that had blue Christmas lights strung around the railing and large picturesque windows on all sides. One window had a Christmas tree standing in front of it, the white lights twinkling.

I brought my hand to my mouth and couldn't stop the tears from flowing. These men had turned me into a crier.

Olly scooped me up into his arms and carried me toward the wooden stairs. They wound their way around the base of one of the trees and up onto the deck.

"Asher designed this." Olly slid open the door and walked inside the house. He put me down, and I took in the room.

The living room was large, with sliding windows on two walls. The sleek, white kitchen was open to the living room, which was decorated in blues. I really couldn't wait to see where we'd be sleeping. My guess was the stairs leading up to another level was where the bed was.

"It's gorgeous." I turned back toward my guys standing in front of the tree.

I could think of no better way to spend my Christmas than with four men who looked at me like I was their entire world. I hoped they knew they were my entire world too.

ANGEL BABY & THE HOLY GRAIL

A CELESTIAL ACADEMY NOVELLA

CHAPTER 1

DANICA

I sat with a box in my lap and waited impatiently to get permission to rip it open. Not that I needed permission, I was a grown-ass woman. A *married* grown-ass woman. Some might not have agreed with my assessment that I was grown and a woman, but the men sitting around me sure did.

It would be rude of me to just tear into the gifts while we were waiting on Olly to get his ass out of the bedroom. *What is he doing in there?*

"Give me a hint." I smoothed my hands over the shiny blue and silver striped paper. "As your wife, I demand a hint."

"Oh, is that how it's going to be now?" Reve bent over the back of the couch and kissed me as I tilted my head back to see him. "There are four of us versus one of you."

I cocked an eyebrow and he hopped over the back of the couch and sat next to me, grabbing the present out of my clutches. He gave it a good shake and I snatched it back.

"One pussy, four dicks. Would be a shame to be last in line for it." I smirked as he rolled his eyes.

"Last in line for what?" Olly finally came out of the bedroom, his hair still wet from his shower.

"Her pussy. There's a line for it now." Asher sat on the other side of me with his coffee and took a sip. "I don't need to wait in line for it, I'll just take your ass."

I groaned and shoved at his shoulder, nearly causing him to spill his coffee on the brand-new couch in our island treehouse.

I still couldn't believe we had our own oasis with no one else around. I had thanked them by passing out from exhaustion as soon as my head hit the pillows.

"I'm sorry I fell asleep last night." I looked over at Tobias who was sitting cross-legged on the floor next to the tree. He had been whispering such naughty things in my ear during the treehouse tour and then I had gone and fallen asleep.

"Let's open some presents." Tobias rubbed his hands together. "We have the whole week to punish you for falling asleep on us last night."

He grinned at me and I bounced in my seat as Reve handed me my present back. I loved Christmas, and it was even more special now that I had spent Christmas Eve marrying the four men I loved.

Olly kept looking at his phone, and I narrowed my eyes when he looked over at me. "What's so interesting on there?"

"Nothing." He threw the phone upside down next to him on the floor and took the box Asher had put in his lap. "I thought we said no gifts for each other."

"I believe my response to that ridiculous notion was a grunt." Asher smirked and then grew serious. "Open it."

I sat forward in my seat, already knowing what was inside since he had talked to me about it. My heart was nearly exploding from anticipation.

Olly opened the shoe-sized box and then threw out the abundance of tissue paper. He pulled out a black ring box and stared at it silently.

My heartbeat was thudding in my ears as Asher took it from him and opened it. Inside was a band that had a dark woodgrain pattern in the titanium.

Before Asher could say anything, Olly was up and out the door, leaving all of us with our jaws hitting the floor.

"Fuck." Asher snapped the ring box shut and stared at the door that had just closed behind Olly. "I don't understand."

"Go after him, you idiot." Tobias threw a balled-up piece of wrapping paper at him. "He's been acting strange this morning."

Asher stood and shoved the ring box in his pocket before following Olly. I leaned forward and scooped Olly's phone up off the floor.

"He put a password on it." I frowned down at it before putting it back. "Do you think it's because he didn't want this?"

"No. He was the one that suggested we all get married in the first place." Reve moved my gifts to the side and scooted closer to me.

"I don't want any of you to feel like you're obligated to be with me because of some stupid prophecy that didn't even come true."

"What do you mean? You saved the light from the dark." Reve took my hand and brought it to his mouth, kissing my knuckles.

I rolled my eyes. "I did nothing except get myself killed."

"Do you think your dad would have killed her if it hadn't been for you? He did love her at some point. It's hard to stop loving a person." Tobias put his new Dodger's baseball cap on backwards and looked up at me from his spot on the floor. "You might not have directly saved the world, but you played a role."

I looked down into Toby's brown eyes and knew he was right. It just felt like I hadn't done anything while so many others had given their lives.

Reve stood and stretched his arms over his head, revealing a small sliver of his tattooed stomach. "Sometimes it only takes the smallest gesture or choice to change the world."

CHAPTER 2

OLIVER

I knew he was following me. I felt him as I trudged across the sand and down the beach. I was ruining everything, just like usual.

I stopped at the edge of the water and let out a scream of frustration. My throat burned as I fell to my knees in the water and looked up at the sky.

It was His fucking fault that I was such an idiot, and now I was being punished for it. I hadn't even given a second thought to the missing Holy Grail until the morning before when Michael had texted me.

It had somehow made its way back to Earth, and now they wanted me to find it. Find it or be summoned back to Heaven for good.

I shook my head and grabbed a shell that was stuck in the sand, shucking it out as far as possible.

"Angel baby." Asher stood next to me, his feet sinking in to the sand as the wave went back out. "I thought we were on the same page."

I ran my hands over my head, getting sand in my hair. Another wave rolled in and I stood, walking out farther. The waves hit my shins. It made me feel dizzy as the water rushed back out.

"I'll just go back if you aren't going to talk to me. I'm sure Toby and

Reve are giving Dani the presents in their pants." He chuckled, and maybe I would have too if my life wasn't at stake.

If I was sent back to Heaven, I didn't know if I could handle it.

"Why does everything have to be a fucking joke to you?" I turned around and nearly fell backward in the water.

"It's not. I was just stating the facts." He stood in front of me, a serious look on his face. A line formed between his eyebrows. "Why are you throwing a tantrum? It's unlike you."

I rolled my eyes and went to walk away, but he looped a hand around the back of my neck and pulled me to him, putting his forehead on mine. My breathing was heavy with frustration and I put my hands on his chest, clutching his shirt tightly.

"I was issued an order by Michael." I shut my eyes as his fingers played with the hair at the back of my neck. "The Holy Grail is back on Earth and I have a week to find it or I'm going back to Heaven."

His hand stilled for a moment before running up the back of my head. "Do you know where it is?"

I shrugged. "He said it was in Las Vegas somewhere. Apparently, he can sense it's there but is too busy to go find it himself. How can I possibly find it in only a week?" I opened my eyes to find his slate blue ones staring intently at me.

"We'll find it."

"I don't want to ruin your honeymoon." I was going to need to leave soon to start my search.

The Holy Grail wouldn't be easy to locate. When I had first taken it from the artifact room in Heaven, it had called to me, but since then, it had been silent.

"What will ruin our honeymoon is if you get sent back." Asher stepped away and took my hand. "Let's go for a walk. There's something I saw on Google Maps I wanted to check out. Then we'll worry about that damn cup."

I let him pull me to where the sand was just barely hit by the waves and we walked down the beach hand in hand. I stole glances at him as we walked, wondering what was running through his head.

Asher still didn't do well with change or surprises, and I had just dropped a big surprise in his lap. One that left us with a lot of uncertainty. Could I even accept his ring when my future on Earth was a big fat question mark?

It didn't seem fair to him.

I wanted to accept it. We couldn't officially get married since we were angels, but it was just a piece of paper anyway.

"Where are you taking me?" We came to a stream leading out into the ocean and Asher turned and headed in the direction it was coming from.

"You'll see." He wrapped his arm around my waist and we continued into the trees. There was a path that wound its way through the thick tropical foliage.

The sound of running water became louder and louder. I smiled as we came into a clearing. "A waterfall?" I had never actually seen a real one up close before.

There was a pool of water that had a waterfall cascading off a twenty-foot high drop.

"Come on." Instead of going to the pool, he led me up a steep incline, letting go of my hand so we could use the boulders to climb. "I guess we could have flown up here."

We stood at the top of the fall and Asher took off his shirt. My eyes traveled along the hard planes of his body. His muscles were long and hardened due to construction work.

"Flying takes the fun out of it." I took my own shirt off and then looked over the ledge. "Is the pool deep enough?"

"I guess we'll find out. What's the worst that could happen?" He chuckled and took my hand. "Come on."

We stood just to the left of the fall and excitement filled my belly. "On the count of three?"

We counted down together and then jumped, our hands losing each other as we hit the water. It was deeper than it had looked. I surfaced, running a hand over my face to get the water out of my eyes.

Asher came up right in front of me. "You look sexy as fuck all wet." He wrapped a leg around me but then a panicked look came over his face. "Fuck!"

He dove under the water and I tried to see what he was doing. I should have been concerned with how long he was underwater, but angels had superior breathing, so three minutes was nothing to worry about.

He finally surfaced, his hand darting into the air with the ring box. "Fuck me. It came out of my pocket."

He went to swim away, but I took his arm. "Ask me."

"Right now?" He ran a hand down his face to get the water off it.

"Yes. Right now."

He let out a puff of air and then opened the ring box, looking inside it at the ring. "I never thought that I'd fall in love with a woman, let alone a man and a woman." He took the ring out and tossed the box to the shore. "But I did, and I can't imagine my life without you in it. We might not have started out on the best of terms, but somehow, you managed to break through to my shriveled heart and find a home there."

I told myself not to get emotional, but Asher was starting to get emotional. His eyes met mine, holding me in a stare that said a million words. He wasn't always good at expressing himself, but his words meant more than he'd ever know.

"Marry me, angel baby. I don't just want Danica forever, I want you forever."

I nodded because, for once, I was at a loss for words. I held out my right hand to him and he chuckled, shaking his head, grabbing for my left. He slipped the ring on next to the matching one we had from Danica.

"I love you, you asshole." I pulled him to me and kissed him hard.

He groaned against my lips and his hands went to my back, rubbing up between my shoulders. I pulled my lips away, breathing deeply. He knew that was the one spot that made me harder than a rock.

"Asher... we can't-"

"Why the fuck not? This is a private island." He grabbed my hand and swam around the waterfall to an alcove behind it. "I may have done some scouting while you guys were still asleep this morning."

I looked around the small cave that had a blanket and candles. "You planned this."

"Dani helped. I meant to propose tonight, but I couldn't wait." He pulled me toward him and buried his face in my neck.

His scruff scratched against me and I tilted my head to the side as he kissed my sensitive skin. "Ash... what if we can't find it?"

"Hmm?" He slid his hands to my shorts and pushed them down, placing his palm over my cock. "Let's not think about that right now."

I sighed as he moved us closer to the ledge so we could stand on the bottom. He gripped me and began working me until I was panting. "Fuck, that feels good."

My eyes felt heavy, and he hooked a leg around my thigh and brought me closer, his dick connecting with mine. He gripped us both. "I love it when you say the word *fuck*."

"You're corrupting me." I groaned and shut my eyes as his grip tightened. "Do you remember the first time we did this?"

He kissed along my jaw. "How could I forget?" His lips pressed against mine in a soft kiss.

The memory of us coming together in the shower in Shanghai made my dick pulse. I gripped the back of his head and deepened our kiss, our tongues exploring each other's mouths.

Asher pulled away and released our dicks. My body shuddered at the sudden loss of contact. "Where do you think you're going?"

I watched as he lifted himself out of the water and took off his shorts. "Come here."

I cocked a brow as he bent over in front of me, giving a full view of where I wanted to be. He turned back around with a bottle of lube and grinned.

He lowered onto the blanket on his knees and squirted a generous amount of lube on his hand. I put my arms on the ledge and watched as he stuck his ass in the air, his chest on the blanket, and began preparing himself.

The urge to rush to him and take over was intense, and I pressed my palm into my erection, trying to calm it down. Watching him stretching himself for me was one of the most erotic things I'd ever watched.

"Angel baby, are you just going to stare or are you going to get up here and take what's yours?" He groaned as he inserted a third finger. "I'm ready for you."

Without a word, I pulled myself out of the water. Asher's eyes locked on me as I shucked my shorts. I grabbed the lube, enjoying the cool sensation as it hit the sensitive skin of my dick.

Asher began stroking his cock as he watched me. I moved behind him and ran my hand down his back, causing goosebumps to spread across his skin.

I rubbed my tip against his entrance and then slowly pushed inside, the pressure immediately squeezing me like a vice. I grasped his hips as I buried myself to the hilt and he pushed back against me.

"You feel so good." My balls were already tightening, and I willed them to not spill so soon. "Tell me what you want, Asher."

His hand worked faster and he moaned, the sound echoing in the cave along with the sound of the waterfall. "I want you to fuck me so hard I see stars."

I pulled out most of the way and then slammed back into him. He cried out and then let out a whimper. "Like that?"

"Yes." His voice shook and he looked back over his shoulder at me. "Fuck me just like that, baby."

I began thrusting, his eyes locked on me. I wasn't going to last long with his dark blue eyes staring back at me.

Our grunts and groans filled the cave. I wrapped an arm around him and pulled him to me, his back against my front. He twisted enough for me to take his lips in a bruising kiss.

His hand worked faster and he cried out against my lips, ropes of his cum jetting out onto the blanket. The sight sent me over the edge and my orgasm spiraled down my spine as I came.

We sat there panting for a few minutes before I pulled out and Asher handed me a towel. He was always prepared for everything.

I stood and dipped the rag in the water, cleaning myself, then cleaning him up. "I needed that."

He snorted a laugh and pulled me to him for a hug. "I could tell."

CHAPTER 3

ASHER

I hated the knot that had formed in my stomach. There I was thinking everything was going to normalize and calm down, and another curve ball was thrown our way. Almost losing Danica was hard enough, but the possibility of losing Oliver was too much.

When we got back to the treehouse and everyone freaked out over us being engaged, I snuck into the bedroom for a few minutes to myself. I still couldn't get used to being around so many people when my anxiety was high, despite it being almost a year since they'd come into my life.

I was fine at the moment, but in all likelihood, I would never be okay.

I squatted next to my bag and pulled out my flask that I had for emergencies and took a swig. I had promised myself that I was going to try to cut back on drinking, but desperate times called for desperate measures.

"He just told us."

I jumped and fell backwards, spilling some alcohol on my hand and bare chest. "Fuck, Reve. You should fucking know by now not to do that!"

We had this conversation before about his invisibility, and how suddenly appearing or talking might lead to me wringing his neck or stabbing him in the gut.

He snatched the flask from me and took a swig. He cringed and put the cap back on. "I thought you were going to stop."

"I am." I snatched it back and put it in my bag. "It's not like I can just stop after decades of drowning in it."

"Sure you can."

"Have you ever had a drinking problem?" I zipped up my bag a little too hard and was lucky the zipper didn't break. "Because unless you have, don't tell me how easy it is."

He held up his hands. "Sorry, just trying to help."

I stood and turned to face him. "Did you need something?"

He frowned and crossed his arms over his tattooed chest. It was hard not to stare at his tattoos; they were a mix of intricate portraits, scenes, and symbols. I had a hard enough time with getting the wings on my back done.

"I came to check on you." He took a step forward and I backed up. "You know, you're going to have to get used to all of us caring about you."

I rolled my eyes. "I don't need anyone to care about me. I'm fine."

"If you say so. Just know that I'm here for you." He went to his bag and pulled out a pair of really short swim trunks. "We're going to spend the day at the beach and then go home tomorrow morning."

I looked away when he stripped off the pajama bottoms he had been wearing. "Dude."

"It's not like you haven't seen it or *accidently* touched it before." He laughed.

The bedroom door opened and Dani stepped in, a smile lighting up her face. "There you two are." She looped her arms around my neck and kissed me. "Is that why you came in here?"

Her face fell with a look that made my stomach twist. I put my hands on her waist and pulled her back into a kiss. She moaned but then pulled her lips from mine.

"Yes." I shut my eyes and she traced my bottom lip with her finger.

"It's going to be fine. We'll find the grail and put everything behind us." She sounded so sure that things would return to normal.

I thought they already had, but it seemed the universe wanted to keep tripping us up.

Even though I didn't feel like it, they dragged me down to the beach where umbrellas and chairs were set up. I had to give it to Toby; he had thought of everything.

"Did Michael say where to go in Vegas?" Reve opened a bottle of beer and then frowned at it. "Maybe we should all quit drinking."

"Don't let my issues spoil your fun." I settled into a chair and closed my eyes. "You shouldn't have to give up something just because of my inability to control myself."

Danica sat down on the side of my lounge chair and put a hand on my cheek. I didn't need to have my eyes open to know it was her. "Reve has a point. We should be more supportive."

I pushed my glasses up to look at her. She was practically glowing in the sun with her smooth tanned skin and navy bikini.

"You aren't supposed to be drinking anyways." Tobias plucked the can of hard seltzer out of her hand and took a drink of it. "I think the occasional drink wouldn't hurt him."

"Thanks, Dad." I rolled my eyes and put my glasses back in place. "What are we going to do if we can't find the grail?"

Olly had gone for a quick dip in the ocean so he was out of earshot.

"We'll find it." Danica sounded convinced we would.

"I'm more concerned about how it got back here. The shaman is still in Inferna, so who or what has it?" Reve took a football from the beach bag and tossed it in the air. "I guess it doesn't matter. Let's enjoy the rest of our day."

He and Toby ran off to play catch, leaving me alone with Danica. I sat up and pulled her into my lap. "Thank you."

"For what?" She took off my glasses and wrapped her arms around my neck.

We had been slowly working up to her sitting longer and longer in my lap. She wasn't the best at using her angel soothing yet, but was getting better each day.

"For giving me a family." Tears filled her eyes and I cupped her cheek. "I never thought I'd have one."

She put her hand over mine. "I never imagined I'd have four partners that make me want to be a better woman." She kissed my palm. "If we can even count me as one."

I laid back, her hands bracing on my chest and then rolled over so she was under me. "You are definitely a woman." I kissed down her neck to her bikini top.

I rested my head on her chest as she played with my hair. "I'll take your word for it."

"I got married to Lena when I was eighteen and she was seventeen. We were both miles off from your maturity." I hadn't talked much about my life before becoming an angel. Sometimes, I thought I could handle sharing it, and other times, the pain was too much.

"Were you high school sweethearts?" I shut my eyes and felt a warmth spread through my body as she massaged my scalp. My body relaxed into hers.

"Her dad owned the construction company I worked for. We ran off when he told us we couldn't be together because I wasn't good enough." Her hand stilled on my head for a moment. "I was a farmer boy, not good enough for a proper city girl."

She moved her hands to my upper back and I groaned. I always had a hard time controlling my dick when she touched where my wings came out. We all did.

"Who's a proper city girl?" Olly sat down on the chair next to us, water dripping from his hair still. "Danica is far from proper."

"You got that right." Reve plopped down in the sand. "I was thinking... I have a few contacts in Vegas I can call before we head there. They're demons though, if that's okay with you all."

"You guys should really just stay here. I don't want to ruin your honeymoon." Olly put his face in his hands. "I'm such a fuck-up."

"You've made some mistakes, but you've grown a lot since I've known you." Toby sat next to him and put his arm around his shoulders. "We can always come back here another time."

"School starts again in two weeks." He moved his hands and met my eyes. The sadness in them made me hold in my breath. "I got myself into the mess, I should get myself out."

"Us not being together would really ruin our honeymoon." Danica pushed at me and I sat up. "We do this together." She grabbed her things. "Now, I don't know about you four, but I'm hungry, and not just for lunch."

She sauntered away, shaking her ass in a seductive walk that certainly got my dick's attention. I was the first out of my seat and running to catch up.

CHAPTER 4

REVE

I slid out of bed from between Toby and Dani and unplugged my cell phone. I had meant to make phone calls the afternoon and evening before, but we had a little too much fun in the treehouse after spending the morning at the beach.

I shut the bedroom door quietly behind me and walked to the large floor-to-ceiling windows overlooking the ocean. The moon reflected off the water and reminded me of home. The sky showed the faintest signs of sunrise.

Scrolling through my contacts, I worried that other demons wouldn't even want to talk to me. I had let Inferna be taken over by a lunatic woman and then renounced the throne once she was dead. I would have never been happy back in Inferna, though.

I found the contact I was looking for and brought the phone to my ear.

I tried to keep my knowledge of non-registered demons to myself for many reasons. Michael's registration system was a new phenomenon in an attempt to keep demons from running amuck. He didn't trust us, but he also didn't know us.

Lucifer had quite a few of us spread across the globe, remedying the issue of too many souls being sent to hell. It was a necessary evil he had to put into place since no one understood the dire situation beneath the surface of Inferna.

It was filling up much too quickly.

Besides the dream demons that had joined Lucifer's cause, there were quite a few incubus and succubus demons, and different types of shifters. We still answered to Lucifer, but Michael had us under strict guidelines.

A little less strict for me, but checking in once a week was a gross invasion of my privacy.

"What do you want?" The gruff voice sounded annoyed, and in the background, I heard music thumping.

"Felix, how's life?" I sat down in a chair. "I have a proposition for you."

"I have no complaints. A proposition? Do continue." A door shut and the noise in the background disappeared.

Felix was one of a dozen fox shifters whose job it was to teach excessive gamblers a lesson by stealing their money. Half the money was kept by them and the other half went to Lucifer.

"We're looking for an artifact that is rumored to be in Vegas." I cut straight to the point because I wasn't fond of talking to foxes longer than necessary. "Have you heard or seen anything?"

The phone was silent, and I looked at the screen to see if the call had disconnected. I shifted in my seat as a solid minute passed before Felix sighed.

"The vampires have it," he whispered.

I sat up straighter in my chair. "What do you mean the *vampires* have it? There shouldn't be any vampires here."

"They've been here for a while. They own and operate the largest hotel and casino here. I don't know much about it because they kicked me out when I was on a job." He must have opened the door to the room he was in because music could be heard again. "I have to go."

He hung up without another word and I stared at the phone in disbelief. "Fuck." I rubbed a hand over my face.

"What's wrong?" Danica got a bottle of water out of the refrigerator and sat on the arm of my chair. "I missed you in my dreams."

I set my phone on the side table and put my hand on her thigh. She tilted her head back and took a drink of water. The long line of her neck was calling to me.

"Too much going on in my head to give you a good dream." I took the water bottle from her and took a drink. "I think I know where the grail is."

Her eyes went wide and she slid down into my lap. "Where?"

"The *Claret*." I twirled her hair around my finger. "With vampires."

"We should call-"

"No!" She jumped and I lowered my voice back down. "If we get your father involved then Michael will get involved."

"I don't understand why Michael being involved would be a bad thing. He has resources we could use."

"He calls the shots with demons. If he finds out there are vampires here that aren't registered... what if he shuts us all down and sends us back to Inferna?" I wanted to believe I would be exempt if it came to that, but Michael was all business.

If he decided demons no longer benefitted Earth, we would be goners. The number of demons was far less than the number of angels. There would be no stopping him on following through with it.

"He won't. At least not you. I won't let him." She kissed my cheek and then passed a thumb over one of my nipple rings. "I wish you still had your tongue ring."

I pushed my head back against the cushion as she moved to straddle me. "Didn't you get enough last night?"

Danica's libido was something they would one day write books about.

"Are you complaining?" She lowered her lips to my neck and trailed them to my ear, nipping the lobe. "Because I can always go wake up one of the others."

"Fuck no." I squeezed the round globes of her ass as she began grinding against me. "I just don't want your pussy to be sore."

"Angel perk." She kissed her way down to my nipple and sucked it into her mouth, drawing a moan from me. "I want to taste you."

My dick was as hard as a rock as she pressed her palm against it and switched to my other nipple. Her tongue flicked the barbell, and I bucked my hips as it sent a zing straight to my cock. I pushed my hands into her hair and then pulled her lips up to mine.

Our tongues explored each other and she pulled away, panting with half-lidded eyes. She stood and dropped to her knees in front of me. I licked my lips in anticipation as she looked up at me with her big brown eyes.

"Take off your top, I want to see your tits as you suck me off." There was nothing hotter than watching them bounce as she took my cock over and over between her lips.

She pulled the tank off and threw it in my face. I inhaled her sweet flowery scent and then threw it on the floor. She wrapped her fingers around the top of my boxers and pulled them off.

I shut my eyes as her tongue licked around the crown. She worked her fist at my base as she teased my shaft with kisses and small nips.

The bedroom door opened and clicked softly closed. I didn't need to turn my head to see who it was. Had it been Asher and Olly, they would have immediately made a comment or a sexual sounding noise.

We had all walked in on each other having sex. It was hard not to when you shared a house. We mostly operated on the code that if it was already going on, we couldn't join unless Dani said something.

Unless Toby walked in. He was a watcher.

"Oh, fuck." I groaned as she took me all the way to the back of her throat. I didn't know how she did it, but it felt amazing.

I ran my fingers through her hair as she bobbed her head up and down. Toby knelt behind Dani without a word and pulled her panties off. He probably had enough of watching from earlier.

He ran his hand down her spine and then massaged her ass which she had pushed back toward him. He had a wicked glint in his eye and I just hoped she didn't bite my dick off with whatever he was up to.

His palm hit her ass, the sound of it seeming louder than it was in the quiet room. She moaned as she sucked me, the vibrations almost sending me over the edge. He spanked her again and she let go of me and breathed against my thigh.

I resisted the urge to stroke myself the last few pumps. My balls were already tingling like they were about to explode.

Toby lowered his mouth to her ass cheeks and she whimpered as he kissed where his palm had just stung her sensitive flesh.

"I want to try something." Toby moved his hand between her leg. "Do you trust me?"

I didn't know what was left to try besides eating or fucking each other's asses. "What did you have in mind?"

Dani was rocking back and forth as Toby began fingering her. I smoothed her hair and groaned as she took me in her hand.

"She's ready to have both of us." He reached forward with his other hand and tweaked one of her nipples, causing her to cry out. "She's taking four fingers right now."

I wrapped my hand around Dani's and stopped her from getting me off. I didn't need to blow my load hearing Toby talking about taking her in the pussy at the same time.

"Dani?" I cupped her chin and lifted it. "Do you think you can handle the both of us in that tight cunt of yours?"

Her eyes closed and she dug her nails into my thighs as her entire body shook with release. "Yes! Oh, God, yes!"

Toby laid down on the rug and pulled her on top of him. She was still shaking from her orgasm as she slid onto his cock. She began rocking on top of him, throwing her head back and jutting her chest out.

I wasn't going to last long.

Toby pulled her forward and then slipped out of her. I slid in easily and groaned as her wet heat engulfed me. She was so wet I shuddered at the sensation.

Toby pressed the tip of his dick against mine at her entrance and slowly slid in. She let out a strangled groan as he became fully sheathed right alongside me.

We remained still until Dani began rocking her hips. I began moving in short thrusts, clenching my jaw to keep from shouting out how fucking good it was. It was ten times better than anal.

Her wet heat surrounded me and the added friction and pressure from Tobias's dick was almost too much.

Her shoulders finally relaxed and I took that as my cue to increase my pace. Toby began thrusting up, his dick sliding along mine. The sounds coming from Dani were raw and unhinged.

I reached around her and pinched a nipple and found her clit with my other hand. She cried out and fell forward as her orgasm hit. Her pussy gripped me and I thrust one last time before my seed exploded out of my dick.

"Holy fuck!" Tobias thrust his hips up with force and I felt his dick shudder with release.

We collapsed into a tangle of bodies on the rug, not caring that we were making a mess. I wiped the sweat from my forehead and felt envious that angels didn't sweat.

I looked to the window where the sky had turned a gorgeous purple color. I would never stop being amazed at how the sun changed the entire look of Earth. I had been on Earth longer than I had lived in Inferna, but it still made me stop what I was doing and appreciate it.

The bedroom door slammed open and I turned my head to find Asher standing in the doorway, panting. "He's gone."

CHAPTER 5

DANICA

I zipped my suitcase closed and took one last look around the bedroom. We could come back anytime, but it still stung to have to leave so soon. It was like we couldn't catch a break.

Oliver was gone, and I felt somewhat responsible for him taking off on his own. If I would have just stayed in bed, maybe he wouldn't have taken off.

Tobias wrapped his arms around me and kissed the side of my head. "He'll be fine. It's not like he doesn't know how to fight."

"I know, but I still worry." I carried my bag out onto the balcony.

"I've secured us a suite at the *Claret*." Reve slid his phone in his back pocket and took my bag. "We ready to roll?"

Without a word, Asher took off, his wings stirring the air and sending my hair flying everywhere. "I worry more about him than Olly."

I pulled my hair into a quick messy bun and took Reve's hand. He could fly on his own, but not at the same speed as the rest of us.

My wings extended, and I pumped them a few times. I was still getting used to the feeling of them. They weren't heavy, but they sometimes had a mind of their own if I wasn't completely focused. It happened more than I cared to admit.

We flew after Tobias and I fought to keep my eyes open. It slowed me down if they were closed.

The *Claret* had an approved angel landing zone like most Las Vegas hotels and we quickly made it to the door to the stairwell.

"Wait here. I'll go check in." Reve took off down the stairs.

"Where do you think Asher went?" I sat down on a step and pulled up the group text where Asher had sent Olly about ten texts. "Olly isn't answering."

"He could be anywhere. He looked like he was asleep when I got up this morning, but maybe he had been awake and heard Reve mention this place." Tobias sat down next to me and put an arm around my waist.

"I hope not." I didn't know much about vampires, but from what Reve had shared, they were manipulative and always trying to get ahead. "How can there actually be vampires?"

It was a hard thing to wrap my head around. It was one thing to be Lucifer's daughter and know for certain there were angels, but to know there was a whole other world that could come to Earth? None of us would know since they appeared human.

I shuddered.

Tobias rubbed his thumb over the small line of skin between my pants and top, and I put my head on his shoulder.

"I sometimes have a hard time wrapping my head around things too. Not just the existence of another world, but everything that lives there. I still doubt the existence of prophecies and curses though." He sighed. "I'd like to think what we have is more than just the fulfillment of a prophecy."

"I wouldn't have married you if I didn't feel a connection." I shrugged. "Besides, it's not like the prophecy was correct. I didn't even do anything to save the light or whatever."

Tobias took my chin and made me look at him. "Stop saying that. Your dad was able to kill her because of you. You were his motivation." He kissed me gently. "I wish you wouldn't have died in the process."

"I don't feel like I died. I felt like I've become who I was always meant to be." I made a gagging noise. "I sound old."

Tobias laughed and stood, helping me stand too. Reve rejoined us and handed me the card key. "I was able to get us the honeymoon executive suite. Once we take care of this whole magical cup business, we can party it up."

"I can't wait to see your moves on the dancefloor. Dancing the waltz is one thing, but twerking is in a class of its own." I laughed.

Reve dropped his bag between the set of stairs. "You don't think I can twerk?" He raised his eyebrow and dropped into a squat with his hands on his thighs. "I've had centuries to perfect the bounce of my ass."

"I feel like this is a commercial for what happens in Vegas stays in Vegas." Tobias groaned in annoyance as Reve began popping his booty.

I laughed so hard tears came to my eyes. "Let's go, so we can enjoy ourselves."

The honeymoon executive suite lived up to its name. It was bigger than some people's houses and had a living room, kitchen, two bedrooms, and two and a half bathrooms. It also had a massive balcony that overlooked the strip with a large hot tub.

"This is nothing like the treehouse, but it'll do." I came out of the master bedroom to find Tobias and Reve talking with Asher. "What's wrong?"

Asher turned toward me with a frown. "Fucking Olly, that's what's wrong. He isn't answering his phone and he's blocking himself from being found."

I pulled him into a hug, and he wrapped his arms around me. "It's going to be fine. Let me see if I can pick up on anything."

I wasn't the most skilled at using my archangel abilities, but I had been getting better at locating the guys from long distances.

I backed up a step and shut my eyes, focusing on the feeling Olly usually gave me when he was around. There were three other angels, but none of them were him.

"We need to talk to the three angels here. They have to know something and I want to know why they haven't reported vampires." I doubted they were clueless about who ran the hotel and casino.

"Maybe they don't know." Tobias rubbed his scruff. "You can't sense demons, can you?"

"Well, no. But with Reve, I..." I shut my mouth because it was an awkward conversation to have about what I felt around Reve.

"Spit it out, Danica." Reve crossed his arms.

"I feel a darkness." I cringed as his frown deepened and hurt filled his eyes. "It's only when you're close, so I'd have to be near vampires to know."

Tobias smacked Reve on the back. "She might feel your darkness, but she was feeling your dick in the best way possible this morning."

"Can we focus on Olly? He might be in danger." Asher shot daggers at Tobias and then went to the door. "Let's go."

We went down to the casino. It was loud and smelled of stale cigarette smoke. I didn't understand how people could spend all day cooped up in a place like this.

The *Claret* was different from other casinos I'd seen on TV. It was darker with red and gold accents. It had women dressed like they were going to a movie premier and men that looked like they had walked straight out of a *James Bond* movie.

I looked down at my jean shorts, crop top, and flip flops. "We stand out."

"There are plenty of tourists in here." Reve raised his chin toward a card table that mostly had high rollers, but also had one tourist in a Las Vegas t-shirt and cargo shorts.

I reached out with my angel sensing and easily spotted an angel security guard by two large ornate doors. He had his arms crossed over his chest and sunglasses over his eyes. I grabbed Reve's hand and walked toward the man.

"Can I help you?" His eyes raked my body and his frown deepened. "Are you even twenty-one?"

I ignored his second question and stood taller. "We're looking for another angel, about this tall." I held my hand up past six feet. "Boyishly good-looking. You wouldn't have missed him."

The guard raised an eyebrow under his glasses. "Even if I had seen him, why would I tell you?"

"I'll have you know that I'm-" Asher stepped forward and elbowed me gently in the side.

"She's a neurotic girlfriend. Please, man, I can't listen to her whining about missing him anymore."

I wanted to wring Asher's neck, but the guard laughed. "It'll cost you."

Asher pulled out his wallet and flipped it open. "How much?"

Tobias made a noise in his throat and I knew he was holding back what he wanted to say to the angel. I was holding back myself, but this angel was compromised. Money was probably a factor.

"Two thousand."

"One."

"Fifteen hundred or we'll escort you out."

I squeezed Reve's hand harder and two other angels stepped to the sides of us. What the hell was going on in this casino?

Asher counted out fifteen hundred dollar bills and smacked them in the angel's hand. He made a big show of recounting them and then nodded to the other two.

"Follow us."

I had a bad feeling about what we were about to walk into.

CHAPTER 6

TOBIAS

*T*he *Claret* reeked of trouble from the second I laid eyes on the casino. Something felt off about it, but I couldn't quite put my finger on what it was exactly.

Angels working as guards was not unheard of, it was part of being a guardian, but these three were batting for the Giants instead of the Dodgers.

We followed behind the two angels through the casino and to a staircase that was roped off. I felt like I was in some kind of mafia movie, being led to my execution.

At the top of the staircase we turned right and walked down a long corridor that was covered in shiny black stone with wall sconces that gave off red light. We came to a door, and one of the angels leading us looked up and into a camera. The door clicked and opened into a room about the size of a small bedroom.

"Arms out. We don't allow any weapons here."

I gave Asher a warning glance because I knew he was carrying his seraph blade. I wouldn't put it past him to stab both of them and then try to break through the other door.

They put our weapons in a plastic bin and then secured it in a locked box in the wall. Maybe we hadn't thought this through all the way.

"Why are you working for vampires?" Danica asked as they headed for the door on the other side of the room. "Does Michael-"

One of the men grabbed her and slammed her against the wall, holding her by the throat. We all lunged forward, but the second angel pulled a gun and pointed it straight at me. "Don't move."

"We won't hesitate to let him kill you, and he really enjoys angel blood." Danica whimpered against his hold. "One wrong move in there and we tell him who you are."

She nodded and the angel released her. She rubbed at her neck and glared at him but kept her mouth shut.

With the gun still pointed at me, we were led through another series of dark doors and hallways until we came into a large room that was just like the first hallways we had walked down. Everything was black except for the red lights. I nearly choked on my saliva as my eyes tried to communicate with my brain.

There were couches and tables spread around the room with small stages. Some were empty, but many had women, men, or a combination of several dancing and fucking.

"Jesus Christ. What the fuck is this?" Asher balled his fists at his side and I clutched onto the back of his shirt as he moved forward so he didn't do anything rash.

"Welcome to Thirst." A beautiful woman with long black hair that fell down to cover her naked breasts greeted us.

We followed her as she led us across a floor that was so shiny that the red light hitting it made it look like blood.

"Is this like a sex club or something?" Danica took a seat on a crescent-shaped couch we were led to. "Where's our friend?"

I sat down next to her and put my arm around her waist, squeezing it in warning. Now was not the time to test what these people were made of.

Asher stood next to the couch with his arms crossed. One of the angels left with the woman and we were left staring at the angel who had shoved Danica against the wall.

I wanted to kill him.

"Your friend caused quite the commotion earlier today." He looked at Asher and frowned. "Sit, before I make you sit."

Reve tugged him by the hem of his shirt and he let out a slew of curses. He was barely holding onto his emotions. His brows were drawn inward and his jaw was clenched. I didn't want to see what these people would do if he lost his cool.

We sat in silence, avoiding looking at any of the entertainment, until the woman returned with a tray of drinks. "Mr. Sangre will be ready for you shortly."

I took my drink in my hand and eyed it suspiciously before bringing it to my nose. It smelled fine, but I wasn't keen on drinking alcohol from a vampire's lair.

Even though they hadn't said it outright, I'm pretty sure that's where we were.

"Sangre?" Reve sniffed his drink and then drank it in one gulp. I wasn't sure if he had a death wish or had some poison sniffing ability.

"Zayden Sangre is the owner of this establishment." The woman eyed us curiously and then turned on her spiked heel to head back to the bar in the corner.

"Fuck." Reve pinched the bridge of his nose. "My sister was engaged to his cousin back before..."

"That's a good thing, right?" Asher put his glass down, not even smelling it like the rest of us. Maybe he knew it was whiskey and sniffing it would only make him want to drink it.

"Val is nothing like the rest of his family. They remind me of the mafia." He took Danica's drink and drank it. "My father was building a case to present to the council when everything happened."

"Are you okay?" Danica took the glass back from him once it was empty. "I've never seen you drink so much in such a short time. Should we be worried about this Zayden guy?"

Reve shifted in his seat. "I might have slept with his sisters."

I tried to school my reaction. I wanted to laugh as Danica's eyes widened and her mouth opened slightly.

"Sisters? Please tell me you didn't sleep with them at the same time." She held up a hand. "Never mind. I don't want to know."

"I do." I sat forward. "You dirty dog."

"Not at the same time, but their rooms were connected with a bathroom." He cringed as Danica smacked his arm.

"Mr. Sangre is ready for you now." A different woman came to a stop in front of us, her breasts on full display.

I had a hard time not looking at them. Danica was the first to stand and step into our line of sight as the woman turned and headed toward yet another door.

She turned and looked at us with a glare that said for us to keep our eyes off any breasts. The patrons and performers turned to look at us as we passed.

I caught up to Danica and laced our fingers. She was shaking slightly, but had an impassive look on her face. She was worried about what we were going to walk into.

We entered another room that had four gaming tables with men and a few women playing poker. The room reeked of cigar smoke, and if I wasn't mistaken, it smelled faintly of blood.

"Oliver!" Asher tried to lunge forward, spotting Oliver sitting chained to a chair on the far side of the room, but was stopped by a man that was seven feet tall.

"Where do you think you're going?" The man had hands as big as Asher's head and gripped him by the shoulder. "You're to wait right here until you're summoned."

"You motherfucker! If you don't let me go, I'm going to-"

"Gentlemen. What seems to be the problem?" A man dressed in a solid black suit stood from one of the card tables and adjusted his red tie. His eyes landed on Danica and the set line of his mouth turned into a grin. "Well, hello there."

I bit down on my inner cheek as he took her hand and kissed her knuckles. She yanked her hand back and wiped it on her shorts. I did a silent fist pump.

"Zayden." Reve spoke through clenched teeth and Zayden looked at him, faking surprise at seeing him. He had surely seen all four of us walk in.

"Reve. What an unpleasant surprise." He spoke with a faint lisp, but then I noticed he had fangs. "I'm guessing you're here to get the archangel?"

"We are." I stuck out my hand, trying to save the situation, and he shook it, squeezing a little too firmly.

"We are also looking for something that belongs to us." Danica shut her eyes for a moment. "It's my favorite wine cup."

I groaned internally as Zayden refocused his attention on her. "I'm well aware of what you and your little harem are after. Your friend has agreed to be our drink of choice for the next few days. I feel inclined to ask you to offer the same."

"Fat chance in hell." Asher gasped as the man holding him from escaping squeezed his shoulder.

The vampire cocked a brow and smirked. "Grab her."

Two suited men grabbed Danica while several others surrounded us. Reve disappeared and I felt a little better with our situation until Zayden wrapped his arm around me from behind and brought a knife to my throat.

"Oh, Reve. You should know better than to make a move like that." He backed us up until he was against the door with two men flanking our sides.

He was smart, I'd give him that.

Asher was being held against the floor with the giant man's foot on his chest and he clawed at his ankle, trying to break free. The card players at the tables were watching as if this was a normal occurrence as Danica was dragged to a door and thrown inside.

"Let her go." The knife dug into my neck, and I felt its sting and the subsequent drops of blood.

Zayden chuckled. "Now why would I do that when I can have two archangels to snack on?"

Whatever Reve was doing, he needed to hurry the fuck up before Asher and I were killed. One of the men fisted a handful of my hair and tilted my head to the side.

"Mmm. Your blood doesn't smell as good as your friend's over there, but it'll do for now." Zayden bit into my neck and I yelped.

My body started to relax, despite my brain screaming for it not to. His fangs left me suddenly and I dropped to my hands and knees as everyone in the room stood abruptly.

"Well, fuck, Reve. I guess you do still have it in you." Zayden held his hands up as all eyes landed on him. "Fine, fine. You can have them back."

Asher was already sprinting across the room to the door, but when he tried it, it was locked. "Open the fucking door."

Oliver stood, rubbing his wrists, and shot a deadly glare across the room. He walked to the door and unlocked it himself.

"Where's the cup?" Reve grabbed my arm and pulled me to my feet, still invisible. "It doesn't belong to you."

"It's in my office. Down the hall, to the left." Zayden crossed his arms. "I want something in return."

"I'll spare your life." Reve's voice was deadly. "We also want our stay in your fine establishment comped."

Zayden snorted. "If I didn't know any better, I'd say that there is still a king that lies under the surface of that pussy-whipped exterior of yours."

"You'll understand once you find someone of your own." Reve pushed me toward the door Asher and Oliver had rushed into.

I had never quite understood what Reve had meant when he said an alpha dream demon was always king until watching him in action. He put Zayden in his place quite quickly.

I could still hear Zayden's laugh as we left the room.

CHAPTER 7

DANICA

*T*here were so many hallways, I felt like I was a rat in a maze. I should have been more scared than I was, but oddly enough I felt a sense of excitement.

When I died, it felt like I was being reborn into a better version of myself. A version of myself that couldn't die, had awesome wings, and special abilities. It made my impulse control even more difficult to manage when there was little to fear.

I knew the Holy Grail was nearby; I felt it. I opened a door off the hall and my eyes widened. It looked straight out of a BDSM manual.

I quickly shut the door and opened the door next to it. My skin tingled and a faint ringing hit my ears. It was like the cup was singing to me.

The office was large with a dark mahogany desk, dark leather couch, and bookcases filled with books. There was a door that I only assumed led into the sex dungeon, and then another door that I wasn't keen on looking in.

I rounded the desk and tried opening the drawer the grail was in, but it was locked. I focused on the lock like Olly had taught me and heard a faint click.

No more lock-picking kit for me. I *was* the lock pick now.

I slid open the drawer and frowned. There were three glass bottles of blood. I scrunched my nose and picked up one that had the letter A written on it. One didn't have any label. The third had the letter L.

The hair on the back of my neck stood on end and I popped the cork and sniffed. I don't know how I knew, but something told me it was my father's blood. I did the same to the bottle with an A, but I didn't recognize it as anything other than archangel blood.

I looked around the room again and opened the second door, finding an opulent bathroom that looked like something straight out of a mansion. I took all three bottles of blood and dumped them down the sink, running the water to rinse out the bottles and ensure the blood was completely gone.

I didn't know what effect archangel blood had on vampires, but it couldn't be good. If it could almost bring down the barrier between Earth and Inferna, it was extremely powerful.

The office door slammed open and I jumped, dropping one of the cleaned bottles and causing it to shatter across the black marble floor.

"Dani!" Asher came to a halt in the doorway and breathed a sigh of relief. "What are you doing?"

"He had archangel blood, including my father's. I was dumping it. What the hell happened?" I stepped carefully over the shards of glass and put my hand on his bruised cheek.

It would heal soon, but I didn't want to see any of my men suffering. My hand warmed, and a shimmering golden light traveled from my hand to his cheek, the bruise disappearing.

"Reve worked his dream demon magic. I forget just how powerful he is until he does something like that." Asher put his hand over mine.

"I should get this back to the artifact room sooner rather than later." Olly was standing in the middle of the room with the Holy Grail in his hand.

He was lit up like a Christmas tree, and the cup was emitting a golden light. It was as if the grail was celebrating the fact that it was finally home.

"Let's go before that Zayden guy discovers you dumped out all his angel blood." Asher took our hands. "Let's get out of here."

~

IT SEEMED a little too good to be true getting the Holy Grail back. Maybe I had just grown accustomed to everything ending with blood being spilled.

"So, let me get this straight." I pulled my legs up on the couch in the living room of our suite and tapped my lips with my finger. "Instead of spending your honeymoon here, in our luxurious suite with me, you two are going to go and watch the Raiders?"

They both looked at each other and then back at me. "You could come with us?"

"You don't even like the Raiders." Asher was flipping through the movies on the TV. "But if you two want to go off on a date and leave me here alone with Dani, by all means, go right ahead."

"I don't like the Raiders, but this is the playoffs. Their first year here in Vegas and they already made it. It's amazing." Tobias crossed his arms. "You'd understand if you cared about football."

While he was wearing normal clothing, Reve was decked out in a jersey and backward baseball hat. It had only taken ten minutes of us being back in the room before he announced he was going to the game.

"We'll make it up to you later." Reve walked to the door. "Let's go. We don't want to be late."

Tobias and Reve left on their man date and Asher turned off the TV. He scooted over next to me on the couch and put his hand on my foot.

"Wifey." His grin made my heart swell, and I giggled. "What should we do in their absence?"

"There are a few things I can think of..." I sucked in a breath as he moved his hand up my bare leg to the edge of my shorts. "What about your fiancé?"

"What about him?" He ran a finger back down my leg and I put my legs across his lap. "We can have a little fun until he gets back. Get you nice and ready for both of us."

I whimpered as he leaned down and trailed kisses from my knee to the bottom of my shorts. He wasted no time unbuttoning them and sliding them off with my panties. I slid one of my legs off the couch, opening myself to his touch and mouth.

"Fuck, Dani." He swiped a finger along my slit and brought it to his mouth. "I'm going to devour you."

I was already breathing heavily as he moved onto the floor on his knees. He lifted my leg and kissed the arch of my foot. I was going to combust.

"Asher," I whimpered and shivered as he sucked the sensitive flesh of my ankle.

"Why don't you take off your top and bra? I want you to pinch your nipples for me." He draped my leg over his shoulder and watched as I did as he asked.

I rolled one of my nipples between my fingers and Asher licked his lips. His eyes darkened, and he watched me with a hunger I hadn't seen from him in a while.

He ran his fingers lightly across my skin and heat pooled between my legs. These men were the reason I never got enough. One touch and they lit me up.

"You're such a tease." I groaned as his tongue made its way north until he got to the apex of my thighs. "Asher, please, just-"

He spread my lips with his thumbs and blew on the sensitive flesh. I shuddered and my hands fell to the cushions and dug into the fabric.

His tongue lightly flicked my clit and I closed my eyes, trying not to squirm as he drove me crazy. I was already ready for him to be inside me, but he had other plans as he slid two fingers in.

"I'm a little disappointed I missed your first time having two dicks in your pussy at once." He curled his fingers inside me and I whimpered as he increased his pace. "Did it feel amazing?"

"Yes." I was panting and moved my hips to match the thrust of his fingers. "So amazing."

His tongue flicked out again and I cried out, nearly coming off the couch as he circled my clit before sucking it into his mouth. I clinched around his fingers as my orgasm washed over me.

My brain was still fuzzy as he picked me up over his shoulder and smacked my ass on the way to the bedroom. I didn't care where he was taking me, but I needed him inside me.

He threw me on the bed and stripped out of his clothes. My eyes watched greedily as he went to his bag and dug around inside.

"What are you doing?" There was nothing we needed besides his dick inside of me.

He turned around with a bottle of lube and a small black object. I situated myself against the pillows and my body burned as he threw the bottle onto the bed next to me and then rolled a ring with a nub over his shaft.

The faint sound of a vibrator came from the ring and I shivered with anticipation as he climbed on the bed and kissed me. He moved his lips down my neck and then took one of my nipples between his teeth, biting with just the right amount of pressure to make my toes curl.

He lined up with my entrance, thrusting in with one smooth stroke. He grinded against me, the vibrating nub of the cock ring rubbing against my clit.

"I'm going to die," I moaned as he pulled away and thrust again.

I don't know why we'd never tried a cock ring before, but now I felt like they had all been holding out on me. I shuddered as it hit against my clit over and over.

"I want you on top." He stopped mid thrust so my clit wouldn't be stimulated and kissed me. "Just... don't lean forward on me."

"Are you sure?" I cupped his cheek and bit my lip to keep from crying out as he circled his hips.

He rolled us so I was on top and I braced my hands on his chest. He shut his eyes for a moment and then opened them, thrusting his hips up as I grinded against him, keeping the vibrating nub against my clit.

"Fuck." Asher jacked his hips off the mattress and came inside me, his body shaking with his release.

I squeezed around him and the vibrator hit me in just the right way, sending me over the edge. I threw my head back and rode the waves of my orgasm until it started to burn and I had to scoot back.

"That was hot." I jumped at Olly's voice from behind me and turned to look over my shoulder at him. "The grail is back under lock and key."

I rolled off of Asher and laid next to him, trying to catch my breath. Olly came to stand next to the bed and gave me a heated look before his eyes traveled down my body.

I groaned as he unbuttoned his pants and he paused with his zipper halfway down. "Are you too worn out?"

"Never." I propped myself up on my elbows as he stripped out of his clothes and lowered between my legs.

Asher turned on his side and watched as Olly slid in and took my lips. He tugged at my bottom lip with his teeth and I dug my nails into his back.

"So sexy." Asher rose to his knees and squirted some lube onto two fingers.

As Olly increased his pace, Asher kissed his shoulder and his hand disappeared behind him. Olly gasped against my mouth.

I arched my back as another orgasm ripped through me. I didn't know if there was a limit to how many orgasms a woman could handle in a day, but I felt like I was approaching it.

Asher's brows were furrowed in concentration as he fingered Olly. Olly's thrusts grew erratic and he buried his face into my neck as he came.

His body weight settled on top of me and his fingers went into my hair as he kissed my neck.

"Everything is good now?" Asher laid back on his side again.

Olly lifted his head and Asher kissed him softly. "Everything's good. I tried to get in to see the creator to apologize again, but Azrael wouldn't let me see him."

"It's done with now. I'm sure your apology is accepted, even if you didn't get to say it in person." I squirmed out from under him. "I'm going to take a shower and get ready to go out."

They both scrambled after me and my heart felt full, knowing I'd always have four guys by my side.

EPILOGUE

DANICA

One Year Later

"Good morning, Danica. You're calling rather early. What's wrong?" I heard the rustling of paper on the other end of the phone. My dad read the paper almost daily, mainly to catch up on business news.

I sniffled. I didn't know why I thought it was a good idea to call him first. When the plus sign appeared on the pregnancy test and confirmed what I already knew, he was the first person that came to mind.

"Dad, I'm pregnant."

Silence.

I blew out a breath as silence filled the other end of the line. Was he upset? I was barely twenty, and maybe he thought I was too young to be having babies.

"What?" His voice was hushed. "Repeat that."

"I'm pregnant. I'm going to be a mom. You're going to be a grandpa..."

"Danica... I... wow. I'm going to be a grandpa?" He fumbled over his words and I wished I would have waited to tell him in person, but I needed moral support.

"Don't be mad." I grabbed some toilet paper and blotted at my eyes, which were leaking. "I know I'm young, but I have so many years ahead of me and four men to help. Just don't be-"

"Be mad? How could I possibly be mad that I'm going to be a grandpa? I'm just... in shock."

His words made me cry even more and then I laughed. "How is this even possible?"

He cleared his throat. "Well, there's four of them and I'm assuming you have sex with them."

"Dad," I groaned and laughed. I didn't want my dad mentioning sex to me. "Angels can't get each other pregnant."

"I haven't heard of an archangel and a regular angel conceiving, but there also isn't another female archangel."

We were both quiet until I sighed. "So it might be Reve's."

"It's possible. Does it matter?" He sounded sad. "The only way Lia can get pregnant is with Ric. I've come to terms with that. Not that Lia has ever expressed interest in having children."

"I hadn't either." There was a knock on the door. "Dad, I have to go."

"I love you, Danica. If those assholes don't wait on you hand and foot from here on out, let me know and I'll put them in their place."

"Thanks Dad, I love you too." I ended the call with a laugh and quickly wrapped the pregnancy test in toilet paper and shoved it in my pocket.

I TRIED to steady my hands as I sliced a tomato for our dinner. The guys were on the rooftop barbecuing hamburgers and I was preparing the toppings. I had insisted they go bond with each other because I needed some time alone.

I shouldn't have been so nervous about telling them, but a small part of me still felt like I was living in a fantasy world that could be ripped away at any second.

I was twenty with four husbands who adored me and was winning at life for once. Well, life as an angel. An angel that Heaven was still figuring out a role for.

Maybe I could be the angel of dicks. I was good at handling four of them.

Once the burger toppings were spread out on a platter, I put them on the table and waited with a swirling feeling in my stomach.

Olly popped his head in through the door leading to the roof. "Dani! Bring the buns up here and we'll grill them. The burgers are just about done."

"I put them in the oven to warm up already." This was going to completely ruin their dinner.

I put a few bowls of chips on the table and sat down and waited. Any minute now they would find out they were going to be fathers. How was I going to manage being a mother when I could hardly take care of myself?

I shut my eyes and took a deep breath, focusing on the energy inside me. I hadn't really needed a pregnancy test to confirm my suspicions in the first place. I had felt it a little over three weeks ago, but then yesterday, I felt the heartbeat.

The door clanged open and I jumped slightly as laughter filled the large space. I gripped the stool and plastered a smile on my face as they came down the stairs with the hamburgers and beers in hand.

Asher had a non-alcoholic beer since he was six months sober. At first, everyone had the same beer too, but he insisted after a month that if they didn't start drinking again he would.

Tobias put the hamburgers in the middle of the table and they sat down. "Where are the buns? Please tell me you didn't burn them again."

"I left them in the oven."

"I'll get them." Asher jumped up and put an oven mitt on.

I had set it to warm and he pushed the off button before opening the door. I was going to puke.

"Do you want something to drink?" Reve looked at me and stood. He tipped his bottle back and finished the small amount in the bottom of his bottle. "There's one Diet Dr. Pepper left from your weekly allotment."

My eyes were locked on Asher's back as he pulled the cookie sheet out of the oven.

"Dani? Did you hear me?" Reve waved his hand in front of me.

"There is only one hamburger bun in here." Asher put the tray on the stove and then turned to look at me. "Did you burn the rest? I guess we could go low carb tonight."

I heard a stool move back to my left.

"Danica?" Tobias seemed to be the only one who caught on.

The others just stared at me like I was drunk or high. Neither of which I had been in a long time.

I shut my eyes and then turned my head toward him. His eyes teared up as he stared back at me, waiting for me to confirm. I hadn't thought about how he would feel about this.

"What's going on?" Olly pushed back from the table. "I'm confused."

"She has a bun in the oven." Tobias kept his eyes locked on me.

I covered my face as my emotions spilled over.

I'm pregnant.

Tobias wrapped his arms around me, laughing. "Holy shit. Are you sure?"

I nodded against his chest and was passed off to Reve. He kissed the side of my head and then let me go. "We were wondering if it would be possible. This is great, hon."

Olly and Asher were glued to their spots and staring at me with wide eyes. The potholder Asher was still holding fell to the ground.

"I'm going to be a father?" He looked ready to bolt, so I walked to him and cupped his cheek. "Of... a real-life baby?"

I snorted, tilting my head up so he could plant a kiss on my lips. He wrapped his arms around me and nuzzled his face in my neck.

"I know nothing about how to take care of a baby." Olly's whisper drew all of our attention. He was pale and looked like he might pass out. When I had imagined this whole scene in my head, I had expected Asher to be the one to freak out about it, not Olly.

"You'll learn." Tobias rounded the table and put a hand on his shoulder. "Breathe."

Olly took a few deep breaths as I went to him and wrapped my arms around him, putting my head on his chest. He set his chin on my head and I rubbed his back.

"As long as Olly doesn't fly over any bodies of water with the baby, I think he'll make a great dad." Reve snorted and then grunted when Asher smacked him in the back of the head.

I laughed and sat back down at the table. I stared around the table at my four guys and knew that we would be great parents. We had become a family that loved and supported each other, and now we'd get to share that love with our child.

Printed in Dunstable, United Kingdom